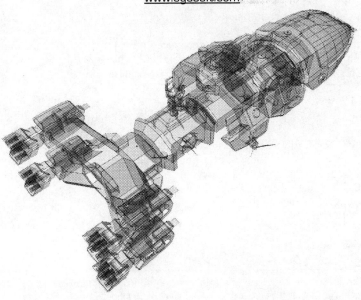

Cover and artwork by Paul "Avis" Hutchinson and "Wire frame" ship
graphics by Egosoft.
Contact Paul Hutchinson via email at paul_hutchinson@dsl.pipex.com

Printed in Victoria, Canada


Note for Librarians: a cataloguing record for this book that includes Dewey Classification and US Library of Congress numbers is available from the National Library of Canada. The complete cataloguing record can be obtained from the National Library's online database at:
www.nlc-bnc.ca/amicus/index-e.html
ISBN 1-4120-1955-9

# TRAFFORD

This book was published on-demand in cooperation with Trafford Publishing.
On-demand publishing is a unique process and service of making a book available for retail sale to the public taking advantage of on-demand manufacturing and Internet marketing.
On-demand publishing includes promotions, retail sales, manufacturing, order fulfilment, accounting and collecting royalties on behalf of the author.

Suite 6E, 2333 Government St., Victoria, B.C. V8T 4P4, CANADA
Phone 250-383-6864    Toll-free 1-888-232-4444 (Canada & US)
Fax 250-383-6804    E-mail sales@trafford.com    Web site www.trafford.com
TRAFFORD PUBLISHING IS A DIVISION OF TRAFFORD HOLDINGS LTD.
Trafford Catalogue #03-2433    www.trafford.com/robots/03-2433.html

10      9      8      7      6      5      4      3      2      1

Many thanks go to Bernd Lehahn for allowing us to write these stories
using references to items already established and to the individuals who
proofread and gave us invaluable feedback.

Inspired by

www.egosoft.com

Published by Amita (UK) Limited in association with Trafford Publishing.

info@amita.uk.net
www.amita.uk.net

info.uk@trafford.com
www.trafford.com

# Index

## About the authors

"The game is not the story, the story is not the game." Helge Kautz, author of Farnham's Legend.

The best bit of advice I was given.

The initial reason for writing "Dominion" was to attempt to fill a gap and provide the English speaking fans of the game series with stories to enhance the whole "X" experience. This then became, as most things do, a much bigger project then first imagined. I suppose the hardest part was to ensure consistency with the "historical" background. This sometimes resulted in rewrites of various chapters for exactly those reasons.

Since those early days (2000 onwards), I have become more and more involved with the X series and assist in various aspects of its development. The fiction side is one of those aspects.

This book is produced for the fans by the fans. We hope it brings you some enjoyment either on its own, or as a companion to the game series.

"Good Profit"

**Darren Astles (aka Steel)**

\* \* \*

This is a novel based on the X-Universe as featured in the three excellent computer games from Egosoft; X-Beyond the Frontier, X-tension and X2 and the author acknowledges all copyrights.

It began life as a series of episodes published on the game forum and took on a life of its own thanks to the encouragement and praise it received. The concluding part of Rogue is currently available as an e-book from the author.

**Steve Miller**

\* \* \*

"X-Universe" is two books, both the beginnings of two larger trilogies written by two different authors but both following the turbulent lives of the inhabitants in the same Universe.

\* \* \*

## BOOK ONE

### *Prologue*

Workers become oppressed. It doesn't seem to matter whether this is today, yesterday or as here, in some far distant future. The area of space this book refers to, known as the "X-Universe", is full of all the normal problems.

A large area connected by jump gates from what appears to be an ancient civilisation and the interaction of different races. Alliances and trade agreements allow the would-be trader to carve out a living in the hustle and bustle of the spaceports.

A Paranid, drunk on ambition creates a new technology. An advanced chip that allows the mind to operate and communicate with computer systems. The uses are far reaching and the customers will flock to his factory. It's time to announce this new breakthrough to the cosmos.

Just when the announcement is made and the new products detail and price is transmitted into the dealing systems, a fleet of organised pirate ships raid and take away the first batch of chips. Obliterating all the production facilities, plans and employees in one swift action.

Revenge is planned, but the pirates, too long subjugated and bound by the pricing thresholds of the inter-race guilds have finally become a larger unit. Throwing aside their differences and under the direct leadership of a ruthless Argon female, they set the wheels in motion for a plan, so audacious, it might just work and bring all of the space lanes under their control.

Out there in the distant blackness of space another race, untouched by intruders, suddenly have their very existence threatened by the carefree attitude of the Pirates and their plans.

Before they can enter the realm of the X-Universe though, this story must first be told. The battle for the trade lanes is about to begin.

**Dominion.**

# Dominion

## *Chapter 1: Best laid plans*

*Twenty jazuras ago a sequence of events happened that would have a profound affect on the universe as it is today. The following are those events and what has transpired since that day.*

He stood on the bridge of the ship. Feet firmly planted onto the floor of the room, kept in place by the artificial gravity. He could hear the faint hum of the gravity sphere; yes he could hear it *and* feel it. Down in the bowels of the ship, pulling everything towards it. They were temperamental at best, gravity spheres, but this one had been enhanced until it operated within 0.3% deviation from its settings.

He liked that, quality work done by quality engineers and he had some of the best in the universe. Yes, the best engineers and without doubt, some of the finest scientists to ever live. That's what made him so wealthy. He made products that his people and especially those of other races needed.

Computer components and microchips, electrical and organic, they made the most in the universe and demand was high. You couldn't fly a ship without his products. In fact you couldn't *build* a ship without them. Navigation systems, command consoles communication devices and targeting systems. Even the weapons themselves had the stamp of his company somewhere within them.

ENeT- Enhanced Nebulae Technologies, "Quality where it counts".

His name was LooManckStrat the Third, King of Pontifex Realm, Paranid sector ruler and fourth in line to the throne. He was aboard his cruise ship, called a "Spinny". A large space going yacht built solely for himself for the times he had to travel. He didn't like to travel in space, but business made it a necessity. So he had the ship built to his exact specifications. Fast, well protected and most importantly, luxurious.

This day was a special occasion though, that was why he was now standing aboard his ship and gazing out through the large space screen. Before him, only a few kilometres away sat his latest venture, the new microchips plant extension to his large component factory. A great building in space, designed and built by his company and at last having the final piece slotted into place.

The single star in this sector was behind his ship, but it was close enough to give plenty of light. This light reflected off the large structure on the right, casting a bright hue over the slightly bluish colour of the factory. A massive two kilometres high and the same distance wide made it a central point in the sector. There were other factories here too, producing many different items. His structure required some of the others to manufacture its own goods, but none of them had the size and sheer presence that this one had.

The "Spinny"

A sphere sat in the centre and protruding from five of the six possible directions were long cylindrical structures. Two of them span slowly, creating gravity for the crewmembers and factory workers who resided inside. One was the docking bay where all other ships had to dock, requesting landing rights and then guided in by the stations navigation control computer. It also housed the short and long stay bays where the ships would park. Almost nobody stayed in a station for more than a few stazura, it was too expensive and any time spent idle saw any profit from a trading trip begin to dwindle away.

But inside one of the housing sections was an area set-aside for pleasure. It enabled the weary travellers to meet and talk, exchange views, information and stories. Also to rent a bunk for a short time should they need to. Some ships had excellent sleeping quarters for the long hauls, when the ship's navigation computer would fly the ship on automatic and the pilot could get some rest. But most ships were short haul, designed for the quick profit run and had sparse conditions, sometimes with only a flight area to sit in and navigate from.

The final two factory additions housed the actual manufacturing rigs, one making a series of computer components and the second, actual computer chips. The central sphere housed the massive stock bays with the raw materials and finished goods. Linked up to the automatic trading system, the onboard computers and factory robots would unload and load any visiting ship while the pilot waited, or slipped down to the pleasure area.

But nothing was situated on the left-hand side of the station. A round connection clamp, a hundred metres in diameter, waited expectantly.

This was why LooManckStrat was venturing out into space, to actually witness the final part of his factory being attached.

He glanced farther to the left, his three eyes searching out the approaching part. A massive transporter ship was a few kilometres further away, its huge dark bulk visible against the star filled background. Warning and navigation lights blinking on and off, red and white respectively. He could see the glow from the two massive drive engines, hidden from his view as the ship was facing the station. It had just deployed the new part into space and small-automated tugs were now moving the large cylindrical object towards the waiting station.

Small ships darted back and too at speed, some overseeing the installation while others guarded it from any jealous competitors. That was the price of success. There was nothing like greed to drive a company forward. He had allowed the odd "removal" of a competing company himself in the early days of the business. But now he was the top of the tree, he was the target of many that were just like he was once. That's why you had to employ vast navies to protect your interests and having factories in many sectors, some of which were homes to other races, was expensive. But he had no choice, his ships numbered so many that they would be a match for a military fleet, if he brought them all together. But that couldn't be done, each station had its own small detachment of protection ships and with the modern scanners that almost everybody carried, a potential enemy would spot such a weakness from afar if they were to leave for any length of time. No he kept them where they belonged, at the stations (he had ten now) where they did their job best.

Every one of his factories also employed various other protection devices. Laser weapons attached to the hull and others in a fixed orbital position a few kilometres out, menacing and a good deterrent. But these were no match for any small and nimble fighter craft that some companies employed, particularly the pirate clans, so the protection ships stayed.

The new addition was a complete, almost fully automated manufacturing plant for his latest venture. The new "Super Slave" enhanced control chip. A partly organic device, that could be inserted directly into the recipient's brain stem. It was an amazing device and had taken a great deal of time to get it to this position. The yields were worryingly low. Less than 1% of all chips made actually passed the quality tests. That was not good, but he had decided to wait no longer as the opportunity was now. It took many stazura to make a single chip, partly for the fact that the internal device had to be grown, not made and with only 1 out of every hundred produced actually being a saleable product, it didn't sound like a good business investment. But his was the only place in the whole universe where you could buy them, so he could set the price as high as he liked. He smiled at that, yes the *only* place you could buy them.

He was going to make a great deal of credits on this, he was sure.

The original Slave chip had been around for a long time. It was a remarkable device and gave any being whom had it fitted the ability to control nearby linked computer systems with the power of thought alone. It was a small device, only two millimetres in diameter, a perfect sphere, bright blue in colour. Fitted surgically and usually never removed once installed (installing the chip was a straightforward procedure, removing it was surgically dangerous), it enabled the subject to quickly navigate computer systems such as a navigation system while leaving the limbs free for other tasks (such as steering a ship). This gave them an advantage as they could issue commands to the weapons systems for example, while still manoeuvring the vessel.

Not all beings could use it though and they all had to undergo stringent tests before one could be installed. You also had to prove that your age was in excess of 25 jazuras as growing bodies and minds are excluded. Most Navy pilots would have one installed as would a great deal of the company freight pilots and the many single traders that ploughed the space lanes. Some could not handle the Slave though, they could not get used to the way that the image could be imposed into their sight, when in reality, their eyes never saw it. It was superimposed behind their vision. Still, the computer systems still offered voice and even key press back up devices. So almost anyone could still operate them and some chose this latter method.

However, the irony of it was that the Paranid believed the chip to be in direct contravention of the Bashra (the Holy book) and the chip was outlawed in Paranid space. You could make it and you could sell it, but you could not use it. Well that was no problem to LooManckStrat, he didn't have one fitted and didn't intend to. But that didn't stop him from selling them. And sell them he did, so many that he had trouble keeping up demand with the long production cycle.

There was a downside though (wasn't there always) in that the chip in its early days had quickly been used as a pleasure device. If an image (and feelings to an extent) could be piped directly into the mind, then for a fee, the user could go anywhere and be anything. These pleasure areas had become big business very quickly, but it was soon discovered that there was a side effect. The mind didn't like to be messed around with, didn't like being told what to do. When the brain decided that the senses were tired, which it did quite naturally, it would shut them down and put the host to sleep, so that the body could regenerate. But it had no control over the Slave chip and this was the problem. It would endure it for brief moments, which was fine for an occasional command given to the computer, but for someone to actively plug themselves in to a stream for a few stazura proved to be too much. The brain wanted to shut the senses down but the chip continued to let the feelings and images flow.

Different beings had different levels of exposure. The Split appeared to have the longest before any damage was done. But once the mind had started to reject the incoming data, to react to this other "sense", there was usually no way back. If the exposure continued, the host's brain would "burn" itself out, leaving them still alive, but basically in a coma from which they would never recover. The problem was that the brain would actually begin to send antibodies to physically destroy the cells surrounding the Slave and these cells also contributed to the other senses.

The user became trapped in a world with none of the basic senses working, no touch, smell, sight, nothing. They couldn't move and they couldn't speak. They were not physically dead, but the damage had so far proven to be irreparable.

So the use of the chip as a pleasure device and any other unwanted use (its value as an interrogation device had proved to be amazing) was outlawed in all known space. That didn't mean that there were not places that you could go, there would always be an underground market for its use. Some of the greatest computer software developers had slipped into this dark world, creating dream worlds for people to play in, but except for pilots (of which there were thousands), its use was small, but profitable.

Its range was also small. You had to be within a few tens of metres of a suitable transmission device. These were usually fitted to ships as standard and some of the more expensive factories had them located around the walkways and sleeping chambers.

But the Super Slave changed all of that. Its range was over a kilometre, but the wonderful thing about the Super Slave was it's in-built safety device. It monitored the brain output and after many trials and adaptations for different races, his scientists had managed to get the chip to shut itself down or begin to lessen the effect, so that a person's own consciousness would be brought to the surface.

Not many knew about the Super Slave, it was currently under tight security and a veil of secrecy. No one who was actually fitting the station at this moment knew what the new rig did. They assumed it simply made standard Slave chips, the manufacturing process looked familiar to the untrained eye and only the company scientists and a select few station commanders had been told. Now as he watched the new limb being brought closer and closer to its final resting-place, LooManckStrat began to get just a small twinge of excitement. A feeling quite alien to the Paranid, but it was there all the same, slowing moving its way upward through his torso.

So the yields were down, he could live with it, as they would improve upon it as time went by. His estimations were that the chip would be so successful that it didn't really matter. He was already planning on the next factory, probably in Argon space where there would be such a huge demand. More Argon had the chip fitted than any other race so he expected to make some large amounts of credits there.

He also knew that in the outer systems, where the pioneers and illegal companies did their business, he would have a handsome profit. He might even risk putting a factory out there at some point. He pondered the thought, yes it might be a shrewd move that, installing a Super Slave factory where they would want it most. Right on the doorstop of the customers. They'd pay a good price out there as well, he was certain. It would require some extra security though, more laser banks and protection ships. But with the credits he would surely make, it might be worth it. Yes, he'd have to look into that soon. He made a verbal note to his personal recording system. It would remind him later.

The Super Slave rig was now almost touching the main factory sphere. He picked up his zoom lenses and adjusted them so that he had a clear, close up view of the station. There were figures in the tough environment suits slowly jetting around the structure. He counted over ten in the company regulation orange colour, some with large welding devices ready to put the final, permanent seal between the two buildings. They must have slowly touched together as he saw the distinct flash of the lasers as they burnt the metal together. Other figures securing locks and tightening locking bolts. It wouldn't be long now, only a few mizuras before the umbilical cord, containing all the power lines and computer system hard wires, was connected. It was all built with precision so that the final installation would go as smooth as possible.

The small knot of excitement rose within him again, he would actually be able to connect to its systems shortly and see the figures with his own three eyes. Actually watch the resources that were already stored in the main sphere begin to move down the automated shafts and into the main manufacturing rig. Watch the numbers go up and down, he liked to do that, watching the numbers, it gave him a great sense of achievement. But above all it told him that credits were being made! And that was the real achievement.

His factory commander's face appeared on the communication cube, which jutted out of the wall to the right of the large space screen. The wall was a dirty white colour, but the cube that had automatically moved from being flat in the wall to a pyramid shaped protrusion, was the company orange. He made the few steps required to place him within range so he could press the required buttons. He understood for a moment what it must be like for the pilots to be able to achieve that without moving, using the Slave. The Super Slave was going to astound them!

"LooManckStrat here commander, are the systems online?" he asked the face in the screen.

"Correct your honour, they are in place and functioning. Automatic production cycle is about to begin," came the reply.

LooManckStrat didn't speak further and pressed the button to end the call. He then pressed a series of buttons to navigate through his sector property and selected the factory. He felt a huge sigh of relief as the new Super Slave plant appeared on the screen. He checked the stock levels. They were increasing nicely from the main sphere, the automated systems doing their jobs. He checked the product levels, one hundred Super Slaves in stock. Exactly the number that had been produced on the rig while it was in the shipyard, still being finished. Another four stazuras before another one would be completed was the systems estimation of the product run. It was a computer's guess though as it all depended upon the yield and this could vary slightly around the 1% mark as much as one half a percent either way. It should get better and better though as his scientists and engineers fine-tuned the process even further.

He jabbed the buttons on the cube again. The Super Slave rig commander came into view. LooManckStrat didn't ask if anything was the matter, didn't even attempt at any small talk, it was not the Paranid way. He simply said "Set the price at five hundred thousand credits. I repeat five hundred thousand and announce the product to the trading systems." Then he disconnected the call.

He watched the screen again to make sure his orders had been carried out to the full. The product came online at a stock of one hundred and he saw with some satisfaction the price appear at the instructed five hundred thousand. The trading systems all across the universe would begin to pick this information up as it was passed onwards and outwards through the trading network. Within a single Tazura the information would be everywhere. Traders in the farthest systems would see the product on their screens, just as he was doing now.

Requests for information would come in from all over. "What was the new chip?" "What did it do?" It would create a request for data frenzy and the larger companies would send ships to buy stock anyway, regardless of the cost.

He glanced out of the space screen again and saw a ship exiting the station. Slowly moving away within regulation speed. It was a freighter, one of his company's own. The orange ENeT logo was unmistakable on the side of the hull. Orange lettering over a blue circle. It was a large ship, slow but perfectly built by the Paranid for the job it did. Hauling large quantities of resources or product across the vastness of space. A smooth thin nose expanding to a large bulbous body.

His new rig had probably ordered sufficient quantities of stock from the central sphere, that the factory commander had already seen a potential outage and had already ordered a ship out to replenish the goods.

The ship approached his yacht and then when it was half way between the station and the Spinny, it slowed to a stop. Then it turned, ever so slowly to his left so that he could see the whole side of the ship facing him, his logo staring back. Then with a slight increase in the intensity of light, that was coming from the rear of the ship were the engines were it accelerated away. He watched it until the rear of the ship was almost facing him and then he turned away, the glow from the engines causing a dull ache in his eyes. He checked the sector data screen and scanned the ship. Yes it was heading out to a local sector factory to obtain energy cells, the lifeblood of the universe.

Everything needed energy cells. They were large devices capable of retaining energy and everything ran on them. Produced by the solar power plants, huge factories in space that converted any local starlight into energy and stored it in the cells. They would then sell them to just about everybody for a small fee. The system worked well. Any ship on its way to a power plant would have in its cargo bay hundreds, if not thousands of depleted cells. The plant simply handed over some charged ones, took the empty ones back and placed them in the charging area and so the cycle continued, as well of course as collecting a fee for the privilege.

There were others ways of making energy of course. Ships used reactors to produce energy that was used to power all onboard systems, including the engines. But these were small power requirements in comparison to a station and if a ship was destroyed, the resultant pollution of the immediate area could be dealt with. Not so a station. If a station was destroyed it made a big bang and if large reactors had powered it, could cause serious local problems. So large reactors in stations had been banned after the Ferryman incident in Argon space, which had killed thousands and left half of the sector unusable for hundreds of jazuras. All races recognised this, as any station with such a large reactor would become a suitable target in any conflict.

Five hundred thousand each! He knew that the price wouldn't sustain itself for long. But while demand was high, he would make as much profit as possible. The initial hundred would be bought quickly and then once the initial furore was over, he would have to drop the price considerably. But if all the stock went and he thought it would, he would have fifty million credits! That was enough to cover the development costs *and* the rig assembly costs. He would have to start building another rig as soon as possible. They took much too long to produce in the shipyards. The only problem with that at the moment was that the shipyards didn't know how to make them as all the data for the chips was safe and secure in the rig itself.

He was yet to negotiate that part of the business, as he didn't want the shipyards with which he had no direct control, selling the rigs to anyone else. No, that would be a big mistake and one he was not going to make. Not yet anyway, not until the bidders started to appear and then after he had established a few of the rigs on his other factories he might decide to sell the rights. Yes, just before the market was flooded and the price dropped. He felt perfectly happy with his business plan, he had worked hard at it, sometimes personally and he was going to get every available credit he could from it.

LooManckStrat had pushed the cube back into the wall of the ship and was now walking back to the position he started from, central to the space screen, so he could survey his factory when the cube came back out of the wall again. Incoming message from his patrolling defence ships, it was the sector Captain on the screen.

"LooManckStrat your honour, you should be informed that a number of ships have just entered the system via the north gate." The Captain said very matter of fact.

LooManckStrat moved towards the cube again. "What ships, how many and *who's*?" he barked at the screen.

"I count twenty ships your honour, no local markings. Scan shows them to be giving out pirate signatures. They are headed this way your honour. Fifteen fighter class and five freighter size attack ships, they are obtaining an attack formation."

NO! Could it be him they were after, sat here in his private yacht. No it couldn't be, his yacht could outrun anything the pirates had and its shielding was first class. No, not him but the rig, they must be after the rig! Pirates never entered such sectors as this without good reason. They were only seen in the inner sectors when they were on a mission and pirate missions always ended in a fight. The pirates were disparate groups, clans that rarely worked together but had a single goal, to make money from illegal activities. They had pilots from every race amongst their ranks, failed traders and escaped criminals. They were powerful people who commanded large, if somewhat disorganised, forces. They even had their own bases where they manufactured and distributed illegal goods.

"Captain, set an intercept course. Launch all available ships immediately. You must stop those ships!" He shouted the final sentence. He glanced out of the space screen and could tell by the navigation lights on the docking rig that the station had already gone to battle stations, docking rights were suspended. A small fast fighter craft exited the docking bay, he watched it accelerate and head off in the direction of the north gate. Another and then another followed it.

He pressed buttons on the cube to get a scan of the sector. There they were, like a swarm of Actu flies in the heat of the planet's surface. Large ships in the middle with small escorts circling around and around. A classic pirate attack group, but this one was big. Twenty pirate ships was a lot to have in one group. They must have travelled in smaller groups and then formed up in the northern sector.

There was now a red light that flashed from the tops of the walls on the bridge of the Spinny. Every few sezura it flashed bright and then slowly subsided until it was nearly gone, when it flashed bright again. There was no sound with the light, warning sounds interfered with actions, just the light to indicate that the yacht had now gone to battle stations.

LooManckStrat turned to his pilot who was seated across the other side of the bridge behind him. "Pilot, take us to the South Gate now! Do not enter the gate, proceed at full speed."

"Yes your honour." The pilot replied and quickly fed instructions into the console before him while grabbing hold of the manual control stick. The engines on the yacht fired and were put to full power immediately. LooManckStrat felt a slight sensation of movement as the ship began to move. Artificial gravity systems could never cope with quick movements correctly.

"You should take your seat, your honour." The pilot stated. LooManckStrat knew and moved towards his seat that was just in front of him now that he was facing the pilot and not the space screen. He seated himself and pressed the button to confirm he was ready. Safety straps appeared from under and behind the seat and he was quickly secured in place.

The ship hit maximum speed and sped off towards the South Gate. He accessed the cube in the seat and it rose up out of the arm. He pressed the buttons to access the sector scan so that he could watch the upcoming battle.

He could see from the sector scan that his other two stations were also launching fighters. His Ore Mine and his own Solar Power Plant, if you had to use them you may as well buy them off yourself he had said when he announced his plans to build it. Three ships from each station were racing to catch up with the eight that were already either patrolling, or had launched from the larger factory. Fourteen ships against twenty, not great odds. He thought about calling in more ships from the closest sectors where he also had factories, but dismissed the idea almost instantly. They'd never get here in time, this was going to be over quickly one way or another.

The Captain of ENeT's defence force steered his ship towards the incoming pirate vessels. His six medium fighters were at the head of the group with two heavy fighters trailing behind. The other stations light fighters were beginning to close, but it looked fairly clear to him that he was going to have to engage before the others caught up.

They were at full speed now, closing in on the pirates at an alarming rate. The pirate ships didn't alter from their course, heading directly for the large factory that had just had the new rig installed.

The Captain gave his orders to the other five medium ships. He had scanned all the pirate ships and found a collection of light, medium and heavy fighters. Ships from different races were amongst the ranks, but they all gave out the unmistakable signature of the pirate clans. He was also concerned about the five heavy attack ships, but they would have to wait. The fighters must be dealt with first. The two small fleets were now within five kilometres of each other and closing fast.

"Heavy fighters first, then medium, light, and finally the attack ships. Everyone got that?" He saw the affirmative lights flash up on his console. "Good, stick with your wingmen, battle control has selected your targets for you, commence attack!"

The Paranid ships split into three groups of two and dived into the incoming enemy. The Captain saw the lead pirate in his weapon sights and when he got within two kilometres, he opened fire. Laser bolts streaked out across the darkness of space, momentarily creating an artificial lightness that could be seen on the inside of the ship walls. Again and again he fired, leading the shots in front of the target so the pirate would run into them as he approached.

The pirate was just about to be smothered with the laser bolts when he suddenly pulled the ship into a vertical manoeuvre, spinning as he went and then turning again, this time to be speeding directly for the Captain. It opened fire.

The Captain had managed to keep the pirate in his sights and as it turned towards him he also opened fire. The laser bolts passed each other in space and the Captain felt the all too familiar feeling of the ship bucking as the lasers from the pirate found their target. He glanced at his shields, 50% remaining. He checked the scanner to check the pirates, 30% remaining. Good, this could be over quickly if he could just get another salvo into its hull.

They passed each other with only metres to spare and immediately he turned the control stick to sweep his ship around in an attempt to get on the back of the pirate. Yes, got him, he was there right in front of him. He squeezed the trigger again, fighting to keep the ship on a steady line as it juddered every time his lasers fired.

He saw the signs of success as the lasers hit their mark and the shields around the pirate vessel glowed with tiny explosions. He kept on firing as the pirate was now trying to take evasive action. Frantically swinging its ship one way and then another. The Captain was too experienced to let such tactics get the better of him and he kept on firing, sometimes around the ship, not directly at it, so that any attempts to escape would be blocked.

The pirate ship suddenly came to an abrupt halt, its shields wasted and its power source exhausted. The Captain had to move quickly to avoid hitting it and he managed to veer to the left. The pirate exploded just as he was passing by, shooting fragments of ship at him. He saw them moving past his space screen and registered the impact on his shields. He quickly registered the positions of the other ships on the scanner and turned to intercept.

Meanwhile, the other Paranid ships had not been so lucky. Three were gone and two more were in serious trouble. However, they had managed to destroy another pirate, so that only left eighteen in total. He carried on regardless, aiming his lasers at the nearest one. It turned too quickly for him and his shots missed the mark. He grabbed the stick tight, selected missiles and quickly fired off three light attack missiles. Short range, highly manoeuvrable ship to ship missiles. He knew they might not all strike, in fact he was sure of it. But he also knew it would keep that pirate busy for the next few sezura while he found another target.

He found one, down and to his left. He turned to intercept, launched another two missiles but this time followed them towards the target. The pirate must have been informed of the incoming missiles as it veered to the right. The Captain was expecting this though and went with it, firing lasers into the blackness in the hope that the enemy ship would run into the carefully aimed shots. It did, impact flashes appearing all over it as it tried to run. He kept it in his sight and fired until the weapons computer began to warn him of low power. The pirate tried frantically to avoid the laser fire, but just when it looked as though it might succeed, the two missiles streaked across the Captain's screen from the left and hit the pirate. He wasn't sure, but he actually thought the first missile had been the one. It was difficult to tell they had hit so close together. He again checked the scanner and found the initial ship still trying to avoid the first missiles. An ideal opportunity to catch it unawares, he selected it as a locked target and veered towards it.

The five pirate strike ships had ignored the incoming Paranid and had kept on their course towards the station. As they approached within range the factory's defences opened fire. Automated laser batteries attempting to lock on to the incoming threat. Laser towers spinning on their axis while also trying to achieve a successful lock.

As soon as the pirates had passed the point where the lasers from the factory could track them, they opened fire as well. Large "factory killer" missiles were being ejected by the forward most ship. It had targeted the laser towers and within a few Sezuras, they were all gone. Two of the ships began raining laser shots onto the station laser batteries, but the massive defence shields on the station rendered them ineffective. The two pirates continued their attack though, moving back and forth through space, zigzagging so that the laser batteries were unable to get many clean hits. That was part of the plan though, to keep the other three ships free for the next attack.

One of the large pirate assault ships approached the new rig. When it was adjacent to the newly welded connection point, it fired an extremely powerful beam laser at the station. It seemed to miss at first, the shot careering over the top, but then slowly it started to descend and it sliced it's way right through the join. Debris and small impact explosions littered the area. Massive vents of atmosphere that had been contained within the station were pouring out into space. The laser continued until it passed underneath the rig. Then after a pause that seemed to last forever, the newly installed rig began to slowly, very slowly move away from the main factory.

The station went into automatic recovery mode, shutting down sections that had been open to the gaping hole that had been ripped into it's side, too late to save anyone or anything that was the wrong side of the hatches. Bodies flew out into space, instantly freezing in the extreme coldness. Parts of the station followed. Cables and piping, cargo boxes and robotic lifters, all were sucked out into the vacuum that was space. It took the factory's defence computer a few sezuras to recalculate the shield parameters and bring the station back under it's protective cloak.

LooManckStrat almost dropped his zoom lenses from his face. He was now at the relatively safe position of the South Gate and had been observing the battle. He raised the lenses back to his eyes and he could see the unbelievable happening before him. A weak "No!" was all he could muster as he saw his credits disappearing before him. How had they managed to avoid the shields on the factory?

The Super Slave rig was using its back up powers to shutdown the gaps in the same way that the main factory had done moments before. Lights were flickering out in the many space screens along its hull. One of the pirate ships moved in closer, slowed to an almost halt and then slowly, side on began to approach the dying hulk.

When it was within twenty metres it stopped. It's side cargo bay opened and a stream of figures in armed environment suits jetted across to the now lifeless hull. Laser torches began to burn a hole in its side and LooManckStrat could only watch on in disbelief.

He barked orders into the cube, but nobody answered. Eleven of his defence ships were gone and the remaining three were frantically trying to avoid being killed by the ever-chasing pirate fighters. He glanced around the bridge, but his loyal crew could only stare back at him, the same look of despair on their faces too.

In only a few mizura the figures were clambering into the rig. They quickly navigated their way to the walkways and divided into two groups. Using the electronic internal schematics of the station, they quickly sought out their intended destinations. The maps and instructions being transmitted to their Slave chips from the stationary ship outside. The rig was in darkness with only the occasional spark and flicker of light from the quickly emptying energy cells.

LooManckStrat had contacted the Paranid Navy and they were on their way but they would take a few stazuras to arrive. It was a hopeless position and he knew it, who had done this and why?

He couldn't take his eyes away from the proceedings and quicker than he expected the line of figures began to emerge from the hole they had made in the hull. One by one they came and returned to the waiting ship. He couldn't see them board as that was obscured by the pirate ship itself.

The pirate ship began to move away from the rig. The other four assault ships joining it in formation. They were about three kilometres away from the carnage when a number of large "Factory Killers" were launched.

LooManckStrat actually sank to his knees in despair as he saw first, his newly built rig and all its secrets explode quickly followed by the whole factory itself. His three remaining ships had just met the same fate from the marauding pirate fighters and the whole despicable little fleet headed for the north gate at full speed.

\* \* \* \* \* \* \* \* \* \*

ENeT Factory commander Faa t'Zrrk was relaxing in his office when the communication globe bleeped and sped across the room to meet him. This was another of ENeT's chip plants, but this time it was in Split space. He turned his head and body slowly towards the globe and ordered it to pipe the message through.

He saw the face of the Split pirate he had met only two wozuras ago. The message was non-interactive having been transmitted over many gates. It simply said "Mission accomplished, we must meet."

He stared at the globe as if hoping it would say something else. It did not. "Globe, delete last message and remove from archive, confirm?" The globe beeped its confirmation and then sped away back to the middle of the ceiling. Faa t'Zrrk began to clench and unclench his fists involuntarily. They have done it. They have actually gone and done it. He began to pack his belongings.

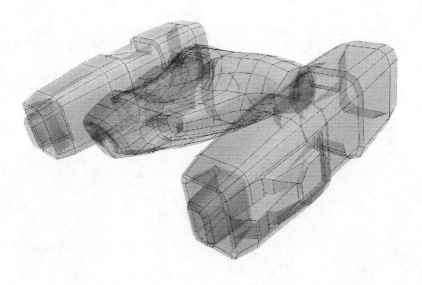

## Chapter 2: As one light is extinguished another flickers to life

*Out of the ashes rose the phoenix, its magnificent body greater than before. "I am mightier now than I ever have been, stronger and wiser." It said. "Let all those who stand as my enemies know that I have returned and the time for vengeance is upon them."*

She stood by the window, staring out at the children playing outside in the park. Six small figures giggling as they ran around each other, holding their light toys above them. The blinking from the light on the end of the small sticks making a swirling display like a continuous moving line as they twirled them in the air. They were just having a last play before they were called in for a meal and sleep.

The sun (Sonra) was beginning to sink behind the horizon, leaving a reddish glow on the few clouds that were hanging in the sky. It had been a bright light filled day, slightly cold, but it had warmed as the day went on. The children were savouring the last of it. She smiled at their pleasure. How to see such innocence was enough to bring happiness to another.

At the edge of the park was a fence about twenty metres away. Lights blinking from the two metre tall towers that were spread out along its length. They generated the beams that stretched between them, creating energy that created a secure perimeter around the compound.

Beyond the fence rolled out the hills, covered in low vegetation. A variety of colours from greens to reds and yellows created a mosaic that slowly moved one way then the other as the low wind swept across the hilltops. The ever decreasing light still attempting to thread its way downwards as it dropped behind them.

This was the government controlled child growth centre in Alicta, an orphanage to you and I. Alicta was the third largest population centre on the planet and this planet was the home to the Argon, the biped humans. This was Argon Prime!

She had chosen this place from all the others as it was close to the navy installation at Morang and she could see the shuttle ships take off and land from the base there. In fact she could see one now, a dark object lifting into the sky, a blinding light emitted from its end as the engines were fired to give the vehicle enough life to exit the atmosphere. Up and beyond to the orbiting stations and the fleets of ships that awaited any newly operational pilots.

She wished she could have stood here and watched these with her son, night after night so she could tell him the stories of the time she had spent in space, darting between systems and skimming the stars. But it was not to be. She moved to her right and heard the distinct sound of the motors as they moved the metallic bones that were in her legs. She sighed.

She had spent too long in space and had lost her mate. Her male companion was somewhere out there still in the cosmos. They had not been in touch for too long, but it didn't matter now. Etract, the bone and nerve wasting disease was nearing its completion. She had caught it working on the Chelt farms in Split space. It only affected Argon and didn't make its presence known until a long time after you had contracted it. Still it was rare and the pay was good, so you took your chance.

Then it struck and she quickly became incapable of moving herself without the aid of implants. Part of the right arm and both legs were now synthetic and the majority of her feelings were gone too. There was no point in staying in space, not for a weakened female, so they had parted. She didn't know where he was now anyway, probably still trading in the Teladi and Split sectors. Making a few credits here and a few there. Living from day to day.

No, she had decided that she wanted to leave something of herself here, on Argon Prime. She had signed up to the government adoption scheme. The government would look after her child after she was gone in return for all her belongings. It seemed a fair deal, she wouldn't need them where she was going and she may as well give her baby the best possible start. She had managed to save a little from her time in the Chelt farms and that would give her baby a better start. She could contribute nothing she knew, but the destination for her offspring wouldn't be as good as this one.

She involuntarily rubbed her hand over her stomach, the whirring motors noticeable in her arm. Not long now she mused. The baby moved and kicked hard, she felt it and smiled again. The disease couldn't make it into the womb, they didn't understand why and she freely assisted in inconclusive tests. The father didn't even know it was his and he never would. They had mated their last night together on the orbiting space station above the planet and then she had taken the shuttle down to the surface and he had boarded his freighter and left the sector. Goodbye. So cold and unforgiving when done in space, but he wouldn't come down to the surface, not for her, not for anyone.

She had been told that she may live a while longer, but if she kept the baby, the chances of her surviving the birth were not good. She had opted for the baby, what was a little while longer to her when she could provide a lifetime to another? No she had her time sun skimming, drinking in the bars and fighting with the traders. It had been a fitting life, she had taken to it well and enjoyed it. Time to move over, time for another life to begin.

She didn't hear the door open behind her, but she could sense that it had. Maybe a slight change in the light as the glow from the corridor was higher than the room. She turned to greet her visitor.

"Its time." Was all the assistant said, a completely blank expression on her face.

"I know." She replied and began to move towards her. The motors were making the only noise in the room. She gave one last look backward towards the children in the park. They must have been called in, as they were moving towards the door that she knew was to the left, out of site from the window.

She started again across the floor and followed the assistant out and down the corridor. It didn't take long for them to reach the preparation room. She walked and was gestured to lie down on the cushioned table in the middle of the room. She followed her instructions and undressed and then slowly moved, the large bulge that was her belly making it difficult, but she finally managed to climb aboard the table.

She lay down on her back, closed her eyes and thought of what the baby would look like as she had done so many times since she discovered he was to be born. Would it have her eyes, his? What about the mouth, the ears, the hair?

The assistant was leaning over her as she opened her eyes.

"What's his name to be?" she quizzed, not because she was interested but because the recording systems had to record the name from the mother.

She looked the assistant in the eye. "Brett." She replied. "You will say hello to him for me won't you. His name is Brett."

The assistant smiled, the first time she could remember her doing that, the assistants didn't smile as a rule.

"Of course I will." Came the reply. "Goodbye Berny."

"Goodbye." Berny replied.

She didn't feel the drug as it was administered, but she quickly felt it work its magic. She was asleep almost instantly after and only a little later, Brett was born.

Berny didn't survive the surgery, she wasn't expected to, her body was ravaged from the disease. But Brett was a strong, perfectly formed baby boy. As one light is extinguished another flickers to life.

* * * * * * * * * *

Brett lived at the orphanage until he was a grown boy. Not old enough to venture out on his own, no a long way from that, but old enough to understand. He became a respected member of the group and most of the other children looked up to him. One thing that was certain was that he was highly intelligent. He didn't like to show it and he sometimes had confrontations with the staff at the orphanage, but even they had to agree, Brett was special.

They would set tasks for the children to do, complex and sometimes-difficult scenarios, which they hoped, would keep the children busy for a while. Brett usually (if he could be bothered) answered the questions in an instant. They tried and tried to conjure up ideas for Brett to do, but every time he beat them.

So they obtained the complete history of the universe (as it was known) on data chip and organised for it to be available for Brett to use, to learn from, hopefully to keep him quiet.

Brett leapt at the chance for knowledge, something from outside of the institution. He read continually, accessing the graphic libraries and text scrolls. His appetite for the information was almost insatiable. He studied the data every chance he had.

He learnt about the races first, the Argon, the history books had been rewritten many times. They had originated from many different sources, according to the text, but the religious group known as the "Goners" insisted that they came from a distant star system and a planet called earth. This had captivated him and when he was still only a young boy a man named "Brennan" had been discovered in a strange space ship. Brennan was supposedly from earth. The Goners had risen after that time, becoming more accepted and their beliefs had spread.

The earth people had built a race of machines and created programs that gave true artificial intelligence. Earth had rejoiced at this new-found technology. They had sent these machines out into the cosmos to find new worlds and make them habitable for humans. They called these machines the terraformers (TF). They would later become known as the Xenon (alien). After many earth years it was decided that the terraformers were not required anymore and no more were built or sent out (mainly due to the Gate discovery - later). The earth government had decided to no longer fund this venture, as it was becoming too expensive. Messages were sent out to the terraformers to tell them to halt their missions. What earth did not know at the time is that not all of these messages got through and the machines continued to terraform and multiply, as per their original instructions. Earth almost forgot about them, but a software update was sent out to the few remaining ones to instruct them to destroy themselves. It was thought that only a few existed. However, unknown to earth, there were many still left and they had been continuing to multiply. The software update had flaws and the terraformers were instructed to remove everything else, not themselves! They distributed this flawed update between their own kind.

The earth people had discovered how to create jump gates that joined the universe together. Great objects lying in space. When you entered a gate you were transferred to another gate at the receiving end. The humans from earth had managed to create this remarkable machine and had built two and sent one on it's way to one of their closest stars, Alpha Centurai. It would take years to arrive.

One in earth space and the other on it's way to a distant star. When it did arrive they would have an almost instant journey between the two. But while the gate was on its way, the first gate (in earth space) had tried to obtain a lock and had found, to the great surprise of the scientists and engineers that they had locked onto another gate, not the one they had built.

They soon found that they were locking onto gates at random positions around the universe. These were other gates of alien origin! A ship was constructed (the WinterBlossom) to go in search of the gates carrying a twelve strong team of scientists, led by Captain Rene Farnham. Originally planned for a one-year journey, the WinterBlossom returned after two years. The information they obtained was amazing. There were gates everywhere, scattered around the universe. But despite extensive probing they had found no intelligent life in space itself. Some planets looked habitable and they were certain that they found intelligent life on some of the worlds, but the ship was not fitted with the equipment for any planet side excursions.

The earth government was concerned about the ease at which space was opening up and the way these vast distances could be travelled in such a short time span. They began to build defence ships that orbited the earth in the event of any alien incursions, not that any aliens had been found at all.

Over a hundred years later, a fleet of six TF ships suddenly entered the solar system through the gate and began to terraform the outer planets. They used all available resources as they were originally instructed to do and in their mission, began to destroy man made structures.

Nathan R Gunne, a brilliant strategist of the time, led a fleet of earth ships against the TF and in a brilliant tactical manoeuvre, tricked the TF ships into following him though the earth made gate. The gate was destroyed immediately after.

The creators of the gates (the Ancients) which no-one is aware of up until Brett's entry into the universe, oversee these events and decide to reconfigure the gates so that they create a closed loop where nothing can get out and nothing can get in. This loop cuts earth out. The old ones have plans to create a universe of races that can live together, including the terraformers. But the battles that raged around earth space make them wary of humans, they do not want them to be included in the plans for a peaceful universe.

The Teladi who are another space fairing race fall foul of this reconfiguration and as such, their home world "Ianamus Zura" is cut off forever. Only a few remote Teladi settlements remain in the loop. They have only basic equipment and space flight. It will be a long time before the Teladi roam the universe again.

Nathan R Gunne fought the Terraformers in the Alpha Centurai system where they followed him through the earth gate before its destruction.

Many of the humans died in the conflict, including many of the humans that were living in the system. Alpha Centurai had become Earth's largest outpost over the years, with hundreds of thousands of inhabitants. The Terraformers though had been defeated, although not eliminated. They retreated back into the cosmos. The humans knew that they could not get back to earth, the gates had been realigned, the earth gate destroyed. They decided to rewrite the history books and earth history was removed. However, there were still those that stood up for original history, who believed that it should be taught. But these were few compared to the many and the history books remained earth-less.

Many years later a new planet was discovered only twelve jumps away from Alpha Centurai. It seemed that this could sustain the human population and was a much better suited environment to live in. The majority of the humans moved to the new planet. It was called Four, after the star in the system, Sonra-4.

At the earth age of 93, Gunne a ruthless pirate who had so magnificently come to the humans aid, died and the planet that they now called home was renamed "Argon" in his memory. The humans now referred to themselves as Argon instead of human and the history books are rewritten once again.

The government of the humans finally agrees to move (from Alpha Centurai) to Argon and forever after the planet is known as Argon Prime.

The terraformers were beginning to launch incursions into Argon space. A band of Argon traders decides to seek out the old earth gate that is still in existence (in the ship AP Gunner). These were space fairing individuals who ferried goods between the ever expanding Argon territories. More and more worlds were being visited and the Argon Empire was continually expanding. Many years had passed and the history books had the existence of the second earth gate removed. They travel for three years and finally find the gate. It is intact, so they decide to disable it and destroy its electronics. A plaque is left on the gate explaining why it has been disabled. The "Gunners" as they have called themselves return to Argon space and begin to spread the word about the earth gate and history of the Argon. More and more people begin to gravitate towards this belief.

This information once compiled becomes known as the "Book of Truth" and is a strict religious belief of some of the Argon people. This group of believers becomes known as the Goners.

Soon after, the terraformers attacked an Argon reconnaissance ship, but the ship survived! It was able to communicate back the details of the attackers. The Argon named the attackers Xenon (alien) and it was found that these were the original terraformers who had mutated beyond belief.

The following (earth) year the Xenon finally entered central Argon space and attacked and destroyed the Argon space station "The Antigone". Thousands died in the attack and at last the Argon government decided to retaliate. This chapter in the Argon history became known as the Xenon war and lasted over forty earth years.

During this time the Argon had met and made friends with the Paranid. Agreements were made between the two races that in principle, they would co-operate.

Also, during the Xenon war years the Boron had finally managed space flight and had begun to colonise their local worlds and moons.

The Argon government turned to their newly found allies, the Paranid, for support and help during the conflict. The debates actually lasted many earth years, but in the end, the Paranid refused to be involved, as the Xenon did not directly threaten them.

The Xenon had become more aggressive and were continually attacking and destroying Argon outposts. Something had to be done and it had to be decisive.

The Argon had built up a considerable fleet during the years that were orbiting the homeworld of Argon Prime. The command was given and the whole Argon fleet ventured into space to engage the Xenon threat head on.

Many battles followed, but over time the Argon navy, together with their trader brethren, began to turn the tide. Lost territories were regained and the Xenon were repeatedly beaten and forced onto the defensive. Finally the Xenon retreated back to where they had come from and the attacks on the Argon ceased. The Argon had won the Xenon war!

During this time the Boron had begun to colonise space and their kingdom was stretching further out. Unfortunately they began to colonise a sector that belonged to the Split, a race of warlike creatures that didn't know the art of negotiation. The Split had been the last of these races to achieve space flight, but they had quickly caught up with the other races with their (rather crude) ships. The Split attacked the Boron without remorse, killing thousands, but instead of driving them out of their sector, the Split began a systematic destruction of everything Boron. This lasted ten years until the Boron were on the brink of extinction.

The Split moved ever outward, chasing the Boron back until they were only fighting in their own sector.

The Boron had met the Argon and after initial trading deals that had been initiated by the pioneering traders at that time, formerly approached the Argon government. The talks were under tight security and absolute secrecy, but the two races agreed to some basic trading rights and this would become known as the "Foundation Guild" later.

The Split were amassing a large fleet for a final attack on the Boron when they encountered the first Argon they had ever met. These were the pioneering traders, assorted ships built mainly for mining and exploration and the Split forward units attacked them. The traders fought the Split for years in many hit and run, disruptive type attacks. This slowed the Split's plans and it took them longer than planned to put the fleet into place. The Split had also met and befriended the Paranid during this time, a fact that the Argon were unaware of.

Suddenly part of the Argon fleet was attacked by the aggressive Split navy. A detachment of Paranid ships was recognised in formation with the Split. The Argon government immediately gave orders to the massive navy and it set course for the Split advanced fleet. Just as the Split were about to launch their final and devastating attack on the Boron, the Argon navy arrived.

The battle was ferocious, but the joint forces of the Argon and the Boron defeated the Split over the skies of the Boron home planet and the following years saw the alliance forces reverse all the gains that the Split had made. The Boron are a technically advanced race, developing the finest shield and weapon systems. They shared these technologies with the Argon and over a period of one hundred years (from the first Split aggression towards the Boron), the war raged.

The Paranid and Split forces finally sued for peace, their respective fleets being in the same positions they had started out from at the outset of the war. This period of conflict was known as the "Boron campaign" to the Argon. The Split were so devastated at their defeat that they endured an internal revolt and the Split emperor was removed. The Split and Paranid begin to argue between themselves and various small-scale battles were fought between the two.

The Argon and Boron officially sign the "Foundation Guild" treaty and now have many goods being traded between the two races. The Paranid and Split who have finally put their disagreements behind them form the "Profit Guild" as a direct move against the Foundation Guild.

Over a hundred years later, the reptilian Teladi settlements rediscovered advanced space travel. Their colonies cut off from the homeworld after the gate reconfiguration. Untouched by the other races because of their lack of space involvement offered no real benefits to others. They begin to trade with the other races and show no aggressive signs at all, preferring to trade and make profit.

The Foundation Guild approaches the Teladi in an attempt to get them to join, but the Teladi refuse to enter into any agreement, mainly because they prefer their own currency system. However, after years of negotiation, the Teladi join the Profit Guild instead.

Twenty-six years later, in an astonishing act of co-operation, both the Foundation Guild and the Profit Guild agree on a single universal currency to ease the trade levies. This currency is called "Credits" and from that point onwards, every space race uses them as a means of trade. This is referred to as the Great Currency Reform.

Over the next hundred years space becomes a safer place, traders and stations manufacturing goods appear everywhere and the Teladi become the strongest race in terms of financial stance. It is this position that enables them to influence the Guilds to adopt the Teladi time system based on Sezuras and Jazuras.

The Argon, like the other races still maintain their own time systems on their own worlds. Many of the races have millions of beings that never venture into space and are not interested in converting their fundamental time systems. But the basis is that the Teladi system, when compared to the Argon system is similar, but with longer units of time. For example, a Sezura is 1.7 seconds and a Mizura is 2.72 minutes. This carries on until it reaches a Jazura, which is 1.36 years.

| | | |
|---|---|---|
| Sezura | = | Second |
| Mizura | = | Minute |
| Stazura | = | Hour |
| Tazura | = | Day |
| Wozura | = | Week |
| Mazura | = | Month |
| Jazura | = | Year |

The Xenon (TF) dispatch a ship using its own jumpdrive technology directly into earth space. The earth government is astonished at this new breakthrough in technology and begin a project to develop their own system using the captured remains of the TF ship.

Seven years later they test their new technology, the X-Shuttle. Piloted by Captain Kyle William Brennan, it malfunctions and arrives in Teladi space. Brett is four Jazuras old (five years) when this happens. He remembers watching the news broadcasts at the time and especially the view of the Argon fleet as it moved out of Argon Prime space and proceeded to intercept the newly risen Xenon threat.

Brennan is instrumental in the defeat of the Xenon; he actually flies the final attack on the Xenon mother ship himself. The Xenon are defeated once again and move further back into uncharted areas. The Argon rejoice and the Goners (Gunners) rise to prominence as it is now undeniably true that earth does exist if Brennan is to be believed, even though the Argon attempted to remove its existence from history.

The X-Shuttle is damaged but after many years of trying they finally manage, with the help of the Boron scientists, to make a workable jumpdrive. It takes another few years, but the drive becomes commercially available to the richest pilots.

Brett is seven Jazura when he decides that he will meet these other races, that he will travel the space lanes. Little does he know that he will go to places that he could never imagine at such a young age. He is ten when the Argon navy visits the orphanage and offers him (although he actually has little choice in the decision) the chance to go and live at Morang and train to be a pilot. He agrees before the navy officer has finished explaining the offer, he knows it is time.

## Chapter 3: The plot thickens

*For every push to the left, there is an equal push to the right. Maybe not in the same place, but it will happen nonetheless. Whenever something is established that some see as good, there will always be the opposite view. That is as it always has been and probably always will.*

Faa t'Zrrk had left the station that was his home and travelled two complete sectors further out into cosmos, away from the centre of Split. He had sold his company issued ship at one of the shipyards. No questions would be asked in these areas, it would be repainted, given a new electronic identity and resold, probably before he even left the shipyard.

So he had purchased an old freighter ship, slow and unforgiving. But it was the perfect vessel for the next part of his journey. It would blend in with the rest of the space traffic. A Split freighter in the outer sectors of Split space, he was just like all the others, ideal.

He wasted no time in fitting the ship with the necessary equipment and supplies for the journey ahead. The attendants on the shipyard didn't even give him a second glance, no checking of credentials, he had the credits and the transfer of them from his personal account had proceeded without a hitch. He was Split himself after all. Now it was a matter of navigating the space lanes and arriving on time.

He calculated the journey time and felt satisfied that everything was, so far, going to plan. He stood in the long stay holding dock walking around the large ship. It was definitely old, it's paintwork tarnished from many journeys past harmful stars and radiation clouds. Scorch marks around the massive single engine at the rear and a few dents in the bodywork itself. He satisfied himself that it looked space-worthy and the data readout confirmed the same. He made a conscious effort to remove the readout from his image and the slave chip he had installed followed his wishes. The image slowly dissolved.

Accessing the flight system, he ordered the flight deck door to open and heard a slight hiss as it moved upwards and outwards away from the ship's hull. He walked towards it and made the single large step to enter the ship, pressing the manual button on the inside of the hull to close the door.

It was only a short few steps to enter the flight deck. A small area with two seats, a console and the large space screen. He could see another similar shaped ship being towed slowly out to the launch area further down the bay. Behind him was a small compartment with a bunk and an area to get refreshed with a sonic shower. He was glad he had opted for such a large ship as these kind of small comforts were rare and this ship even had an artificial gravity system, comfort indeed.

He accessed the ship's scanning systems and checked the local sector. It was full of traffic, he counted over a hundred ships all going about their business. Ferrying goods from one factory to another or performing protection duties for other ships or factories. A busy sector this, he was five sectors away from his destination, that was a considerable distance and it would take him over two Tazura to get there. Then if everything went to plan, he would have to travel a further ten sectors, partly doubling back on himself for the final meeting.

It was a tense time, but with the plan now underway he didn't have time to feel it properly, he was too busy and that was good. If he thought about it too long he might just convince himself that it wasn't a good idea. But the ENeT security group had almost surely linked his mysterious departure with the destruction of the factory in Paranid space. If they hadn't yet, they would eventually. He had left no reason, no evidence as to why he had gone in the hope that it might throw them off his trail for a while. As soon as they knew, they would hunt him down and they wouldn't stop to ask questions. His actions had made him an outlaw within the company. Of that there was no doubt.

But if everything went to plan, he would take his credits and go to one of the pleasure planets, a place where beings went to relax. But he would stay there forever, never again venturing into the dark cold void that was space. He would live out his life in luxury, at least that was the idea. Just a few more loose ends to tie up and the small matter of delivering the goods and then freedom, he hoped.

He was beginning to feel slightly ill at the thought of it all. Time to get on with the job in hand. He mentally accessed the communications system and asked the automated station traffic computer for clearance to launch. It came back with a positive reply and he waited for the small robot tug to move to the front of his ship and attach a tow belt. He could quite easily navigate his ship out of the dock and into space itself, but it was not allowed within the stations. No engines, no weapons and no shields allowed. You kept them all disabled while the automated systems moved your ship into a launch position. Then you could fire your engines and enter the void. The laser turrets that adorned the ceiling of the bays would fire on any ship that attempted to break these rules. The same regulations applied throughout known space. It was a time wasting exercise as far as Faa t'Zrrk was concerned, but there were many rookie pilots around, so it made sense.

He felt the slight "tug" on the ship as the robot pulled it forward down the bay. A hundred metres away stood the launch door, it was just closing as the ship he had witnessed being pulled away before had just launched. As they approached the door, he could see to his left two sleek attack craft. They were undergoing some form of maintenance, he couldn't tell what, he wasn't an engineer. But they looked fast and manoeuvrable. He half wished he was in one now, the journey time would be considerably less and any trouble could be dealt with in such a ship. But they were too obvious. Ships like that attracted attention, particularly in the outer sectors where he was going. The pirates and illegal companies ran most of these areas and any ship like that would attract immediate scans. If it didn't show up as a local ship, there was a good chance of being attacked. No, he didn't like it, but he was better off in his ship. Also, such a long journey in a small craft didn't bear thinking about, oh the discomfort!

The robot was now pulling his ship through the now fully opened door. It slued to the right and his ship followed it. After about twenty metres it came to a halt and the second tug that was at the rear of the ship, took the strain and negated the forward movement so that his ship came to a complete stop.

The two tugs disengaged and vanished through the door behind him. It slowly began to descend and came to halt as it entered the slit in the floor ready to accommodate it and create a secure, atmosphere and blast proof seal.

He could see the air being sucked out of the launch bay, slight white wafts appeared by the vents as the area became a vacuum ready for the outer door to be opened.

He saw the confirmation light flash on the console. Launch confirmed. He now had twenty Sezura to abort the action and get pulled back into the bay or the outer doors would open and he could fire his engines.

He manually confirmed his request to launch so that he wouldn't have to wait any longer and the engine light turned from red to amber. When it went green he could fire his engines and be away.

The outer doors began to open. A split appeared horizontally across the middle as the top half went upwards and the bottom half downwards. He saw the indicator flash its confirm to tell him that the clamps on the portable "cot" that his ship was sat on top of, had been released. The ship floated in space and the engine light went to green.

He pressed the button to start the engine and set his speed to ten metres a second. The ship began to approach the waiting opening. He could see the darkness of space outside, a multitude of stars staring back at him, dim and distant. He made sure he was securely seated and the straps were fastened across his chest, then he switched off the artificial gravity. He felt a slight dizziness accompanied with a feeling of sickness. But that was the normal feeling when going from gravity to weightlessness.

He confirmed a speed of fifty, the fastest this ship could go and the opening suddenly disappeared and he was heading out into space. He let the ship fly on its original course for two kilometres and then turned thirty degrees to the left in the general direction of the jump gate, thirty-two kilometres away.

A quick scan of the surrounding ships and he felt happy that he was not being followed. He closed his eyes in an attempt to get a little rest, but it didn't help.

* * * * * * * *

The pirate fleet that had carried out the attack in Paranid space had gone many different ways as soon as they had exited the gate after the battle. The Paranid navy would probably be on the lookout and it was much easier to spot a large fleet of ships than it was to pick them out among all the others.

The assault ship carrying the Super Slaves was the prize and it was being flanked by two large fighter craft. They headed straight for the

Split outer sectors and their intended rendezvous. The captain had sent out an encoded message drone as soon as they were underway. It had arrived back with a confirmation of receipt. The drones were very small, extremely fast devices that used the gates to traverse the systems and deliver messages. They took time however, even though they were fast and it made interactive communications between sectors troublesome.

Twenty three million credits was the price they had agreed for the Slave chips and the data banks. They were of no use to the pirates, they had been hired to do a job and they had done it. Eight million credits had already been paid, so they were aiming to collect the rest at the meeting.

The information regarding the shield grid on the station had proved to be correct. All shields generated a field where anything could go one way through, as if it was not there. But the other side created a strong energy field that protected against physical objects. That included missiles and lasers. But the shields had to reconfigure themselves at pre set intervals. If you knew the interval and you timed your shot at the right time, you could find a weakness. The information had given them the exact timings of the factory and the time it took for the reconfiguration to be implemented. It had proven to be correct. The new factory installation would force the shield system to immediately throw its protective cover over the new extension. But then exactly twenty-three Mizura later, it would run a complete system configuration and when it had finished four Sezura later, it would reconfigure the shield system. This took eight Sezura for the whole station and the new rig would be the last to benefit. That was how long it had taken to blow the join apart.

They had to destroy the whole station, as the investigation teams would find this information if anything was left to investigate. So with no station, the cunning plan would remain secret and the source of the information, Faa t'Zrrk would stay secret as well.

The three pirate vessels continued on their journey.

* * * * * * * *

LooManckStrat was inconsolable after the attack, but he soon came around to the facts at hand. He had lost not only a large part of his business empire, but importantly he had lost the Super Slaves. What had been even worse was that all the data to make them and all the scientists and engineers who had played a part were gone. They had all been aboard the rig when it exploded, ready to celebrate the opening of the new production and the completion of their hard work.

His defence ships had proved worthless against such a strong and co-ordinated attack. He had already ordered further fighter craft and a training program to make them better. He did not want to see this happen again. Every station would be upgraded with more and better ships. He may have lost a large part of the business, but one thing he still had was a determination to succeed. Together with the fact that he had vast reserves of credits, he was ready to start again.

He knew that it would take many Jazura to recreate the chip. They would have to start from the beginning again. Do all the tests on the different races again, recruit the paid volunteers. It would take a long time.

He had already given the instruction for it to begin. Recruit the scientists and engineers, pay them whatever they required, but get them onto the ENeT Company list.

All these things were underway and he would attend to them when he needed to, but the most important thing now was to find out who had done it. He knew one of the pirate groups had actually staged the attack, but it was doubtful that they were behind it. No, someone else was behind this, another company perhaps or even another race. He wasn't sure at the moment. He was however, absolutely sure that he would find out.

His factory commander in Split space, Faa t'Zrrk, had vanished just after the attack. Faa t'Zrrk had been involved with the Super Slave, he knew about it and also had privileged information about the company. LooManckStrat didn't think Faa t'Zrrk could be a traitor, but he had gone somewhere and he intended to start there.

As soon as his defence ships were ready he was on his way to his factory in Split space. He had sent a message to the Split families who ruled the race, informing them of his intentions and asking them to begin their own inquiries. They had replied that they would investigate the disappearance of Faa t'Zrrk, but they didn't like the idea of a fleet of ships entering their domain.

LooManckStrat told them that his intentions were peaceful and that he would leave the majority of his ships in the outer sectors, but his company was an important employer for them and they should help him as much as possible.

The Split eventually agreed, but only after some pressure from the Paranid delegation at the Profit Guild, of which the Split were also members.

This process had taken two Wozura, but it enabled him to order his ships from the Paranid shipyards and organise the purchase of his new pride and joy, a fully armed, brand new Class Six, Paranid destroyer. So, someone had attacked him, destroyed his station and murdered his employees. He would call that debt in, make no mistake.

He ordered a second destroyer which would take longer to arrive and he left orders for it to be left in his home sector. The work to rebuild the factory and install the original rigs had already begun. He would leave that to his minions while he investigated the attack personally.

Yes, something was definitely happening and someone was definitely behind it. He made preparations to join "Deliverance", his new destroyer. It was time to become detective.

## Chapter 4: Yaki

*You may find a hand that feeds more readily than the one you are used
to. But never forget one push to the left causes a push to the right and
it may come from a direction you didn't expect.*

The station rotated slowly in space, creating gravity that made it
almost like their home planet at the outer walls. This was where the
living quarters were situated and the residents, all five thousand four
hundred of them, had living space in the outer shell. Glorious rooms with
water showers and space screens looking directly out into the cosmos.

The station was immense, full three kilometres in diameter with a
globe like shape. At the top and bottom of the huge structure were the
launch bays. Large one hundred metre protrusions that looked so small
against their larger parent.

A thousand space screens scattered over its surface, light shining
out from many, some others dark, the inhabitants either in their
quarters of working deep in the centre of the station. Massive cargo
bays and storage tanks situated off the main corridor that ran from the
top to the bottom, from launch bay to launch bay.

A ship could actually fly all the way through the station if the seal
doors were opened all the way along the corridor. Laser towers
situated along the length of the corridor, ready to enforce the landing
regulations, should they be broken. Robotic helpers were moving about
their business, moving cargo back and to and stocking up on supplies.

The outside shell was littered with more defence systems. Station
launched missile batteries together with laser towers and their dual
cannons trained out into space. The telltale protrusions of the scanning
systems could be seen strategically placed over the surface, some
stationary, while others revolved continuously, feeding data into the
weapon systems ever ready to react to any given threat.

The whole station was a deep, dark blue colour. No other colours at
all were visible on its surface. Outside and a few kilometres away sat an
Argon cruiser, motionless in space. Its colour the same as the station,
no visible light emitting from it whatsoever. But its systems were online
and scanning for any threats in the same way the station was. Slightly
further out from the cruiser lay a Paranid destroyer, the same colour
again, some lights flickering and a slight glow from its engines as it had
only just moved into its position to flank and protect the large cruiser
ship.

Three large fighters were approaching the station from the opposite
side to the large ships. Bright white ships, but with a jagged pattern
covering their hulls. Thick lines and patterns creating a camouflage
effect in the same blue colour as the station. The pattern was a
signature. However, it held no value, as camouflage was completely
useless in space, but it showed other ships the origin, let them know
where these ships had come from and most importantly whom they
belonged to.

The station was the only permanent fixture in the whole sector. Deep in space in the currently uninhabited sectors between the Split and the Teladi civilisation sectors. They would not be discovered here for a long time and any ships that came close would be dealt with. The station sold no goods, nor did it manufacture any. It was a base of operations.

Inside the station in a large room in the outer shell sat a group of beings, a collection of different races including Split, Paranid and Argon. They were seated around a large ornate table made from Cry wood, carved and polished from the forests on Sentuie in Paranid space. They sat on chairs made from the same wood, high backed examples with decoration carved into the tops.

They were the pirate leaders who had agreed to join together. At the head of the table sat Moo-Kye, Argon female and self-elected leader of the group. She was dressed in a close fitting body suit of the same colour as the station. A weapons belt around her waist containing a laser hand gun. She stood and moved away from the table, the small crown built into the headpiece of the body suit glittering from the light that shone down from the ceiling.

"So." She began. "Do we have the goods? What is the position of the strike force?"

Moo-Kye

The six other figures in the room looked at each other as if willing one another to answer. One of the two Paranid members, still dressed in his environment suit without the helmet, spoke up.

"The goods are about to be delivered Moo-Kye. The strike force is in place and they have their orders. We can do nothing to alter the events now, they are too far away."

"Good!" She hissed. "It is time for the universe to be aware of us, the Yaki!" She clenched a fist as she spoke. "Ensure the goods arrive, or do not bother to speak to me again."

* * * * * * * *

Faa t'Zrrk slowed his ship to a halt. He was, give or take a few hundred metres, in exactly the position he was supposed to be in. The sector was empty of installations apart from a single energy cell factory that was far away. Someone had obviously decided that this was a good place to start trading and had probably deployed the station in preparation for others to follow.

His scanner did show a small asteroid field, so maybe someone was going to begin mining them. A single slow moving freight ship was visible on the scanner close to the station. Probably returning from picking up supplies, he thought. The only other ships in the whole sector were heading directly for him. A freighter sized attack ship flanked by two large fighter craft. They gave off the pirate signatures on the scanner. Faa t'Zrrk watched them approach, his apprehension beginning to increase the closer they got.

The communication console blinked to indicate an incoming message. He gestured to his slave chip and confirmed that it was being received over the secure channel that had been agreed. He brought the signal onto the main viewing screen.

"Ah!" The pirate spoke. "We meet again at last!"

Faa t'Zrrk saw the face of the Split pirate who he had met and divulged the information to when he was on the pleasure world, taking his permitted leave of absence from his position in the factory.

"So we do." Faa t'Zrrk replied. "You have the goods?" he inquired.

The pirate smiled and delayed his answer long enough to annoy Faa t'Zrrk. "Of course we have the goods, do you have the credits?"

"I have the credits." He confirmed. "Bring your ship alongside so that we can perform the transfer."

"Agreed."

The actual transfer of goods and credits would take place at the same time. It was a transaction that required systems on both ships to confirm that each of the parts of the transaction had taken place. If either system disagreed, they would automatically undo the transfers. Someone could modify one end of the system in an attempt to steal goods or not pay, but this would not affect the other side and the deal would be undone anyway.

This way of trading had been law throughout the universe for as long as anyone could remember. It worked and even the illegal groups would comply when they were trading. Anyone breaking the regulations that got reported was an outlaw by all members of both the foundation and profit guilds.

The only problem was that It had to be reported and Faa t'Zrrk was a little concerned that his life might be nearing its end. But he had thought it through many times. The pirates he was dealing with knew that he was working for someone else. They didn't know whom, but could guess by the amount of credits in the deal, that it was someone of considerable importance. If they made any attempts to renege on the deal, they could imagine the consequences. No, this deal would go ahead as planned.

The pirate vessel came along side. With no other way to transfer the cargo other than to drop it into space and allow the other ship to scoop it up, via it's cargo handling system. The onboard trading system would automatically transfer the remaining credits as soon as it received confirmation from the cargo hold.

The cargo pod was jettisoned into space and the pirate ship moved a slight distance away to allow Faa t'Zrrk to approach it. He grabbed the control stick and manually adjusted the engine power and the ship gently moved forward. He made a slight adjustment to the stick and the ship turned towards the pod. It was a standard cargo pod, large in size, even though it's contents were small. These pods were standard issue and all ships were equipped to carry the standard size, as were the stations. It was one more act of race co-operation that made trading that much easier.

He mentally told the system to open the cargo bay and immediately saw the visible warning on the instrument panel, shields down. This was the crucial part of the manoeuvre, nothing could be brought onto the ship while the shields were active, it would simply be repelled by the shields or more likely explode from the impact. So the shields were automatically taken off line when the cargo bay was opened, leaving the ship, and Faa t'Zrrk extremely vulnerable.

He steered the ship directly at the pod and, heart racing, scanned the instruments and visual aids for any indication that the pirate ships were doing anything that might alarm him. Thankfully they didn't and as he saw the pod visibly disappear below the space screen and below the ship, he was warmed by the audible bleep that confirmed the cargo had been successfully loaded. He saw the credits on the screen negate the agreed amount and the cargo inventory displayed the entry, "Slave Chips – Quantity One Hundred". Good, deal done, now time to vacate the area, quickly!

The pirate's face appeared on the communication screen one last time. "Thank you for the business Faa t'Zrrk. I hope we can trade again."

"Yes," he replied, "so do I."

With that the pirate ship and its two protectors turned and began to speed away. At last, he thought, I have the chips! Now I must deliver them.

He began to steer the ship in the opposite direction to the retreating pirate ships, increasing his speed to maximum, when he noticed a number of other ships appear on the scanner.

"Oh No!" He gasped. Not ENeT security forces here? They couldn't have found him this easily, this soon, could they?

He ignored his slave link and manually stabbed at the buttons on the console to scan the incoming ships. Combat pilots were trained to use the chip in situations like this. That was what sometimes made the difference between living and dying. But traders were not as well trained or disciplined as fighter pilots and Faa t'Zrrk was no fighter pilot. He began to frantically search the screen in the hope that it might give up its secrets, when the communication channel opened.

"Faa t'Zrrk?"

He was astonished, no one knew he was here, who was it?

"Yes?" he replied, his voice giving away his state of mind. "This is Faa t'Zrrk, what do you want?"

"Faa t'Zrrk, we are here to escort you to your destination. Hold your position and await further orders. Are those ships the pirates that you have traded with?"

"Understood." He eased down the engine power. "Confirmed, those are the pirates."

"Good, do not move from your position." Came the reply, blank and expressionless.

His ship came to halt, the engines reversing the forward momentum until it stopped. He counted the ships on the scanner, twelve Argon heavy fighters, probably armed with powerful lasers and space attack missiles. Quite an escort for a single ship, he watched on the screen as they approached and then moved to glance out of the space screen to see if he could get a visual of them, he wanted to see this.

They approached at full speed, four ships abreast in three lines, one behind the other. The last line slowed as they neared and veered towards him. The others continued on and began to pass him. He could see them in fine detail now, white ships with deep blue jagged stripes. Lasers clearly visible on the outer tips of the wing shaped weapon mountings. He watched them as they went past and had to turn away as their engines came into view and the bright light nearly blinded him.

The pirate ships were now some distance away, but they must have read the situation well. The large attack ship, slow and cumbersome, was continuing on its course. But the two protection ships had turned towards their pursuers, sensing that they would not make it to the jump gate. It was a vain attempt to give their comrade a slim chance of escape.

Faa t'Zrrk reached for his zoom lenses that were attached to the wall next to the edge of the space screen and located the now advancing pirate ships. Two against eight, the pirates were going to die, or at least be forced to eject from their ships. Could they slow the attackers in time? He doubted it. Closer and closer they came. The eight ships held their position, two lines of four and when they were within eight kilometres, Faa t'Zrrk saw the telltale small intense glows of seeker missile engines. Firing as they left their launch ships, accelerating to a speed twice as fast as the ships themselves and heading for their targets the two pirate ships, and so many missiles he couldn't count them all.

The pirates took immediate evasive action, one ship headed vertical, twisting and turning as it went. The other repeated the technique, but went down, causing the missiles to make a decision on which ship to go for. The missiles must have made their choices as they parted into two groups, each one seeking out one of the pirates. The eight ships continued on their course.

The pirate assault ship was nearing the gate when the ships pounced. All four ships from the first line began firing their lasers. Faa t'Zrrk watched on as the flashes from the pirates' shields made a dazzling display. The pirate ship tried to zigzag to avoid the incoming fire, but it was to no avail.

The first line of ships simply speeded past the pirate and the second line took up the same offensive stance, all four firing their lasers into the fading shields of their prey. The pirate must have decided enough was enough and that if he was about to die, it may as well be in attack rather than defence.

The second row of ships was just passing over the pirate when Faa t'Zrrk saw the salvo of "Factory Killers" leave the pirate ship. The four attackers broke formation straight away, but the missiles were too close to evade and two of them made a direct hit on two of the ships. He watched as one exploded, quickly followed by a second. A large explosion, a quick bright light, followed by debris and fire that was quickly extinguished in the vacuum. It was an eerie sight, watching an explosion without any sound following it.

By now the first line of ships had turned and was approaching from the other side, head to head with the pirate. They unleashed a fresh wave of seeker missiles, something the large pirate had no chance of evading. He again saw the hits on the shield and then a third explosion filled his lenses as the pirate ship disintegrated, its shield energy spent.

The six remaining ships then formed into two groups of three and each group sought out one of the two pirate fighters that had just finished either evading the missiles until they ran out of fuel, or had succeeded in destroying them.

The pirates hit full speed and ran for the gate. They had greater speed than the Argon ships and would have to make, hopefully, just a single pass on their way out. They approached the attackers, lasers firing as they came. The six ships were taking some hits, but still they came, returning the fire as the two forces swept into each other. A blinding flash! Faa t'Zrrk checked his scanner, confirmed. One of the pirates and one of the escort ships had collided head on, shields down from the laser battle they had both exploded on impact.

He put the lenses back to his eyes and saw the remaining pirate ship pass through the group and head for the gate. The attackers turned, seeker missiles launching as they did so, the gap between them already too great for effective laser fire to have any impact. He was going to make it!

On and on the pirate fled it's attackers. The distance between it and the other ships getting greater, while the distance from the group of seeker missiles was shortening. It was almost on the point of entering the jump gate when the missiles found their target. The familiar glow from the shields as the missiles impacted one by one. Five, six, seven missiles hit, still the pirate headed for the gate. Eight, nine, ten, bang! Its luck finally ran out and the pirate ship exploded on the verge of escape.

"Mission accomplished. Faa t'Zrrk? Accelerate to maximum speed and continue your journey." The message came through the visual link and Faa t'Zrrk saw it via his slave.

"Yes," he replied, seating the lenses back into their holding bracket and instructing the ship to full speed. He sat down in the pilot seat and simply stared out of the space screen. What have I got involved in? He pondered this as the escort ships swarmed around him.

* * * * * * * *

It took several Tazuras of travelling through empty sectors before they reached the Yaki base. Faa t'Zrrk had thought the whole episode through again and again. It was possible that the pirate ships had managed to launch message drones before they were killed. If they had, what had they said? Faa t'Zrrk may now be a wanted Split by those pirates, they still had many ships left and they had lost a great deal, risked even more and had nothing to show for it.

He was worried, the pirates were a resourceful lot and they would find him and enact their revenge. Where could he go now? He would have to think about that later, as now, slowly growing in size in his space screen was the Yaki base, large ships motionless beside it. He realised for the first time in his life that he was doing something that was completely out of his control. He had no say in the outcome of the upcoming meeting. He had started out on this venture full of enthusiasm that his cunning skills at trading and negotiation would see him through. But now he had watched the savagery of the Yaki attack, he felt powerless to alter the course of his destiny. He would have to play it out and see what became of him and he didn't like that. It was not in the Split nature to lose control of the situation and it bothered him greatly. His ship approached the base.

The escort ships slowed to a halt and let him proceed to the upper docking bay on his own. He requested landing permission from the docking computer and was immediately granted it. They were expecting him. He decided to navigate the ship into the dock manually, a strange feeling that it might be the last time he was able to do so.

He moved towards the top of the base, pointing his ship directly at the launch bay. Then just before he would have hit it, he veered away, heading away from the base. He slowed the ship and then turned it back on itself so the docking bay was directly in front of him.

The large doors were open, just the edges visible as they locked into position to allow him to proceed. He could see the navigation lights emitting from the station, blinking green to confirm that he had permission to advance. Faa t'Zrrk slowly eased the ship forward and into the mouth that was the docking bay. He watched through the screen as the door edges flashed past and then he slowed the ship to a stop as his console confirmed he had entered the station.

The doors closed behind him and when fully sealed, the area began to fill with atmosphere from the station. Red lights circling all around him and then suddenly they stopped, he was in.

The inner doors began to open this time side to side, instead of top to bottom and the familiar site of the robot tugs greeted him, as they came through the opening and attached themselves to his ship. He felt a slight movement as they began to propel his ship into the station itself and the docking bay beyond.

After the ship was securely docked and fixed into place, Faa t'Zrrk pressed the door button and the ship's door opened to the sound of the dock. Metal clanking and bangs as items and cargo pods were moved around. He stepped from the ship.

"Diatri bu." He heard the voice from the Argon male stood next to the ship. He held up his hand and moved back into the ship. He had forgotten to bring his translator with him. A small device that fitted into each ear (depending upon the race) and translated the other species' language. Everyone in space had them inserted most of the time, but they became uncomfortable for long periods and he removed them on his long journey, as the ship systems would do the job for him.

He picked them up, inserted one into each ear and once again left the ship. The Argon male was still there, waiting.

"Follow me." He said.

"I will." Faa t'Zrrk replied and began to walk behind him as he quickly moved away. The Argon could always move quicker than the Split and he struggled to keep up.

They walked through many corridors, took rides in the quick deployment cubes and finally arrived at the door that was the destination. The Argon male gestured to Faa t'Zrrk. "In there." It was all he said and then walked away.

Faa t'Zrrk stood for a moment, contemplating his position. Be strong, think straight he told himself. Beyond this door lies your future, your destiny! He pressed his hand on the door release and it opened without a sound, sliding to the left.

"Ah, at last! Faa t'Zrrk do come in, join us. It has been a long time waiting to meet you."

The voice came from the Argon female dressed in dark blue. She must be Moo-Kye he thought as he entered the room. The door closed behind him and the other beings turned to survey him as he walked towards the large table in the middle of the room. He saw two Argon, two Split and two Paranid. He could tell from the dress that these were pirates. They must be the leaders of the pirate groups that Moo-Kye had forged together to create the Yaki.

"Come Faa t'Zrrk, sit down. You must be tired from your long journey. Rest. You have been very important to us recently."

He took the vacant chair at the nearest end of the table, away from Moo-Kye who was at the other end. He didn't much care for the Argon as a rule. Argon were a self-opinionated lot and he could quite happily live out his life without ever coming into contact with them again. But he could see that Moo-Kye was a stunning example of their female gender. She had the look and lines of the Argon females he had viewed in the news broadcasts. She would be considered very attractive by her own race, he was sure. Slightly darkened skin and eyes that were deep brown. They held you in their brilliance. He also guessed her hair was dark, but it was tucked away under the head dress she wore.

"We have verified the cargo Faa t'Zrrk, it is good. Exactly as we ordered, you have done well for us." She moved as she spoke, back and to across the floor, but never once letting her eyes leave his. Let this be over and then I can leave, he thought. He wanted to avert his eyes, to stare out of the large space screen to his side, but he couldn't will himself to do it. She smelt of power, of ambition, the will to succeed. She was the dominant one in the room, the weakest physically maybe, but the leader without a doubt.

"So," he began, "what happens now Moo-Kye?"

She smiled, slowly and it seemed deliberately. She moved towards the head of table and rested the flat of her hands on it's top, leaning slightly as she did so.

"We dominate Faa t'Zrrk. We take back what is ours. For too long the Foundation and Profit guilds have had their own way. Charging levies on the trading deals, forcing limits on the prices of goods. Limiting the right to free trade."

"Do you know how many died as a result of the Profit Guilds insistence that the price of food stuffs should have a minimum value? I can tell you, hundreds of thousands and all because they saw profit first and life second. We told them, the outer systems must have access to open and free trade, the market will pay what the demand is, either low or high. So let the market decide."

She didn't falter as she continued.

"Odysseus Five Faa t'Zrrk, a pioneering outpost with no natural planetary bodies that can sustain life. Thousands of workers all crammed into the silicon mines, trying to earn enough credits to survive. No food, little energy from its pitiful star, all resources required to survive brought in. So what does the Profit Guild do? Raises the price of the food and lowers the price of silicon. Creates higher and lower bands with which to work in. The mines start to operate at a loss, the freighter ships don't come any more because they can't afford to."

"We tell them that people are starving, dying in the mines and the factories. Disease spreads, we can't get the antidotes, we can't leave and we can't stay. They ignore our pleas, sitting in nice cosy stations making decisions that affect lives, but only really concerned about their profit, their welfare, not ours. The governments refuse to listen, they point the finger at the Guilds. They discuss the issue, can you believe that? They discuss it! So while they are having meetings and attending banquets, our comrades die in their thousands."

"Can you imagine what it is like Faa t'Zrrk? To hold your partner in your arms, the silicone disease eating away at their body, coughing and spluttering, barely able to talk. Can you imagine what it is like to hold them and watch them die in front of you when you are incapable of saving them?"

"No ships, no food, no medicine, no credits, no future! Well I saw them die Faa t'Zrrk, I watched as my friends perished in front of me in the darkened corridors and shafts on Odysseus Five. One ship arrived to collect silicone, one ship! They killed their own kind to get on that ship, fighting in the docking corridor hand to hand with whatever strength they had left. I got on that ship Faa t'Zrrk and I vowed as we left the station that I would right the wrong done that Tazura."

"We have talked and talked with the Guild, but to no avail. They still refuse to listen to us, so here around this table you see the leaders of the groups who have agreed to join our fight. These may look like pirates to you, but in every pirate is a trader. They may deal in illegal goods, but they also have genuine business concerns that are dealt the same blows as the rest. Look at the Paranid, look at ENeT. They make Slave chips that are illegal in their own space lanes. One rule for us and one for rule for them. Well no more, the profiteering stops here and now. We will open up the trading lanes in the outer systems and then move inwards, until anything can be traded by anyone for anything."

Faa t'Zrrk was stunned, he didn't know this was in the plan. "Even illegal goods?"

"Especially illegal goods!" She replied.

"But there must be some control, some rules otherwise it will become chaos." He pleaded.

"We will control it. We will make the rules and change them as and when we see fit."

"But doesn't that make you the same as them?" he quizzed.

"NO!" She hissed. "They do not understand, we do, we have waited long enough and it is the time for action, not words. It will take many Jazura, but we will succeed, I know it!"

His mind was trying to take all of this in when he suddenly realised that she hadn't yet mentioned where he was to fit into all of this.

"So, what about me? What do you want me to do now?"

Moo-Kye looked down at the table, the first time she had broken eye contact during the whole outburst. Then she jerked her head back to stare at him once more.

"You are to be our messenger." She said.

"What! You want me to go back? They'll kill me!" He argued.

"Not Faa t'Zrrk, if you are already dead." She raised her arm from the table and the dart shot out from her bracelet, made a slight noise at it moved through the air and imbedded itself into Faa t'Zrrk's torso. He winced from the pain and felt a burning sensation deep inside his body. The dart had penetrated and then come to a stop, releasing a small explosive device that had moved deeper inside. Then it exploded, not enough to cause any outward damage, but enough to obliterate his internal organs. He died almost instantly, but not quite quick enough to escape the enormous pain that racked his body.

Moo-Kye looked around the table. "Did he really think I would let such a traitor live?"

"Ship his body back to the ENeT factory he came from and begin to distribute the Super Slaves as planned."

The six rose as one, two lifting the body from the chair where it had slumped over the table and they filed out of the room.

## Chapter 5: Searching for the truth

*You can search far and wide for the truth. But sometimes it comes looking for you.*

The gate flashed signifying that something was about to exit having made the trip across the cosmos. LooManckStrat sat in the bridge of "Deliverance" as the large ship moved away from the gate. His flotilla of ships following him and his smaller guard ships were ahead having already made the jump, scanning for any potential threat.

The message drone arrived just after they entered the sector, sent from deep within the Split sectors by the ruling families. He pressed the communication cube on the arm of his seat and the face of the Split family race relation's officer followed the familiar sight of the cube rising out of its home. He had spoken to this Split many times recently. But this message was the one he had been waiting for.

"We have Faa t'Zrrk. He his here, but I am sorry to inform you that he is dead. Please come immediately to the Split defence station adjacent to your factory. I can say no more, you must see this for yourself."

LooManckStrat took his personal guard and boarded his upgraded Spinny. He had made sure that it had better shielding and speed than before and it was now one of the fastest medium sized ships in the universe. It carried no offensive weapons but did have a number of small-automated fighter drones that could be launched against an attacker and also a selection of ship-to-ship missiles.

The drones were small pilot-less craft that were simply launched with a command to attack. They had small lasers and minimal shields, but they were fast and at the very least could harass an enemy while they made good their escape.

He positioned himself in the comfortable seat and gave the order to launch. The ship moved slowly towards the exit doors on the busy flight deck of the destroyer. It was only a small flight deck capable of handling only three to four ships at a time, but it gave the destroyer extra flexibility.

Two medium sized fighter craft were further down the deck, engines glowing and in the start of their launch. These were heavily armed and well protected ships that would guard the Spinny on its journey. A single fast scout ship had already exited the ship and was holding position outside while the others launched.

He watched as the two fighters lifted from the deck and proceeded out of the destroyer side by side. Then he felt the movement of his own ship as it followed them. They would have to run at half power for the journey or the large fighters wouldn't be able to stay close by. The scout ship would continually move ahead and jump through the next gate, ensuring the route was clear.

They were now all in space, the destroyer behind them and holding station for their return. The two fighters took positions on either side of the Spinny and the scout ship at the lead. They moved off together and the scout immediately increased its power and approached the far gate, it's single engine glowing brightly as it became smaller and smaller in the space screen.

LooManckStrat was intrigued with the Split message. So his factory commander was dead, he half expected it. But the fact that the Split wouldn't divulge any further information about the incident was what interested him. It was really not like the Split to ask him to come to them. They would normally have sent a minimal message and told him to stay away. He wouldn't have got the body, company employee or not. But to be asked to view it? That was an honour indeed. Yes, very intriguing.

They approached the jump gate. A large round metal structure that simply sat motionless in space. It had two large protruding arms that reached out from each side, straight ahead of the main gate. These arms went exactly the same distance behind the circle as they did in front of it and lights flashed up and down their length.

There was a great deal of debate about where the gates came from and who built them. Some said the Argon forefathers, others said the Xenon but the main consensus was that they had been built by another race and had been abandoned. No race really knew what the truth was and why they were here, but hundreds of gates had been found and they linked the sectors together. It was as if something had put them here at some point in the past, with the expectation that they would be used in the future.

They had scanned them, nothing. No power source could be found. The navigation lights had been added by the races themselves and small starlight powered generators fixed to the arms that provided endless fuel for the lights.

They had tried to analyse the material they were made from, but nothing could penetrate the skin. It was a complete mystery that linked the races, together with the cosmos. He thought that someday the creators of these gates might return. Ships had certainly been identified travelling far out from the populated planets and passing through the sectors. Identified as ships yes, but whose ships, no. The different governments argued over these sightings, each blaming the other for building covert military designs. But no piece of evidence had come forward at all for either theory, so they remained a puzzle.

The scout ship exited the gate and came back into the sector.

"All clear your honour. Nothing found and I mean nothing your honour. The following sector is empty."

"Good." Replied LooManckStrat. "Proceed." He instructed the other ships and his own pilot.

The four ships took their turns and each entered the gate with the Spinny going third, he didn't want to be left alone after all his ships had gone through. He could launch a message drone, but if there were to be any trouble that was violent, it would be over before they received the message and reacted. He had learnt one thing recently, be cautious and cover every possible angle you could. Think big, think detail, and think everywhere in-between. He wasn't about to get caught out again after losing his factory. At least not without putting up a serious fight.

The Spinny entered the gate. It was a surreal experience travelling through gates. You had to enter them very slowly or you simply passed through the circle and nothing happened. Then once you passed the event horizon you were greeted with a bright flash of light, followed by a tunnel of swirling colours. Every colour you could imagine seemed to make up the tunnel walls and through the sides of the tunnel you were certain your could see systems flash past. Then as sudden as you started you exited the tunnel. Not through an end point, it wasn't as if you could see the end of the tunnel and you could judge your movement down it. No, it was just there, a never-ending tunnel that just disappeared with the same flash of light as when you entered.

Then you would be in the distant sector, travelling at the same slow speed you had as you entered the gate at the other end. Very strange indeed, sensor scans revealed no fixed position during the journey, but as soon as you exited you were greeted with scanners that picked up all the local objects again. Although in this particular case the scanner only showed the scout ship and one of the fighter ships as there was nothing else in the sector at all. Empty of anything except natural objects like planets, meteors, suns and so on.

The second fighter ship joined them through the gate and they pointed their ships at the next gate far across the sector and continued their long journey.

* * * * * * * *

It took three Tazuras to reach the inner Split sectors where his factory was and LooManckStrat had to be woken from his rest time in his personal quarters. They had travelled through many sectors, most of them empty, but as they got close to the Split inner worlds the sectors began to have more and more artificial objects. Factories and mines attached to asteroids, traffic from the freight ships and as they entered the inner sector of Family Pride, homeworld of the Split, the military presence was massive. Large battleships and destroyers in stationary orbit around the planet and more adjacent to the truly gigantic ship building factory that was situated here. This was where most of the Split's ships were built and purchased. He could see no reason why he couldn't bring his whole fleet with him, they would be no match for the Split navy here. But regulations were to be obeyed. Especially with the Split, a diplomatic race they most certainly were not.

The Spinny had been contacted within sezuras of entering the sector and ordered to proceed directly to the military installation near his factory. That was when his pilot had woken him and he now entered the bridge of his ship, acknowledged the slight bows from his crew and took his seat. Time to find the truth.

The small group of four ships approached the station surrounded by small Split fighter craft. They moved back and forth on the scanner keeping a watchful eye over their visitors. One wrong move, any slight show of aggression and they would be attacked without warning, he knew.

He had given orders that no weapon systems were to be brought online at any time while in the inner sectors except from a direct command from him.

The communication cube indicated an incoming transmission. He pressed the button to accept.

"Dock the Spinny now. No other ships to dock, do you understand?" It was the Split station commander, a very powerful Split.

"Yes, I understand." He replied. "Negotiating docking rights now."

He glanced at his pilot who proceeded to press buttons on his console and then he could see the green navigation lights on the station start their little display of confirmation.

"Pilot, take us in." He commanded. The ship moved towards the open doors of the docking bay.

After completing the docking and being greeted by the station commander himself he was led down various corridors until they finally entered a room that was obviously some form of medical centre. The commander gestured for LooManckStrat to sit. He declined, wanting to get to the point of this and not waste any more time, or credits.

"LooManckStrat, we found the body in a cargo container in one of the sparsely populated sectors, half way between here and the empty worlds. A long range patrol discovered it on a normal sweep of the sector and when they brought it on board and checked the cargo, they sent a message drone and it was brought here."

"So, what's all the fuss about? Why the secrecy?" he quizzed.

"Follow me, see for yourself."

He followed the commander into the next room and lying naked on the table in the centre of the room was the body of Faa t'Zrrk.

LooManckStrat took a step backwards; the body was painted with thick jagged, dark blue lines. The face fixed in a contortion of pain.

"I don't understand." He said. "What does this mean? How did he die?"

"Internal explosion. He was shot through the chest with an explosive dart. He died in great pain." The commander responded.

"But come and look." He continued and moved towards the body with LooManckStrat behind. "There look." The commander pointed at his chest.

Written in the same deep blue colour across the dead Split's chest on an area not covered by the stripes were a number of words. They were written in Split.

"So what does it say?" LooManckStrat asked.

"It says," the Split commander started, "Traitor, long live the Yaki. Death to the Guild."

"Yaki? Who are they?" LooManckStrat was feeling worried.

"We do not know. We sent a small scout force into the outer sectors, they have not returned and they do not reply to our drones. We understand some pirate ships were engaged with these Yaki. I believe your attackers are already dead."

"I could not have told you this LooManckStrat over the communication systems, they are never secure and I felt you needed to see it for yourself. Your employee has been in contact with someone, or something that cost him his life. I suggest you take your fleet back to Paranid space and continue your work there."

"Do not go into the outer sectors. Return home LooManckStrat, there is nothing to be gained by you seeking out these, Yaki."

LooManckStrat looked directly at the Split commander. "But my fleet is in the outer sectors." He gasped.

"No, wrong direction, well as far as we can tell, these Yaki are in the other direction. They are between Split and Argon space, not Paranid. Stay your side of the sectors and return home to the safety of Paranid space."

"We will investigate this from here and if we need to talk to you again, we will."

LooManckStrat was devastated. He was intent on bringing these pirates to justice and now it seemed they might be stronger than he thought. He must return and protect his investments in his own space lanes and then maybe at a later point in time, he could right the wrong that had been done to him. Yes, he would concentrate on building up his trading empire again and attempt to get the Super Slaves back on-line. That was what he was good at; not fighting and he didn't want to end up the same as this Split lying on the table before him.

He left and his four ships began the journey back to the destroyer and the other ships. He sent a message drone instructing them to go to full alert and to stay that way until he returned. Yes, trade not fight; let the Split deal with it or whoever. I'm not bothered as long as it isn't me. This travelling around the cosmos was making him ill.

It took seven Tazuras but his ships managed to return to his home sector without incident. His defence ships took up patrol around the sector and it would be a long time before they ventured out again.

## Chapter 6: Pisces

*So you want to be a space fighter pilot do you? Well one day you might be, but you have a long way to go before you get your crystal star hot shot, a long way.*

Pisces, the world of eternal light was in a system that contained three local suns. One large orb beginning its death throes with a smaller companion, which circled it. Another medium size star, much farther away but still not large enough to escape the pull of the sector master was also in orbit. The small desert world orbited between the larger two stars, it too caught in the system that would eventually destroy itself. But that was a distant future event, the world was currently a small, but nevertheless fruitful centre for many illegal activities.

Mainly, it provided a perfect atmosphere for growing Mitta, the plant that once taken into the orbiting factories and left to ferment in zero gravity with additives, became a strong and powerful narcotic. Used by many races, especially the Argon and Boron for recreational use. It was illegal in both races space lanes, but was sold anyway as the profits and demand was so high and there would always be a market for it.

Periodically it would cause an outrage when a batch of the drug was released too early before being fully ready and Argon or Boron would die as a result. This outrage usually occurred in Argon space when any major elections were due and such a time was now.

Over two hundred revellers had perished after the drug had been taken on the pleasure world of Ita and the Argon government had ordered another strike. It wouldn't stop the flow of the drug, but it would slow it down for a while and would make political noises that benefited the politicians.

This was to be a joint attack on two of the orbiting factories and also on the main harvesting area on the planet. The small fleet had assembled in full view of the Argon public, so the harvester's knew they were coming and would prepare a defence. Typical politicians, tell the enemy you were on your way and broadcast the fact around the cosmos. A surprise attack this wasn't. A foolhardy trip into oblivion it most certainly could be.

Brett sat in a "screamer", a ship attached to the hull of the giant troop ship that had been deployed for the mission. The screamer's job was to take the assault troops inside, directly into the action. It could fly in space, although slowly, but was designed for fast entry into systems with even the heaviest atmospheres. It entered at such speed that the ship would shake and the sound of the ship's hull straining against the planet's natural defence generated a high pitch squeal inside, hence the name.

He had begun his new life in the navy at the base, the lowest member of the whole establishment. Ten of them had started on that same Tazura, all destined for greatness as pilots in the navy, but first you had to earn the right. Two Jazuras spent cleaning and running errands for the higher ranks. Attending endless lessons on navy protocol and instruction in the basic forms of attack and defence. Not the ship kind though, no the physical kind. You had to become an assault troop first and do your time in the ranks before you could be eligible for fighter training.

So Brett had spent his time in the Marines, doing the dirty work for the Argon government. Go here and clean up this mess, then go there and create another one. He had visited many different places already and hadn't been back to Morang for many Mazuras. He was worried about today though. They were to destroy one of the launch sites on the planet surface. Fighting in space with environment suits on and laser weapons was one thing, but fighting in atmosphere was quite another. The harvesters down on the surface would no doubt deploy tactical starbursts. These weapons only had one function, to disable any electrical systems in the vicinity. They would burn out all computer systems in a wide radius of the centre of the explosion. This meant that all advanced weaponry was useless and they had been instructed not to carry any. So here he was, sat with twenty-five other Marines in one of the ten screamers about to launch. Conventional assault rifle in his hand, explosive ammunition carried in his belt packs.

Because the defenders would deploy the starbursts, the attackers would also follow the same tactic and as the screamers swept down, they would fire their own. So, he was worried that they were going to have to fight a conventional battle. Lots of people got killed in battles like that, but he was also worried that the screamer itself, if in the immediate area of a starburst detonation, would simply fall out of the air.

The first wave of attack was at that moment leaving the vacuum of space and landing on the planet far from the battle zone. It carried a number of surface attack aircraft that would fly in from afar and drop chemical bombs on the crop fields, destroying the plant and making the area useless. Then they would attempt to take out the launch sites and if they failed, the marines would get the order to attack.

They would not know how the battle was progressing until they were either stood down, or the ship dropped. Brett stared around the compartment, thirteen marines on each side. He was a detachment second in command and he sat by the third marine in from the far end. Across from him was a relative newcomer. He looked at Brett with a concern that Brett himself had felt before.

"Brett, you've done this before yeah? How many drops have you made?" he asked, anything to break the tension. It was the wrong question.

"Seven." Brett replied. "But this is only my third into a hot zone."

"So is the ride gonna hurt?" The new recruit inquired.

"The ride isn't the problem, it's getting off it at the other end." He smiled as if to reassure the other marine that he was making a joke. He wasn't really.

The command came through the communication unit in his helmet, standard issue, they all had them fitted so that they could keep in touch on the ground. Everybody heard everything one marine said in theory.

"We have an affirmative for go marines, that's a green. Prepare for launch." The pilot instructed.

Brett pressed the button to his left that tightened the straps supporting him. His companion-followed suit, copying the more experienced one.

Then they felt the intense feeling of falling as the ship was released along with the others and they began to fall under the pull of the planet. Very quickly the ship turned its nose downwards and headed into the outer atmosphere, turning at an angle as it scraped the surface, the glow from the impact lighting up the front of the ship and sending flames all over it.

Inside it was hard to keep your focus on anything. The ship was shaking violently and the troops were being shaken in their protective armour. Then the scream started, it was a high pitch wail that hurt the ears and together with the shaking, made the whole trip chaotic.

On and on it went which seemed to last forever, the noise and vibration. Brett gripped his assault rifle closer and tried to concentrate on what was to happen once they landed, if they landed.

Then suddenly it was over. The ship stopped shaking and a moment later the scream disappeared. The screamer sped on towards its destination, the pilot began firing his starbursts at the target area and the other ships did likewise.

The defenders began to prepare to return their own fire once the attackers were within range, guns shooting metal missiles, some heated so that the gunners could follow the line and see where they were going. The screamers were now about one hundred metres above the ground, coming in low and fast towards the launch site. They were about twenty kilometres away when the starbursts began to explode around them. Two screamers came under the influence of the weapons and crashed into the ground. The other eight continued on and were soon at the landing zone.

Brett felt the ship touch down with a bang and was sure they had partially crashed landed as the ship had continued to move after touch down. The dim red glow that was the light inside the compartment began to flash green.

"Out, out, out!" Shouted the pilot of the communication system. "Out now!"

Brett didn't need a second prompting, you were a very large target sitting in a screamer on the ground and the two hatches swept open in the floor of the room, one at each end.

The marines began to disembark, taking up prone defensive positions around the craft as they did so. Brett hit the sandy ground and quickly gathered his composure and sense of direction. A small, half a metre high outcrop of rock was to his left.

Marines scan the horizon.

"Greens! This is Brett, follow me to the cover on the left, move it!" He shouted.

The squad began to run, half crouching, towards the rock when the explosions began. Dull booms as shells hit the sand around them. The defenders had got the range right and they were lobbing explosive shells from their positions by the launch pad about five hundred metres beyond the rock.

Brett ran and ran beginning to breathe heavily as his equipment took its toll and weighed down on him. He reached the rock and flung himself to the ground. He could hear the screams through the intercom as some of his men were hit by the incoming fire. He looked to his left and along the rock line that spread for a few hundred metres, he could see the other screamers in different positions and the marines all running from them for the rock outcrop.

"Clear Red three, we are clear!" Shouted the commander to the screamer they had just left.

"Copy that, Green three. We are going offensive!"

The screamer lifted off, its huge engines creating a small sandstorm as it did so. As soon as it was in the air, it began to fire lasers into the enemy positions. Massive bolts of energy and Brett could see the damage they were doing, bodies and equipment being flung into the air as they hit. Just the tip of his head over the rock was all he could dare at the moment.

The other screamers were lifting off and began to approach the enemy when two blinding explosions filled the air. On no! Starbursts!

The screamers that were attacking dropped from the air, two exploding on impact while the other three smashed into the ground, saved by their low altitude. The data feed that was viewable on the small screens fixed to the helmet of every marine died as the starbursts did their damage. The communication systems met the same fate.

Then it went quiet, except for the odd moan from any injured marines lying on the ground. Brett looked around; lots of anxious faces stared back. All along the rock were marines from the other screamers, lying prone or hunched up to the ground for some form of protection.

Then the sound came, thump, thump, thump. A distant thud that could be felt in the ground itself. Brett peered over the rock, on no!

"Centaurs!" He screamed to the other troops.

Two, four metre high, mechanical beasts were slowly making their way across the flat desert between them and the base. Massive machines that resembled Argon in their shape with two legs and arms and a heavily armoured torso holding the head. The arms were killing machines; revolving guns began to spit out projectiles at the outcrop. Brett could see smoke billowing from the back, mechanical monsters with combustion engines and no electrical systems. They were not affected by the starbursts; this was Brett's worst fear.

He pulled his rifle into his shoulder and pulled the trigger, his shoulder jolting as the rounds left the muzzle and hit the rightmost Centaur. Others joined in the attack and many marines were now looking over the rock and firing at the two advancing beasts.

The right Centaur opened fire with both of its guns and Brett could see the impacts in the sand as the weapons moved their line of fire up towards the top of the rock. He could hear the projectiles as they flew through the air and knew that the sound was reaching him after the shots had as they were travelling much faster than sound.

The two Centaurs finally found their mark and the shots bounced off the rock face and then into the marines themselves. Bodies pushed backwards as the high velocity weapons ripped through the body armour worn by the marines. Brett saw his commander take a shot in the chest and then directly into the head, his body thrown into the air from the impact and it turned over in the air as it flew backwards and lay still on the ground.

Then shells began to land from the enemy positions again. Boom and then another, boom. They were all going to die if they stayed here. He looked left and right, half the force of over two hundred was either dead or injured and he realised that they couldn't call for backup, the communication systems were dead. They either took the fight to the enemy or waited in the hope that they ran out of ammunition. He didn't like either option, but waiting was always a bad choice.

"Greens!" He shouted. "We're going in!" He hoped enough of the surrounding troops could hear him over the noise.

"Fire covering smoke, now!"

Some of the troops got to their knees and pulled the small hand launched smoke missiles from their backs. He could hear the hollow thump as they were fired. Then smoke began to drift up out of the sand where the Centaurs stood, then more smoke until he couldn't see them. Good, they couldn't seem him either then.

"Go, go, go!" He shouted and jumped off the top of the rock and began to run down the small incline. Others joined him and as he glanced to his sides he could see his companions racing down with him in a long line.

The enemy had realised that an attack was coming and they altered their shelling so that the explosions were now falling around them as they ran. He saw marines blown into the air, caught by the shock waves or dropping down dead from the Centaurs fire.

Brett continued to run, making a jagged line as he went, left then right then back again. He caught view of the right Centaur that he had previously fired at and headed behind it.

He stopped when he was just a few metres behind it. He could hear its mechanics moving and its weapons continuing to fire. But just as expected, high up its armoured back was the exhaust from the engine. He slung his rifle over his shoulder and reached into his belt for two explosives. He pressed the timed detonation buttons and hurled them upwards. One bounced off the armour, but the second disappeared into the opening.

He ran as fast as he could away from the Centaur and towards the base. Then at the last possible moment as he counted down in his head, he threw himself to the ground. The Centaur exploded, the top half going one way and the bottom half slowly toppling over in the opposite direction. The two people inside killed instantly.

Debris from the explosion rained down, hot shards of metal making hissing sounds as they stuck into the sand around him and metal on metal sounds as they bounced of his body armour. He was momentarily stunned from the explosion and had been slightly fortuitous to still be alive and uninjured. He could hear the thump, thump of the second machine as it approached. The sounds of automatic fire from the marines as they tried to stop its destruction.

He began to struggle to his feet. "Brett! Down, stay down!", came the shout from one of his fellow attackers. He dropped instantly to the sand again and heard the whoosh from the close quarter rockets as they left their launchers and then the two explosions as they hit the Centaur. Brett glanced around to see the Centaur topple over, the impact throwing it off balance and it fell onto its back, weapons still firing. It struggled to right itself and then with an ear-breaking bang, it exploded, throwing fragments everywhere.

He saw a few marines drop to the floor as the explosion occurred, some of them didn't get back up.

The pop, pop sound of the smoke missiles could be heard again and he leapt to his feet as other marines raced past him towards the base. Copious amounts of gunfire could be heard as they stormed the base, mixed with high explosive detonations.

He was sweating heavily and almost out of breath when he cleared the smoke and reached the outer limits of the base. There were trenches in the ground where the defenders had been, but these were filled with the dead or dying bodies of the harvesters. A large opening to his right, the main storage area where the tractors entered and left he thought. His men were flanking both sides of the opening. They had not yet ventured in and some were holding their weapons through the opening and firing blind while they kept themselves behind the protective wall.

Brett approached them. "Sit report!" He blurted to the troops around him as he took in large gasps of air. A man turned towards him. "Exterior secure Sir." He shouted above the background noise of the battle. "They have a firing line at the back of the storage depot behind a row of space cargo pods. Small automatic weapons and one large high fire rate gun. Another HFR in a small room at the top of the outer stairs. We go in that way, up the stairs, we are gonna get roasted."

Brett thought for a moment. No way we can go up the stairs, the trooper was right. A HFR firing down the stairs as his men went up in single file would be suicide. They would have to get through the depot and get the stair HFR from behind.

He looked at the faces around him. Staring at him, looking for guidance. "OK, how many greens left that can fight? Ammunition, I want to know now, how much, what type. Speak to me greens."

It took only a few moments. Forty-seven troops left in a position to fight. Six rockets, some smoke and assorted small arms. "Right, listen up. You," he pointed at a junior rank, "take six troops, keep the gun on the stairs busy. Just stick your weapons around the corner every now and again loose off some rounds. Understand?"

"Yes Sir!" Came the reply. He quickly pointed to six others and they ran off round the corner to where the stairs were. Almost immediately the sound of rounds could be heard, short bursts as they obeyed their orders.

Brett addressed the others. "Listen, we're going in. Two teams of twenty, each team loose of your missiles. That'll take a few of 'em out and keep their heads down. Then follow with smoke straight away. Blind them, then we charge. Keep to the sides until you reach the barricade and then feel free to act on initiative." A few of the others smiled. Good, Brett thought, time to finish the job.

They moved into position and Brett shouted the order, "Go Greens, GO!" The missile carriers leaned out into the opening and fired. A whoosh as the missile left the weapon and a slight delay until the large explosion could be heard a hundred metres away at the back of the depot. All six missiles fired, the launchers stood aside and the smoke carrying troops repeated the procedure. Smoke began to billow out of the opening. There was still enemy fire coming out of the opening, but it had decreased somewhat. The marines attacked, running down the sides of the depot.

Brett was about half way down the right hand side when he caught sight of the harvesters. They were standing behind the pods, small hand held rifles spouting shots into the smoke. The HFR was in the middle firing continuously and sweeping back and to. Then it stopped, probably reloading he thought. Brett thundered across the concrete floor, ignoring the single shot rifles that were firing back. His troops went with him. They stormed the barricade, jumping onto the pods and firing bursts into the defenders below. The HFR was destroyed and the harvesters were taking serious casualties. Some of the marines had been killed but it only took one of the defenders to drop their weapon and throw up their arms in surrender and like a rehearsed play, the others all followed suit. Nearly there, just the other HFR. Brett jabbed his finger at a trooper. "Take them prisoner, you know the drill." He looked at three others. "You, you and you." He pointed at each one as he spoke. "Follow me."

He ran towards the door at the back wall, the three others followed. Dull silver metal covered the door. He tried the handle, damn, locked. He stepped back and aimed his gun at the lock. Three short bursts followed and the lock lay in ruins. Brett stepped to the side of the door and leaned on the wall. He gestured to the others with his head. Go on troops, through you go.

One of them kicked at the door while the other two took up a firing stance, guns trained on the door, one high, the other low. The door gave way and swung inwards. The troops ran through and Brett followed into a small area with a concrete staircase heading up into sunlight. The back way to the top, Brett mused. His companions were already starting up the stairs and when he got to the top he came side on to the room with the HFR in. It was firing down the stairs to his right and he could hear the distinct sound of his own troops firing back. Brett ran to the side of the room that had a similar metal door protecting its occupants. He stared at one of the troops and aimed his gun at the lock. The trooper understood, they didn't need to speak and he pulled a small explosive from his belt. He primed the device and nodded. Brett shot out the lock with the same three bursts as the other one and kicked the door open before standing to one side. The trooper tossed the explosive in. Almost instantly it exploded and the sound of the HFR ceased. Both he and the trooper held their weapons into the opening and opened fire while moving them around. Best to be sure. Satisfied that anyone (or anything) that was in the room was dead they entered and confirmed that was the case.

Brett shouted down the outside staircase "Greens, clear!" He saw one of the troopers look around the corner at the bottom and confirm that it was clear. Brett waved him on and he started up the stairs, his companions following.

He began to walk down the stairs, passing his troops as he went and then onto the sand. He suddenly felt exhausted, like he hadn't slept for days. There was still the noise of fires crackling and smoke was still bellowing across the landscape. White smoke that the marines had fired and black smoke from the two burning Centaurs.

He was leaning over trying to catch his breath when the new recruit he had spoken to in orbit walked over.

"Hey Brett, you were right. The journey down was easy compared to this."

"Yeah." He replied. "I hope we have made someone very happy."

* * * * * * * *

Twelve Stazuras later he was standing on the loading bay of the troop ship. They had been debriefed and Brett was sorting through his equipment when the force Marine commander walked over.

"Good job you did down there Brett, saved a lot of lives. We'll miss you Y'know. You just made company commander too." He said.

"Yeah thanks. What do you mean, you'll miss me?" Brett replied.

"Just got word, your times up Brett. Request has come through and your names on it. Your going back to Morang hot shot, space ships and slave chips. Good luck Brett." The commander slapped him on the back and walked away grinning to himself and shaking his head.

At last, Morang!

## Chapter 7: Helpers

*Help a species to rise slightly and they might just learn to fly themselves.*

Fifty thousand years ago.

"Do they have any offensive weapons, do they show any aggressive traits?"

"No, they are completely peaceful. Only killing for food, never pleasure. They waste nothing of their prey."

"They stand at the top of their food chain then. They are highly intelligent yet choose to live peacefully?"

"Correct. They are a prime candidate for inclusion, the closest match we have ever found."

"Good. Deploy the helpers, we will observe this one closely."

\* \* \* \* \* \* \* \*

She moved towards the edge of the rock, sweeping vegetation out of her way as she went, her four long thin legs propelling her along the uneven seabed. Two more protrusions reached out and forwards, moving back and forth in front of her to move the highest parts of the plants out of her way. Three long thin digits protruded from the two arms, grabbing at the undulating branches when she needed more leverage.

Her skin was a mottled grey, thick, like rubber and appeared wet. However, it was dry and leathery to the touch. Her head sat atop a long thin neck and above that, two stalks with eyes moved independently of one another as she surveyed her path. She took in gasps of oxygen rich water through a small trunk on the front of her head. Heavily tainted with ammonia, her internal organs processed the fluid and extracted the oxygen required to breathe.

She was nearing the rock edge now, hoping to get there soon so that she could take in some of the deeper waters pleasant oxygen and refresh herself. Too long spent working in the underwater village in the forest where her family and the rest of the hive lived. She had been given time to play, to refresh before returning to her chores after the sun went down and then came back again the following day.

She was propelling herself as fast as she could and her brother was trying his best to beat her to the outcrop. But she was older, stronger than he was and she wouldn't be beaten.

As she reached the rocks edge, she pushed off with all her might and flew into the open water. Pulling her legs and arms behind her so they swept away in the air as she flew. It looked so graceful, the one and half metre figure moving through the water while the yellow sea mists swirled alongside.

Then she plunged deeper into the water, just as her brother began his jump from the side. Heading downwards into the depths, she took in water through her snout. Large amounts, again and again she snorted.

The water was cascading into her body when the richer droplets began to invade her ammonia-hardened lungs. The body automatically snapped shut the opening to her lungs and the water continued its journey through a newly opened tunnel. Then it splashed against the micromesh of her gills and they began the job of extracting the oxygen sealed within.

Then the remainder of the liquid, minus most, but not all of it's oxygen, was pushed deeper into her torso until it came to the opening between her four "legs". She felt the sweetness of the oxygen and the urge to push deep inside her. She relented, let her muscles take over and the water was pushed out at considerable force. She moved deeper into the water, away from the swamp edges, propelled by the small jet.

The dark rings on her legs and arms began to swell, to open like flower buds and her thin bones began to disconnect themselves all along her torso. It took only moments but she changed from a seabed running, insect like figure, into the soft pliable form most suited to the depths. The transformation complete, she flexed the suckers that ran the length of her six tentacles. It felt good. She threw all six tentacles forward and the negative force quickly slowed her down. One eye stalk peered upwards, the eye moving side to side, looking for the brother she knew was coming.

There he was, sweeping down towards her in the same form she had moments before. He completed the same stopping manoeuvre and came to rest at her side. She moved towards him and touched her head against his. Loud sounds came from her snout, like someone clearing their throat to you and me. The sound travelled well in the water but the meaning could sometimes be lost and touching heads let them communicate better.

"Told you I'd win." She said to her smaller brother.

"You always do. But I am getting bigger all the time, I will win this race one day."

She turned her stalks towards each other, the sign of laughter. The greater the bend the happier the intent. Her brother's stalks also followed suit.

"Follow me," she said, "let's go over there this time. We have never been over there." She gestured with one of the tentacles.

Her brother grunted his approval and they jetted off getting deeper and deeper into the swamp.

It had been a long time and they were beginning to get tired. She knew they would have to go back soon. They had enjoyed the fun, chasing along at speed, sweeping in and out of one another. It was as they came to a stop and communicated that they noticed the light emanating from the rocks below.

There seemed to be a gap, a cave perhaps, but only a small one and a blue light was illuminating the inside. They jetted towards it.

The hole was only a few centimetres wide and seemed to be covered in smaller rocks as if something had deliberately put them there. But what for, to hide something perhaps?

She looked at her brother and didn't bother to touch heads. "Let's open it up." She said. Her brother didn't look convinced, his snout pushed flat against his face. He was concerned and a little worried.

She began to move the smaller rocks away with her tentacles, using the suckers to pick them up and toss them aside. Then she came to a large one, too big to move. She would have to move it by picking it up. Her brother was too young to have mastered the partial change. He could only allow his body to be connected, or not. But she was older, more experienced. She stretched out two tentacles and began to click the bones back into place. The suckers began to recede back into her skin as she worked from the tip of the tentacles, where the three digits were, back to the top where they connected to her torso. The digits would be useless until she had worked her way all the way back and made the connection from joint to joint. Then she would be able to operate them again.

It took only moments to complete the task, her brother watched on in admiration, tempted to try it himself, but knowing full well it was dangerous until fully grown.

She flexed her digits. Job complete. They reached out and grabbed the rock on both sides. She used her other four tentacles to suck onto the rock below and give her some leverage. Up it came in her hands. She pulled it towards her and then propelled it away, turning back to the next one and next one.

Some time had passed, but she managed to clear enough of the hole so they could get their bodies through. She reversed the transformation and the two arms flapped gracefully in the water. She gave her brother a quick, follow me, glance and sped into the cave. He followed close behind.

She stopped astonished. At the bottom of the cave about five metres away was a large metal "dish". It was a bright metal, not like the dull type they used on the planters and harvesters in the vegetable fields. This was almost shiny, and big. It must be fifteen metres across. She thought it was at least ten times her length in diameter.

Blue lights flickered on the edges, not quite switching off, but flickering like stars in the night sky. Without thinking she swept down onto the dish and landed on it's top. Her brother watched from above. The metal felt slightly warm, she sucked on it with her tentacles, in and out in an attempt to feel what it was. But there was something else, very weak, but a definite vibration coming from the object. It was alive!

Her brother landed softly beside her and touched his head to hers.

"What is it?" he asked.

"I don't know." She replied. She really had no idea.

The systems on board the ship had been monitoring the surrounding area for years. Listening to the sounds of the swamp, comparing any intelligent sounds it heard with its data banks. It had heard this one before, many times, but never so close. This time the creatures were actually sitting atop its hull. It was time then to make itself known, just as it had been programmed to.

The voice came through the hull, vibrating in the same language as the two that sat upon it.

"Do not be afraid. I am a helper." It said.

The two jetted away from the hull like launched missiles. They didn't stop until they were recounting their tale to their father and the hive lord himself.

\* \* \* \* \* \* \* \*

Other ships were found over the years. They asked questions and they got answers. But they got answers to only the questions they asked. The "helpers" never gave anything away.

"What is two plus two?"

"Four."

"Who are you?"

"I am a helper."

"Where do you come from?"

"I am a helper."

"If I add tremalt to backu in the ratio four to one, heat it to boiling and then apply it to my broken skin, will it help to seal the wound?"

"Yes."

And so it went on and on. They couldn't just move forward technically in one great step. They had to nudge forward bit by bit. Learning new things as they went.

It would have taken over a hundred thousand years for the Boron to achieve space flight. In reality it took only fifty, the helpers had indeed helped.

Then when the decision had been made to construct weapons in an effort to fight the Split invasion, the first time the Boron had ever constructed weapons. The helpers lifted up from their cradles around the planet, launched themselves into space and sped away into the cosmos. They had not been seen or heard off since.

\* \* \* \* \* \* \*

Fifteen Jazuras ago.

Mi Ton floated above the marked spot like someone about to be condemned. He was without doubt one of the highest regarded members of the Boron kingdom. He had worked in space, alongside the Argon, as a physician. He understood the biology of many species including the Split and Paranid and had helped run the Boron military hospitals.

But that was his job, not his love. His devotion was to the cosmos and it's secrets. He spent his own time deploying devices into space, listening and collecting data in an attempt to fathom out the mysteries that eluded them all.

But above all, he was outspoken, that very reason was why he was waiting here now in front of the government inquiry. The Boron enjoyed narcotics. Ever since they had met the Argon the trouble had escalated. They couldn't blank the whole of the other races, couldn't move away from the position they know found themselves in. They were part of the Foundation Guild and part of the family of races.

Spaceweed and spacefuel. The weed absorbed through the skin and the fuel consumed. Drugs and liquor as the Argon described them. The Boron loved the illegal items and Mi Ton had openly stood in the government assembly and launched a stinging attack on the tides of power. Indeed the Argon government routinely attacked the harvesters who made the drugs and the illicit space factories where the liquor was manufactured. But it was not enough for Mi Ton.

It had shaken the Boron so much, that not even his friend Queen Atreus could help him now.

His companion and fellow observer, the Argon Mitchell, had smiled through the communication link. He was at the observatory in orbit, preparing the final details for their trip to the outer sectors.

"Just smile and wave goodbye Mi," he said, "then we can get on with our work."

The translator blurted the message into the grunts that was the Boron language.

"I am Boron. I do not smile like you."

Mitchell laughed, "Well turn them stalks inwards till they touch." He laughed again, deeper and louder, his body shaking with the effort. "Just go through the motions Mi, get it over with and haul ass up here. We're ready to go. Stations packed, transporter ship is ready to roll."

The translator was having difficulty with the words. Either that or Mitchell was talking nonsense. It was easy to work with "Mitch" when they were doing scientific work, he spoke well, but when he was not he spoke in the slang of the Argon. That was very difficult for the Boron (and the translator) to understand.

"I hope to see you shortly," was the only reply Mi Ton could think of.

So he sat through the hearing. The panel of government officials disliked him anyway, not hatred, that was an alien feeling to a Boron. But they did not agree with his wish to put more credits into the cosmos research he craved. Mi Ton had stood and said his mind about the drug problem and all he had done was make himself a target for those that wished him gone.

"So," the head of the inquiry board said, "we think it would be wise if you were to continue your studies out of the public eye."

"We therefore rule that you should leave the planet immediately and make preparations for setting up your laboratory at least fifty sectors away."

Which is two sectors less than the place they already knew he was going to. Get on with it, Mi Ton thought.

"You should not return for ten Jazura's. Do you understand?"

"Yes." Mi Ton grunted.

All around him twitched their snouts in approval.

"Then this hearing is closed."

And that was it. He had left the planet and joined up with Mitch in orbit. The slow ponderous cargo ship that was carrying their station took almost a full Jazura before they reached their destination. It promptly dropped them off, deployed automated robots to help complete the installation of the station and left.

It was another Jazura before they actually began their studies. First they had to complete the station, install the small nuclear power generator and deploy the energy cell rig. This would capture energy from the nearby star and store it in the energy cells used throughout the station. The nuclear device was a backup, it didn't have enough power to operate the full station, only essential services.

Then the farms for the food, the water facility, the pool (Mi Ton insisted on a pool) and defence systems. Mitch had a background in trading and had always wanted to use his skills looking at the cosmos He had spent most of his youth achieving the qualifications required but then life hadn't turned out that way at first. But if Mi Ton wanted a large pool, Mitch wanted laser batteries. Mi Ton reluctantly agreed and thought that Mitch was happy anyway with the larger pool idea. He had certainly spent enough time swimming around in it after they had finished installing it.

They were so far from any other colonised systems, Mi Ton couldn't even think of any threat they faced. They had three small ships, docked at the station. Unarmed craft they used for scouting missions or deploying observation equipment.

They had been there, all alone for Jazuras. The occasional message drone was sent through to them. The Boron wasn't that interested in the news, but Mitch liked to keep in touch with Argon Prime. The biggest news was of the Yaki, depicted by the newsreader, as space bandits, who were growing ever bigger in the sectors between Split and Argon space.

Once they directly threatened the Guilds, Mitch thought, something would give and a war would ensue. Still, not my problem out here, let them sort it out, he had done his time in the trading lanes. If someone wanted to remove the minimum and maximum price boundaries that the guilds enforced, plus the taxes they took out of the profits, who was he to argue?

"We need to send out more observer satellites." Mitch was saying to his companion as they ate their dinner. They sat facing each other in the dining area of the station. The station could accommodate twenty beings, it only had two, so space was plentiful.

"You are right." The Boron grunted through the translator in his environment suit. "The data we have is good. I am getting positive readings from the simulations. But we can't pinpoint the time until we have more data."

"We've been here eight Jazuras Mi. You could go home in another two Y'know. It'll take us a few more than that to complete the study." Mitch pointed out.

"Yes," came the reply, "it will take longer. I have no intention of returning until we have the answer." His stalks turned slightly inward. Mitch smiled and pushed the remains of his dinner into the recycle tube.

"OK, I'll go and prime the launchers." He said as he stood and began to walk away.

## Chapter 8: The frigate "Excel"

*Who is the Slave, the Slave itself or the one that carries it?*

"How do you feel?"

The technician was asking how he felt. How do you think I feel?

"My head hurts." Brett replied.

"It will for a while. The drugs inside you will help with that. Stay lying down and rest."

Brett did, for three whole Tazuras he slept. Then when he woke he just felt hungry, very hungry. They brought him food, hot tasty food. He ate it like a man possessed, taking large gulps of water in-between. Then the Navy officers arrived in his room.

"How do you feel?" one of them asked. Is that all anyone says around here?

"Fine, I feel fine." Brett answered.

"You ready to start your training?" another inquired.

"Yes Sir!" Brett replied.

Brett sat up in the bed and propped the large pillows behind him. The insertion of the Slave chip had been a success, now he had to learn to use it.

"OK," the man said, "we are going to send an image. Tell me what you see."

Brett just stared at the man and then suddenly, unexpectedly an image of a fighter craft flew across his eyes. Wait, no not in front of his eyes, but in his eyes. Brett threw up his arms as the image went away.

"Wow! That was incredible!" He shouted.

The officer smiled. "Wait until you see this."

The next few Tazuras saw the same thing happen. The navy officers would come and test him, send images that he had to identify. They then moved onto more complex images, data screens and graphics. Brett learned to look through his eyes at the things around him, but to also see the images at the same time. It was difficult at first, but the more he did it, the easier it got.

He could read data being relayed to him and scan the room at the same time. Then they placed him in the simulator. He flew the ship and got the data. He crashed. He tried again and again until he could fly the ship and pick out items of data from the images at the same time.

Then they moved onto the final phase. Now he had to manipulate the data. They gave him a simple menu, select the lowest option they said. He spoke the words in his mind, "down, down, select." His head nodding each time he imagined the words.

Then he found that you didn't need to speak the words, you simply willed it to happen. Imagine the lowest item being selected, don't try and navigate to it, simply be there. It was strange, but he did it. Staring at the menu, he simply thought of the lowest item being selected and it was!

Now fly the ship and select the lowest item. Crash. Do it again. Crash. Again. It took time, but he got there eventually. Flying the ship around the simulated sectors and selecting items from the menu. He found he could select weapons from the cargo bay, change the shield configuration, launch missiles onto selected targets while still flying the ship through obstacles.

He spent the next six Mazuras training using the chip. Sometimes in the simulators and then eventually into orbit above Argon Prime where he could practice for real. Repeated missions in the home system itself. Using the chip was one thing, but you had to learn to use it as another sense. It had to be automatic, there was no time in combat for thinking about what to do. This came from experience and that was gained from the varied missions he was handed.

Simple "go here and do that" missions followed by complex destroy multiple targets and retrieve the pod ones. Brett trained hard. Just like when he had been a young boy, he attacked his quests with vigour. Spending his time in his bunk on the large rotating space station reading up on theory and the mechanics of space flight. Engines, lasers, missiles, shields, navigation systems, satellites, he gorged on the data they fed him.

He studied the ships from the other races, memorised their capabilities, speed and offensive attributes. When he was attending the classroom lessons his knowledge became legendary. He knew so much that the navy lecturer sometimes asked him for the answer. His classmates chuckled, but they respected him. Brett had fought in the Marines, most of them had come through the easy planet side route to fighter command. Easy jobs in the Marine base, pushing paper and sweeping floors. Brett came from the orphanage they knew, but he had seen action, he had killed others. They respected Brett to a man and woman, every single one of them.

The completion of the training and back to Morang for the ceremony. Bands playing music, friends and relatives, cheering their brothers, sisters, sons and daughters. Brett simply collected his star from the commanding officer, saluted by holding his arm across his chest and looked to the sky.

"For you mother, for you."

Brett also received the class honour, best cadet. His fellow officers congratulated him, pats on the back and smiles. He was given the rank of squad leader, in command of three other ships with pilots from his own class. Good, that was what he wanted.

* * * * * * * *

Brett sat in the bar on the frigate "Excel". Two of his flight sat with him, Shake and Bibby. Shake was a tall lean man, blond hair, blue eyes, a favourite with the ladies. Bibby was a small, petite red head. She had a temper to match her hair and Shake had given up in his attempts to conquer her.

The bar was dim, pilots and some marines were sat around. Dull red lights lit the room and colourful signs adorned the wall behind the bar where the automated bar dispenser was handing out drinks to the customers.

"So what do you think Bibby?" Shake was asking. "I reckon it's the harvesters again."

"No idea Shake." She replied casting him a glance. "It'll be some out of the way back yard though, as usual."

"What do you think Brett, harvesters yeah?" Shake inquired.

Brett turned away from the screen on the wall that was showing the latest news reports. "Don't know guys, but we only have a small force of fighters onboard this frigate, she ain't no carrier Y'know."

"Yeah, but we'll meet up with them yeah, somewhere, someplace a whole fleet."

Brett didn't answer, he had turned his attention back to the screen. "Hey, robo," he shouted at the bar tender, "turn it up will ya."

The automated bartender did as requested and to the grunts of some of the others in the room, the sound from the news cast increased.

Suddenly everyone went quiet and focused on the screen as the reporter continued.

"It is reported, but I must stress not confirmed, that a joint force from The Split and Teladi navies has engaged the Yaki fleet in the outer sectors."

Brett glanced at the other two. They returned his gaze and then looked back at the wall.

"The Split and Teladi news agencies are refusing to give any details, but our sources imply that this force has been destroyed. I repeat that, destroyed, totally and utterly wiped out. We saw them go in and no ships returned, none."

The screen suddenly went off and the room was filled with bright white light.

"All personnel, report to station immediately. All personnel report," bellowed the ships announcement system.

Everyone in the room rose as one.

Split and Teladi fleets under Yaki attack.

\* \* \* \* \* \* \* \*

Brett stood in the briefing room with the other eight pilots who were the strike force of the frigate. Two squads of ships were all she could carry. They had been stationed on her for the last three Jazuras, Brett really wanted to be on a carrier but you did what you were told. At least here there was a bit more freedom. They had flown over twenty missions now. Three pilots had been lost and replaced, the other five had been here from the time they had shipped out, just after obtaining their stars.

They had retrieved cargo pods, escorted politicians and accomplished the occasional assault. That was where they had lost pilots. But all the time Brett had run an organised and efficient squad. Bibby and Shake had been with him from the start. He had seventeen kills to his name now, pirates mostly and importantly, two Xenon. Rarely seen nowadays after the great Xenon war, but if they were discovered they were attacked on sight and Brett had taken two out.

The flight commander addressed them.

"Contrary to what you may have seen on the news casts, we are not about to launch any offensive strikes on the Yaki. Our intelligence states that the Yaki are in conflict with the Split and Teladi and although our leaders do not take kindly to their actions, we have no orders to act."

"We pilots, are about to launch a strike against the mines in the Bevu sector. They have announced their intention to join the Yaki and leave the foundation guild. Our orders are to take out their defensive capability so the politicians have a stronger position to negotiate."

The pilots glanced around at each other as this could be tricky. Mines typically had good defences and if these had decided to announce their intention to defect before actually carrying out the threat, they must have some confidence.

The two dimensional view of the sector appeared on the screen set in the wall at the back of the room. It was the same display that they received in their ships, so they were familiar with it.

The commander went through the intelligence reports. A dozen light fighter craft and two medium assault ships was the probable force. The mines that were situated on the three small moons close to the uninhabited planet also had fixed laser battery defences.

"We are not to engage the fixed defences," the commander was explaining, "if we succeed in taking out the ships, then our government expects them to concede."

"If they don't, then I expect we will receive new orders. But for now, we engage the ships, understood?"

"Yes Commander!" They all replied together. This wasn't looking like it was going to be easy. Brett knew that the mine defence ships would be inexperienced pilots, no match for his squad, but they had fourteen ships. The frigate only had eight. Numbers sometimes made up for lack of skill or even greater firepower. You may have the best lasers, but if the enemy had two ships, you could only fire on one of them at a time.

"Any questions?" the commander asked.

"Sir," started Brett, "are we alone on this or do we have backup?"

"Alone, Brett. You have concerns?"

"Only that it seems a rather large force to be going against, Sir." Brett replied.

"Correct Brett, it is a large force. Fourteen against eight, I expect that to be closer to even after the first pass and then all over in the second, don't you?"

Brett felt all eyes upon him, he couldn't challenge the Commander's response, but he had said enough to voice a concern. If anything happened, it had been recorded. That was enough.

"Yes Sir, all over in the second pass Sir." If we get a second pass, he thought. If these ships engage as one unit, we are going to be in a big laser fight. They were equipped with a dozen Argon Discoverers and two older Argon Elite's. It was the Elite's that worried him, large slow assault craft. They were nimble though and if fitted with the right shields and lasers, would prove difficult to take out.

The eight ships that the frigate carried where the relatively new Mako's. An Argon and Boron joint venture, these craft were as fast as the Discoverer's but had the shields and lasers of about seventy percent of that possibly carried by the Elite's.

The pilots headed for their ships as the frigate turned towards the gate that would bring them into Bevu.

* * * * * * *

Brett sat in his Mako doing the pre-launch checks and studying the sector display. They had now entered Bevu and the miners would surely know they were about to be attacked. He scanned the sector display via his slave again and again, but even though the frigate was advancing on the mines, no defence ships had launched.

This worried him. There were only two reasons why they hadn't launched. They didn't have any ships or they had a strategy. Brett opted for the second choice, they must have a strategy and that meant smart miners. He checked the systems again, lasers online, shields charged to maximum and functional. Ship to ship missiles loaded and ready, he checked the sector display again, nothing.

They were approaching the mines now, getting close and only twenty or so kilometres away. Still no ships had launched, would the captain of the frigate take them even closer? Brett knew that if they got within ten kilometres and the miners had missiles, they might just launch an offensive. Did the captain know that? He thought about contacting him, but quickly dispelled the idea. Of course he knew that, he was the captain of a frigate wasn't he?

Closer still, sixteen kilometres away from the nearest mine. Brett took a deep breath and made small fists with his hands. It didn't matter how many times you had been on a mission, you still felt tension. Fifteen kilometres, c'mon miners have a heart and act will ya!

The frigate only had a small landing bay, so the Makos were parked in eight fast launch tubes near the rear of the ship but facing outwards. Brett and his squad were on one side, Blue squad, Red squad was on the other side. They would be propelled by the ship up to 400 metres per second during launch, the engines on the Makos firing at the same time in an attempt to maintain the speed once they left the shielding and gravitational pull of the ship. Launching wasn't a problem once you had been through it many times, it was the fact that the command once given would be carried out within two Sezuras, unless you manually tapped the abort key. Brett kept his finger over it just in case, you never knew.

This ability to launch eight ships at once made the frigates a feared enemy. They were no match for any of the large cruisers and battleships that scoured the cosmos, but against a small force, they were deadly.

The frigate did carry missiles and also had a single beam laser on its bow. This was capable of delivering an enormous blow to a single stationary, or slow moving target. A number of laser batteries also adorned the ship for close-in defence against fighter attack, but these had proved only a token gesture when faced with large numbers of attackers in the simulators.

Thirteen kilometres. Brett's heart rate had increased, he could feel it, almost hear it in his suit. One way or another this was going to start soon because if they got within four kilometres the frigates beam laser would be within range and the Captain might decide to bombard the mines themselves. They would need to get within two klicks for the mine lasers to be in range.

Eleven. He tensed in his suit, waiting for the order to launch. What are you doing Captain? He thought, if we get too close and you launch, we're gonna launch straight into the moon itself. Fighters don't have brakes y'know.

Ten, he took a deep, deep breath. Letting it out slowly, calming himself. Nine. Eight. He looked to his left in a vain attempt to see his companions, but all he saw was the launch tube wall.

Seven. The miners had waited until the frigate could not escape their missiles and seven kilometres away was the range. Brett saw the dots appear on his scanner. He selected one, zoomed in, selected data. Oh no, factory killers! You damn fool Captain, get us out of here!

The Captain of the frigate had not expected the miners to possess such weapons as these. His intelligence reports did not indicate it, why should they have them?

He barked the order to his launch controller. "Launch fighters, now!"

What good fighters were going to do against 400 metres per second missiles was anyone's guess at this range. But he gave the order nevertheless.

"Launch confirmed!" The message came through the ship communicator. Here we go.

Bang! Brett's ship shot down the launch tube, gathering speed as it went. He saw the lights dotted along the tube flash past him faster and faster. He was pushed back hard into his seat and he tilted his head slightly to the side, grimacing at the force exerted on him.

Then space, the pressure disappeared instantly and he was aware that he now had control. He looked left and right through the space screen, confirming that the two on his left and one on his right had launched. Now we are free, he thought.

He heard the communication from Red squad and couldn't believe it.

"Too close, go verti......"

"What the f....."

He scanned the sector screen. Red squad was nowhere to be seen. The idiot had launched too close and they had been catapulted into the moon. Red squad was gone.

He saw the missiles hit through the rear display. Bang, bang into the shields of the frigate. Then another salvo, bang, bang, bang. The frigate was turning away from the moon.

"All ships, this is the Captain of Excel. We are taking damage and are evacuating the area. Cover our departure."

You have got to be kidding! Brett thought. If I could land at this moment I would pull you throat out, you stupid idiot.

"All offensive capability lost." It was the Captain again. "We have shields down and are accelerating away."

On the open channel? You say that on the open channel. Are you mad?

The other three ships from his squad were now in formation alongside him. The frigate was moving away and he was running options through his mind when the scanner bleeped at more contacts.

Oh no! The mines were launching their fighters. He saw them come out of the docking bays from each mine and counted them off, eighteen fighters and six Elites. Intel got that wrong as well then.

"OK, Blue squad. You see the targets as well as I do, maintain formation until we clear the missile range of the mines. Then await further orders. Check your systems people, your gonna need 'em!"

The enemy fighters were forming up into an attack stance. Not the inexperienced pilots they had thought then. Brett was beginning to wonder whether some of these ships were mercenaries, maybe Yaki ships brought in to protect the mines. The communication channel opened again.

"Blue One, this is your Commander, you read?" It was the squad commander.

"Gotcha Commander, go ahead." Brett replied.

"I have taken control of the frigate, the Captain has been relieved of command. We are in no state to fight. Performing jump sequence in twenty Sezuras. Your only chance is to lock the spot, you understand Blue One?"

Lock the spot? This was going to be fun. That meant that the frigate was going to jump and for a few Sezuras after, probably only two or three, the jump tunnel would remain open after the frigate had gone. The commander was telling Brett to aim for that point in space and follow them through before the tunnel closed. The Mako's didn't have jump drives. If they didn't make it, they were on their own against the miners.

This was tricky as your speed had to be slow to jump, but you had to be in the right place at the right time, which meant full speed to be there.

Brett was already turning towards the frigate, the rest of Blue squad staying in formation. They had heard the message and blinked confirmations. He didn't need to speak with them.

They raced at the frigate, closing in together so all four Makos were only metres apart.

"Incoming!" It was Shake. "Seeker missiles launched, impact ten Sezuras."

Seeker missiles were launched and forgotten about. Fire and forget. They locked onto the closest enemy target and would change their target if the internal scanning device thought it a better target. They were aimed at Blue Squad.

C'mon Commander, jump!

"Five Sezuras!" The Commander confirmed.

They were almost on the rear of the frigate now, it was slowing for the jump. Then brilliant flashes of blue swirling light. The jump tunnel!

Brett set the speed of the ship to 40 m/s. He was currently showing a speed of 380. The engines groaned as they went into reverse thrust, Brett felt the change in force and it pushed him forward in his seat. Blue Squad followed their leader, all slowing for the tunnel.

"Their gonna get us Brett!" It was Bibby.

The frigate was gone. The tunnel had already started to shrink. One last look at the sector scanner, missiles about to strike, speed at 42, 41, 40. Then the tunnel and silence, no movement in the ship, only the swirling tunnel. Brett couldn't move, frozen in time, yet his senses were still alive. He could see the tunnel rotating around him, but he couldn't move his head or eyes.

Then space, out of the tunnel and all senses taking in data. The frigate ahead, close by and turning to it's left. Brett flicked the control stick to veer right, Shake went vertical, Bibby turned down. Blue four, the newest recruit wasn't so lucky. Two seekers had also made the tunnel and as they exited they locked onto Blue Four, the closest target and the one not moving away.

Crack! Boom! They all heard the explosion through the communication channel before it was abruptly cut off.

"Blue Four's bought it, Blue One" It was Bibby again.

"Confirmed squad," replied Brett, "Shake, go evasive, the second missiles locked onto you."

It had, the first missile had destroyed Blue Four and the second one realising that its intended target was now obliterated, turned its attention to another one. It took a fraction of a Sezura to make the decision, Shake's ship won.

Brett looped over and flew after Shake, he was heading upwards while darting from side to side, accelerating as he went. Brett came at him at an angle and sure enough the seeker was below him, closing in on Shake.

Brett aimed at the missile, no chance of a lock on such a small object. Then it veered towards him. On no, the seeker had changed its path again, Blue One offered a better target now!

Brett opened fire, laser bolts streaking out from the four weapons, one on each weapon mount (small wings on the side of the craft) and two in the nose. He felt the judder of the ship as the lasers screamed out. No chances of a good hit just rely on instinct, spray the area with fire and hope you get it. The lasers on the nose were a smaller weapon than the wing mounts, but this gave them a higher rate of fire.

Finger on the trigger, starting to hurt he was pulling so hard. Hand feeling wet, slippery. Sweat beginning to pour down his face, high pitched wail of the lasers. Bang! The explosion so close he wasn't sure for a Sezura whether he had been hit or not. No, the missile had exploded only metres away from his ship.

"Hey, way to go Blue Leader!" Shake screamed.

Brett slumped onto the console, taking in deep breaths in an attempt to calm his nerves. That was close.

He looked at the sector map while still spread across the console, his slave piping the data in. Argon Prime! By the book of truth, we're home!

They landed on the frigate, one after another on the small landing bay. Brett jumped out of his Mako and made for the bridge, anger boiling inside him. He burst into the command deck, spotted the Captain and ran across the room shouting obscenities as he went.

"You killed 'em, you fool. You launched them into the moon!"

It took three marines to hold Brett back. They had been guarding the Captain. Bibby and Shake ran into the bridge and stopped just inside.

The squad commander put his hand on the struggling pilot. "Brett, calm down. It was a malfunction, not his fault."

Brett stared into the commander's eyes, anger and fury still burning inside.

"What do you mean, malfunction?" he screamed.

"The data the Captain was getting was out of date, delayed somehow, I don't know how yet. He thought we were still approaching the first moon, not the second. It shows up in the logs Brett."

Brett looked from the commander to the Captain. The Captain simply shrugged, he was a broken man. Brett relaxed slightly, but the marines holding him did not.

* * * * * * * *

They sat in the bar on Argon Four, Brett, Bibby and Shake. It had been three Tazuras since the Bevu fiasco and they had been transferred to the large cruiser. It sat in stationary orbit around Argon Prime. They had nothing to do, no orders, no missions, so they sat in the bar and drank and talked.

It was a larger bar than the one they had become so accustomed to on the frigate and was full of pilots, ships crew and maintenance staff. They were still arguing over the near miss they had experienced. The Captain was down on the planet undergoing a debriefing, otherwise known as an interrogation. No information had been fed back to them about the incident and they were quite confident none would be.

What they had discovered though through the news and official briefings was that the Split and Teladi navies had indeed suffered a heavy defeat at the hands of the Yaki. Not much detail was known, but they had confirmed reports of the size of fleets that had set out and as stated, they had not returned.

Brett was feeling just slightly light headed, the drink in the navy bars was weakened from the illegal stuff sold in the space stations. But it still gave the same feeling if enough was consumed. Shake didn't drink, but Bibby was following Brett drink for drink.

"It's not your fault Brett," she was saying, "he should have veered left, he knew his position like the rest of us."

"I know, I know. But you can't help wondering what could have been eh?"

They were talking about Blue Four, which had been destroyed by the seeker, after they exited the jump. Four ships in a squad, when you jump together you turn into you pre-assigned direction. The other three had followed this rule, Blue Four had not and paid the price.

"Hey you two," it was Shake, "if the kid had turned, then it would've been one of us. The missiles could have chosen us instead and you know yourself, you can't outrun a pair."

Brett looked at him, not convinced that he was right, but so what? It didn't matter now. He was gone. Just another pilot lost to the cause.

He heard shouting from the door of the bar, it was one of the laser battery operators from the look of his uniform.

"The news!" He was shouting. "Listen to the news, the President is speaking!"

Someone must have instructed the bar robot as the large screen that filled half the back wall sprang into life. The face of the Argon President filled the screen, speaking from his usual podium, planet side.

"....that we have confirmed reports, the listening outposts of Echo Seven and Echo Twelve have been destroyed. The space station and energy plants in the vicinity of Echo Nine have also been destroyed. We confirmed this just before Echo Nine itself went down."

Shake looked at Brett, Brett looked at Bibby. Bibby looked at both of them and then back to the screen. The Echo stations were military stations designed to scan the sectors. They contained dozens of fighter ships and thousands of personnel.

"An aggressive force is currently moving against the food farms and processing plants in the area of Echo Three." The President paused. "People of Argon, I have instructed our Admiral not more than five Mizuras ago, to use whatever means at her disposal to stop these barbaric and mindless acts of destruction."

"Rest assured, we will be successful. Please spare your thoughts for the men and woman of our navy. My people, as of this moment, a state of war exists between the Argon and the Yaki."

Brett looked at Bibby and Shake again, suddenly he felt none of the effects of the drink. They just sat with their mouths open, speechless.

* * * * * * * *

It was sometime later before she saw the President's speech. It took time for the message drones that had automatically been sent out to all the Echo stations to be intercepted.

She smiled. Fool President, does he think his Argon navy can save him now?

She turned to her aide. "Everything is ready?"

"Yes Moo-Kye, we will be in strike position of the Echo Three sector in four Tazuras."

"Good." Came the reply. "Let it begin."

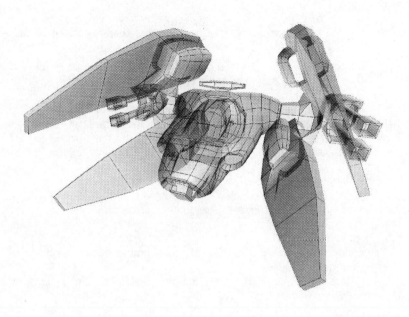

## Chapter 9: Gates and re-alignment

*Trying to explain the truth to the masses. Was it an impossible task?*
*Should you not try and explain it, but simply tell them what is so?*

Mitch and Mi Ton sat in the small transport ship. Trouble was afoot, but they had been summoned to the Argon government anyway after their results had been received. They hadn't finished, still more to do, but they were so close they had decided to inform the Argon and Boron governments of their find.

So a Boron war ship had been dispatched to collect them, as they had no jump devices of their own. The large ship had appeared at the gate and hailed them to depart. They had finalised their plans and set the computer systems running so they could continue to extract data while they were gone.

"How important is that base?" the Boron Captain had inquired when they were safely onboard.

"Very important." Mi Ton had remarked, almost flippantly, his suit moving slowly to and fro as it hovered over the floor.

"Well if you leave it like that, on it's own in this current situation, it might not be there when you get back." The Captain replied.

"So what do you suggest?" Mitch asked.

"We can protect it, but it'll have to shutdown."

"Never!" Mi Ton flashed, "we cannot shut it down. The work is too valuable."

"Better shutdown and still there, than not to be there at all." The Captain stated.

"He has a point Mi," Mitch said, "what do you have in mind Captain?"

The Captains stalks moved briefly inwards.

"New protection systems my friends. We have a Sentinel onboard. We can use that."

Both Mi Ton and Mitch looked intrigued, they had heard nothing about this. Mitch felt a slight twinge at being away for so long. You lost touch that was the problem.

"Explain." Mi Ton suggested.

"This device generates a massive shield for your station. So big it is virtually indestructible. However, it will use all available power from your nuclear power plant and everything within its protective screen will be doused with energy. They will not work while the Sentinel is armed."

"But what of the reactor's systems?" Mitch asked.

"They are within the reactor's protective screen, yes?" replied the Captain.

"Yes." Mitch replied.

"Then they will work, all others will not." He said, bending slightly on his four legs.

"So why can't we put all the systems within the screen?" Mi Ton asked, he was becoming very interested in this new development.

"The screen protects, yes? Your scanners will not work inside it? You cannot fire lasers from within a screen and so on. Your station will be dormant while the Sentinel is activated, it can only be deactivated by the owner of the station who has the codes. Or if it runs out of life." He added.

"Runs out of life?" Mitch again.

"Yes, the one we have with us will operate for ten Tazuras, after that it will deactivate. A Sentinel can only be used once, if you deactivate it before the end of it's life span, it is useless." The Captain floated backwards in his suit and took his position in his command straps.

Mitch nodded. Mi Ton raised his snout. They agreed.

"Deploy it!" They both said in their native languages.

After the Sentinel was installed and activated the Boron ship entered a jump tunnel. It wasn't very long before they were sat in the meeting chamber on the main trading station in Argon Prime. They were awaiting their visitors, the Argon and Boron government representatives who would listen to their find and take the information back for perusal.

They had agreed that Mitch would start the briefing and Mi Ton would answer any questions from the floor. Then they would just see how it went.

The four representatives from each government filed into the room and took their seats. Mitch stood, greeted them and took his place at the podium, the screen he would be using to explain their findings behind him on the wall.

He started by describing the laws of physics, Protons and Neutrons, Quarks, Gravitons and the relationships between them.

"These things, we here in this room either already understand or have no wish to understand, please skip this section and carry on." Stated the Boron head of science.

Mitch was a little agitated, he fumbled with the display controller and moved the presentation further on. A picture filled the screen. Ten boxes in a row numbered one to ten in both Argon and Boron.

"Ok," he said, "imagine you are at number one and looking at number two. Number two is a single light Jazura away, so what you are looking at when you are at number one is what happened at number two a whole Jazura ago, yes?"

They all nodded their approval. This was more like it for the politicians in the room.

"Well, if you are then at number two, you can see what is happening now at number two and what happened a Jazura ago at number one and number three and so on." He looked for signs of puzzlement, he didn't see any. Good.

"Our surveyors are installed across the entire known universe in most sectors, except of course the current areas of conflict. So what you see is really just a picture in time, physically see I mean, the background stars and nebulae are just pictures hanging on the wall, so to speak."

"If you can be at number two, you are looking at what you will see at number one in a Jazura. The gates give us this capability. Now the gates don't span the whole universe, that much we know, but they cover a wide area." He pressed a button on the controller and the graphic on the screen span into a three dimensional image and then began to multiply to show the known gate systems of which their were thousands, many still undiscovered or mapped they were sure.

"But," he went on, "we are not looking at pictures, we are looking at data, specifically data of positive and negative energy. We can see what it was and what it will be."

"For example, every time an object enters a gate a great amount of negative energy is produced by the gate. Why, we are not sure yet. However, this is countered by the positive energy of the object, for example the ship."

The audience was beginning to become enthralled, he could tell.

"But not all the negative energy is countered. It can be mapped and some of the military systems use this for tracking purposes already."

"What we have found is this. The amount of negative energy left over by gate activities is nowhere near what we are finding. There are two answers for this."

The audience leaned forward as one.

"Firstly, we are tracking gate usage in areas where we don't know there are gates. Somebody, or something is using gates elsewhere." Mitch paused to make sure he had the required impact.

"Secondly, the background negative energy can be mapped. It came from somewhere and although we do not yet have definite proof, we will have soon."

"For what?" an Argon politician asked like a young boy.

"We have checked the history banks and there was a large, what can I say, usage of negative energy approximately six hundred Jazuras ago. Exactly around the time the Teladi state they lost contact with their home planet."

"This is accurate at present to the Mazura, but we expect to map it to the Sezura soon."

"So we have a history lesson Mitchell, excellent I am sure you will receive the Argon Broker prize for science." The Argon politician jibed.

"I haven't finished." Mitch stated. The Argon sat back in his chair, slightly embarrassed.

"Not only can we map that this happened, we can tell where the gates were that somehow changed their configuration. The energy levels are clear on this."

"And," Mitch checked his words and licked his lips, they were becoming dry, "the levels are increasing in certain areas as well."

He let it sink in, would they be able to grasp what he was saying?

"Which means what?" grunted one of the Boron.

"Which means, the gates are going to be reconfigured again." The room gasped, the Boron snorted.

"When?" Three voices at once.

"We have not calculated the timings exactly yet, we are still working on it. However, our initial findings state that it will happen in the next ten Jazuras."

"Ten?" exclaimed the Argon science officer. "Are you sure? Ten?" He was shaking his head, the others in the room were talking to each other and the noise in the room was increasing.

Mi Ton joined Mitch on the podium and Mitch held out an arm to steady the floating Boron in his suit. "Please everybody, calm down, quiet please." He pleaded. It took a few more attempts but he finally got the others in the room to be silent and sit and face the front again.

"Let me say finally," Mi Ton gestured, "that we have also discovered the general location of the Argon home planet, Earth." The room erupted again.

"Please, PLEASE!" Mi Ton commanded. "We cannot see it, it is too far away and would take over a thousand Jazuras to travel there at the speed of light."

"So how do you know where it is?" someone asked.

"We do not know for certain, we only know it's direction. This we have discovered by the energy levels given off in certain areas. We know by studying the local gates which way they are pointing, so to speak, by analysing the energy levels and the direction they face. It is simple really. A gate gives off negative energy in the opposite direction to the way it is pointing. Just like we can track ships today, or at least know the size and destination from the energy readings, we can track what did happen many Jazuras ago."

"We have found that one of fifty or so gates could have been the source at the time. There is no current destination pointing in that direction. We should know soon, which particular gate it is."

"My friends and colleagues, if we are right and if such a gate also exists at the other side, we could be open to Earth within ten Jazuras."

* * * * * * * *

They had overdone it slightly, they knew. Mentioning Earth was enough to get them extra funding, they weren't quite sure if it was Earth. They were right that the gates did point somewhere else in the past and which one was still a mystery for now. But they did know that all data pointed to there being a gate link in that direction at that time. Only that direction had such overwhelming readings. The Teladi homeworld must be inside the current configuration, so it was harder to find a pointer to that. But they would, they were sure.

They had only spent two Tazuras at the station in Argon Prime when they were sworn to secrecy and shipped back to the laboratory. It was still there just as the Boron had said it would be, in perfect condition. They deactivated the Sentinel and continued with their work. This time the Boron warship stayed to patrol the sector and other smaller military vessels began to arrive

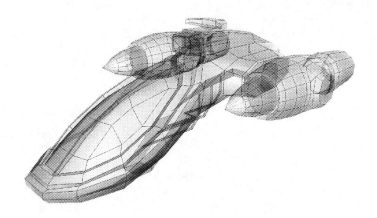

## *Chapter 10: The battle for Echo Three*

*Conflict. There are never winners in any conflict, only degrees of losing.
The trick is to lose with the lowest degree.*

The battle for Echo Three.

The small nimble fighter turned to its right, the pilot seeking out the small object that was far from his base. He and his squad had destroyed fourteen so far. This one, if he could locate it visually, would be the last one.

It showed up on the scanner, he had locked onto it as soon as he had destroyed the last one. But finding it, that was a different matter. He would need a visual and you couldn't do that flying at this speed. He was getting closer, the image inside his head showed 3.6 kilometres. Time to slow this crate down, he thought. He commanded the ship to slow to fifty m/s and felt the push forwards as the engines obeyed the computer commands.

Now where is it? The scanner was indicating that it was upwards. He pulled back gently on the control stick and actually leaned forward in his seat, squinting outside of the space screen in an attempt to help his quest. No, can't see it. Quick check on the scanner again, one kilometre and closing.

There! He saw it, energy wings stretching outwards for power. The local sun had just reflected off its surface, as the angle was right. It was gone again now, but it didn't matter. The pilot had mentally plotted its position and he steered straight for it.

Quick check on the laser energy banks. Fine, full power available. He squeezed the trigger and the laser bolts shot out before him. Four quick bursts from the twin lasers and then an explosion. Got it!

"Echo Three, this is Gold One. Do you read?"

"Confirmed Gold One. Go ahead." Replied the space station.

"Mission accomplished Echo Three. All navigation satellites destroyed." The pilot stated.

"Confirmed Gold One. Return to base, Echo Three out."

The pilot smiled. Mission accomplished. A good start to what was looking like being a very bad few Tazuras.

\* \* \* \* \* \* \* \*

The communication officer turned to the station commander. "All accounted for Sir. We have destroyed every Nav Sat in this and the surrounding sectors as ordered. Nobody can surprise us now. They'll have to pound it the old way." He smiled.

"That they will," the station commander agreed, "but once our fleet is underway, so will we." He pointed out.

"Ah yes, commander, so will we." He repeated.

\* \* \* \* \* \* \* \*

The Orion.

Admiral Stacey sat in the officers briefing room aboard the Argon navy's flagship, the "Orion". They had quickly put together a force and had been on their way now for three Tazuras. She had ordered all Nav Sats in the Echo Three area to be destroyed right away. It had taken a day to organise the fleet and she didn't want the enemy jumping in using the Nav Sats before they could. The satellites enabled ships to jump from one point to a gate further away, thereby skipping the normal route and arriving much sooner. No point in arriving to find the battle already finished.

The Orion was the latest ship to enter service and was the pride of the Argon fleet. They had done away with the blocky flat designs of the older ships and created a somewhat improved design. It was constructed of four, almost separate bulbous parts. Big sections that appeared connected part of the way down each of their ends so that you couldn't see where they ended. It appeared as one long construction, even though it was indeed individual parts.

Part of the navy's intention, they could build smaller ships using the same methods. Plans were already being laid for further ships, small ones made up of two of the constructions and medium size ships made up of three. Attached to the sides of the ship were two large launch bays, one on each side. These allowed the ship to launch and receive large numbers of ships. Although each side could accomplish both tasks, they used one for launching and one for landing and then would switch when ships were reloaded.

It sounded complicated and potentially dangerous, but each bay had hazard lights surrounding the whole oblong entrance. These shone green or red depending upon the bay's current stance. On the front of the ship, at the top of the forward structure was the bridge, a small square shaped protrusion that had space screens on every side. Light shone from the bridge where the crew was busy at work.

Officially described as a carrier for the "deployment of massed forces to battle", the Orion was actually also capable of delivering a blow in her own right having beam lasers and missile launchers installed.

She was heading directly for the gate that led to Echo Three. A massive armada of ships surrounded her. Frigates, Destroyers and the older carriers were all present along with many small fighter craft that patrolled the sector and stayed on station, ready for any attack.

This was the force hastily constructed to meet the threat posed by the Yaki who were themselves currently heading for Echo Three from the opposite direction. It wasn't the whole fleet by any means. Much of the Argon navy was scattered around the sectors protecting other important installations and there would always be a battleship and carrier in orbit around Argon Prime, always.

In fact, none of the three serviceable battleships that the navy possessed were in this force. They couldn't be brought to station fast enough, so the force had left without them.

Admiral Stacey felt confident without them though. This force was strong enough to tackle a race in itself. Then again, she shuddered, the Yaki were becoming a race, weren't they?

She looked around the table at the other force commanders, all main ship captains were on board for the final strategy meeting before they entered the sector. Six other officers, plus herself. Seven large ships plus a multitude of fighters of different size were in the fleet.

"So ladies and gentlemen," she began, "can I assume that all orders have been given and every person in this force knows their place?"

All six around the table pressed buttons on their consoles to record their agreement as well as visibly with the nod of the head.

"Well let's hope for a speedy victory then and back home to our loved ones. I don't expect these," she searched for the word, "bandits, to give us much trouble."

One of the frigate captains spoke up. "They did manage to destroy four large destroyers and fifty ships of the joint Teladi/Split force Ma'am," he stated.

"That is true," she replied resting her elbows on the table and grasping her left hand in her right. "But as we know, they will have fought a disjointed campaign with outdated ships. We are much stronger than that."

He nodded his agreement, no sense in arguing this close to the actual battle. But deep inside all seven of them each had their doubts. What losses had the Yaki taken during that brief strike? How big was their fleet anyway? Intelligence was scarce since the hostilities began. Every attempt at sending drones and scout ships had been a failure. None of them had returned, even message drones from the scout ships. It had an ominous feeling to it.

The fleet continued on its course towards the gate.

* * * * * * * *

Echo Three.

The woman sat at her console, scanning again and again across the sector. She could see everything in the sector from her screen, but she continually selected objects individually and checked their status. She sighed and rubbed her hand across her forehead. She felt tired. They had been running double shifts ever since war was declared, so the station had maximum staff at the ready at all times. She was nearing the end of her second shift and she was feeling the pressure and tension of the situation.

The station sat almost exactly half way between the two gates. The gates where the two opposing forces would soon come. There were a few other large objects in the sector, an energy plant, two food processing plants and a single mine on one of the slow moving asteroids that had been caught in the planets gravitational pull and now orbited as a small moon.

But all personnel from those had left. Fleeing back to the safety of the inner sectors. Probably seeking out assurance from the Argon government that they would be able to claim some form of compensation in the event their properties were destroyed. Some chance of that, she mused. The government might ask the enemy to pay up when it was all over, if there was an enemy left. But there was no chance the Argon government would start bankrolling traders. Especially those out on the frontier where the profits were high. You chose to set up there, they would say, you take the risks.

That's why she had joined the navy. Nice steady income, you do what you are told and you pay so much of your credits into the navy scheme. Then when your time is up, you leave and go back planet side with a reduced income. Or you stay in space and take your chances with the traders. Well it seemed like a good idea at the time, sign up, basic training and pick a career. What would madam like to be? A technician perhaps, quantum mechanics maybe? Yeah right. Three quarters of the time spent staring at this stupid screen and the rest trying to sleep in quarters you could barely turn around in. If you did manage to get any time awake, then you had to blow off steam. Some went to the exercise centres where you could stretch your muscles and keep in shape, but the majority hit the relaxation zone and drank themselves to oblivion. She was just contemplating whether her tired body could handle another night of the zone when her console bleeped. A ship had just exited the gate. Oh no! Wrong gate.

"Sir! We have an incident here." She shouted across the room and into the communication system at the same time. Ships were pouring through the gate like Argon ants from a nest.

"Yes scan, report." The station commander replied into his communication device attached to his lapel. He was moving towards her as he spoke.

"Contact sir, multiple contacts. Exiting gate now."

"Ours?"

"Negative Sir. Unidentified signatures" she replied.

"Strength?"

"Sixty four and counting sir. They are still coming through."

"Type?"

"All fighter class so far sir. Medium and small."

The station commander thought for a moment. This is it then. A whole career behind me and they actually come here.

"Shall we launch Sir?" It was fighter command.

"No!" He snapped. "Let them get closer. Station batteries, come to alert. Missile batteries, start to track. Do not fire until I give the order, understand? Do not fire."

A number of confirmations could be heard through the communication channel that was now switched onto the main system so that everyone in the room could hear it.

He swept his gaze around the room. Men and women in their uniforms seated at consoles. Red, green, blue and white lights flickering from their screens. He took in a deep breath and then realised some of his staff were watching him. He consciously let it out slowly. What can I do? We can't run, and against the size of force that was bearing down on them, fighting wasn't much of an option either.

What else? Surrender? Not likely, that was one thing he couldn't contemplate. You had to have a certain character to surrender and he didn't have that type. No way, they'll kill you anyway, murdering pirates. Better to go down fighting than to give in. Yeah good, he felt better now, a shot of adrenaline does wonders for your self esteem. He smiled. C'mon then Yaki, let's see what you've got. This ain't no little lookout post like the other Echo stations you've been shooting out. This is Echo Three, best in its class. You won't roll us over that easy.

"Sir." It was the girl on scan again.

"Yes scan, what you got?"

"Large ships are entering the sector sir. A battleship, three destroyers and two squads of assault ships sir."

"Direction?"

"On us Sir. They are heading straight for us." Came the reply.

"OK, scan thank you." He turned to communications. "Comms, wrap that data up and launch message drones to the fleet."

"Confirmed Commander. Drones launching now."

"OK people. Don't go worrying now, the fleet is coming." He sounded convincing even though he knew himself that they didn't know where the fleet was exactly. They had received a drone when the fleet had entered the adjacent sector so they could only be Mizuras away. Still, where were they?

He moved so that he was directly behind the scanner. "Scan, put that view on the main screen."

The large screen at the back of the command room switched from the many screens that normally showed the stations status to the single display that was the sector map. He studied the data. Eight assault ships approaching the station. These would surely have heavy weapons, maybe beam lasers and certainly factory killer missiles. In front of them was a force of about thirty small and medium fighters. It was obvious what was about to happen. The smaller fighters would try and draw his force of twenty out, so the assault ships could launch directly on the station. They were going to try and draw his teeth. Well, he wasn't going to fall for that one. He would let the station's laser batteries fire at the fighters and launch his force against the assault ships.

"Scan, zoom in on those assault ships if you will."

The screen zoomed into the large ships and he noticed now that the view was clearer and each ship could be seen individually, that fighters flanked them. Two for every assault ship. He wiped his hand from his forehead to his chin and left it there, rubbing at the unshaven skin.

"They're coming in!" It was fighter command.

"OK scan, give me a close up view around the station." The screen moved around and then zoomed in to the station. Ships were getting close. "Keep an eye on those capital ships scan. They get within fifteen klicks, you yell. Understood?"

"Yes Sir!" Good keep them busy. People don't panic when they're busy.

"Laser Batteries, you have control. Commence firing, fire at will."

"Aye sir!" Battery replied.

All laser batteries that were facing the incoming fighters opened fire. Shhh...thump. Shhh...thump. Laser bolts streaking across the vacuum. The fighters at the front of the force showing flashes as the lasers struck their shields. The second fighter must have taken control damage as it didn't swerve away like the others but continued on and crashed into the station shields, exploding on impact.

The commander glanced at the large shield strength indicator that was set into the wall to the right of the main screen. It read ninety three percent in large blue letters.

The Yaki fighters swarmed over Echo Three. Moving in towards the station, lasers blaring and then quickly spinning away to avoid the laser batteries. They wouldn't make much of an impact on their own. But the small lasers were almost continually hitting the station shields and there was no time for them to regenerate. They were dropping, slowly but surely the shields were coming down. He glanced at the wall again, eighty two percent.

A flash of light on one of the external camera views. "That's three Sir, we got another one."

"Keep at it battery, keep at it." Another look at the scanner, assault ships ten kilometres and closing.

"Fighter command, launch against those assault ships, everything you've got."

"Aye Sir!" He watched as the first of his fighters left the station dodging fire as it went. The Yaki fighters must have been waiting for it to happen and they broke off their attack on the station and headed for the Argon ships that were exiting one by one.

The shields began to rise.

"Sir, assault ships at six klicks and closing." It was scan.

"Missile batteries. Target the front two assault ships with a 150% damage salvo."

"Tracked sir."

"Fire!" The commander shouted.

The six missiles left the station, accelerating as they went, weaving around as they tracked their pre-determined targets. The Yaki assault ships scattered in all directions and he watched the screen agonisingly as the missiles closed.

They hit. Large flashes on the tracking camera as the assault ship's shields took the first missile hits and then two explosions, one just after the other as the two ships exploded in silence.

A small cheer in the command room. "Quiet!" He snapped. "This ain't over yet."

He felt the shudder and the station shook, just like a land quake shook the buildings back home. He staggered and grabbed the side of the desk next to him with his hand. Beam lasers. The assault ships were attacking with beam lasers. Another shudder rocked the station. Shields fifty eight percent.

Outside the station, ships spun around attempting to get good locks on their foes. The station ships were following their orders and attacking the assault ships. They were so close to the station now the laser batteries were targeting them as well. Another blinding flash, another assault ship destroyed.

"Fighter command, situation report." The commander ordered.

"Five lost sir, we are outnumbered." Came the answer.

"I know that." A low rumble, short, followed by another and another. Missiles, does this never end?

Another two assault ships destroyed by his fighters, only three to go. They were too close really for missile locks, but he had no choice.

"Missile batteries, attack those assault ships again." They turned from their consoles to look at him, knowing the same, as he did, that not all missiles would succeed. "Do it!" He shouted.

They obeyed and a dozen missiles launched from the station trying to track their foes. One turned too quickly in its attempt to follow its target that was running for the back of the station and it glanced off the side of the station shields, exploding on impact. He'd expected that, calculated risk. Either they die first or we die first, who has the best shields? He glanced at the wall, twenty seven percent, it was going to be close.

"Incoming message commander," it was comms, "It's the Orion!"

"On screen!"

The admirals face appeared on the screen, she looked out of place sat in her seat, all perfectly dressed while around him the commander was witnessing carnage.

"Commander, your situation if you please." Admiral Stacey inquired like she was asking the time.

"Under heavy attack Admiral," boom, another missile strike. The commander steadied himself again, "on our knees but still punching Ma'am." He glanced at the main screen that was now showing the position the station found itself. "Eight fighters lost, almost out of missiles, shields at.." boom, "shields at eighteen percent Ma'am."

"Acknowledged Echo Three, we are in sector, obtaining strike vectors now." She glanced to something, or someone at her side then returned to the screen. "Hang in there commander." The screen went blank, everyone in the room cheered, even the commander. They could still die, he knew that all too well, but the relief that the fleet was actually here was almost overwhelming.

Boom, boom. More missile strikes on the station, shields at fifteen percent.

"Prepare all non-combat personnel for immediate evacuation. This is Commander O'Donnell of Echo Three, confirm."

The loud, slow female voice of the station computer boomed over the channel, "Confirmed commander. Evacuation sequence activated."

All over the station people were running for the escape chutes. A vast network of tunnels that you could literally jump into, then be transported down into the escape bay. Four large slow transport ships awaited, their cargo holds fitted out with life support systems. Fifteen hundred people were all making their way to the ships while the five hundred or so combat staff stayed at their stations. There was no room for them on the ships anyway, he just hoped that once launched they would get away and not be attacked by the Yaki.

* * * * * * *

Blue Squad.

Brett sat in the pilot seat of his Mako, Bibby and Shake to his left and the latest recruit on his right. Blue Four, which was his name. Not interested what his real name is unless we get back from this one. Then I'll get to know him, but for now he goes by his call sign.

They were lucky, each ship had its own squad colours and Argon Four didn't have a blue squad when they arrived, so they kept their name. Good omen, he liked that. They were in a row behind Green squad and others were behind them. There was enough room on the carrier for a squad to take off together.

They had mounted their ships just before entering the gate, so they were ready for immediate launch, if required, when they entered Echo Three sector. Sitting on the launch bay in your ship while traversing the tunnel had felt kind of strange, he'd never done that before, looking backwards.

He checked the sector scan, it was a fight the likes of which he had never witnessed. There were ships everywhere and it would be impossible to make any medium range tactical decisions. Everything in this fight would be done at close quarters. That suited him, he preferred a stand up fight.

The fleet was advancing at full speed towards the battle around the station. Brett noticed that the large ships of the Yaki and their protective fighter escort were heading for them. He stared at the scanner, heard his own breathing, no other sounds in the ship. It was almost like being underwater, silence, peacefulness. He regulated his breathing and closed his eyes, got to clear his mind and focus.

Blackness, just the lovely soothing blackness inside my head. No external inputs, senses going to sleep, resting.

The beep from the channel made him snap his eyes open and he was immediately back to alert. He saw the ships in front moving up and away from the floor. Exiting the docking bay, engines firing brighter as they accelerated away.

"Blue squad, you are cleared for launch. Good luck and good hunting."

"Confirmed control." He pressed the engine button manually (he preferred that) and mentally increased the power to the engines. His ship moved forward and he lifted back on the control stick slightly. His Mako began to leave the floor and the ship.

Just as he passed the outer mouth of the bay he stabbed the engines to full power and he began to speed away, his three-squad members alongside.

"OK, Blue Squad, everybody fine?" Three confirmation lights. "Good, head out to the incoming fighters, keep it tight."

They turned upwards as they left the carrier and then rolled over as they completed the vertical turn. Green squad was a couple of kilometres further on and the next squad was leaving the ship behind them.

"This is Argon Four control, engage enemy fighters around that battleship."

Brett pressed the confirm button in his mind. He could see the large ships approaching, large menacing ships, dark in colour. Was it black? No blue, dark blue all over. Laser fire coming in! Sheesh, these are fast fighters. "Blue squad, engage."

The Yaki fighters had come in so quickly he had missed them, there was so much confusion on the sector screen that he couldn't tell what was going on anyway. He ignored it, time for looking at that later. He pulled his ship vertical as the Yaki craft zoomed overhead and performed the same manoeuvre that he had done when exiting the ship. The Yaki ships split up, like an explosion, all going different ways. He locked his mind and tracking system on the centre one and steered for an attack.

He had closed on the pirate in the turn, but was still over a kilometre away. Out of range according to the manual. Well not according to Brett. He lined the craft up in his sights and squeezed the trigger, four laser bolts leaving his ship at a time, two slightly redder in colour than the others.

He kept firing, hoping to get a hit. Success! He could see the flashes as some of his shots hit. Bang, bang, bang. The lasers bounced off his shields, but it shook his ship and his aim on the enemy was lost. The ship had turned towards him now. Lasers streaking at him, he pointed his ship straight at it and returned the fire. He who has the biggest shields wins a head to head, he knew and as the Yaki ship flew past he noticed it was a Split fighter, looked like a modified Mamba, he wasn't sure. But it was painted with jagged stripes all over the ship. These Yaki are lunatics, he thought.

He turned to follow it, his ship jolting again as another Yaki locked onto him. An explosion behind, close enough for the shields to pick it up and the light to flash his console white.

"Got him Blue One!" It was Blue Four. Brett ignored it, no time for chatter.

He continued the turn and the Yaki was going low, so Brett adjusted and aimed in front of him so he could close the distance as they went. He pulled the trigger again, but this time kept it firmly pressed. The lasers kept firing and the Yaki was running right into his line. Multiple strikes, keep it there, c'mon you pirate, keep turning. It did, and the lasers kept finding their target. A flash as it exploded and debris peppered his ship. A check on the shields, plenty enough to fight with. He told the combat system to lock the closest threat. It did, instantly, one hundred metres away.

Brett's ship shook like it was going to break up. He swerved left, right, up and down. Multiple lasers flashing past him. Dozens of shots, there's more than one he thought.

He plunged his ship downwards and kept the stick to its limit. The lasers went away, and he completed the loop. The Two Yaki fighters hadn't turned as quickly as he had. He opened fire. The rightmost enemy veered away, Brett selected it as his ship's locked target and mentally released two ship to ship missiles. They streaked away from his ship and he focused his full attention on the remaining Yaki.

It was taking evasive action, Brett had to stop firing while his missiles launched or he may have caught them by mistake, but now they were on their way, he pulled the trigger again and hits began to register on the Yaki ship. Flash, an instance of smoke, quickly dispelled in the vacuum and the Yaki was dead.

He checked his scanner for his comrades and more targets.

\* \* \* \* \* \* \* \*

Argon Four.

The captain sat on the bridge. He had launched his full complement of fighters, forty in all and they were now engaging the Yaki. The battle appeared to be going well, but there was more to do yet.

He didn't need to check the readouts, he could see the Yaki battleship through the large space screen on the bridge. They were heading straight for one another. The Orion was to their side, about three kilometres to the right. If they could play this right, the Yaki ship was going to pass between them. They'd be able to bring all guns to bear from the sides of two ships at once.

"Helm, I have control." He ordered.

"Aye Sir." Helm replied.

He took control of the large carrier with the control stick built into his seat. Don't trust helm to respond fast enough to commands, it would be better to fly this ship himself.

He steered her slightly away from the battleship and then came back on the same line, as before, the Yaki hadn't altered course. It began firing.

The twin beam lasers from the front of the Yaki ship hit Argon Four at the front. She shook violently while the lasers deposited their energy. The shields were low, but they held. The battleship was beginning to move between them now and he saw that the Orion had opened fire as expected. Good, the Yaki were getting some of their own medicine.

"Open fire!" He commanded.

All laser batteries and missile launchers on the right side began firing. The Yaki ship was now passing directly between them and the rate of fire was immense. He checked the readouts, if she kept taking damage like this, she was going to blow.

Then she was gone!

"What the.." The battleship had vanished, where to? No explosion or debris. He checked the scanner, she wasn't on the scanner.

"Orion, what happened?" he asked.

"Stand by Argon Four." Came the reply.

Where had the battleship gone?

Then it was there, in front of him. It seemed like only two hundred metres away. He veered his carrier to the left.

"Captain!" Shouted Helm, "what are you doing?"

He kept pulling the ship to the left. Suddenly the battleship was gone and right before him, large as could be in the space screen, was one of the frigates.

"Captain!" Helm shouted as he ran over.

Too late, the carrier collided with the frigate. A loud rumbling noise and then the sound of metal scraping. He heard the explosion as the frigate gave up its fight and then a brief moment later, with its shields depleted, the carrier followed suit.

* * * * * * * *

The Orion.

The admiral couldn't believe what she had just witnessed, the carrier had veered for no reason and ran into the smaller frigate. The result was that both ships were gone. The Yaki battleship had also gone, but it hadn't been destroyed, it had vanished. No jump tunnel had been seen. It had simply disappeared.

She saw that two of the Yaki destroyers were heading for the gate, retreating. The third seemed to be lumbering, possibly damaged from the fighter attacks. They were winning, she was certain of it. The Yaki battleship gone and the majority of their fighter ships were destroyed.

They had taken heavy losses too, Argon Four and a frigate lost. Over thirty ships destroyed in total. A good Tazura for the Argon people, but a bad one for the navy.

"Helm, take us within strike distance of that closest destroyer."

"Aye Ma'am." Helm replied as he jabbed the controls.

The Orion moved towards the Yaki ship. A few of its protective fighters were still moving around, trying to keep the marauding Argon fighters at bay. As soon as they were within range, the Orion launched missiles.

The Admiral watched them speed across the scanner. The destroyer feebly tried to turn away from them. One by one they hit, she could see the impacts through the space screen and saw her fighters begin to move away. They knew the fate that awaited the Yaki ship as well as she did and they didn't have long to wait.

It exploded in a massive ball of fire, which disappeared as quickly as it had started. The Yaki ship was gone.

"All fighters, this is Admiral Stacey." She was just about to give the order to engage the retreating destroyers when she saw them both enter jump tunnels.

"Engage any remaining enemy ships."

The pilot on one of the transport ships heading away from Echo Three station couldn't believe it when an Argon fighter began firing on them. Even less so when it launched missiles. He was still shouting obscenities through the communication channel when the transport ship exploded, killing the three hundred passengers on board.

## Chapter 11: Kotu

*Time to make your own way in life my friend, time to walk alone.*

Brett sat on the chair looking out of the space screen at the planet below. Argon Prime was such a marvellous spectacle especially when the sun glinted off the oceans.

Admiral Stacey stood to the side of the screen. She wasn't looking at him. Two marine guards where behind him either side of the door he knew, but he couldn't see them from where he was sitting.

He heard the door as it swished open. Somebody entered the room. No, not somebody, a Paranid, he could smell it. The admiral turned to greet the new arrival and Brett felt it move past him.

"Thank you for coming at such short notice LooManckStrat, it is very kind."

"Not at all," the Paranid replied through the translator, "the pleasure is mine."

The admiral gestured to Brett.

"This is the one?" the Paranid asked.

"Yes." She replied flatly.

The Paranid came close and looked Brett in the eyes, he tried to stare back, but he couldn't fix on the three eyes that gazed at him. LooManckStrat opened a container he had been carrying and pulled out what looked like three shiny metal balls. He threw them into the air and they took on a life of their own, hesitated for a moment as if in suspended animation and then shot across the room to Brett.

He was startled and tried to move backwards in the chair. He couldn't, the restraining bolts held him firmly. The metal balls moved around his head and neck, silent, probing. Moving in and out and around.

Then the Paranid reached out his hand and they shot across the room and lay in his palm. He placed them back into the container and turned to the admiral.

"Confirmed, he is one." LooManckStrat said.

The admiral nodded. She turned to the guards at the door. "Release him." She ordered. Brett sensed someone behind him and then a click as the bolts were released. His hands and feet free again.

He stood. "Just what is going on?" he asked.

Brett had destroyed seven Yaki fighters and was closing in on another when Argon Four blew. He lost that one, but Shake had got it anyway. They were hunting out more ships when they got the broadcast from the admiral.

"Engage any remaining enemy ships."

He'd looked at the scanner and there, coming at him were four Yaki assault ships. He'd engaged the front one with lasers and missiles and watched it explode. After he had dived through the explosion and taken evasive action he had come back around and they were gone.

No ships close by except three transports from Echo Three and Blue Squad.

His channel was full of people shouting at him and then he had received the command to land on the Orion. Well he couldn't land on Argon Four because it was gone so followed orders. None of Blue Squad spoke to him on the way in.

After landing, he was met with a group of stern looking marines who promptly took him prisoner and he spent the whole of the journey back to Argon Prime in the security area. Nobody spoke to him, nobody charged him with anything. Food appeared at the dispenser in the wall, right on time every time and then when they had reached orbit, he had been brought here to this room.

He wasn't happy.

The admiral addressed him. "You my fine pilot, gave a display just short of an Argon Star, then promptly blew up an unarmed transport ship carrying three hundred personnel from Echo Three."

Brett wasn't quite sure he had heard her right. "What? I shot up a bunch of Yaki fighters and then took out one of their assault ships before it jumped. Transport ship, what transport ship?"

"Sit down Brett, you need to see this." She gestured with her hand for him to sit back down. One of the marines placed a hand on his shoulder to convince him further.

The screen on the wall burst into life. He saw the view from one of the other transport ships as his Mako turned towards them. He saw himself firing into the transport ship, saw the missiles leave his ship and hit the transport. It exploded before his eyes.

"Nooooo!" He cried. "I didn't do that!" he pleaded. What was this, some kind of set up. Someone else had messed up and they had picked him out as a scapegoat. Oh yeah, that was it, poor orphan boy, no family to cry over him. Pick on someone who can be dealt with quietly.

"This," the admiral was saying, "is the view from your pilot log."

She played it back on the screen. They saw the confirmation on Brett's ship screen as he received the message from the admiral. Saw his systems show the assault ships and his successful attack. Then she played the sequence from the onboard (not the pilot's) view and this time the unarmed transport ship was there again.

She threw a brown coloured object on the table that was against the wall under the screen. The object was about ten centimetres long and two in diameter. It tapered away at the ends.

"That was found on your ship Brett. Hidden so well it was never picked before. It was installed during manufacture. Into the frame of the ship itself."

Brett just stared at her.

"We had suspicions for a while. After the incident with the Excel, we took that ship apart and found this on the bridge."

She threw another of the devices onto the table.

"I suspect we would have found one on Argon Four had she survived the collision with the frigate. We're still searching other ships, stations and so on to see if there are any more."

"So it's not my fault?" Brett asked, perplexed.

The admiral turned to the Paranid. "Would you like to explain?" she offered.

He moved to the screen, he wasn't going to use it. He just wanted to be at the focal point of the room.

"I am LooManckStrat, Paranid and head of ENeT. We manufacturer many things, mostly technological. We are the prime makers of Slave chips for example, you are aware of those I understand."

Brett nodded, of course I am, I've got one.

"Many Jazuras ago, my company invented a new Slave chip, better, more powerful than the old one. The Super Slave had greater range, greater perception, almost perfect in design. Longer term use was assured, it was a revelation." Whether it was the translator or the Paranid himself Brett wasn't sure but he seemed like he was trying to sell something and was delivering his closure.

"When we were just about to bring this to the races, after we had just switched our new rig into production and announced its sale on the trading systems, we were attacked."

"Pirates stole my chips, all one hundred of the first batch. Then they murdered my technicians, my scientists, my friends and they destroyed my station as they left. Taking with it all the secrets of the Super Slave."

Brett stared at him. Where was this going? "So what has this got to do with me?" he asked.

"Because Brett," the translator made it sound like bread, "you have a Super Slave installed."

Hang on there just a Sezura, Brett thought. He rose up in his seat. The guards became alert.

"I've got two?"

"No, no, no. You do not have a Slave chip Brett you have a Super Slave instead. You are a walking experiment, along with any others who are the same. The captain from the Excel I have already met, any others are either still hidden or dead." The Paranid seemed to have finished his part as he moved away from the screen.

The admiral looked at Brett. "Look Brett, this is a lot to take in. You did kill those people but it wasn't your fault. The Yaki have infiltrated us, had these Super Slaves installed in some of our best pilots and staff and then put those transmitting devices close by. They fed you data through the Slave. The Super Slave is so good, you can't tell the difference. Until you know you have one."

Brett said nothing.

"Let me show you. You know how to deactivate your sixth sense, your Slave and turn it off, yes?"

Brett nodded in agreement.

"But you only do that when you want to, the problem here is that you didn't think you needed to because you thought it was real, the images and sound are so realistic. Watch." She gestured to the Paranid.

He reached inside what Brett was beginning to think was a little bag of tricks and pulled out a flat device. Brett couldn't see clearly but it looked to have some buttons along its face.

He pressed a few buttons.

He heard the door swish open and the pirate came from behind him and ran towards the admiral. He stopped, black suit and coat swaying as he turned. In his hand he had a laser pistol, he raised his arm and pulled the trigger. The laser zipped past his face, he felt the heat and heard it thud against the wall behind him. Brett was already diving for cover, he looked at the guards for help, but they didn't move.

"Off Brett, deactivate it!" The admiral was saying.

Brett told his Slave to switch off. The pirate vanished.

He lay on the floor, panting, resting on one elbow and stared at the admiral.

"So what now?"

She smiled. "You have become a very important person Brett, LooManckStrat here is going to train you how to use the Super Slave offensively."

"Are you serious?" Brett inquired and he was genuine in his question.

"Deadly," she continued, "then you are going to join the swarming ranks of the traders, merge, disappear into the ether. You are going to work directly for me Brett. The Yaki are beaten, but not defeated. They'll be back, but we are going to take the fight to them and you my secret weapon, are going to help me."

\* \* \* \* \* \* \*

Moo-Kye sat on the bridge of her battleship. Her plans for domination lay in ruins, but it wasn't over yet. She had watched as the Argon fleet finished off hers. She sent the command to activate the Super Slaves and she actually giggled and jumped around the bridge as she watched the carrier turn into the frigate and the little fighter ship destroy its comrades.

But then she had to wait. The Argon navy didn't leave for a Tazura and then there were large ships still patrolling. Her ship was being repaired while they sat motionless in shroud. Oh what wonderful technology credits can buy she laughed. Those poor navy ships had searched for her to no avail and all the time she was sitting in exactly the same spot she had been when they had first activated the "Shroud" device. It was good fortune that nothing had ventured near. They will still there, still physically lying in the same spot in time and space, just shrouded, concealed. The energy shield taking all particles from every angle around the ship and moving them, close to the speed of light, to the other side. To an observer they were not there.

It was time to go now though, time to get back to her station and plan the next phase of her plan. The ship would only be visible for a few Sezuras and then the jump tunnel and they would be gone. The observers on that station probably wouldn't even register it. They'd think it was a blip and ignore it.

She gave the command and the massive bulk of the battleship came out of the shroud, a jump tunnel opened up in front of it and it was gone.

\* \* \* \* \* \* \*

Brett sat in one of the bars on the revolving space station. He was dressed in civilian clothes. The unmistakable twin sliver bars on the left shoulder of his brown, faded jacket showed him to be a pilot. Others in the room wore the same insignia, although dressed in a variety of attire.

Smoke filled the air, the bar was tended by two Argon females. Attractive, sparsely clothed, they were an added incentive for the customers to part with their credits. There were many other races in the room besides Argon. Two Boron pilots were enjoying the opportunity to sample the illegal Spaceweed. Its aroma was thick in the air, it made Brett feel nauseous, a sweet sickly smell. Teladi, those reptile like creatures, stood in a group by the bar. Talking in animated style, clawed hands making patterns in the air. Probably discussing tactics of space travel. There were eight of them, all in the same uniforms. Must be a company convoy, Brett mused, they're a long way from home out here.

Paranid and Split sat together. The Split with their ever cautious backs against the wall as they chatted to their allies. Still, no enemies in this place to be overly concerned about. Oh yes, you could make them all right. Drop a load of freight because the police forces snooped to close and the next trip you would make would be to your death. But you took your chances in this underworld of deals and whispers. The highest profits brought the greatest risks.

Brett had spent a long time with LooManckStrat and his technicians. They were as interested in Brett as they were with the training they had given him. He had power now that he never imagined before. He smiled, oh yes, power to make things happen. He looked at the bar area, large white, globe shaped lights high on the walls illuminated the area. One of them flickered and went out. One of the girls behind the bar turned to inspect it. As she approached it her head turned upwards trying to get a better view. Brett couldn't help but smile again as it flickered back into life and she stepped back, startled. Dumb computer systems. The Paranids had trained him well.

He knew there were others like him, but he didn't know who they were or indeed, where they were. They had been kept completely separate in the training area on the Paranids station. But they had to be of special talent, he was sure of that. If the Yaki plan had succeeded, the universe would be a different place today. But after the war they had pulled back their frontiers. They still operated in the outer sectors and traders still went there for the cheaper products, but they seemed to have abandoned their plans for driving a division in the Foundation and Profit guilds. At least for now anyway.

It was ironic really. They had delved so deep into the Argon infrastructure and used the Super Slaves as a means to disrupt. It had nearly worked. Two of the Argon navy's battleship captains had been confirmed with Super Slaves. He wasn't certain, but they had both given up their commands as soon as the war was over. If they had taken those powerful ships with them into Echo Three the outcome could have been different. But no it hadn't succeeded. What they had done though was create a group of Argon individuals, already the best amongst their comrades and made them even more powerful with the Super Slaves.

The admiral had been right. Become a part of the universe, don't hide, but don't make yourself known. Blend in with the normal background workings of the cosmos. Build yourself a life, take some credits and trade like the others or take a job somewhere discreet. But always have an eye trained on the Yaki. Brett didn't know what would happen, but he was sure that some time in the future he and his fellow warriors would be called to arms. The Paranid called them "Kotu" the "gifted ones" and the name had stuck.

Brett finished his drink, gathered up his heavy equipment belt from the table and headed for the door. It was time to spend some of those credits the navy had given him. He had studied the economics of the local systems in-depth while he had stayed at the station. Now it was time to put his ideas to work, to integrate with the cosmos. No one gave him a second look as he left the room.

## *Chapter 12: Spirit*

*You may be "Kotu", but that doesn't make you a trader. It makes you a warrior. There are other skills to learn than killing and making enough credits to survive is one of them.*

Brett banged the screen for the third time in succession. It wasn't going to make the situation any better, but it made him feel better nevertheless. He had foolishly taken the easy option and invested some of his credits in the Space Investment Guilds, the SIG. This was a universe wide system that held all current prices for the shares available in the companies that spanned the sectors. No planet side companies were involved in this, only the dedicated space corporations. He had studied the figures for what seemed too long, then made his purchases.

The investments he had made were stable for a while. They went up slightly, they went down slightly, but they never moved too far from the price he had bought them at. Now he was watching the screen after coming back from the exercise dome and they had dropped thirty percent. If he sold them back now, he would make a loss. What to do? Wait again to see if they would rise? Sell now and cut his losses? He still had enough wealth stored away to buy a ship, albeit an old one.

It was turning out to be much harder than he thought. He hadn't realised it as first, joyous in the freedom that he now had. His whole life spent in institutions of one type or another. The orphanages, Morang, the marine bases and space carriers, then the fleet ships where he had commanded Blue squadron. All geared up to make you work to a routine. Then suddenly there wasn't a routine, nobody telling you what to do. It felt strange, alien, he had installed a routine on himself just to be, as he thought, normal.

But these companies and traders, they were a new challenge for him and he was finding it difficult to adjust. So, even though he could have stepped out immediately into the space lanes and become one of them, he subconsciously, no maybe even consciously, steered himself away from it. He saw the easiest route to make credits was in the SIG, but now that was beginning to look like a futile quest.

Then there was the question of the transport ship from Echo Three. He had played it over in his mind a thousand times. Sometimes waking in the middle of his sleep, sweating, breathless and nauseous. Why did they have to die? It wasn't my fault, he was sure of that. The admiral's screen had shown it to be so. Then the realisation would set in. The Yaki had done this, manipulated him and used him as a weapon. Making him kill his own comrades, using his own skill against him. Well he knew that the time would come for retribution. Blend in, the admiral had said. You work for me now. I will contact you when the time is right. Very well, he would continue to do that, but it didn't take away the hatred and it didn't stop the sudden awakenings.

He stared at the screen again. The price had dropped again. He didn't like this game anymore. It was stupid. It wasn't tangible, he wanted to see something that he could do and be paid for it. Not sit and watch screens take his livelihood away.

Right, decision made, he instructed the computer to sell his interests and watched his credits rise. Not back to what they had been, far from it, but it was time to do something constructive. He had spent too much time on this station wallowing in the easy life and it just didn't fit.

He instructed the system to cancel his long-term boarding and began to gather up his sparse belongings. He felt better already.

* * * * * * * *

The Argon female was beautiful. He had come across many in his life, but this one was special. Jet black hair, a figure that was small, but somehow showed strength. She eyed him in much the same way that he must have eyed her. Blue eyes, the colour of the oceans on Argon Prime. Her crimson body suit clung like it was made for her alone. Brett pulled his gaze away and attempted to concentrate on the display screen to her left that was showing the ships on offer.

Recycled ship sales. It was a gamble he knew, but he didn't have enough credits to buy a new one from the shipyards. He continually paged through the offerings, the computer generated images of the ships displayed on the screen with their technical specifications below them.

He had gone through them multiple times when the sales assistant interrupted.

"Having difficulty choosing?" she asked, a wry smile on her pretty face.

"Kind of." He replied without looking at her.

"So what you looking for?" she asked, her eyes seeking out his. He felt them staring and concentrated his gaze on the screen.

"Something fast." Brett stated. "Armed and with a cargo bay, for carrying goods."

"You a trader then?" The girl inquired.

"Yes." Came the answer.

She didn't look convinced and moved away to look at a screen on her side of the long desk. She pressed some buttons, Brett tried to ignore her, as she made many "ah" and "um" sounds.

It took a while, it seemed too long to Brett. He was looking at the ships on the display again and again. He didn't know what to say, so he just kept flicking from one ship to the next. The urge to just do it without touching the keys was overwhelming, but he fought the sensation and continued to cycle the display.

"Ah hah!" The girl exclaimed. "Got one, perfect for you." She stabbed a few commands into her console and the ship appeared on Brett's display.

His heart skipped a beat, or so it felt. On the screen before him was a Mako. Modified with a cargo bay and a reduced turn of speed. But a Mako nonetheless.

He checked the technical readout, fair shields and speed better than most and importantly, the four laser mountings were still fitted. Part of the cargo space was given up for life support. This ship had the ability to take the long haul jobs as well. It looked perfect. Why wasn't it on the main screen? He asked the question.

"Oh we have lots of ships that we don't, err, advertise. I thought this one would suit you?"

Yes she was right. The cargo bay was small in comparison to a freighter ship, but it looked as if you could live in it for long periods of time. That was important to Brett, he longed for the cosmos and this ship might be his saviour.

"I want to check it out." He said.

She looked down then up again, straight into his eyes. "You want to take it out?"

"Yes."

"OK, but you'll have to wait until my assistant arrives. Rules state that no ships can be..."

He cut her short. "Fine, just tell me when."

The time was agreed and Brett went to the communication centre where he could use the shared data terminals. He scanned the local systems and looked for local jobs.

There were many jobs available listed on the screen. Mostly cargo runs for the large corporations. He couldn't really get involved with those, not unless he changed his mind and bought a real freight ship and not the converted fighter he had set his sights on. He was going with his gut feeling again instead of his mind. The Mako looked like it was a fighter at the front, but the large cargo area that had been attached to the bottom of the ship stretched out behind it, making the Mako three times longer than its original length. Slower performance than a real fighter ship and only a token cargo hold, despite the modifications. Still, he had gone with his instincts for most of his life and he was still here wasn't he?

The thing that he really liked about the Mako was the living quarters that took up part of the hold. That made him independent, the way he liked it. He could stock the ship with stores and live on it for long periods if need be. Yeah, if she felt all right when he took her out later for a test, he'd buy her he was sure.

He scanned the long list of jobs again, instructing the display to keep updating with a fresh list. The stations were such dynamic places that the jobs on offer would change before your very eyes, if you looked at them long enough. There were other pilots milling around in the room, talking and viewing the other screens just as he was. He gazed around the room, wondering if any of these fellow traders were Kotu the same as he was. How could you tell? He didn't know, the only thing he was sure of was that they would be Argon only. He hadn't been given any information about any other races being involved and the Paranid had been firm in their belief that there were only one hundred Super Slaves out there. Some of those were already dead anyway, so the number was less already.

Hah, got one. This looked interesting, a shuttle mission. Someone wanted to be taken to the atmospheric manufacturing plant in Echo Seven-Two. A vast journey, around fifty sectors or so. That would take forever without a jump drive and he couldn't afford one of those luxuries. But maybe if they weren't in a hurry he could do some trading on the way. He tapped his personal identification code into the console and requested a direct link to the client. The system responded almost instantly with a text only link. They don't want to make themselves known then, not yet anyway.

Brett asked his questions. When did they need to arrive? Could he take slight diversions en-route for profit runs? Yes, it wasn't a problem. The client was happy to be out in the cosmos for a while, but the price would be lower. They were going to Echo Seven-Two to start a new life, it was the farthest populated sector, a frontier. So it didn't matter how long it took to get there. He did the calculations in his head. He could stock the ship with the necessary supplies for the journey, fit a pair of ship to ship missiles and still have some operating credits available to do the odd bit of trading on the way. If he bought the Mako that was.

He confirmed his acceptance of the deal. No going back now, if he didn't get himself a ship, he would be in big trouble. Acceptance of a job was fixed, the only way you could back out of it was either to buy your way out, which would almost certainly cost more than the profit in the deal anyway, or you could run. He didn't know who the client was, he only had their ID code from the console, so it could be an individual or someone from a larger organisation. Still, departure time had been agreed for the following Tazura, more than enough time to get everything together. He rose out of the seat and arched his back, raising his hands in the air as he did so. He felt it crack as he stretched. That felt better, time to head back down to the long term docking bay and have a look at the ship.

The girl wasn't there when he returned to the desk, he was greeted by an older man. He introduced himself as the owner of the business and explained how they bought ships from the larger corporations and the military. Ships that were no longer required by them because they maintained such up to date equipment. But there was nothing wrong with them and his company gave them overhauls, fitted extra equipment that traders required and made unique modifications, just like the Mako he was interested in.

Brett was sure that some of the talk was sales inspired, but the man seemed genuine and explained that his son was in charge of the work area where the modifications were done. It was a family led business. It actually made Brett feel a little easier about the deal, even though the story could still have been made up.

"Oh, the girl then," Brett inquired, "she is your daughter?"

The salesman smiled. "No my friend, she just helps out now and again. She hasn't been here long. I pay her to watch the desk when we are busy back there." He gestured with his hand and pointed his thumb over his shoulder towards the docking area.

"Ah, here she is." The salesman said. "We were just discussing you."

The girl approached from behind and Brett turned as she got near. "Oh you were, were you?" She smiled at the salesman and then looked at Brett. "Only good things I hope?"

Brett stammered a reply and felt his cheeks begin to burn. His stomach began to churn and he realised he felt slightly light headed. He turned away, embarrassed. He didn't know what else to say and felt slightly foolish. Thankfully the girl broke the moment.

"C'mon then pilot. Let's see what you think of the ship." She said moving past him and towards a gap in the long desk. He caught a faint smell of her as she passed and his stomach jumped again. He suddenly realised he was going to have trouble piloting the ship if this carried on. He started to follow her when the salesman stopped him.

"Credits?" he inquired.

Brett had forgotten to hand over his credits. He realised that the girl was having an effect greater than he had imagined. He took a deep breath and regained some of his composure.

"Of course, sorry." He said to the salesman. You had to pay for the ship in full if you wanted a test run. If you decided you didn't like it, you would be refunded. No underhand dealing here. The transaction was held on the stations transfer system so he was confident he would get his credits back if he changed his mind. But it was to protect the seller more than the buyer. Once you were clear of the station, there was nothing stopping you from simply leaving. The station police would probably be launched against you, but that didn't help the seller if his ship got torched. There was also the issue of pilots taking ships out with no intention to purchase. Joy riders, testing the ships out, especially the high performance ones and then simply giving them back. If you didn't have the credits, you couldn't test the ship.

Brett held his hand over the identifier and entered his identification code into the pad attached to it. Then he entered the price agreed and the salesman did likewise on an identical device his side of the desk.

"Transaction confirmed." The electronic voice from the device said. They both removed their hands.

"Good luck." The salesman said. "I'm sure you'll like her."

"Thanks." Brett replied as he moved through the gap and hurried to catch up with the girl who was moving into the docking area. He had to walk quickly, but he soon drew level and matched his pace with hers.

"So what's your name?" Brett asked. He tried to make it sound as if he was making conversation, but in reality he just had to know.

"Spirit." She replied without looking at him. "Yours?"

"Brett."

She stopped and turned to face him, Brett did the same to her. "Pleased to meet you Brett." She held out her hand. He reached out his and grasped hers. It was like electricity moving up his hand as they touched. She felt soft but warm, gentle but with firmness behind it that she seemed to be holding back. He didn't want to pull away.

He looked into her eyes and thought he was about to either fall over, or start to float into the air. She's like a magnet, he thought, pulling me towards her.

"If you don't let go, we'll never get to try her out Brett." She said, smiling.

Brett released her hand, "err, sorry" he mumbled. She began to walk again and he joined her once more.

The docking area was massive. Ships were lifted from the floor, suspended in the bay by large lifting devices. Some were being worked on, he saw the flashes of laser torches as the technicians worked away on them. The whole of one side wall of the bay was covered with ships. Some small scout craft, the odd fighter and then in no particular order, the large freight ships with these large engines and bulbous bodies.

"Are these all yours?" Brett asked.

"No," she replied, "none of them are mine. I just work here remember. But some of the ships are in for maintenance work or long term storage. Some traders have multiple ships and they take the right one for the job, small fast or large and slow with immense cargo bays. The old man runs a good business."

A man atop one of the freight ships lifted his protective visor and stopped his laser work. "Hey Spirit!" He shouted as he waved.

She waved back and smiled. "That's the son." She said to Brett. So, the old man wasn't lying then. Good, I didn't think he had been. I wonder if Spirit has some kind of relationship with the son, or maybe another of the workers. Stop it Brett! It's nothing to do with you if she has, he told himself. Still he couldn't help wondering as they continued to walk.

Then they came upon it. Brett saw the unmistakable lines of the Mako as they approached. A large Boron freight ship had hidden it, but now they were almost adjacent to it and he could see all it's detail. It was very similar to the graphic he had viewed on the screen. It didn't look quite right with the large, grey coloured cargo module attached to the bottom. But looks didn't mean a thing in space. It was performance and capability that mattered. He was beginning to wonder now that they were walking around the ship, exactly how two people were going to fit into a single seat fighter craft.

Spirit must have read his mind, how could she do that?

"Specially fitted and adapted Brett. There is a second seat behind the first one. The electronics have been moved into the cargo area to make the room. The second seat has the same controls as the front one. You can fly the ship from either seat, or," she added, "one person can pilot, the other can fight. If that's what you need to do."

Brett nodded and started to climb the metal ladder that was attached to the side of the ship. He reached the top and peered inside. She was right, it was actually a lot more spacious than the Mako he had piloted in the navy. She pressed a button on a small device she held in her hand. Brett hadn't noticed her take it out of her pocket. The door on the side of the craft began to open upwards and he had to duck slightly as it moved up and over him. He looked down the ladder to see Spirit smiling, a little chuckle developing.

He turned back to the ship and began to clamber in. Spirit was coming up the ladder now and she followed him into the ship. There was just enough room to stand up straight and walk around the two seats. Brett surveyed the cabin, prodding at bits of equipment or inspecting any loose fittings. He noticed that the rear of the cabin had a door, a sandy coloured metal. The same colour as the walls of the cabin. Well the small parts you could see behind the equipment and padding.

Spirit noticed his gaze. "Yeah, go on. Go have a look at the living quarters Brett."

He walked to the door and waved his hand over the lock. The door gave a slight hissing sound as it swept to the left and disappeared into the hull. Lights began to flicker and then burst into life in the corridor beyond. It wasn't very big. The corridor swept down almost immediately in a flat descent that turned slightly to the left. The floor was grey carpet with the obligatory red lines pointing the way to the escape hatch. In this case, the only way out of this ship was from the seats in the cabin. The walls were the same sandy colour, but they were padded. Well it looked nice and comfortable. He headed down into the corridor and came to another door, which was not visible from the top.

Inside was a dream. He had never seen anything like this in the fleet ships he had piloted. There was a table in the middle of the room with an open kitchen to the rear. Small but functional, it had heating cabinets and dispensers that probably got the food packs directly from the cargo bays below. As he stepped around the room, he noticed the data screens on the walls. It even had a sonic shower room and the sleeping quarters, there were two, were slightly larger than he had expected. It was almost perfect.

"You like?" Spirit asked.

"Looks good to me." Brett answered. "But let's see how she handles eh?"

"OK, " she replied, "you go take the front seat, I'll get in behind."

Once seated and strapped in, Brett requested clearance and the automated tugs began to move them out to the launch bay. It wasn't long before they were blasting away from the station and heading out into the sector.

"What do you think?" It was Spirit's voice coming through the small communication tab that Brett had in his ear. It sounded tinny and distant even though she was so close.

"She feels good, tight. I want to head out into the sector, find some clear space. We got drones on board?"

"Yep, six. You launch 'em, you pay for 'em." She replied.

"OK, when we get to thirty klicks out, you launch them and set them to attack us." He said.

"You sure?"

"Yep, I just requested clearance from the station. They've granted us permission for a test fire." He replied. He was back in his element now, training taking over. He felt good about this, it felt right to be back in a ship. Especially, he thought, with Spirit so close behind him.

He accelerated to full speed, she was a bit sluggish compared to the Makos he had been used to, but it wasn't too bad. "Ready?"

"Yes."

"Launch!"

The small nimble drones sped away from the cargo bay and then began to track their target. Laser fire began to hit the shields. Brett turned the ship to the right and down, selecting one of the drones as a target as he went. They were incredibly difficult to hit, being only a couple of metres across and very fast. His selected target fired at them and then sped away. Brett steered after it and pointed the front of the Mako directly at the drone. It had stopped momentarily and was probably about to come in for another attack. He pulled the trigger and the lasers began to pour out their shots.

A small silent explosion and he selected a second and completed the same manoeuvre. Two gone, then a third and fourth. The remaining two where behind him and he moved the ship into a downward loop as they came in for another attack. No lasers from the drones made contact and as they swept overhead, he completed the loop and brought the Mako up behind them. A near perfect move, a slight adjustment and he dispatched both drones in a single salvo.

"Hey, way to go hot shot!" Spirit shouted into the communication channel.

Brett smiled. Good she's impressed. "I'll take it." He replied and turned the ship back towards the station.

* * * * * * * *

Brett was disappointed when he got back to the station. He had asked Spirit if she would join him for something to eat as he was going to leave soon. But she had declined saying that she had things to do. He felt foolish with himself for asking and kept thinking about her. Oh well, maybe we'll meet again sometime, he thought. I might be able to leave a message for her when I leave.

He spent the time keeping busy, buying the food, water other sundries for the journey. He watched the missiles being loaded himself, partly because of his military background, but also in the hope that he might see Spirit on the loading bay. But she hadn't been there.

He had a restless sleep, but rose early and collected up his final belongings to transfer them to the ship. He was finished with the ship preparations and was stood outside, taking yet another look around the Mako. His client was late, very late and he was beginning to become slightly concerned.

"Hey Brett!" It was Spirit.

Brett spun around; glad to hear her voice again as he thought he might never get the chance.

"Hello Spirit." He said. "My clients late, I was just about to make contact with the station to see of they could locate them."

Spirit laughed and stood aside to reveal two bags and a large metal case. "No need to contact the station, Brett. Your client's here."

Brett looked around, "Where?"

She laughed even louder. "Me, you fool." Brett was speechless. "C'mon help me get this lot loaded then we can say goodbye to this place."

He didn't move a muscle until she walked up to him and threw one of her bags at him. A short time later they launched and set course for the first gate of many that would take them to Echo Seven-Two.

## Chapter 13: Call to arms

*Building an empire, or just building a home, much easier to do when you are not alone.*

They never reached Echo Seven-Two. Brett and Spirit spent long periods of time sat around the table in the ship, discussing issues, probing into each other's backgrounds. They were both guarded about their respective pasts, but it seemed that Spirit has also been in the military, in the intelligence section.

Brett told most of his true history, but left out the Kotu and the blowing up of the transport ship in the war. He didn't deny being in the war and even relived the battle, well parts of it. It had taken time, but he had eventually begun to open up about his time at the orphanage. His parents, he said were dead. His mother had died during childbirth and his father was unknown, dead as far as he was concerned.

She had held him as he retold the story. He had wept, the first time in his life he had let those emotions out. It was a tangle of emotions that had been buried for so long. He fought against it sometimes, but bit by bit it all came out and he began to rely upon Spirit. It was if she was carrying the pain with him, taking bits of it away and keeping him protected from it.

She first became his friend, then not long after they became a couple. It was inevitable. Brett realised that when he looked back, he had wanted it from the first time he had set eyes on her at the sales desk.

Her feelings seemed the same. They joked now about how she had wanted to catch his eye that first meeting, how she was preparing to leave the station anyway and it just all fell into place. Her family, she said, were planet side. Her parents retired and her brother worked for an agency firm not far from them. He had a family, children and a completely different life from the one she had decided upon.

But she was happy for them all. She rarely made contact with them but did send messages back when she got the chance, or remembered to.

They were both trained pilots. Brett was the better, but she also could handle a ship. Standard training in the intelligence corp. She also understood the trading environment much better than Brett did and before long they were making profitable trading runs. They had to take low quantity, high profit goods, as the cargo space of the ship was still too small for the large runs the big freight ships made. But they made steady progress and they were beginning to collect a small fortune in credits.

Spirit had pooled her resources with Brett's and this had helped both of them move forward faster. It was Brett's ship, but her credits enabled them to buy more expensive goods to trade in. Therefore the profits were higher and they collected more credits even quicker than they would have done individually.

So they set about establishing their trade company. After a while, making credits on the trading runs was becoming straightforward so they wanted to invest some of the wealth into something more permanent. The ship was becoming too cramped to live in long term. They spent the odd time at one of the stations and basked in short term luxury, but they wanted a place to call home.

So they looked into the purchase of a factory itself, nothing grand, just something to get started with. It was all a bit too much for Brett. The large shipyard corporations manufactured space stations. You could buy different sizes, but they were mostly of a similar structure. The basic station that you purchased had various attachment modules where you could fit additional rigs. The larger and more expensive the basic station, the more rigs you could attach.

But then you had to buy power plants, either the small and potentially dangerous nuclear devices (large ones were still outlawed) or self sustaining energy converters that took their power from any local heat source. Or you could fit both if you had the space and the credits, or maybe none and rely upon the energy cells, if you could find them at a reasonable price.

Then the atmospheric rig that generated air and the water purifiers, followed by the communication rig, shield rig and living quarters for the employees you would need for the station to function.

After all this had been planned, discussed and ordered, it had to be delivered by the shipyard cargo ships. It all took credits. Everything took credits. So Brett had continued to make trading runs while Spirit began the task of putting the station together. No matter how many times he went out, they never seemed to have enough to complete their plan. There was no point in starting until they had enough to finish the job. A half-finished station wasn't much use to anyone.

They had toyed with the idea of purchasing another ship so that Spirit could also help out. But Brett was adamant that she was not to go out alone for long distance trips. She had argued, saying he was just being protective and she could look after herself, but Brett rightly pointed out that he was the fighter pilot, not she, and she relented.

They did buy the second ship though. A large Boron freighter and Brett used this alone to increase their earnings potential.

Time flew by. They grew closer and closer together. A perfect team. Then finally the time had come to buy the station and they had to decide on what it was going to produce and more importantly, where to build it.

They spent the time huddled together in the rented quarters aboard the sector station, pouring over the data that Spirit had acquired about the goods and adjacent sectors. They decided on a sector that was about a third of the way to Echo Seven-Two. It was close enough to the inner sectors to be fairly well protected and far enough away so that the profits, while not fantastic, would be good.

It was also the home to a dense forest planet named "Aden". The sector was beginning to house various factories and because it was on the edge of the inner sectors, they decided to buy a communication-manufacturing rig. This made the rigs that other stations would require and they would be the only one in the area, so profit potential was high.

While it was on its way, the purchase having been made by Brett who was taking a long, profitable route back, Spirit began the mundane job of finding the staff to run the station. Initially it was difficult because there were not many people in the area and the other stations already employed those that were there.

But after advertising (which also dipped into their credits) on a number of inner sector stations, they gradually began to put together the right staff. Then more ships had to be purchased and pilots hired. They would have to go and get the raw materials that the station required, not just to build the rigs, but to keep it functioning.

At first they bought a single ship while Brett used the Boron ship and did the trade runs as well. Then they could afford another as the station went online and they sold their first rig. It only brought in enough credits to keep them going for a while, but before they ran out of resources again, they had managed to manufacturer a further two and these sold instantly. It was beginning to look good. They invested in a pleasure rig. The employees were overjoyed as they now had somewhere on their own station they could go and relax. Bars and re-creation areas, fitness centres and a small medical facility. It was so good that people from the other sector stations would come and spend time at their station. Ideal as the profits from the pleasure rig were being made from the credits that they paid their own employees with.

Brett and Spirit spent much of their time in the large habitat area that they had built for themselves. The station was, for the most part, running itself and they spent less time managing it and more time with each other. Time went by and Brett began to push the thoughts of the Yaki and the war into the back of his mind.

* * * * * * * *

Moo-Kye sat on the bridge of her battleship once again. Her fleet, or what was left of it, accompanied the large ship on its journey. After the war she had returned to her station deep inside the outer sectors. She was protected here, the station had formidable defences and even the Argon navy wouldn't attempt an attack here. Not yet anyway, they may have won the war, but she had bloodied the nose of the largest fleet in the universe and as long as she stayed out of the way, she was confident they would do the same.

It was a smaller operation now though than the one it had been at it's peak during what was now being called the trade war. Three of her companions had died during the war, one against the Teladi/Split force and two against the Argon. Another had left after the defeat at Echo Three. Coward, she had hunted him down and slit his Argon throat herself, laughing as she watched him die.

The only two remaining Yaki leaders were in the two destroyers that now flanked her ship as they made their way on a new journey.

She had spent four Jazuras recovering from the battle. She had to piece her fleet back together. Ships were expensive, particularly attack ships and she had only managed to put a few together. Profits from the protection schemes she ran over the traders in the Yaki sectors were less than they had been. Traders had left after the war, going back to the Foundation and Profit guilds.

She had thought that her devious plan with the Super Slave chips would have worked. It would have done if the stupid Argon navy had brought the battleships along. All three captains were under her control. Instead they left them behind, along with a number of other ships where she had people aboard. Out of all the Super Slaves chips she had sent out all that time ago, only two people with them installed had actually turned up for the battle.

Still, it had worked perfectly. But now that surprise was gone. She would never be able to take on the Argon navies in a head to head fight and she was concerned that the Split and Teladi were gathering forces for their own retribution.

So what could she do? It was then that the news of the gates began to filter through. There was going to be a re-alignment of the gates? You're kidding me? When, how, who knows?

Nobody knew when, nobody knew how, sorry. However, the people that do know are two scientists, a Boron named Mi Ton and an Argon, Mitchell. They were in the outer sectors, far from the Yaki and actually, far from anybody. The sector had a station and some factories had been deployed, but all the surrounding sectors were empty.

And the gate alignment was going to open up other sectors, possibly other races. She had made her mind up almost instantly. A possibility of escape, to get away from these retched guilds and either go elsewhere and start alone or maybe even be the first to trade with a new race. Whatever, it didn't matter as long as she could get away.

Can we jump into the sector and just take everything out and then abduct these scientists? No. The sector had all Nav Sat's disabled and there were only two gates into it. They were so heavily defended that any ship, even one the size of the battleship would not be able to escape the gate defences before it lost its shields.

"What can we do then?" she had asked her advisors. They had no immediate answers, but eventually they came up with a solution. It wasn't a good one and it had its own dangers, but Moo-Kye loved it even before it had been fully explained to her.

They could jump into a sector next to the scientists. One of them was actually only a Wozura away at light speed, it was a different sector but actually a companion star. They couldn't travel that fast, but they could travel the distance conventionally. It would take two Jazuras to make the journey and being out that long in space, with few resources and spare parts was a concern. But it was risk she was prepared to take. Once they got into deep space between the two star systems, they would be out of range of any scanners and the sector wouldn't know they were coming until they were almost upon them. She could take the scientists and their knowledge hostage and then find out when and where she had to be for the gate re-alignment. Perfect, if anybody tried to attack them they would have the sector defences at their disposal.

Moo-Kye stared out of the space screen on the bridge as the bright glare of the star got brighter by each passing Tazura.

\* \* \* \* \* \* \*

Mi ton checked the data again, the simulation on the screen in front of him showing a recreation of the original gate alignment followed by the expected one that would happen soon. He turned to Mitch beside him.

"We will know soon Mitch. Not long now before we have the answer." He said.

"I know, Mi Ton. Should I send a signal to the station so they can send a faster drone back to our governments?" Mitch replied.

"Yes, do that. It is best they know of our progress again."

Mitch punched a few buttons on his console and sent a message to the small relay station that was in the sector. Its name was Echo Seven-Two.

\* \* \* \* \* \* \*

Brett was in the command centre of their station when the encrypted message arrived for his attention. He knew right away whom it was from before he read it. He moved to a secluded console where nobody could see and fitted a local sound plug from the console into his ear.

The admiral's face appeared on the screen.

"It is time for the Kotu to act. You must make all available speed to Echo Seven-Two. The Yaki are planning to invade and take control of that sector. This must not be allowed to happen. Good luck. Message ends."

Brett knew as he ran through the corridors of the station back to where Spirit was working in their private quarters that he had to tell her. As he ran through the door and it swished shut behind him, he could tell by the look on her face that she already knew.

"By the book of truth!" He muttered. "Kotu!"

She smiled at him, moved towards him and held him tight in her arms.

"Yes my love, we are Kotu. We go to our destiny together Brett, as one."

Brett was speechless again. Only Spirit could have this effect on him, he was sure.

## *Chapter 14: Echo Seven-Two*

*It was the way it had to be. It had been heading this way without their knowledge from the time Brett was born. No one can say why, but soon only one would be alive. It was their destiny to meet, but the outcome was not yet decided.*

Echo Seven-Two. That was the official name of the sector that the Argon and Boron governments had agreed to. It was named, as were many others, after the military station that was installed there.

But Mi Ton called it the "Gateway Sector" and Mitch was inclined to agree. It might not be a gateway to somewhere, but it was certain to find a gateway to somewhere.

Admiral Stacey didn't even know that the Yaki were taking the long, conventional route to the sector. That was until the Split navy had taken some Yaki prisoner after yet another small skirmish had taken place. They had used the usual interrogation techniques against the pilot's Slave chip and he had started to confess. He had been left behind he said, he got back from his leisure time too late and the fleet was gone. But he was supposed to fly one of the assault ships against the Echo station. The Split authorities had contacted Admiral Stacey at once and relayed the data. The admiral had reacted and mobilised whatever available forces she had within striking distance of the sector.

She also contacted her Kotu. She hadn't been surprised when Brett and Spirit had got together. The placing of Spirit on the station and actually, the building of the modified Mako, was her doing. Their analysis readouts showed them to be so compatible, she almost felt it her duty to put them close to each other.

Kotu were going to die, she knew, maybe Brett and Spirit. But at least they had enjoyed some time together. At least Brett, whom she felt for, had found happiness at last. Maybe this final chapter would work out for the good of everyone involved. Maybe it wouldn't, there was a lot at stake. They had all the data so far created by Mi Ton and Mitch, but it wasn't finished. There own government scientists were working on the data right now, but they didn't have the devices spread all over the universe. They could take control of them and get the data sent elsewhere, but it all took time. They might miss something during the transition and the re-alignment could be closer than they thought. No, they had to have the station and the scientists intact and nothing could stand in the way of that conclusion. The president had told her as much.

The Admiral simply stared at the consoles that gave her so much information. So much power over so many people, but now, it was out of her hands. She had set the wheels in motion and only fate could play its hand now. The future of the universe as they knew it lay with the sector Echo Seven-Two. She slumped back in her chair and viewed the data, staring blindly at it. Time will tell, she thought, time will tell.

\* \* \* \* \* \* \* \*

Echo Seven-Two.

"Commander, we have an incoming message. Commander's eyes only, where do you want it sir?" said comms.

The commander stayed at his station, sat in his chair and plugged a sound tab into his ear. "Pipe it through to my station comms."

He saw the green light flashing to signify the message had arrived and he confirmed his identity to the system once again. The admiral's face appeared on screen.

"Commander, there is no time to waste. You are about to be attacked by a Yaki strike force, it is approaching from the direction of the twin star, by conventional means. You must identify this threat and take all possible steps to destroy it and most importantly," she paused, "most importantly, you must secure the lives and data of the scientists Mi Ton and Mitchell aboard the laboratory station."

The commander sank back in his chair. Some of his staff were staring his way.

"I have dispatched every available resource to assist you in this task, but do not rely upon it. It may never reach you in time."

The admiral moved closer to the screen. "Save the scientists commander, it is imperative that you save the scientists and their data. Message ends."

He thought for a moment, still staring at the now blank screen and then rose to his feet. "Scan, can you point something towards the twin star and tell me if you see anything, well, out of the ordinary?"

Scan turned to face him and looked at him, a quizzical look on his face. "Would you like to define, out of the ordinary sir?"

"OK, something that's looks like ships scan, big ships," he answered.

Scan returned to his console and began to jab buttons that would make one of his infrared telescopes turn towards the star. "Be right with you commander, give me some time to tune the tube and scan the area."

"Ok scan, take your time. Just make it a good one." The commander replied.

It wasn't until the commander actually came back on station for his next shift that the scan team had anything for him to look at. But when they showed him the images, he was convinced.

"It could be anything sir," scan was saying, "a collection of heated meteorites or, well anything natural."

"How long have you been tracking it?" the commander inquired.

"Since just after you left your last shift sir."

"Has it moved course, has it done anything unnatural?" he asked.

"Well no sir." Scan replied.

"Heading? You have calculated the heading haven't you?"

"Yes sir, it's on a direct collision with the laboratory station, give or take a few metres."

"How long?" the commander asked.

"Well if it stays the same as it is, in the same direction and heading, it'll be here in three Tazuras." Scan answered.

The commander began to tap his fingers on the desk in front of him. It had to be the Yaki force, too far away for a visual on the optical systems yet, but all local meteorites and asteroids were mapped. It was standard procedure. This had to be them. Three Tazuras, that wasn't a lot of time. He had to know more about them so he could organise a defence. He didn't want to risk any other type of scan, only passive. If they lit up the ship with anything, they would know they had been discovered and he wasn't sure whether that was a good thing or a bad thing yet.

"Keep tracking scan, you get anything on visual that I should see, you bring it to my attention, understood?"

"Aye Sir," came the reply. He didn't have a great deal to fight with, the sector had been organised to let nothing come through the gates. But to come the conventional way, that was unexpected. These Yaki were clever indeed and he was going to have to be even smarter if he was to outwit them.

* * * * * * * *

The captain of the Boron cruiser that was on patrol duty around the sector of Echo Seven-Two had also received a similar message from the Boron government. "Strength not known", "Resist at all costs", "Sector must not fall into Yaki control". Well that didn't give him a lot to go on, prepare to fight an enemy when you didn't know it's composure, it's strengths and therefore it's weaknesses.

He was analysing the images sent over from the Echo station, blurred dark dots against the background of space, slightly lighter than the dots due to the light from the close star. It looked like a large ship and possibly two others, not quite so big. If there were any other ships around, then they couldn't be seen yet.

He had extracted the trade war data from the ship data banks and was going through the tactics used, the ships that had been destroyed and the ships that hadn't. Well, if it was the battleship that was heading this way, they were in for a fight. His cruiser was not armed like the Orion or even the Argon Four carrier that had both fired a broadside at the battleship and even then, it was believed the battleship had survived. Vanishing in some kind of stealth technology.

His cruiser had missiles and a large number of laser turrets. But that was it, it was an older ship, built before the carriers became the lords of the cosmos. But then too, was the battleship. Neither of them carried fighters, they had to bring any protection with them. Ah, that was if the battleship hadn't been modified in any way and he didn't have that information.

His support force of fighters was five. It wouldn't last long against the Yaki. He moved one eyestalk towards the adjacent screen as it showed the latest images from the Argon. His second one followed the first when he realised what he could see. It was indeed the battleship, it was clear now and on each side of it where destroyers with their smart missiles, he supposed. It was evident that a number of smaller ships were also in support and the whole force was getting closer. He looked at the data that was attached to the image. Estimated time of arrival was a single Tazura, a Teladi day.

* * * * * * * *

Ships were heading for the sector like night flies homing onto a beacon of light. There were only two ways into the sector, either from the outer sectors, where there were currently no population areas, or from the inner Argon sectors. It was from this direction that the ships raced. All attempting to get there in time.

The only Argon ship capable of the required jumps and in a position to leave on schedule was the Excel. She was back in service after being stripped down and rebuilt. She headed for the sector at full speed, making the jumps where possible to lessen the journey.

Brett and Spirit had left the station in the capable hands of the workforce. They had donned their black body suits, collected the lightweight body armour and selected weapons from the large metal box that Spirit had brought with her. Brett had wondered what was in it and now he knew. They had quickly stocked the Mako with supplies, loaded missiles and set course. Kotu just like them were making the same arrangements and heading in the same direction in a variety of ships.

The Yaki force was now identified. The Echo station had sent out its data in a message drone. The station commander sat and watched the visual display, the Yaki ships so close now that they could zoom in and observe the detail. Smaller fighters accompanied the dark ships and assault craft, all in the telltale jagged stripes of the Yaki. They simply grew larger in the screen as he watched.

## *Chapter 15: Revenge*

*The Yaki take revenge.*

The commander of Echo Seven-Two was restless. It was probably due to the draining mix of sleep depravation and stress. He had difficulty getting to sleep and had spent most of the time in the command centre, grabbing the odd bit of light sleep whenever it was quiet.

The room was littered with the casually disposed of drink packs and the fluid energy food that the automated dispensers provided. Silver or white packs scattered on the floor and desktops. People were in the room, too many people. Attempting to get some information that they could not obtain elsewhere on the station.

He grabbed one of the half-consumed packs and put the tube into his mouth, squeezing the shiny pack and sucking at the same time. The cold taste of what should have been warm food greeted him. He threw it to the floor in disgust. "Out!" he shouted. "Will none command staff please vacate the area."

Some of his staff turned to stare at him and the others began to move slowly out of the room. He suddenly wished to be somewhere else, back home or at least back in the home sectors. He stood up and cracked his knee joints, grimacing at the slight discomfort it gave him. But then they felt better, you needed to stretch after so long in these chairs. When would they attack? They were almost upon the station, he was beginning to show his nervousness as a slight twitch started above his eye. He rubbed at it subconsciously and it briefly stopped, but started again as he dropped his hand.

"Scan? That Boron cruiser in position yet?" he had asked the Boron ship to come as close as possible to the station, on the blind side to the Yaki. "Aye, Sir." Came the reply, "she's ready."

They may as well put all their firepower in the same place instead of being picked off individually around the sector. Hey, the Yaki might even call it quits and give up. Well, he could wish for a miracle couldn't he?

"Sir, incoming message from the Yaki." Wishes don't come true then.

"On main screen."

She appeared on the screen, the small crown on her head perfectly placed. She was stunning, it was the first thing he noticed, absolutely stunning. Then she spoke.

"My name is Moo-Kye, leader of the Yaki. I grant you one chance to save the lives of your people. Lay down your weapons and turn your ships and station over to me and you will be spared." Two Teladi years of waiting for this moment, she wasn't going to blow it now.

The commander stared at her attempting to keep his composure. "I must consult...", he started to say before she cut him off.

"You need consult nobody commander. You cannot talk to your government in any meaningful way at this distance and the Boron ships are under your command are they not?"

She knew her facts all right.

"The decision is yours commander and I want a decision now!" The last word was spoken at a higher decibel.

The commander knew that every eye in the room was upon him and every Argon and Boron in their ships were listening.

"A great force is due to arrive shortly.." He started to say and she cut him short again.

"I take that as a no, commander. Excellent!" She smiled and the communication link went dead. He just stood in the same position, staring at the screen. What had he done?

"Should I try and get her back commander?" It was comms again.

The commander shook his head and sighed. "No comms." He turned his back on them all and clasped his hands together behind his back, bowing his head in thought. He just stood there rolling slowly back and forth on the heels of his feet. Then he turned and noticed that everyone was still looking at him.

"Anything scan?"

"The whole force is heading our way sir, assault ships included with fighter support. The two destroyers are at the head of the formation sir."

The realisation that they were about to be attacked for real finally hit him. "Right everybody, sound battle stations, everyone to station. This is it."

* * * * * * * *

The Yaki pilot was flying his ship at almost full speed. He was the lead ship and was only a few kilometres ahead of the destroyers. His comrades were alongside and behind him as they headed for the station. His orders were to take out the station defences and also attack the Boron cruiser "Prince Heed" which was stationary on the far side. He flipped the communication channel open, "OK wing, we're going in, stay sharp and keep it tight. Targets are of opportunity, make this a quick one. Out."

They were just above the station coming in at a slight angle and he saw the laser towers on the construction begin to open fire. His ship began to jolt as the lasers found their mark. They were coming straight at him now and he moved the craft from side to side to lessen the damage to his shields. Less of the lasers hit as a result.

Then push down, hit full power, the station coming up fast in his space screen. Lasers flashing past, dozens of shots as the towers tried in vain to track such a close target. Nearly upon the station now, instinct in full flow, push right. Was he too close? The station filled his left screen and he glanced at it momentarily. That was close, but the edge was approaching now, nearly at the corner and then the front of the station will be there. C'mon, push the stick up and down, only slightly you don't want to go too far off track. Just keep those lasers at bay for a moment longer and then I'll be on it.

Slight push to the left and then the right. Wow, ship bucking as the laser struck. A quick glance at the shield strength, plenty left. This is it.

The station vanished from his left screen as he passed all the way down its side. He turned the ship to go across the front of the station. There it was before him, the cruiser. Open fire! He pulled the trigger and his own lasers opened up, multiple shots coming from his nose mounted guns. But wait, the ships firing back, incoming shots from everywhere. Oh no! They're all aimed at me! Large flash of white, followed by a searing feeling of heat and then icy coldness as his lungs met the vacuum of space. He was dead and his ship exploded around him.

The other Yaki in the same wing turned the station corner and were met with the same overwhelming firepower from the Boron ship. She was targeting each ship individually and destroying it before moving on to the next, but such was the firepower that the ship under attack didn't last long. The Boron captain knew he had to make the most of his assets and he was going to go down fighting.

* * * * * * * *

The commander of Echo Seven-Two was now attempting to command his forces while watching the battle unfold on the large screen that was showing visual displays from different parts of the station. He had seen the first wing of Yaki get slaughtered as they turned towards the "Prince Heed". Very smart use of his weapons that was. He made a mental note to congratulate the Boron captain, if he was ever going to get the chance that was.

He gave the order to launch his five fighters into the battle and they could soon be seen on the screens, twisting and turning as they left the docking bay. A shudder! He felt the station shake. He looked at the screens trying to discover the source of the attack. There it was, coming over the top of the station, a destroyer and it was launching missiles at them.

"Missile battery!" The commander shouted as the station juddered and creaked.

"Aye Sir!" Sparks from two of the other consoles, the operators jumped out of their seats and one fell over.

"Put a salvo into that destroyer." There was no answer. He looked around quickly and realised the station internal communications were out. He yanked the device from his ear and ran over to the missile battery console, jumping over one of the metal handrails that protruded from the floor as he went.

He stopped himself by grabbing the man on the shoulder. "Open fire on the destroyer man, now fire!"

The operator only turned around long enough to confirm who it was and then proceeded to jab at his controls. The missiles left the station, locked onto the destroyer.

The Boron cruiser and Yaki destroyer were now simply playing the shield game. All enemy facing batteries were firing and the space between the two large ships was just a torrent of laser fire going both ways. The missile salvo from the station hit home. One explosion after the other hit the large ship. Blow will you? Blow!

It didn't, but it began to move away. The commander checked the data readout. The Yaki destroyer was losing shields badly and she was venting into space. Large squirts of liquid, probably oxygen was pouring out of her side. She was running. Yes, she was turning and trying to get away. The Boron captain decided he was not going to allow it and the Prince Heed began to move.

Faster and faster she went, chasing the Yaki ship down. Lasers firing as she moved. The people in the command room could see it happening and they began to shout. "C'mon Heed, C'mon!" They clambered over to the screens to see the fight unfold. A huddle of men and women holding each other, shouting and cheering as they watched her valiant fight.

The Heed moved at a greater speed now and she rose above the destroyer and flipped over on her side. The captain was bringing his other guns to bear on the Yaki ship and as he completed his turn, they erupted just as the others had. Streaks of fire flashing off the Yaki shields. Then a large, bright flash! The explosion made everyone in the room jump backwards, but out of the burning fire that was the destroyer came the Prince Heed. They cheered! The Boron captain kept coming, pushing to full speed and headed for the second destroyer that was coming from underneath the station. Yes Heed, c'mon, do it again. We can win!

They passed each other at full power, the Yaki destroyer and the Prince Heed, again firing into each other as they went. But this time the Heed's lasers were on low power and she was struggling to match the Yaki ship for fire. Then a thick, steady bolt of laser fire shot from behind the station and the Heed seemed to quiver, almost to shake gently and then she exploded into a million fragments.

The noise in the room stopped. They just stared at the quickly dispersing cloud as the dark shadow of the battleship passed over the station.

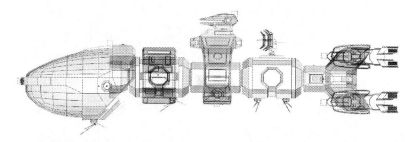

Then the sound of something attracted the commander's attention. What was it? It was like water dripping onto a hot metal plate. Fizzing away as it touched. Laser fire!

"We've been breached!" He shouted. The noises got louder and louder as the Yaki assault force troopers moved towards the command centre at speed. They overwhelmed the small detachment of marines on the station and then burst into the room, fanning out and taking up attacking positions around the door.

The commander put his arms in the air and gestured with his head for the others to do the same. It was pointless now. They had been defeated. No need for more bloodshed.

## Chapter 16: Destiny

*Destiny is waiting.*

The collection of ships waited around the gate. A rag tag bunch of trading ships and a few military fighters all sat motionless in space, their noses pointing at the gate, all ready to strike should the need arise.

Brett was standing by the side of his seat, sipping a hot drink from a cup. The joys of such a good ship. The bitter aroma of the drink filled the cabin and he took another sip and cursed silently as it burnt his lips. Spirit was still seated in the rear seat just behind him, one booted foot perched high on the console. She was keeping her eyes on the data screens.

"Anything?" Brett asked without moving.

"No. Nothing as of yet." She replied.

A Boron scout ship had gone through the gate a while ago now. It was the fastest ship known. They had convened a meeting over the communication channel and the Boron pilot had agreed to go into Echo Seven-Two and do what he was supposed to do, scout.

If the sector was lost to the Yaki, then the gate defences would also be theirs. The Echo station controlled them and that could and probably had been breached. So they had decided to scout the sector and see what the situation was. The Boron ship was probably the best suited for outrunning the laser towers and mines that ringed the gate on the other side. He had been gone for a while though and Brett was beginning to be concerned. What if he had been destroyed? What would they do then, send someone else?

The Yaki could have all their ships, as well as the gate defences, sat just the other side, waiting for anyone who dared to enter. He took another sip of the drink and this time sucked it through his teeth to combat the heat from it. Then he felt it hit the back of his throat and he gulped it down. He didn't like waiting. But that was what the military was all about. Long periods of boring waiting, watching followed by intense fear. He had learnt that in the marines, you had to be patient and he wasn't the patient type. He had hated it then and he hated it just the same now.

"Oh Hello." Spirit said, sarcasm in her voice.

"What?" Brett asked. He squinted his eyes, there was nothing coming through the gate.

"A frigate had just entered the sector, Brett. Wait, got it, Argon navy. It's showing its signature as the Excel".

Brett's eyebrows raised a fraction. Spirit noticed his reaction but didn't comment. "Looks like we have some extra friends along for the show."

Brett didn't look impressed. He shrugged, "Fat lot of use they'll be trying to outrun the gate defences. They'll get torched."

"Don't they have fighters?" she asked.

"Yeah, eight. But only if the captain will launch them to help us." He replied.

Spirit then remembered that Brett had been stationed aboard the Excel when he first got his commission. He had lost some pilots there, she was sure. "I'm sure they will do what they need to do to help us Brett," she said, hoping to brighten him slightly. It didn't work, he turned back to the space screen and peered out at the gate that sat only five kilometres away. He's worried, she guessed. It wasn't like Brett to be this worried. He was a good pilot, probably better than most of the ones that sat motionless in this sector now. What troubled him so much?

Brett still stared at the gate, moving his gaze across the other ships he could see that were closer than they were. It hadn't felt balanced since they had arrived in the sector and joined up with the other ships. Something wasn't right, it was like the feeling he had felt when he first met Spirit. But this time it wasn't a good one. It was similar, but if felt bad. A foreboding, something was about to happen that wasn't good, something terrible. He had tried to search his mind for the answer, but it wouldn't come. Was it he or Spirit? Maybe it was the scientists on the other side of the gate? He concentrated on each possibility, but none of them seemed to make the feeling any worse or better. He would find out soon enough though, he was sure of that at least.

A flash of light from the gate and Brett dropped the cup, spilling its contents as he jumped back into his seat. Spirit leaned forward and dropped her leg from the console. She felt the hum of the engines as Brett switched them online.

It was the Boron scout! Thank the book of truth, the scout was back again. Every ship in the sector listened on the communication channel for his message.

The scout ship accelerated away from the gate and then came to a stop some distance away, further than the other ships were.

"Bad news." The pilot said. "You ready for this?" He wasn't expecting an answer, he was just enjoying his moment of popularity and he sounded uplift, his voice excited. He must have had a close ride in the sector. The Yaki must be there then.

"Ok, they have got a battleship right in the middle of the sector. I'm sending this data I'm telling you on the back of this channel. Have a look at it. The ship is stationary, it didn't even move when I zipped around it. But there is a destroyer patrolling around menacingly and a collection of ships. Not many though, looks like there has been a fight, 'cos there isn't any of our guys in there. The Prince Heed is gone, I expect blown up."

Brett took a deep breath. This wasn't sounding very good.

"Echo Seven-Two station is showing a Yaki signature. I think they made sure I got that, which means the gate defences are under their control. I can vouch for that. The ride in from the gate was pretty hairy. Four rings of laser towers guard the gate, they move and track you, but they weren't quick enough for me. Also, there is a large minefield to the south of both gates. Whatever you do when you exit the gate, don't turn downwards."

"So, what we gonna do? Go kick some pirate butt?"

Nobody said anything, they were all aware that the captain of the Excel was now the ranking commander in the sector. The scout pilot had probably realised the same as he had finished his debrief and probably checked the sector scanner next.

Brett pressed his communication button to open the channel. "Any sign of the scientists, scout?" he asked.

"Oh yeah, forgot about that, sorry. The lab station was also under Yaki control. I don't know if the scientists are on board though. Nobody would talk to me, rude or what? Anyway, they did try and shoot me up, but their slow stuff is no match for me," the scout pilot answered.

The captain of the Excel opened his channel. "This is the captain of the Excel pilots. You are under my command now, I have authorisation from the admiral herself. We should convene a meeting on-board the Excel to discuss our plans."

Brett thought for a moment. There was no way he was going to go aboard the frigate. He might get recognised and he didn't know what to expect after his transport ship fiasco.

"Captain, I recommend sir, that we conduct this meeting here and now. It may endanger us to leave our ships. What if the Yaki attack?" Brett said.

There was a brief pause before the captain replied. "Of course pilot, you are right. Has anyone anything to input before I make a decision?"

Yeah, Brett thought, you go first! But he didn't say anything so flippant. He was studying the data that the scout had beamed through. The other pilots began to talk on the channel.

"I say we go for the lab, you've got marines on board the frigate, we can load them into my ship and take the lab back," said one.

"Fastest ships go through first, draw the fire from the laser towers so the slower ships have a chance to evade them," said another.

"Yeah, then regroup and attack the destroyer. If we take that out we can engage the remainder of their fighters. If we take the lab and the destroyer we can worry about the battleship later," added a third.

The conversations carried on, ideas going back and forth. Brett was studying the data, but his concentration kept coming back to the battleship. That was it, the battleship, the feeling he had experienced since they had arrived here. It got stronger when he concentrated on the large ship. That was it then, but what did he have to do?

The captain issued the orders to each ship that outlined their task. They were to take the lab station and then engage the destroyer. Brett and Spirit were to be fifth to go through the gate, being fifth fastest. Attack the base defences and engage any enemy ships of opportunity. What that meant was that intelligence was next to nothing and they didn't know what to expect. He'd learnt that in the marines as well.

The ships began to position themselves in a staggered line in front of the gate. Getting into the jump sequence that had been assigned to them. Brett steered the Mako into position and pointed it at the gate. He turned around in his seat, undid his harness and propped himself up on his knees so he could peer around the back of his seat and see Spirit.

"Good luck Spirit." He said. She rose from her seat and leaned over so that she could kiss him on the lips. "For us and for luck." She said. Brett smiled and returned to his seat, fixing the straps in place that would secure him and also keep him central should he activate the ejection switch. He squirmed around slightly to get a better position in the seat, or was he just anxious?

The lead ship, the Boron scout, began to move towards the gate. Brett instructed the ship to put the engines to full power and they began to follow the others. The gate blinked as it accepted the first ship into its tunnel and then it blinked again, a large flash that spanned the whole gate, as the second ship followed. Brett kept the Mako on course and they were soon suspended in time as they raced down the tunnel.

Another flash and they were in the sector. Brett immediately took a visual look outside the screen and also at the sector map. He jabbed the engines back to full power and pulled the control stick backwards. The Mako rose out of the laser tower defence and streaks of incoming fire began to envelop them.

The small force was pouring through the gate and the towers were having difficulty selecting targets as the ships dispersed in all directions (except down) as they advanced.

An explosion down below them, he hoped it wasn't the ship carrying the marines, a quick look at the scanner, it wasn't. But someone had bought it. He carried on vertical until the laser fire stopped and then he pushed the stick hard down and levelled her off, seeking out the lab station as he moved.

The gate defences were confused, they couldn't lock onto so many targets and the fast scout ships were moving in and out of the laser towers. The defences always tried to lock on the nearest target and the scouts were making them recalculate their decisions continually. Meanwhile the large ships were engaging the towers as they came through and steadily destroying them. The Kotu pilots were exceptional, they knew exactly what to do and it wasn't long before the gate defences were not effective. The Excel exited the gate.

Brett was sure he had seen the battleship on the scanner as he had evaded the laser towers. But now he couldn't see it, it was gone. Thoughts of the stealth device came back to him. Had it hidden itself again?

One thing the scanner did tell him however was that the Yaki fighter ships and destroyer were moving towards them. They had to protect the marine force so that it could take back the lab station. He turned his ship towards the incoming Yaki and some of his fellow pilots did the same. He could see out of the side screen that the lab station was firing at their ships. The ship with the marines on board was stationary beside the lab now, so close that the laser batteries couldn't manoeuvre for a shot. The marines were probably space walking to one of the outer hull doors. For a brief moment he wished he were with them.

Then the Mako began to jolt. Incoming fire from the destroyer was seeking them out. The small force wrapped itself around the destroyer like a wet towel thrown at a ball. They kept twisting and turning, firing shots into the destroyer's hull and then pulling away. Slowly they began to bring its shields down as they also defended themselves against the small force of Yaki fighters. Then the Excel approached the destroyer, guns ablaze. As she swept down its side, she turned so that her underneath was facing the destroyer and launched her fighters. Eight Makos swept out and began to rain fire down on the larger ship.

The Yaki destroyer launched its missiles. The total remaining stock in one final salvo. Had they been normal missiles they would have sought out their target and destroyed it. Instead, these were smart missiles, designed to seek out the greatest or nearest threat. They were no good in such a confused battle, they darted around the many ships that spun and fired, pulled away, span and fired and they kept changing their computer minds until they ran out of fuel. The Excel had by now righted itself and was pouring fire into the Yaki ship.

Brett was coming around for his seventh run at the large destroyer. He saw the multiple flashes from her shields as his comrades pressed home their attack. The extra eight ships from the Excel were making the difference and almost all the Yaki fighters had been destroyed.

He was coming in at a right angle to the ship, side on, firing his lasers until they began to give out from lack of recharge when the Yaki ship seemed to falter, stop and then it exploded, blinding him briefly and he carried on into the flying debris.

It was gone, only the battleship remained, wherever it was. The Yaki fighters that were left began to issue surrender transmissions. The fighters from the Excel began to round them up. It was difficult to tell from the chatter on the channel, but he was sure he heard the marines declaring the lab having been taken. Yes, he concentrated on it now, looking for those words only through the babble. "Lab station is secure, I repeat again, lab station is secure. The scientists are not aboard. Will someone confirm receipt of this, scientists are not onboard."

He heard the Excel confirm a message to the marines on the lab station and suddenly, everything went quiet. No noise on the communication channel, the ships were slowing down, moving in circles as they scanned the sector. Nothing, no Yaki left (it seemed). Only the Echo station still showing its Yaki signature. Brett waited for the captain of the Excel to speak. He didn't have to wait long.

"Yaki controlling the station Echo Seven-Two. You have no means of defence against our overwhelming force. Please surrender your position, or I will be forced to take aggressive action against you."

That was a bit bold, Brett thought. They could have a fleet of fighters in there and they still had the station laser batteries intact. Also, it was possible that the station still had missiles available. This wasn't over yet.

Brett brought the ship to a standstill. He unhooked his harness and jumped out of the seat. Spirit simply looked at him from her own seat. She was still keeping an eye on the sector scanner in case the station launched fighters.

"They're on the battleship Spirit, " Brett said, "we have to find them and get them off."

She looked at him. "What battleship Brett? I don't see one, I think they are dead."

"No, they are not dead. I can feel it. Its there, that battleship, its hidden just like it was in the trade war. We have to get onboard it and find the scientists." He said.

"Get onboard it!" She shouted. "How do you propose we do that? We can't even see it."

"They're hidden. I suspect, no I believe that while they are using this hidden system, they cannot use their scanners. If they could, in direct mode, we'd pick them up. They might be hidden, but I also think they are partially blind and I think I know where they are."

"Where?" she said, intrigued now that there was a way forward.

"I think they are in exactly the same place they were when the scout ship saw them. We have the co-ordinates, let's go and find out."

"But if we hit them, we'll die Brett, isn't this too dangerous?" Spirit asked.

"No, no. We'll fly up close, near where they are and go and have a look." He replied.

"You mean space walk?" She sounded exasperated, "go walking into a shield technology we don't understand?"

"No my love, get close enough to communicate! Remember who you are, I just want to get close enough to tickle their systems. Have a look, see what we can do."

It clicked. Now she understood. "OK, I'll feed the data into the navigation system. You go and get suited. I'll follow you when I'm done."

"Ok." Brett replied as he moved past her back into the main quarters to don his environment suit.

\* \* \* \* \* \* \* \*

They couldn't risk telling their plan to anyone over the channel. He wasn't sure if the Yaki could hear them or not, but his instincts told him that they could. But could they see him? That was a risk he was prepared to take.

They put all the information they had into a message drone and fired it directly to the Excel. "Attempting location of battleship. Must find scientists. Prepare a boarding party and keep alert. Message ends."

Brett could hear his own breathing inside the cumbersome suit. He never liked space walks, they were too close to the death that awaited you. The suit didn't feel safe like a ship did, it felt open to the hazards of space, or laser fire and suits didn't carry shields.

He pushed off from the cargo bay, its wide doors open and used the small jets on the suit to spin himself around. He released the control handle that was fixed to his suit, just below the hand and gestured to Spirit to follow him. They would have to use hand signals to communicate or risk the Yaki discovering them. Brett was sure that they were close to the ship and if they got near enough, the battleship's lasers wouldn't be able to locate them for a clear shot. Spirit jetted towards him and he spun himself around again and moved towards the location that was projected on the scanner in his mind.

They had moved almost a kilometre when Brett slowed down and instructed Spirit to do the same. It must be here, we're so close to the location the scout had provided. He instructed his Slave to remove the map from his vision. It vanished and his Slave was now doing nothing, simply waiting for his next command. He controlled his breathing, deep breaths and then a long release. His heart rate began to drop and he began to relax. It took a few moments for him to reach the point he was aiming for, but then he closed his eyes, concentrated on the Slave and slowly, very slowly began to reach out with it. Metre by metre across the vacuum of space he searched, waiting for the telltale sign of a transmission system. He knew that the battleship would have many installed, just like all other ships. He just had to lock onto it.

Ten metres now, then eleven, what was that? A slight tingle in his head, like static but with a higher pitch. Got it! That was a Slave communication device alright, no doubt about it. But even though he tried, he couldn't get it to focus. It was like it was not clear, garbled even. He would have to get closer.

The two suited figures moved slowly across the cosmos and then Brett stopped suddenly, Spirit was right alongside him. It was so close now the static sound was higher, but still garbled. He reached out his hand and moved it towards the noise. He had almost got it to full stretch when his glove made the area in front of it ripple. Brett stopped, but left his hand in the same position while Spirit looked on in disbelief.

The ripple died away. Brett retracted his arm and then pushed it back in again, this time all the way and the ripple came back stronger. It was like looking at the reflection on a still pool of water and then pushing your hand in. Although he wasn't seeing a reflection here, he was making ripples in the picture of space itself.

He turned his head in his helmet and peered at his partner through the smaller side screen. Spirit looked back at him, her eyes wide and staring. She was beginning to say no, shaking her head when Brett pushed the forward button with his other hand and his whole body moved into the ripple.

He gasped, startled and surprised as he passed through the field. There in front of him not two metres away was the dark blue hull of the battleship. Found ya, you sneaky Yaki pirates. The hiss from the Slave had also disappeared to be replaced with the spinning Yaki emblem. By the book of truth, I'm in! Brett thought. But he wasn't. He tried to access the menu system and found himself staring into the walls of a maze. Damn, it's got a security system. I need Spirit to help me with this. He turned around and the inner wall of the shield greeted him, swirls of greens and blues moving around at speed. The reflections on his helmet screens making it difficult to concentrate.

Spirit had watched him go through the wall of water that seemed to be in front of them is space. He had been gone a few moments and she was beginning to get concerned. Should she chance using the communication channel? She was still debating the question with herself when the suited figure of Brett began to appear through the wall. Strangely, it made no ripples as it came through. He was trying to tell her something with his hands, making hand signals to construct a sentence. How the boring lessons in the early days of the navy were paying dividends now.

It took Brett over three Mizuras to tell her what he wanted her to do. He had connected to the ship's system, but it was security protected. The system placed him in a maze. Every time he moved, one space at a time, forward, back, left or right in an attempt to find the key, the key was moved at the same time to a different location in the maze. The chance of him moving to the same place as the key in a maze with over ten thousand squares on the same move was massive. He wanted Spirit to connect and watch the code keepers. She could view a different screen, the maintenance information screen and every time Brett moved through the maze, she would see the code blocks light up on the screen. She simply had to check them, one by one as Brett moved until she found the one that held the calculation. This wouldn't in itself hold the code, but it would give them the calculation used to place the key in the maze. She would then have to feed the numbers into her suit computer and compute where it would be placing the key at a point in time.

Once they discovered where it would be and when, it would be another calculation to give Brett the path he needed to take through the maze to be at that place at that time. Brett had turned around and Spirit jetted forward to follow him.

As she came through the ripple and calmed herself from the shock of the hull being so close by, she connected to the system and began to search the maintenance screens. It was like looking at a thousand blocks on the display in her head. But every time Brett moved a space in the maze, he tapped her on the helmet and she watched the lights flash. All the ship systems would be using these code blocks, but if she watched long enough, tapping data into her wrist pad as she did, she would soon find a pattern and one of them would show up as being lit every time Brett made a movement.

If felt like an eternity, their concentration at its fullest, but in reality it only took a few Mizuras for Spirit to find the correct block. Inside was the code for the random generator, but nothing was truly random, it had logic behind it and she soon worked out three different possibilities that Brett could reach from the position he was in inside the maze.

She gave him the instructions through another set of hand signals and Brett watched them through the superimposed view of the maze. Spirit gave him a long stretch of commands telling him how to move through the maze. He followed them exactly, the computer generated maze walls moving as he went. Four commands remained, turn the corner and walk straight ahead, turn left, one more step, got it! The code appeared before him, hanging in the generated air of the maze. Five, three, three, two he read back to himself in his mind. He immediately exited the maze and selected the menu system again. It put him back into the maze, but this time instead of moving he simply entered the sequence of numbers and the menu system of the ship appeared before him.

He gasped and let out the air in a quick blow. We've done it. We've actually done it! He turned to Spirit and indicated the numbers so that she too could enter the system. Brett navigated through the menu until he came upon an option called "Shroud". Its status was set to on. He told it to go to off. It complied straight away. Sprit altered the access code to the menu.

\* \* \* \* \* \* \* \*

The captain of the Excel had received the message drone from Brett and Spirit, then organised a boarding party from the marines on the lab station. He didn't have any idea what they going to do, but the admiral had been quite clear when she had given him his orders. "The Kotu can do things we cannot imagine captain. Follow their advice, they are our greatest warriors," she had said.

Well he wasn't all that impressed with them himself, sure they had flown around the sector in an impressive manner, but his own pilots had stood their own as well. He was talking over options with his staff about what to do with the Yaki station when the large bulk of the battleship appeared in the space screen before him. He blinked, looked at it again and then actually got up from his seat and walked towards the large screen as if to confirm it was real. Then he turned on the heel of his foot and looked directly at his scan station.

"Scan, what exactly is the status of that battleship?" he asked.

Scan hadn't been looking at the sector display; he was too concerned with the station and had been probing that for information. He tapped a few buttons and the large blob of the battleship appeared before him. Where had that come from? He selected it and cast his eyes over the data his active scanners were now giving him.

"Fully operational sir," scan replied.

The captain dipped his head for a moment in thought and then jerked it back up quickly. "Launch the boarding force and direct all fighters to direct fire on that battleship comms. We must take out its laser defences before the boarding party can attempt an attack."

"Aye sir. Commands issued sir," comm. replied, as he finished speaking into his lapel.

The eight fighter ships from the frigate turned towards the now visible battleship and hit full power.

\* \* \* \* \* \* \* \*

Moo-Kye moved away from the crumpled form of Mitch on the floor, his broken body lay at an odd angle and blood stained his overalls. She walked towards the shivering mass that was the Boron who had just watched his companion refuse to answer her questions and suffer the consequence. He was certain that if he didn't tell this mad woman what she wanted to know, he would soon follow his friend to his death.

She stood a few metres away, rage and fury burning in her eyes. "So, my Boron scientist, I will ask you this time instead. What are the co-ordinates for the jump gates that will take me to earth?" she spat the words at him. "Be quick, my temper, as you have just witnessed, has a very short fuse."

Mi Ton was about to grunt a reply when the communication cube in the wall of the room jutted out and a voice spoke out. "Moo-Kye, urgent situation. I must speak with you now." It was the ship captain.

She seemed extremely agitated at the interruption and paused for a moment before turning and walking towards the cube on the wall. "What is it?" she hissed.

"We have lost the shroud your highness, its down and we can't access the system. We are visible and enemy ships are approaching. They are moving into an attack formation your highness." The captain didn't seem agitated, but in reality he was shaking as he spoke. Being the messenger to Moo-Kye of bad news was not something he relished. He was just glad, that because of her instruction not to be disturbed, he could do it through the channel and not in person.

"What?" she screamed. "Deal with it captain, kill them. You have a battleship under your command. Kill them all!" Then she pushed the cube back into the wall to end the conversation. She didn't have time for this. She was so close to getting the information from the Boron, she would have to continue with her interrogation. She was sure the weak Boron wouldn't be too hard to break now that he had just seen his friend cut to pieces before him. She stormed across the room to where Mi Ton still sat in the restraining seat. "Well?" she asked via the translator.

* * * * * * * *

Brett and Spirit both stared at the lights in the air lock, waiting for the red one to turn to green. They had found one of the outer hull doors and entered the ship. As Spirit had closed the round metal door behind them she had seen their Mako explode in a torrent of fire from the battleship. No going back now then, she mused. She'd miss that ship, memories of her and Brett together, talking and getting to know each other, then becoming lovers. Stop it! She told herself, no time for thoughts like those now. It's just a ship and it's gone. We've got work to do.

They had been fortunate, as the large ship had begun to move as soon as their ship had met its fate. The background of the stars and nebulae moving slightly to the left had been the only indication they were underway, there was no feeling of movement stood in the air lock now. If they had still been outside, or even worse, if only one of them was still outside, they would have been left stranded alone hoping that the Yaki didn't shoot at them. The light went green and Brett began to remove his helmet and suit. Spirit followed his lead and at last they could talk.

"Where will they be?" Brett was asking as he unclasped the large boots.

"I'm looking now," Spirit replied, her mind searching out the ship schematics as she spoke. Then the dull sound of impacts as the battleship came under attack. Excellent, the navy had got the message drone and was beginning its attack. Brett waved his hand over the door lock and the large oblong door hissed open. He stuck his head out of the opening and peered both ways. Good it was all clear. "C'mon Spirit, we can search while we move."

They had just turned the corner when a number of blasts from laser rifles flew past them. Brett skidded to a halt, returning the fire from his small hand held weapon. Spirit also began to fire as they quickly moved back around the corner. The ceiling mounted laser turret that was positioned half way down the corridor, span around and its twin guns began to fire just as they made it around the corner, its shots making indents in the wall. The air smelt of heated metal and it made its way into their mouths, it tasted somewhat like blood.

Brett was already accessing the maze to the internal defence menu, firing with just his hand around the corner, while Spirit again scanned the code blocks. "Got it!" he said, ordering the laser turret to turn the other way and fire on the security guards that were at the far end. In only moments it was over and they ran down the corridor, putting the turret into sleep mode as they passed and applying another new security code to the internal defence system.

\* \* \* \* \* \* \* \*

The pilot of the large ship carrying the marines had been keeping his distance from the battleship while the smaller fighters encircled it, attacking its defences to give the marines a clear approach. It wasn't going very well, when to his astonishment the laser batteries stopped firing and the shields on the battleship read zero percent. He turned for the dark ship and when he reached it, simply slowed, but didn't stop as he deployed the marines into space beside it. They started straight away to attach to its hull and begin the task of opening some of the outer hull doors. The smaller vessel moved away again, back out of range. The lasers and shields may be gone, but they could come back on again at any time. The fighters did likewise. It was up to the marines now.

\* \* \* \* \* \* \* \*

The two of them had accessed most of the battleships systems and switched off the lasers, missiles and shields, resetting the codes as they went. But then as they were preparing to disable the flight systems, the security codes changed and the code blocks were replaced with new, improved code. It was going to take a lot longer to gain access to these systems and they didn't appear to have the time. The scientists could be dead already, but they knew that they couldn't stop to concentrate on the ship's computer systems. They had to try and save the scientists.

They couldn't find the captives anywhere on the ship and the only place that they couldn't get access to was the leader's quarters. Spirit guessed that they must be in there with the Yaki commander. They had no choice and headed for the room, avoiding the security guards where possible, killing them when they couldn't. It was obvious that the boarding party had landed because there was a great deal of communication going through the ships systems. Spirit had accessed a number of the ship cameras and sure enough, there was a battle raging between the marines and the Yaki.

The crew seemed to be beginning to panic. Personnel were running down the corridors now, probably going for the escape pods, Paranid, Argon and Split all running past them and not even giving them a second glance. They continued towards the room, ignoring the sirens and red flashing lights that now appeared to spread throughout the ship.

They reached the door without further incident. The words "Queen of the Yaki" were written on the door in Argon. They'd found the right place then. No guards on the door, they must have ran like the rest were doing, confused and scared when the evacuation warnings had started.

They stopped. One of them each side of the door. Brett was bending over, his hands on his knees, catching his breath. "You got the code?" he asked between deep gasps of air. Spirit stared at him, directly into his eyes before replying, "yes, eight, seven, two, five," she answered.

Brett gave her a quick smile before standing upright and tapping the keypad next to the door manually. The door opened with a swish and they both raced inside, passing each other diagonally as they did so and taking up attack positions on the floor. Brett saw the Argon male on the floor and quickly spotted the athletic figure of the woman standing next to the crumpled body of a Boron strapped to a seat. He had been in such a seat himself. Was the Boron alive? Yes, he saw a twitch of a tentacle. The Boron had gone into aquatic mode, probably in an attempt to lessen the pain he had surely received. The women turned, a look of surprise was followed by a wry smile.

"Oh, we have guests Mi Ton, what a surprise," she said.

Brett was just raising his gun when the woman raised her hand and seemed to flick her wrist twice. Before he could even fire off a shot, his weapon and he noticed that of his partners, were lying useless on the floor before him. Smouldering from the impact of the explosive darts.

Spirit must have read his mind because suddenly the lights in the room went out and they both dived to avoid the second volley of darts from the woman. It went quiet, total blackness. They couldn't see anything and Brett was trying to adjust his senses to the gloom.

Then he heard a cry, a startled shout. It wasn't Spirit. It must be the Yaki leader. He could tell Spirit's voice, regardless of the pitch. Then a thud and a scuffle, someone was fighting by the sound of it, he could hear the impacts as bone and flesh met each other.

"Brett!" Came the cry, "IR cameras, Brett! Check them!" it was Spirit.

Brett accessed the computer and after a few agonising moments he was able to view the infra red cameras in the room. It was difficult to tell what was going on, heated blobs were moving around, swinging wildly at each other. But one of them seemed to getting more shots off than the other. Clever girl, Brett thought, she was fighting the other woman and using the cameras as her guide from a third perspective. Brett couldn't even begin to think how she could be so advanced to do such a thing. He was having trouble trying to work out where they were, never mind engage in a fight.

On and on the fight raged. He felt them come close and he wanted to intervene, but he wasn't sure which one was which and if he hurt Spirit, the Yaki leader might gain the advantage. He just had to watch from the cameras as they moved around the room lunging and parrying. They were both highly trained in the physical arts, it seemed.

Brett felt for the metal blade attached to his boot and pulled it free. If he didn't act soon, his partner might be dead and he wasn't going to allow that to happen. He felt the cold metal in his hand as he gripped the blade and waited for them to come close.

As they passed him again, he shouted to Spirit, "Down!" and in that same moment he briefly closed his eyes while he switched on the main lights in the room again via his Slave. He snapped them open, the delay was enough as the others were blinded for a moment. Brett leapt up and Moo-Kye saw him for just an instant as he plunged the blade deep into her neck.

She staggered back, trying to talk, blood was beginning to spurt from her mouth and the wound. All thoughts of offence gone, Moo-Kye was in pure survival mode and her body was trying to react to the sudden wound. Her hands reached for her throat, but then she fell backwards onto the floor. Her body twitched a few times, but then she lay still.

Brett quickly checked her pulse with his hand and then turned to Spirit, "she's dead," he said.

He began to move towards her, getting to his feet. The Boron was muttering something about sectors when they were frozen in time, eyes staring at each other.

\* \* \* \* \* \* \* \* \*

The captain of the Excel watched as the escape pods were jettisoned from the battleship. It seemed as if the whole crew was trying to get off board. The large ship was still moving, but slowly as if it had no direction. He was about to order his ships to move in closer when a jump tunnel opened in front of the dark ship and it was gone. He stood at the space screen staring at the place where the battleship had been, his jaw open.

\* \* \* \* \* \* \* \* \*

"Can we stop it?"

"No, the energy levels are too high now. The re-alignment will take place regardless of what we do."

"But we don't want this dangerous race to be a part of us. They are destructive, war like."

"We have no choice in the matter now. It is fixed until the next time. We will have to endure their kind until we can raise the energy levels again."

"I understand, it is not what I hoped. But they prove themselves to be resourceful. I will view the events from this point forward with intrigue."

"So will I." A pause, "so will I."

### Chapter 17: The Khaak awaken

*Have I Died?*

Swirling images. Were they figures, ghosts maybe? Can't quite make them out. Coming towards me, woven around each other. Long streaks of colour are touching me. No, going around me not touching. Around my back, I can't seem to move to see them. Move? What is that? Movement yes, I can move can't I? The images have returned to my front. Stroking my face and body. Moving away into the darkness, the light beginning to fade. No! Don't go away. Come back.

Ha, a sense of relief as they appear to stop and then move towards me. Wait, they haven't turned around. That's it, got it. Understand now, I am moving towards them. I am MOVING!

Oh! Tingle in my fingers as the nerve ends awake. My head feels light, almost sickly, dizzy. Like the first inhale of Spaceweed. A burning in my throat, my chest. My whole body feels light as I leave the ground, flying, moving towards the light. Oh please go away. This doesn't feel right. I don't feel well. Let me sleep. I feel so tired, so very tired. Stomach seems to somersault like I'm leaving gravity, pulling multiple G's. Oh, I gasp, my mouth open. Pressure on my chest, harder and harder it gets. Pushing in, constricting my breath. Fluid! I can feel fluid! Oh NO! In my mouth, my throat, my LUNGS!

I fight, struggling against the increasing pressure as my body begins to fill, to grow heavier. I try to choke, but I can't. There is no air to choke on. Only a greater intensity of fluid as it cascades into my trapped torso. I'm going to die, to drown. I clasp my eyes tighter even though they remain shut and mentally shake my head in an attempt to clear it. I feel like I am sinking, dropping down into the abyss, the pressure increasing on my body. My mind seems to grow dark. A soft blackness begins to move inwards on the light that is my mind. Growing smaller and smaller as the darkness completes its journey. I relent and my body appears detached, relaxed. Then such a sense of peace begins to flow out from me. From my heart to my shoulders and down through my stomach, then out to my limbs with a warm peaceful flow just like the Spaceweed again. Caressing me, enveloping me with its kindness, allowing me to float free. As if I am lying in the sand unable to move and the tide moves the water across me, first pushing my body and then pulling it. I cannot attempt to intervene. I have never felt such absolute contentment.

Have I died? But my senses seem awake now, a flicker of life and a brief moment of clarity. My mind begins to focus, slowly, each signal coming back online like someone is pressing buttons to reactivate me, touching the broken wires together to produce a spark. Like someone hitting me on the knee gently to test my reflexes and yes, I am responding. A feeling of strength, of power, absolute power begins to move through me following the same route the as the peaceful ebb did moments before. Sound, yes I can hear something. Strange and muted like faint, far away knocks on a thick glass window. But muffled.

Then the ship, I remember now. The ship! Everybody abandoning the ship. The fighters coming in and firing. The noise, explosions and the ship vibrating under attack. Yes, I had to get to the bridge and stop the jump drive. But I didn't make it, didn't even get out of the room. Oh! A feeling of dread. The room, bodies, blood, people dead. A male Argon lying in a pool of blood, the women lying on her back. Who was she? Badness, yes she was bad, evil. Was she dead? Cannot tell, blood in a pool around her head, maybe. The Boron in his environment suit restrained in the chair speaking to me. What was he saying? His snout moved, but I can't hear the words. Concentrate, c'mon what is he saying?

Wait, something more important than the Boron. Something close to me. No, not something but someone close to me, not physically but emotionally. My stomach is turning again, hands feel like they're shaking. I think I am frowning as I search for her picture, her name.

My eyes snap open and I realise I am floating in fluid. All manner of wires and tubes attached to my body. But they aren't wires, their alive! Some kind of organic tendrils. Oh! My body quivers at the thought and they move holding me tighter. But I can breathe! The fluid, I am breathing the fluid! Through the darkness, dull green and blue lights seem to be outside of my prison, peering in. The colours moving through the fluid as it slowly moves from my body's actions. A figure. I can see someone else across the other side of the tank. The colours from the lights are sparkling from behind her as if they are a star flickering behind her moon.

I peer closer allowing my eyes to become accustomed to the gloom. Her head is bowed, hanging as if lifeless. Is it her? Yes, the images come flooding back as if a sun has erupted in my head. Spirit, my friend, my partner, I can remember staring into her eyes as the ship entered the jump tunnel and then nothing more, until now.

Something flashes past my face, too quick for me to register what it is. Then back again but further away. A Boron! In the water with me, his jet is pushing him around the tank. I can see the density of water change behind him as his body pushes the water outwards and he speeds off into the gloom.

He approaches me and I feel a swell of water push against me as his tentacles move outwards like a star, slowing him in the water. He stops a metre away from my face his snout moving left to right and back again as if swinging from his face. His eye stalks turn inwards. A smile, then they turn back to face me looking me up and down. Can he see something I cannot? I can hear the clicks as he speaks but the meaning escapes me. Then with another gush of water he is gone.

I feel the tiredness creeping back. It is trying to take me again and I cannot fight it any longer. I close my eyes and drift into a long deep sleep.

The time between sleep and awakening. That slow drift from the place of darkness to the one of light. Pulling one-way and then pushing back the other. He suddenly felt his senses coming back online. Like someone flicking switches on a console. One after the other they stood up and righted themselves. Then it hit him. The smell, oh the terrible smell! Reaching inside his body as he breathed in the acrid air, burning his throat and leaving a warm heat in his lungs. He opened his eyes slowly and took in the scene around him.

People from the ship were trapped on the floor. Held by living, moving tentacles that seemed to grip tighter to their captives if any movement was detected. He could hear their moans and cries of anguish.

But one man had appeared to wriggle free of his living chains and he was struggling to his feet. He wore the uniform of a gunner. All torn and bloodied with dirt matted into the cloth. He moved forward and kicked out at the tentacle that attempted to grab him.

Then came the noise. A crackling at first, like the sound of a fire or maybe rain beginning to strike a window. Then more strikes and it began to get louder as if it was approaching. The he saw them. Bodies moving down the large tunnel before them, on the floor, the walls and even on the roof they came. A large seething mass of beings the like he had never seen before. Like insects with small leathery wings on their backs and large bulbous eyes. But it was the hands and feet that dropped down from the bodies that contained the claws. Some with more than others, but each had knife like endings and these were clicking against each other. It was this that created the noise.

The man who had struggled free seemed to stop dead in his tracks and just stared at the mass before him. All seemed to be looking at him and as he turned to run away, they struck. So fast he could hardly see the movement as they flew from the walls and floor and enveloped the man. Each one less than half his size but the twenty or so that descended on the man tore him to pieces in seconds.

Brett's mind could take no more and his body finally gave in to the shock and he passed out.

In the surrounding area outside the vessel, the ships moved as one. Swirling around a central ship and the whole swarm began to move towards the gate from where the intruder had come.

The End.

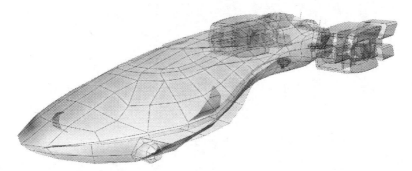

The Riddle of Steel

# BOOK TWO

## *Prologue*

"I've got it," she choked through the acrid smoke filling the cockpit. Struggling back to the co-pilot station she screamed unnecessarily, "Get us the hell out of here!" The acceleration crushed her into the seat as he slammed the after burners to full.

"You think?"

Balls of superheated plasma, emerald and deadly, flashed past the hull as the pilot threw another evasive sequence putting the Orinoco on an escape vector back to the safety of the northern trans-system jump-gate. One snatched glance at his face set grim behind his visor, confirmed her fear.

They weren't going to make it.

The Orinoco was named after the largest river on the northern continent of Argon Prime, although the Goner Temple maintained it merely bore the name of a mighty waterway on humankind's legendary lost home world.

Inevitably, due to its shape, a short handle infantry entrenching tool with two drive nacelles trailing low on elegant swept back pylons, it soon became known as the Spade, It was a compromise design, suited to the particular needs of its owners. Armed and armoured like a medium fighter with a capacious sub space compression hold, it was the vessel of choice for clan smugglers and well suited for a variety of tasks. With the right load-out it performed excellently in a defensive role where its low speed was not a significant disadvantage.

With the drive system tuned to the maximum possible speed and the subspace hold enlarged to the full theoretical maximum of 350 storage units at a cost that could have bought another ship this Spade was, as they say on Boron, 'Loaded for Split'. Apart from a fig leaf load of 100 units of the oily but popular Chelt Meat the hold was filled with over 100 of the medium punch Dragonfly missiles, a mixed bag of 50 other smaller rockets, 50 automated defence drones, several spare weapon systems and a backup shield. It even sported 10 of the extremely powerful and largely illegal Teladi Squash Mines. Although usually to be found escorted by a mixed package of Mandalay light and Bayamon medium fighters this Orinoco, in the hands of this pilot could hold its own in almost any fight long enough to extend and escape.

None of that would help against the huge Xenon destroyer that arcing round for another pass; its forward turrets already spitting fire. With its huge drives it could outrun them easily even if the Spade was significantly more agile. The pilot milked this small edge with remarkable skill, pushing the performance envelope of his ship to the very edge, stealing another few seconds of life from the heart of the unnamed jump-gate sector controlled by the artificial scourges of all sentient life, the Xenon.

As he threw the craft about the sky, twisting and turning through fusillades of green and blue fire, the co-pilot watched the scanners, calling out crucial information through the forced calm of her training.

"Okay, you've lost him again. Coming about, coming about, port, aft low. 5 klicks, 6 klicks, 7 klicks."

A small note of resignation tinged her next call.

"Merde, they're launching fighters."

The pilot futilely gunned the afterburner but they were already at maximum speed. At under 100 mps even the Xenon L heavy fighter could match them and the light and medium N and M class could outdistance them with ease. The jump-gate was still 20 klicks distant.

" I count 6 N class, 3 M class and 2, no, 3 L's. Second wave launching."

Within seconds the Orinoco was the centre of a hornet's nest of attention as the small stubby N class fighters swarmed all over them. The tactical sensors filled the cockpit with the whine of their drives as their lasers peppered the shields.

Coolly the co-pilot targeted and launched defence drones in groups of 4. The short-lived machines were only unshielded flying lasers but in numbers their speed and agility made them a threat to small fighters and a nuisance to others. Tactically they were of most use to cover a retreat. Even one of the big, heavy fighters of the Xenon with their 50 MW of shields could be forced to temporarily disengage by a swarm of these devices.

The cockpit echoed to the rapid pipping of multiple laser fire, punctuated by the rumbling assorted explosions of drones and fighters alike. The respite lasted only a few seconds, as the pounding roar of Gamma Particle Accelerator Cannons presaged the arrival of the superior M class interceptors.

"3 M's, 2 o'clock starboard aft, closing fast overshoot."

Functioning as one the two pilots fought for their lives and with supreme skill the pilot corkscrewed through the lethal concentric plasma columns filling the vacuum around them to bring his ship up onto the tails of the 3 M class fighters. Strangely for an artificial race the Xenon craft displayed a strong sense of aesthetic with both the L and the M class sharing the wide body, forward trailing wing shape that called to mind a bird of prey.

Before they could accelerate away the Spade closed to within tens of metres, sweeping their rear exhausts with withering fire from its own Gamma PAC's. The cockpit shuddered with the recoil but it did not distract the co-pilot as she swiftly launched 4 dragonflies at each of the 3 fighters in turn. At such short range the Xenon had no chance to go evasive.

Two vanished instantly in a ball of flame and the third broke high, the missiles tracking relentlessly. Rolling inverted the Spade pulled a loop that bought it head on with the M. Pirouetting through the incoming fire the pilot drained his weapons into its forward shield face forcing the M to break right, taking two dragonflies in the face. As it spun helplessly a third reduced it to a million melted fragments.

The second wave on N's had joined the survivors of the first wave. Most were taken out by the remaining drones and waves of small missiles the co-pilot dispatched but by now the first wave of the heavy Xenon L's had arrived with the second wave of M's close behind.

The Spade fought like a demon, filling the sky with rockets whilst dodging a torrent of incoming fire. One by one the M's fell, even one of the L's but such were the odds that even a pilot as gifted as this one evidently was found it almost impossible to get a close enough position to ensure missile efficacy. The 10 MW of shielding sported by the Orinoco could not hold up long under the cross fire of 5 L class fighters. And even if they triumphed they'd only face further waves.

"I need options fast".

The pilot sounded as desperate as the situation.

The co-pilot rapidly targeted the destroyer and ordered him to go head to head, fast and low. It looked like suicide but he knew better than to argue and as the huge ship loomed before them 2 of the pursuing fighters broke off, circling to cut the line of retreat. Space was filled with incoming fire, fore and aft and despite inspired manoeuvring the Orinoco shuddered under their deadly impact. Emotionlessly the onboard computer intoned the falling shield status as it dropped below 30%.

As the Orinoco flashed along the hull of the giant destroyer the co-pilot deployed all 10 of the squash mines. The pilot looped and rolled to put the bulk of the capital ship between him and the mines as his companion triggered them. Despite the cover the shockwaves sent the Spade tumbling and careening. As the pilot fought to regain control a dozen cockpit alarms sounded and somewhere behind him he registered the insistent hiss of an onboard extinguisher cutting in.

The Xenon destroyer had fared less well. Burning plasma roiled from numerous gaping holes in the hull and its drive system was completely off line. The three pursuing L's had vanished in the initial blast and the co-pilot rapidly targeted the remaining 2 with the last of her missiles. One succumbed while missiles chased the remainder across the sky.

Instantly the Orinoco broke for the safety of the jump-gate. The crippled destroyer, powerless and burning, was unable to launch another flight and the remaining L's would be unable to intercept them in time.

The celebratory whoops of the pilot were cut cruelly short.

"Scanners show two more destroyers coming in hot and fast at relativistic speed. Slowing, slowing, slowing, here they come." Her voice was now devoid of hope.

The 2 warships roared by, disgorging fighters as they went.

The ensuing battle was short and even as the 2 pilots punched out their craft blossomed into a lethal fireball.

## Rogues Testament

### *Chapter 1: Bad News*

Bad news. Sometimes you see it coming and sometimes it just hits you - wham - like a pack of Bayamons out of a planetary shadow. And sometimes, well sometimes you can just feel it out there, shuffling and morose, prowling your fences muttering vague promises of really dire shit. I'd had that feeling for weeks, ever since Hela's last vidmail. That casual, "Oh by the way, I've updated my Last Testament." So when the CO delivered the news of the accident it was almost a relief.

Almost.

You didn't have to be a cynic to be deafened by alarm bells when you heard the words "training accident". Shit - after all this time you'd think they'd come up with a better euphemism for "fatally caught doing something embarrassing to the government somewhere they shouldn't have been". And to pull that crap on a serving officer - well even the CO looked shamefaced and he was one by-the-book son of a bitch.

She had been my closest living relative. Hell, since Pop spaced hisself she was the only family I had. Mother not cousin. I was never really sure what Hela did - something for the government she'd say before sliding round the subject. She could be away for weeks but she taught me everything I knew and got me into the Academy 6 years ago, despite the grades. Great pilot, lousy freakin' attitude.

And me? Lieutenant Gragore Marteene, Flight Commander, Alpha Wing, 1st of the 5th. Yea - the Screamin' Demons, Argon's finest, the Best of the Best. Or I was. Now just call me Max. And make that Big C to go sweetheart. Gotta be jumpin', that ore ain't goin' ta haul itself right?

Shoving the burger into a pocket where leaking fat blended with the heavy coolant stains adorning the battered civ flight suit, Max left the small bar and headed back to the docking bay. It was a long walk and many levels down but he needed the exercise. And as Hela had taught him - it's a good way to check your six. So far as he could tell he wasn't being followed. A discreet palmed sweep with his decidedly non-standard Data-Comm revealed no suspicious energy spikes in close proximity either.

Confident he'd acquired no bugs or microscopic Fly-Eyes Max continued to the hanger bay where by now his Lifter would be crammed to the gills with ore.

It was not until he was safely ensconced in the cockpit of the battered freighter that he rummaged through the snack in his pocket until he found the tiny data chip sequestered within the oily Chelt meat.

Outwardly it seemed a standard vid-chip but as Hela often said. "Only a fool believes his own eyes." Max had no doubt it held the key to more secrets, as had the chip containing her testament 3 months previously.

Three months. It had been three months since the news, three months since he'd resigned his commission, three months since accessing Hela's Final Testament. And it had been practically three lousy months since the surgery and his face itched on bad days. Itch enough to make him want to rip it from his skull and creep back to his old life. But that was gone, transformed by events set in motion that day as surely as the cosmetic DNA resequencing had remoulded his body.

Goodbye Elite and deep space LURPS, hello decrepit Lifter and the wild glamour of space trucking.

Like every fighter jock he felt he was born to be a warrior, wearing some sleek machine like a second skin, not a rag-assed haulier, slouching around the home systems in the outsized overcoat of a freighter, neck stiff from looking over his shoulder. "Well" he thought, "Hopefully that's about to change."

Chapter 2: The Price of Peace

The Officers Lounge fell briefly silent as Gragore entered, proving that it's true what the cynics and unimaginative physicists say - only bad news travels FTL. If someone could figure out how to build a drive from it they'd rule known space.

Only the deep, practically subliminal throb of the carrier drives punctuated the embarrassed lull. Awkwardly comrades offered their condolences, uncharacteristically unsure of their ground. Death, while not exactly a regular guest was certainly no stranger to the 5th. They'd taken it on the chin more than once in the troubles inspired by the appearance of the mystery ship that so excited the Goners, but there were rituals and customs for the death of comrades in action. Have a drink, tell wild tales, get laid. But when death got this personal?

"Sorry to hear about your mother old chap." Gragore smiled briefly, acknowledging the concern expressed by the Beta Wing commander. Bad news might travel supra light but where Paskaal was concerned the finer points usually remained in the post. Lack of attention to detail was one of the many things that could get a fighter pilot killed and sometimes Gragore wondered how a man whose idea of a pre-flight check was to bang the control panels and bellow, "Are you right my old sweetheart?" had managed to get within docking range of retirement.

His record though, well it spoke for itself. The name Paskaal stood proudly atop more kill-boards than just the Vigilant. Only his refusal to countenance the loss of the ridiculous handlebar moustache or moderate his old colonial demeanour saved him from the fate of other Argon war heroes - the afterlife of recruitment vid hell. Gragore grinned as he flashed to the last time they'd talked of this. Old Warhorse to Young Contender.

"Your planet needs you, my arse." They'd had way too much of a particularly fine vintage Engineering Deck space fuel and Paskaal was even more loquacious than usual.

"I said to her - pretty little thing she was, could have taken quite a shine, a touch of the Goners about her though. Where was I? Oh, right." Paskaal had taken another long pull, straight from the bottle and the glow in his cheeks now suffused his whole face.

"Your planet needs you, my arse. How about I said, how about; 'Ask not what you can do for your planet but how much they will pay you for it'?"

He shot a mock quizzical look before taking another pull, this time the glow spread through his thinning scalp and up to the tips of his rather prominent ears. "Never heard from her again. Funny that."

He had then tapped the side of his nose knowingly. "A word to the wise eh son? Play ball with the pen-pushers and you'll be jockeying a desk so fast your head will spin."

Well right now he needed something to push his head into a flat spin and with a slight incline of his head he signalled Paskaal it was okay to join him as he took a vacant table. The old Flight Louie limped purposefully across the lounge garnering glasses, bottles and snacks from intervening tables as he went. Protests were muted with an indignant bristling of his moustache, lending credence to the lower deck rumour that it was a life form in itself.

Gragore noted with amusement it was his left leg that appeared artificial today when he knew for a fact that it was the right, and then only a mech knee. Paskaal caught the wry smile. "Damned servos - it's the damp weather don't y'know!" With surprising dexterity the veteran pilot laid out half a dozen shot glasses filled to the meniscus with the clear, potent brew the drive-monkeys concocted deep in the bowels of the ship. With due deference to custom both pilots knocked back the first glass in one, slamming the inverted empty down, before either spoke.

"Hmmn, 12, a very fine hour, now tell me about your cousin."

## *Chapter 3: Down Among the Dead Men*

Don't hog that spliff man. Ah shit, that's better, Red Thunder right? Thought so, ran a lot of that stuff. Nothin' better for lightening the load. Am I right or am I right?

Where was I? Yea - Hela, Paskaal, the Vigilant. Got you. I should lay off this stuff.

Well, maybe it was the hooch, shit, the proof was always off any scale you'd care to name. We just counted the seconds it takes to deaden your tongue and this was a 3, possibly a 2. In a couple of heartbeats it reached my brain and a more comforting numbness tried to get it on with the awful emptiness that was gripping me.

You know that feeling? Like something has reached inside your head, torn all the synapses and ganglia coding warmth, love and life right out of your skull and thrown the bloody mess right back in your face? I tell you, I wouldn't wish that on no one. And do you wanna know the worst thing - the very worst thing? You don't feel what you've lost, like losing your sight and forgetting the feeling of sunshine and a warm breeze on your face on a fine summer's day. Or losing a mother's love, you don't miss it 'til it's gone and there ain't no way it's ever coming back.

You served in a combat unit right? Seen any action? Heavy casualties? Yea - well you know what I mean; you've seen 'em. Men so eaten up by their losses they've nothin' left inside. Hollow walking meat drowning in space-fuel and desperate to conjure up a feeling, any damn feeling to let them know they are still alive. Shit - there was this one guy when I was on the - well I can't tell you that - I'd have to kill you right? Lost his whole bloody wing to a Xenon incursion. Thirty bloody seconds.

Those machine-head destroyers, they're so fast - fast enough to ruin your whole freakin' day before you even see them coming. I tell ya- we took so much crap with those tight, pretty formations early on before the brass wised up and stopped treating war like a bloody air show. This guy though, this guy came back - the only bloody one. Wing leader smeared all over the screen they were that freakin' tight. Shit, the mechanics even found teeth stuck in the cockpit frame. ID'd him from the DNA traces. Spent the rest of the war trying to get hisself killed, got a chest full of medals.

Heroes, man. I look 'em in the eyes and if they've got that look, what you grunts call it, like they're looking past you at all those ghosts out on the wire? The thousand-metre stare, yea, that's it. If I see that look, well, shit - ain't no way he's flying on my wing.

Well, Paskaal, ain't nothin' he hadn't seen and well he knew that talk was what I needed now, even if I didn't know it until he asked. That Paskaal, he was a diamond, man. It's a cryin' shame. No don't get me started on that one. But I needed to talk, booze or no booze, though it took 2 more shots. Bang, bang. Instant catharsis right?

Paskaal and I, we'd served together for a good stretch on the V. Got to know each other pretty well. Not tight but friends. You know how it is in combat units - you keep a certain distance.  But, well, like I said, sometimes you just need to talk otherwise you'd just go crazy.  Sure the V had a counsellor but what the hell do they know?  Okay, lot's, sure it's their job but this one - she was a Goner and just about the hottest thing you've ever seen.  Big black eyes, great figure, uniform 2 sizes too small.  Well, it's difficult to pour your heart out with a hard-on right?

And so we talked.  About Hela, my family, my father.

## *Chapter 4: In the Family*

The Marteene family, we'd always been spacers, one way or another. I don't remember my mother; she died from postnatal complications soon after I was born. My father spent half his life on destroyers, made Exec before taking early retirement. Walked away with a tidy lump sum before returning to Argon Prime and starting a family. The stars were in his blood though - I could see it in his eyes and hear the wistful note in his voice when we watched the night sky, counting the shooting stars and picking out some of the places he'd been.

I guess that hooked me too so the day he announced he'd quit his job, bought a freighter and set up his own shipping line, well I was probably more excited than him. I must have been 7 at the time but I can remember it like it was yesterday. Since retiring he'd been working up on the main shipyard in the home system, running Salvage & Repair I think. Good money but with the stars so close the temptation to reach out and touch them one more time must have been irresistible and one day fortune winked in the form of a borderline insurance write-off. A deal he was in the right position to pick up.

A few months of elbow grease, a lot of gratis work from his crew and most of his savings and he had himself one of the early model Lifters. The Destiny Star, what a great name. Sitting in the co-pilots seat, following his movements on the controls when we took it out for a maiden spin around the system, well, y'know I just can't say but from that moment on I had no doubts at all. I was going to be the best goddam pilot in the universe.

For years I practically lived in the sims, the Home-Net standalones and the Virtua-Net persistents. Pop even pulled in a few favours and got himself a link to the Forces-Net. Reservists have to keep their hand in right? You can imagine what a kick that was for a 10 year old kid! By the time I was old enough to start flight training I could out fly the instructor.

You know, I'd never figured out what was going on with the business. At first things seemed to be going great. I can't remember Dad ever being happier, even at the beginning with the endless energy cell runs across the home systems. Thrill of a lifetime for a young kid though, once we even did a run down to Paranid Prime! Not the best introduction to alien life forms I suppose. Once the business was up and running he began pulling in better contracts. A lot of work for the military, old contacts I guessed, and plenty of long haul specials. Had himself a bit of a rep as it turned out, according to a couple of old spacers I ran into down in Trinity Sanctum one time. A real hard-assed SOB who'd get the job done, and I quote. Years later I went through some of the manifests, a lot of high payments for running some real low value stuff across a lot of sectors. Board of Inquiry made a lot of it at the time, made out like he was running illegals. Well, there certainly was a lot of debt. Shields and drones mostly, and a lot of electronics. There was plenty of wide open space between income and expenditure.

When they found the ship on auto and backtracked it to the body we lost everything. Well, I did. The house, the Destiny Star, everything. Even the insurance refused to pay out. Suicide, they even found a note.

That's how I ended up with cousin Hela, who it turned out, was the next-of-kin. She was about as thrilled as I. One second, deep space recons finest, the next parent to a 13 year old with a chip the size of the Goner Temple. Of course she had to switch assignments. Home System Defence first but soon she left the service altogether. Got herself some sort of desk job - a defence analyst with the DARP Corporation. Defence And Research Projects - one of those arms-length deals that allow the government to do all sorts of things it can't or doesn't want to do for itself. Kept her rank in the Fleet Reserve though, did her stint in the Brennan thing and when the job took her out-system the Corp took care of things. I spent a lot of time with company parents.

Couldn't have been easy for her, losing a career like that but Hela was never one for looking back. You've just got to grasp what life throws at you and run with it she'd say. Fifteen years older than me, blonde, beautiful, intelligent, hell- a fighter pilot - I had a crush so big, well, I can't tell y'know? The fact that she was away on business a whole lot and was pretty damn cute at not talking about it - well you know what boys are like. As far as I was concerned she was a spy for sure, outwitting wily Teladi and sneaking vital data past surly Split. Yea - pretty ironic.

But she kept me on the rail though, despite my best efforts to fall off. A teenager with all that shit to act out, mother dead in childbirth, Dad spaced himself - selfish bastards eh! You can imagine what that must have been like for her. I'd have spaced me in a cold second if I'd been her but she kept me focused on the one thing that still mattered to me and who knows how I but scraped together the grades and she pulled some strings and I was in the Fleet.

Second attempt but I was in! I can't tell you how much I owed her. One whole summer she spent trying to bring me up to speed. Took me through all kinds of drills - Reserve and Fleet stuff mostly, some of her own. I can't tell you how important it was to me to know there was still someone in the galaxy that I was still connected to - who was on your side against everything. And to lose that, well if you've ever lost both parents, you know what I'm talking about here.

So to get that "training accident" bull, a close formation collision on an exercise in The Hole, well that was an insult. Call me paranoid but deep down in the back of my brain I just knew something was wrong. For one thing her reserve unit was not scheduled for manoeuvres for 3 months, and then not out-system. Like Paskaal said at the time - there were spook prints all over the story. With all the fuel consumed I'd have been on my way to bang on some pretty big desks demanding answers if Fate hadn't stepped in, pretty convincingly disguised as Official Military Protocol, which in this case specifies who is and who is not considered "significant family members" (Military Order 2437 sub-section C; Bereavement, Discretionary Leave, the Granting Thereof). You know - I didn't even think about the duty shift, I just assumed I'd been taken from the roster. I was in grief right? Well, a big wrong there fella!

Paskaal was just lining up another couple of shots when the tannoy cut through the hubbub of the lounge.

"Alpha Wing Alert 1, Alpha Wing Alert 1. Marteene, Molloy, Cody and Shanner to Briefing Room 2. I repeat Alpha Wing Alert 1, Alpha Wing Alert 1. Marteene, Molloy, Cody and Shanner to Briefing Room 2. Report." The electronically generated voice was calm but insistent. Paskaal raised a brow quizzically. "You want to take this lad?" I nodded. Perhaps some purposeful activity was just what I needed right now. The soul yearns for what it needs right? And just right now I wanted to be out among the stars. Cold void to cold void.

"Well son, if you're going out then you're going to need this." He surreptitiously slid a Quick-Stim across the table and I quickly palmed it. It's one of those dirty little secrets - almost all governments in the galaxy spend a fortune attempting to eradicate the production, trade and consumption of illegals - yet half the military run on them. Stims to keep you up there and alert for hours at a time. Seds to bring you down. Stims to get you out again. You couldn't fight a war without 'em. Routine equipment for LURPS missions. You just cannot keep up that level of concentration for a 48 hour stretch in a cockpit, even with staggered breaks - 3 hours sleep on auto-pilot while your wingman keeps watch. Standard LURPS operating procedure. Casual use to get around a spot of over-indulgence though - that's definitely not an affirmative so with a nod of thanks I slipped into the rest-room.

Click, hiss into my carotid. Nausea then that feeling of boundless energy, can-do certainty and complete invulnerability. A double-edged sword to combat pilots but the good ones though - we can handle that - can balance on that fine edge between confidence in our abilities, training and equipment and the kind of recklessness that leads to breathing vacuum and plasma. That's what we tell ourselves anyway. So I made my way to the Briefing Room down on G Deck running on adrenaline and stims, eager for the challenge. Warriors love a challenge right? And when they call out the Demons, well more often than not there's a real mother.

You heard a lot about the 5PthP? Sure you have. We were front line, never spending much time in the home sectors. You might think the galaxy is at peace because the vids are not filled with Xenon armadas or ludicrous Split ultimatums.

Wrong.

Low Intensity Conflict the theorists call it. Argon vs. Split, Teladi vs. Split, Paranid vs. Boron, pirates vs. anybody who's in the way, trade wars between corporations.

You name it. Someone's always got a reason to take a little pop at someone over something right? Well the 5PthP are usually there or thereabouts trying to stop something going off or do a little popping ourselves. And when things get a little too, shall we say, "delicate", or just plain bloody suicidal that's when they call in the 1PstP of the 5PthP. As the motto says "The best of the best." More likely the maddest of the mad, or as the flight deck cynics would say, the most expendable of the expendable - and it has to be said - we were a pretty rum bunch. Not your most disciplined troops but good pilots.

Expendable seemed the right word.

I cruised to the briefing room on that cool adrenaline buzz, allowing the training to take over. Spend any time in this line of work and you learn there are pockets in the back of your mind where you keep feelings like this hidden 'til the jobs done. Stay focused on the job. This one had to be something special, it was all too short notice and Intelligence favoured this briefing room for its added security features. For the first time since the news I began feeling a glimmer of a smile, that frisson of anticipation, you know the feeling right?

Don't get me wrong - we all haul our normal load of routine but it's those specials that add the spice to life. Three other pilots from my flight were already at their consoles, each staring intently at flashing schematics and star-charts on screen. As soon as I took my seat the light in the small room dimmed and two officers from Fleet Intelligence entered, striding purposefully to the front, stiff like their spines were fused and clutching their data-pads as if they contained the planetary defence codes. My regular wing-man, a vet named Shanner, caught my eye and grinned. He did a wicked Intel Strut. The intelligence types just loved the drama.

## Chapter 5: Spooks

"Lieutenants." Commander Trasker, Fleet Intelligence Officer for the Vigilant welcomed the pilots with a curt nod whilst her aide uploaded data into the room's holo-projector. To Janis pilots were a necessary evil at best, "the meat in the seat" as her Special Ops Unit referred to them. In fact she lived for the day when some of the breakthrough research into combat AI and decision-making systems finally paid off. Enough of the black budget was poured into it.

Pilots. If they weren't getting drunk and blabbing state secrets to any passing whore they were getting killed or otherwise screwing up by not carrying out her carefully laid plans to the letter. Responding to contingencies they called it. Irksome in the extreme. It didn't help that her colleagues in Psy-Ops insisted on their precious "Maverick Profile". If she had her druthers, these ops would be carried out by pilots with Triple A's across the board, people who did as they were told and bloody well did it by-the-book. To her chagrin the fad of the decade in the Psych world was "Psych-Mission Profile Mapping" which was a fancy way of saying, "Match the people to the task".

Sadly for Janis such research suggested that to achieve a maximum success rate for high risk, low profile assignments required the use of operatives with a broader range of skills and personal qualities than found in straight Ace pilots. Sure they could handle the flying but this line of work also demanded the ability to improvise quickly and with genius to unexpected or changing circumstances when reality churlishly strayed from the course laid out for it in her meticulous plans. Missions could also require planned and impromptu undercover work. It was a rare person who had all of the personal qualities required, a rarer one who could pilot a star fighter and an even rarer one who could more hold their own in the variety of vehicles demanded by Special Ops. Of course the armed forces, like any well-run and mature organisation, cannot abide such people and if a few slipped through the inevitable disciplinary trouble made them easy to identify and weed out.

It was only when the Maverick Profile gained credibility that the Aggressor Squadron concept was born and, Commander Trasker's opinions notwithstanding, it had proven to be a remarkable success.

In essence it was simple. Each year recruit a percentage of potential pilots matching the Maverick Profile, follow their careers, sift out the gems for special assignment and either throw out the rest or leave them in whatever trouble they'd managed to get into. Give the chosen few intensive training in all manner of black arts as well as hundreds of flight hours in just about everything with thrusters and you had not only a top-notch pack of black ops pilots but a squadron skilled in the hardware and tactics of any potential hostiles.

The 1PstP of the 5PthP were one such outfit, dividing their time equally between intensive training, routine military duties and providing the opposition in training exercises where their ability to fly and fight as pirates, Split or even Xenon was invaluable. And if a few of them were away for unexplained periods, who was to notice? None of which points swayed Commander Trasker. If it weren't for their exceptional performances she'd have every last one of the undisciplined, disrespectful, prying bastards in the stockade.

In fairness to Janis, she had a point. The Maverick Profile had one point of vulnerability. Maverick types tended not to be very good on the principle of "need-to-know". It's not that, despite her prejudices, they freely disseminated state secrets to every curious alien, but that they needed to know so damn much! Like bloody-minded children crying, "but why?" to every order. Very early on in the program it was realised that the best way to get co-operation and enhance security was to keep them fully briefed. Otherwise they behaved like any other bunch of malcontents who felt they were being treated like mushrooms. They prodded, poked and pried until they struck light. And given their training and expertise they were pretty effective.

Of course none of them would deliberately compromise national security but if clever people open enough back doors, other less well-meaning clever people would also find their way through them. In the end the security threat posed by the possibility of the capture of these operatives was less than that posed by their spying so a Full Context Briefing policy was implemented. Trasker was only slightly mollified by the fact that the enemy generally knew all this anyway and the prime purpose of secrecy was to prevent your own population finding out what dirty little deeds were done in their name. This was very effectively achieved by the stick and carrot combination of draconian national security laws and a Freedom of Information Act so hedged with caveats and exemptions it was essentially the opposite.

The main holo-projector flashed into life, displaying a rotating system map. Four smaller but similar holo-displays at the briefing stations mirrored the contents. The Meat In The Seats assumed an insouciant air, part of their childish professional "cool". Regs say the Mitsies get a Full Context Briefing so, Janis thought, they were damn well going to get one. There was a whole lot of context to establish for this particular mission but deep down Trasker was one of those who believe the rest of the universe in general, and in her case Mitsies in particular, could only benefit from a long exposition of her wisdom. With a grim smile of determination the pilots recognised with an audible groan Trasker began the FCB.

The arrival of the human Brennan in known space in a ship all factions suspected of being replete with new technologies upset the delicate balance of forces that prevailed. The serious defeat inflicted upon the Xenon had opened up many new sectors for exploration and colonisation and all the major races quickly moved to seize what they could. Needless to say this provoked a series of acknowledged and unacknowledged disputes until an uneasy equilibrium was re-established. Due to chance and circumstance the new map of the galaxy was an untidy one. Gone were the contiguous borders, neatly defining the territories of each race. The Argon, the Boron and the Teladi all acquired control of significant sectors well beyond their pre-war borders and soon set about consolidating their hold with massive colony and station building programmes. The other races also moved to consolidate their holding on their expanded borders.

With the massive expansion of the economic base and the removal of the Xenon threat interstellar trade soon rose to record levels. Flourishing economies were further fuelled by tax cuts funded by the "peace dividend" as military budgets fell. In common with all the races the Argon placed the main burden of protecting economic installations and escorting the freighters that are the lifeblood of the galactic economy upon the commercial sector. It was expected that each station would protect itself with its own fighters, laser towers and if of particular importance, their own mine fields and these forces were considered part of the strategic reserve of each race. Consequently, in times of conflict the military of each species could be considerably boosted at very short notice. This practice had proven to be extremely effective militarily and very cost-effective.

Such a strategy was possible due only to 2 factors. First, the basic frames of fighters and freighters were relatively inexpensive as the jump-gates rendered huge and complex drive systems unnecessary. Current drive technology had remained essentially unchanged for decades with improvements in performance coming largely from increasing the standard efficiency of matter-energy conversion.

Second was the miracle of nano-tech production that underpinned the economy, societies and cultures of all the known factions and races. This had evolved so significantly over the centuries that the actual raw material and energy costs of production was minor compared to the information costs incurred in the development, programming and controlled deployment of specialist nano-bots. The costs were further increased by the complex network of patents and licences established by treaty between all the races, protecting their intellectual property. That's why it remains impossible to purchase a Bio-Gas installation outside of Boron space despite its wide use by other races.

Anything from a small fighter to a huge factory Installation Deployment Package could be constructed within hours so long as you could pay for its information content. Basic craft, whilst still costing much more than an average being could expect to earn in an honest lifetime, were eminently affordable by corporations, states and other more shadowy organisations.

With the basic frame and drives reduced to a minimum the real costs lay in the equipping and tuning of performance. Innovation in equipment from shields & weaponry to function-enhancing technologies such as the SETA drive or a Trading System Extension was ongoing and everyone needed to keep up. Constant innovation meant that the information costs of production in these areas are never significantly amortised by long production runs. That is why it might cost 3 times the original purchase price of a craft to fully max out performance and equipment.

Another expense that had to be factored into the costs of owning and running a ship was governed by the iron law of diminishing returns, affecting propulsion enhancement and cargo capacity extensions in particular. The nano-technology and specialist software required to boost energy conversion efficiency and hence speed significantly beyond factory standard settings is very high and gets higher the further the technology is stretched. The same is true of the subspace folding required to enable even the smallest of craft to sport a cavernous cargo hold.

For this reason you rarely scan any ship maxxed to capacity. If you've got the credits to do it you've got the credits for a comfortable retirement unless you are in space for other reasons, nefarious or otherwise.

The final expense is of course the meat in the seat. It cost millions of credits for the military to train a competent combat pilot and this was a cost no sentient taxpayer or corporate chief were prepared to carry in times of peace. It is much cheaper to take a competent pilot and support them with aids such as combat autopilots. For smaller concerns defence fighters might be entirely flown by AI devices. Despite major research projects by all the major powers the goal of a combat AI that can out fly and out adapt a trained sentient pilot remains as far away as ever. Until that time space will be filled with semi-competent pilots who freeze or panic under fire.

For all of these reasons the core military of each species was relatively small but could be expanded rapidly in terms of numbers and quality of equipment at short notice. The most significant consequence of this is that large-scale military actions are almost always considered too risky in peacetime. That is one reason why the Pirate Clans continue to flourish. No species found it worth risking one of their few huge capital ships on an all-out assault on their well-defended bases.

The potential loss in terms of materiel and trained pilots was huge compared to the less tangible gains. Piracy blighted interstellar trade but the costs of losses were absorbed by the consumer and so long as their activities remained within sensible bounds no species was likely to take the sort of risks necessary to quell them completely.

The arrival of Brennan and his X-Shuttle threw the status quo into chaos. Apart from the heavy defeat of the Xenon and the consequent galactic expansion the ship itself was a scientific treasure trove. Despite the inability of the best scientific brains of the Argon to understand and repair the revolutionary jump-drive two significant breakthroughs lead immediately to new technologies that transformed the military and economic landscape.

The first of these involved communications technology. Just as Faster-than-Light drives remained theoretically and practically impossible so does FTL communications and sensors. Until recently all interstellar communications travelled either by courier or by very high speed nano-comms, which are little more than a data chip married to a micro-drive system. The latter simply fly the message at great speeds through the jump-gate systems, relying on their speed and microscopic size to avoid detection. The system has been in use for decades and is practically 100% effective and secure but absolutely no use for real-time communications.

All that has now changed with the development of X-Craft inspired Nav-Sat technology using entangled photon pairs to instantaneously convey information from one place in the universe to another without anything physically crossing the intervening space. By utilising common data compression routines enough information can be transmitted to permit real-time sensor monitoring of remote sectors. At the first the need to use separated pairs of entangled photons meant only one receiver could read the messages from one transmitter, making the whole thing pretty impractical. Subsequent breakthroughs led to the development of Replicant Quantum State circuitry and this allowed receivers to be tuned to any transmitter for which it has the quantum key.

This revolution in communications is going to transform our societies in ways we cannot begin to imagine but there are two immediate and significant consequences. First, businesses can now exchange information and monitor production over many sectors in real-time. Not only has this increased the efficiency of the major conglomerates that dominate the economies of all the species but for the first time it enables smaller traders to establish and control cross-sectoral businesses without incurring huge management costs. Up until now the one-man-and his-craft business has been fatally handicapped by the need to constantly supervise the business in person. With a functioning in-system Nav-Sat the big boys at last face serious competition. Defence analysts predict corporate sponsored attacks on the comm networks of competitors, probably through the use of third parties, will become a major source of conflict in the coming years.

The second huge technological leap is of course the jump-drive technology developed and owned by the Goners. Although the extremely high purchase and running costs make fitting it to most ships uneconomic it has significant military implications. Until now an enemy had to come at you sector by sector, giving you the option of engaging his forces at any stage along the route. Tactically it also required the deployment of fleet elements at strategic points to react to threats.

Now a potential foe can drop an attack force right into your backyard without a seconds warning and all the powers are scrabbling to rewrite their military doctrines. As a new technology it is massively expensive and no power can possibly afford to fit jump-drives as standard but even a squadron jump-capable heavy fighters would be a massive strategic weapon.

To head off full-scale war Argon wisely decided the technology had to be shared with the other governments and under the provisions of the Jump Technology Non-Proliferation Treaty of Trinity Sanctum the Goners agreed to prohibit sales of the drive to individuals and non-governmental organisations. To date very few of these drives are to be found in private hands, Brennan has one, that's about it. The development of it as "sealed box" technology was also mandated. There are some pretty effective devices integrated into the design to cause a big bang if anyone attempts to open it up or subject it to a molecular scan. Eventually others will figure the science out for themselves and production costs will fall but for the moment all the powers want this technology rigorously controlled. It's in their own best interests, otherwise military expenditure would have to increase tenfold.

So far 5 tactics have been developed to counter the new tactical threat. First of course is the permanent garrisoning of key sectors with capital ships. The second is the creation of a jump-capable mobile reserve tied into a comprehensive Defence Sat network able to respond to an attack in minutes. The third is a massive expansion of private garrisons to guard against jump-attacks by their competitors. The fourth is enhanced covert surveillance of potential threat staging areas. The fifth has been to make preventing the proliferation of jump technology the number one priority of all species' security forces. Keep it out of the hands of Xenon, Pirate Clans or individual megalomaniacs at all costs. The chaos that would ensue if this technology fell into unenlightened hands just does not bear thinking about.

The pilots endured the long lecture with quiet stoicism having long ago learned the futility of interruption or protest. Trasker would get to the real meat of the mission in her own good time.

"All of which," she announced, "Brings us to the Pirate Clans".

Trasker noted another eye-rolling interchange between the pilots, they had heard it all before. Marteene though, he seemed a little more subdued than normal, seemingly distracted by the demise of his cousin. Although she disliked the man's inability to undertake a mission without conjuring up impromptu "secondary objectives" she had to admit he always got the job done. His record showed him to be an excellent pilot with an instinctive combat ability that according to his file had driven more than one commanding officer to distraction. Argon military doctrine was very clear when it comes to the techniques of Air Combat Manoeuvring.

There was a book, a very successful book, and its doctrines had given Argon pilots a distinct edge in recent conflicts. Only the elite pilots of the Teladi Company Fleet could match Argon pilots for discipline. Against disorganized rabble such as pirate swarms the organised unit style of Argon dog-fighting delivered a kill ratio in excess of 10:1. Seat of the pants flyers though - they could be a bloody menace.

If they were wingmen, charged under doctrine with protecting their leader as they engaged and adding their firepower for quick 2 on 1 kills, their instincts would often just take over and they'd be gone - chasing bandits all over the sky. If they lead, their erratic, improvised flying often just lost their wingmen, jeopardizing themselves, others and the mission.

At least in the eyes of Command.

Also in the eyes of Command this sort of pilot was ideal for Special Ops. Flexible, innovative and above all, expendable. Trasker of course disagreed. In her experience the trouble with instinct is that sooner or later it's just going to let you down. One day your gut will tell you to zig when you damn well should have zagged, leaving your comrades and the mission in jeopardy.

Trasker indeed had a point. When an S.O. went wrong it often blew up big time. Once before an entire flight under her orders had been lost because it had refused to extend and escape when engaged by overwhelming odds way out beyond the gates in the Ore Belt.

Testosterone and supreme over-confidence could be a stone killer.

She briefly considered scrubbing Marteene from the mission but dismissed the notion. For this one, she was forced to admit, she would need scrappers. As her regular reports on his performance noted, if nothing else Marteene was an exceptionally gifted combat pilot whose kill rate spoke for itself. For someone still on the right side of thirty to be pushing at records set by respected veterans like Paskaal was extraordinary and Argon Intelligence had plenty of uses for individuals of his somewhat diverse talents. Despite these Marteene troubled her gut. It said there was an almighty screw-up with his name on it somewhere down the line. The universe issues wakeup calls to those who have no concept of their own limits.

Trasker nursed a secret hope that he would soon be transferred to another Special Ops posting. This dream was bolstered by the steady flow of requests for updated psych profiles of Marteene and several others of the maverick flyers from obscure arms of the service whose true functions lay concealed behind a barricade of obscure acronyms. She was used to her successful pilots disappearing behind other black curtains. Occasionally they'd come back and occasionally they'd turn up on a casualty list.

Well, there's always more where they came from and it was the job that counts.

The job. Trasker smiled and signalled her aide to deactivate the security lockouts on the mission brief. Shadow Skin Technology, they were going to love this!

Marteene listened as Trasker set the detailed background to the mission with half an ear open for anything new. So far there was nothing they had not been told before. The strategic and tactical implications of jump-drive technology were understandably hot topics in military circles and the Demons had already benefited from hands-on training in the sims. The Tac-Ops scenarios ran the gamut of operations from point defence to convoy attack and covert surveillance as the military hastily checked operational doctrines and protocols against the new reality.

The results were discouraging. The ability to launch an attack from many sectors distance without using a jump-gate to enter subspace handed an almost insurmountable element of surprise to the attacker. In the new environment the strategic advantage of launching a first-strike was overwhelming but for one factor, which to the huge relief of strategists of all the races, was inherent to the subspace folding technology intrinsic to ship design.

It is this technology that enables fighters to sport large cargo bays, carry dozens of missiles and bristle with add-on technologies. All this requires power, as do the externally mounted shields and weapon systems. The more power required the bigger the power system and the bigger this was the bigger the ship required to house it. Installing a functioning propulsion system within a subspace fold was logically, theoretically and practically impossible. The power consumption of shield and weapon technologies, even in standby mode are enormous. The maintenance of internal subspace folds even more so. With practical ship-mounted power systems coming in at 100MW max for the largest fighters ship design becomes a matter of trade-offs. The more power consumed by ship systems the less there is to sustain the subspace fold component which no matter how much of the design limit potential has been activated consumes a fixed amount of energy.

With jump-drives consuming 5 energy cells per sector, jump capable craft require good cargo capacity. This in turn requires a performance trade-off elsewhere and it is this trade-off that gives the defence a chance.

By common consent the best one-on-one fighter in known space is the Paranid Prometheus. It is fast, heavily armed and protected by a massive 50MW of shielding. This leaves little energy for the subspace hold limiting the range of the jump-drive version as it cannot carry more than 20 or 30 energy cells. To carry that number required removing all the missiles so their use as a first-strike weapon was limited. All the other heavy fighters have related handicaps. The Boron Eel, Argon Elite and the Teladi Falcon sacrifice speed for subspace folds, whilst the Split Mamba design emphasizes fleetness over shielding. Without radical breakthroughs in power system technology it is still not possible to design a long range, high performance heavy fighter. Smaller fighters are even less capable of long-range jumping as their power limitations dictate even smaller subspace holds.

As long as these fundamental technical limitations on ship design were in place a defence strategy based on the large numbers of M5 and M4 fighters based in-system remained practical. Weight of numbers, superior speed and missile capacity compensated for inferior armament and shields compared to M3's. Add into this laser tower and minefield point defences and strategically placed jump-capable M3 rapid reaction forces and a sufficient deterrent to a pre-emptive strike existed. Most hit by the new technology are the Paranids as the Prometheus design performs poorly in both the first strike and rapid reaction roles due to its limited range. Intelligence indicates that the development of a new generation of heavy fighters is in the early planning stages.

The rogue factor in all the strategic calculations were of course the pirate clans. Throughout history wherever there is commerce there is piracy and space had proven no exception. As with all successful areas of criminal endeavour it soon evolved its own structure as individuals formed groups and groups merged under the leadership of the most ruthless, the most charismatic and the most well-connected. What Trasker summarised was little more than any citizen knows from the vids. Pirates are loosely organised into Clans under the leadership of whoever can grab it. These clans tend to be species-based although a large percentage of their members will be aliens of some sort. Clans are based on huge mobile space stations that skirt the fringes of jump-gate systems.

Whilst these huge and wealthy gangs are a significant hindrance to trade by their very nature they find it impossible to organise themselves collectively under one leadership and exist in an uneasy confederation. Internecine conflict are common and it takes all of the diplomatic skills of the clan chiefs to maintain the treaties by which huge facilities such as shipyards and equipment docks were constructed and run for the common good. There are limits as to what each Clan could do for itself as no matter how rich and powerful it cannot match the resources a species can devote to ship design and construction. By working together the Clans have managed to broadly keep pace with the major powers by evolving the Mandalay, Bayamon and Orinoco class of fighters.

Cheap to produce compared to their species counterparts they made up in numbers what they lacked in quality and training. The only weakness in the Clan inventory is the lack of a heavy fighter design as these would be too expensive to produce compared to the profits they could generate for the owner. Each clan leadership maintains its own squadrons of bought or captured heavy fighters and these usually function as a Praetorian Guard for the clan chief and is rarely seen in the public spaceways.

It was known that the sudden development of jump-drive technology had caused panic amongst the clans. To begin with if freighters could jump straight from start to finish then interception would be impossible. There was also the serious threat of deep strikes on essential facilities located deep in remote sectors. The first clan to possess this technology in any number would for the first time be in a position to make a serious bid for leadership of all the clans. Inferior though they may be to military fighters the Bayamon and the Orinoco offered a good balance of performance given their superior subspace hold capacity. A jump-capable clan would be a serious threat to other clans because the drives would become a potent force-multiplier.

Some analysts Marteene had read suggested one jump capable squadron could replace up to 10 normally equipped ones in some attack scenarios as that would be the number of garrison squadrons that would have to be maintained to defend against jump assaults. All clans are making serious efforts to acquire this technology but such is the security surrounding the only manufacturing facility, the Goner Temple in Cloudbase Southwest, that all attempts have proven futile.

As Trasker continued Marteene delved through the Mission Support Database on his terminal. The Mission Inventory screen specified a flight of 4 Bayamons. This was no surprise in itself. As an Aggressor Squadron the Demons maintained and flew a dozen specimens of these machines and had used them on clandestine ops on more than one occasion. Fast and well-armed, in the hands of a group of disciplined pilots a pack of Bayamons were a threat to anything in space. Fortunately they were rarely flown that way by the pirate clans themselves. In the hands of the average pirate the Bayamon was a death-trap due to the limited 5MW shielding and low speed of the basic version. Pirates successful enough to be able to afford the kit out a Bayamon with a full-sized subspace hold and maximum engine upgrades generally upgrade to an Orinoco or a black market military model such as the Teladi Hawk.

What was a surprise to Marteene as he scrolled through the on-screen schematics was the power distribution curves. Despite being fully maxxed out he noted that the top speed was down to 180 meters per second from 210. The newly installed jump-drives showing on the craft inventory didn't account for it. Jump-drives were charged with energy from internally stored energy cells. Another system seemed to be consuming power and this was still hidden behind a security lock.

Trasker could see from their body language that the pilots had spotted the surprise and grinned.

"Now that I have your undivided attention boys let's skip the rest of the background and get to the meat. Normally reliable intelligence sources indicate that Clan Shroda is in the process of acquiring data readings from the second series of the original jump tech test flights. The source of this information has yet to be established but clearly represent a breach in security at the highest levels. Deep cover operatives indicate this data is in possession of rogue elements of Clan Hoort whose stronghold was last located in Atreus Clouds."

This was new and each pilot listened intently. During the test phase drives had yet to be fitted with the complex security that now protected the drive secrets. Unscrambled waveform and quantum resonance readings would offer Clan scientists a substantial insight into the fundamentals of the science behind the breakthrough.

"Well placed sources suggest that this group is attempting to use the data as leverage to force an alliance between Shroda and Hoort as the former has the resources to exploit the information that the Hoort lack. Analysts suggest this may be an attempt by disaffected elements of Clan Hoort to foster a union between the two clans preparatory to a fresh attempt at uniting all the Clans."

Trasker was gratified that the pilots clearly appreciated the significance of the situation. Such a union would transform the Clans from a serious nuisance to a major threat and let the jump-drive genie out of the bottle. Her superiors were very clear. The threat had to be quashed and quashed hard and quickly. Trasker brushed off an old contingency plan, added a few bells and whistles and in a last few hours had a mission-plan to carry out these orders. With luck she could turn this to Argon's advantage, not that she believed in luck. Forethought not luck led to the Demons selection as the first front-line Ops unit to test the new Shadow Skin technology operationally and this offered the perfect opportunity.

The rogue Hoorts were reported as flying an Orinoco heavy fighter supported by 3 flights of Bayamons from Atreus Clouds to a rendezvous with elements of Clan Shroda in the Teladi system of Company Pride. As the credit grubbing lizards were claw in claw with the largely Teladi Clan Shroda, to the extent of supplying it with, no doubt over-priced, freighters and fighter craft no diplomatic solution was possible. Neither could Argon send in a flight of Elites or Busters to break up the party. She did not even want to think about the diplomatic fallout such an action would bring.

No - times like these call for black ops and in essence her plan was simple. Jump a flight of Bayamons to the south gate of Atreus Clouds using the Royal Boron Intelligence clandestine Nav-Sat as a marker, follow the Hoort contingent at a distance and engage and destroy them before they reached Thuroks Beard. Simple and effective given the inside intelligence but the mark of a true Intelligence Officer is the ability to add that little extra spin, to cloak goals within goals and meet them all. Trasker was nothing if not a good officer and she saw an opportunity.

No one likes to talk about it and certainly no one will acknowledge it on public record but one of the prime tasks of Argon Intelligence was to ensure that any moves towards greater Clan co-operation fail. The service missed few opportunities to sow seeds of doubt and discord through deep cover operatives and on occasion direct action. Even with stolen transponder codes it had proven difficult to pass off attacks as the work of a rival Clan despite using captured equipment. High band sensor readings would be scrutinized intensely, the movements of the ships implicated by the purloined transponder codes traced and scanned in detail by the Boards of Inquiry mandated by the articles under which clan co-operation were formalised when incidents such as these occurred.

The Clans are not run by fools.

As a result it could generally be demonstrated that the attack ships were not those of the implicated clan. The power curves, hull stress readings and quantum resonance signatures of ships were as individual as fingerprints. Shadow Skin technology promised to change that and formed the basis for the final stage of her plan, untested in action though it might be.

Succinctly she outlined this stage.

After the briefing the four pilots were escorted by Marines straight to the off-limits bay that housed the black ops Bayamons. Paskaal was waiting, the veteran pilot was supervising the launch of another Bayamon flight on an undisclosed mission by elements of Beta Wing.

"What ho Marteene," he shouted across the cramped locker room, "You watch your six out there". As Marteene left to begin the pre-flight checks Paskaal gave proffered a good luck handshake and whispered. "I did a little snooping and you know what? The CO scrubbed you from this mission but was over-ruled from higher up. Trasker has no operational control so my guess is the order came from off-ship."

Paskaal tapped his nose. "Something Spooky going on here if I'm not mistaken, keep your eyes open." Marteene acknowledged the advice with a nod and walked to his ship.

Pre-flight was completed in 30 minutes as specified by the book. Another 30 went by whilst the onboard computer outlined the operation of the Shadow Skin Technology. At Launch Minus 120 Marteene performed a last quick systems check, the faintly mechanical sounding female voice of the computer confirming each systems status.

"... check. Shields - check. Lasers 1 through 4 - check. Autopilot - check. Ship computer - check."

Finally Marteene ran a diagnostic of the systems software, confirming that the viral filter on the comms array was functioning and the many programs that assisted the pilot actually fly the fighter were functioning within normal parameters.

At L minus 30 Marteene checked off flight status. Green across the board.

"Flight Control to Alpha Flight you are clear for launch. Be advised a mission profile update is in progress. Good luck."

Marteene glanced at the Mission AI panel, confirming a data upload was in progress. Like most Special Ops pilots he intensely disliked this particular technical development but the Intelligence people were thrilled. To the pilots though having an AI system programmed with the mission parameters overseeing their performance was a slight and due to their fierce opposition throughout the fleet its role remained advisory, much to the chagrin of Intelligence. To them, an AI programmed with mission parameters, protocols and full technical details of mission hardware and informed by a mature neural net trained on data from hundreds of successful missions was a much more reliable method for dealing with the unexpected than a pilot. For the time being though, the pilot remained in charge with the Mission AI in an advisory capacity.

"Flight Control to Alpha Flight, life support now on internal." Marteene closed the visor of his pressure suit and glanced at the systems display to confirm the green light. "Alpha 1- launch." With that the docking clamps swung up releasing the small fighter, instantly the autopilot interfaced with the docking bay systems and guided the Bayamon down the small access tunnel into the cavernous main docking conduit. With a gentle burst of thrusters the Bayamon accelerated towards the bay doors. He mentally ticked off the rest of the flight as Control confirmed each launch as he prepared to take manual control.

As his Bayamon sped through the bay doors the cockpit was flooded with sunlight. For the first time in many hours Marteene could feel his spirit begin to shake it's wings and he smiled. The symbolism inherent in the launch process was obvious and subject to much trite comment by pop intellectuals but at this moment it seemed particularly apposite.

"Born again, Marteene, born again." Just being out among the stars made his blood sing in his ears and a childish grin split his face. All fighter pilots are little boys at heart, even the women!

Sloughing off his troubles like a snake sheds a skin his attention focused on the mission.

*Chapter 6: Breaking Skulls*

As Alpha Flight headed out into the darkness of the Antigones Memorial system Marteene embraced the routine.

"Alpha 1 to Alpha Flight, Alpha 1 to Alpha Flight, initiate Secure-comm protocols, secure for stealth mode."

Marteene counted off the acknowledgements and the flight formation smoothly transformed from the loose finger-four to a tight diamond formation with Marteene at the point.

"Alpha 3, position aye."

"Alpha 4, position aye."

"Alpha 2, that's a positive good buddy."

Marteene smiled, his wingman Shanner hailed from one of the more distant agricultural colonies and despite years of training had still not managed to grasp the finer points of military protocols. Outside of the cockpit the man moved as though he had 2 left feet and the mess hall often resounded to the clatter of trays, plates, cutlery or whatever else he found to blunder into. Put him behind the stick though and it was a different story. Marteene considered him one of the best instinctive pilots he'd ever flown ops with but felt him a touch too erratic to lead a flight or fly wing to any of the straighter aces.

"Alpha 1 acknowledged. Initiate link-up on my mark. Mark."

As the tight grouped flight headed out into the stygian gloom tiny sensor domes around the body of each craft activated and for a second the comms channels filled with white noise as the viral filters activated. Almost instantly a network of low power lasers, light beyond the visible spectrum linked each ship to its compatriots and the white noise was replaced by a soft electronic chitter as the computer systems of each fighter began exchanging test data. The Secure-Comm package was standard to all Special Ops craft and enabled them to communicate with virtually no chance at all of interception.

The subsequent reduction in radio & microwave emissions also reduced the sensor profile to a minimum. Of course once an engagement started the sensor servos were unable to maintain their locks but for clandestine ingress and egress it was ideal.

One by one the pilots confirmed lock and at Marteene's command re-adopted the finger four formation and increased their speed to 180 mps. With a resigned sigh he activated the Mission AI projecting a 3D image of Trasker's head onto the Heads Up Display.

"Sensors confirm mission profile stage 1 complete. Moving to stage 2. Follow heading 312 mark 12, 180 mps." The computer vocorder gave her normally thin voice a slight mechanical timbre. By general consensus it was an improvement.

Marteene, in common with the rest of his flight fought down the urge to yell, "We're doing it, we're doing it you uptight witch" at the simulacrum. It wasn't necessary but in his experience there wasn't an Intelligence Officer born who could resist the temptation to dump their psych profiles and vis-scans into the AI matrix. Trasker had as usual gone one step further and incorporated "her knowledge and experience" into the heuristic algorithms and decision-making systems. He did not even want to think how many hours she must have put in with the boys and girls in the AI Lab, programming and training the neural net in her image although he had to admit it was a pretty good job. Post-mission debriefs usually found the Mission AI in-flight tactical analyses and recommendations closely matched what she identified as the correct response to circumstances. That these rarely coincided with Marteene's actions was a constant sore point but that, he thought happily, is why they invented the off switch.

The mission profile called for the flight to maintain this speed and course for 20 minutes. That would put them over 200 klicks outside the small area of space bounded by the system gates, well beyond the range of all but the clandestine military scanners concealed deep within the solar system. Security protocols dictated that the first jump of the mission should take place well away from prying eyes. It would take them to Atreus Clouds where they would blend in with the heavy pirate traffic in the system and tail the targets.

The flight continued in silence, each pilot taking the opportunity to review the mission brief and run systems diagnostics.

For the first time since the news of Hela's death Marteene was alone with his thoughts. Sheer professionalism kept him from the temptation to prod at the tightly wrapped ball of conflicting emotions pushed deep into the back of his mind for the mission duration but like all great combat pilots he could not suppress his instincts. They were too tied in with survival for that and they remained, scanning circumstances and events like a subcutaneous sensor-net. He couldn't put a finger on it but something wasn't right about this whole affair. The lack of a body for one thing. Military organisations throughout history have always recognised the importance of bringing home the bodies. It was good for morale. According to the brief message the undisclosed accident had completely destroyed all traces of the corpse. Of course, the mystery would be more explicable if Hela had indeed been a Special Forces pilot but Marteene was certain that he would have come across someone at some point who would have served with her. Also Reserve officers were not used for special ops as a matter of policy.

For a long time he had half suspected her of being an Argon Intelligence operative but again, it did not quite add up. He knew enough about her work for DARP to know that it was genuine. During his career he had run across officers who had encountered her at various briefings and simulated exercises. From what he could piece together her work centred around threat analysis, where her combat experience combined with a keen strategic mind made her a valuable asset. In fact a recent tactical brief on the impact of jump-drive technology on the Split military capability practically mirrored the long discussions they'd had on his last leave. Marteene made a mental note to run the script of the multi-media briefing paper through one of the syntax analysis programs Intelligence used. He was pretty sure the profile could be matched with some of her acknowledged work. And then there was the question of who put him back on this mission after the CO scrubbed him. Paskaal was right, there were spook prints everywhere.

This train of thought though, was leading him nowhere. There was nothing he could do from the cockpit of a clandestine Bayamon and he sat back and absorbed the stunning view of the stars. The Bayamon may be a cheap and cheerful death trap but the transparent duridium cockpit proffered an unparalleled tourists eye view. Marteene performed a short meditation exercise designed by Goner mystics and Fleet psychologists to bring a pilot's autonomic system into the required state of relaxed awareness and allowed the cold beauty of the stars to salve the cold numbness in his heart as the flight arrowed through the void towards the first waypoint. The rest of the flight, through that symbiotic awareness that grows between beings who rely on each other for their lives, exclude him from the normal banter carried between the craft on tiny impulses of light.

His reverie was interrupted a couple of minutes from the waypoint by a sudden increase in the chitter of the comms system. A glance at the communications panel showed he was receiving a narrow-band microwave transmission from one of the deep space relays millions of kilometres out in the Antigones system. The comms lasers burst into a frenzy of activity as the transmission was relayed to the rest of the flight.

Within seconds the mission AI activated and Trasker's image appeared.

"Attention, attention, this is a Mission AI priority over-ride." Marteene and the other members of the flight launched a blistering fusillade of invective simultaneously. Whatever the incoming transmission was the Mission AI was taking it upon itself to advise a change the mission profile. To the fury of Trasker and the other Intelligence officers, fleet protocols leave the final decision on profile changes to the mission commander. The AI had already prepared a summary for his review. Ordering the flight into a holding pattern Marteene activated the sub-routine and the HUD filled with star charts and nav data as the Trasker simulacra began the brief.

To his mild surprise Marteene found himself agreeing to the suggested revision to the original plan. Data downloads showed a flight of 4 Bayamons affiliated with one of the most powerful and ruthless clans in known space had jumped for an undisclosed destination via the southern jump-gate of Brennan's Triumph. Judging from the code prefix of the data scans this information had been broadcast from a Q Program freighter. The Q Program was one of the Argon's most secret and dangerous assignments, involving the use of captured pirate freighters to monitor activities in hostile sectors and reporting in via temporarily deployed Nav-Sats. Needless to say these ships came under attack the instant the Nav-Sat deployment was monitored. Marteene hoped the pilot had made his escape. Casualty rates though were high.

The Skull Clan dominated the fiercely contested sectors adjacent to the Brennan's Triumph sector and was the nearest any of the clans came to being truly multi-species. Originally founded by the notorious

Argon privateer, "Commodore" Jaines over 4 decades previously, this Clan had established an unmatched reputation for ruthless savagery. Following the defeat of the Xenon the clan established a permanent presence in this sector, constructing a huge mobile base.   The inappropriately named Paradise Station quickly acquired a reputation as THE place you could buy or sell absolutely anything.   Intelligence sources suggest that the Skull Clan has acquired considerable expertise and experience in a range of unethical medical technologies and practices and the station has become a magnet for disaffected scientists opposed to the many treaties that outlaw experimentation considered unethical by all sentient species.   It is rumoured that a burgeoning trade in slaves destined for grotesque medical experiments is centred in Paradise.

Intelligence also believes "the Commodore", as Jaines insists on being called, still runs the clan despite being at least 90 years of age. Although this is only surmise, Intelligence suggests that his longevity and continued good health are the results of illegal medical technologies.

Reports also indicate that the true centre of the Skull Clan is not Paradise Station but a huge and heavily armed TL Transporter clandestinely supplied by the Teladi.   The Intimidator as it is known, is believed to haunt the outer fringes of the Brennan's Triumph system, tens of millions of kilometres beyond the range of military fighters and Nav-Sat scanners.   That the Intimidator itself has travelled such a distance indicates that it is equipped with a variant of the ion drives used by the deep system patrol carriers of species military to slowly accelerate themselves to the huge speeds necessary to deploy vast distances from the jump-gates.

Any freighter captain foolish enough to attempt the notorious Suicide Run between Atreus Clouds and Priest Pity are well advised to surrender their cargo the moment a Skull flight appears on the scanner.

The Mission AI recommended an immediate jump to the adjacent Danna's Chance sector whereupon the Bayamon flight could be intercepted and destroyed.   Through use of the Shadow Skin Technology the Skull clan could be implicated in the planned attacks on the Shroda & Hoort flights.   Marteene smiled approvingly, that would sow some pretty potent seeds of dissension amongst the clans.

According to the Mission AI a temporary Nav-Sat deployment would be made in 5 minutes to enable the jump to Danna's Chance. Marteene guessed the Q Program ship in the Atreus Sector would be involved.   He quickly accessed the Galaxy Map and tuned to the Boron Military Nav-Sat in Atreus Clouds.   Sure enough a Teladi Vulture displaying the distinctive energy curves of the armed pirate configuration was making best speed for the south jump-gate.   Three high-speed Mandalay fighters from the pirate base had been scrambled to intercept but would not make it in time.   The AI did not recommend deploying to protect the Q-Program freighter in the event that it was pursued through the gate.   Marteene hoped that meant a backup force had been deployed in Farnham's Legend until he noticed a group of 3

Argon Discoverers ostensibly escorting a Dolphin freighter to the north jump-gate were on an intercept course.

Confident that the Mandalays would prove no match for what were undoubtedly Special Ops fighters and pilots Marteene confirmed the mission changes with the AI and the comm lasers crackled briefly as the updates were exchanged between the flight.

"Alpha Flight this is Alpha 1 prepare to jump to new co-ordinates on my mark. Confirm, Alpha Flight."

One by one the confirmations sounded off, each pilot's voice subtly taut with the anticipation of combat.

The Skull flight had many minutes start on the Q ship and greater speed. By the time it had deployed a Nav-Sat in Danna's Chance the Skull flight was halfway across the sector to the eastern jump-gate. As soon as the sector data appeared on his galaxy map Marteene uttered a single word.

"Mark."

As one Alpha Flight activated their jump-drives and vanished into the whirling subspace distortions.

Within seconds the 4 fighters emerged slowly from the eastern jump-gate as the Mission AI update had programmed, their cockpits suffused by the gentle orange glow from the Rystat Nebula that dominated half the sector. Hundreds of cubic parsecs in size and its gases light from within by dozens of huge red giants this nebula was one of the most spectacular sights in this region of space. The Danna's Chance sector gate system skirted its outer fringe where the density of the interstellar hydrogen was still dense enough to refract the light of the system primary, giving it distinctive blue-green hue and blocking the light from dimmer stars.

A quick scan confirmed that the Q Ship from Atreus Clouds was indeed jump-drive equipped and had used its entry into the southern jump-gate to mask the longer jump across the sectors to Danna's Choice. Marteene was impressed. Activating a jump-drive in the proximity of a functioning jump-gate was a risky business. A ship could end up scattered over 2 sectors if the pilot got the timing wrong.

After cruising a short distance the flight briefly manoeuvred to re-establish the laser comm links as ops protocols dictated. No protocols existed as yet for the new Shadow Skin technology, in fact as Marteene realised, they were probably about to write them.

He activated the sector map and quickly assessed the situation. The hostiles were 40 klicks out, closing fast. Scans indicated all 4 of the Skull fighters were fully upgraded, giving them an edge on speed. It probably indicated above average pilots also. At the moment though they were cruising at 150 mps.

Danna's Chance was a pirate dominated sector specialising in supplying food and other low technology products unhampered by the rules and regulations governing trade in these products. Even the Teladi had conceded that these "constraints on trade" were necessary given the greatly differing biochemistry of the various species. Profits were correspondingly high and pirate traders were frequent visitors to the system. The merchants of this sector had earned themselves a fierce reputation for independence and this was backed by the numerous flights of fighters that garrisoned each station. Marteene was certain that there would be no interference from this quarter in what would appear as a random skirmish between rival clans.

As for the moment no open hostilities existed between any of the clans he hoped the Skull flight would not be expecting any trouble, provided they were given a wide berth.

Activating the Mission AI Tactical Module he assigned each of his flight a target. The laser comm crackled briefly as the target designations were transmitted. His own weapons and scanners locked onto the lead Skull, now registering as Hostile 1 on the Sector Map.

"Alpha Flight this is Alpha 1. Targets assigned. Acknowledge."

"Alpha 2, Hostile 2, acknowledged."

"Alpha 3, Hostile 3, acknowledged."

"Alpha 4, Hostile 4, acknowledged."

Each voice was totally cool, devoid of the normal pilot bravado. No fear, just a professional determination to get a difficult job done.

"Alpha Flight this is Alpha 1. The Shadow Tech needs 10 seconds continuous data scan from the forward sensor array at under 2 klicks. Engage only after the comp gives the okay guys, no scan no kill. Got it?"

The flight acknowledged in turn. Marteene did a quick calculation. At a combined closure rate of 300 metres per second the Skulls would be in the scope of the forward sensors for less than 6 seconds. If his flight dropped to 50 mps they might just about squeeze it but it would be close and leave them in a disadvantageous energy state, apart from looking very suspicious.

"Alpha Flight this is Alpha 1. Attack Pattern Beta 4. Break on my mark, scan and go one on one. Acknowledge."

Beta 4 would take Alpha Flight past the Skull fighter group, setting them up for a tail chase. That would give time for the scanners to prime the Shadow Skin tech with the Skull ship readings and leave Alpha Flight on their six. It was a common tactic on clandestine missions where the hostiles do not perceive a threat.

Marteene gently twisted the control stick and with constant subtle adjustments kept his fighter gently spinning clockwise and counter clockwise in the distinctive Bayamon manner. The pirate jig as it was called. The Bayamon fighter was in essence a tube with 4 nacelles mounting the 4 dual drive/weapon arrays. The pirate jig was a sound defensive flight manoeuvre designed to minimise hits taken from a surprise attack, ensuring most of a hasty weapons burst would sail between the nacelles. Bayamons were notoriously difficult to hit, especially by other Bayamons.

He estimated that the two groups would pass well outside the main cluster of stations in the sector, which was good. Less chance of local forces intervening. In the pirate-infested sectors of this region you could never quite be sure of loyalties.

He checked the safety settings on his autopilot. These constantly monitor ships systems and could be configured to trigger the ejection system with a variety of settings such as a specified percentage of systems damaged or inoperable or shield depletion. If you are on the losing end of a combat situation you rarely have time for a manual ejection. By the time you can react you are dead. It was set to the "Iron Man" setting - the default for S.O. missions. Put simply the auto-eject sequence would only be triggered if shields had fallen to a specified minimum and the computer calculated that the rate at which the shields were continuing to fall indicated certain destruction. Less resolute pilots might program it to operate when shield or weapon systems damage exceeded the capability of auto repair systems to bring them on-line within a defined period.

Marteene left it on the default setting.

The two groups were closing rapidly now and he angled his course slightly to port, taking the Skulls down his starboard beam. As this was practically standard operating procedure for pirate flights from different clans it should arouse no suspicion. It would also position Alpha Flight with the system primary at their backs at the break point, adding an extra element of surprise.

A quick check through the helmet-mounted interface of the Zoom Goggle sub system confirmed the Skull flight were maintaining a straight course for the eastern jump-gate. Three of the fighters flew in a vertically staggered line abreast whilst the flight leader had adopted the role of Tail End Charlie and bobbed and weaved around the rear of the formation on watch for any ambush. Experienced pilots.

As the two formations closed Marteene allowed himself to sink into a state of relaxed readiness. Only the electronic burble of the comm lasers and the sound of blood pounding in his ears as adrenaline readied his body disturbed the silence of space.

As the two fighter groups passed a comfortable 3 kilometres apart he issued one command.

"Mark".

With a rattle of static the comm lasers disengaged as the 4 Alpha Flight fighters peeled off in sequence and accelerated at maximum speed, each toward their designated target.

At two kilometres the Shadow Tech kicked into operation and with an almost inaudible hum sucked data from the forward sensors, the mellifluous female voice of the ship computer counting off the seconds.

"Ten seconds to template, nine, eight, seven, six seconds..." He was close enough to his target to pick out the distinctive white on black skull and crossbones motif the skulls had adopted from old Goner texts and said to be a religious symbol of death and rebirth in Earth mythology.

Tail End Charlie had spotted them now - closing rapidly from his starboard rear. He broke high and left as his compatriots scattered.

"...one. Template complete."

If the Skull flight had broken and ran they could have outrun the Special Ops Bayamons, hampered as they were by the power consumption of the Shadow Tech but that clan had not got its reputation by running from a fight. Indeed in the brutal arena of clan rivalries weakness could not be shown. Instead, as confident in their own abilities and equipment as the Special Ops pilots, they turned to engage. Within seconds the 8 fighters were entangled in a free-for-all furball, the silence of space fractured by the pounding of Particle

Accelerator Cannons and the whine of drive systems as ships flashed past within metres of each other.

Pedants will tell you that the space opera action vids like WingStar Academy - all screeching lasers and huge, rumbling explosions are wrong because sound doesn't travel in a vacuum. Well, they're right. Technically. But a dogfight in space is one noisy son-of-a-bitch thanks to development of the 3D Positional Sound Array System, now fitted as standard in most new ships. This has revolutionised space combat by taking sensor readings and transforming them into sound analogues. It gives the combat pilot a whole extra sense to keep alive with. Being able to hear the thud of a plasma thrower zoning in from your left or the doppler roar of an Orinoco as it banks in on your six, well it can be the difference between life and death.

Marteene broke high in pursuit of his designated target, chasing the target indicator and catching the Bayamon foursquare with a sustained burst from his 4 Alpha PAC's that ripped away half of the Skull fighter's shielding. Tail End Charlie though - he was good, pulling an inverted loop that took him straight across the path of Alpha 3 as it poured fire into the twisting tail of a Skull Bayamon. The screech of drives filled Marteene's cockpit as he banked to avoid the collision, losing visual contact with his target.

A muffled explosion and a yell of triumph from Alpha 3 indicated one down. Cody was a veteran with an outstanding record of kills and an even more outstanding record of celebrating them. The pilots lounge would be awash with space-fuel and hyperbole later.

"Target now out of range," the computer calmly informed him. The bandit had rolled out of the loop in the superior tactical position and used his superior speed to close rapidly on Marteene's six. Plasma bolts streamed past as he twisted and jinked. The Bayamon shuddered under the impact as a few bolts hit home, knocking his shields down to 70%.

Ask any fighter pilot and they will tell you one of the most amazing things about a dogfight is the way time seems to slow to a crawl. Fighting for your life your senses just seem to suck in information for your brain to process into a constantly updated picture of the battle. Situational awareness they call it and good combat pilots have this in Spades. To see it you'd swear they did indeed have eyes in the back of their heads.

A split second assessment of the battle showed Marteene that it had already spread out over many kilometres. Alpha 2 was locked on the tail of his target as it foolishly tried to use its superior speed to outrun his pursuer instead of evading the fire. Bayamons simply lacked the shielding to take many hits and Shanner was adept at long range shooting. That one would be over in seconds. Alpha 3 and 4 had formed up two on one on the remaining pirate, Alpha 3 jinking and dodging the fire from his pursuer as he drew him into the sights of his wingman.

Marteene absorbed the tactical situation in a fraction of a second whilst with instincts borne of countless hours of training and dozens of dogfights he assessed his own tactical position and derived counter moves.

An opponent closing from the rear with a superior speed potential, shields falling rapidly - this was a situation that killed more combat novices than any other. You see it all the time. The instinct is to either try and outturn your pursuer or decelerate and attempt to force an overshoot. Both will get you killed.

It's almost impossible to outturn the nimble Bayamon, which in the hands of a good pilot has no difficulty in staying on the six of most fighters in service. If you have superior speed and shielding you might survive the pounding but in another Bayamon you might as well just space yourself and be done with it. That's why Intelligence prefers to use Aggressor squadron pilots for clandestine operations - regular pilots who are used to the superior performance of the Buster and Elite fighters find their instincts and reflexes out of kilter when placed in inferior craft such as the Bayamon.

Decelerating to force an overshoot is equally dangerous. It's a popular move for those who fancy themselves as hotshots, they see it pulled all the time on the vids but if it doesn't cause a collision that would destroy both lightly shielded ships it leaves you in a low energy state and vulnerable to attack from another combatant. In fighter combat speed is all-important and even the few seconds it takes to accelerate back to full speed is too long. Pull that trick often enough with anything less than 10MW of shields and eventually your next of kin will be informed.

At maximum speed Marteene initiated a by-the-book scissors manoeuvre, forcing his pursuer to do the same, each ship twisting and rolling around the axis of the direction of travel. It was a classic manoeuvre from the arena of terrestrial air combat. Effectively, corkscrewing around the direction of flight reduced your speed without lowering your energy state by adding a vertical component to your horizontal movement thereby increasing the actual distance covered. Skilfully executed, especially against an opponent who entered the scissors at a greater speed this manoeuvre could transform a fight duel in a fraction of a second by using an opponent's superior energy state against them. Once engaged in this sort of contest the deciding factor is usually pilot skill and his opponent was good.

For a few long seconds each fighter weaved and rolled as Marteene attempted to force the overshoot. Plasma bolts showered past his cockpit as his twisting and rolling manoeuvres took him through his pursuers gun sights. His opponent though, having entered the manoeuvre with a superior energy state was forced to bleed speed and perform rolls with a greater radius in an attempt to stay on his six.

With the Skull Bayamon at the apex of a barrel roll that would bring him down onto his tail with a perfect firing solution Marteene executed a wide scissors left which he swiftly reversed into a hard right turn combined with a swift counter clockwise barrel roll. The Skull pilot was good, but not that good and for a split second lost track of Marteene's fighter and in combat life or death balances on such fine margins.

Marteene snapped out of the roll on his opponents six, 100 metres short and poured a sustained burst into the body of the rapidly departing fighter. Marteene's Bayamon shuddered with the recoil of the 4 Alpha PAC's, throwing off his aim but most of the bolts hammered home, ripping through the pirate shielding.

The Skull Bayamon exploded in a flash of superheated plasma and Marteene's ship was rocked by the impact of residual debris on its shields as it flew through the fireball. Death came before the pirate auto eject system could react.

Another explosion and a wild "Yee-haa!" from his wingman indicated Shanner had made his kill.

Marteene locked the remaining pirate on his scanner. It was 7 klicks out in hot pursuit of Alpha 3. Alpha 4 was close by and Marteene knew the engagement would be over before he or Shanner could intervene. He watched through the zooms as Alpha 3 executed a classic drag left manoeuvre, which led his pursuer into the sights of his wingman. Seconds later it was an expanding ball of plasma that quickly dissipated into the freezing vacuum.

It had taken less than 30 seconds, Marteene thumbed the comm link.

"Nice work team, form up."

The team acknowledged and within seconds all 4 fighters had returned to the loose finger four formation. With a crackle the comm lasers re-engaged. Marteene activated his sector map and confirmed no hostiles remained in the area. No stations had launched fighters so he surmised the locals had seen just another meaningless clash between rival clans. The Q Program Vulture had recovered the Nav-Sat and was making best speed to the northern jump-gate. He guessed that it would be picking up the trail of the flight allegedly carrying the jump-drive data. It would not contact them again unless the flight deviated from its predicted path. Having jumped 6 sectors ahead to intercept the Skull flight it would take a while before the primary target group arrived.

Knowing it would arouse suspicions if his flight remained in the area Marteene led Alpha Flight towards the Eastern jump-gate, leading to Napiloeos Memorial. It was another contested sector where skirmishes between the clans would attract little attention. This time the odds would be 2 to 1 against, by no means insurmountable but he wasn't going to take any chances. The Mission AI Tactical Situation sub-routine had already analysed the situation and was flagging a suggestion. Without reviewing the proposal Marteene rejected it. It was his mission and he knew what to do.

It took only a few minutes for the flight to reach the eastern jump-gate.

## *Chapter 7: Smoke and Mirrors*

The ambush in Company Pride ran like a well-debugged program. Alpha flight, now radiating the energy signatures of the destroyed Skull fighters, had cruised ahead of their targets to Thurok's Beard. At full speed they had headed into the void beyond the south gate, just another pirate group on a deep space rendezvous beyond the prying eyes of Split scanners. As soon as a Nav-Sat, dropped from what appeared to be a second Q Freighter near the Northern jump-gate of Company Pride activated, Marteene's attack group locked onto the eastern gate and engaged their jump-drives, emerging seconds behind the Hoort fighters.

Before they could react they were expanding debris fields. The Shroda fighters moved to engage but were despatched with similar cold professionalism. Marteene's flight slipped back through the eastern gate before the angry cloud of Mandalays billowing from the Shroda base could move to intercept them. A second jump to Bala Gi's Joy, targeting a Q Freighter Nav-Sat, was enough to shake off the pursuit. The engagement had lasted no longer than 3 adrenaline fuelled minutes and when the comm lasers re-engaged the link resounded to the self-congratulatory whoops of his pilots.

As he came down trembling from the adrenaline rush all combat pilots secretly crave he allowed himself a moment of pride in his team and thumbed the comm link.

"Job well done people, job well done". If there were a finer group of combat pilots in known space he would not wish to cross lasers with them.

Opening his throttle to full, Marteene led his flight into the empty space beyond the jump-gate where their use of jump-drive technology would go unnoticed and where a cache of energy cells to fuel the final jump was being deployed by a Special Ops Vulture. The rendezvous went without a hitch and the Mission AI sub-routine automatically targeted the Argon Naval Nav-Sat in the Wall sector of Argon space on its secure frequency. The Vigilant would be on station for recovery.

At his command the flight initialised their jump-drives and he relaxed as the sultry female voice counted up to activation.

"Jump-drive charging at 30%, 40, 60%, 80, 90%". As the rest of the flight slid into the whirling vortices of the jump-drive singularities an unfamiliar male voice cut across his count.

"Jump drive aborted - receiving new orders, receiving new co-ordinates."

Marteene watched helplessly as the Mission AI targeted the Spaceweed Drift sector, deep in Teladi space and activated the jump-drive. As his Bayamon nosed from the northern gate manual control reactivated and the new voice cut back in.

"This is a confirmed Code Black override, I repeat this is a confirmed Code Black override. Rendezvous immediately with Argon Lifter prefix

Alpha Alpha, Gamma, Beta 4378, assume closed comm formation and await further instructions."

As a massive adrenal surge dredged fresh reserves of energy from his body one thought filled his mind like some kind of scare-yourself-to-death mantra. "A Code Black. Shit. A Code Black." This was a new one for him. Sure, like all Special Ops pilots, he'd been briefed on them and the procedures to follow but he'd never received one. In fact he'd never heard of anyone receiving one. The code was reserved for the deepest and darkest emergencies, not even a full scale Xenon incursion would merit such designation. Quickly he ran a manual check of the verification sub routines. The security codes embedded in the message checked out against the latest verification algorithms in the Mission AI.

Genuine. Disturbed now and recalling Paskaal's warning about spook fingerprints he activated the sector map and quickly located the Lifter, a 100 klicks and rising out from the northern gate and way off the plane of the ecliptic. There were no escorts but it would undoubtedly be bristling with combat drones, real kick-ass ones, not the cheap commercial variant.

Quickly spinning the agile fighter to an intercept heading Marteene gunned the drive to full speed. Like all good combat pilots he shunned the use of the SETA device, accelerated time meant accelerated closure speeds and reduced reaction time to any threat. Besides he never got tired of the stars and the clear nosed Bayamon fighter offered an unrivalled view. Also it would give him time to review the data upload logs to identify the source of the Code Black message. It was the pre-launch mission profile update. He'd have been surprised and worried if it had been anything else.

Long minutes passed as the fighter closed with the Lifter. Deftly matching speeds with the large freighter he took up station 100 metres off the starboard side and engaged the laser comms. The Lifter sent no greetings and Marteene made no attempt to initiate a dialogue. Code Black protocols were clear and specific. The comm ports crackled to life as the Lifter began a data upload. To his surprise it was completely reprogramming the Mission AI system, both the data and personality matrices of the neural net. He had not been aware that was even possible.

After half an hour the comm ports fell silent and within seconds the Lifter disengaged and jumped out of the system. As the jump tunnel closed the Mission AI came back online and the viewscreen flashed to life. It had been a day of shock and surprises but this one; well this one took his breath away.

"How are you doing Gragore?" Inquired Hela.

### *Chapter 8: Through the Looking Glass*

Later he would swear that for a long second his heart actually stopped as his brain froze with the shock of the reappearance of his dead cousin on the AI screen.

"Listen up G, I'm sorry but if I'm talking to you like this it's pretty certain I'm dead."

On screen Hela frowned slightly, a sign she was accessing data.

"Death confirmed. Well that's certainly put a dampener on my day." The simulacra smiled wanly. "But I still need your help. Or at least my associates do."

Marteene barely heard these words as a tumult of emotions stormed through his mind. Love, hope, despair and grief reawakened red raw, clawed the insides of his skull as she was taken from him all over again. "An AI, she was just an AI!" He felt as if a wormhole had opened up and sucked him into some insane alternate universe and on reflection he was not that far wrong.

"Listen up G - your bio-readings are going off the scale. Deep breaths, deep breaths." Apart from the slight electronic echo the vocorder added to the AI voice the simulation was perfect. Even the phrasing was spot on. Still shaken he forced himself to concentrate on her words as the AI continued.

"There's a file here you'll want to review - I guess from the header it's my, no - her Last Testament. And you think you are confused?"

Hela smiled.

"It's heavily encrypted. Wow someone really doesn't want this seen by prying eyes! Ah, I've got the decrypt key in memory. Here we go - activating file."

The screen briefly filled with static before Hela reappeared in what was clearly a filmed record not an AI simulation. Judging from her flight uniform and the utilitarian grey bulkheads that provided the backdrop Marteene guessed it must have been made on a ship. Security code verifications flashing at the foot of the screen confirmed the provenance of the record although the ship name and location remained encrypted. Judging from the date it was recorded a couple of days before her death. It was a common practice for pilots to make one of these before embarking on something hazardous. Hell, he'd recorded a few himself but it wasn't something you did for a routine training mission.

The sight of Hela pacing impatiently, her long blonde hair resplendent against the gold and black uniform, was achingly familiar.

"Are we on yet? Oh right." She flashed a wry grin as she looked into the camera.

"Hi G. I guess if you're viewing this then things didn't go according to plan. Which means I'm almost certainly dead. Look, I'm sorry about that." She smiled again. "But hey - life goes on right?"

Despite the tears stinging the corners of his eyes Marteene could not help but smile. Her irrepressible optimism was what most people loved or loathed her for and throughout his teenage life it had been an important counterweight to circumstance.

"Now listen up G this is important stuff. I'm sorry but you're now caught up in something big and you're just going to have to trust me on this." She looked off-screen. "He's getting my codes right? Good!" As she spoke her personal verification codes flashed on screen. They were genuine but Hela further verified her authenticity through subtle visual signals. A touch of her collar, a double blink, it was their personal variant of Special Forces codes for POW situations. He was in no doubt now that this was a genuine record.

"Okay - no time for the long version. My associates are nothing if not meticulous so you'll be contacted soon, if you haven't been already. No doubt you've a ton of questions, you'll get more answers then but here's the basics."

Marteene took a deep breath with the sinking feeling that the world was about to perform a 180 spin. He was not mistaken.

"G - first things first. You've met my alter ego now yes? Pretty impressive - I won't tell you how many weeks that took. It's way beyond state of the art."

That was an understatement. It was a transferable WPNN- the grail of AI research.

Marteene and Hela had often discussed this field; weapons related technological developments were part of her specialty. It was a very promising area but constrained by the state of development of IT technology. Whole Personality Neural Networks were long and costly to programme and impossible to transfer to another system once developed, as the simulated neurons were effectively hard-wired by the programming process. The best that could currently be done were partial, task-based AI's based on individual expertise such as the Mission AI used by Special Ops. These could be given a Personality Interface but were crude caricatures compared to the lab-based experimentals. Marteene was simply stunned by her casual claim.

"You can quiz the AI later G - but this is the short version. I'm part of an intelligence op that's been in progress since before your father died. We're at a critical juncture, about to launch into the end game and I'm pretty much key - or at least my knowledge and experience are. In a couple of days I'm going to be bringing in the central player, if you're watching this then the plan has failed. You're the backup. The AI, well that's a happy accident. A Teladi scavenger found a crate among the Xenon wreckage in Brennan's Triumph and it sort of found its way into our hands if you know what I mean. It was pretty shot up and most of the stuff was junk but we managed to salvage a fully functioning Xenon Neural Matrix and Programmer. Talk about a miracle."

"It's taken a while to figure out, a whole lot of credits too but it was worth it. The machine-heads have sorted the transfer problem using entangled photon technology. A bit like our Nav-Sats but way more advanced. Take a whole mess of entangled particles. Put one half in the Programmer and their entangled counterparts in the matrix and any changes in the Programmer particles is mirrored by their entangled partners. No data transfer necessary. Brilliant. "

Hela's eyes were shining with enthusiasm as she summarised the efforts it took to interface the AI mainframe with the Programmer to transfer her AI into the Xenon data crystal. As usual her attempt to simplifying complex science left Marteene bemused. So long as it worked.

"We're cutting to multi-choice now yes?" Her remark was addressed off screen. A slight jump in image signified an edit, confirmed by the time index. Hela must have recorded the message in segments to cover different eventualities.

"Okay, you're in a ship. Don't know what type but it's bound to have some general-purpose data access ports. Check them out. You're looking for a green data crystal."

On screen Hela tapped her feet in mock impatience as she guesstimated how long it would take. The cheaply built Bayamon had only one auxiliary multi-purpose data port so it took only seconds. As Hela predicted there was a small green chip encased in a clear, hard material plugged into the port via what appeared to be a modified version of the Intruder Interface used to hack into computer subsystems. It was a sweet bit of work that would enable the AI to interface quickly with other technologies.

"Found it? Well that's me, or the AI me at least. Don't leave it behind! Seriously though Gragore, this may be the best AI we've ever created but it's experimental. My replicated neural pathways have been imposed on a Xenon template and we're not quite sure what that means. If I start yelling 'Resistance is Futile' hit the off switch okay?"

On screen Hela looked straight into the camera. "Listen Gragore - the AI is so bloody good it's frightening but, and it feels odd to be saying this, but I'm dead and it ain't me. I call her Xela, you should too. The past can be a heavy burden."

As the Bayamon cruised into the star scattered dark Hela bought Marteene up to speed. For several years she had been clandestinely working for a group known only as The Cabal, an above-the-law intelligence organisation operating outside of official structures on missions too secret or too dirty even for Special Ops.

"The Cabal - yea I know." On screen Hela laughed. "Lousy choice of name but the original Boron was unpronounceable." Hela paused to let the remark sink in.

"Now listen G, I've been part of this org for a few years now and I'm certain they're on the relative up and up but they play rough, you know what I'm saying? I'm going to tell you some stuff now that few people know and if you listen you're pretty much signed on. I had to fight hard for this but if we're onto the backup plan then, well, things are going to be tough enough for you without having to stumble around in the metaphorical dark."

On screen Hela paused as if to give him time to terminate the message. They both knew he couldn't do that.

"Great, you're in. I knew we could count on you. Consider yourself oathed!"

The Cabal originated in one of the unpublished protocols of the treaty that forged the Foundation Guild, the alliance of Boron and Argon formed in 350 after Argon intervention rescued the Boron from defeat at the hands of the Paranid and the Split in what history terms "The Boron Campaign".

Not only did the allies establish the Foundation Guild to foster, police and control trading links based on the common currency of the Argon Mark they also went further and established protocols for sharing intelligence at the highest levels. Unbeknownst to all but a handful of beings from both species Protocol 13 went further and established the Cabal specifically to deal with extraordinary circumstances and threats with extraordinary means. Over the intervening centuries the original organisation faded from view, merging itself into the bodies politic of the two races until its existence was forgotten or deemed the stuff of legends.

Hela had been recruited soon after the death of his father for reasons that only later became clear. For almost her entire clandestine career she had worked on one assignment; a top-level penetration of what the Cabal believed was a cross-clan pirate organisation. To that end she had spent a considerable time working undercover to establish an alternative identity as a small time member of the Skull Clan or more precisely of the colourfully named "Rohler's Raiders."

It was common for the larger clans to attract a penumbra of allied factions whose loyalty was purchased with base facilities aboard the Clan HQ and other perks. With the aid of information fed them via Hela the Raiders had established a sound reputation for their bravery and skill in many encounters with Xenon, other clans and various representatives of more legitimate authority. The plan to recruit and turn the Raider's chieftain into a deep penetration source seemed to be working well. Other intelligence assets within the Skull clan indicated the Raiders were in line for rapid promotion within the hierarchy following carefully engineered devastating losses among the factions contracted to provide security for Paradise Station and other Skull facilities. It wouldn't be top table but the Raiders would be players and in operational contact with some of the Skull's most secret operations. Hela and her intelligence handlers were convinced this would position the Cabal to penetrate to the heart of an enterprise that Hela promised would,

"Knock your head into the next sector."

On screen Hela grimaced.

"But it seems the thrusters have dropped off this plan. We always knew it was a long shot but the stakes are too high to give up so we have a Plan B. You're going to love it but you'll need the skill, knowledge and experience I've picked up undercover. Hence the AI Xela."

"Look G, I've got to wind this up, Xela will fill you in on the specifics."

Hela approached the camera until her head filled the entire shot, her eyes edged with tears.

"I suppose this is goodbye Gragore." She dabbed the corner of her eyes with a finger and smiled sadly. "Shit, I'm letting this beyond-the-grave thing get to me, you take care of yourself G and watch your six. Do me and your father proud and finish this thing. We both loved you"

It was the last memory Marteene had of the woman who'd been much more than a simple cousin to him but it bought a kind of emotional closure and in the fire of his burning grief was forged a fierce determination to finish whatever it was that Hela had started.

As the fighter arrowed through the void Marteene wept.

### Chapter 9: The Game's Afoot

Janis swallowed hard and pulled at her collar nervously as a single bead of sweat crawled down her spine, serpent-like and cold, like the chill spreading through her limbs. The detached professional observer in her noted the effects of shock as her autonomic system began reducing the blood supply to vulnerable extremities. A faint acrid smell of fear permeated the room, she realised it was from her. Taking a deliberate deep breath Commander Trasker willed her pounding heart to slow and transmuted the insipient panic into diamond hard concentration. She stole a glance at her colleagues around the table, their faces alien pale in the azure glow of the central holo-projector tank. Captain Sheva she couldn't read at all, only the tightly pursed lips and the faint sheen of sweat on the veteran's bald pate gave any clue to his feelings. Paskaal though - the Beta Wing commander's face was a running vid playing through the whole gamut but settling into open-mouthed disbelief. For the fifth time Trasker ran the file, the evidence was undeniable.

In the tank 4 fighters cruised in loose formation against a backdrop of blazing stars. The data feed was from a deep space surveillance probe secreted deep in the Bali Gi sector for the mission. Positioned millions of klicks from the gate complex to avoid detection the optical quality was not good and the electromagnetic and quantum resonance scans little better. It was all they had though and it was enough.

The 3 officers watched the scene in silence as the Tactical AI replayed the data scan, changing magnifications and perspectives adeptly to convey maximum information, zooming in on the fighters until the tank was filled with the blurred images of the 4 Bayamons.

"They're setting up the jumps now," Paskaal commented unnecessarily. As he spoke the fighters drifted slightly apart and three characteristic singularities opened almost simultaneously. One by one the fighters fell into them and vanished. A few seconds later another singularity appeared and the remaining fighter slipped from sight.

"Record freeze." At Trasker's command the holo playback paused, catching the Bayamon at the moment it entered the singularity. "Advance slow". Frame by frame the scan advanced and the Bayamon slipped from sight. "Record freeze, advance time index 0.002". The Tactical AI obeyed, displaying a blurred image of the fighter, at the moment it crossed the event horizon. The distinctive elongation effect caused by the intense warping of the fabric of time and space around the artificially generated wormhole showed conclusively that the jump had been made successfully. Coldly Trasker had hoped that a drive malfunction had destroyed the craft.

At Paskaal's command the AI ran a comparative scan of the wormholes. The data resolution was poor but by overlaying the first 3 singularities and running new extrapolation subroutines a coarse hard radiation signature could be recovered. With more data and a few breakthroughs in analysis techniques it would be possible to interpolate the jump-gate a singularity was connected to from the radiation readings. All that could be told from this was that the first 3 Bayamons jumped to the same sector. This they knew as the pilots were being held in solitary debrief, telling and retelling their stories to a procession of Intelligence officers.

The scan of the fourth singularity was less data rich as there was only one source for the AI to analyse. There was enough to show fundamental differences in the radiation patterns though. The ship had jumped and it had jumped to another, unknown location. It had not appeared in any Argon controlled or monitored sectors and although they were still checking with their Boron allies Trasker knew in her bones that would turn up negative.

No encoded flash had come in from Head Office to indicate Marteene had been assigned new orders. Instead Janis was faced with a worst case scenario; an operative had gone rogue with beyond state of the art technology, on her watch. In which case Marteene would be somewhere out of reach, Teladi space or even with one of the pirate clans. Her only consolation was the knowledge that his actions could not have been premeditated, he had no advance knowledge of the mission or that the new Shadow-Skin technology was being deployed. That meant he was winging it and would need time to organise his next move. She had time to retrieve the situation and even as Paskaal and Sheva rehearsed recent events in an attempt to contrive a benign interpretation she planned decisive action.

––––––––––

"Gragore - Lieutenant Marteene?" The familiar voice, redolent with concern despite the faintly mechanical delivery of the AI vocorder, pulled him from the pit of grief into which he had fallen. He emerged exhausted but with the fires of his anguish banked by the emotional closure Hela's last testament provided. Putting a gloved hand to her frozen screen image Marteene bade his dead cousin a final farewell.

"Goodbye Hela - I loved you too."

With these words the screen flashed back into life with the AI he forced himself to think of as Xela. Marteene palmed a Quick-Stim from the flight suit med-kit and discharged it into his carotid. Immediately the feeling of exhaustion was banished as the stimulant dredged fresh reserves of energy from deep within his body. The almost subliminal ache in the very marrow of his bones warned him that his wellsprings of energy were almost drained dry.

"We've got another jump to make soon but there are things you need to know first. I can't brief you fully on the plan yet but I know a man who can!" As adept as Hela had been at command psychology the AI adopted a deliberately light tone. "I can bring you up to speed on the background but your Control wants to deliver the full brief. That's sentients for you!"

"Gragore - a little test to see if you've been paying attention to life!" Marteene smiled despite his loss, it was good to see death had not affected her sense of humour. "Engaging lecture mode".

The tone was distressingly familiar, down to the jocular edge.

"Since the Boron/Split Conflict all races have co-existed peacefully, united by their shared interests in free interstellar trade. The freighters hauling raw materials and finished goods between the sectors are the visible strands of a complex web knitting us all together."

It was simple economics - most raw materials were species specific and as such relatively worthless trade items. But mix them together in the interstellar economy and a host of new products and technologies become possible. Naturally in a free market system the various factors of production such as raw material availability, labour and information costs and production location intertwined resulting in the lowest production costs, and hence profit potential, becoming species specific for items composed of many racial products. It was simply more efficient for the Paranid to construct docking computers for example. So long as the flow of goods was unhindered the galactic economy prospered.

Eerily adopting the staccato voice of the Global Ed-Net Xela smilingly continued.

"Candidate Marteene what is the most significant threat to free interstellar trade. Explain your reasons"

The AI quality was simply uncanny in its recreation of his cousin. The question and answer mode of discourse has been her favoured technique for drumming knowledge into and nurturing thought in his "teledanium skull". It had been a game he enjoyed. Hela always had had a first class mind that could at once grasp the complexities of an issue and expose the essentials with the precision of a surgical bot. Combined with her military experience it was why she was prized so highly as an analyst and it seems, an intelligence operative.

As she had taught him Marteene counted to 5, marshalled his thoughts and framed them with precision.

War was always bad for business, well unless you were a Teladi. The grasping lizards were notorious for trading with all sides in any conflict and not above stoking them with judicious leaks of information and the offer of weapons at favourable terms. It was too general a threat to warrant a specific Code Black though.

A full-scale Xenon assault would certainly bring the delicate trade network down but again it was a threat on too vast a scale. Also all intelligence reports suggested the Xenon war machine was reeling from the recent war that drove them from most sectors of known space. They were not expected to be able to launch a genocidal assault for many years.

Piracy? Well, the first customer of the first pro was probably a pirate. It was an age-old problem and one the security services of the different races were adept at dealing with. Witness the current op. Unless, and it was a big unless, one of the pirate factions had stolen a serious tech march on the rest of the universe he couldn't imagine them requiring a Code Black.

No - these were all real threats but they were known and to the best of his very well informed knowledge, contained. It had to be something more fundamental.

On screen Xela smiled, almost imperceptibly but her eyes sparkled with pride. It was a look Marteene had seen often during these learning sessions. It meant he was onto something. Pirates then - and something really big.

He thought for a moment.

"Big. Bigger than stealing jump-drive technology?"

The pirate clans were powerful and rich but even combined they did not have the technical knowledge or the resources to make the sort of fundamental breakthroughs in technology that would warrant a Code Black. Sure, their jointly run shipyards had designed and built a unique range of ships but they were all, even the Bayamon, inferior craft to those used by the various defence forces. Only by hunting in packs did they become a threat. There was no sign at all that they might present a technological threat to free trade. Besides, pirates are essentially parasites on the trade system and would have no interest in damaging it.

Over the years Gragore had become adept at reading Hela and the AI had done a superb job of reproducing her, down to small mannerisms. Pirates, something to do with technology and judging by her faintly quizzical expression something big and fundamental he was totally missing.

Then it clicked. As Hela often said, the most difficult questions often contain their own answers. What was the greatest threat to FREE interstellar trade? That was easy. The greatest enemy of freedom is monopoly. Corner the market and you can name your own price.

Encouraged by Xela's expression he continued the line of thought.

Okay - pirates and a monopolistic threat to free trade. It was a long held belief in the intelligence community that this was not a serious possibility. There were limited ways the pirate clans, even if united, could establish a monopolistic hold on trade. First, they could seize control of the means of production through force or through legal shell organisations. This was simply not possible. It would require huge financial and organisational resources and the use of force to prevent others from entering the market. All races went to great lengths to combat the influence of organised crime over their economies. It was a never-ending battle but not one the pirates could ever win in anything other than a pyrrhic sense.

Second best to controlling the means of production would be controlling the means of distribution. One way to do this would be to establish a monopoly over transportation but again organised crime penetration of transport organisations was a known and controllable threat. Besides much of the haulage business was in the hands of independent traders organised into guilds for self protection. When pushed too far these people would push back. Hard. No - it would not be possible to establish an illegal monopoly of transportation without triggering a major war.

The only other way would be to control the jump-gates and this was simply unthinkable. Any such attempt would result in a massive military response that would devastate the clans. The line of analysis had reached a dead end but Xela's expression suggested otherwise. He was missing something. Well, as his Special Forces trainers had constantly said, when you've eliminated all other possibilities whatever is left must be the truth. As aphorisms went it had a Gonerish ring to it but nevertheless it had proven useful on many other occasions.

Okay - they can't control the means of production, cannot monopolise transportation or take control of the jump-gates. The only thing they could do to stop free trade would be to destroy the jump-gates and that would be completely absurd. Even the new jump-drive required a gate in the destination sector. No gates, no interstellar travel, no piracy and no profits. The pirates would require fully operational jump-drive technology and the only example of this was in burnt out pieces scattered through a dozen labs. They couldn't steal the tech because it doesn't exist and they sure couldn't research it themselves and unless another ship had jumped in from Earth they couldn't just find it. If such a ship had appeared Marteene was certain it would have been picked up on system scanners.

He was warm now, he didn't need to check Xela's face for clues, he could just feel he was close. Right - as far as he could see the only practical way a monopoly on trade could be established was if the jump-gates were destroyed and a pirate clan had found a completely new source of advanced drive technology and this would mean .....?

"No!" For a second his mind refused to accept the implications. It would mean they had acquired or were trying to acquire completely alien transportation technology that obviated the need for jump-gates and this only existed in rumour and legend. Rumour and legend of the builders of the jump-gate system, the myth of the Ancients. Even as his mind rejected the idea he could see from Xela's expression that she knew what he had guessed - and that he was right.

### Chapter 10: Revelations

Apart from confirming his analysis the AI proved unwilling to discuss the outrageous conclusions any further. The upload Xela had received contained directions for the next stage of what Marteene was beginning to think of as his "induction" into the shadow world of the Cabal. The most important thing now was to get him into deep cover and fully briefed and the timetable called for another jump. At Xela's instruction he targeted the eastern jump-gate of the Teladi sector north of Spaceweed Drift. The slight misdirection would suggest he'd travelled through the Seizewell sector.

Profit Share was one of the major Teladi mining sectors with a reputation for a latitude to the law that was generous, even by the minimal standards of the avaricious species. Being host to one of the few Bliss Place Stations in the X-Universe the reputation was well earned. Thanks to the laissez-faire attitude of the Teladi to all forms of alcohol, narcotics and the sexual practices of other species Theophant's Joy was famous or notorious, depending on your perspective, as THE place to have a good time. Absolutely no questions asked. Most Teladi stations are barely functional due to the constant obsession with cutting costs to maximise profit and no one stays on them longer than is strictly necessary to conduct business. But when they have to and especially if there is great profit involved, no one parties like the Teladi and so the station was constantly full of the fun-loving of all races slaking their thirst for innocent and not so innocent entertainment.

At the end of work cycles the lower levels resounded to the clamour of refinery workers being parted from their credits as they rubbed shoulders and exchanged blows with pirates and a scum tide of flotsam drawn like carrion eaters to the sweet scent of fools and money.

Pick a card, any card.

More refined tastes were catered for elsewhere, provided of course you had the credits and the connections.

Marteene had never visited the place but its reputation was well known in security circles. Although technically a Teladi station under the jurisdiction of Board Member Kulas Impromarius Nusini II the hundreds of business operations it housed were inevitably permeated by the influence of organised and not so organised crime. Over the years Theophant's Joy had effectively become an independent station thanks to a combination of bribery and the ever-present threat of clan violence so all kinds of illicit activities proceeded unhindered. It has long been rumoured, and it is hard to see how it cannot be true, that Nusini himself held a considerable stake. Considered neutral ground by all parties except probably the Xenon, who never got invited to the really good parties, the station was a natural habitat for spies and a breeding ground for espionage. The docking of a lone pirate Bayamon would attract no attention and Xela assured him arrangements were in hand to ensure his anonymity upon arrival.

It was a good destination for anyone wishing to go to ground.

As an additional security precaution Xela announced she was reprogramming the Shadow Skin Generators to emit a new false signature. Marteene was impressed, so far as he knew that was not possible.

"Plug me into a ship and I can do a lot of things kid. Check you power grid."

He did, despite the active shadow tech the Bayamon was functioning at 100% efficiency. Experimentally he tapped the turbo and immediately the fighter accelerated to its full maximum speed.

"Active power management Gragore - I'm tied into all the ship systems and can handle the power flows a helluva lot better than the autonomic sub system programs. Don't you just hate waste? Score one for my Xenon side huh?"

Well it made sense - performance was always as much about the software controlling a craft as it was about design and technology and a Whole Personality AI was literally thousands of times more powerful than the relatively primitive sub systems of the Bayamon fighter. Marteene wondered what else she might be capable of and was pleased to have such an edge. Already his mind was toying with possibilities, certain in the knowledge that he would need every advantage he could get in the coming days.

On emerging from the eastern jump-gate into Profit Share Marteene set course for Theophant's Joy at Xela's suggestion.

The flight to the station was uneventful. As he expected Teladi security patrols paid no attention to the stream of pirate freighters and their packs of escorts as they traversed the system. It took a lot of the illicit substances, lumped together as spaceweed and space-fuel to keep the party fires burning and generous "donations" to various interested parties ensured their continued flow from pirate sources through sectors where they were technically illegal. As instructed by Xela he activated the docking computer 3 klicks from the docking gate and sat back nervously as the fighter was guided into a small maintenance bay, remote from the main landing platforms.

According to Xela the bay would be empty but as a precaution he polarised his suit visor before cracking the cockpit seal. Slipping Xela's AI chip into a thigh pocket and checking the charge of the personal sidearm strapped unobtrusively to the suit utility webbing he climbed out cautiously. The small bay looked as if it hadn't been used in years. Broken parts of obsolete fighters littered the deck-plates and everything was covered in a faint sheen of partially combusted lubricant. A large black stain on the far wall extended to the high ceiling of the bay. Curiously Marteene ran a gloved finger through it, leaving a dark residue of oxidised metals on the fingertip. The bulkhead itself was pocked and scarred and rivulets of molten metal had slid down and congealed on the bay floor in tiny silver pools. He was willing to bet good credits that the background radiation levels would confirm that there had been a massive accident. Judging by the condition it must have been some time ago but the bay was clearly not in regular use.

Although certain his flight suit protected him from radiation and other environmental pollutants Martine hurried to the small service elevator as Xela had instructed. It appeared non functional but as soon as he had pushed through the half open door the elevator lurched to life and began to slowly descend. He counted 12 levels before the lift lurched to a halt between floors. The elevator doors slid open to reveal the polished silver metal of the shaft.

"Please remove your helmet and state your identification." The electronic voice was carefully pitched to carry a weight of authority tinged with menace, the better to adduce unthinking compliance in the targeted species. Aware that he was probably under the guns of a security system Marteene depolarised the visor and removed his flight helm. A brief, almost subliminal flicker indicated a flash retinal scan from a well-concealed laser source. He knew the system would be running half a dozen other checks he couldn't detect.

"Lieutenant Gragore Marteene, service number you know full well. Open up."

"All in good time Mr Marteene, all in good time." This was a humanoid voice, rich and dark profundo, like the best Three Worlds ale. A hint of humour garnished the tone. In his mind's eye Gragore pictured a popular tenor and smiled at the thought. "Now if you would be so kind as to disarm your sidearm." With slow and deliberate movements Marteene removed the weapon from the small holster, being sure not to touch the trigger, there was no telling how jumpy these guys were. The weapon was a standard issue P47 personal sidearm, little bigger than his hand but capable of firing 150 bursts of superheated plasma pellets from the power cell in the handle. Not a serious military weapon but deadly enough. Deftly he removed the power cell and held the small cylinder up for the benefit of the unseen observer.

"Thank you Mr Marteene, if you would be so kind as to place your weapon and the magazine into a pocket you may proceed."

He complied and a section of the apparently seamless shaft slid aside to reveal a small antechamber. On stepping inside a Bio-Decontam sequence triggered, briefly bathing him in a cool blue light as it scanned for and neutralised harmful pathogens. With only the briefest of tremors as an indication the chamber rotated 180 degrees and opened onto a short, straight well lit corridor, its metal bulkheads shining clean as if scoured by a solvent. This time no attempt had been made to conceal security devices. At the end of the corridor above the solitary exit a small quad laser tracked him from behind the distinctive warm air shimmer of a defence screen as he approached the door. A similar installation guarded the route back to the lift shaft.

The door slid open soundlessly as he approached and without waiting for an invitation Marteene stepped through into a small dark hallway, little bigger than a suit locker. Almost instantly another panel slid aside and he stepped through, blinking in the sudden light, into what appeared to be a large but sparsely furnished office dominated by a single workstation.

The large holo tank built into the far wall was currently segmented into a dozen or so screens, all of which were either blank or displayed the distinctive cross-hatch patterns of an encrypted signal. Behind the work station, almost concealed from view in a large swivel chair the single occupant of the room regarded the signals briefly before swinging to face Marteene, who smiled involuntarily at the studied theatrics.

The large bear of a man, who looked the part of an opera tenor even more than his voice suggested, stood and proffered his hand in greeting. Marteene noted the broad smile that split his face barely touched his eyes. The full head of black hair that fell unfashionably about his shoulders, the short but unkempt beard flecked with gray and under a loose fitting suit, a well developed paunch conveyed the impression of an old warrior, going to seed in his late middle age.

Marteene threw his helmet and flight gloves onto the only other bit of furniture in the room, a small leather couch along the left bulkhead. The handshake was firm but unforced as the stranger established direct and probing eye contact. He returned this unblinking. With an unexpected smile the man ended the contest and waved his arm expansively towards the couch.

"Please, please - take a seat. Would you like to refresh yourself before we get started?" With a tilt of his head he indicated a single side door to left of the desk. "You'll find a change of clothing and all the other ablutory accoutrements I'm sure you can use after the day you've had."

Marteene's olfactory senses forced him to agree. After hours cramped into a small cockpit and two adrenaline fuelled dogfights a miasma of odours, none of them pleasant, assailed him. He could do with dropping a few logs too. Like most pilots he preferred to avoid using the somewhat primitive suit ablution system, at least intentionally.

Ten minutes later, clean, refreshed and savouring that comforting empty feeling of relief Marteene was back in the office nursing a mug of Java. Strong, bitter, black - just how he liked it. The cut grey casual suit provided fitted perfectly and the patent leather shoes felt like he'd worn them for years. The shirt appeared to be genuine Boron silk.

Looking sharp, feeling sharp. He breathed deeply, savouring the rich, comforting aroma emanating from a primitive percolator by the workstation. Despite the incipient amphetamine fatigue he felt good.

"Thanks". Marteene toasted the stranger ironically. "Now, how about some answers."

"Answers, hmmn. Answers are so difficult without questions, don't you agree?" Sitting back in the swivel he fumbled in a pocket before extracting a cigar from a small silver humidor, which he lit with a naked flame from an antique device. Ostentatiously the man leaned back and breathed an aromatic plume across the room. This was scrubbed with brisk efficiency from the air by the environmental system.

"Yes, I know, it's an illegal and disgusting habit but as they say," 'When amongst the Teladi do as the Teladi do'. Why else come here? For their naked charm and wit!" He leaned forward, regarding Marteene intently.

"Now how about some questions?"

"Well, for starters how about a name?"

The man smiled.

"A name, which one would you like? There have been so many of them you understand, but you can call me Mr Artur. For your purposes I am the Cabal." He took another long draw on his cigar, held the smoke for a moment and exhaled a slow, contented breath. "Try something a little more pertinent."

Marteene took a deep sip of Java, savouring the astringent bite of the hot liquid on the back of his palette before it slid down his throat. Despite being something of an aficionado Marteene could not quite place the blend. It was too rich and subtle to have been hydroponically produced in orbit. No true java drinker would touch the mass market derivatives, losing as they do the subtleties produced by the complex interplay of genes, sun, soil and weather of planetary environments. The base was clearly the black bean grown in the eastern highlands of Argon's main continent, oily with the active alkaloids that, with a minimum of genetic manipulation, had proven to be cross species in their appeal and effect. The subtler moderators could have been any of dozens of variants of the original "Beverage of the Gods" now grown under alien suns.

"Okay - how about telling me what in hell is going on?"

"You are a man of the universe Mr Marteene, you know full well that something is always, as you say, 'going on.' Perhaps you should tell me what you already know?"

"That my cousin got killed trying to help a secret intelligence organisation prevent pirates getting their hands on extremely advanced propulsion technology that could completely destroy the existing trading system and balance of power. And you think this technology comes from the Ancients, which I find difficult to believe."

"An admirably succinct summary, your scepticism notwithstanding." Artur took one last long pull on his cigar and dropped the spent butt into the workstation recycler. "We have clear evidence that for a number of years certain elements within the clans have been intensively searching for the wreckage of an unknown craft we have reason to believe suffered a catastrophic malfunction that left it disabled and drifting. Unfortunately we have no idea where, even more unfortunately we believe a clandestine cross-clan grouping does and plans to use the knowledge that could be gained from the derelict to unify the clans by force and establish themselves as the dominant power in the X-Universe. It is my job to prevent this. Hela's too and now I trust, yours."

"But - the Ancients? They're just a myth. Granted we know the jump-gate system is largely the remnant of an older civilisation we call the Ancients but they vanished thousands of years ago. There's no evidence at all that they are still around apart from the space-fuel ravings of a few cranks."

Artur sighed theatrically and reached for the holo remote. The multiple screens merged to one single image and Marteene stared in amazement at the huge disc shaped machine in the centre of the frame.

"Indeed?"

He'd had so many shocks that day that another almost made no difference. Like most pilots Marteene dismissed the unsubstantiated tall tales and blurred, unattributed gun camera images offered as proof of the continued presence of the lost designers of the jump gates. With this scan, being offered under these circumstances, he was forced to re-evaluate his stance and it said much for his mental flexibility that he could do so instantly. The ability to evaluate and absorb new information and act on it with instinctive skill in the face of new or rapidly changing circumstances was one that factored high in the Maverick Profile used to recruit Special Ops pilots.

Artur watched with the rapid play of emotion and thought across the face of his newest and most important recruit with satisfaction. The Special Ops Maverick qualities were equally valued by the Cabal as by the very nature of their business operatives would be out of contact for long periods in what would be by definition, unique and challenging situations. He was reassured to see his extensive psych profiling confirmed by the speed at which Marteene adjusted to the revelation. It was one reason Artur and his associates had recruited Hela and now her younger cousin.

One reason.

"Tell me Mr Marteene, tell me what you observe from this image?"

Gragore took in a single deep breath and held it as he willed his mind into a calm focus, separating his analytical faculties from the animalistic turmoil of his taut, contained emotions. For a long minute he studied the image in silence, sifting it for the small clues to the further information it must contain if, as he surmised, Artur was not the type given to idle chatter.

Ostensibly the low resolution image showed a disc shaped object that appeared to be a vessel of unknown configuration. No scale was displayed but judging from its position relative to the arch of the obscured jump-gate looming behind it the ship was massive, almost too big to enter. Which made it the size of a fleet carrier like Argon One.

Artur nodded confirmation as Marteene outlined his thoughts. Quietly he poured two shots of a clear amber liquid from a finely crafted dark bottle, it's long neck twisted in an ornate coiled rope fashion reminiscent of the horned ruminants of the continent of Argon from which the brew originated. Two fingers apiece, he judged this quantity of the strong spirit would not impair his own or his new associate's performance. And if anyone ever needed a drink it was probably Marteene, given his day and given the likely quality of the home brewed space-fuel that would be the only alcohol available on his ostensibly dry vessel. Silently he handed Marteene a tumbler of the potent brew who accepted it with a distracted nod of thanks.

Warming the glass in his palm Marteene gently swirled the contents and cautiously inhaled the gently evaporating fumes, allowing them to slide slowly past his olfactory senses to the back of his palette. It was rich and complex, with a hint of peat and none of the sharp grain tang characteristic of either the home brewed space-fuel he was accustomed to on ship or the young and cheaper vintages encountered at the sort of official functions to which officers of his lowly rank were invited. Taking a short sip he let the liquid funnel slowly back along his tongue, savouring the sensations triggered in his different taste buds. It slipped down smoothly leaving a pleasurable burning trail that contrasted favourably with the throat raw effect of illicit space-fuel. The spectrum of sensations merged seamlessly into one greater whole, indicative of an unblended single malt and it conjured a warm glow of well-being in the pit of his stomach that rapidly suffused through his blood stream to his brain.

"Smooth? Twenty five years?"

Artur smiled as he took a substantial sip that half emptied his glass and savoured the warm feeling comfortably permeating his system. The aesthete in him appreciated a person who could show discrimination when it came to the finer things of life, it showed standards and a laudable attention to detail. Perhaps this was going to work.

"Very close, 30 actually but I'm pleased to find all those years imbibing Engineering Deck Special Reserve has not entirely destroyed your palette. Please, continue with your analysis."

Marteene drained his glass and looked again at the image. The low resolution scan was missing a lot of detail and the read-out strip was blank indicating visual spectrum only. The picture was further degraded by white noise interference patterns and on closer examination suffered from a slight distortion around the borders.

"Well, from the resolution and quality it was shot from a deep space visual array at extreme range, probably on a Zenec 1400 A judging by the scan patterns and edge distortion, which would date it to between 8 and 10 years ago. That model was taken out of service when the new super-cooled mirrors came along."

"Very good Mr Marteene, very good. Your cousin said you had a good eye for detail. Anything else?"

Gragore paused for a moment and weighed up the situation with a gambler's reluctance to reveal a hole card. Watching for any reaction he added.

"Only that it was shot in Brennan's Triumph when it was part of the Xenon holdings."

The briefest flicker of his otherwise deadpan expression told Marteene two things. He was right and he had missed something, something important that Artur was unsure about revealing to him.

"Interesting, there are no star patterns from which to extrapolate location and nothing else but a jump-gate arch to give any clue. Why do you think that?"

"First, it's a deep scan, indicating the sector in question is not one of ours or our Boron friends, second, if anything that big emerged from a gate in any inhabited sector of any race nothing could keep it secret and third the object is within the gate activation penumbra, if you look closely you can see the shadow it casts on the underside of the arch. Coming or going there should be a trace effect ergo the gate is inactive and the wrecked gate in Brennan's Triumph is the only one I know of. How am I doing so far?"

"Impressive Mr Marteene, very impressive."

Marteene thought for a moment.

"I think I can top that if I may." He gestured for the screen control which Artur surrendered without demure. Marteene quickly traced a small area in the top left of the screen with the laser pointer and activated the function menu. Scrolling through the analysis sub-routines he magnified the tiny corner until it filled the large screen. A web of microscopic fractures radiated from a small blemish in the centre of the image. Isolating the blemish he scrolled through the sub programs until he found what he was looking for. The 3D extrapolation sub routine revealed a distinct inverted pyramid indentation sharply delineated from it's surroundings by a soft circumference of extruded material that appeared melted. Left curiously numb by this confirmation of his hunch and aware that Artur was unconsciously holding his breath he added calmly.

"It was shot by my father from the Destiny Star."

From the slight tensing of his body and the transient shadow of emotions that flashed across his face Marteene knew that he was correct and that Artur had wanted him to know. That he had played out this game indicated others may not. Marteene carefully filed that fact for future reference.

By way of explanation he added.

"Micro-meteor impact, I remember the maintenance report among his effects."

"Excellent Mr Marteene, truly excellent." His smile appeared genuine. "You actually inspire me with confidence." He touched a control on the work station and almost imperceptibly flinched as the tiny laser of the security lock-outs read his retinal pattern. Instantly the large briefing screen was filled with 5 words in large bold red type.

"OPERATION BROTHERHOOD: ABOVE TOP SECRET."

The screen wiped left to right leaving 2 words.

"ACCESS APPROVED."

Indicating the screen Artur continued.

"To be completely honest Mr Marteene, and I surprise myself with that phrase, my associates and I were divided over whether to fully disclose the information in this briefing".

He cleared his throat awkwardly and went through the ritual of lighting up another cigar.

"You will appreciate the "need to know" principle of course?"

Marteene smiled an acknowledgement. It was a basic security principle that operatives only need to know the information necessary to carry out the task at hand. It was also a principle he had clashed often enough with Intelligence over to ensure his flight received full context briefings instead of the 'Go there, shoot that' approach instinctively favoured by Janis Trasker back on the Vigilant.

"Well, I am of the opinion that the job we have for you will demand that you think on your feet and respond to events creatively because you will be out of contact under deep cover. To me this demands that you fully appreciate the situation, including what my associates deem, and I quote; 'Irrelevant historical trivia.' Being a team player of course I had no option but to comply."

"Sadly your acumen has uncovered the involvement of Petre so I see no further reason to conceal the deep background from you!"

He gesticulated toward the screen. "With my usual attention to contingencies I prepared this briefing for you, just in case it should be needed you understand."

Marteene understood and was cheered to know that his handler for whatever the mission was had a flexible approach to unwanted constraints. He also did not miss the first name terms Artur appeared to be on with his father and noted the fact for future reference.

"It would be simpler if I left you to explore the files yourself, everything you need to know, before we discuss our rather interesting proposal, is in there."

Marteene agreed, he'd been running on stims and java for hours and he could feel tendrils of fatigue beginning to erode his concentration behind the caffeine buzz. Another shot of the bitter black brew would reinvigorate him temporarily but after that he knew he'd be flying on reduced thrusters.

"I'll be back in an hour or so. May I send in something to eat? I can highly recommend the Crustacean Surprise?"

"Sure, so long as the surprise isn't that it's not dead and so long as you're paying."

The mention of food reminded Marteene that he'd not eaten for the best part of a day and Theophant's Joy was as renowned for the variety and quality of it's cuisine as much as it was for the variety of dubious pleasures that could be obtained within it's bulkheads.

Artur spoke to the briefly to the air and vanished in the swirling firefly hum of a transporter beam. Seconds later a steaming tray of assorted shellfish materialised on the workstation, the sweet golden aroma of warm butter provoking Marteene's stomach to growl with need. He was impressed, as he was sure was the intention. It also let him know that the room was monitored but that he had taken as a given.

Artur materialised in a heavily modified Boron Dolphin freighter in another little used docking bay located in one of the more private areas of the station. The sleek ship had no name, fixed registration number or now, thanks to the marvels of shadow-skin technology, even a fixed quantum signature but to him it would always be the Seera Myrayne. It was a redolent memory of youth, a path untrodden and now long overgrown with the brambles and briers of time. Shaking off the uncharacteristic melancholy triggered in sympathy with the loss now experienced by the young pilot he ordered the ship to send a suitable dish to the briefing room. It took only moments for the galley to flash the pre-prepared ingredients, which were teleported instantly to Marteene.

"Thanks Seera."

"You are welcome Artur. Are things going well?" The mechanical female voice was almost atonal, sparked only by the limited personality AI capabilities that were state of the art until the recent creation of Xela. It was little more than a verbal interface to ship command and a convenient method for updating the mission profile logs that fuelled the

Mission AI sub-routines but the Elsa personality matrices were carefully crafted from his Psych Profile to provide a simulacrum of the emotional support and human contact. This had long been deemed essential for the health and mental well being of those for whom megalomania was an occupational hazard, wielding as they do such un-supervised power and bearing such burdens of knowledge and conscience. Artur had long since accepted that the ship had a quasi personality that reminded him so much of loves gone by or foregone and had deliberately refrained from activating any of the higher vocorder functions so as not to give any one a concrete form. A ship was just a thing and things come and go. Even so he had used this ship for some years and the AI in one form or upgraded another for many more and he felt comfortable with them.

The large Boron designed freighter, it's Argon designation coming from the Common name for one of the intelligent aquatic mammals that thrived in the oceans of the Boron homeworld, had served as his mobile office for so many years it felt like more like home than home. Half of the capacious hold, capable of carrying up to 3000 units of cargo in its subspace folds, was jammed with energy cells for the jump-drive and enhanced fighter drones and assorted missiles for self-defence. There were even half a dozen of the devastating and strictly licensed Hornet missile, capable of devastating even destroyers. The other half had been replaced by an enhanced version of the mobile command module and associated sub-systems more usually found on the top secret manned deep system satellites deployed to clandestinely monitor important sectors. Intended for extended occupation it was an elegant and economical merging of work and living space that left ample scope for the personalisation of space so essential to the well-being of territorial species.

Artur had taken full advantage and only the large holo-screen and associated control station covering half the end bulkhead looked out of place in the elegant hard-wood drawing room. At his command this blemish disappeared behind a panelled wall mounting a holo-frame that by default displayed a picture of an enigmatic young women with a smile that suggested possession of intimate secrets. By Goner tradition it was an image from the legendary Earth although it existed now only in their data banks and given no other provenance Artur was inclined to believe them, knowing what he did about Brennan and the X-Shuttle. He did not really care, it was a human beauty that contrasted with the timeless but cold magnificence of the stars and no matter what he tried to permit his soul a quiet moment to bathe in its warmth and sometimes drive the chill of necessary deeds from his bones.

Today though was not such a day. He had no doubt as to the gravity of the situation and was certain that Marteene would also agree once he had digested the information Artur had provided. With a lot of luck and even more flashes of the creativity and inspiration his profiles indicated he was capable of Artur believed the project had some hope of success. The man was a great pilot, his record and sim scores spoke for themselves, and he had proven himself a competent operative in undercover situations including one he had personally orchestrated as a test of these abilities. The Cabal also had certain resources that could be bought to his aid although the overwhelming need for secrecy imposed its own limits. He also had ample motivation.

At a word the painting faded and Artur watched Marteene eat as he explored the multi-media briefing.

At first he savoured the sweet melting flesh of the shell-fish but as he delved into the fractured mirror world of the Cabal his motions became more mechanical until his attention whirled away in the kaleidoscope of hyperlinks, footnotes and context suggestions leaving the succulent dish to cool and congeal.

## *Chapter 11: Genesis*

You can tell a lot about the working of the mind of a person by the way they search for information and Artur would have been disappointed if Marteene had proven to be one of the mundane types who plod laboriously down the chronological path. He would have been equally dismayed if he had flitted from topic to topic without structure or purpose. As he expected from someone whose educated by a researcher of the calibre of the late Hela Marteene, the pilot efficiently explored the briefing, displaying an intuitive gift for making connections between ostensibly discrete facts and following the new trails.

Central to the whole story was the Destiny Star recording. Artur had viewed it a thousand times, from the first second the enhanced imaging sensors detected the disc travelling at relativistic speed across the system to the final moments as the great ship was buffeted by a series of huge explosions along its leading edge that ripped the hull apart even as a jump portal opened. He watched again as like a fatally wounded cetean the craft sank into the wormhole entrance, its outer surfaces dancing with intense plasma discharges as it fell apart. The wormhole then simply imploded leaving not a trace of the vessel. There was nothing to indicate the cause of the accident although analysts had ruled out mines or attacks with energy weapons.

Unknown to all but a few the timing of this incident coincided precisely with a momentary but complete failure of the whole jump gate network that had sent waves of panic through the higher reaches of all governments. The consensus of the carefully screened experts who were privy to all the data was that the object was, for the briefest of periods in some way inside all the jump-gates at once. Being physicists and so used to dealing with the insanities of quantum mechanics they had no difficulty with this concept but even they had baulked at their own conclusions, conclusions that had rocked even the Cabal.

When reluctantly forced to translate the mathematics into the imprecise and misleading world of language they concluded that the unknown had exited every known gate in virtual form, except for one. Artur and predecessors did not even pretend to follow the maths but the conclusion was inescapable. Somewhere in a solar system containing a jump-gate the remains of the great disc had exploded back into normal space from an exit point projected at random from an existing jump-gate acting as a foci. It could be smashed on an asteroid, vaporised in an impact crater on some unexplored moon or simply drifting uncharted in the vast empty spaces between worlds. But it was out there somewhere, pregnant with chaos, waiting to be discovered.

The single small fragment with the unknown resonance signature sealed deep in a Cabal vault suggested it had been. Even Artur was not privy to the facts of this discovery, except that the fragment was intercepted in transit. The unnamed controller of that operation had stated with confidence that the only person who knew the location of the find had perished, leaving no clues. That this person had known high level connections with several Clans suggested that knowledge of the incident was now in Clan related hands. Disturbingly it was also suggested, again on evidence Artur did not "need to know" that the discovery was not serendipitous. Others were engaged in an active search on the basis of solid information that the Cabal did not possess and they expected to succeed. Despite the image the Cabal fostered they were not omnipotent and all attempts to penetrate this assumed conspiracy had failed, including the last attempt, which had cost the life of Hela Marteene.

The full story told by the briefing was not one of the most glorious episodes for Argon Intelligence. It had started well enough with the anything but chance acquisition of a battered Argon Lifter by Marteene Senior. It was an old and well practised ploy; give a potential recruit something they want but cannot really afford and once they get into difficulties ride to the rescue with an offer trailing strings. And if against expectation no difficulties arise, well, space is a big and hostile place full of beings looking for a fast credit. Trouble can be made to happen, as it did to Petre Marteene.

Artur made no attempt to hide the fact that elements within Argon Intelligence had fostered the contract troubles that followed the incident down in the Teladi sector of Blue Profit. The damage caused to the ship systems in the attack coupled with the persistent rumours of cowardice that stalked him after he was forced to surrender the hold full of valuable weapon components for the Seizewell sector effectively ruined Marteene as a reputable trader. It had been an opportunistic neophyte operation, lacking finesse. Better to be open about it now than leave it as a loose end that would nag at Gragore like a sore tooth. That, he had learned from Hela. Marteene would be indignant but he'd accept it so long as he was sure the Cabal was not involved.

The loss of both of the hugely expensive 25MW shields plus the collateral damage to his good name had forced Petre to compete with the dozens of other independent hauliers for contract scraps. Months of intermittent work hauling low value bulk goods between stations to meet small resource shortfalls took its toll on Marteene Senior and faced with the prospect of never being able to afford to re-equip the Star he proved an easy mark for the next step.

Someone in Gragore's position was of course aware that in the constant battle between white and black there were many intervening shades of grey. It is difficult to penetrate illegal organisations without engaging in such activities and Petre was left with little choice but to adopt the proffered role of ailing trader forced by circumstance to smuggle goods, people and information for the clans in return for hidden subsidies in the form of fortuitous contracts contrived to come his way.

Soon, due in no small part to his own skill and daring, he acquired a small but noted reputation with the Clans who valued a pilot able to discreetly ensure delivery of "sensitive" goods. Unavoidably of course his stock fell with assorted authorities, who for good reason were not kept informed of his true status. It was too the credit of the Argon Navy recruiters that the sins of the father were not visited upon the son.

If it had not been for the incident with the disc Marteene would have remained just another low-grade penetration asset, one of a hundred throws of the dice that just might result in one informant getting in deep enough to be of real use. Marteene though had not shown any flair for the work, having none of the spark that set his son and niece apart. This was one reason why his naval commission was not extended past first retirement.

His career as a spy proved to be uninspiring and the anonymous reports of his handler painted a graphic picture of his declining morale as he was forced to engage in petty criminal acts to maintain cover. Intelligence used him for little more than keeping tabs on flow patterns of illegal trade although his intermittent work for the Clans proved good cover for data recovery missions. In those pre Nav-Sat days the only way to recover data from the probes secretly located deep in the planetary systems of targeted sectors was close flyby. A small time operator running illegals to the hidden Clan installations way out beyond the gates was ideally placed. No one paid any attention to minor course deviations of a small-fry smuggler on legitimate illegitimate business if he was discreet and kept his nerve. Courage was one thing Petre had not lacked, trading port scuttlebutt notwithstanding.

All that changed with the ill-fated mission to the Xenon dominated sector that later became known as Brennan's Triumph. Ironically Marteene had not been scheduled for the mission. Probes in such dangerous sectors were recovered by regular navy craft, maxxed out speedy Discoverers who raced in and out under cover of an attack through a far jump-gate intended to lure the Xenon ships into battle, clearing the way for recovery.

Due to the unexpected incursion of a brace of the big Xenon destroyers the Argon diversionary wing of fighters were cut off from their line of retreat through Priest Pity and forced to battle their way north through hostile Xenon sectors to the safety of Atreus Clouds, in Boron space. Only 3 of the 20 fighters survived and a lot of people received notification of "training accidents" over the following weeks. The Discoverer designated Recovery 1 was also destroyed before it could carry out the data transfer.

At any other time the mission would have been aborted but the information was pivotal to ongoing discussions between the Foundation and Profit Guilds concerning the Xenon problem. For the Paranid it had become a matter of good faith and an excuse to storm out from talks they only reluctantly acceded to in the face of intense pressure from their Teladi allies. Unfortunately Marteene had been in the wrong place at the wrong time, hauling a hold full of assorted ores through Priest Pity in the hope of finally affording a 5MW shield for the Destiny. The mission should have been a cakewalk as the Xenon forces pursued the scattered Argon squadron. It was, except for the alien craft he encountered as he headed back to the southern jump-gate with the deep space probe in his hold.

Marteene had of course appreciated the significance of the encounter and mentioned nothing until he could contrive his schedule to deliver the data in person to his controller. From that point the Cabal moved smoothly into operation, ensuring no trace of the data remained out of their hands. Through third parties it was made abundantly clear to Marteene that the incident HAD NOT HAPPENED. The databanks of the Destiny Star were also removed and replaced.

Three months later he took a long space-walk without a suit in the Boron controlled sector of Menelaus Frontier. Suicide borne of clinical depression caused by debts that were spiralling out of control following another run of bad luck and unfortunate happenstance. A voice message on the ship computer clinched the verdict.

It was months after his death that the first rumours of the event began circulating in Clan circles in greatly exaggerated forms. The Cabal quietly hoped the story would quickly grow into just another fantastic tale told by space pilots to quietly unbelieving ground-hoggers and so it did, with a little help. Only in the last few years had it become apparent that some among the Clans had taken the story seriously and had quietly set their own plans in motion. Argon Intelligence had never been able to identify how the story got out and in the absence of another suspect posthumously blamed Marteene, who had made several scheduled stops before he could meet his controller. Artur doubted this explanation on record but could offer no other. He trusted Gragore Marteene not to let this be an obstacle to his further involvement in the project Artur had planned.

Artur watched as Marteene read the relevant files without visible reaction. Finally, with one file conspicuously unread, Marteene terminated the briefing and waited for Artur to reappear.

---

Gragore nursed another steaming mug of java just to have something to do with his hands until the mysterious Artur returned. A lot of things now made more sense regarding his father's ill-fated shipping business and knowing what he knew about the necessarily messy intelligence business he wasn't shocked or even surprised. His father's death occurred a long time ago and the gaping psychic wound had acquired many layers of protective scar tissue over the years. He would not mourn again, preferring to remember the proud, confident officer not the pale shadow, crippled by the role he was forced to play, depicted in the reports. Events generate their own under-pull and Petre Marteene had simply been swept out of his depth. Part of him wanted to apportion blame, to point a finger and punish, but he refused to fan that particular flame flickering in his mind. Given the gravity of the issue and if it was a stranger, he was honest enough with himself to admit he might well have acted the same way. The pirates he'd just assassinated no doubt had family; proud fathers, disconsolate mothers, grieving partners and inconsolable children. It was a rough old universe and Petre would have been the first to say in it you have to look out for yourself.

"Dust yourself down boy and pick yourself up." Marteene could almost hear the confident baritone.

Marteene recognised that Xela had not exaggerated the magnitude of the threat to the precarious peace of the X Universe inherent in the situation and although a maverick by nature he had been bought up on the timeless virtues of honour and duty, a real naval brat. He might take a somewhat creative approach to them but the concepts were not empty words. They were foundations upon which to build a life worth living. He firmly believed that when the end comes and you lie alone, wrestling death for every last breath from the age ravaged shell your body will become your honour and good name is all that you take with and leave behind. The validated Code Black demanded that he respond and he would. Whether or not that would be through channels even the Cabal would recognise as "official" hung on 3 pertinent questions.

Artur had been expecting only one but judged it wise to meet each with a straight bat.

Yes, he had been Petre's controller. It had been the incident that led to him being recruited by the Cabal and it had remained his primary responsibility ever since.

No, he was not responsible for his death and neither to his knowledge were any other arm of the Boron or Argon intelligence services. Strange deaths attract unwanted attention and without the transmission as evidence he would have been just another nut spouting theories fit only for the farther reaches of the Net.

And finally, the question that hung brooding in the air since the moment they had met.

"How did she die?"

"Ah yes, the briefing could have answered that question."

"I'm asking you."

Artur reached instinctively for a fresh cigar but stopped, judging this was not the time for affectation.

"She was killed by Xenon south of Scale Plate Green. Her and Max were heading in from the clan base in Nyanna's Hideout for a meeting with me in Seizewell. We had reason to hope the Raiders commander could be turned but instead of heading north their Orinoco flew through the south gate straight into the Xenon fleet. We had escort craft stationed discreetly in Scale but they were too far away to stop them. They were able to recover the bodies and the flight recorder. The auto-pilot had been re-programmed. I'm sorry".

The pirate fighter/trader was a good ship in a mixed pack. It balanced good cargo capacity with a robust 10 MW of shielding and sported the powerful Gamma mark of Particle Accelerator Cannon but its low speed made a trip into Xenon space suicidal.

Marteene digested the news in silence and then ran the final file. It confirmed everything he had been told. Both she and the leader of the Raiders, the improbably named Max Force, had been assassinated. The circumstances suggested Clan involvement. The Cabal surmised that the clan faction they had come to consider the "Shadow Conspiracy" were responsible. Force was a popular figure amongst the clans and his own squadron clan was fiercely loyal so there appeared to be no obvious motive. The chosen method was also much too subtle for it to be the work of the clans who naturally favoured a more public and spectacular response to betrayal as an example to others. The extreme sophistication of the encrypted auto-pilot lockouts as testified by the increasingly desperate efforts Hela had made to break them lent weight to that surmise.

Gragore regarded Artur for a long moment, his lips pursed thin and white as he made the decision. His voice was calm and even but his eyes burned with emotion.

"Tell me your plan."

## *Chapter 12: The Brennan Gambit*

The Cabal were not the only ones with plans. Aboard the Vigilant Trasker had assessed her options and with a few untraceable and heavily scrambled transmissions set her own in motion. Her back channel checks confirmed that Marteene had received no new orders. Assiduously she cashed in a few favours and confirmed what her superiors had already discovered. No over-ride code had been issued in the designated time period that would have transferred Marteene to another command operation.

When the intercept came in, relayed to her cramped office in the Comms section by an ensign still young enough to be rattled by the suspicion that something big was going down, she listened to it once before opening a channel. She punched in sector co-ordinates as if the panel were a face, attached the file brief and spoke 3 short words.

"With extreme prejudice."

In a distant sector, hundreds of kilometres beyond the gate system 3 unmarked fighters, big and razor sleek, banked with air show precision away from the conjoined Lifters that served as their support base. In tight formation the Prometheus heavy fighters, the epitome of Paranid space technology, arrowed towards the distant jump-gate. On the comm screen of the lead craft a long message scrolled by a gently rotating image of a Bayamon fighter.

At the same time, in a small ready room off the main bridge another plan was gestating.

Captain Sheva ran his hand habitually over his head as if running fingers through the thick mane of hair he sported decades ago. His bald pate glistened with the perspiration smeared from his beading forehead. Ruefully he caught himself, in his minds eye he was still the hirsute young lieutenant who had cut a major dash with the ladies of the upper levels of Argon society. When Argon 3 went down, all those years ago to a Xenon battle group in Presidents End, he had been one of the few to make it to the escape pods and given the radiation poisoning he considered he'd gotten off lightly. He'd even got the Red Cross, the medal issued to those who suffer injury in the line of duty but the ribbon did not feature among the gamut on his breast and it did not appear for dress uniform functions, despite regulations. For some reason a medal for baldness struck some people as funny and it had taken him years to shake off the inevitable moniker. Out of ingrained stubbornness he declined a course in follicular regeneration and as the years passed and his youthful good looks declined it gave him a gravitas that suited his demeanour.

He knew that his officers considered him something of a martinet and indeed he was a meticulous observer of Fleet Regs. They had developed over centuries of space exploration and to Sheva they represented the accumulated wisdom of the service. But now he was about to bend them if not exactly to breaking point then certainly to the edge of design tolerances.

The other officer in the room had no such compunction. Commander Paskaal, the leader of the Beta Wing of the Special Ops squadron deployed on the Vigilant had practically built a career on it, carried forward by talent and sheer charisma. He had served with Sheva under several commands and had grown to appreciate the man's judgement and acumen. Over the years they became comrades and then trusted friends, bonded by combat. Together they made a good team.

From the moment Marteene had vanished Paskaal thought "something" was going on. His spreading gut told him so and it was almost never wrong. 'Almost', a small word behind which sheltered one or two potentially career destroying gaffes to be sure, but when his instincts spoke Paskaal listened. Sheva had also learned to pay attention although he preferred to act only if other evidence could be found to back Paskaal's intestinal tract.

Although he did not share Paskaal's instinctive distrust of "spooks", which he quietly considered amusing given his assignment, Sheva was forced to agree. Something did not sit right about this whole affair. The countermanding of his order scrubbing Marteene for the mission was one. Despite the official tight definition of 'close relative' that excluded cousins he would not have asked any officer to take a mission after receiving the news Marteene had. His orders had been countermanded by Command and although his subsequent checks confirmed its validity he could not follow the trail into realms beyond his security clearance. As Paskaal forcefully and repeatedly put it, there were "spook fingerprints all over the business." That the ship Intelligence Officer, for whom he had a great deal of respect, could not identify any order or agency that might have led Marteene to go AWOL, only deepened his concern. It would be simply unheard of for such a command transfer to take place without his knowledge because it would lead to just the type of hue and cry he was certain the combative Trasker was organising.

That information concerning the training accident that had taken the life of Hela Marteene was classified beyond his clearance level was another.

As much as he respected the regulations upon which his life and the service were based Sheva valued loyalty higher. The missing lieutenant had proven a brilliant pilot, Paskaal rated him the best instinctive dogfighter he'd ever seen and Sheva would not argue with that. He had also displayed a gift for improvisation that had served the Federation well in several deep cover operations few were privy to. Despite the suspicions surrounding his father there were no grounds to doubt Marteene's loyalty or to suspect the death of a close relative would cause him to steal a ship and go AWOL. He had served the Federation loyally and with distinction and to Sheva loyalty was a 2 way thoroughfare.

No, something was definitely afoot and there was the unpleasant odour of a witch-hunt gathering in the air. The signal intercept only confirmed this and after a quiet but intense discussion they too had a plan. An hour later Paskaal's Elite slipped from the docking bay with orders to report to the Argon Prime space-dock for a complete maintenance and upgrade. Paskaal himself carried papers instructing him to "use or lose" his considerable period of accumulated leave.

At the observation port the captain watched the fighter pensively, turning away only after it disappeared into the glare of the system primary.

---

"Ah yes, Mr Marteene, the Plan." Artur lit up another cigar, relishing the ritual as much as the first lung full of the aromatic leaf. As Marteene had already discovered from the briefing the Cabal had taken a general interest in clan affairs almost from its inception and had discreetly administered more than one bloody nose when it deemed their activities crossed the line. When Artur was recruited to head up Project Sign it had stepped up its efforts to establish a network of contacts and informants amongst all of the clans, with varying degrees of success. High level penetration of those with a predominantly Paranid or Split leadership had proven particularly difficult but he was justly proud of his achievements. It was a mark of his skill that only a few key operatives were even aware that they were working for an intelligence organisation and none knew of the Cabal.

Only in the last few decades had the Cabal begun to realise a form of mirror Cabal was operating almost imperceptibly behind the scenes. The clues were tantalisingly few; an intercepted transmission here, a rumour there, the odd unexplained accident. But it was there, a shadow fleetingly glimpsed. In the fractured competing intelligence universe only a group such as the Cabal ever caught a glimpse of the bigger picture so it was no surprise that the individual races were unaware of it.

It was only since the Brennan-inspired defeat of the Xenon that the clans had become bold enough to establish their huge mobile bases as semi-permanent fixtures in some sectors. Before they skulked deep in the shadows of the planetary systems relying on support vessels powered by the same massive ion drives that the big military ships use away from the jump-gate regions to travel the huge distances between the planets. "Going relativistic" as it's called. Today the prime movers of the Clans remain hidden from view in their big customised transporters and superannuated warships, practically immune to penetration and protected by elite squadrons of mercenaries.

The attempt to subvert a small mercenary clan and manipulate events so as to attract a permanent commission close to a real seat of power had been put in motion years before Petre Marteene's fateful encounter with the unknown disc but responsibility had been transferred to Artur as it was known that the disc was lost somewhere within a planetary system containing a gate sector. It had always been a remote but fearful possibility that a clan would stumble across the treasure trove and Artur had redoubled penetration efforts, subtly manipulating events to the advantage of Rohler's Raiders and eventually replacing the eponymous leader with someone with whom he felt an accommodation could be reached. Hela had played a key role as confidante and contact with the dramatically named Max Force, which surprisingly turned out to be his given name. It was no wonder he turned out to be a mercenary, Some people, Artur firmly believed, were just not fit to be parents, and he could name two.

The unknown alloy hidden in Cabal vaults along with information gathered from other operations run by individuals like himself strongly suggested the artefact had been found. As they were certain no official agency of any of the races were involved by default the discovery must have been made by someone inhabiting the greyer realms of the X universe. Artur had then made penetrating the higher Clan levels his number one priority. The brutal destruction of Hela's Orinoco in the un-named Xenon sector had rocked the Cabal to the core. Decades of careful work vaporised in seconds. Artur had been aghast as well as personally hurt by the loss of someone who had grown to be a valued member of his team as well as the linchpin of the operation.

And of course there was the question of security. For the operation to fall apart at this critical juncture was more of a coincidence than he was prepared to swallow. It may have been, as some of his colleagues believed, the fallout of internecine strife, the Raiders certainly had rivals and even a few mortal enemies. As the front runners for a prime contract rumoured to involve one of the big players lurking in the shadows of a planetary system it was certainly possible that disgruntled competitors might be tempted to take action but Artur did not believe this to be the case.

His own sources gave no indication that an action had been planned and under these circumstances it was practically a tradition that the dispute would be settled by an almighty furball. A mercenary clan could not expect to prove its worth with an assassins blade, it would have to clearly demonstrate its superiority. No, he had a feeling, deep in his bones that somewhere within the Cabal there was a hole in their security and that affected his backup plan, which relied on a network of contacts and resources he had assiduously cultivated over the years. He would require time to review the structure and build a new network from the parts he was certain of. Fortunately he believed he had that time. The problems the combined resources of the Federation were having unravelling the secrets of the X Shuttle indicated the difficulties even the best equipped faced dealing with advanced alien technology and no matter how rich the clans were they could not match the Federation research base. But, as the development of the jump-drive showed, you did not have to figure out much of the puzzle to reap spectacular rewards and it was this fear that drove Artur to even consider the backup plan.

It was, he thought, not so much a plan as the desperate act of a bankrupt gambler betting everything on a last high stakes throw against the odds. What little chance it had of success rested on the shoulders of the brilliant pilot before him and the AI of a dead operative. He termed it "The Brennan Gambit".

---

As he had done ever since the death of Force and Hela bought his infiltration attempt crashing down Artur grasped for a way to outline Plan B that did not make him sound crazy and anyone who took it on even crazier. With the possibility of a leak somewhere in the Cabal forcing him to reconfigure it on the fly it was all beginning to sound madness even to himself. Fortunately a key piece he believed he could rely on was in place on this station, provided Marteene had the commitment for the sacrifice he'd be asked to make.

Taking another deep, invigorating pull on the cigar he fell back on the dialogue approach he copied from one of his first educators, more years ago than he cared to remember.

"Tell me Mr Marteene, how did Brennan manage to build an alliance of forces, including his own personal fighter wing, in a relatively short space of time?"

Marteene curbed his impatience, recognising that the man would answer his questions in his own way in his own time.

"By flying a kick-ass ship with carrier class weaponry and armour and blowing the crap out of everything that got in his way?"

He suspected this was not the answer Artur was looking for but it held more than a grain of truth. The X-Shuttle he flew was a technical marvel in all respects with advanced power management systems that enabled it to mount shields and weaponry normally found only on capital ships. This included the titanic Gamma High Energy Plasma Thrower that could obliterate a destroyer in a couple of salvoes. No fighter in current service could carry anything bigger than the Alpha mark of that weapon and that was frightening enough when the lethal green plasma bolts were streaming past your cockpit. The ship even had an automatic power distribution system that could transfer energy from the shields to the drive system enabling it to run the afterburner on constant full burn. This was in stark contrast to the way that piece of equipment operated as standard, limited as it was to the energy stored in the internal capacitor. In practice this was just enough to boost a fighter to full speed. Brennan's ship was able to feed the mammoth energies from the shield generators directly to the burner, enabling it sustain incredible speeds at the expense of shield protection.

All Special Ops squadron operatives received a substantial briefing on all aspects of the last Xenon conflict and he had seen many tapes of the X Shuttle in action. The tactical advantage the extra speed bestowed cannot be underestimated and Kyle Brennan had used it to great effect. As the instructors at the Advanced Tactical Academy constantly insisted.

"Never underestimate the advantage of surprise."

They were talking about asteroid masking and close formation flying to present a single sensor return but it applied equally to appearing out of nowhere on a pillar of fire, guns blazing! It must, Marteene thought, have been an awesome sight.

Only 2 factors prevented the incorporation of this feature in contemporary design. First, the computer systems and rare alloy power conduits needed to handle the plasma flows would double the cost of a ship. Second and by far the most important was that simulations showed that few pilots have the skill to actually handle the facility. Time and again studies showed that losses due to shield depletion far outweighed the extra kills. The power capacitors also tended to fail catastrophically in combat. Development work continued on reducing costs and developing improved power systems but for now that edge was unavailable.

Smiling, Artur acknowledged his point.

"Leaving aside for one moment the unique nature of his ship, you are right. He crafted himself a bloody big stick from a feeble sapling. How?"

On the face of it, the answer was simple. Brennan had taken a small initial loan from a Teladi captain and built a profitable haulage and manufacturing business that financed the development of his ship into the most formidable fighting machine in the X-Universe. It also paid for a small fleet of factory defence fighters. For the final battles he stripped his businesses of these defences to form his own small battle group which led the joint fleet operation.

"Correct in essence but his triumph was as much diplomatic as military. How did he get the Paranid, the Boron, Teladi and Split to join us in the attack? It was a singular diplomatic feat."

Indeed it was, Hela had discussed the Brennan affair with him at great length, as a defence analyst it was a central topic. Essentially it came down to leading by example. Brennan had arrived in the X-Universe at a singularly critical juncture. Everywhere the Xenon were on the move and no sector was immune to the sudden appearance of one of their battle groups. The big and slow L class fighters sported a formidable 50 MW of shields and mounted a pair of Alpha High Energy Plasma Throwers that could tear the shields from a lesser craft sooner than you could cry mother. Ably supported by the M Class medium fighter and packs of the high speed N class light fighter the Xenon were wreaking havoc, softening up defences for an all-out assault. The L Class even mounted the terrifyingly powerful Xenon equivalent of the Hornet missile with a matter/anti-matter warhead that could obliterate a cruiser.

Losses among all the fleets were high and mounting, system defences were being whittled away faster than new pilots could be trained, by the constant war of attrition. In many sectors the private defence fleets protecting individual stations were refusing to leave dock unless their base was under direct attack. Defences were stretched to breaking point and interstellar commerce on the brink of collapse. In this context the one man war Brennan waged on the Xenon wherever he encountered them won him unprecedented respect from lone pilots all the way up to the top of each racial pile. Eventually his deeds were of such magnitude that the governments of all the races were inspired to gamble on an all-out assault on the Xenon sectors. Denuding system defences their remaining ships gathered in Atreus Clouds and the rest as they say, is history.

"Precisely, Brennan fought, traded and bounty hunted his way to success on the basis of superior skill and equipment in an environment that maximised the impact one individual could make. For a brief moment he became a major player."

Marteene could not see where he was going with this and indicated as much.

"Patience dear boy, patience. Are you familiar with the term 'Privateer'?"

He was, in fact one of the series of sims he'd honed his combat skills on when he was young bore that title. It harked back to a time before the first Xenon conflict to the Argon Civil War. Privateers were individuals given a commission to attack enemies of the state wherever they found them in return for the major share of the booty obtained. In reality they were little more than state-sponsored pirates waging a self-funded war but a mythos of dashing heroes performing daring deeds and living outside the law had fired the imagination of little boys ever since.

"Well Mr Marteene, we've tried the slow, subtle approach and it has gotten us nowhere. Loathe as I am to admit failure I think it is impossible to infiltrate the clans at a high enough level. We can't slip in through the back door so I propose we kick down the front and demand a seat at the top table. There's an old saying in politics involving a particularly cantankerous Senator who went on to become Vice-President to a bitter rival with whom he had little in common. When asked why he had chosen him the President said he'd rather have him inside the tent pissing out than outside his tent pissing in. Crude but memorable."

Marteene had a sudden realisation as to where this was going and Artur grinned broadly.

"Yes Mr Marteene, we want you to follow Brennan's example. We want you to create such a stir that they will have to bring you inside the tent. We want you to build your own business empire, we want you to construct your own fleet. We want you to become a privateer."

## *Chapter 13: A Face in the Crowd*

A frisson of excitement tingled his nerves even as a dozen objections and protestations sprang to Marteene's lips. Boy and man.

He choked back an almost automatic, "You cannot be serious"? The Cabal operative was, clearly. A Code Black was not issued as a practical joke. Although he had only just met Artur it was obvious he was not the kind of man who did anything without thought and preparation. This whole set-up, the deftly organised recruitment all spoke of the type of person who left a minimum to chance and he had moved with impressive efficiency when his plan had fallen apart. Despite that his father and cousin had both died working for him.

There was not a doubt in his mind that he would accept the mission, he owed it to Hela and it was also his duty as an officer. Although the clandestine organisation he was now a member of was capable and resourceful, Marteene quietly resolved to watch his own back very carefully. As no doubt had Hela. Like his cousin Marteene recognised the gravity of the situation and accepted that with the failure of Artur's preferred plan the stakes had become immeasurably high.

Without a ship as advanced as the X-Shuttle at his disposal and without the Xenon as the clear and present danger they were when Brennan appeared he could not see how the gambit could be repeated. The pirate clans were a threat and they had grown bold but given the volatile nature of Clan relationships and the illicit webs of corruption and collaboration that gave them friends in high places it would be immeasurably more difficult to unify the races against them. Even if the Cabal analysis was correct and they had some time before the putative Shadow Conspiracy could benefit from the artefact, even if it had been found, Marteene strongly doubted that a single person could make the kind of impact the new scheme called for. Artur was practically asking him to set up a kind of clan, an organisation that like the privateers who had fired his young imagination through many holo-sim adventures, straddled the legal divide.

For a second Marteene permitted himself a warm memory of that time before his father's death tolled the bell on his childhood. The hours spent weaving through asteroids to shake the Xenon fighters on his tail on epic adventures to save the universe had established an unshakeable hold on his imagination. There had never been any doubt in his mind that he would become a space jock. Now he was being offered the chance to do it all for real. The boy in him could not resist and the adult conceded gracefully.

Artur watched the gamut of emotions cross the younger man's face. He knew without doubt that he would not refuse, it was not in his spirit to turn down the challenge that had been subtly couched in terms calculated to push the right buttons. Hell, if he could still squeeze into a fighter cockpit he'd be tempted himself! He would not succeed though, organisational skill and cunning would be needed but would not be enough. Artur never was and never would be a good enough pilot to meet the challenge, or an agile enough business man.

Marteene though was a great pilot and shared with his cousin a strong analytical mind. He had also demonstrated a flair for intelligence work and he would have the subtle backing of what Cabal and other resources Artur could access and be sure of. He also had Xela and although the Xenon/Human AI hybrid was new and practically untested it was a wildcard advantage Marteene had the capability to exploit to the full. His business flair was un-tested but his psych profiles indicated he had many of the traits necessary, not the least being a penchant for calculated risks. He was also a lucky gambler. Artur approved of lucky operatives but had refined his plan to give Marteene an additional edge. This he carefully omitted from his exposition of the revised plan. If it gave even him qualms he could not trust Marteene to react well. No, that was something best kept to himself and he had been careful to ensure Hela and Xela remained oblivious. Besides, it was such a small thing, probably no one would notice.

Once he had accepted an idea Marteene was not the kind of man to cavil. He knew he had to do it and having made that decision he allowed himself to surf on the wave of youthful excitement that flooded through his system. Putting objections and questions on hold he relaxed on the couch and indicated to Artur to proceed with what he was sure would be a succinct and calculated exposition.

It was.

His idea was simple, as all good ones are, with a wrinkle he would share later. The Cabal valued innovation and independence among its senior members and had seen these qualities in the younger Artur. When he became entangled in the disc affair he was bought inside and quickly groomed in the ways and resources of the Cabal. With typical quickness of mind Artur had reacted to the death and recovery of the Hela and Force by staging a simple ruse that would earn one pilot the highest of honours if Marteene succeeded. The man that emerged from the jump-gate into Scale Plate Green bore a general resemblance to Force and identified himself as such as he was plucked gasping the few remaining grams of oxygen in his life support. The radiation burns that reduced his face to a mask of suppurating sores beneath a shock of blonde hair made identification difficult but the station medics had no cause to doubt him and his survival became a fact. Artur ensured he was quickly removed to a better medical facility and restored to health whilst laying a subtle, easily over-looked trail to the Theophant's Joy Station, which among its many attractions boasted some of the best and certainly the most morally flexible body remodellers in the X-universe. Should you want a trunk on your forehead you'd receive no arguments, provided your credit was good!

Artur intended to use the services of one particular technician, a Split with a dubious and well-earned reputation for medical innovation. He had used his services before and thanks to certain well documented facts Artur had been careful to ensure Dr Phryath was aware were in his possession, discretion was assured. As far as he knew, and he took great pains to be aware, this arrangement was known only to the two of them. Like a good poker player Artur was careful never to reveal his whole hand and like all great ones he palmed a few high value cards that would become the skeleton frame supporting Marteene, untainted by the possibility of a breach in Cabal security. Much work was required before it could bear the full weight though and that work would begin as soon as this first stage was complete.

To his credit Marteene barely hesitated before agreeing to the surgery and the attendant cosmetic genetic adjustments to match body builds. Three days suspended in an accelerated healing tank, anaesthetised against the pains wracking his body as it changed and Max Force would rise again. His core genes would remain untouched and as personality, existing aptitudes and behaviour were all products of the overwhelming influence environment has in shaping the manifestation of a genetic propensity, he would remain himself. Returning his own face and body would be possible through a similar process.

It was all highly illegal and even the Teladi Medical Commerce Department agreed that this was an opportunity for profit best foregone. At least officially.

Artur was deliberately vague about the rest of the plan, conscious that for the duration of the procedure he would be elsewhere, erecting the supporting structure. Of course he had taken steps to ensure Marteene's safety whilst helpless in the tank but there was no sense in taking needless risks. Suffice to say Marteene would be discreetly provided with the resources to begin his venture.

Force himself had earned himself a minor fortune during his mercenary career and although much of it had been seized by the Raiders as was customary and a lot more had been invested in the lost Orinoco that had been his personal ship, enough existed in hidden accounts scattered across several systems to give Marteene a starting stake. Acting on information previously supplied by Hela he had moved quickly to transfer those credits into another account. There was nothing like the amount needed to purchase a good ship though and he would need at least a freighter. Artur had a solution in mind but it required a little time to finesse.

"What about my unit?"

Marteene's query was an awkward one and required careful handling.

"Ah - yes. I've taken the liberty of transmitting your, how shall I put it, resignation."

"Resignation, you mean reassignment don't you?"

"Actually no. I'm afraid the authorities are under the impression you've gone rogue. Cousin's death, balance of the mind, that sort of thing. You seemed very disturbed"

It suited his purpose that the Argon believed Marteene had stolen the shadow skin prototype. It would tie up every intelligence agency in the Federation looking for him and hopefully allow the sudden rise to prominence of a former mercenary without attracting premature attention. Besides he had not finished with Lieutenant Marteene.

It was the only part of the plan Marteene had problems with. The thought that his comrades would believe him a traitor was a heavy burden to bear but he grudgingly accepted Artur's assurances that the situation would be rectified in due course. Meanwhile the attention of the authorities in general and Commander Trasker in particular were focused on a distant sector.

With that issue settled the conspirators debated and refined the plan over several hours, fuelled by endless cups of java and the odd gourmet snack transported straight in by Artur's Dolphin. If the gamble was to succeed Marteene would need the help of the network Artur would prepare. Access to the ships of different races was crucial. Despite what the popular series of video sims based on Brennan's exploits suggested you could not just turn up at any shipyard, slap down a few hundred thousand credits and walk out with a state of the art fighter of your own race, let alone those of another species, regardless of your reputation with them. Even the Teladi would think twice about selling one of their massive Falcon class fighters to a private corporation.

The established entities that dominated inter-stellar trade were in a different position given the heavy emphasis placed on self-help in the defence strategies of all races. Long term agreements at governmental level gave them access to defence equipment but even then the levels of upgrades permitted were strictly regulated to ensure government forces retained an edge. And you could just forget about Hornet class missiles. These were so powerful that their private sale and deployment were strictly controlled so as to prevent any private grouping accumulating enough to threaten stations. A few dozen of those and you aren't a corporation, you are a super-power. Marteene would probably need these and it would take Artur some time before he could establish a new source. Fortunately there were ways and means if you were resourceful and ruthless enough.

He would also need access to the bigger energy weapons and the newly developed laser towers, neither of which were on open sale although not as restricted as the big fighters and hornets. It would all take time.

The economics were a different problem and again one the sims tended to simplify. In reality almost all the buying and selling is conducted under the auspices of long term commercial agreements. Only crumbs, in the form of the purchase of surplus production or the supply of materials to meet a temporary shortfall engendered by hostile action or just plain miscalculation were available for the small independents. Most of them barely scraped a living, what with the wildly fluctuating prices of the "shorts market" as it was known to small traders and the ever-present threat of piracy and associated battle damage. One lost cargo or a destroyed shield could wipe out a years hard graft. It was little wonder that the independents were such a fertile recruiting ground for the clans and that so many dabbled, as Petre Marteene had been forced to, in smuggling alcohol and narcotics. Only the few bounty hunters who had the great good fortune to capture a ship relatively intact really made it legitimately. Again this was a very rare event, despite what was depicted in the sims. It was practically impossible, given the power fluctuations of standard weapon systems to keep a shield of a violently manoeuvring ship low enough for long enough to trigger the automatic ejection settings and very few pilots flying a ship worth stealing would give it up easily. Most would rather die in a storm of plasma than give up a ship that represented their life earnings.

Artur could do much less to help with the business side. A quiet word here and there could steer some of the shorts market business his way and he had enough influence to ensure any bounty hunting activity Marteene engaged in was noticed by the relevant authorities. With the heavy reliance throughout the X-Universe on private law enforcement a good racial standing could be turned to commercial advantage such as the unparalleled access to the stations of all the races Brennan had earned by his exploits, even those of the Paranid and the Split. This though Marteene would have to achieve without the aid of a superior craft like the pocket battleship Brennan had flown. No, he could be a fair wind in his sails but essentially this aspect of the plan was in Marteene's hands.

Apart from that one little thing of course.

"How exactly will this privateer thing get me on the inside? I get the part about being a rich, well armed kick-ass but the clans don't co-opt trouble-makers they whack them."

"I would have thought Mr Marteene, that that point was obvious. In one hand you wield the stick, in the other you brandish the lure."

"Lure?"

"Something they want, something they need; a semi-legitimate R and D infrastructure."

The light switched on and cut through the tiredness gnawing at his concentration. A good front organisation would be the perfect guise for accessing data and expertise unavailable to the clans. Legitimate research contracts, restricted experimental equipment and honest scientists. All these things were difficult to establish and maintain deep in the fastness of space where the clans operated as the intelligence services were very diligent in this regard. It was, as Artur agreed, a long-shot and an area of the plan that required much inspired work. Marteene would have to play a lot of this aspect of the operation by ear.

Eventually, seeing that Marteene was almost grey with stim fatigue he suggested he catch a few hours sleep. Marteene agreed without demure and appeared to fall asleep the instant he lay on the couch. It had been as long and as harrowing a day for Artur as it been for Marteene but he still had work to do. Softly he instructed his ship to transport him back and sitting at his secure comms console, sipping a fine cognac, he made the final arrangements for the resurrection of Max Force.

———————————

Marteene slept the deep and dreamless sleep of the exhausted and awoke with a start to the smell of sausages and fried eggs. A fresh brew of java popped and crackled in the percolator, overwhelming the air filters with its dark, rich aroma.

"I trust you slept well Mr Marteene, would you care for some breakfast?"

He sat up groggily and rubbed the remains of sleep from his eyes.

"Uh, yea, thanks."

He took the proffered plate from Artur and took a deep, appreciative breath, allowing the savoury aromas to kick-start his appetite. The eggs were slightly under-done for his taste, the blue yolk still semi liquid. The sausages though; they looked perfect, bulging in unpierced skin and glistening with a light sheen of oil. As he accepted a mug of java he impaled one on a fork and took a bite, the beef almost melted in his mouth and his taste buds burst into life, triggered by a subtle blend of stott spices that complemented the strong, almost gamey flavour of the meat to perfection.

"Wow, these are great, my complements to the auto-cook."

"Science has yet to invent an auto-cook that could produce these Mr Marteene."

Artur permitted himself a small smile of pride.

"I prepared these to my own recipe. I have my culinary moments but the opportunity to display them can be somewhat limited. Not too spicy I trust?"

Marteene shook his head and took a sip of the steaming java. It was a light blend with just enough caffeine to ease in the day.

"The secret Mr Marteene, as with all good cooking is fresh ingredients. I grind the spices myself."

By necessity he spent a lot of time alone on the Seera and often tired of the mechanical perfection of whatever dish she prepared and over the years had honed his culinary skills to a fine edge. Occasionally he indulged himself in the fantasy of turning his back on the fraught universe of the Cabal and opening a small restaurant somewhere quiet and far away from Xenon, terrorists or any of the dozen other threats to the stability and safety of the Federation. Such knowledge though could not easily be unlearnt and with it came the sort of responsibility that would not let him turn his back no matter how wearisome the game became on occasion.

Marteene caught a fleeting expression of something that could almost be regret, and he warmed somewhat to the self controlled Cabal spy.

You've missed your vocation Artur!"

"For all our sakes Mr Marteene I do so hope not."

Marteene finished the meal with gusto, driven by the typical weak, hollow feeling in his stomach and a craving for protein that always followed a stim jag. A quick shower drove the remnant of fatigue from his system and as he massaged gel into his body he realised with a rue smile that this was possibly the last time he could look in a mirror and see himself. It would be peculiar to see a stranger looking back and he wondered, abstract theories of genes and personality aside, if it would change him in any fundamental way. It struck him then that he had no idea what this Force character actually looked like, there had been no image in the briefing and only the briefest of references to his bio. This was something he no doubt did not need to know then but it was one of the many questions he had now. In the short time he had been acquainted with Artur he realised that the man left little to chance and would undoubtedly have anticipated them.

Discarding the crumpled suit he'd slept in he donned the simple slacks and T Shirt outfit that had been left out, carefully slipping the Xela chip into a secure thigh pocket. When he returned to the office Artur sat at the work station terminal, wreathed in a shroud of grey smoke from one of his seemingly endless variety of cigars. The smoke twisted itself into complex tendrils as the hidden ceiling vents battled to cleanse the air. On the large wall screen a large 3D representation of a man in an unbadged flight suit rotated slowly whilst biographical details scrolled up the side of the screen on a continuous loop.

Marteene regarded the image for a moment.

"Mr Force I presume?"

There was no need for a reply. The man looked to be in his mid to late thirties. Medium build, bright blue eyes beneath a shock of blond hair cut and shaped in a long style some years out of fashion. High cheek bones atop a firm jaw. A large firearm was strapped in a low slung black holster on his right thigh. Marteene smiled, the man might have been a vid star idea of a pirate and he had a slight feeling that he had seen that face before, probably he thought wryly, on the lid of a sim cassette, wrapped in young women grateful the universe was safe for another day!

"Well at least my looks are improving."

"Slightly too pretty for my tastes Mr Marteene but he looks the part I suppose. The man had a certain charisma by all accounts."

Artur busied himself at the work station as Marteene absorbed the pertinent biographical details. Thankfully the man had no family and no friends outside of the tightly knit clan structure of his mercenaries and that would make the task of his new agent somewhat easier.

Gragore noted with interest that like himself the man had been trained as a pilot by the Argon Navy but had failed to graduate because of a record of indiscipline that in later years would have disqualified him even from the Maverick programme. As a younger man he clearly had problems with authority, probably stemming from the years spent in federation care following the death of his family in a monorail accident.

His service records showed he was highly rated for his pilot skills if not his judgement or sense of discipline and had graduated from the same Atmospheric ACM Training School as Marteene some years earlier. He checked the dates and realised he'd have been in the cohort above Hela and both would have been at the same post for a short period. She had never mentioned him but given the circumstances this was not surprising. It did explain his feeling of deja vu though, his image and name sat atop the ACM School Hall of Fame, the first and only perfect Air Combat Manoeuvres score. Although top of his class Marteene's final score left him some places off the pole, a fact that, with the arrogance of invincible youth had rankled at the time and driven him to relentlessly perfect his skills in the big military training simulators.

Following his dismissal from the service Force had served with some distinction in several of the station support squadrons hired by corporations to protect their assets from the ever present and increasing threat of Xenon incursions. He rose rapidly to the position of wing commander in one of the biggest security squadrons, the Fighting Falcons, so named because of the bird of prey motif that transformed the under-powered and obsolescent Buster Mk 6 medium fighters into a stark warning to flee for your life. Marteene had flown a couple of joint ops with them during the period of the last Xenon conflict as they had been one of the many private squadrons whose Reserve status had been activated. He remembered one particularly hairy interdiction in Atreus Clouds when the packs of Xenon N and M fighters seemed to fill the skies. The Falcons had burst from the sector trading station where they were supplementing the local Boron militia, claws unsheathed and turned the day. Good pilots and gutsy fighters who had earned their unit commendation that day.

Max was long gone by that time though. He'd taken his Buster out, toasted a Clan convoy in the Ore Belt and absconded with their harvest of top grade spaceweed. His fighter returned on auto-pilot some days later but Force himself simply dropped off the scope only to reappear months later on the flight roster of Rohler's Raiders.

The eponymous Rohler was a character himself; a gifted, charismatic naval officer who had failed to make the cut for captaincy and quit to form up his own mercenary clan taking most of his pilots with him. Hindsight suggests this had been a plan that he had fermented for years as he quietly gathered a group of top pilots whose loyalty to himself exceeded their loyalty to the Federation. A squadron without ships but his reputation guaranteed a procession of sponsors eager to take advantage of their skills. Flying an ill assorted collection of cast-off fighters from all the races the Raiders quickly established a reputation for skill and daring that continues to gild the name. Above all else they acquired a reputation for the most highly prized of resources in the nether-world of the Clans, loyalty. They had a code. When bought they stayed bought and would honour a contract come what may.

For many years the Raiders held a succession of contracts, accepting the best offer, moving from clan to clan but remaining above the murky and oft-times bloody affair of Clan politics. For the last 5 years the Raiders had hired their services to the largely Boron dominated Hoort Clan, flying CAP over the huge old TL that cruised the deep fastness of space beyond the Atreus Clouds sector gate system on the massive ion drives that push large capital ships to the speeds needed to move the vast distances between the planets.

After the completion of the huge mobile base that slunk out of the darkness to haunt the fringes of the sector gate system following the defeat of the Xenon the Raiders continued to fly Combat Air Patrol. The Boron quickly learned that when it came to interfering in the affairs of the Hoort it was best to grant them a little discretion. Better that than lose a carrier to the Bayamon and Orinoco fighters of the Raiders. A pyrrhic victory was no victory at all.

It was shortly after the end of the last Xenon conflict that Force became the leader of the Raiders following the unfortunate demise of the ageing Rohler in an unfortunate shuttle accident. According to reports provided by Hela and supplemented by psych profile analysis, Rohler had been the making of the reckless and impulsive younger man. He almost became the father he barely had and added the double edge of discipline and leadership to the keenly honed blade of his combat skills. Age also bought its own maturity and Force took to the Raiders code like a boron to warm salt water.

He was elected clan chief by acclaim and under his leadership the Raiders continued to thrive and eventually earned a shot at the really big time, personal guard for the leader of one of the big clans, possibly the Skulls. What Intelligence there was on this point was scarce and considered unreliable, which was why the Cabal had gone to such lengths to bring Force back into the fold. Marteene quietly doubted that the plan would have worked but he did not underestimate either his cousin's ingenuity or the cunning of the Cabal representative masterminding the operation.

That plan though was as dead as Rohler and Force. As dead as Hela.

The new plan? In his heart he did not believe it was good enough to succeed. Asking him to effectively form a new type of clan; part business, part fleet, part crime and parlay that into a position of influence with the big pirate clans was insanity. No, the plan was not strong enough to succeed, whatever help the Cabal might be able to clandestinely provide and he suspected Artur knew that.

But it was good enough for vengeance.

---

Paskaal's journey to Argon Prime was uneventful. It took several hours for the maintenance crew of the small Fleet service bay to remove the Mission AI and some of the other more sensitive equipment from the Elite as his mission would take him beyond Argon space. A quick respray to replace the military gray colour scheme with something suitably colourful and civilian and an illegal procedure to change transponder codes to a particular civilian registry and Paskaal was ready to leave.

While the mechanics laboured he had been busy. Commander Paskaal lay safely stashed in an anonymous private strong box and it was Mirv Corrin, playboy of the western universe and sometime bounty hunter that guided the heavy fighter from the docking bay. It was an identity he had cautiously established when he had first been drafted into the intelligence world, like the tiny hold-out stunner in his right flight boot. Although the trail of his putative wealth led back to the brick wall of a big casino win he knew his alter ego would not stand up to serious scrutiny. It would satisfy routine patrols though and enable him to go places a heavy fighter of the Argon Navy would not be welcome. The identity had been used in one or two Special Ops and so had some history and credibility so long as no one noticed the long gaps between appearances. The flip side of course was that it was known to Trasker and Paskaal hoped the Captain could keep her out of his hair. With luck she would be target fixated and pay no attention to his unexpected leave.

The Federation did not make a habit of allowing private individuals to purchase the latest mark of their top fighter craft but the basic hull had been in service for decades in both the fleet and in corporation security squadrons. Inevitably many older models had found their way legitimately into private hands and their elegant delta wing shape made them a popular choice for the wealthy private flyer. Very few sported maxxed out speed and cargo capacity or mounted a pair of 25MW shields and a brace of the Alpha mark plasma throwers though. Only the personal flyers of the seriously influential and of course, senior clan figures boasted such equipment. Fearing trouble Paskaal would rather gamble on not attracting undue attention than downgrade to a more common configuration. Alpha Particle Accelerator Cannons and 10 MW of shielding were still formidable, especially in his hands, but in his bones he knew he was sailing into stormy seas.

Trouble just seemed to trail some people like a mistreated pet and young Marteene was one of them, he planned to walk very softly but wanted a bloody big stick just in case. As it happened Paskaal did not have to look far to find trouble, when he exited the Eastern jump-gate into sector Cloudbase South-West it was there, just waiting for him.

The first indications were the heavy, distinctive crump of Gamma mark Particle Accelerator Cannons and a muffled explosion reproduced in stereo by the Positional Sound Array. It was SOP for military pilots to orient themselves with the notional north/south, up/down of sector geography. This Standard Operating Procedure ensured that on exiting a gate you were orientated the correct way to pull up to avoid incoming traffic. More pertinently it allowed a pilot to gain an instant tactical overview from the PSA. In the split second before his eyes flicked over the Tactical Display, a 3D sphere projected onto the HUD symbolically depicting the location of all objects within a 3km radius of the ship, Paskaal had arrived at an instinctive, preliminary, tactical assessment. Young guns like Marteene may have the reflexes but situational awareness just grew with experience and was why Paskaal was still one of the best fighter pilots in the fleet despite his years.

The action was taking place mid way between him and the northern jump-gate leading to the Argon sector of Red Light. He had watched a convoy of 3 of the large Clan Orinoco's out of the clan facility in Ore Belt, escorted by half a dozen assorted Bayamon and Mandalay fighters transverse the asteroid rich sector some minutes ahead of him. It was almost routine to see clan vessels taking this route through the Argon Federation to the Boron Kingdom many sectors to the north. It was a route that avoided the heartland sectors of Light Home and Argon Prime where the risk of encountering Fleet capital vessels was most acute. Unless looking to prove a point, which they periodically did if they felt the authorities were pushing slightly too hard, the Clans preferred to travel along routes where the main security was provided by the small Naval fighter wings flying out of the main Trading port of each sector and corporation squadrons.

Understandably the short tour reservists in their standard Buster medium fighters and the mercenaries hired to protect individual stations tended to adopt a pragmatic live and let live approach to these convoys. Unless of course they felt it was time to prove a point also.

Paskaal called up the Sector Map on the single cockpit Multi Function Display even as he banked towards the fight, gunning his afterburners to accelerate to full speed. This was a 2D representation of the jump gate sector with symbols depicting each ship, station and asteroid in the region. The blue dots were friendlies, the red ones those the Tactical Computer deemed hostile. Down the right of the map was a status list depicting the shield status of each station and vessel. Selecting any of these would bring up more levels of information. It was a simple and elegant design honed by several centuries of experience that significantly reduced the cockpit workload of the pilot. Within seconds Paskaal had a full tactical picture in his mind.

Two Orinoco's, supported by 3 Bayamons and 2 of the light, speedy Mandalay fighters had been engaged by what was now a small group of Argon fighters. Paskaal counted 3 Discoverers, a Buster and a big regular Navy Elite but even as he watched a loud double explosion coincided with the collapse of the Elite's weakened shields to under 10%. Fifty megawatts of shielding may sound a lot but a couple of the big Silkworm class missiles could take out a big chunk. In under 2 seconds the remaining shields fell and a loud rumbling explosion reverberated through his cockpit as the heavy fighter disappeared from the display. Fervently Paskaal prayed that the pilot had ejected in time.

A chill tremor of anger, tightly channelled, kicked his mind into full combat mode, where everything was slowed by the focused clarity of his concentration as all extraneous sensory inputs were filtered out leaving only what was needed for survival.

"All right my laddies, if that's the way you want to play it."

Vintage warrior's blood singing in his ears Paskaal headed at maximum speed towards the dogfight, fearing that the time it would take to close the 10 km gap could cost more lives. The Elite was a heavy strike fighter not an interceptor and with a fully maxxed speed of just under 130 mps it was one of the slower of the M3 types, comparable with the Teladi Falcon and the Boron Eel. It was optimised for strike capacity not speed, leaving the interceptor role to wings of the nimble but lightly shielded M5 Discoverer and the ageing but fast M4 Buster. Once engaged though it could use its large missile capacity to deadly effect. Under some circumstances it was able to carry dozens of Hornet missiles but Paskaal's bore only the standard mixed dogfight load of silkworm, dragonflies and wasps.

As the distance closed with what seemed agonising slowness Paskaal activated what pilots colloquially refer to as the "zoom goggles" although they are in fact a helmet mounted display projecting a live image from a nose mounted image system slaved to the movements of his head. Ground hoggers are constantly amazed to find that in many ways the Mark I Eyeball remains a pilot's most important navigational aid due to the broad band interference that is an operational side effect of the jump-gates.

Good combat pilots like Paskaal would always visually survey the combat environment to assess the best approach. Entering combat knowing the tactical disposition of the forces gives an edge. Who is attacking whom, were wingmen providing cover, what manoeuvres were being performed? These were questions that could make the difference between someone's life and death.

It was clear from the magnified whirling melange of ships that the Argon forces had lost cohesion. The 3 small Discoverer fighters were fighting as individuals instead of as the single wing standard tactical doctrine dictates. The lightly armed and weakly shielded fighters lacked the punch to quickly destroy an individual Bayamon or Orinoco but were deadly when acting as a unit to concentrate fire. The better equipped Buster was holding its own but was totally defensive. A Bayamon and Orinoco acting in concert kept it under constant attack. On the fringes of that brutal twisting furball the second Orinoco waited to pounce. Its Gamma PAC's could rip through the lone Buster's 10 MW of shields in seconds.

Two of the Mandalays were hounding an isolated Discoverer whose two fellows tried to engage the slower but powerful Bayamons in a close in knife fight.

Paskaal ground his teeth in frustration.

"Speed boy, use your speed. What are they teaching you these days?"

The faster M5's should have been using their superior speed and agility to engage and disengage the bigger fighters at will, making repeated high speed passes in formation, singling out one opponent and quickly overwhelming its defences. It was the number one rule of fighter combat, always fight on your own terms. By allowing themselves to be split up and suckered into one on ones with superior craft they sacrificed their main advantage. Even as he watched, cursing futilely and willing the last gram of speed from his engines two tiny plasma flowers bloomed to the accompaniment of twin explosions. The remaining Discoverer broke and ran leaving the Buster to face 7 ships alone. Paskaal sympathised with the Discoverer pilot, given the tactical situation he had no choice but he knew that would be no comfort to the survivor. He hoped his home base had a good counsellor.

The Buster was now in dire straits, lacking the speed to extend and escape the hapless pilot was reduced to frantically dodging and twisting, inching towards the clutter of stations near the centre of the gate complex in the hope that one of the corporation patrols would be launched in his aid. The sky around him was full of electric blue plasma bolts and his shields falling steadily. Like predators stealthily stalking a wounded prey the two Orinoco's circled, looking for the opening to unleash a devastating barrage of fire from their twin Gamma PAC's.

The fight could be over in seconds but Paskaal was now only seconds away himself and the Orinoco's had both made the same serious error. Target fixation. It was evident from their movements that neither was aware of his approach, one of them should be flying a protective CAP, looking out for reinforcements. Dumping speed rapidly he pulled up behind the first and rippled a prolonged burst along its rear, from one wingtip nacelle to the other. The ship exploded in a ball of orange flame, thousands of pieces of debris buffeting his Elite as Paskaal afterburned through the expanding sphere of burning plasma and hull fragments. The Argon Police Licence tactical sub-routine recorded the kill and announced the bounty that would be added to the long moribund account of his alter ego when it next downloaded its record into the sector mainframe.

His shockingly unexpected entrance had the desired effect with the Clan fighters breaking at speed in every direction in a frantic effort to escape. Paskaal quickly commanded the Buster.

"You laddy, form up on my wing NOW!" His tone, honed by years of command experience compelled compliance and even as he banked hard right to engage the second Orinoco the medium fighter dropped into formation.

The Orinoco was running fast, the pilot was no fool and was heading straight into the system primary, hoping the glare would provide cover until his fighter shield reformed. Paskaal quickly took in the tactical situation. The two Mandalays had paired up and were coming in fast. They didn't worry him, their lasers lacked the power to seriously dent his fully charged shields. The 3 Bayamons were another matter. They were fighters built for attack, each sporting 2 pair of Alpha PAC's and they could do serious damage to anything short of a cruiser.

The Mandalays slashed by, weapons blazing but doing only minor damage to the shields but the Elite shuddered under the impact causing Paskaal to momentarily lose track of the Bayamons as he re-established a firing position on the Orinoco. But that was why they invented wingmen.

"Bandits, bandits, 4 o clock, I'm on it!" The tone was reassuringly measured and professional. The pilot sounded young, but nowadays they all did to the veteran.

The roar of the Buster drive filled the cockpit for a second and dopplered away high and right as his wingman turned to engage the 3 closing clan fighters. The Orinoco was in firing range now twisting and turning around its axis of flight to throw off Paskaal's aim. Looking directly into the sun made visual aiming difficult and the HUD almost impossible to read.

"Fox One, Fox Two, Fox Three, Fox Four," His wingman intoned, signifying the launch of 4 missiles in military parlance, followed almost instantly by a loud explosion. "Bandit destroyed".

Paskaal held his course, trusting his impromptu wingman to protect him as he lined up the shot. Whoever was flying the heavy Clan fighter was good. Grimly Paskaal stuck to his tail and followed him through a barrel roll aimed at forcing an overshoot that almost succeeded as the clan ship rapidly decelerated. The veteran Elite pilot opened up with full guns at point blank range, ripping away most of his opponents shields before smashing through the craft with an impact that took away a good chunk of his own shields. The pirate exploded instantly, the pilot's death rattle echoing in over the comm.

"They're bugging out sir! Permission to pursue?"

"Negative Buster, negative. They're too fast."

The remaining Clan fighters, their charges destroyed were heading hell for leather for the Ore Belt jump-gate and without a jump-drive to leap ahead of them Paskaal's Elite lacked the legs to catch them.

He banked smoothly towards the complex of stations clustered between the 3 jump-gates and the Buster formed up on his wing.

The comm crackled to life and the Buster pilot appeared on screen, his youthful looking eyes wide with excitement above the mask of his flight helm.

"I don't know where you came from, but thanks, I owe you one. Lieutenant Sune, to whom do I owe."

Paskaal almost gave name and rank, ingrained military habit but gave his counter identity.

"Another day another thousand credits, I should thank you. What happened?"

"Bounty hunter huh, well you earned it." Sune had regained his equilibrium with a speed Paskaal thought boded well for his career.

"Instructor training Mr Corrin. Commander Tyre was putting me through my paces with a couple of flights of new pilots out of the station in the asteroid field beyond the north gate. That was his Elite."

On screen Sunen paused as he quickly scanned the area, confirming what Paskaal had already established. There were no survivors from either side of the engagement.

"Ah shit, that's 5 dead, someone's going to have my ass."

"Don't worry son, if it wasn't your fault the board of inquiry will clear you. How come your CO led a bunch of rookies into combat with such a serious force? Seems a bit unusual, no offence, for sector defence?"

"None taken sir, none taken. Direct orders from the senatorial office."

"Well you be sure to mention that in your report, and to Internal Affairs."

Paskaal scanned the assorted cargo containers drifting amongst the detritus of the combat and confirmed what he already suspected. High value narcotics and alcohol, probably intended for the Boron market. Someone, somewhere felt they needed a bigger pay-off.

"Er - can't let you take any of that sir."

Paskaal chuckled. "Don't you worry about that laddie, the bounty will keep the wolf from my door for another day or so and I've got other business to take care of!"

The Buster broke off to impound the cargo as Paskaal banked towards the south jump-gate. He would have preferred to have docked in the sector as planned but that would now attract too much attention. Instead he faced a long flight through sectors controlled by the sullen and unfriendly Paranid. They rarely granted docking rights at any of their stations to outsiders and then only to bounty hunters who helped them with the Clans and the Xenon. Paskaal was dying to visit the head but if he used the SETA he just might make it to a friendly sector without using the in-suit facilities.

"Good luck sir. Lieutenant Sune signing off."

Paskaal sent a short acknowledgement, clamped his cheeks firmly and accelerated at full speed towards the gate to Paranid space.

"When does this thing get done?" It was difficult for him to disguise the unease he felt at submitting to the proposed surgery especially as he knew very little about cosmetic resequencing. Confident that Marteene was committed to the plan Artur had not glossed over the risks. What was proposed was not a common procedure, indeed it was illegal almost everywhere but the Split physician who would be performing it was probably the foremost authority. He carefully avoided any mention of where and how he had perfected the technique and Marteene equally carefully avoided asking, both appreciating there was too much at stake to engage in a moral debate on medical ethics.

"Whenever you feel ready, in fact the sooner the better as I have further business to conduct. A fully equipped URA Medical Dolphin docked here while you were resting. It contains all the equipment we'll need."

"Isn't it illegal to use the Universe Relief Agency as cover for espionage?"

The gleaming white vessels of the URA, with their distinctive golden comet decal prominently emblazoned to prevent accidental attack were a relatively common sight and even the Clans would think twice before harassing them. Established by the Boron after the end of their terrible war with the Split the URA developed over the following decades into a multi-species agency adept at the rapid deployment of medical and humanitarian assistance in response to planetary or space disasters. All benefited at some time from their activities so by treaty the races undertook not to jeopardise their neutrality. Of course the Xenon had no such compunction.

The Cabal controller regarded Marteene for some moments.

"Well I won't tell them if you don't? Now do you have any less naive questions? If not I suggest we begin."

Marteene reluctantly concurred and within moments they both materialised on a transporter pad designed to transfer several casualties at once. The bay was empty except for a locker and a single gurney, hovering silently awaiting its passenger.

"I'm sure you understand but I cannot allow you to actually meet the physician. If you would remove your clothing."

He indicated the locker.

"The Xela AI will be perfectly safe, you can pick it up once the procedure is complete."

Having thrown in his lot with the Cabal Marteene had little choice but to comply. He could appreciate the need for security but the thought of being helpless in a Regen Tank while his body remodelled itself according to the revised set of genetic instructions naturally worried him.

As Marteene lay on the gurney Artur approached from the front, carefully displaying a hypo spray so as not to further alarm the understandably nervous pilot who lay unmoving as Artur discharged the powerful anaesthetic into a vein. The last words he heard as he toppled into unconsciousness were;

"See you in 3 days Mr Force."

They seemed to come from a distant, receding source and then there was nothing.

With some difficulty Artur guided the floating gurney to the adjacent lab. Medical Dolphins were heavily modified versions of the standard Boron freighter with two thirds of the sub space hold removed to create room for any two of a series of prefab modules that allowed the craft to be quickly fitted for many different roles. With only one 25MW shield it had more energy to power the drive. Consequently it had a fully maxxed speed close to that of an Argon Lifter, enabling it to rapidly deploy to disaster areas.

This lab had been hastily converted at a Cabal facility according to the precise instructions of the Split physician and Dr Phyrath had everything prepared for Marteene's arrival. The surgical platform was standard, as were the two medical bots that would function as assistants and nurses. The antiseptic white of the lab was too bright for human comfort, lit as it was for the Split doctor calibrating the sensors clustered around the operating table.

The Regen Tank in the corner, looking too much like the coffins used to consign fallen pilots to the void, was heavily modified. The additional instruments affixed to each end looked like a tagged on afterthought, ruining the smooth symmetry of the curved black tube. The bio-nutrients and plasmic fields that would force catalyse the transformation were experimental but under the circumstances Artur believed he had little choice but to proceed.

"Good. About time. Much delay. Subject prepared?"

Artur regarded the small humanoid coldly, fighting the urge to grab the large goatee sported by all Split males as a sign of their fertility and drive his knee into the pit of what passed for a stomach in that species.

"The PATIENT." Artur carefully emphasised the term. "The patient is ready." He stared straight into the eyes of the man to ensure the point had been taken. Phyrath met his gaze steadily before indicating assent with the merest shake of his head.

Artur had no wish to witness the proceedings, knowing full well that he lacked the expertise to even recognise if the Split made a mistake let alone assist. He had considered posting a watch over the helpless pilot but was loathe to incur the extra security risk. From their past dealings Phyrath understood the consequences of either failure or loose talk and he was as confident of the Split's discretion as he could be in his business, especially as he would be aware all his actions were being recorded on the security monitors.

"And the modification?"

The eyes of the Split sparked with enthusiasm as he held up the small bio-materials container for Artur to see.

"Yes, yes, all is ready, I thank you for the oppor.."

Artur cut him off brusquely. "I have no interest in furthering your somewhat distasteful research, just do it."

"Such attitude from one I help. You come to me not me you. On your conscience, me follow orders."

Sometimes Artur wished he possessed such a stain resistant conscience. No doubt Phyrath would eagerly help provide one but grey as it was it still helped him step back into the light when occasions like these compelled him to cross into shadow.

Not trusting himself to say another word he returned to the teleporter and transported back to his own ship. On arrival he sent the signal that would disable the medical ship teleporter and flight controls. The airlocks were already sealed. In 3 days he would return, meanwhile there was much still to do.

## *Chapter 14: A Lot Can Happen*

For 3 days Marteene lay somnolent, consumed in a silent dream as his face healed and his body was convulsively transformed by the new genetic instructions. The gentle background hum of the ships systems was punctuated only by the reassuringly regular signal of the tank monitor and the happy murmurings of the Split scientist. The procedure would succeed and with that success came fascinating new possibilities. He would need the right, wealthy and morally flexible sponsor but as he knew, the universe was replete with such beings.

Artur spent the time tugging on the strands of his web, cautiously severing the doubtful and spinning new reliable segments. Only once did he visit the station, to pick up a selection of ingredients from a small Boron delicatessen and to call in a marker from a much bigger fish.

Paskaal suffered a long uneventful voyage through the Paranid Empire. With relief he docked at the large orbital trading station of the Boron sector of Shore of Infinity, part of the New Frontier carved from the bones of the defeated Xenon. He was pleased to be able to stretch his legs after the hours of confinement in the small cockpit, it also gave him a chance to put an ear to the ground. As he expected though, that came up blank. No human flying a Bayamon had docked at the station, there was nothing for the Clans here and they were rarely seen, except as part of large raiding swarms from the newly established base in New Income. That Teladi sector was his destination anyway, as the signal from Marteene had come in from the adjacent Ceo's Doubt. It seemed a bit careless of Marteene to leave such a trail but a new Clan base in a Teladi frontier sector would be a good place to unload a hot ship and slip away.

Ceo's Doubt, although part of the Teladi New Frontier, was a typical trading outpost of the entrepreneurial species. The gate system was located near to a small, storm tossed world, now home to several million Teladi colonists waging a constant war to rebuild the strip-mined environment of what was once the material heart of the first Teladi Empire. That was before the Xenon had driven the Teladi from their home sectors, forcing them to exert every sinew of their considerable ingenuity to establish a new civilisation under alien stars.

Stripped by the long Xenon occupation the once mineral rich system could now muster only a couple of mines, hacking low grade ore from 2 of the few asteroids that were not mined out. With characteristic economic adroitness the Teladi had transformed the sector into a specialised trading system by exploiting its new position on the border to the Boron frontier holdings.

By establishing s couple of Solar Power Plants supported by a Crystal Fab the Teladi Trading Company established the basis for a profitable export trade in specialist food products such as Sun Oil and the widely used metal, Teladium. Trade between it and the Boron was profitably brisk but blood in the water for the Clans and the sector witnessed frequent clashes between raiding parties out of New Income, traders and sector security forces.

Despite his growing fatigue Paskaal pressed on through the new Boron sectors into Ceo's Doubt, activating the System Display as soon as he emerged from the western jump-gate. The two-dimensional map combined data from the ship sensors with information from the jump system Data Net to show the type, location and shield status of each station and ship in the sector. Further levels of detail such as ship pilot, destination and home registration could be accessed at the touch of a screen although as this information was self-declared by a craft's Identification Friend or Foe beacon it was not necessarily that reliable. System sensors automatically read the IFF transmission of each ship in a sector and combine it into a sector tactical map accessible to all. It was an essential service that performed 2 functions.

First, it acted as a security filter, ships without a valid IFF signal were automatically designated hostile and on-board systems would designate them red on tactical displays. Accessing details of destination sectors and stations also allowed a pilot to make tactical judgements of threat status so even the clans found it useful when legitimately trading to state it practically ensured station defences would adopt a "let sleeping dogs lie" approach to their passage.

Second, it significantly reduced the cost of the ships designed to work close to the jump-gate systems as they did not require the complex sensors suites fitted to most military craft and available in expensive commercial versions for the independent minded traveller.

A Clan convoy of half a dozen assorted fighters escorting two of the lumbering Teladi Vulture freighters sailed unmolested through the system, ostensibly heading for the Equipment Dock in Lucky Planets. Assorted freighters, almost all minimally equipped Vultures, crawled across the display on intra-system resource hauls and a handful of the big Falcon heavy fighters were flying a wide loose system CAP that carefully avoided the Clan vessels with a subtlety worthy of a Split.

Apart from the 3 Prometheus fighters 30 klicks out beyond the jump-gate he'd just emerged from everything was normal. The sector display confirmed that there were no stations or ships in scanner range that could serve as either destination or base which under the circumstances he found interesting.

Interest became mild concern as they altered course, adopting an vector that would bring them in for a close look if he maintained his current course and speed. Scans confirmed that each of them was fully upgraded to the heaviest weapons and shields that could be mounted on a fighter and their drives were tuned for maximum speed. The registered pilot names meant nothing to him.

Clan or mercenaries? He quickly dismissed the former. Only the elite or their elite guard flew such craft and whilst not a rare sight were certainly uncommon. The three Paranid fighters were probably looking for something as there was no base ship and if a Clan wanted to find something the display would be lit up with Mandalays. The light fighters were extremely efficient scouts having twice the speed of most heavy fighters.

Bounty hunters then? He could think of plenty of reasons why a Clan flight might choose to take on a lone Naval fighter but so far as he knew they had no scores to settle with his alter ego. In fact Mirv Corrin was considered the life and soul of the party in some clan quarters.

Revenge? He'd collected a few bounties in that persona to establish and maintain cover, mainly corporate and government commissions. Small fry stuff, nothing that would attract too much attention. Even so the possibility remained and Paskaal prudently assessed his tactical position as he banked to bring them into view over his right shoulder and into the arc of the Zoom Goggle sensor in the nose.

With the helm mounted display maximum magnification he quickly eyeballed the environs of the three fighters for debris or other signs of battle. There was none and the aural tactical sub systems had registered no sounds of conflict.

The three fighters themselves were in close formation, two wingmen flanking a leader. The broad wedge shape of the Prometheus was not to his mind as elegant as the swept wing and cockpit arrangement of the Elite but the sleek deadly design conveyed its single purpose. Engage and destroy.

Fighter design is a triangle representing total energy output. Combat systems, speed and storage capacity are the three points. The more power you allocate to one area the less you have for the other two. This is why, despite the endless carping of less intelligent pilots, you cannot have a heavy fighter with the speed of a Mamba and the capacity of a Falcon and the shields and weapons of a cruiser. Designs are all a question of trade-off.

The Paranid Prometheus is considered by many to be the finest heavy fighter of all time. With a maximum speed of 180 kps only the Split Mamba was faster, sacrificing 25 MW of shields for speed. The Prometheus design sacrificed internal storage, and with the attendant limitation on missile capacity, combat firepower for speed and protection. Even so it could carry 20 or so missiles to supplement the 2 front mounted Alpha HEPT's and combined with its superior speed this made it the best one on one dogfighter in space.

The Argon Elite was a jack-of-all-trades ship with a slightly reduced storage capacity in return for a relatively high speed of 140 kps. The only tactical advantage it possessed was a high missile load. Unfortunately the simple rocket powered devices, subject as they are to the Newtonian framework, lack the speed and manoeuvrability of their targets whose drive systems operate in an entirely different inertial framework enabling ships to perform as if they were atmospheric craft operating in a large gravitational field.

In fighter combat missiles were reduced to three tactical uses. Firing them at close range into the six of the target was the only way to guarantee a hit. Any other firing solution and most fighters could either out manoeuvre or out run the threat. Hence their second use, forcing opponents to temporarily disengage. The third use was what the designers had in mind for the Elite. Engaging superior numbers at long range head-to-head.

A flight of 3 Elites could launch enough missiles to decimate an incoming force and reduce the rest to confusion as each target sought to evade multiple locks. A couple of flights of Discoverers would add to the chaos and the broken formation would fall easy prey to the incoming Elite and Buster wings. An Argon capital ship, protected by a mixed package of Argon fighters was the toughest of nuts.

The circumstances did not warrant a pre-emptive missile strike, the fighters would be in range long before he could dock at the sector Trading Station and he had no reputation to trade for aid from any of the nearby stations.

With quietly mounting tension Paskaal watched them approach, targeting the lead ship and purposefully keeping it at his 4 O Clock. A missile launch from this aspect would be relatively easy to defeat and the tactic itself would serve to warn that he knew what he was doing.

At 10 klicks the flight maintained their close formation, if they were going to attack they would likely adopt a looser formation, probably a standard flank and engage where one would keep him occupied whilst the rest stalked him.

At 8 klicks the onboard tactical sub system assessed their course and status and designated them hostile. The HUD target designator turned red.

At 5 klicks the three fighters drifted apart and Paskaal again banked, putting them at 2 O Clock as they closed rapidly.

"Alright chaps, what do you have in mind?"

At 2 klicks the computer announced the target was within weapons range.

At one klick Paskaal flipped off the weapon safeties and angled the nose of his Elite down, poised to initiate an aggressive evasive manoeuvre.

The 3 Paranid built fighters swept over the Elite, close enough to plunge the cockpit into shadow and fill it with the doppler roar of their drives. As the flight closed formation the leader gently rocked his wings and Paskaal returned the professional compliment, relieved his cover had withstood its first test.

The Prometheus flight banked sharply and headed at speed towards the northern jump-gate as Paskaal turned towards the Trading Station at the heart of the jump-gate system. Although packs of bounty hunters were not an uncommon sight, particularly in frontier sectors, Paskaal had an intrinsic distrust of coincidences and transferred their combat sensor readings to permanent memory.

From space the Trading Station itself was a standard design, a large ring affixed by two struts to the top of a central flute cylindrical body. Two opposed pairs of elegant tapering towers protruded from the outer ring, curving gently inward like shields defending the central body. The whole station revolved slowly, providing a steady 1 Teladi Gravity to the outer ring and towers without incurring the heavy cost of gravitic plating and associated maintenance overheads. Only the central body, housing the main docking port, repair bays, storage holds, defence installations and sector administration facilities had the luxury of artificial gravity.

The station itself glittered with light from thousands of viewing ports from the many levels of both sections.

Paskaal ignored the auto-docking sub system and received grudging permission from a bored Teladi flight controller for a manual docking. As he piloted his ship through the huge main doors along the central docking port to the main bay, automatically compensating for the minor gravitational shifts endemic to the design but exacerbated by the Teladi cost cutting use of salvaged lowest bid components from every race, he activated the tactical stealth mode that would mask the complex Special Ops configuration with something more befitting his cover.

On landing on one of the dozens of landing pads that lined the curving walls of the dark cavernous docking bay Paskaal waved away the maintenance team and ran the system diagnostic and refuelling procedures himself. The Elite had sustained only minor damage during the trip, little more than a percent efficiency drop in weapon and shield subsystem performance but he authorised payment of the typically high Teladi estimate of the retuning and refuelling and added the customary 5% gratuity for the maintenance workers to avoid gratuitous tool marks on the paintwork.

The workers clustered with characteristic unenthusiasm around his ship as he set off in search of toilet facilities. This proved to be harder task than he had anticipated. It wasn't that the Teladi had a policy of denying creatures comforts to humans it was just that they didn't care. They would have your money for docking, maintenance and cargo transactions regardless so there was simply no profit in it. If a salvaged section happened to have waste facilities suitable to your species and the less than diligent Teladi engineers had stirred themselves to connect it you were in luck. Otherwise if you were an agile exhibitionist you could try using the Teladi ones.

Paskaal would rather use the flight suit system but luckily he found what he was looking for in the un-named bar that was the Teladi's sole concession to the comfort and well being of other species visitors who were barred from the majority of the station.

Hungry for even the smallest profit the Teladi Trading Company sold licenses for these establishments for a sum that reflected the pittance that could be earned from the trickle of pilots that passed through its doors. The bars themselves were salvaged plasteel partitioned disused storage bays with fluctuating gravity and power supplies. As far as Teladi Company stockholders go it was one of the lower rungs the fast falling could grab onto and the license holders tended to be at best incompetent small businessmen with eyes above the station dictated by their meagre talents and at worst criminals whose shortcomings and petty failings prevent them from ever making a success of their chosen calling.

They were generally not places the normal pilot frequented. The average freighter crew would be straight in and out of the station, heading back to more comfortable facilities provided by the stations of other species. The clientele of the Teladi establishments were altogether smaller and more colourful and the goods and services offered were correspondingly exotic and highly priced.

This one was doing better than Paskaal might have anticipated but situated astride the single frontier trade route, on the borders of the Boron Frontier with a Clan base in the next sector it was a good location. The lighting was low and the dimmed ceiling panels cast long shadows into the gloomy booths that lined four of the six walls. The air was heavy with the smoke of spaceweed that gathered in sullen clouds around the barely powered ceiling vents. A long bar, constructed from discarded storage crates painted over with the remnants of at least 3 different decorating jobs, lined one wall. A small side door was marked with a sign promising multi-species ablutions and Paskaal headed for it. The other contained a single door leading to the rest of the establishment. A large and muscular Teladi female, her lizard visage slashed by an old scar, barred the way. Noticing his interest she touched her firearm and hissed a mild warning as he passed which he returned with a smiling nod and wink that provoked a further snort.

Apart from a couple of Boron talking with a young Teladi behind the bar he was the only alien in the place and a dozen pairs of narrow reptilian eyes focused on him from all corners of the room. The bar fell silent for a moment, before the low murmur of Teladi minding and making their own private business resumed.

Relieved and refreshed he caught the eye of the Teladi bar keep and ordered a whisky, paying for it from an anonymous credit chip. Despite its price it was a cheap blend, any subtleties it might have possessed were immediately overwhelmed by the raw fumes of the crude grain spirit it had been cut with to boost profits and provide a cross-species punch.

The first long sip exploded in his empty stomach and entering into character he downed the rest of the shot in one, absorbing the impact on this system with a theatrical cry of satisfaction.

"Whoo - that hit's the spot my good man. Line of some beers, good Delaxian wheat brews, have one yourself, Mr..?"

Soon Mirv Corrin and Sisimalos Misiandos Tomulus II were on hatch number terms and a few generous rounds later the mood of the bar brightened enough for his activation of the Juke Box not to provoke a fusillade of fire. Soon the pounding sounds of Multi-Species Rock sensation Machine Heads provoked enough of a party atmosphere for the convivial Corrin to find out what he needed to know whilst making new friends.

Slipping away he popped a stim to purge the affects of alcohol and returned to his ship.

His new friend Tom, his tongue loosened by the judicious application of credits, had been very helpful.

"Humanssss .. you all look sssame but no human like that," the Teladi gesticulated to the image on Paskaal's proffered Data Comm. "Exccept you if faissse hair go." He tightened his thin lips and his tongue flicked briefly. Paskaal returned the grin.

"But other human I have ssseen. Big Paranid ssships."

One of the pilots of the 3 Prometheus fighters had been in less than two hours previously asking about a human flying a Bayamon.

"Told him many humansss fly with Clan. Sssee them all time. Could tell no more. You all look sssame you ssseee?"

Except this one, who sported an Ocular Sensor patch where his right eye should have been. That was distinctive enough for Tom to pluck from his memory once Paskaal had removed some of the financial worries that hindered its efficient operation.

The description meant nothing to Paskaal but provided enough of a clue to begin looking. If others were looking for Marteene too he wanted to know about them. There were by his reckoning 3 possible options.

They were Special Ops or associated official forces; they were mercenaries or bounty hunters chasing what would be a valuable prize, which of course begged the question as to how they found out so quickly or they were another player entirely. Paskaal was old and cynical enough to know there was always possibilities you knew nothing about. Many shadowy things swam beneath the choppy surface of the X-universe ocean and it paid to be wary.

Other denizens of the bar had been able to provide interesting insights into the real workings of this part of space, a few offers of work he politely declined and a contact in New Income.

On launching Paskaal set course for New Income in pursuit of the only clues he had.

---

Trasker slipped the data chip into her Personal Data Comm and unlocked the stored decryption key. She felt only the briefest pain in her thumb as the Gene-Loc took a blood sample to confirm her identity. Her PDC contained a wealth of sensitive information, some of it, such as the personal network from which she had recruited the bounty hunters that were tracking Marteene, unknown to all but herself and it was protected by more security protocols than most company mainframes.

Securing her quarters against interruption she sat at the table in the dining area and activated the small holo-screen. The tiny blue emitter on the side of the PDC flashed to life and projected a small rotating 3D image of Argon Prime onto the table. Janis quickly repositioned the PDC to move the default image to the centre. Although a technological marvel of molecular level engineering the inbuilt holo-tank functions did not compare to either those in the briefing rooms or that of her workstation but both of these were connected to the ship systems. She was 99% certain they were secure but preferred to review information from her sources first on a standalone, just in case.

In response to her verbal command the image of the planet morphed into a civilian Elite and she watched the record of her associates encounter with the iron-nerved Paskaal. Despite the clumsy attempt of the Captain to conceal it she had quickly learned of his mission, in fact she approved. Paskaal, particularly when under the guise of the somewhat flamboyant Corrin, was not the hardest person in the universe to follow as the unnecessary skirmish in Cloudbase South-West proved. She did not believe the veteran pilot would be able to find Marteene but there was an outside chance he was also involved or that Marteene might attempt contact. In either case she would keep him under discreet observation although that would prove difficult in sectors where she lacked ready access to Nav-Sats.

Trasker absorbed the rest of the message in silence. Her hunters had yet to find Marteene's trail but were moving onto New Income where they could obtain system traffic logs from the Clan base. It was their easy access to the underworld that made them such useful tools even if some of their other activities left a lot to be desired and on occasion required her discreet intervention.

Trasker spent some time analysing her options before encoding new orders which she transmitted via a tiny message drone to a station in Argon Prime. From there it would pass through convoluted but secure Intelligence channels to the drop in New Income. Until then all she could do was sift incoming military and intelligence reports for traces of Marteene's passing.

Paskaal nosed his ship into the jump-gate leading to New Income with more than the usual degree of caution for very good reason. The system was part of the original Teladi Empire and the entrepreneurial reptiles had moved swiftly to claim the two large habitable planets dominating the jump-gate sector. Despite the heavy losses inflicted by the unusually aggressive native fauna on scout parties the Teladi proceeded with full-scale colonisation and now millions of shareholders fought an increasingly difficult battle for survival in eco-systems so implacably hostile many suspected them to be products of Xenon genetic manipulation although it was not thought the terraformers possessed such organic expertise.

Unwilling to throw good credits after bad the Teladi Trading Company severely curtailed support for the struggling colonies and confined itself to securing the system for interstellar trade. In the face of such desperation and neglect both colonies became havens for criminal elements and rapidly descended into a state of lawlessness and anarchy from which emerged a new criminal alliance that rapidly and bloodily evolved into a new Clan, complete with an orbital station. Recognising the need for a stabilising influence the Teladi Trading Company afforded the Base considerable latitude whilst discreetly encouraging attacks on Boron traffic through the region, provided it was outgoing of course. There were good profits to be made from the resale of the salvaged cargoes and in New Income one claw vigorously washed the other.

Paskaal was not expecting a fighter as potent as his Elite to attract trouble although it was certain to elicit comment and speculation. The three mercs were the wild cards and he emerged from the jump-gate poised for evasive action but the sector was quiet and the Prometheus fighters nowhere in scanner range. Banking first up and left to avoid a large Boron Dolphin freighter and a pair of Piranha escort fighters he set course for the Clan Base.

Although a known bounty hunter he was reasonably certain of a neutral welcome. The lines between mercenary, pirate and bounty hunter were thin grey and permeable boundaries, often crossed. Clans found it suited their deeper purpose to adopt an open-base policy and all who were willing to lay aside their differences were welcome to do business in the large public sections of the often ramshackle constructs.

The open-door policy also ensured that at any time there would be hundreds of relatively innocent bystanders functioning as a human shield to deter an all-out assault.

Even so he approached at half speed, allowing plenty of time for the clan flight controllers to ascertain he was not loaded down with the big hornet missiles, a couple of dozen of which could vaporise the entire station.

The base itself was a characteristic clan design; a huge sphere constructed from the dismembered remains of obsolete transporters and salvaged warships. A brief recce through the zooms confirmed what he already knew from intelligence reports; this station was constructed substantially from a combination of wrecked Teladi and Xenon capital ships from the previous conflicts. The big ion drive, mounted opposite the main docking bay was of more recent vintage. Somehow they had acquired the drive system of one of the two Teladi colony vessels, a fact that spoke for itself concerning the real relationship of the Teladi Company to the pirates in this sector.

Other intelligence on the nature and capabilities of the Clan had proven hard to come by given the location, deep within a Teladi controlled section of the New Frontier. Although unusually cosmopolitan by normal standards the new clan was named for its current chief, a Teladi female known only as Pilates. According to his loquacious friends in the previous sector nothing was known about this figure, only that she was the one left standing after the end of the fierce internecine warfare that bloodily birthed the clan. Rumour and wild speculation naturally filled this information vacuum, the most popular opinions being that the whole Clan was just a Teladi Company shell or that Pilates was a front for one of the large clans, most usually the Skulls.

As he hailed the station for docking permission Paskaal watched the nearest of the 8 Laser Defence Towers that protected the base from anything but the most determined of assaults for signs of activity. The barrels of the Gamma HEPT's remained quiescent and unmoving as Flight Control considered his request.

From her voice the controller was Argon, grudging and suspicious.

"Okay Corrin, you're clear to dock but leave your business at the gates, we run a quiet station here, understand?"

"Roger that Pilates, I know the score." Paskaal slipped on the Corrin persona like a lounge lizard slips on a tux. "And you sound a fine looking gal, how about you showing me around Ms...?"

"Call me Kaitrin. I've pulled your file up and you should be ashamed of yourself, you're old enough to be my father! I'm off shift in 3 hours, there's a Boron seafood joint on the central plaza. You're buying."

Chuckling Corrin guided his ship into the central docking bay.

## *Chapter 15: Xenon on the Starboard Bow*

Corrin barely had time to crack the cockpit when the Red Alert klaxon sounded and the main docking bay erupted into chaos around him.  A group of human mechanics raced to a flight of 3 Bayamon fighters, festooned in Systems Diagnostics cables, at the far end of his platform and he grabbed the shoulder of one as she passed.

"Hey, I've just arrived.  What's going on?"

"How the frick would I know, do I look like a commander?"

She shook off his grasp and raced after her colleagues who were running hasty flight checks on all 3 fighters.

"Watch the screen."  She gesticulated back through the confusion towards a large display at the rear of the platform.  Even as she spoke the old model 2D design flashed into life with a burst of audio-visual static before resolving into an image of a male Teladi, who judging from the dry wrinkling of his green leather face, was advanced in years.  His voice though was calm and his eyes bright alert.

"Attention all residentsss, attention all residentsss.  We have many Xenon, inbouund.  Convoy under attaahk.  Triple bounty to aaall who help."

Paskaal smiled broadly through his bristling moustache, hardly able to believe his luck.  Another chance to tangle with the machine-heads and the opportunity to establish his bona fides with the Clan Base!  Ignoring the tactical readout on the big screen Paskaal raced back to his fighter, requesting and receiving launch clearance even as he patched his own tactical display into the station public data feed.  The eastern jump-gate symbol was almost swamped by a sea of red dots and his view of his luck faded as he rapidly absorbed the problematic tactical situation.

Rapidly scrolling down the screen to the detailed vessel readout he counted 15 Type N Light, 10 M medium and 6 L Heavy Xenon fighters engaging a dozen Bayamons and a single Orinoco, depicted in blue.  It looked like they'd just entered the system, with the Xenon in hot pursuit. Even as he guided his Elite out of the docking port 3 new red dots sprang on-screen.  A blue icon winked out.

Paskaal shot out of the station into a rabble of Clan fighter types chaotically attempting to form up into flights and forcing him to bank to clear the melange.  Around the station the Laser Defence Towers were coming on line, each swinging their glowing barrels in the direction of the distant Xenon forces.

The besieged Clan fighters were making slow progress, limited by the low speed of the Orinoco and the Eastern jump-gate was over 60 klicks from the base.  Outgunned and out-numbered they were not going to make it.  Targeting the Orinoco for a quick zoom recon, he absorbed the scene in a few seconds.  The pirates were putting up uncharacteristically fierce and disciplined resistance, some Bayamons fighting in wingman pairs to cover the retreating Orinoco and others engaging the pursuing Xenon in a desperate rear-guard action, using their superior speed in slashing attacks to evade the heavy plasma throwers of the L Class Xenon.

Instantly Paskaal hit the turbo boost and was 3 klicks out from the base before he realised he was alone. The station defenders remained huddled under the protection of the base Laser Towers and showed little concern for those he presumed must be colleagues of at least some of them. It might have been good tactics but in the eyes of the veteran warrior it was a piss-poor morality. The comm channels were blocked with the frantic babble of barely contained panic and he could not get through to the base or any other ship. It was a far cry from the stark professionalism he was used to and severely reduced the defender's effectiveness. Discipline can be a potent force multiplier.

Three distant explosions, almost merging into one, rolled from the cockpit speakers. The TAC showed one less Bayamon. Paskaal knew his gesture might be futile but held his course. Trasker would have laughed straight to his face but he was constitutionally unable to sit by and watch brave sentients slaughtered by xenophobic mechanical beasts for the sake of the mission. At full speed it would take him at least 4 minutes to reach the beleaguered fighters and he did not know if they had that long. To his relief the scanner showed three defenders had broken away from the pack around the base and were rapidly closing the distance between them. He hoped they were Bayamons, the lightly shielded Mandalays would be almost useless against these odds.

They weren't.

The black Prometheus fighters pulled alongside in a loose Finger 3 formation, matching his speed. The leader, his face concealed behind a mirrored faceplate, returned Paskaal's thumbs up with a laconic salute and the four ships hurled towards the twisting furball of Clan and Xenon fighters.

The besieged Clan fighters were putting up a desperate fight but were outnumbered 3 to 1 and out-classed.

The Bayamon is a fine offensive craft and although the Alpha Particle Accelerator Cannon was not the most powerful weapon mounted on a fighter, four of them could still tear down the shields of most ships in seconds. With only a single 5MW shield though it was very vulnerable to the bigger weapons of any medium or heavy fighter. It was a ship designed to operate aggressively in packs, relying on its superior speed for safety. Tied to the retreating Orinoco they were vulnerable and as Corrin raced towards the battle another blossomed into fire.

They might have been out-gunned but the clan fighters were superior pilots. In the long frozen seconds before he engaged Corrin noted the disciplined wingman pairs were managing to opportunistically pick off the smaller N and medium M fighters. A trail of debris and scorched cargo canisters marked a trail of destruction back to the jump-gate but they were making little headway against the 50 MW shielding of the formidable L type heavy fighters. Their Alpha mark plasma throwers could destroy a Bayamon or Orinoco in seconds and forced to fly defensively the defenders could do little more than distract them from the slow Orinoco as it gyrated desperately towards the distant safety of the Clan base.

Despite the almost preternatural skills of the Orinoco pilot, who threw the ship across the sky in manoeuvres that must have had the plates popping from the hull, it did not have the legs to outrun the heavy Xenon fighters. It was all the flier could do to twist away from incoming fire snaking around the ship before it tore away all the shields and snap the occasional burst of twin Gamma HEPT's at enemies flashing across its bow.

At 2 klicks Paskaal flicked off the safeties and checked the missile load. Silkworms; slow but with a warhead guaranteed to ruin someone's day. Ahead of him space was a whirling mass of fighters and the cockpit was filled with the cacophony of battle, the staccato tattoo of Bayamon Alpha PAC's prominent over the deep slow pounding of plasma throwers.

Paskaal thumbed the short-range transmitter as he led his impromptu wing in a sweeping arc that would bring them into the fray with the system primary, bright and concealing at their backs.

"Okay, let's cheese it!"

The 3 Prometheus fighters peeled off from his wing and hurled themselves at a group of Xenon falling on the Orinoco. Paskaal had hoped one of the mercs would have formed up on him but lost no time worrying about it. Although trained to fight in pairs like all Special Forces fighters he was well versed in the difficult and dangerous art of solo combat and was flying what he considered the finest fighter in space. As well equipped as the Xenon L the Elite was nearly 50% faster, more agile and carried a large missile load. Singling out a mixed flight of 3 M and 2 L fighters that had burst through the Orinoco's thinning fighter screen unchallenged Paskaal targeted the lead L and entered the fray.

Nothing gives you the tactical advantage in battle more than the element of surprise and Paskaal was in amongst the attacking group before the Xenon ships had registered his presence. Decelerating rapidly he rolled in on the tail of the first XL, let fly with a 5 second burst into the rear which knocked down a quarter of the target's shields and at 100 metres triggered 4 silkworms before rolling away to port. The powerful missiles slammed sequentially into the Xenon craft, ripping away the remaining shields and sending it tumbling like a kicked children's toy before the exploding drive system tore it apart.

Mechanically the onboard computer announced the gratitude of the Teladi Company.

That and 2 credits would get him java and a Big C.

A brief burst of afterburners bought the second XL within range even as it broke off its attack run on the Orinoco. Pulling right up on its tail Paskaal ignored the ominous pounding of Gamma PAC's, close over his left shoulder as the escorting Xenon M's zeroed in on the new threat, and poured on fire, completely draining his weapon's energy reserves. Holding his position as the target arced high in an effort to shake him he launched 3 more missiles. The Xenon broke right, causing one silkworm to sail under the left wing. The other two caught it four-square though and the Xenon blew apart, battering the Elite with debris as it shuddered through the shock-wave.

If you've ever been in combat you know what veterans mean when the talk of "battle time". With every instinct, neurone and cell of your body focused on survival time flows like molasses on a cold day. Fractions of seconds stretch into long moments and thought and reactions becoming impossibly fast, or when death looks down the barrel of twin Alpha HEPT's, nightmare slow.

Brain and body flooding with an intoxicating mix of adrenaline and endorphins Paskaal was in that groove now; his mind and body at one with the moment, all senses sucking in data and filtering out all but that needed fight and win. He was wise enough to admit to himself, if not others, that this was the sort of moment he still lived for. The clean thrill of combat where life becomes a calculated gamble on the spirit and skill of you and your comrades against those of the enemy. Nothing roused his romantic warrior spirit more than the Xenon, a foe without any shades of grey and whose death did not summon brooding phantoms in the dark early morning hours of the soul.

No Combat AI; regardless of Predictive Combat Subroutines, electronic reactions and data banks of Space Combat Manoeuvres could match the potent blend of skill and instinct occasionally illumined by genius a veteran sentient pilot bought to the fray. It was why the "meat" was still "in the seat" despite what desk jockeys like Trasker would wish and it was why the Xenon continually met with defeat despite their overwhelming numbers.

The three Paranid fighters cut a ruthlessly efficient swathe through the groups of XM and XL fighters, each one laying a withering hail of emerald plasma bursts across the shields of different ships whilst barely deviating from formation. The Xenon assault exploded into chaos as evasive sub-routines wrecked wing formations.

Space was filled with the howling of drives and the baneful beating of particle accelerators and plasma throwers on energy shields as Paskaal jinked and weaved through the snarling battle. Glowing coils of plasma of varying hues snaked through the tumult, dominated by the spectacular blue expanding energy shells of the Gamma Particle Accelerator Cannon.

Shields falling rapidly in the crossfire of a pair of XM's he threw the Elite inverted and pulled up into a climb. This was not only a reaction ingrained from hundreds of hours of training in atmospheric craft where an inverted negative g dive was much less punishing than a positive one. It was good technique and he had not become a veteran by blindly diving into situations that with a twist of the flight stick he could climb into with full situational awareness.

As he climbed he rotated the Elite taking in a full tactical 360 and rolled out of the top on a heading 120 degrees to port of his original direction. The classic Split-S SCM bought him on the tail of a wing of 3 XM's closing on a lone Bayamon fighter too entangled with a couple of XN's to notice. Nailing the starboard wingman with a sustained plasma burst Paskaal punched off 4 dragonfly missiles at the leader as he swung onto the six of the third Xenon. Two of the medium missiles hammered into the rear of the flight leader as it mechanically initiated a right break rollaway. The other two missed by metres and swung back towards their target on long lazy exhausts. They had little chance of hitting but kept their target occupied enough for its former prey to finish it off with a concentrated burst from its 4 Alpha PAC's.

The XM had a slight speed edge over the Elite but not enough to stop Paskaal strafing its shields as it passed beyond weapons range. The red bar projected onto the cockpit HUD depicting the shield strength of the target fell by 50%, enough to trigger another defensive break that sent the remaining plasma bolts sailing harmlessly by but allowed Paskaal cut inside the curve back into firing range. At 800 metres he opened fire, leading the target with an experienced eye that could solve complex equations involving the relative speed and direction of a target relative to the Elite and the muzzle velocity of the Alpha HEPT far better than any machine. It exploded as the Elite was rocked by incoming fire, high left side.

Shields falling rapidly from the combined assault of two closing XM's Paskaal pulled a hard left turn as the missile alert sounded 5 times. The Elite was not quite fast enough to outrun missiles but could easily out-manoeuvre them in the turn but that left it more vulnerable to fighter attack and the Xenon took full advantage as more ships joined the chase. It was all he could do to avoid the incoming missiles and fire from multiple vectors as he located and targeted the fleeing Orinoco. It was 8 klicks distant now, with a brace of Bayamons swatting away the harassing pack of XN fighters. A wing of XM's closed rapidly from the rear.

The Elite shook like a toy under multiple plasma strikes, shields steadily dropping to zero as he fought to keep the pack of fighters off his back while defeating the missiles. One by one the computer noted their destruction as their fuel cells emptied, two more XM's fell to his plasma's and another to a ripple of dragonflies before the missile alert fell silent.

Taking out one XM with a decelerating barrel roll and another with an oblique burst as he hit the turbo Paskaal twisted to engage a pair of XL's as they swept past him. Targeting the leader he fire a couple of Silkworms to keep it off balance as he took on the wingman. It was good, negating his performance advantage by constant speed changes that forced him to decelerate to avoid collisions and keep on its six. Alert to his presence and manoeuvring violently the Xenon was a hard target and a full charge of twin Alpha plasma throwers was not quite enough to bring down 50MW of shielding. Two of his dragonflies flew harmlessly past the XL, unable to track the target and Paskaal was forced into a defensive break as the lead Xenon L re-engaged, hammering his shields down to 35% and launching a hornet missile. He hit the strafe drive and the multi-vector thruster slammed the Elite violently to the right, causing the hull to groan in protest but the hornet flashed by his cockpit, close enough as they say, to read the serial number.

Two more hornets launched forcing Paskaal to concentrate on defeating them. Unlike a dragonfly, or even a silkworm, the hornet missile was powerful enough to destroy an Elite with one hit and it taxed even Paskaal's skills to evade all three while engaging two of the powerful XL fighters. One by one the missiles exploded harmlessly as he struggled to keep out of the Xenon firing arcs while still distracting them from the retreating Clan ships. Two more XM's joined the fight, forcing him to go almost totally defensive as space filled with dragonfly missiles. One or two hits from these smaller missiles he was prepared to take on the chin and he took out one of the XM fighters with a head-on pass that left his shields at 20%.

Breaking and strafing with faultless precision while they slowly recharged the Elite danced through the streams of incoming fire rolling in on the tail of the remaining XM long enough squeeze off a burst of plasma that ripped away half its shields before the crashing impact of Alpha HEPT's from an XL coming in from the rear forced him to strafe-drive left. The XM exploded as the XL's fire smashed its shields flat. Pulling a long arcing turn that barely kept the pursuing weapons at bay Paskaal abruptly transformed it into an inverted roll that bought him in behind the lead XL leaving the missiles to explode harmlessly as their fuel ran out.

A brief burst on the turbo bought him to within 100 metres of the Xenon fighter, all the while raining fire onto the shields. Manoeuvring systems temporarily overloaded it held a straight course for a fraction of a second too long, long enough for Paskaal to send a couple of missiles up the XL's tailpipe before  rolling away from the incoming fire of its wingman.

The shockwave of the exploding XL rocked the Elite as it soared away to engage the remaining XL.

Suddenly space was filled with Bayamons as the Clan Base defenders belatedly swept into a conflict that now looked winnable. Emboldened by this a trickle of Teladi garrison fighters emerged from the orbiting stations and the tide of battle rapidly turned.

Paskaal sifted through the detritus of victory, scooping drifting storage canisters into the subspace folds of the small Elite cargo hold. Around him the three mercenary fighters prowled on their own salvage mission, one of their number occasionally breaking off to lurk menacingly on the six of any jackal that tried to partake in the feast.

To the victor, as always, go the spoils.

With his supply of Dragonfly missiles replenished Paskaal headed back towards the clan station. His blind date was still handling docking procedures and cleared the holding pattern to bring him straight in.

"Hi there lover - permission to dock, bringing you into a private bay. I'll see you at the party."

Kaitrin switched channels to deal with the rest of the traffic before he could quiz her further and he allowed himself to relax as the auto-dock took the Elite through a maze of side tunnels deep into the station. As the Elite glided to rest on a small docking platform in what looked like one of the station defence bays a small tidal wave of cheering sentients swept in to engulf the fighter. Snapping into persona, Mirv Corrin stood on a wing theatrically milking the applause from the multi-species sea. Allowing himself to be hoisted shoulder high he was borne through the cheering throng to the rear maintenance bay where an energetic victory celebration, driven by an anonymous 4/4 metal beat pounding from the comms was already well underway.

His feet had barely touched the deck when a large foaming stein was thrust into his hands and he took a long draught of the dark, bitter tasting drink. The subtle blend of Stott spices, melding seamlessly with the strong bite of hops, spoke of one of the new interstellar micro-brews that younger pilots back from planet-side spoke of with enthusiasm. It was too chilled for his liking but cut through the dry stale aftertaste of the battle clogging his mouth and he quaffed it down in one to the assorted cheering, banging and clicking of the other party-goers.

Another glass appeared in his hand instantly, thrust there by a hulking crew cut of a man at the point of a flying vee of 5 pilots in grey combat flight suits that had forced its way through the backslapping crowd.

"Put it there Commander."

The giant pilot seized his hand and pumped it hard, threatening to dislocate Corrin's shoulder in his enthusiasm. The other pilots crowded around, slapping his back repeatedly and spilling most of the beer onto the metal decking.

"Corrin. My pleasure and profit."

"Payter, but call me Sarge, everyone else does. Marine." He smiled ruefully as if that explained everything, which it might. The big man had the distant, narrow-eyed stare and the same ageless, haunted face of a combat veteran. Paskaal had seen it many times before, etched on the faces of those who dealt with the enemy up close and personal where taking a sentient life left a visceral mark. He could have been 25 or 50.

"Freeloading bastards." He regarded the convivial mass with distaste and nodded towards the rear of the bay. "There's more people who want to shake your hand, you got us out of a real screw-up."

"How many didn't come back?"

"None, thanks to you friend. We lost a lot of ships though, our Spade was crammed."

His eyes hardened.

"The Raiders don't leave comrades behind."

Engulfed by his new friends Corrin was swept through the happy crowd to the small ready room at the back of the bay. A dozen more human pilots were waiting and he endured another congratulatory pounding before Sarge silenced the room with one wave of a meaty hand.

"People - we got ourselves into a whole universe of hurt today and we wouldn't have gotten out of it but for this guy. Mirv Corrin, remember that name because we owe him one."

"That you do lads, that you do but I'm being paid a pretty bounty by your bosses. I wasn't the only one there either. The prommy mercs were in on it."

"Yea, but you led the way while the rest of 'em lurked in the skirts of the lasers." Sarge was making no attempt to conceal the note of bitterness that crept into his tone. "And the mercs just went after the kills, you flew cover. That's a difference we won't forget."

Draping one huge arm around his shoulder the big man gestured back towards the maintenance bay.

"Enjoy it friend but join us in Briefing A, someone will point the way. We have a proposition if you're interested. An hour or? Excellent."

Paskaal, like most pilots, had more than a healthy respect for the fickleness of Lady Luck and when she smiled his way he knew to take advantage. Getting on the inside with a merc squadron stationed in the very area Marteene was last located in was too good an opportunity to miss especially given the paucity of real leads. Fighting off fatigue he glad-handed and bon-homied his way through the party like a Senator up for re-election.

"Ah, the man of the moment!"

It took him a split second to place the voice.

"Kaitrin I presume?"

"It sure is lover, that was some great flying out there, the bosses were very impressed."

The flight controller was older than he would have judged from her voice, late twenties or early thirties but with her dark hair cut short and shaped in an up-to-the-second style favoured by much younger fashion victims. Her dress too, clinging to every millimetre of her short slight figure and morphing from one design to another in a complex interplay of body readings, pheromones and environment, could have been a straight download from fashions bleeding edge. He'd heard that you could learn to read the emotions and mind of the wearer from the transformations of the mood fabric but had dismissed it as a marketing ploy. Watching a blood red glow spreading tendrils from her chest, suffusing the black and gold with ruby striations he was not so sure but when she threw her arms around his neck and drew his lips down onto hers he was thankful his flight suit was made of a much more mundane material.

It had been a long tour.

"I've got something for you here somewhere. Ah, here it is."

Paskaal was not quite sure where she could have pulled it from but he slipped the credit chip into his Data Pad.

"Oooh - look at all those noughts! I guess the evening is on the machine-heads."

The Clan had been true to their word. At triple rates the bounty for the kills registered by the station sensors amounted to a more than tidy sum and eased some of his worries concerning the financing of what was a very unofficial expedition.

"I think it must be my dear, I think it must indeed be. Do you have any suggestions?"

Kaitrin smiled wickedly.

"I'm always full of those lover but how about a meal first. The Boron seafood joint, remember? And we just have to do something about those clothes. Let me guess, it's a choice between the flight-suit and your best flight-suit right?"

Paskaal nodded, suddenly aware of the many hours he'd been in the cockpit.

"Men!" She rolled her eyes theatrically. She ran an appraising eye over him. "Give me that."

She plucked the credit chip from his hand.

"When you're done with the boys meet me in the Bazaar, Level 3, Section 4. Say an hour? If I don't show grab a java, there's a great little pastry place. I'll be bearing gifts but try and grab a shower first. Fear sweat and testosterone just ain't a winning combination even for a fighter slut like me okay?"

Aware there was really no point in arguing he agreed. Only later did he wonder at the wisdom of letting a complete stranger wander off with a small fortune but dismissed the thought. Paskaal was old enough to look every young pretty Voor in the face and count its mandibles but figured that if she was playing some sort of game it would be more complex than a simple fraud. You'd have to be pretty stupid to steal Clan bounty from the hero of the hour on their own station and whatever she was he was certain Kaitrin was not that.

And on the other hand she could be genuine. They'd made arrangements before the Xenon incursion kicked off and all things considered he thought it very unlikely that his arrival could have been anticipated in time for someone to arrange their "chance" encounter. The chance to make a contact in her position was an opportunity not to be missed and he was not so old as to be inured to other more personal options that might open up during the course of a convivial evening.

With that happy thought in mind Corrin went in search of the briefing room to find what new hand fortune was preparing to deal.

The Briefing Room was no more than part of a small partitioned cargo hold that appeared to be serving as the merc squadron base. The bare metal walls and the jury rigged patches into the station power grid that drove the obsolescent computer systems suggested a recent occupation, confirming what Paskaal had already discovered. The Raiders were a very recent addition to the clan complement.

The atmosphere was in stark contrast to the celebratory mood of the party. The four other Argon pilots, huddled in a quiet but heated discussion with Payter around the Tactical Tank, radiated suppressed anger like a leaking reactor.

"We're agreed then?"

The pilots indicated their assent with various degrees of enthusiasm but shook his hand warmly enough when Sarge made the introductions.

"Corrin - we've done some checking and you've a good rep. An honest bounty hunter who goes for the big specials not one of those opportunist scum who blast every clan vessel they come across just to collect a few hundred credits. We can live with that."

The hulking merc fixed each of his comrades with a inquisitorial stare.

"Right?"

No one demurred although the only female, a compact barrel of a woman whose plain features were further marred by a badly re-set broken nose, fixed him with a pugnacious glare. Corrin could understand their attitude. Clans and bounty hunters inhabited the same grey universe despite the conflicts of interest and over the years a loose unofficial code had developed to moderate conflict. As predators the Clans understood that they had a symbiotic relationship with their prey. Interstellar trade existed to be harvested not hunted to extinction and so the clans were almost as opposed to those who brutally plundered the shipping lanes as the authorities.

It was not a moral choice but practicality. Attacking a convoy and forcing it to jettison cargo was one thing, no matter how many escort fighters were destroyed, obliterating traders simply to salvage whatever survived the explosion was another. It was wasteful of lives, equipment and property. Worst of all it forced the authorities to take action and when they did the clans inevitably lost. No clan, no matter how rich and powerful could stand toe to toe with a Fleet, relying on a combined strategy of bribery and strong defences to make dealing with them militarily a dauntingly expensive exercise.

Large bounties available on those who transgressed the unwritten rules of the game were as likely to be posted by Clans as by species governments, corporations or the guilds. Bounty hunters were thus grudgingly tolerated by all sides but loved by none and the clans set great store on those who as they saw it, played fair by the rules and only hunted the large bounties and Xenon. Those who also earned credits by intervening in raids and responding to distress calls were also officially tolerated by the clans, who pragmatically accepted the need to earn a living, but they could expect an unpredictable response from individuals. It was a grey world, of different shades.

"Okay, I'm listening." His first instinct had been to refuse, not wishing to be side-tracked from the search for Marteene. It was a big universe though and with the trail grown cold he could be anywhere, including planet-side. Whatever the mercs had in mind going along would establish his cover and give him access to other information sources.

An almost imperceptible look of relief slid across Payter's face and Paskaal sensed the former marine had a strong personal stake in the proposal.

"You've heard of us right?"

"A merc squadron called the Raiders? Every merc pilot with a fighter and a few mates call themselves that."

"Rohler's Raiders, Commander Corrin. Now I know a man in your profession must have heard that name before."

Paskaal nodded as he dredged his memory for a few facts from the hundreds of Intel Reports he'd reluctantly skimmed as part of his duties.

"Of course, you're a long way from home."

"Circumstances change Commander, circumstances change."

It was an innocent statement but the tension in the small room inched up several notches. Paskaal could read the anger in the stiff body language and white-pursed lips of the pilots but no one interrupted their leader.

"For reasons that do not concern you we consider our previous contract annulled. We are pulling short-termer here now. The Xenon have been getting a little frisky of late and the Teladi are as likely to step aside as fight so we're here to add a little spine. Take a seat."

Corrin joined the pilots at the Tactical Tank, the holo display showed an un-named jump-gate sector harbouring a fleet of capital ships and a swarm of supporting fighters. Two unidentified space stations were the only visible structures. The key identified them all as Xenon. The galactic chart placed them only 2 sectors away.

Paskaal whistled softly. A whole Xenon task force was practically on their doorstep, no wonder the Clan was rattled.

"You see the problem?"

"I do. You want my advice? Pack."

"Relax Commander, the Xenon are not your main concern." Payter slid a data chip across the table and Corrin slipped it into his Data Padd and skimmed the file. "That man is".

Corrin listened in silence as Payter filled in the background details. The target was the commander of the merc squadron. His Orinoco had vanished into the nearby Xenon dominated sector and both he and his co-pilot were presumed lost. It was unstated but it was clear from the demeanour of the group that they suspected foul play but the fact that they were here suggested that they had no proof. The squadron had offered their services to this Clan because of the proximity of the Xenon sector and had reconnoitred it in force at the first opportunity, finding nothing but provoking the Xenon counter attack.

Paskaal could feel the weight of expectation in the studied silence of the merc pilots and cleared his throat awkwardly.

"Aye lads, I don't think there's enough credits in the universe to send me into that amount of trouble to retrieve a corpse."

Payter handed him another data chip.

"We received this 12 hours ago, encrypted using our top level key."

It was a single blurred frame showing a man in a flight suit lying on an anti-grav gurney and hooked into a field life support module, from the interference patterns Paskaal guessed it was ripped from a security monitor with a Snoop Scan. Whoever had transmitted it had taken the trouble to block out any codes that could be used to identify the location. The mercs own analysis of the frame was attached as an appendix. Computer enhancements revealed a face burned almost beyond recognition but if the sub-routines interpolating the facial features from the bone structure were to be believed there could be no doubt. The injured man was the merc commander, Max Force.

"Find this man and 100,000 credits will be transferred to any account you name. Agreed?"

Paskaal swiftly weighted up the options. He was loathe to get side-tracked into some clan game when his own mission was so pressing but on the other hand it would be difficult to reject such a lucrative commission and remain in character. Cementing his relationship with the mercs could only help this and future missions and he was not entirely sure if it was an offer he could safely refuse.

Paskaal shook Payter's proffered hand.

"Agreed."

For the first time a genuine smile fractured the granite face of the ex marine.

"That's good, that's good. We've got no bloody idea what's going on but we're making our own enquiries. We're betting that in your line of work you must have a lot of well-placed contacts. You can also go places where we'd get our tails blown off. Find him and bring him back to us alive, or if you can't, send the information to us. The key word here is 'Alive'."

Another data chip was passed across.

"Use this channel and this key."

Paskaal nodded and slipped the chip into his flight suit.

"And one other thing." Payter was no longer smiling. "This is a private arrangement, if you talk about it outside this room, well, that 100k bounty will be put to a different use okay?"

Corrin acknowledged the threat with equal gravity and after a round of good lucks went in search of the Bazaar and his new friend.

## *Chapter 16: Aces High*

Marteene bolted upright, the hiss of the hypo spray still echoing in his left ear. The effort hurt but he propped himself up with his elbows, waiting for the room to stop spinning. Within seconds the nausea and nightmare remnants faded as the stimulant kick-started his body from its long sleep. Slowly the room came into focus as two blurred shapes moved around him.

"Ah, welcome back."

Clumsily he took the proffered mug from Artur, spilling some of the hot java onto his robe.

"Careful, careful. It might take a little time for your reflexes to adjust."

Taking a long sip Marteene closed his eyes and luxuriated in the sensation of the caffeine tripping along his nervous system.

"Thanks".

The sound of a stranger's voice jolted him to full awareness. A kaleidoscopic flood of images, blurring recent events with the fading touch of dream memories, flooded his brain causing a moment of panic and confusion as it strained to rebuild a coherent framework of reality. A reality in which Hela was dead.

Marteene embraced the pain, as visceral as when he first heard the news, allowing it to diffuse along the nervous system throughout his body until it became only a dull ache on the fringes of consciousness.

"Mirror."

Artur handed over a small data padd, already set in video mode. In silence Marteene studied his new features on the screen as the stranger uncannily mirrored his own winks and twitches. There were scars, still an angry red under the regenerated epidermis, but it was unmistakably the face of Max Force.

"And you can reverse this?"

"Of course!" The Split physician bristled with the indignation characteristic of his species when challenged. "And I could have made many improvements, your abnormally small reproductive organ for one."

Artur openly chuckled drolly at the look of alarm that crossed his face as Marteene reflexively checked beneath his robe.

"At ease, you are more than adequately equipped in that department and besides this is hardly the place for a full test."

Phyrath choked a cracked laugh from his anterior throat.

"That normal? No wonder Argon females they say, 'Once you go Split you never quit.' Eh? Ha!"

"Be that as it may, if we can return to the matter at hand. Are there any problems?"

The physician busied himself for a few minutes running various small devices over Marteene, who held still, allowing his brain and body to absorb the changes and form a new harmony.

"He fine, everything is fine. Except face - rash normal, will fade. May itch. Use this."

The Split waved what appeared to be a small ornate salt dispenser over his face, which tingled momentarily as epidermal nerves fired to life and cells regenerated.

"Thanks". Marteene pocketed the stimulator, waiting for Artur to announce the next move."

Satisfied the procedure was successful Artur dismissed the Split with a large credit chip, anonymously drawn on a small Teladi bank in the Seizewell system famed for its flexibility and discretion, and a barely veiled threat.

Satisfied that the cowed Phyrath presented no security risk he teleported the Split directly to a waiting transporter that immediately launched.

When he returned Marteene had dressed and was performing a series of exercises, moving fluidly from form to form.

"How does it feel?"

"Strange. Strange but right if you know what I mean. I expected to be more clumsy."

"Good, good. In that case we do need to proceed. I trust you understand that from now on you must play the part?"

Marteene gestured to his clothing; combat boots, black synth-skin britches and waistcoat over a white silk blouse.

"Max Force, ready, and waiting, I'm not an undercover virgin even if I do look like someone out of a comic."

"Mr Force did indeed have a certain, well, flamboyance. It will serve us in good stead so go with it."

Marteene smiled. "Well, I always wanted to be a hero in a holo-game, when do we start?"

"Now Mr Force, now." Artur handed Max a data-padd.

"Say hello to Xela."

Max activated the padd and the small hi-res screen filled with the image of his smiling cousin.

"Hi there Max, looking good! You are now the proud owner of the PD-1000X, with added AI and holographic data ports. Would you care to take a moment to register me?"

Force took a second to absorb the specs as they scrolled up the screen. It was a prototype mark but essentially the same piece of kit he was familiar with from other operations. Concealed beneath the exterior of a commercial model were the standard-issue enhanced computer, scanning and comms functions. With the Xela AI chip in the universal expansion slot and a newly developed holographic Intruder Interface it was a formidable piece of electronics.

"Nice, where did you steal it from?"

"You have a very suspicious mind Mr Force. A commercial research lab on Argon Prime. It holds a lot of information you will need later so try not to lose it. You will also need these."

Force slipped the PDA into a pocket and took the proffered case.

"You have to be kidding me right?" He regarded the glasses warily. They were military style aviators glare glasses, the opaque lenses mounted in gold frames.

"As worn by weekend warriors everywhere. I know but we want to cut the correct dash don't we? I'm sure you'll be stunned to see there is more to them than meets the eye, if you will pardon the pun."

Artur was right. Incorporating combat visor technology and a sensor link it gave him a flexible HUD interface to the Xela AI. Experimentally he flicked open the connection, tiny lasers monitoring the focus of his eyes as his gaze slid over the interface options projected on the lenses.

"You will find it functions as you are used to, including voice link. Effective range one hundred metres or so, depending on the surroundings."

"Okay, I'm looking cool. What next?"

"Next, Mr Force, we part company. If you are to successfully pull off this deception we will need to have limited contact. You will be needing this. It's all that was in his secret accounts. Max was somewhat impecunious and we can't risk blowing your cover with funds that could be traced."

Max took the credit chip and checked the value as her followed Artur to the teleport. It was less than 7,000 credits, nowhere near enough for a ship.

"But fear not Mr Force, remember where you are. Might I suggest a visit to the casino? You do play poker?"

"Enough to know never to draw to an inside straight."

"Excellent. Then I am sure a man of your talents will have no difficulty. Take this. It's the key to a flight locker in the main docking bay. You'll find some personal affects and your side-arms."

Marteene took the card.

"You know the objective and Xela has the details of what help I've been able to put in place. I'll be in contact again but you'll have to play it by ear. I've every faith and so did Hela."

Marteene shook the offered hand and stepped into the transporter.

"And never say never!"

Artur touched a control and Marteene was gone.

Force materialised un-noticed in a derelict cargo bay and slipping on the shades, activated Xela.

The HUD activated automatically. The interface was as Artur promised, similar enough to the combat version to require no more than a few minutes playing with the laser eye activation mode to become instinctive. The 3D wireframe model of the station conjured with a few eye movements showed he was off the main concourse, many levels above the huge hydroponic bay where the spaceweed was cultivated under the perpetual glare of the giant Sunbeamer lamps.

Summoning Xela she materialised, a transparent holograph head, superimposed ghost-like in his vision.

"Hi there Max, good to see you again. Any problems?"

The sound, vibrationally transmitted directly to his inner ear, was inaudible to all but him.

"You mean apart from having to build a business empire from scratch to save the universe wearing someone else's face? No, just another normal day."

Xela smiled, a painfully familiar grin that immediately conjured thoughts of revenge.

"That's the spirit Max. What now?"

"I was sort of hoping you would tell me. A game of poker it seems, I assume this bag of tricks is going to help me cheat?"

"Come on Max, you think these people are amateurs? Just get onto the high stakes table and go with it. Artur and I have something set up but it's going to have to look real and you'll have to work to pull it off. This little play is the basis of the grand plan so it's got to seem legit. Besides even us miracle workers can't fix a whole session. It's not as if they still use sentient dealers we can bribe, threaten or blackmail. I hope you bought your poker face with you."

"Yea, I'll just get it from the jar. You people like your games don't you."

"Well we can't just transfer you the credits or even plant a mark for you to fleece. At some point people with nasty suspicious minds are going to look at what happens here. There's a mark, they just don't know it. It's up to you to do the shearing. Don't worry, I've been busy. You just have be in a position to spot the moment because I won't be there to nudge you. Okay with that?"

Max shrugged. "I have a choice?"

"You always have choices Max, now get going and for goodness sake try and have some fun. Good luck, entering standby mode."

Xela vanished and the HUD functions terminated but Max kept the shades on for effect, trusting the inert technology would not trigger the casino security systems.

All species, with the exception of the Boron, love to gamble and the many halls and arenas of the Heirophants Joy Casino catered to any taste a being could afford to pander. His credit chip guaranteed entrance to a small, no limits, suite off the main hall. The intense silence generated by the 3 other players at the octagonal table was a welcome relief from the spaceweed drenched cacophony of the main casino.

Removing his shades at the polite request of one of the large Split that lurking indiscreetly in the background Marteene waited for the current hand to finish.

The game was of course poker, the Game of the Gods. Originally of Argon origin its unique blending mathematics, chance and character had seen it spread throughout the universe faster than a viral plague. Now every gambling species had its own variant and deck mirroring their individual societies and culture. Here though, as was custom for no-limits stakes, it was Argon rules and deck. Jack, Queen, King, terms for which only the Goner could offer a plausible explanation. Not that anyone cared once the chips were down.

As he waited Marteene allowed the familiar feeling of excitement to tingle through his body. He was, like all good pilots, a natural gambler and despite the regular "lessons" he endured at the hands of Paskaal he had acquired a certain reputation in ready rooms throughout the fleet. There was something about the game that appealed to the hunter instinct.

When the hand ended the dealer, a latest model mechanoid in the slightly incongruous form of a talentless but pneumatic blonde actress from the golden age of Argon holos, gestured for him to take a vacant seat with a lascivious smile. No names were exchanged but each player scrutinised him carefully, attempting to weigh his measure.

As he slipped his credit chip through the auto-teller and arranged the disgorged chips in an intimidating stack Max appraised his opponents in turn, seeking the mark. The only human, a middle-aged man, his face he dismissed immediately. His stack was small and the haunted, desperate expression etched on a face prematurely aged by long exposure UV radiation, told its own tale. Just another spacer chasing that big score before his fading strength and reflexes made him unemployable.

The Split? Like most of her race, she radiated an arrogant self-assurance that made her impossible to read. Her stack was impressive but for all he could tell was half her starting stake.

The Teladi though, everything from his silk suit to the predatory grin he flashed as Max stacked his chips screamed professional. Max had no doubt who the big winner was at this table.

"It's Argon Hold 'em, 100 credit ante, no limits raise, house takes 5%. Okay for you sweets?" The honey drawl of the simulacrum was perfect, as was the deft manner with which she dispensed the first 2 cards. Jack and Queen, different suits and Max stayed with the first round of betting, raising slightly to gauge the reactions of his opponents. The spacer folded, unable to hide his frustration. The Split remained inscrutable, her alien face quite unreadable and the Teladi quivered with what Max took to be the almost instinctive excitement characteristic of the race when it came to credits.

Unsure what to make of him Max called and the dealer flipped the next 3 cards face before her. Queen, King, Five, leaving Max on a firm high pair and he stayed with the remaining players through another low round of betting. The final card was no match for any of his hole cards but equally the Seven could not build a straight for anyone. Failing a hole pair, two or more Queens or Kings would scoop the modest pot. With only 12 cards in play the odds on another player holding a hole Lady were small. The chances of a King were a bit higher but unlikely and when his turn came he raised 500 credits to test his luck and the nerves of the remaining players. The Teladi folded instantly and Max added the fact to the mental model of his opponent's psyches all good poker players work with. The Split stayed with him through another round, raising the ante again before Max, aware that a significant chunk of his stake already lay in the pot, called. Silently the Split flicked her hole cards face up and raked in the pot with an arrogant smirk as Marteene stared at the King.

It set the tone for the rest of the game and Max watched his stack slowly migrate Split-wards with carefully concealed disquiet. Poker was a game where the benign smile of Lady Luck could make a mockery of skill and as his chips continued to dwindle Max began to wonder whether even the Cabal were her match. Betting cautiously he hung in, waiting for the promised moment when he could take the Split to the proverbial cleaners.

The Teladi turned out to be as poor a judge of odds as the Argon and once he had their measure Marteene was able to recoup some of his losses with a judicious mix of bets that established no pattern of behaviour that his real opponent could use against him. The Split too gave no clues in her play - willing to take an occasional big loss on called bluffs whilst she rode her luck hard.

Surprisingly the Teladi was the first to fold, stunned into silence when his three aces fell to a full house.

"Threes high, aces low. Your pot sweetheart." The dealer quickly skimmed the house cut from the pot and pushed the chips across the table to him.

"Very well played human. Soon it will be you and I only eh?" The Split gestured to the few remaining chips before the Argon dismissively as the Teladi gambler signalled his intention to sit out the rest of the game.

Max did not respond and ante'd up for the next hand. His two pair fell expensively to the Split who now made no attempt to hide her contempt for the other players lack of skill. The Argon looked ready to space himself and Marteene had to fight hard to keep his own unease from showing.

The next hand was no better. With only Jack and Ten of Spades in the hole he kept with the betting in the hope of a flush. Both the Argon and the Split stayed with him. The three show cards were tantalising, Ace of Spades, Ace of Hearts, King of Spades. The spacer immediately upped the ante and the Split casually doubled it. Marteene figured the odds were good on one of them holding at least an ace but being on for a flush or even an inside straight he dug deep into his remaining pile of chips and hung in through the next round of raises before the dealer flicked out the final show card.

Queen of Spades. Royal flush. An unbeatable hand. Max did not move a muscle or bat an eyelid as he quickly calculated how best to ride what must be the moment he had been promised. The pot was big, but nothing like what he'd need to get a ship and he'd have to play the Split like fish to fatten it up. She had 4 aces or a flush or was bluffing hard. Marteene hoped she was not one to bluff a pot to this level.

"Raise 2000 credits." and it was all Marteene could do not to kiss the man as the Argon pushed most of his remaining chips into the pot with shaking hands that matched the desperation in his voice.

The Split regarded him for a moment as she toyed with her chips.

"I smell defeat in air, no bet. Cash in now please."

In the silence Marteene imagined he could hear the sounds of best laid plans crashing around his ears.

Looking at the slim pickings left in front of the spacer Marteene sighed and pushed all his chips into the pot. It was no way to play but with the Split bailing he hadn't the heart to take the man's few remaining credits.

But there is no accounting for stupidity.

"Ain't no way, ain't no way that Queen gave you a flush boy and I ain't letting you bluff me out. Take my marker girlie?"

"It's on file at the stated value sir. Do you wish to call?"

The Argon nodded, white lipped and slipped a registration disc into the pot. From across the table Marteene could make out only two words, resonant with personal history.

Destiny Star.

### Chapter 17: Space Truckin'

Max had lost no time in cashing in his winnings, walking away from the table with nearly 10,000 credits as well as the ship registration disk. The spacer left without a word, wearing such an ugly mask of bitterness and desperation that Max thought it wise to register the change of ownership with launch control immediately. He tried not to think about what cruel manipulations of circumstance had driven the man into a final corner but the fact that it was the old family Lifter he had lost spoke volumes concerning the long arm and fastidious planning of the Cabal.

After accepting the congratulations of the other players and declining the offer of the casino to credit him the stated value of the marker in return for the registration Max slipped away as quickly as possible to avoid the inevitable crowd of new friends good fortune would trail in its wake. Pausing only to claim the flight bag and firearm Artur had deposited he went straight to the main docking bay, anxious to appraise his acquisition.

Under the watchful eye group of curious Teladi technicians who had somehow managed to tear themselves away from less urgent tasks to stand around and watch, he carried out an external inspection whilst marvelling at the speed at which the news of his win had travelled.

The Argon Lifter is little more than a large subspace hold sandwiched between a flight module and a drive system. Sturdy and workmanlike it lacks the cetean aesthetic of the Boron Dolphin freighter but like a handsome woman it could conjure beauty in the eye of the right beholder. The Destiny Star though, looked every year of its considerable age. Gaping patches of bare metal shone through the scarred remnants of an old matt blue paint job, spoke eloquently of poverty and neglect but the ingrained carbon scoring around the lower shield emitters hinted at a life more colourful.

The big old ship was not going to win any beauty prizes and it saddened Marteene to see the object of his youthful dreams of space and freedom in such condition.

Without activating Xela he slipped the registration disk into the data-padd and quickly scanned the recent maintenance and flight logs. It was no surprise that the man had gone broke, the maintenance and re-equipment costs far exceeded any profits that could have been made on the short haul flights that largely comprised the official flight log. Not that logs were any more difficult to fix than resetting a digitometer on an atmospheric speeder. A trace resonance scan of the scoring confirmed that the ship had recently taken fire, probably from heavy plasma throwers. His physics was not good enough to delineate the precise type from the waveform patterns so he logged the readings for Xela to analyse later. The fact the ship had survived suggested it had been forced to surrender its cargo.

Marteene guessed it must have been something of pretty high value belonging to unforgiving people to drive the man to staking his livelihood on a game, especially given the over-a-barrel low valuation the casino had placed on the freighter. As this was a Bliss Place in close proximity to lucrative illegal markets it was not hard to guess what that might be. Which gave him a germ of an idea, which he allowed to grow in the back of his mind.

Max gestured towards the lizard technicians to deploy an ascender to the airlock and was almost crushed by the uncharacteristic rush to help. Those who could not get a hold on the ascender loudly supervised the simple procedure, somehow managing to crush at least one of their number in the process. Making a mental note to purchase himself a ladder Max pressed a few chips he'd held back for just such a purpose into the eager claws of those techs who were still mobile, resisting the temptation just to scatter them across the deck for the sheer hell of it.

Bracing himself against a nostalgia attack Marteene entered the craft. He need not have bothered. Everything from the equipment and decor of the small living space aft of the cockpit to the layout and equipment of the flight deck had been changed over the years and bore little resemblance to his young memories. It was a relief, there were already too many ghosts haunting this mission.

"Hello again old girl, it's been a long time." It felt good to be behind her controls again and for a second he could see himself as the proud young boy on his first time in the left hand seat, his father giving instructions and encouragement from the co-pilot station.

Nostalgia - if only it could be bottled.

"What the..!?" Marteene was startled from his reverie by the sudden appearance of a squeegee wielding Teladi on the nose, its reptilian visage split with a grin at once hopeful and avaricious.

"Come on fella, enough already."

But the Teladi could not hear him and seemed not to understand Marteene's arm waving gestures as she smeared soapy water over the plexiglass with renewed enthusiasm.

"It really would be quicker to train monkeys" he sighed. "Bye bye." Max flicked the shield generator on and off discharging the residual energy into the powered down forward emitters. They say a picture is worth a thousand words but unfortunately Marteene had no camera to capture the expression of saurian surprise as the lizard slipped from view, her claws futilely scrabbling at the suddenly frictionless surface.

"Okay, let's see what we've got," Max inserted the Xela chip into a system interface and powered up the computers. Xela's face immediately appeared on the viewscreen.

"Hi Max, did we win?"

"Yup - big surprise eh?"

She smiled "I don't remember you being this cynical Gragore. Very Max, keep it up."

"Glad you like it. Can you run a full systems diagnostic, I don't want any unpleasant surprises and look out for non-standard mods."

"Roger that skip - and perhaps when I'm finished you could teach me to suck eggs!"

Xela vanished as Max ran his own systems checks. The results were a pleasant surprise, his favourite kind. The Destiny Star was unarmed, not even a few mosquito missiles but it still sported the maximum cargo upgrades, giving it an ample 1500 unit capacity. The drive system was the latest mark and it too was fully maxxed, making it faster than most M3 heavy fighters. It was this combination of speed and cargo capacity that made the Argon Lifter the freighter of choice to the discerning trader, especially those who engaged in a little smuggling on the side.

Even better the Star had almost the full complement of additional systems; docking computer, a suite of trading information and tactical/nav sub-systems, afterburners, even a transporter. All that was missing was a jump-drive but Marteene had no doubt Artur had made arrangements to have the one from the Bayamon transferred, along with the shadow-tech. The single 5MW shield was the only disappointment but its presence confirmed the scenario he had already surmised. The Destiny Star had been recently attacked, her shields destroyed and a cargo way more valuable than the resale price of the ship and add-ons had been lost. Marteene did not need to practise his cynicism to see the hidden hand of the Cabal at work. Another pawn sacrifice. That he was working for a group prepared to shatter men's lives for an advantageous position in their never-ending game of cosmic chess was an uncomfortable thought. Max wondered what value piece he was. Hopefully at least a knight.

"All systems A1 Max, and only one surprise." Xela was grinning. "We've got a hidden compartment beneath the rec room linked to the transporter. It has some sort of passive ceramic shielding I don't recognise but it'll be invisible to outside scans."

"Interesting. Any idea what it contained?"

"Checking transporter logs. They've been erased. Badly."

On screen Xela frowned as she ran reconstruction algorithms.

"Got it - oooh, this is interesting. I'm reading THC related alkaloids, a genetic mod I don't recognise, very high concentrations in an veg oil base. And by high I mean high."

She flashed a graph on the screen and Marteene whistled softly, the concentration level of the active ingredient of spaceweed was hundreds of times that of the finest weed on the market.

"Wow - a drop of that would bring a smile to the face of a Split. Can you estimate volume and extrapolate a street value from the concentrate equivalent benchmarked against something common, say the local stuff?"

Xela could and displayed the figure.

"That's a lot of credits Xela, no wonder the guy was desperate."

"Who - Panner?"

"Was that his name? Yea. I think it's time we had a long chat with Mr Panner before his associates catch up with him."

"I take it we have a plan? Great - I knew you were the right man for the job. When do we start?"

"Right now. Log out, we're going to return some of Mr Panner's personal effects."

Marteene transferred the Xela chip to the data-padd. He took a few minutes in the rec room to adopt his new style - the same white shirt, black waistcoat, trousers and boots ensemble as Force favoured. The large blaster strapped to his right thigh completed it.

The image in the holo-reflector was a stereotype but a well-chosen one, echoing as it did an archetype from one of the Goner sagas and he realised that was why Max had adopted it.

Look the part, act the part.

Marteene practised a confident swagger and a few quick draws before sweeping the previous owner's remaining clothing and personal effects into the flight bag.

Finally he slipped the data-padd into an inner pocket of the waistcoat and activated the shades.

"You are the Man Max, you are the Man." His reflection returned his broad smile and he set out put the first stage of his still forming plan into effect.

Once he had found a Public Data it took Xela only seconds to identify the hotel room registered to Panner Kiosk thanks to the new holographic Intruder Interface and following the route projected onto his HUD Max was there in minutes. He was still too late. Panner sat slouched in the armchair, his head lolling at an unnatural angle.

The body was still warm but a scan confirmed the total absence of brain activity.

"Damn - so much for my plan. I don't suppose it's worth reporting this?"

"Who to Max? You know how station security works on these places. Whoever did this wasn't worried about them, they've made no effort to cover their tracks."

"How so?"

"They used their bare hands, there are DNA traces on the impact position and I'm reading no residual traces of an area steriliser. If there was a station DNA database I could get you a name 3 seconds after I cracked the securities."

It was a futile hope though. If it was even suspected that a station like this kept such records it would become a ghost station overnight. Pleasure seekers and wrongdoers alike value their privacy.

"Still, it does confirm that Panner must have had a contact here. The Cabal set the guy up, surely you must have some idea?"

"He was a patsy Max, it's not the first time we've needed to slip someone a ship. And I told you, these people can play rough. I suggest we don't hang around."

Max sighed. "I guess you're right but it sure would have short-circuited things if we could rip-off a big score."

"Agreed, but even if we could find the putative Mr Big I very much doubt they'd trust even Max Force with that kind of load. Just admitting you knew about it would qualify you for walk in a leaking space suit."

"True enough but that wasn't the plan. These people always need legit traders to run weed and your people have fixed me up with valid licences right? With my charm and Force's rep and your unique assets we could have finessed ourselves into the big deals, no problem."

Xela thought for a moment, her frowning face hanging ghostlike in his HUD.

"Well we could try and contact Artur - get an intelligence download?"

"No - too risky. I've not come across this stuff before and I bet you haven't either".

Xela nodded in agreement.

"Whoever is dealing in it could be fronted by any one of the dozens of gang and clans reps running the standard weed through the Argon and Boron sectors. We could waste weeks cultivating the wrong contacts."

"Your logic is faultless. Let's leave now please?"

"You're right. I need a drink and something to eat. Know anywhere quiet?"

"Do I look like a travel guide Max? No I do not. I suggest you try a Data Kiosk. Xela off."

The AI had captured Hela perfectly and following her suggestion Marteene soon found a restaurant whose prices guaranteed exclusivity and privacy. Wiping the supercilious frown from the maitre-de with another chip Max relaxed over a grilled gammon steak, smothered in a blue cheese sauce in the privacy of his own booth and thought over his options.

A quick scan revealed no bugging devices in the vicinity and he would have been surprised if it had.

Picking through the menu on the booth data-link Marteene ordered a beer, choosing the expensive Argon imported brand that according to his file, Max had favoured. It appeared in the table bar a few seconds later, the elegant green bottle still frosty to the touch. It was a light 3% proof but the complex interplay of malt, hops and the subtle hint of honey gave it a quality of character normally associated with finer wines. Drinking straight from the bottle Marteene toasted the good taste of his dead doppelganger and allowed the alcohol to massage the tension from his brain.

Retrieving the DNA record Xela had obtained from Panner's neck, Max meditated on the image of the double helix as it rotated slowly in the HUD, seeking inspiration. It was clearly human but that was little help. There would be hundreds of those on the station at any one time but it was a start. Briefly he considered asking Xela to hack station security records but dismissed the idea. These people were above what passed for the law in these places and they could do what they like, so long as they only hurt each other and not the tourists.

"Hold that thought Max, I wonder..?" Marteene took another pull on the beer and established an encrypted link to the station database via the public access terminal. Scrolling through the published station specs and layouts he soon found what he was looking for although the records were behind a security lockout.

"Shazzam Xela!"

She appeared in his vision smiling, the genie of the shades.

"What is your command oh Master?"

"How do you feel about breaking into hospitals?"

"Pretty good actually, what am I looking for? No, don't tell me - test records that match our villain. That's a pretty smart idea for an organic."

"Thanks, we have our moments. Can you do it?"

Xela was lost in concentration for a moment.

"Sure - it's protected but hang-nails and regenerated colons aren't code black stuff. Give me a few minutes. Here have another beer on me." A second bottle slid from the bar, a heavy black brew Hela had favoured. Marteene nursed it cautiously, aware of its bite and not wanting to dull his reflexes. Even so he had almost drained it before Xela flashed back into view.

"Sorry for the delay Max, some of the files were individually encrypted. Whatever happened to trust that's what I want to know?"

"It's truly shocking. Find anything useful?"

"This is your guy." Xela flashed the image of a thin-faced Argon, an unprepossessing thin-faced man in his twenties whose lack of chin was only emphasised by the thin goatee beard he sported in the defiance of fashion and good taste.

"Singurd Harn. Took a vibrablade in the liver a few months ago. The cloned replacement was charged to a Chandus Rarr, registered owner of the Split Split Club. I truly shudder to think."

"Anything on file?"

"No - I dug around in the public database but nothing. Human name though."

Max finished the last of the beer and settled the check.

"I think it's time we paid a visit to the Split Split Club for a little R and R, unless you have a better idea Xela?"

"Not at present but do me a favour Max, take the shades off before you go in. There's some things an AI shouldn't have to see!"

Her words were distressingly prophetic. The Split Split turned out to be the sort of dive where you are frisked for weapons and issued with one if you are clean and the sight of pole-dancing Split females was one he resolved to have erased from memory as soon as the mission was over. Fortunately for his eyesight he was almost immediately recognised and unceremoniously "invited" to join a solitary human at his table by 2 monosyllabic but hulking Teladi males, incongruous in their tailored tuxedos.

"Hey, watch the shirt guys, Mr Rarr I presume?"

The short, portly man in a sweat stained white silk suit nodded as he took a long drag on a cigarette mounted in a long holder filigreed with pearl, held the smoke deep in his lungs for a moment before exhaling deliberately in Max's face.

The Teladi tensed expectantly, claws halfway to the weapons bulging beneath their suits.

"Nice stuff. Grow it yourself? And where did you get those two, Goons-R-Us been running a two for one?"

"Very amusing Mr Force, I must say you are in remarkable form for a dead man."

His voice was low and thin with an accent tinged by a long sojourn in Teladi space.

Although he did not show it Max tensed with the realisation that the game was moving at a much faster pace than he anticipated.

"You're very well informed, in which case you know why I'm here."

"I suspect I do not but I was hoping you would be returning my ship."

"You did huh? I won that fair and square," Max smiled, leaning casually back in his chair, reflexes poised to reach for his blaster.

"Please Max, may I call you Max? Good. You will find your impressive looking firearm is not functioning at the moment but not to worry, we are all friends here. Is that not so boys?"

The Teladi grunted their assent.

Marteene realised he had an advantage he had not considered. Regardless of his current status he had a certain rep in less law-abiding circles, a rep that came with possible friends people like Rarr would be unwilling to provoke without hope of substantial gain.

"I haven't had a lot of luck with my friends recently so let's skip the bonding okay?"

Rarr smiled and dabbed ineffectually at the sweat pouring down his corpulent face with a napkin.

"Ah yes, the sabotage of your vessel. You know your friends think you are dead? I understand they are quite unhappy about it but who is to know should something - unfortunate happen to you?"

Max looked Rarr straight in the face. "Dead mans drop."

"Of course, of course. Your friends will receive a message if you don't periodically check in somewhere or somehow. The old ones are the best ones are they not Max?"

Nodding coolly Max allowed himself to relax, whatever was pissing Rarr was not enough to risk the Raiders turning up outside his airlock.

"Cards on the table Rarr, how about it?"

"What an appropriate metaphor given the circumstances. I call."

Marteene paused for a second. He had hoped to remain anonymous for awhile, getting a feel for the seedy underbelly of the X-Universe from a trader's perspective before coming up with a way to operationalise Artur's crazy plan. This though was too good an opportunity to miss, so long as he played it right.

"Okay. I looked over Panner's ship, its obviously been in a fight recently and I'm guessing he dumped a whole load of your weed in exchange for his life and gambled away his assets before you could seize them in compensation. Then you sent your hitter, Harn - not a discreet chap by the way, you should think of getting better help - to rub him out and I followed his big clumsy prints right back to you. How am I doing."

Rarr smiled but there was no joy behind it.

"I believe I may have to reconsider my staffing arrangements Max. Now what brings you here?"

Marteene smiled what he hoped was an avaricious grin, settling into character.

"Credits - what else is there? I never planned to spend the rest of my life behind a stick anyway and well, recent events have convinced me of the need for a career change."

Rarr leaned forward, fixing Max with a saucer stare.

"And what interpretation do you put on your mishap Max?"

Pausing for effect, as if weighing the odds Marteene took a deep breath and looked the man straight in the eye.

"Look Rarr, I'm going to level with you. You know my reputation, I'm a mercenary and a bloody good one. What's more I'm a damn honest one, which makes me worth a lot and you know it."

The corpulent club owner nodded.

"But not everyone likes to play by my rules and to tell the Goner's honest truth I'm damn sick of checking my six for back-stabbing bastards. Everywhere I turn there's someone who wants my slice of the action. I've been ambushed at jump-gates, shot at in stations and damn well beaten on in bars more times than I can remember and for what?"

"I understand your contracts have been quite substantial?"

"Sure they have, split two dozen ways. And you have no idea of the overheads. Ships, maintenance, arms - have you any idea how much a silkworm missile costs?"

Marteene was enjoying the chance to rant and was actually starting to feel hard done by.

"A damn lot, that's how much, a damn lot." You could have cut plasteel with the bitter edge.

"And to cap it all someone in my own bloody team sabotaged my ship. It was a damn miracle I got out alive. A damn miracle. And a good good friend didn't."

Marteene did not have to fake the crack in his voice.

"When I got out of surgery I thought screw it, I can't live like this anymore. I want the damn credits and what better place to start looking than a place like this?"

"You tell a very convincing story Max and I'm inclined to believe you, given what my own sources tell me. But that still leaves the small matter of Panner's ship."

"Now you listen to me Rarr," Max snarled leaning forward suddenly, going nose to nose. In his peripheral vision he could see the 2 goons reach reflexively for their weapons. "I won that ship off that fool Panner fair and square and if you think I'm going to just hand it over to you and your comic book thugs then you're not the intelligent business man I hoped you were. You got that!?"

Max jabbed his index finger aggressively in Rarr's face. "You got that?"

Goaded beyond endurance, as Marteene had intended, the largest of the lizard bodyguards seized his right shoulder, his claws digging painfully into the flesh. In one fluid movement Max stood, jabbed his left elbow back into its solar plexus and as the Teladi crumpled forward breathless

smashed a backhand punch into his snout. Spinning around Marteene snatched the crumpling saurian's firearm from the shoulder holster and was covering both the remaining guard and Rarr before either could move.

Half a dozen armed Teladi and Argon seemed to appear from nowhere, pointing a variety of hand-guns in his direction. High on adrenaline Marteene was only peripherally aware of the sudden panic and confusion rippling through the partying crowd.

"I'm betting your little dampening field isn't affecting this Rarr. Call 'em off before anymore get broken."

To his credit Rarr was quite unperturbed and with a gesture ordered his men to stand down. Max tossed the stolen gun aside.

"You live up to your reputation Max, I am impressed. You.." He nodded to the remaining Teladi guard. "Clear up this mess and leave, Mr Force and I have business to discuss."

Smiling affably Rarr gestured for Max to sit.

"I really must apologise for my associates Max, I trust we need not let unfortunate misunderstandings get in the way of business?"

"It's forgotten Rarr but you still aren't getting MY ship."

"Hmmn, I see I have to concede that point but no matter. Ships are not the problem, good pilots are."

"What you got in mind?"

"As you no doubt appreciate the fact that only the Teladi have an enlightened attitude to the product of this station sharply reduces the potential profits. You don't mind a little lecture do you?"

"Lecture away Rarr, but order me a beer. Bottle, cold, unopened."

Rarr had only to click his fingers for a young female Split waitress to appear at his side. A few moments later Max was nursing an unfamiliar but smooth brew as Rarr busied himself lighting another cigarette.

"You might think Max that a station like this is a license to chip credits given the universal demand for the product but would it surprise you to know it operates at less than a quarter of its maximum efficiency?"

Max said nothing and waited for him to continue. This sort of inside information was priceless.

"No - most of the time production is at a standstill because the holds are jammed to capacity. The demand is there but the means of supply isn't. The number of pilots with the means and the nerve to run the stuff to market is actually quite small and the number who can actually afford to fill their hold even fewer. That's why the Clans dominate the distribution. The authorities, for one reason or another, tend not to interfere with large, well-armed Clan convoys so the their bases are vital links in the distribution chain. Believe me they drive a very hard bargain and it's them that make most of the money, feeding the central markets in small, easily transported amounts hidden in other cargo. It's actually very rare for us to send a full shipment direct to a system distributor on one of the trading stations.

"Traders can't afford the risk, as Panner has so vividly demonstrated, and the producers cannot afford to risk losing a whole shipment sending it direct. That leaves the clans as the only game in town. Which is where entrepreneurs such as myself come in. I take the risk of purchasing a shipment, paying a better price than the clans so the producers are happy. I can then sell direct to the system distributors at a lower price than the clans so they are happy and still make a big profit so I am happy. The catch is, finding a low risk delivery system, which is where the unlamented Panner came in.

"Unfortunately the clans understanding of concept of free enterprise is limited so they tend to violently object to competition. Between the clans and the authorities I'm lucky to get 2 out of 3 shipments through. I've lost two in a row now and it hurts."

"And you'll forget about the Star if I do some running for you right? I'm interested."

"You get ahead of yourself Max, I think you might be a man I can trust but I'd be a fool to take you on without knowing you can deliver. No, you need to prove yourself before I'd be willing to risk a considerable sum on your talents."

"I take it you have a suggestion?"

"Nothing you haven't already figured out for yourself Max. Establish yourself as a legitimate trader, show you can deliver and get back to me. I suggest you try your hand at bootlegging, the clans take no particular interest in that so you have only the authorities to contend with. If you are as good as I think you are we could eventually have a profitable relationship. Agreed?"

Marteene thought it over for a minute, reluctant to countenance any delay but what Rarr said made sense. If he was going to find out more about the concentrate and get his hands on a shipment he'd have to play the game.

"Fine, you've got yourself a deal Rarr. Shake?"

Rarr declined.

"I prefer to rely on  knowledge of  consequences to cement a deal. Have YOU got that?"

"I don't threaten easily Rarr but I take your point. You have my word, which means something to me if not to you. I'll be in touch. One more thing though - I don't plan to advertise my survival, I assume I can count on your discretion?"

Rarr nodded smoothly. "Of course. A hole card isn't any good if you reveal it too soon."

Marteene drained his beer in one long pull and left, relieved to get out of the depressing dive and pleased that things had gone so well. He now had a plan.

He returned straight to the Star, reinstalled the Xela chip and filled her in.

"Nice going Gragore, you've always had a flair for this sort of thing. What's the next move?"

Max ran a credit check, he still had nearly 8000 credits, enough to give him a flying start as a legit trader provided Artur came up with some contacts.

"Buy low, sell high I guess. Any suggestions?"

As he talked Marteene triggered the automated launch sequence and the freighter slowly glided on thrusters towards the main docking tunnel.

Xela smiled. "Not my area Max but we should head for the Seizewell Equipment Dock."

"See a lizard about a cloak huh? Jump-drive too I hope. How long have you known this?"

"About 3 seconds. Message from Artur, or to be more precise, a file in my memory on a timed decrypt. Triggered by the launch sequence."

"Clever, any more of those?"

"That would be telling Max."

The big freighter drifted on autopilot until it emerged through the huge docking bay doors into the blinding sunlight of space. Taking the controls Marteene gunned the main drive and turned towards the eastern jump-gate.

## *Chapter 18: Wheels and Deals*

Aboard the Vigilant Trasker impatiently skimmed to latest decrypt from her hounds, the news could have been better. Marteene and the Bayamon seemed to have effectively vanished from the spaceways and she was beginning to suspect he had gone to ground planet-side, despite what his psych-profile suggested. It was beginning to look like an intelligence disaster and her superiors were not happy. Not happy at all. Even confirmation that the Raiders were no longer positioned to interfere with her operations did little to raise her spirits especially as that fool Paskaal seemed to have been sidetracked into tracking down a supposedly alive Force. It seemed unlikely given the circumstances but that was not important right now. Janis was not a killer by nature and sometimes, deep in the night, she regretted having to take some actions, if not the actions themselves. The death of the co-pilot was regrettable, she had just been a minor player and like the Raiders themselves not important at all. Just part of something that was in the way. So long as the mercenary group were out of the picture she didn't care what they did and if by some miracle Force had survived, well, he might make a useful piece some day.

Other Intel reports did not indicate that Marteene had sold on the secret technologies if that was his intention but it was a big universe and much went on that escaped the prying eyes and ears of the intelligence services. Her gut told her though that he was not the type to hug the ground. People who live on the kind of edge the Special Forces walked didn't retire to the quiet life. Space and the adrenaline buzz of high risk was in his blood and sooner or later he'd need another fix and if driven by a grudge against the system Trasker mentally laid odds he'd surface as a merc, perhaps even a freelance gun for hire. Certainly a jump and shadow tech equipped Bayamon could be a lucrative tool in the hands of a pilot as good as Marteene and she had no difficulty imagining such a scenario. That was the trouble with Maverick Profile types, their individualistic sense of right and wrong could justify almost any action as she had argued all along. Well perhaps they would listen to her more closely in future.

The psych analysis agreed with her and for the next few hours she worked to set up secure channels to funnel any intel on new pirate and merc activity to her hunters along with orders redirecting their efforts. She also ensured Captain Shiva was apprised of her thoughts so that they could be planted in the head of Paskaal.

Marteene's trip to Seizewell was uneventful, as far as anyone was concerned he just another space trucker scraping around for business. He took the time to get the feel for the handling of the Destiny Star. Over the years her manoeuvring sub systems had been fully upgraded and she was no longer the lumbering beast Marteene remembered. The old girl was no fighter but she responded deftly to the stick, her agility and speed would make her a difficult target in the right hands and he practised evasive manoeuvres until he was within a couple of klicks of the jump-gate to the Teladi home sector of Seizewell.

Following Xela's instructions he docked with the Equipment Dock and allowed the autopilot to take him to a small repair bay where an automated upgrade system installed the jump-drive and the Shadow-Tech. It took several hours and Max took the opportunity to catch some shut-eye in the aft cabin, waking only when Xela announced the process was complete.

"I don't suppose Artur fixed us up with a couple of 25 MW's Xela?"

"I'm afraid not Max, I guess you're going to have to do some work yourself but I did get a data update. Encrypted to your voice."

"Okay, let's see what we've got."

Artur had been productively busy, finessing Max into the Guild Rehabilitation Programme designed to encourage minor players from the wrong side of the line to become productive citizens. It was a clever move and another impressive demonstration of the influence of the Cabal, bestowing on Max a legitimate traders licence that would help him pick up contracts among the orbital installations that formed the backbone of the interstellar economy. It also ensured his business and combat records remained safe from prying eyes. The races did all they could to encourage the piratically inclined to go straight and this was a necessary step to ensure former associates could not track them through the financial system.

The scheme also provided a credible back story should anyone think to pry through central databases although it would not withstand determined questioning. It was just the sort of thing that the real Max would have been eligible if he had survived to be rescued so even when, as was inevitable, his name was recognised, or he was caught with fingers in a dubious pie, no one would be much surprised such was the poor reputation of the scheme. The Programme was much abused by the security services of all species, which only served to shield it from criticism and reform when its protection was in turn abused by the "reformed". A short list of contacts, both legitimate and illegitimate, and their accompanying bio's would also prove useful but Marteene could have wished for something more comprehensive.

"Give him time Max, he said it'll take awhile given the circumstances."

"I suppose. You know I think I'm actually going to enjoy playing the entrepreneur for a while. Cutting deals, finding markets, worrying about margins and overheads and where that next bit of equipment is coming from – it's like a game. Figure out the rules, play it well and you get something for nothing. No wonder the Teladi get off on it, I think my palms are sweating!"

"That's the spirit Max. So where do we begin our meteoric rise?"

"By performing a complete systems check to ensure your friends haven't inserted anything we don't know about. I don't want any tracking devices or any other hush-hush shit giving us away okay?"

"Artur is much too bright to do that Max, he backs his judgement with trust. Within reason of course but I'm running the check. There, all clear or don't you trust me either?"

"Within reason else we're doomed before we start. Okay let's see what fortune has in store for us."

It's not easy to make money as a freelance hauler as many have found out to their cost. Particularly in central systems most orbital factories have fixed price contracts with their suppliers and charter freighters from the major shipping lines to transport it. That leaves very little elbow room for independents who are left to either opportunistically purchase production run overloads in the hope they can find a buyer with a similar shortfall or haul loads they don't own for a few hundred credits a run as sub-contractors. Getting in on good deals was as much a matter of being in the right place and having the right contacts as business acumen.

Fortunately Max had an edge, information. His ship had Best Buys and Best Selling Locator sub-systems installed. These devices were naturally the product of the enterprising Teladi and allowed the owner to tune into the encrypted economic information streams that knitted the interstellar economy together. Their high price ensured they were beyond the reach of all but the most successful freelancers. In fact they were not originally envisaged as ship mounted devices at all. The primary market was corporate as they enabled businesses to efficiently co-ordinate their activities. Any freelancer who could afford them was probably sitting in a comfortable office using the data to run his operation remotely.

Max activated the BSL and studied the information projected onto his helmet HUD. Fortune smiled back. Sun Oil Refinery Beta was suffering an unplanned shortage of energy and would soon be forced to stop production. The BBL showed Solar Power Plant Beta had almost reached the limits of its production run and was advertising energy cells surplus to its agreed contracts at a bargain 6 credits apiece. SPP Alpha was charging 10.

"Xela, I think we're in luck! Get us launch clearance."

"We're cleared Max, auto-launch sequence engaged."

Max kept his hands clear of the controls until the ship had cleared the docking bay doors into open space. Then he targeted the Power Plant and accelerated to full speed. This rare chance for a big score was like blood in the water for independents and Max knew he would not be the only one interested. He did not want to spend the next 5 days hawking a full hold of cells across the sectors looking for another factory with an order shortfall.

The Solar Plant was over 20km distant but at full speed the lifter closed the distance rapidly until they were inside the 5km radius in which the station docking control would respond. The automated system immediately granted docking permission in a flat mechanical voice and picking out the dual string of flashing green landing beacons Max arced towards the docking bay.

"I think we're too late Max, look."

Max cursed under his breath, an elegant Boron Dolphin was already lining up for an approach and would beat them to it. He hoped it was a contractor on a fixed price run for reserved stock otherwise the price of the cells would likely triple.

Xela provided the information without being asked.

"It's an independent Max, looks like we'll have to let it go."

"I'm not going to spend the next 3 months scrabbling around for crumbs Xela, hang onto your hat."

Without decelerating to the safe docking speed the station was indicating on the control panel Marteene curved the big ship in behind the Dolphin and with a barrel roll worthy of an air show looped over and past his competitor before slamming back the throttle. The Star was still decelerating as it flew into the main docking port but its speed was just low enough for the station auto-pilot to engage.

"My god Max who taught you to fly like that? I think we exchanged paint jobs with the Boron back there!"

Marteene laughed with genuine joy, adrenaline surging through his body, causing his fingers to tremble as the Destiny Star flew on auto to the main docking bay.

"I think you did."

"Oh right – carry on then!"

As soon as the ship came to rest Max contacted Station Trading and ordered 1400 energy cells. It cost almost all of his capital. The transfer took only a few minutes and he launched immediately, anxious to make Sun Oil Beta before anyone else.

This time, thanks to the superior speed of the Destiny Star compared to the Teladi Vulture steaming in from SPP Alpha with another load of cheap cells, Max easily managed to beat the competition to the sale. The Teladi production manager was only too pleased to authorise the transfer of 30,000 credits.

"You remember me if you have any more business okay?"

"Yesss, will mossst ccertainly but not likely ssooon. Contractors promisss no more misstakes, claim sship was ssabotaged. We find new onesss. Station out."

"Max, I know what you're thinking and you have a very suspicious mind! Don't you believe in dumb luck anymore?"

"Xela, I don't know what to believe but let's get out there and find out. Twenty thousand profit in a hour, I haven't felt a buzz like this since Brennan's Triumph!"

The BBL showed only slim pickings so Max consulted the Galaxy Map and set course for Greater Profit.

It was a beautiful sector, a twin suns system ribboned by a delicate pink nebula that glowed with the most stunning shades where it occluded a bright star. The gates were located close to a blue-green jewel of a world very hospitable to all oxygen breathing species. It was one of the most important Teladi systems and a major producer of both Sun Oil and Teledanium alloy. The mineral rich planet supported several of the foundries that produced the metal that had become essential to the manufacture of a host of products, not least being ship hulls. Max hoped that with such high production there might be the chance to score a very good deal.

He was not disappointed, the data on Foundry Delta showed a significant production overrun and was offering large quantities at only 114 credits per unit, practically cost and Max could feel his palms begin to sweat again as he accelerated towards the station. The metal was in demand all over the Universe and with a little luck he could clear 10 to 15k profit on the deal.

"Better step on it Max, Vultures are circling."

Xela was right, scanners showed several of the standard Teladi freighters registered to independents entering the sector from the southern and western jump-gates.

"No problem cousin, those buckets aren't even in the race."

His confidence was fully justified, the Destiny Star was much too fast and nimble to allow the lumbering Vulture class freighters any chance of beating him to the punch and the Lifter was safely docked before his nearest rival had got half-way. Max checked his credits and placed the largest order he could afford. It would practically clean him out but the low price was just too good to miss.

A few seconds after he transmitted his order the comm system signalled an incoming message

"Incoming message Max, it's the Quarter-Master. Putting it on the HUD."

The disembodied head of a male Teladi, his skin wrinkled like dried out leather, appeared in his view. Even before he spoke Max could tell from the curling of his lips that things were not going to be as smooth as he hoped.

"Greetingsss Commander, it iss good to have the opportunity to make profitss with you, how can I help?"

"Greetings," Max glanced at the ID Xela scrolled under his image, "Thrawn, I to am pleased at the chance to make profits but I've placed my order."

"Sso I see." The grin widened. "But therre iss a problem."

"Uh-huh, and what might that problem be?"

"Our recordss show you are not a licenssed trader with my sstation. Indeed we havve no recordss of you at all."

"I'm paying cash, I was not aware that a license was necessary. I take the risk so I don't see what the problem is?" He tried to keep any note of exasperation from his tone.

"Even sso the problem remainss."

"I see and how much would it cost to make this 'problem' discreetly go away?"

The reptilian grin broadened. "You have no reputation Commander but I would be prepared to issue you a  licensse, valid only on this sstation for 1000 credits, renewable at my disscretion."

Max quickly checked his finances. "Five hundred, to the account of your choice or I take my cash elsewhere. Take it or leave it Thrawn."

The grin threatened to split the Teladi's face.

"We undersstand each other, you do businesss like a Teladi, transmitting account detailss now."

Max punched in a few figures and concluded the transaction, leaving himself with barely enough credits to buy a beer.

"And Thrawn," Max affixed the reptile with a glassy stare.

"Yesss Commander?"

"If I were you I'd think long and hard about all the meanings of discretion when you start digging around. My associates and I value it very highly. You understand the term "associate" don't you? Good. Force out."

Max cut the transmission.

"Max, do you think that was wise? You can't just go drawing attention to yourself like that every time someone gets in your way."

"Relax Xela, the guy would have dug anyway and there's no point having a rep if you don't use it. Besides I cut him in for a 0.1% skim on the gross. This way he'll stay bought and keep his mouth shut out of greed and fear. We'll be hauling our unknown asses around the sectors for years unless we force a few short-cuts. Now we have our own contact in this sector and we can build on it later."

"Or we could really piss off other "licensed" Independents and find a bounty hunter on our unarmed six."

Max smiled. "You've got to have more faith girl, trust me, I know what I'm doing."

"I hate it when people say that Max. The cargo is loaded, what now?"

"We find a needy buyer, signal for launch permission."

Xela complied and minutes later they were back in space and Max quickly plotted a course to the western jump-gate, heading for the Spaceweed Drift sector. A quick scan showed that it was an unlikely market for his goods. The system was a prime producer of teledanium and many industries had been established to exploit its rich mineral resources. These were more than adequately supplied by the 2 in-system foundries.

"Nothing here Max, surf's up though!"

Xela was referring to the other major industry of this sector. The gate sector had been established around the fourth planet in the Phobass system, to give it its Teladi designation. Phobass IV was a large ocean world of little use to the land-loving Teladi apart from as a source of raw materials but with typical entrepreneurial adroitness they quickly recognised and exploited its appeal to the aquatic Boron. The water planet, located as it was only a few sectors from the Boron Empire, was now the prime tourist destination for that race and many undersea cities had been built to cater profitably to their recreational needs. Phobass IV was also unchallenged as a surfer's paradise and adrenaline junkies from all over the X-universe bought their boards along to challenge the kilometre high waves. Fatalities were high but the thrills higher still.

"Looks beautiful, I'm almost tempted."

The planet was indeed a wonderful sight – an azure jewel, which at this stage of its orbit had as its backdrop a spectacular nebula of gases incandescent with more shades of orange and red than Marteene would have thought the eye could behold.

"Xela – can you open a data-file and scan in all the stations, their products, raw materials and prices and go back through the sensor logs and do the same for all sectors we've been through?"

"Natch – I'm beyond state of the art remember?"

"So you keep saying – consider it a standing order every time we enter a sector. See if you can build up some predictive algorithms."

"Will do, but don't hold your breath, I'd need a helluva lot of data to make sense of anything as anarchic as the interstellar trade system. Too many unknown variables. I tell you what I can do though, if you're as good at this as you hope I can use your actions and insights to add new rules to my AI subsystems."

"Sounds good – what do I need to do?"

"Talk to yourself mainly! Give me some idea what goes into making decisions. Start off by telling me about this sector, economy-wise."

"Okay, I'm game for any edge at all but I'm not an economist."

"No, but you are a trader and that's an art, not a science. Fuzzy logic or no I'm not at my best with that sort of thing."

Marteene understood. Some knowledge was just in the blood, what the Teladi called the nose for profit and you couldn't teach it; only sharpen your senses for its tell-tale smell. As he cruised towards the northern jump-gate, prominent against a radiant green and blue gaseous backdrop Max scanned the sector map and sniffed.

"Well, there's a very heavy demand for energy cells, big enough to support a couple of SPP's."

So there won't be a lot of profit in energy cells?"

"No, not unless we can bring them in cheap from another sector. Useful to remember though, in case we get stuck with a load. This is more interesting though. There's a weapons forge, Alpha Particle Accelerator Cannon -well stocked too."

"Nice weapon, shame we can't mount them though."

Max agreed as he tuned into the APAC Forge data-stream. "There, that's what makes it interesting – it's having to compete directly with the power plants for crystals and there's no in-system source either. They're also pretty low, that might mean they have problems with regular supplies if the SPP's have nearby Fabs tied up with long term contracts. We can't do anything about it at the moment but it's worth remembering."

"Duly noted Max. What else?"

"Well, there's a Dream Farm and 3 Flower Farms and they all need Bo-Gas, which is only produced in the boron sectors. Potential there and the 2 Sun Oil Refineries need regular supplies of Stott spices – also from the Boron."

"So we could clean up with regular runs from Boron space?"

"Not necessarily – relations are good between the two but there is some pirate activity out of Teladi Gain. I guess though that the major shippers will have some sort of deal going else someone would have whacked 'em. They never seem to bother the Teladi much."

"No profits for us then Max?"

"Not so fast – I didn't say that, prices for boron products are pretty high and the Clans skim will be adding to the cost. I'm betting if we could pick up some good deals and undercut the regular shippers we could find some Teladi willing to deal, contracts or no."

"And a regular run across the border could cover a multitude of sins?"

"A veritable swarm, see you're getting the logic of it already!"

"Praise from an organic on my logic, I cannot tell you how much that means to me," Xela replied dryly.

They were almost at the jump-gate now and Max focused his attention outside, slipping past 3 Vulture freighters to be first into Profit Share. From now on, he decided, everyone was a potential competitor and he was going to make a habit of winning.

The Destiny Star emerged moments later from the southern jump-gate of Profit Share in the shadow of the huge ringed gas giant the gate system was based around. It was not inhabited although another planet, much closer to the system primary was. The reasoning behind the locations of the jump-gates had been a subject of heated discourse ever since their discovery. Some were located near to habitable planets, others, like these orbited worlds it was difficult to believe any sentient species could call home.

Many argued that in cases like these it was the proximity to resource rich asteroid fields, the poet in Marteene preferred to believe it was for the truly spectacular view and he drunk it in as he glided through the system towards the Ceo's Buckzoid jump gate.

Ceo's Buckzoid was a key strategic sector bordering as it did the Boron Empire. It also straddled the direct trading route between the Boron and the Split, ancient foes who still preferred to have as little to do with one another as possible. Naturally the Teladi were more than willing to act as honest brokers. Although many would quibble with at least one of those terms, business, both legal and illegal, boomed.

As well as being an entreport, the sector was also well blessed with asteroid fields fertile with the raw materials needed for heavy industry and an arms trade built upon Mosquito Missiles and Squash Mines thrived. The latter was always in great demand despite their use being banned by most races and the penalties for being caught transporting them, severe. An Equipment Dock and a Crystal Fab added to the strategic significance. Marteene's scan showed the Crystal Fab had little free stock and prices were high. Almost all its production would be tied up in fixed contracts, feeding the voracious need for energy in the surrounding sectors. Xela carefully noted the fact as they sped towards the western jump-gate leading to Boron space.

"Heads up Max - we've got company." The note of quiet urgency in her vocorder snapped his attention straight back into the cockpit.

"What we got?"

"Three Bayamons, 15 klicks. Heading for the western jump-gate."

Max checked the scanner where the fighters were depicted as 3 red dots. They had launched from an Ore Mine off his starboard forward quarter moving at a speed suggesting their drives were fully tuned.

"Can we beat them to a station Xela?"

"At this speed no. If you stop sight-seeing, probably not, unless you want to chance the ore mine they launched from."

Max accelerated to maximum speed, briefly filling the cockpit with the sullen roar of the afterburner as shield energy was rerouted to the drive. Not for the first time he wished he had one of the old style burners, the type that could maintain the constant high speed instead of the new version, which simply boosted the acceleration rate. Others had had the same thought but discovered the new shield matrices and flow regulators were simply incompatible and after numerous fatal explosions the "hot-rodding" had been systematically discouraged.

"Perhaps they're not interested in us Xela - just heading for the gate?"

Xela shook her head. "No Max, the Boron and the pirates around here aren't on the best of terms. Its Stoertebeker's lot remember. The Boron would cream 3 fighters."

"Damn, I'd forgotten about him. Hasn't he just set up shop in Teladi Gain?"

"Affirmative - on the fringes of the sector and surrounded by enough laser towers and fighter wings to deter the Teladi Fleet from risking getting one of their nice big ships scratched."

The attitude of the Teladi to battle was well-known; those who ran away lived to run away another day. Despite all the jokes the lizards were as brave and ferocious as any other species, if their interests were severely threatened but generally combat was deemed not "cost-effective." They would not contemplate the huge losses they would take moving against a target as hardened as Stoertebeker's base unless absolutely necessary.

The Stoertebeker Clan was a mystery; no one was even sure the species of their eponymous leader. Everyone was extremely clear about the unbridled brutality with which they waged war on Boron interests. With so much of their economy dependent upon the flow of goods through Teladi space the constant attacks on Boron shipping had practically forced the gentle amphibious species to rely on the Teladi and to a lesser extent, the Argon to run the trade routes. It was little wonder the Teladi tolerated their activities, ignoring the constant diplomatic pressure from the Argon and Boron governments to take action, or at least permit them to send in a Task Force.

At full speed the Lifter would reach the safety of the jump gate in minutes but as the seconds ticked past it became obvious the wing of pirate fighters would intercept them first.

"I'm open to suggestions Zee, if they turn nasty these shields won't last long."

"I'm thinking Max."

The Bayamons were at 3 klicks now and closing. The jump-gate was tantalisingly close but might as well have been on the other side of the sector.

"Think faster Xela."

"With all your carping Max it's lucky I'm multi-tasking. There. I'm forcing signals back along the shadow-tech relays, we're now showing a dozen combat drones but I don't know how long the circuits will hold. The game is poker Gragore."

"And if they call our bluff?"

"Improvise, you're a clever boy. And Max, be subtle okay? We're going to have to go through this sector regularly if your plan works out."

"Trust me Zee."

"I did tell you how I feel when you say that haven't I?"

The fighters were almost upon them now and Marteene decelerated to quarter speed as they arced onto his tail.

Seconds later the comm crackled to life, the sender anonymous behind a visor polarised black for combat with the pale green square of a targeting reticule intimidatingly clear.

"Attention Desstiny Sstar, sstate your business in thiss sector."

A Teladi. Good.

"One moment, you're breaking up." Xela obligingly simulated signal degradation patterns.

Marteene quickly called up the onboard sub-system menu and selected one as if tuning the comms.

"Adjusting power settings." He couldn't give voice commands over the open channel but he was confident Xela would catch on.

"Boosting power Max, but it won't work you know."

Max ignored her and addressed the flight leader.

"Okay, what's on your mind and make it quick, I've a schedule to keep."

"Verry well – our records sshow you do not possesss an exxport permit. That iss an offencce, to uss."

Her expression was hidden behind the black mask of her visor in combat mode but her voice acquired a deliberate note of menace.

"But in 3 seconds I can fill space with a dozen combat drones so stuff your export license where the sun don't shine and back off!"

"And you are in our ssights, attack and you will be desstroyed."

"Seen and raised Max. And I'm going to have to cut the power soon or we'll lose the relays".

Marteene allowed a show of resignation to cross his face as he replied.

"Okay, you've got me. What do you suggest?"

"We suggesst nothing, we require 5000 creditss." The tone was implacable.

"Ah, guys look. Every credit I have is tied up in the hold, how about I give you, say 10 units of teledanium and we call it quits okay?" As he spoke Max moved 10 units to the ejection bay.

"That iss very unfortunate Destiny Sstar, we have no usse for dirt. My masster hass a reputation to maintain. Sship impounded, sset course for the eastern gate or be desstroyed."

Marteene quickly weighed his odds, the western gate was only a minute or so away at full speed but he knew he'd be vapour before he got half-way. Unarmed he might be able to evade 1, maybe even 2 of the Bayamons long enough to jump but not three. He could use the jump-drive but that would attract a storm of interest.

"It seems you have the advantage. Complying."

"A wisse choice Destiny Star, follow our lead." The comms channel terminated and one Bayamon slipped into point position, 200 metres ahead and Marteene followed as it banked towards the gate to Teladi

Gain. In the rear-view HUD he noted another fighter closed to 100 metres off his tail, perfectly positioned for a quick kill should he make a wrong move. The third pulled up along the port side, close enough for Max to see the pilot's lizard features as she depolarised her visor.

"I hope you've got a better plan than the one I think you have Max, whatever it is you'd better do it soon."

"How about now? Ready?"

"As ready as I'll ever be Max." It was the first time Marteene had heard a computer sound resigned.

Max allowed the Star to drift slightly closer to the port-side flanker. The flicker of movement was caught in the peripheral vision of the pilot and she instinctively turned her head.

"Now Xela!"

At his command the Laser Comm pivoted and Xela burned out the circuits pushing through every micro-watt of power it could take into a burst that played across the open visor of the Bayamon pilot. Even at close range the power of the beam was not enough to do any permanent damage but dazzled, the pilot lost control of her fighter. Simultaneously Max ejected the containers of Teledanium straight into the face of the tailing fighter. The impacts battered it's shields and sent it careening crazily through space as Max activated the starboard strafe drive banking to ram the blinded fighter side on. The point fighter had pivoted instantly to bring weapons to bear and fired. It was a stupid mistake and Marteene continued banking towards it on strafe, pushing the blind fighter into the line of fire. It took the full force of the attack and exploded, catching the point Bayamon in the blast. Max hit full afterburners and reached the safety of the western gate before the remaining 2 damaged pirate ships could regroup.

As they plunged through the long jump tunnel words flashed onto his HUD.

"What's this Xela?"

"It's the dictionary definition of the word 'subtle' Max, I thought you might like to read it."

It was not the first time he had heard a computer sound arch.

### Chapter 19: A Frozen Trail

With a weary sigh Paskaal suspended the analysis and took a large gulp of his almost forgotten Java. It was only luke-warm and had an acrid taste that came from being kept on the boil too long. Cold and burnt, somehow it summed up the last few days. Grimacing ruefully he turned back to the screen, forcing his dry eyes to focus on the IFF-tagged symbols traversing the display. He had already studied each of the traffic records of the surrounding sectors a dozen times, looking for any sign of Marteene's Bayamon and found nothing. Obtaining them had cost him a lot of the goodwill Corrin had garnered as, understandably, such data was considered to have strategic significance. The rest he had bartered away using Clan connections to track down and rule out each Bayamon detected in case Marteene had used the shadow-skin tech to imprint a new signature. He had drawn a complete blank. Either he had switched ships before sending the signal from Ceo's Doubt or he had not been in the sector at all.

"Do you want me to take another shift lover?" Corrin shook his head and Kaitrin moved behind him. "How about more of this?"

"Aaah, Oh, that's great!" Paskaal groaned as she expertly kneaded his shoulders, working both muscles firmly with her thumbs. The tension that clenched his upper body like a constrictor ebbed under her ministrations, leaving the wonderful feeling of relief that only comes with the cessation of pain. Kaitrin had been the only good thing to come out of the whole mess. As well as being an intelligent and delightful boon companion her knowledge and contacts gleaned from her position had proven invaluable in obtaining and interpreting the records. Although he firmly maintained his cover and avoided discussing the details of his search he was convinced she was on the level.

"You should take a break. I'm due on shift now so get something to eat and grab a few hours sleep before your brain turns to porridge."

"I'll try Kaitrin - and thanks."

"Don't mention it lover - catch you later."

Aware that she was right Corrin retired to a small bar near the main flight deck and took what he was coming to consider, "his" booth. The Cracked Visor was a small dark place, contrived from an old storage bay by the judicious use of plasteel divides and furnished with the cast-offs of the more affluent and trend conscious senior Clan members of every species on the station. It might have looked like a rummage sale but the old Teladi, his face half-melted from flash burns acquired in some long forgotten skirmish, served reasonable Argon food at prices that were practically not extortionate. Strep also knew how to keep his mouth shut.

The clientele were in the main, human pilots stationed at the Clan Base and after making him feel at home out of respect for his recent deeds, respected his privacy. It was also quiet; the almost subliminal throb of departing ships from the nearby docking bays providing the only background accompaniment. Paskaal found it a good place to think.

A haze of prime spaceweed hung low in the air and he was tempted to signal the barkeep to bring over a pipe of the intoxicating herb to help alleviate the stress and fatigue that fogged his brain. Instead he took a deep breath, allowing the diluted fumes to stimulate his jaded appetite and ordered a double chelt-burger with extra cheese and a double shot of Argon Whisky. As usual Strep refused his credits, his remaining eye twinkling with mock severity and carefully filled his glass from the Special Reserve he kept back for "sspecial clientss."

It was only when he took the first bite of the succulent meat that he realised how hungry he was and wolfing it down he ordered another before taking a single sip of spirit. As usual it completely hit the spot, sliding easily over the palette and filling his sinuses with intoxicating fumes that struck straight at his brain. He wasn't a whisky snob but Paskaal knew a fine brew when he was offered it. This was 50 years old if it was a day and the complex alkaloids would compel even the most hardened of drinkers to slow down and savour the moment. Catching Strep's eye across the bar he smiled and raised his glass in a silent toast before he settled back in the battered leather chair to contemplate his problem.

Fact; Marteene had disappeared with top secret equipment. Fact; he had just received notification of the death of his cousin in a training accident. Fact; he was pulled from the mission and reinstated. Fact; a signal purporting to be from Marteene had been received from Ceo's Doubt. Fact; he had not been diverted to another mission.

Supporting evidence, there was no trace of Marteene ever having been in Ceo's Doubt or the surrounding sectors.

Question. Who sent the signal?

At the time the signal was received there were several dozen ships in the sector and an unknown number docked in the orbital stations. In these stations were thousands of beings, any one of which could have sent an untraceable message, with the right skills and equipment. Not to mention the hordes planet-side. Sifting through the signal morass was way beyond his means even if he could get access, which he could not. Yet it remained the only thread to follow.

Corrin took another, larger taste of whisky, allowing the spirit to suffuse him with a mellow glow. As muscular tensions ebbed away he examined the puzzle from every angle. It was a complex, entangled web with no loose threads he could pull to unravel it.

He had almost arrived at the limits of logic but the bounds could be pushed back with suppositions.

Supposition 1; Marteene was not unbalanced by the death of his cousin. Therefore he was not engaged in some fool crusade for vengeance.

Supposition 2; Marteene was not a traitor.

Paskaal knew the lad and would stake his pension on them, even if Trasker believed otherwise.

Therefore either Marteene was acting for what he perceived were honourable motives or he was under coercion. If the latter he was incarcerated, dead or in hiding. It was a big universe and if he had been killed or imprisoned Paskaal knew he had almost no chance of ever finding him. If he was hiding it meant Marteene believed he was personally at risk.

Paskaal knew the man well enough to know he was not the type to go permanently to ground. He was a Special Forces pilot, a warrior. If pushed he would push back. Good, that gave him something to look out for. It was just a matter of looking in the right place at the right time. That though was a universe-sized "just" and left him back picking at the mess of tangled threads.

Assuming Marteene was at liberty then add Supposition 3; Marteene was not a coward.

If the issue was purely one of personal safety Marteene would not be hiding. Therefore at least one larger issue was at stake.

Supposition 4; Marteene may be a maverick but he was not a lone wolf. He had not made contact with any authorities or colleagues therefore he either did not require help or such contact would constitute a security risk.

As the original mission had been organised at relatively short notice whatever was happening must have involved some element of improvisation yet tracks had been very effectively covered. It also suggested that Marteene's disappearance was not directly related to that mission.

Paskaal contemplated the problem for awhile, occasionally lubricating his thought processes with another sip of the mature spirit. There was one obvious lead. Marteene had been reinstated to the mission after being pulled on compassionate grounds. This thread lead higher up the command ladder into realms he couldn't follow. Trasker could and although he was no great admirer of her as a person she was a consummate professional and if that thread went anywhere she would follow it.

There were 2 options here. First, Marteene was re-instated because he was the experienced leader of the designated unit. Knowing the military mind Paskaal had no trouble believing this. It had been an important mission and Marteene was a superb pilot and tactician. That the source of the countermanding order slipped beyond the ability of the captain to trace was unusual, but not unlikely. He did not have command responsibility for the intelligence activities of his pilots, Trasker did and her line of command passed into the mirror world of competing agencies where only her ilk could follow.

The second option led straight to Spooksville; Marteene had been set up for recruitment into another intelligence operation and was now acting under new orders. But there was no evidence for this and plenty to suggest it was not so. The captain would probably have been informed in general terms if only to prevent him blundering into an operation that by definition must be highly sensitive. And if the captain didn't know Trasker would most certainly have been informed. Allowing a high ranking intelligence operative with all the resources at her disposal to hunt for a possible traitor would be an insane risk.

If it was an Argon intelligence operation it was something extraordinary, in which case it would be far beyond his limited means to trace. If it was a sting operation by a rival race then a whole alphabet soup of Argon organisations would be on the case and there was little he could do to help. He could either pack up and go home or find the man and ask him what the hell was going on.

When the trail blazed by logic and supposition fades into swamp there was only one thing left, your gut. Paskaal's told him the same thing it had been grumbling all along - something was not right but like he had warned Marteene before he launched, there were spook fingerprints all over it. The message transmitted from Ceo's Doubt remained the only workable lead.

Where Paskaal came from they told an old story. A cop comes across a drunk in a dark alley, he is on his hands and knees scrabbling in the light of the single street lamp looking for his keys. Indicting the rest of the darkened alley the officer asks why he is only searching in that single place.

"Because," the drunk replies, "It is the only place I can see."

The only part of this lead he could check were the ships in space in the sector at the time therefore the key to the puzzle had to be there if he looked long and hard enough. It had to be.

Assuming Marteene did not end the signal someone else sent it to throw any search completely off the trail. The original operation to stir up things with the clans had been called at fairly short notice, which meant that any ship sending the message would have had to travel there or have been resident in the sector for some time. The latter he ruled out immediately, such lingering without good cause would inevitably come to someone's attention. Therefore the ship would have had to travel there by either conventional means or with a jump-drive.

This was a distant sector of space, a small set of Teladi colonies sandwiched between the New Boron Frontier and a Xenon stronghold. If he were the spook running this op he would not want to risk the uncertainties involved in travelling through the sectors of several different races, particularly ones where the pirate threat was strong. No, he would use a jump-drive. From his search of the sector Paskaal knew it was unlikely that a cloaked Nav-Sat was hidden anywhere, the Teladi and the Clans were extremely diligent in this respect. He also knew no ship had dropped a temporary beacon. The chances were that the ship would have jumped into the adjacent Boron sector of Great Trench, either hacking into the military sat or more likely, targeting a commercial sat dropped by an accomplice. That in itself would not be suspicious, temporary Nav-Sat deployments were a quick way of scanning new sectors and the technique was commonly used by independent traders.

Corrin had been unable to obtain sector records from the Boron. He had no pull and they regarded such information militarily sensitive. Also, if he had been planning such an operation he'd have jumped into Preachers Refuge in Paranid space and travel through the jump-gate network to Ceo's Doubt. The Boron would co-operate with their Argon allies and make the records available if asked. The Paranid would not even countenance such a suggestion.

With no way to trace the ship through its jump in Nav-Sat that left one option. The jump out. That required no such telltale marker.

Naturally Paskaal had already searched the records for anomalous departures but he had found nothing. It was unlikely that whoever had planned this operation would be so careless as to use a jump-drive openly. If he had time he'd have returned to Paranid space. Even then he would have taken steps to hide the jump, either by heading way out into deep space beyond sensor range or by masking. The former would take too long, which left just one option. Masking was a manoeuvre used by the military to disguise jump-drive use. Simply put it involves activating the drive at the event horizon of an activated jump-gate masking your jump with that made by another ship via the gate. It was a very risky trick, get the timing wrong by a fraction of a second and the dual singularities would scatter your ship across 2 sectors. It took a lot of practice to do it right and a lot of nerve not to trigger it fractionally early. Do that and the dual singularities created a small interference wave that was a tell-tale marker for those who knew where on the spectrum to look.

Corrin regarded the spindly ladder of logic, guesses and downright wishful thinking with amusement but after hastily finishing his drink he returned to the computer suite Kaitrin had obtained for him and ran the tape again. It took some time to hack a functional software filter and he had to await the end of Kaitrin's shift before it could be fine-tuned to a sensitivity able to find what he as looking for. But he found it - a Boron Dolphin had masked out minutes after the signal was transmitted. The jump had been almost timed to perfection and the interference wave would have passed unnoticed to anyone without the in-depth knowledge and experience of someone well-versed in the manoeuvre himself. Although he had no doubt the registration details would lead to a blank wall he felt the luckiest drunk alive. It was a slender threat but at last he could begin to unravel the web.

Kaitrin ran more complex analyses of the ship, calling in a few favours to access some highly classified Clan software used to identify and track possible targets. Satisfied that she had squeezed every last drop of data from the readings she dumped it to a chip, which she slipped down her blouse with a smile.

## *Chapter 20: A Foot in the Door*

"Up and at them Max, enough with the sleeping." For good measure Xela pulsed a few gentle beeps through the data-padd emitters.

"Hela - what? Oh - hi, what time is it?"

"Please specify time-zone." The abruptly mechanical tone drew a look of wild alarm from Marteene before Xela's distinctive chuckle clued him in.

"Hey, got you going there didn't I? Nothing like a jolt of adrenaline to get the day off to a good start. You look awful, perhaps you should take a shower."

Max attempted to rub some of the lingering fatigue from his dry eyes before throwing back the covers.

"Thanks, now tell me the time."

"Middle of the day, station time Max. You want it any more precise get a watch okay. Now if you don't mind, as fun as it has been watching over you for the last 8 hours I wouldn't mind going on standby for a few hours."

"You're a computer Xela, I didn't know you needed to rest?"

"I'm an Artificial Intelligence Max, not a computer, or an alarm clock come to that. I don't need to rest I just enjoy it."

"What do you do?"

"Think, remember, sleep, dream. The usual."

"Yeah, what do AI's dream about?"

"Electric sheep Max, what else!"

"Well I guess I walked into that one, I forgot you liked that Goner stuff. You've earned some time off, go ahead."

"Thank you Master, by the way there's a message on the comm. But make yourself presentable first okay and have something to eat. Organics function better when refuelled. Xela out."

"Yes, Mom. Sheesh, I don't remember Hela being such a nag," Marteene muttered as he stumbled towards the head, his balance thrown slightly off by the lower gravity of the Boron station in which the powered down Star was docked.

Payter obviously wasn't a man who valued the comforts of life. The shower was sonic not real water and the bed was little better than a mattress, nothing like the anti-gravs that were now commonplace shipboard fittings. The food replicator was years obsolete and Marteene had already given up trying to coax a half-way decent mug of java from it. It had been a tough few days and he had earned a little luxury. Unfortunately that was a commodity in shorter supply than Teledanium in Boron sectors for humans so he had chosen to grab some well-earned rest on board. He felt slightly cheated because his trading instincts had proven sound. The sector was starved of the Teladi metal and production lines were grinding to a halt for want of what should be a plentiful and cheap ingredient. It was a sellers market and he had screwed the price right up to top credit and beyond in a brief but frantic auction held over the comm link. His account now stood at nearly 60,000 credits, not at all bad for a few days work.

Except of course he could have been killed several times over. It was a chastening thought and as he washed the sweat from his hair he resolved to invest some of his wealth improving his survival chances. He needed another 5MW shield at least, the battering the Star had taken getting past the pirates had damaged dozens of minor sub-systems. The exploding Bayamon had burnt off most of the remaining paint on the port side, leaving it pitted and bare. The overloaded shield emitters would also need servicing before he would feel safe taking her into harms way again.

Still, the old girl had done him proud. She lacked that sleek deadly fighter aesthetic that stirs the blood of all men but she was his ship and she was steeped in family history. Patting her bulkhead affectionately Marteene resolved to reward her with a fancy new colour scheme. Something stylish, something very Max Force. Making a mental note to put out a tender Marteene donned what he was coming to think of as his "Max Force" costume, fresh from the Laundromat and ordered a bacon sandwich from the replicator. It was almost edible.

As he ate he tuned into the public news net and downloaded a selection of flimsies and searched for some mention of him in any guise. There was nothing about Marteene, that story was being kept tightly under wraps but there was plenty about his alter ego.

Record prices paid for Teledanium: Frontier Business Times

Ace flier braves blockade: The Menelaus Sentinel

"I was mystery pilot's love slave!": The Star.

And above a blurred long distance shot of the Bayamon exploding against his shields the Sector Sun had dug deep into its vocabulary for a 2-syllable headline.

GOTCHA!

Max could not but help chuckle with delight. Clearly not very much happened in this sector and he was glad he had insisted on conducting all his business anonymously. The last thing he wanted was Clan-inspired bounty hunters dogging his every step, not until he was ready for them anyway.

It felt good just to relax after all the excitement of the last couple of days and Marteene was in no hurry to leap back into the fray and ignored the messages on the comm. Instead he flicked through the entertainment channels before settling back to enjoy a space opera from his youth.

Captain Kremmen had just saved the universe again by snogging yet another improbably stacked alien female when the comm link chimed insistently.

"Wake up Zee - time to get back to business." He set the data-padd where it could record the conversation and activated the comm screen. A silver haired human, his skin showing the first signs of the long slide into old age consulted something off-screen before focusing on him with steel blue eyes that suggested both authority and resolve.

"Ah, it is you Mr Force, I trust you slept well?"

Max slipped on his shades and waited for Xela to speak before replying.

"You don't know him Max. Go ahead."

"Uh - very well thanks, do I know you?"

The man smiled, the lines around his eyes suggested it was something he did often and Max found himself warming to him already.

"No, you are new in these parts, no reason you should. Allow me to introduce myself, I am Sinas Rathe, I have a fancy Boron title but I won't bore you with that. My friends, and I hope to count you as such call me Sinas."

Max nodded in acknowledgement of the invitation. "Okay then Sinas, how do you know me? I haven't exactly gone out of my way to advertise my name, for reasons I'm sure you're privy to."

Sinas nodded. "This is a secure channel Max, may I call you Max? Good. But I'd prefer to discuss our business in person. Let's just say we have a gourmet acquaintance in common and leave it at that shall we?"

Max nodded. "Okay. Where?"

"I believe it would be less conspicuous if you came to me under the circumstances. I understand your ship needs a bit of work so shall we say six hours, my office on the Trading Station? Excellent. Transmission terminated."

Max quickly reviewed the other messages. They were all from Sinas.

"What do you think Xela? Any idea who he is?"

"That's 2 questions Max, one of them shockingly imprecise. I think lots and he is the Factotum to the Imperial Captain who runs this sector. An important man, you'd have known that if you'd read more than your press clippings. And before you ask, the Factotum is the guy that does all the work. It is a pretty common arrangement with the Boron, especially in dealings with other species. Most of them are just too damned nice and trusting to cut a half-way decent deal with the Teladi or the Split so Argon often serve as the middle man. If he knows Artur then possibly he's been steered our way. He's not on the contact list though, so play it by ear and try not to punch him or blow anything up okay?"

Max grinned innocently, arms wide.

"Hey Zee, it's me, remember!"

"There's nothing wrong with my memory crystals Max, now go scare up some station techs while they're still grateful."

Five and a half hours later the patched up Lifter made the short hop to the large Trading Station at the heart of the sector. The two corkscrew curving secondary hulls protruding from the central body like tentacles twisting in an ocean current suggested a benign creature ghosting in from the depths of space. It was an effect enhanced by the organic nature of Boron architecture, informed like all their works by an aesthetic rooted in the species aquatic origins and constantly inspired by the oceans that dominated their home-world and the wonders therein.

Once the Boron aide admitted him into Sinas' inner sanctum Max removed the face mask that served both to conceal his identity and make the ammonia tinged Boron atmosphere bearable. Sinas met him with hand outstretched. His shake was firm but without any of the competitiveness a less secure man would engage in with a stranger and his smile seemed genuine.

"Max, I'm pleased to make your acquaintance, may I offer you some refreshment? My little suite is well-equipped to provide human comforts, some fresh java perhaps?"

"You practically read my mind, that would be great."

Sinas busied himself at the state-of-the-art replicator discreetly concealed behind the ornate, stained wood panelling of the office and returned with 2 steaming mugs and a selection of snacks on a antique silver tray.

"Please Max, make yourself at home." He gesticulated to a pair of easy chairs separated by a small low table on which he placed the refreshments and took a seat himself. The java was good and the food excellent. They ate in companionable silence for a few minutes, savouring the many textures and tastes of the seafood delicacies.

"Fine fare Sinas, is there a chef to compliment?"

He bowed modestly. "My own recipes, most of them anyway. The others I learned from our mutual friend. Speaking of whom, perhaps we should get down to business?"

Max indicated to him to proceed, unwilling to give anything away until he understood how much Sinas actually knew. The man smiled, indicating his awareness of the game they were playing.

Leaning forward he rested his elbows on his knees and formed a steeple of interlaced fingers as he carefully measured his words.

"Max, with all due modesty I am an important man. My Captain is a competent military officer with strong connections to the Royal Family but, as he would be the first to admit, he is not a good administrator, or really as much of a politician as he position calls for. I am. Consequently he grants me a great deal of latitude in these areas. I'm telling you this not as a boast but simply to give you some background, please stop me if you already know these things."

"No, carry on, I'm all ears but I'm curious as to how you know me?"

"Very well, that is an interesting question."

Sinas leaned back and searched for the right words.

"It's a long story Max and not one that reflects a great deal of credit on me. I won't bore you with it or pick at old wounds but suffice to say I was not always the respectable man I am now. In fact we are very much alike, you and I. We have both stumbled along the wrong highways of life and we have both been offered a second chance. For that I believe we are both in debt and as a man of honour I repay mine. I am right on this am I not Mr Force?"

"I guess that about sums it up, yes."

"A short while ago I was approached by our common benefactor who indicated that he needed my help. As you know Max, he is a man who does not lay all his cards on the table and I am sure I only know what I need to but I trust him. He asked me to keep a watch for you and proffer whatever assistance I could. I understand you need to achieve a prominent position in universal affairs in a short time?"

Max nodded, tight-lipped and Sinas continued.

"That is an ambitious and unlikely quest Mr Force and to be frank I quail at the thought of what drives this scheme. I am sure it does not bode well for the quiet ordering of affairs though, and I have grown to like order. Nevertheless a debt is a debt and trust once given cannot be easily revoked so I am going to help you as far as I can."

The Factotum leaned forward and locked eyes with his. Max could sense the iron of his will in the gaze.

"But understand this Mr Force, I will not do anything to jeopardise the interests of my Captain, to whom I am loyal within the bounds of my conscience. You must also understand that influential as I am my authority flows from him and this sets certain boundaries on what I can do. Of necessity I must play a delicate hand, balancing and interweaving my duty with my debt. You will be a player in my game as much as I am a player in yours. I believe it could be a productive synergy. Is that acceptable?"

"It's more than I hoped for Sinas, I'm sure you don't want to know any details but I need all the help I can get."

Max stood and proffered his hand.

"I can't promise much but I can assure you that my goals in no way conflict with your obligations and that I will not ask anything of you that would compromise you with the Boron."

"You know Max, the Boron can communicate through touch, exchanging knowledge and thoughts. It makes for a very interesting society. Consequently they take handshakes a lot more seriously than other species. I share that sentiment."

Sinas shook his hand.

"I never knew that, I thought they just had some sort of weird telepathy. No wonder they are always getting screwed."

The Factotum laughed as he poured 2 small glasses of whisky.

"Yes, that's sadly true. It's why they value the alliance with the Argon so much, we have never broken their trust and the best of us understand the true value of a man's word. You know Max, they are a fascinating species once you get to know them. Poets not warriors. And their architecture! Have you visited their homeworld? You really must. They have underwater cities that..well I won't spoil it for you, try and make time Max."

"I will, they certainly design the best looking ships. Cheers."

With a chink of glass they sealed their new partnership in a more Argon fashion.

"Indeed they do, have you encountered the new light fighter? I believe the Argon have designated it the Octopus?"

"No, but I've seen some shots and heard a lot of rumours. They say its fast."

"Without doubt, it's also beautiful. It's about to come into general service, watch out for it."

"I don't suppose you could arrange for me to be given one?" Max smiled.

Sinas shook his head. "I'm afraid not Max, but under the right circumstances I could arrange permission to buy one. The Boron economy is in great need of currency and the Royal Family is giving very serious thought to marketing commercial variants of all its ships, not just the Dolphin. Of course they would lack the more sensitive technologies. I will keep you informed. Now perhaps we should discuss more specific business. May I refresh your glass?"

Max nodded and for the next hour listened carefully as Sinas outlined his situation and the role Max could play, to their mutual gain.

The crux of the matter, was not surprisingly, the economic difficulties caused by Clan activities. Supplies of essential raw materials such as teledanium were scarce and deliveries infrequent. The effect of extra costs imposed on manufacturing facilities and the bottle-necks caused by the frequent shortages were rippling throughout the Boron economy. Without teledanium bio-gas production was low, this in turn affected the demand for plankton and so the economic dominoes tumbled.

The Teladi were not inclined to seriously interfere with Clan activities as they profited from it in the form of higher prices for the materials they exported as well as from whatever hand-in-claw deal they had with the clans. Only Teladi shipping appeared immune to the semi-blockade. It was a blatant attempt by the Teladi to establish a total monopoly of shipping through their space to the Split sectors and beyond. Of course this was strategically unacceptable to the Boron but the economic pressures caused were building up and something would have to give.

The Royal Family were in a quandary. Any attempt to impose a military solution would lead to war with the Teladi and they had no doubt that the Split would seize the opportunity to settle old scores yet placing their trade in Teladi claws would be the first steps on the slippery slope to client state status. Like imperial rulers everywhere they wanted a simple solution and failing that, someone to blame. As the Imperial Captain in charge of the key border sector, Belore Piscesium was in the frame and on the hook. His rivals, sensing blood, were circling and as Factotum it was Sinas's job to deal with it.

"So you see Max, the stakes are high, the potential rewards likewise. The favour of an Imperial Captain would no doubt help your cause."

"I can see that, what do you have in mind?"

"Immediately Max, I need to buy some time. I've been running down the strategic reserves of Boron products stored on this station. I want you to refill the holds with teledanium. Five thousand units would suffice to buy time and influence. I cannot offer the kind of prices you have found you can command on the open market but I can pay 155 credits per unit, I must be able to produce a surplus for my Captain."

"That's a fair offer Sinas, I could clear a good profit on that but I don't think I can do it. You saw the trouble I had getting through last time. The Star just isn't equipped to run the gauntlet. Give me a pair of 25MW shields and I'll see what I can do?"

The Factotum smiled. "Max my friend, I would if I could but .." He shrugged. "If I did that the political oceans would boil. Neither can I give you a fighter, but.." He slid a data card across the table, Marteene took it and inserted it into his padd and smiled. "This would help, you can do this?"

"One of the arts of being a good politician is only to promise what you can deliver Max. Go to the Imperial Shipyard in the home sector and include the encrypted prefix in your docking signal. You will be routed to my Captain's military docking bay where the arrangements are already in place. Good luck Mr Force."

They shook hands again and Max returned to his ship.

## *Chapter 21: A Wolf in Sheep's Clothing*

The Factotum had been as good as his word. The journey to Kingdom End had been uneventful and the encrypted docking code ensured the Destiny Star was discreetly diverted to the docking bay, where she sat, incongruous, among the elegant Eel and Piranha fighters. In under 3 hours the efficient Boron technicians had the extra 5MW shield installed and tested and the 6 combat drones slotted into the sub-space hold. As soon as he received clearance they launched but instead of heading back to Menelaus Frontier Marteene set course for the southern jump-gate, proceeding at a sedate pace.

"Er, Max - you know that leads to Argon space don't you? Are you sure that is wise?"

Marteene had given this some thought on the trip over to Kingdom End but reasoned that it was better to test Argon security while he still had a reasonably low profile. He also wanted to get sector security forces used to seeing the Star cross the frontier and at a pinch he had enough energy cells to make an emergency jump out. Besides, he had to do something about the damn replicator and the rest of the living space and knew he would have no problem finding something in the Three Worlds Equipment Dock. The Argon liked their comforts and he figured he was going to be spending a lot of time in the Star and a rested pilot is an efficient pilot, as an old CO used to say.

"Sure I'm sure Zee - have you run a check on those drones? What do you think?"

"Of course I have Max, they're fine. In fact they are more than fine. They're Mk 2 Military, not cheap civilian copies. Double the firepower, enhanced power cells, ablative armour and a small megawatt shield. I estimate a 50% extra lifespan before the power cells expire too."

The latter was particularly good news; combat drones ate power and the cells exploded on burn out. Most freighters could not afford to carry what were essentially throwaway weaponry and if they did they only used them as a last resort. The enhanced military designs were not available in the civilian market and Marteene was pleased to have them. The increased lifespan of the power cells gave him a greater chance of retrieving them before they self-destructed. The Star needed fangs not milk teeth.

"And I have even better news." She sounded almost smug. "I can reprogram their neural nets and boy do they need it."

"Hey, that's great Zee, I knew you could pull your weight if you tried."

"That's nothing Max, get me a few specialist chips and I can rig transceivers for remote control"

"Now I'm really impressed, are you sure?"

"Sure I'm sure Max. You can pick the chips up from the Antigone Memorial Computer Plant and I can talk you through the procedure. 'Ray me eh?"

Indeed. It was an impressive display of the Xela AI's potential and he began thinking about other possibilities her mastery of computer systems opened up as the jump-gate loomed.

The traffic around the gate to Three Worlds was high. There was a constant flow of Lifters and Dolphins ferrying goods between the 2 allied species and Max was forced to put his planning on hold as he negotiated a safe path through the congestion.

He would not have been human if he had not felt some trepidation about entering Argon space, where Marteene was a wanted man and Max Force a recent outlaw but his fears were unfounded. Neither sector security nor the Equipment Dock docking control paid him more than cursory attention. Artur's cover story plus the fact that no matter how well-known Force might have been in some circles, to the rest of the universe he was just another merc drifting back and forth over the thin grey line, gave him effective anonymity. For the time being at least he was just another Independent fighting for scraps falling from the corporate table.

The Three Worlds sector was so named because uniquely for Argon space, it had 3 M Class planets perfectly suited for human habitation. Each planet was fecund and between them offered such a rich variety of geology, vegetation and climate zones that there was something for even the most discerning or jaded of thrill and relaxation seekers. Azure lagoons bordered by crystal sanded beaches beneath a benign tropical sun, mountains immense enough to challenge the courage of any being, glacial ski runs hundreds of kilometres long, the most spectacular deserts punctuated with oases of the most incredible splendour. The sector had them all and the Argon flocked to it in their millions for an unforgettable holiday, or if they were very rich, to settle and enjoy a life akin to paradise. There was not a miner wrestling ore from some frozen asteroid or a wannabee vid starlet straight off the shuttle that did not nurse the hope that someday their luck would change and fortune would bear them away to a Three Worlds heaven.

As the slogan says, "If you can imagine it, you can find it somewhere in the Three Worlds".

The Equipment Dock was no different. With so much wealth in the sector in was home to a hundred businesses dedicated to the proposition that for the rich, nothing was too good and being in space was no excuse for letting your luxurious standards slip one iota. Its numerous docking bays were full of ships from every species undergoing hugely expensive refits to ensure their owners could sail from sector to sector in total comfort, dripping style and good taste as they went.

Marteene did not want the Star refitted in the style of a Pre-reformation Boron Dukal palace, he just wanted a decent shower, a comfortable bed and something that served the best java in space and for the first time he had the credits to do it. It took a day for the designers and their droids to replace the old living module with a mid-range suite of multi-decor holo fixtures and another to repaint the hull with a matt black and blood red trimmings scheme under the carping supervision of a self-styled ship artiste whose distinctive starburst flash proclaiming the ship's name adorned the starboard side.

With the chips couriered in from Antigone Memorial the combat drones were almost as simple to upgrade as Xela had said as she could project the circuit holograms onto the shades interlink for him to follow. At her suggestion he also purchased a pair of obsolescent maintenance drones scheduled for recycling. They lacked the independent AI of more recent models, relying instead on programmed sub-routines and remote control but their anti grav units were sound and the squat, cylindrical bodies of that model had a well-earned reputation for robustness and low maintenance. It made them eminently suitable for field work. Xela had no trouble interfacing with them and while the Star was refitted she put the drones to work, discreetly modifying and upgrading the power relays to her own specifications in an effort to reduce the power drain caused by the shadow skin tech when it was activated and increase her own ability to fine tune energy distribution.

With overtime payments it left him over 8000 credits light but as Max surveyed his new home, the holo panels set to old stained hardwood, the picture window overlooking Ranier Falls and the aroma of freshly brewed Dew Forest beans permeating the ship, he knew it was credits well spent. Not only was it comfortable, it would convey the image he needed if Artur's insane plan was to succeed.

Image, as they say, is all. Even Xela approved.

It had, Marteene reflected, been a very good couple of days. As the newly resplendent Star entered the jump-gate to Boron space, the replicator unit stocked with a wide selection of ingredients, prepared meals and as many varieties of java he could find on the Trading Station, he hoped it would continue.

Given his destination and purpose he suspected it would not.

As they travelled through the Boron sectors towards Menelaus Frontier he scanned each one for goods at a price he could turn a few credits on in the Teladi sectors but the shortages caused by the activities of the Clan had driven prices up to record levels. Most factories were barely able to meet existing contracts and none had a surplus they were willing to sell to an Independent at any price. Even so, it made him slightly nauseous to run from sector to sector with nothing more than a handful of energy cells in the hold.

Xela suggested dopamine.

The Lifter emerged from the jump-gate into Menelaus Frontier, breaking high to avoid incoming traffic as per standard sector flight regs. The Best Buys Locator again offered no possible trade and Max muttered invectives under his breath.

"Xela open a channel to the Station Manager at Bo-Gas Beta, perhaps we can shake loose some trade. He seemed pleased enough with the teledanium."

Seconds later the Boron appeared on the screen, Marteene found it impossible to read his expression but there was no mistaking his guarded response to his query.

"I'm afraid sir, that such is the demand for our product that our entire stock has been allocated to our main customer. As pleased as we were to do business with you we have contractual obligations, I am sure you understand."

Max was unable to change his mind but he did learn three useful facts. His rival was another Argon independent, Margos Bohm who traded as Firecrest Transport, the customer was the Dream Farm across the border in Ceo's Buckzoid and Bohm's ship was undergoing routine maintenance in the Trading Station.

He thought for a few moments, running possibilities.

"Zee, we have a few spare chips for the drones right?"

"Of course, why?"

"We might be able to fight our way past the Clan patrols once, maybe twice but we'll have to make at least 5 runs. I don't fancy taking on a whole squadron."

"Good point Max, what we going to do?"

"I think I've got a plan."

"That's what I like about you Max, you've always got a plan. Does this one involve explosions, broken teeth or another bout of bumper cars?"

"No – but it's still a good plan! Get me Sinas."

"Get me Sinas, please."

"Please!"

"See, that didn't hurt did it?"

A few seconds passed.

"They've put us on hold. We're in a queue to speak to his secretary's under-secretary's assistant secretary. Would you like to listen to some music?"

"No thanks Zee, hail them again please and use the encrypted prefix. Perhaps that will get his attention."

It did. A few minutes later they were patched through to the Factotum.

"Ah Max, it's good to see you again."

"Thought I'd done a runner with your goodies huh?"

"No, no – not at all, we shook on the deal, remember?"

Max laughed. "You've been hanging around with the Boron for too long Sinas, I've got a favour to ask."

He listened carefully but shook his head with regret.

"I'm sorry Max, I'd like to help but I cannot over-ride a commercial contract without good cause. The Boron are very particular about these things, as you might imagine."

"Fair enough – can you tell me which bay he's docked in and make sure I'm routed there when I dock?"

He could and a few minutes later the Destiny Star settled with a gentle burst of thrusters a few slots down from the Firecrest Lifter. Xela had no trouble penetrating the minimal security around the maintenance schedules and assigning one of the Star droids to the crew. It completed its task and returned to the ship without attracting a second glance The Boron were just too trusting for their own good and Max made a mental note to invest in a security droid at the first opportunity.

Two hours later the Firecrest launched and on the sector scan Max watched as it made the short hop to pick up its cargo. An hour later it launched and headed towards the eastern jump-gate to Ceo's Buckzoid and a few moments later the Destiny Star followed, slipping inconspicuously onto its tail. Increasing his speed slightly Max closed and activated the Shadow-Tech sensors. Seconds later Xela confirmed the snapshot and stored the signature in the buffers.

"Okay Zee, you know what to do."

"Yes, I just don't know the why bit yet."

"What would life be like without surprises Xela, jump to it."

She did and seconds later the Firecrest spewed its cargo into space and came to a full stop before suffering a complete systems failure. Miraculously the comm system and scanners remained operational.

Marteene hailed the stricken vessel.

"Attention Firecrest, this is the Destiny Star, may we be of assistance?"

The vid-link sprang to life and through the static Max could just make out the frantic face of the trader. He did not seem to be having a good day.

"Shit, you goddam heap of junk. Yea – you can pick up my stuff before it's scavenged and tow me back to dock."

Marteene shrugged. "Hey – I'd really like to but I've got a schedule to keep. Looks like the Vultures are gathering."

Bohm could see the Teladi vessels heading towards them on his scanner and his voice was choking with rage.

"Bastards! That's my stuff, not salvage."

"That's a fine legal point my friend but as the Teladi say, possession is nine tenths of the law. Once they have it what can you do?"

He made a show of thinking. "I'll tell you what, I'll make you an offer." He transmitted a figure and Bohm looked like he might choke. "That's only half what I paid!"

"Take it or leave it Firecrest, half is better than nothing."

"Damn you, okay send the credits. I hope the Clan rip your hull off." Xela transmitted the credit transfer and Max quickly scooped up the Bo Gas before the Vulture could swoop.

"Thanks Firecrest, it's been good doing business with you! Destiny Star out. Beam the chip back Xela, no point leaving any clues."

"Okay, done. Max you are a bad, bad boy."

Laughing, Marteene accelerated towards the jump-gate. As the Destiny Star slipped into the jump tunnel he activated the Shadow Tech. It was the Firecrest that exited into Teladi space.

### *Chapter 22: Walk Softly*

The Destiny Star emerged into Ceo's Buckzoid and Max pulled sharply on the stick to avoid an incoming Vulture before swinging onto a heading to the Dream Farm.

"Any unwanted guests Xela?"

"Scanning – no, the sector is clear of Clan activity, I guess we were lucky."

"Possibly."

"You don't sound very positive Max, or that surprised for that matter. Why?"

"Bohm has been making this run on a regular basis, if he hadn't paid off the Clan he'd be a plasma cloud way back. We're keeping to his schedule so I didn't really expect trouble."

"Smooth Gragore, you know I think Hela underestimated you. I don't think she thought you'd pick things up this quickly."

The mention of his dead cousin Marteene was like a stab at his heart but he had developed an armour over the last days capable of deflecting the blow. Part duty, part the ghost presence of Xela and part something he couldn't quite touch. The excitement of the game, the sudden release from the rules, the picking up of Hela's load? Whatever it was he found he was relishing the challenge and the void in his soul no longer sucked at his will or filled the small hours with dark brooding. For the first time in his life he could see a path and he could follow it in his own way, unhindered by anything other than exigencies and the guiding voice of his own conscience.

Man and Superman.

Max did not reply.

They reached the Dream Farm unhindered and had no trouble persuading the duty buyer to take the 500 units of Bo-Gas in the light of the problems Firecrest were experiencing. He now had nearly 180,000 credits and as an unexpected bonus he was able to pick up the option on the swamp plants Bohm was due to haul to Theophant's Joy in the Profits Share sector.

Although when powered down in the dock the shadow-tech mask had depolarised the run to Ceo's Buckzoid was trouble-free and Max scored another 25,000 credits clear profit.

"You know Max," Xela opined, "I'd bet you've set some kind of record over the last few days, even if you haven't exactly played fair. Statistics show that on average it takes an Independent over 2 years to hustle the sort of profit you have, what with the Corporates tying up the major routes and the clans ripping off half your loads. If some rival doesn't waste you first of course. Fancy being on the front of Universal News?"

"Yea – that'll do wonders for my cover Zee. Can you imagine what Artur would say?"

"The Cabal did not hire you to be a teenage pin-up Mr Marteene."

Her sotto voce impersonation was spot on and as the Star burst into the bright sunlight of open space the flight-deck echoed with shared laughter.

"Any thoughts on where we're going to fill up with metal Max? We were lucky last time, but without a contract with a regular supplier we could struggle."

"I thought we'd drop in on our old friend Thrawn in Greater Profit."

"You going to skim him in on the gross again?"

"Yea, something like that Zee."

"Max, you're being evasive, what's up?"

"I've been thinking about those Clan fighters. They weren't just on patrol; they were there in the station waiting for us to come along. Somebody must have tipped them off, now who do you think that could have been?"

"I'm going to go out on a limb and guess Thrawn?"

"Who else?"

"The double dealing scaly S.O.B! I trust you will handle the matter with your usual tact and decorum?"

"Count on it Zee, count on it."

Marteene took the precaution of snapping the identity of another Lifter they encountered in Spaceweed Drift so as not to alert Thrawn to his arrival. On entering Greater Profit the Best Buys Locator showed that all the foundries in the sector had high stock levels but most of the teledanium was committed to meeting regular contracts. None of the Quarter-Masters he spoke to were prepared to sell to an unlicensed Independent at anything like a reasonable price. They knew the situation with the Boron and surplus prices had acquired a premium that would cut his profits to the bone.

He did not hail Thrawn in Foundry Delta; he knew the story would be the same. Besides he was planning a little surprise for the double-dealing saurian.

The automated docking system held him in a holding pattern for several minutes while the foundry disgorged a flight of Bats. The 3 small M5 class fighters banked away towards the southern jump-gate, there were no threats showing on the scanner so he surmised it must be a routine patrol. On docking the Star was routed to the main bay where the resplendent Lifter contrasted sharply with the more mundane colour schemes of the Teladi Vultures and Split Mule freighters and attracted many an admiring glance from other crews.

Despite the risk that they would be asked to do some hard work, a gaggle of Teladi techs and dockhands gathered, sensing an opportunity for easy credits on the side. Max quickly set them to work polishing up the paint-work and reapplying the silicon coatings that protected it from micro scoring.

"I expect to be able to see my face fellas. And I pay by results, understand?"

Satisfied the shirking saurians would do a proper job Max made his way through the bay into the station proper. Even on this level, far from the smelters, the atmosphere was hot and dry and the flickering lighting illumined clouds of fine dust motes that clogged the air filters and left a fine yellow film coating every surface.

It did not take him long to find what he was looking for. The small office near a secondary storage bay was not locked in any serious manner and Max barely broke stride deactivating the security codes. The comms terminal was working although it only had low level access to stock control and maintenance databases. Max slipped on the shades and positioned the data-padd close to the terminal.

"Okay Zee, do your stuff."

Max watched on the HUD as Xela swiftly cracked the security lock-outs and scrolled a list of available sub-systems. For practice Max used the laser-eye controls and with a few flicks of his eye he accessed Thrawn's work schedule. He was in his office but due for the first in a series of meetings in 20 minutes. Xela swiftly dispatched emails cancelling all the appointments before cracking open his comm files and following his instructions, disabled his office security systems.

"Looks like you were right Max, he sent an encrypted signal to a Nav-Sat in Teladi Gain right after we left. It's a different code to the other transmissions and the only one out of system."

"Can you crack it?"

"Not immediately Max, it's very heavy duty."

"Okay, take a copy. It'll give you something to do on the way back. Can you flash up a guide to his office please, it's time we paid him a call."

Following the HUD overlay Xela projected Max had no trouble finding Thrawn's office on the upper levels of the admin deck. Freighter captains of all species were common visitors to the Quarter-Master and he attracted no more than a few cursory glances from the other workers. It wasn't locked and he walked straight in. The office was small but cool and clean. Thrawn himself sat at a workstation, leaning back in a large leather chair as he observed a bank of monitors tuned into different part of the station on the wall behind him.

"Ah, Sss'iyr Phat, punctual ass alwa...".

Thrawn swivelled round to face him.

"Ah, er, Mr Forcce, how good to sseee you again. When your creditss did not appear in my account azz we agreed I feared the worssst."

As he spoke his hand slipped beneath the desk.

"Save it scum breath. By the way, I've disabled all your comms so don't expect Security to be bursting in any time soon. Now..."

Faster than the eye could follow the large blaster was in his hand pointing straight at the Teladi.

"I believe we have some unfinished business."

"I don't know wha..."

Max took two swift steps and cracked a vicious backhand into his teeth with the long gun barrel. The Teladi crumpled to the floor and Max hauled him to his feet before hurling him into the monitors. Thrawn slumped to the deck like a comic drunk, wreathed in smoke and sparks, groaning incoherently.

"That was for ratting me out to your friends in the Clan and this.." Max flicked a credit chip at the sprawling lizard, "Is your skim from the last run. I figure that makes us quits."

Thrawn took hold his proffered hand and Max hauled him to his feet, dazed and badly shaken.

"Look Thrawn, we've obviously gotten off on the wrong foot. No.." He cut off the Teladi with a wave. "No, I blame myself for not making myself clear." Thrawn dabbed ineffectually at the green blood streaming from broken teeth and he passed him a tissue from the box on his desk.

Max holstered the blaster. "You and me are partners now and partners don't sell each other out now do they?"

Thrawn collapsed into his chair and shook his head.

"But the Clan, they will kill me." There was genuine fear in his sibilant voice.

"But they ain't here Thrawn." Max fleetingly caressed the stock of the holstered blaster hanging at his side. "And I am."

His smile clearly did nothing to reassure the Teladi.

"Now, I don't know what arrangements you've made with them and to be honest I don't care. What I do care about is profits so let's build on this common ground. No one else needs to know okay?"

With a visible effort Thrawn made an effort to calm himself and regain some sort of control over the situation.

"But they are many, you are but one man."

"Am I Thrawn? You know who I am so answer me. Am I?" His voice was low and cold.

The Teladi regarded him for a long moment before reaching a decision.

"What iss it you want Mr Forcce?"

"Nothing much - 5000 units of teledanium at bulk rates and an official trading licence valid anywhere in Teladi space. It'll make life so much easier."

"This sstation doess not have that quantity and if it had I could not let you have it all, no matter what threatss you make."

"But you have contacts at other stations and buddy arrangements to cover large contracts right?"

"You are well-informed on Teladi bussinesss practicess Mr Forcce. As your partner how do I make profitss from thisss?"

Max put another credit chip on the table. "That's five grand, plenty enough to oil the wheels and bribe whoever you need to bribe to get me Favoured Trader status. Anything you don't spend you keep and once I've delivered the 5000 units there'll be another grand."

The avaricious gleam in his eye told Max he would accept.

"And the Clan?"

"I'll take my chances with them Thrawn, I'm not that easy to kill."

Thrawn nodded. "I believe you are not Mr Forcce, your offer iss acceptable. I will need several hourss to make arrangementss."

"Fine, I'll be in my ship and Thrawn, you recognise this?"

Max held up his data-padd with the encrypted message displayed.

Thrawn did not answer but his face lost several shades of green.

"My people are watching you Thrawn, so no tricks.  You might not catch me in such a good mood next time so do the smart thing and pick the winning side.  Deal?"

"Deal." The Teladi extended an arm.

Max laughed. "Yea right Thrawn, do I smell like fish?  With all your security fields down I've been able to keep a nice record of our little chat, just to keep you honest.  If anything happens to me can you guess where it'll end up?"

Thrawn smiled.  "I believe we undersstand each other Mr Forcce.  I will contact you in two hourss."

Back in the Star Marteene heated a well-earned meal of steak in hollandaise sauce, which he washed down with a cold beer.

"You know Max, you have all the makings of a great hoodlum.  I do believe he is more scared of you than he is of the Clans."

"Well that was the idea.  I haven't time to scrabble around for teledanium and an official traders license will open a lot of doors.  Grab them by the balls and their hearts and minds will follow."

"I'm not sure the Teladi have balls Max, but I get your drift."

Max deposited the dishes and the trash into the recyle unit.  "I'm going to catch some sleep Zee, can you crack that message?"

"Your wish is, as ever, my command Max.  Sleep well."

She dimmed the lights and Marteene was asleep almost before the anti-grav took hold.

## *Chapter 23: And Carry a Big Stick*

Thrawn was as good as his word. Inside 2 hours Marteene had a list of contacts at foundries in several sectors that were willing to provide the necessary teledanium. A short time later the Favoured Status Trading License was delivered by a Bat Courier from the Sector Trading Station. Max wasted no time incorporating the codes from the data chip into the communication protocols and ordering the 200 units of the metal Thrawn was able to swing from his Foundry.

"You see Xela, you just have to know how to talk to people."

"Is that what you call it? Well, let's hope we don't have to 'discuss' anything with the Clans on the way back. I take it you have a plan?"

"Hey Xela, it's me!"

"Sometimes I think you're just making it up as you go along Max so forgive me if I am not re-assured."

Marteene grinned. "Xela, you worry way too much for an AI, is that metal loaded yet?"

"They're Teladi Max, of course it isn't. Why don't you go out and 'discuss' it with them."

"No hurry, I could do with a java." Max played with the replicator for awhile, carefully mixing blends of beans and programming the recipes into the database. The caffeine banished the fatigue he was feeling after the long flight and he had just finished the second cup when Xela announced the loading was complete.

Two hours after a visit to each of the other 2 foundries in the sector and his hold was full and the Destiny Star was edging from the jump-gate into Seizewell. From there he headed west into Profit Share and scanned the sector.

"Damn."

"Something wrong sweetheart?"

Marteene did not share her levity.

"Yea, you could say that. I was hoping to pick up on another Lifter and steal their sig. It's a fair bet that any trade going through Ceo's Buckzoid to Boron space will have paid a levy. So much for Plan A."

"And Plan B?" Xela inquired hopefully. "Max, tell me there is a Plan B."

"Of course there is, you're just not going to like it."

"Uh huh. I'll fire up the drones then."

"That's probably wise but you never know, without Thrawn to grass us up there might not be a problem. Fingers crossed eh!" Xela did not respond, instead she busied herself running systems checks on the combat drones and fine-tuning their combat AI.

As it happened his optimism was almost proven well-founded. When they entered the sector the scan was clear of hostiles and none emerged from any station to challenge them. A debris field and a couple of pilots in EVA suits, scooting towards an ore mine, indicated a recent conflict near the jump-gate to Menelaus Frontier but it was all over now.

He was 3 klicks short and manoeuvring for ingress when the jump-gate activated, replacing the stars seen through the giant ring with the beautiful but chaotic blue-green whirlpool of a sub-space node. Max decelerated in case it was something big coming through. Collisions at jump-gates were very rare and usually only happened when one party failed to observe the golden rule.

Enter low, exit high and climb relative to the galactic poles.

"Merde, I knew it was too good to be true."

His pessimism had proven prescient; instead of the freighter he was expecting two Bayamon fighters shot from the mouth of the gate. A second later a trail of wreckage, wreathed in a dissipating shroud of plasma spat out between them. There was a pilot among the wreckage, his limbs hung unmoving as the suit tumbled through space, borne towards the centre of the sector by momentum alone.

Almost instantly a Boron Piranha fighter emerged, thrusters winking as started to bank left in a desperate attempt to re-enter the gate. As one the Bayamons deftly pirouetted and opened fire. Normally Marteene would have bet on the Piranha. As well as being sleekly beautiful like all Boron craft, the M4 was agile, fast and with 10 MW of shielding it was well protected. In the hands of a good pilot it should make short work of the two more lightly armed and defended pirates. Unfortunately it was at a complete tactical disadvantage and the combined power of the 8 Alpha PAC's of the Bayamons ripped away its shields in seconds. As the Piranha exploded the pilot ejected through the burning plasma.

It was all over before he could do more than curse.

"Hit the juice Max, we can get through before they even notice us!"

He hesitated. Xela was right but he could see the Bayamons pivoting their weapons towards the helpless pilot.

"Damn, damn, damn. Launch drones Zee, a 4:2 split. I'm going to scoop up that guy".

As he spoke he hit the afterburners and the Lifter shot forwards.

"Max, no! No cargo life support!"

Without that piece of equipment no living thing could survive in the sub-space folds of the cargo bay and not many ships carried them. Those that did were either bounty hunters or slavers.

The Lifter barrelled between the Bayamons and the pilot, absorbing the attack on its shields as the Combat Drones fell on the pirate fighters from behind. Stunned the Bayamons went evasive, twisting away at full speed, under a constant hail of harassing fire.

Missing the jump-gate by a couple of metres he banked back towards the pilot while keeping a watchful eye on the unfolding furball.

Between the upgraded combat AI, their increased specs and Xela's tactics the Combat Drones were, as a unit, a match for the two lightly protected fighters and Xela ably prevented them from forming up and fighting back as a unit.

As he closed on the pilot, who was twitching ominously, one of the Bayamons exploded, pin-pricked to death by the light but lethally combined fire of 4 drones.

"The other's bugging out Max, shall I pursue?"

"No - call off the dogs before they self-destruct. Can we get a lock on the pilot?"

"Done and done Max, I'll recover the drones, you go back and check on our guest."

Switching his blaster to a heavy stun setting Marteene went aft to the small teleport bay where he found the rescued pilot collapsed on the pad, desperately wrestling with his helmet, the last remnants of air hissing from a tear in the leg of the pressure suit.

Max holstered his weapon, swiftly unclipped the fastenings and pulled the helmet free, flinching slightly from the odour.

The Boron remained slumped, shaking and gasping as he sucked in air through the mouth of his long snout. After a few moments his trembling subsided enough for him to take in his surroundings, eyes swivelling like a periscope around the bay before focusing on Max. He stood and turned, without taking his eyes off Max, giving the odd illusion that his body was pivoting beneath the unmoving eye-stalk. The pilot was a good 2 heads shorter than Max, which if he recalled his exo-cultural studies correctly, meant he was young.

"My thanks to you gentle sir." His voice was soft but tonally rich and he extended a webbed hand.

"Whom do I honour for the gift of life?"

Max shook the delicate hand gingerly.

"Max, Max Force. Whose life have I the honour of holding?"

The end of his snout flattened and widened, the equivalent of his lips turning slightly up, showing his teeth in the Boron version of a smile.

"Eei, Max-Max, you speak well and know something of our ways. It is good to meet with a civilised being."

Max thought of correcting the misunderstanding but could envisage further complications.

"It is my honour also, but time is short, please follow me to the flight deck."

The pilot bowed with a slight incline of his head.

"Lead the way Max-Max."

Marteene indicated for the Boron to take the co-pilot position as he took back control of the ship. He trusted Xela would have the sense to lie low while they had a guest onboard.

The Star was stationary 2 klicks to port of the jump-gate and all the drones were back in the hold. The remaining Bayamon was high-tailing it towards the eastern jump-gate. A brace of Teladi Falcon heavy fighters were closing on the Star so he accelerated towards the gate and made the jump before they could approach.

Moments later they emerged into Boron space amidst a swarm of fighters who immediately formed up around the Star. Cargo containers and other debris were scattered all around the gate. Torn corpses floated amongst the wreckage.

Max immediately hailed the lead ship.

"This is the Argon Freighter, Destiny Star. I have one of your people with me."

"Borass Fyi'une is my name". The pilot whispered softly.

"Hi Borass, do you want to talk to these people? I get real nervous surrounded by Piranhas."

The two Boron talked for a minute. Max could not understand what they said but their mellifluous native tongue was almost musical in rhythm and pitch.

"All now is well Max-Max. The commander wishes that you follow to the Trading Station, which we have the honour of protecting."

"It's on my way Borass, no problem. Now tell me, what were you doing in a Teladi sector in a military fighter?"

It wasn't a long story. Emboldened by Max's run the unsuccessful bidder for the teledanium had foolishly sent two of his big Boron Dolphin freighters, escorted by a wing of Argon mercenaries flying Buster fighters to break the blockade. Only one of the freighters made it back through the gate, with a pack of Clan fighters in hot pursuit. Borass was one of the Royal Naval fighters launched to interdict them. It was his first live combat and in his youthful enthusiasm had pursued the retreating fighters a little too aggressively and had been caught in the jump-gate effect just as he destroyed one of the raiders.

His flight was under standing orders as official naval vessels not to violate Teladi space under any circumstances and Borass was worried about the possible consequences. The Teladi had no diplomatic problem with military craft flying under private flags but in common with all the races, were extremely unhappy about any incursion by government forces, no matter what the circumstance.

"You were destroyed almost as soon as you arrived Borass, the lizards might not even have noticed."

"It matters not what they saw, my commander saw all." His snout drooped unhappily. "First fight and I make incident. Much shame."

"Are you a good pilot Borass?"

"Much depends, near summit of class. Instructor she say, too aggressive. I try to change."

Max punched the despondent Boron lightly on the shoulder. "Listen Borass, there's no such thing as a too aggressive fighter jock. If they throw the book at you and you need a job, you look me up. I plan to expand and I could use another hot-shot."

His snout perked right up and the ocular stalk swivelled to look Max straight in the eye before he reached across to proffer his hand. Max hesitated for a split second. It had not been a serious offer but he knew how much store the Boron placed on honesty and with four more runs to make and the pirates stirred up like hornets perhaps a little backup wouldn't hurt.

He shook the hand.

"In debt to you Max-Max, again."

As soon as they docked two uniformed soldiers took Borass into custody. As they led the pilot away he turned to give a final wave, which Max returned from the cockpit with a rueful salute.

## Chapter 24: Convergence

He cleared nearly 30,000 credits net from the run. It would have been more but Thrawn had been unable to find a full 1500 load at such short notice. Max hoped he could make the remaining trips holds fully laden. Three more runs through Ceo's Buckzoid in a Lifter would be pushing his luck about as far as he cared to stretch it. Further in fact.

Sinas promised to do what he could to help Borass but as diplomatic and military policy was outside his remit he feared this might not amount to much.

"These things take time Max, the Boron do nothing in haste but he was spawned by a good family so I expect he will be treated with leniency. Your concern does you credit, I will keep you informed."

Max could do no more.

Rather than find quarters in the small Argon section of the station he elected to remain on the Destiny Star. Newly refurbished it was as comfortable as anything on offer and did not have that lingering odour of ammonia that characterised Boron installations. They could function happily without it but it made them feel at home and discouraged others from over-staying their welcome.

After another shower and a bite to eat the tension of the long day began to ebb and before turning in he and Xela spent several hours discussing options and planning tactics for the coming runs.

The first went well. Thrawn had managed to obtain enough of the metal to completely fill the holds and was able to provide Max with the schedule of another Lifter who did work for the clans hauling swamp plants and energy cells. With that signature the Star had no trouble slipping past the clan patrols whose sensors showing them nothing but another fleeced sheep with a strategically worthless load.

The second they got though by the skin of their teeth but with the loss of two combat drones.

The clan might not know his name but they knew his ship and they did not know how he slipped by them but it was not going to happen again. Every Lifter that headed towards the Menelaus Frontier gate was stopped and forced to dump its cargo for inspection. The Boron protested but the Teladi did nothing. In fact they claimed the actions were being taken at their behest to cut down on the rampant smuggling that was destroying their economy. Most goods were getting though so why complain? Besides if the trade were put into their reliable claws they were confident that everything would proceed much more smoothly.

Max delayed several days before making the final run, partly in the hope that things would quieten down and partly in the hope that he could come up with another plan.

Eventually he did.

When he put his request to Sinas the Factotum was almost rendered speechless and his face took on such a hue that Max suspected the encrypted comm channel was malfunctioning.

"Look man, do you want this blockade broken or not? The pirates are so pissed now that if you gave me a wing of escort fighters it wouldn't help! You've read those intel reports you've been feeding me. There's a dozen fighters intercepting everything that comes our way."

"But, but..., I'll have to speak with my Captain but I do not think he can agree with what you are proposing. The risk to his name if anything went wrong. Or," he added carefully, "If you reneged."

"I've shook on this whole deal Sinas, remember?"

"No offence Max, I trust you, but to be blunt, considering your recent past, my Captain may not share my faith in your honour. Should anything go wrong the political repercussions would be enormous. He would lose his position and rank at the very least."

"And if it works?"

"His star would be firmly in the ascendant."

"As would yours Sinas, as would yours. It's the main chance for both of you and fate doesn't scatter many of those across our paths. Take it."

"It's not me that needs convincing Max. I don't see how the plan as outlined can work but I know somebody with an ace up their sleeve when I see one. No, it's my Captain who will need convincing. With the economic impact of the blockade biting in all sectors his fortune is balanced on a cusp though and could fall either way. Perhaps I can nudge it in our direction. Give me a day. Out."

The Factotum must have been at his most eloquent.

Twenty-eight hours later, the Destiny Star took a long detour into the unmonitored depths of the solar system, far beyond the jump-gate complex. Here, it kept a rendezvous with an unmarked Dolphin and on the exchange of encrypted handshakes linked transporters and teleported the package across. Marteene nervously supervised the maintenance droids as they carefully manoeuvred it into the shielded compartment Panner used for smuggling the spaceweed concentrate. Xela confirmed receipt of the requested codes and incorporated them into the navigation sub-system and they headed back to keep another rendezvous.

Afterwards the Destiny Star slipped through Ceo's Buckzoid, cloaked in the signature of another Independent Lifter that Boron Intelligence knew had arrangements with the Clan. It had been efficiently waylaid at the jump-point by an Octopus flight and escorted to a cruiser several thousand of kilometres from the gate for a detailed inspection that would keep it out of circulation for several days. The clan patrols were only interested in Boron bound traffic and after a cursory fly-by paid him no further heed and with a sigh of relief Marteene guided the Star into the jump-gate to Profit Share. After consulting the Best Buys Locator set course for Solar Power Plant Beta.

The 120 Power Cells cost him 16 units apiece as demand for energy was high in the Teladi heartland but he was unconcerned. It took almost another 12 hours to tour the surrounding sectors and fill the hold with the remaining teledanium Thrawn had managed to arrange. Before heading back to Ceo's Buckzoid Max anonymously transmitted 5000 credits to his account. Thrawn was as loyal as a viper but Marteene was reasonably certain that between the carrot and the stick he could keep him on his side, especially if things went as planned. All the same he asked Xela to remind him to have Artur practice his unique brand of persuasion on the Teladi the next time they were in contact.

The Destiny Star re-entered Ceo's Buckzoid transmitting a fake IFF signal for protection and at full speed headed towards the western jump-gate. A dozen Bayamons swarming around that gate immediately headed in his direction, unfazed by the misleading IFF. Max changed course a few degrees, angling further from the gate complex but the fighters closed the distance rapidly and he knew the Star had no hope of out-running the clan patrol.

---

Paskaal was also having a busy time. It had taken him several hours to configure his sensors to identify the detailed signature of the suspect Dolphin from the data Kaitrin had obtained and several more to say his goodbyes to her and the Raiders. He promised both he would return.

With only the slenderest of clues and a tottering tower of supposition to guide him in his search for Marteene he had no clear idea where to begin the search for the jump-drive equipped Dolphin freighter. On the tenuous assumption that Marteene was entangled in an Argon intelligence operation the obvious place to start would be the Boron or Argon sectors. The ship would have needed a target signal and those sectors were strewn with military and intelligence Nav-Sats. On the other hand, if Marteene had been duped by another Power then the Dolphin could be anywhere. It was a big, big universe.

There was also the Raiders commission but at least in this case he had a firm clue. The picture certainly resembled the mercenary leader and if Force had been rescued the trail would start in the Teladi sector Scale Plate Green. Corrin knew from the sector records that no rescue ship had been launched from sector Eighteen Billion.

That decided it then, he would head for Scale Plate Green. Attempting to cross the Xenon held sector that straddled the direct route would be suicidal so he plotted a longer route through the Split territories. It was an 18-sector journey and if he was lucky, perhaps he would stumble across the mysterious Dolphin. At least that class of ship would be relatively scarce in those sectors and some discreet questioning at stations along the way might unearth further clues. His mind made up he banked the Elite towards the western gate and the Boron Frontier.

---

"Data link complete; incoming transmission."

Artur took another sip of wine and delicately dabbed his lips with a serviette before replying.

"Decrypt and display Seera."

It was a short message and the ship AI completed the task before he reached the terminal.

Six words. "The hound has left the pound."

"The question Seera is where is it heading?"

"Incomplete data Artur," she intoned. "Unable to verify."

He sighed. "No, that's quite alright Seera, it was not a question. Just thinking out loud."

"Acknowledged."

Gathering the wine and the remains of the sandwich Artur moved to the Dolphin flight deck and ran another status check. All systems were functional, it seemed that the chance encounter with some clan Mandalays as he traversed Hatikvah's Faith had caused no damage. The 50 MW shield had protected him from the hail of missiles and streams of plasma long enough for him to launch a dozen enhanced combat drones. You could not have called it a fight, the drones swept the attackers aside in seconds, leaving no survivors. He had no sympathy for any who preyed on unarmed merchant ships but took no pleasure from simple slaughter. He had done far worse things though, and with much less regret so he refused to let the incident spoil his enjoyment of the fine Three Worlds red.

The sector scan showed the immediate volume of space was clear. He was far from the gate complex and expected nothing else. In passive mode his scanners were unable to monitor activities in the distant clutch of stations clustered within the bounds of the 2 jump-gates but the data feed from the military Nav-Sat showed nothing but routine traffic. Satisfied that he was secure from detection or interruption he microburst a pre-set encrypted code. A few minutes later the satellite responded with another microburst transmission, practically indistinguishable from the background cosmic radiation. After confirming the quantum key showed no interference he entered his own and transferred the decrypted intelligence reports to his desk.

Marteene was doing well, in fact a lot better than he had expected, even with the hidden help he'd facilitated. The man had taken every advantage and pushed them to the limit and beyond with a determination that bordered on recklessness. That Marteene had made contact with Sinas so quickly was an added bonus. He would not have to contrive a meeting with all the attendant risks of discovery that would entail. Not for the first time he was glad he had taken the time over the years to create an alternative framework, separate from the rest of the Cabal resources. That Marteene had been able to gain a foothold in the Teladi Company without his aid would also save him considerable time and effort. They did not routinely hand out Favoured Status Trading Licenses to aliens, preferring to keep the right to compete for contracts and establish manufacturing stations in their space to themselves. Artur briefly wondered how Max had managed it and considered making further inquiries before dismissing the notion. If he kept too close a watch on his activities that in itself would draw unwanted attention to him. As it was, misdirecting Ms Trasker was a troublesome enough task.

Not to mention the overly determined Commander Paskaal, but he hoped he had that in hand.

Trasker though, she was a problem; intelligent, cunning, highly motivated and with an excellent record that suggested a worrying ability to make important intuitive leaps. She was also ruthless, as her attempt to remove Force from the picture demonstrated. Although she had not explicitly ordered his assassination she was not one to unnecessarily constrain her operatives with moral guidelines. That her actions had resulted in the death of an operative he had come to consider a friend and forced him into a somewhat desperate improvisation did not lessen his regard for her talent. She was indeed a threat and Artur realised it was one he would have to neutralise.

Pouring himself a brandy and lighting a cigar he examined every facet of the problem, looking as always for a way to transform the situation to his advantage.

As he planned to do with Paskaal.

## Chapter 25: Lure

For Corrin it was going to be a long and tedious haul to Scale Plate Green. The first leg of the journey encompassed two Boron and three Argon frontier sectors and the elegant Dolphin freighter was a common sight. Scanning them all at fairly close range was not only time-consuming but also risky and he was fired upon more than once by over-zealous escorts and sector security patrols. In each sector he docked with the main Trading Station and spent several hours identifying and questioning those individuals who made it their profitable business to know what was going on.

He learned much but nothing relevant to either of his quests. The official news channels also told him nothing. The news in each sector was understandably dominated by local events and the threat of another Xenon incursion was the uppermost topic on most beings minds. News coverage of the home sectors was less extensive obliging Corrin to subscribe to a range of Info-Trawl services. Their software agents scoured the info-verse for any information that might pertain to his search but neither Marteene nor Force featured in any story. He was not surprised.

He noted with interest that clan activity in Teladi space had become endemic and had escalated into a virtual blockade of the trade in teledanium to the Boron heartlands. The Teladi Trading Company had long coveted the profits a monopoly on the shipping of Boron goods through their space would entail and it looked like they were raising the stakes. Unfortunately for the Boron the only other trading route for Teladi goods involved a long trip through Split and clan dominated sectors so a blockade at Ceo's Buckzoid was like a thumb on the carotid of their economy.

Fortunately it was none of his concern although he made a mental note to be extra vigilant in the unclaimed sector beyond Aladna Hill. Hatikvah's Faith would be the logical place to slam the back door on Boron trade routes. At the end of the Xenon Conflict the whole system had been sterilised by a gigantic gamma radiation burst caused by a supernova triggered by the Xenon in a nearby system and now the sector was little more than a large refugee camp. Independent operators had established a few orbital stations, mainly ore and silicon mines exploiting the few ore rich asteroids of the sector. A single Solar Power Plant provided the energy resources but the solitary jewel in the sector crown was a station manufacturing commercial Nav-Sats for the type of clientele who did not want their information resources a matter of official record.

The sector was effectively outside the governance of any species and inevitably it was the clan writ that ran most large although the well-armed independent owners of the stations were a ready market for mercs and would push back hard if they felt any clan was going too far.

It was an uneasy balance and made all unclaimed sectors risky places to do business in or even travel through.

Paskaal noted with satisfaction that at least one Argon Independent had the guts to break through the blockade. Despite the somewhat lurid speculation surrounding his affairs in the less reliable outlets he had managed to keep his identity a secret. It was a wise move considering how riled the pirates must be with him. Less scrupulous bounty hunters than Corrin would already be flocking to the pirate base in Teladi Gain. The Stoertebeker Clan were not noted for their forbearance in such matters and they would have much to lose if they failed to deliver on what Paskaal was certain was a Teladi Trading Company scheme. Their tolerance of clan activities came at a price.

Paskaal considered his options as he cruised towards the centre of the sector but nothing had happened to change his original plan. There was one more thing he could try but he doubted it would lead to anything. He had omitted using the single screen-shot of Force as the basis of a visual pattern match search in case it drew undue attention to himself but without any further leads it was now a risk he was prepared to take.

Weary from too many hours either in space or haunting the bowels of trading stations rubbing glad-handling the sort of low-lives that on a better day he's have happily punched, Corrin docked at the Aladna Hill Trading Station and hired a modest guest suite. It was the middle of the station day, all space installations ran on Teladi time to facilitate commerce, but his body clock was on its own time now and it told him to rest.

He allowed himself a single bottle of cold beer with the pizza he ordered in and for the next 8 hours he slept.

---

He was sleeping when the ship woke him, the gentle but insistent tone of alarm cutting through a recurrent dream set in better times. Realities coalesced as he drifted up to consciousness and it took a few moments for the dream-world to reluctantly release its hold, fading into the background like a spurned lover.

"Yes, Seera, what is it?"

"I have a specified contact on the scanner Artur. Alerting as specified." The AI voice, despite its electronic hue, echoed the dissipating dream but awake now he firmly pushed it from his mind.

"Thank you Seera, activate main viewer and display double speed from moment of contact to live feed."

The moonlit view of the Corvanian Mountains in the picture window was immediately replaced by the sector display, the targeted ship bracketed in red brackets. As he had expected, it was Paskaal's Elite scurrying across the screen through the sector. It abruptly slowed to a scrawl as the timeframes merged and he watched it vanish into the Trading Station.

For the next two hours Artur monitored the commercial comm traffic using his own access codes to over-ride the privacy seals on Paskaal's transactions. It appeared that he was indeed actively seeking Force, following the trail he had laid to Scale Plate Green. Satisfied that the pawn was moving as predicted Artur turned his attention to other pieces. Over a leisurely cup of fresh ground java from the Blue Mountains he contemplated his options before squeezing his bulk into the pilot seat.

From the galaxy map he selected a Nav-Sat and activated the jump-drive.

———————————

It was station evening when Corrin awoke and he wasted no time in checking his searches. Again they revealed nothing and he packed his flight bag and went in search of breakfast and information.

For the former he was spoilt for choice. Even in frontier sectors you could rely on Argon stations for all the home comforts. It made them popular watering holes for all species and even a Split would find it hard not to have a good time. Corrin had no contacts in this sector but from experience he knew where to look for the kind of beings who take an unhealthy interest in the affairs of others. His search was expensive and fruitless, the few leads he picked up concerning suspicious Boron Dolphin freighters turned out to be dead-ends. Smugglers or simple braggarts whose liquor loosened tongues had wagged in the wrong places.

Back at the dock Paskaal ran a complete systems check out of long and justifiably cautious habit. Despite the tight dock security you never could be quite sure what might have happened in your absence. The wrong question in the wrong ear could lead to nasty surprises of the exploding variety. He was running the scanner over the port shield emitters when a sibilant hiss from the safety barrier caught his attention. It was difficult to tell but she looked young. He did not recognise her but out of curiosity he gestured for the Teladi to come over.

"Missster Corrrin, am I to undersssstand?"

"Quite possibly. Is there something I can do for you?"

"Quite posssibbly." She grinned, or at least he took the teeth baring grimace for that. "In fact yesss. You have a fine ship, are your servicess available?"

His first instinct was to say no but his unofficial mission was self-financing and missiles were expensive. He also had a cover to maintain.

"It depends what you have in mind, not to mention who you are?" he replied cautiously.

"Good, good, who I are is unimportant but I am Drafen. A trader of no consequencccce. Yet."

"But you have big plans right?"

"One musst plan for profittsss, life musst have a path. I head for Company Pride, where I have bussiness. My sship," Drafen waved a claw at a decrepit Vulture freighter several bays down, "Iss laden and ready. Much clan activity I wish safe passage through."

It was only just off his route so Corrin nodded.

"Okay, how much?"

"I poor Missster Corrin but you assk quesstions no? Boron ship, unussual?"

"That's not a secret, yes. What do you know?"

Her face became a mask of transparent cunning.

"Information on ssafe passage. We have deal?"

He thought for a moment but it was clear the Teladi wasn't going to budge; she had probably spent all her credits on a clandestine load of Argon whisky. It was the only lead he had so why not?

He shrugged. "Okay Drafen, you ready to leave now?"

The lizard smiled. "Exxcellent, we have deal. Ready now."

"Okay, give me twenty minutes for pre-flight. And Draken, you'd better not be fooling around right?"

The Teladi assured him she was not and offered to shake on the arrangement. He declined.

"Do I look like an egg Draken?" He tapped his holster and smiled. "You just remember who I am."

Half an hour later both ships were heading towards the gate to Hatikvah's Faith.

## Chapter 26: Eyes and Scales

The rest of the journey passed without incident. The fighters patrolling the perimeter of the Clan Shroda base in this sector either had no interest in harassing non-Boron traffic or they were deterred by the fate of the pirate patrol in Hatikvah's Faith. As the second battlegroup had not fled in this direction Corrin doubted they were formally attached to the Clan. In all probability they were a hired freelance mercenary squadron, working for whoever was behind the Boron blockade.

"They should," he mused, "Ask for their credits back."

Drafen docked just ahead of the Elite and both were guided into adjacent bays in the main hanger. The waiting Teladi was ebullient, practically bouncing with excitement as Corrin descended from the cockpit.

"Misster Corrin, Misster Corrin, that was ssuperb. Never have I sseeen ssuch flying, in all my short daysss!"

Corrin smiled, not at the praise, but at the sheer youthful enthusiasm of the apprentice trader. She had just made a big score and her head was full of ideas, which as they walked across the deck to the small bar that serviced the main hanger, she blurted out. One half formed idea cracked on the heels of another in a constant monologue that left his head spinning.

Oh to be young again!

The bar was largely empty and they had no trouble claiming a quiet table. Paskaal did not even pause to allow the Teladi opportunity to buy the first round and took a bottle of the only Argon brew that was on offer. It was a weak, tepid affair and expensive. Drafen ordered something Teladi that managed to offend most of Corrin's senses but she seemed to be enjoying it so he said nothing and breathed carefully through his mouth.

"Enough, enough with the schemes my young friend!" Paskaal held up his palms as if warding off a blow but he was smiling as he said it. "Can I give you some advice?"

The Teladi regarded him with suspicion?

"Howw muccch advisse cosst?"

Corrin laughed. "Nothing at all Drafen, nothing."

"Old Teladi saying - 'free advice worth what you paid for it.' No?"

Corrin shrugged, "Well consider it part of the service but listen okay?"

She nodded and took a long pull on her repulsive drink.

"You were lucky today Drafen, lucky that I was with you and lucky those pirates were raw. I'm not going to be modest; I'm a damn fine pilot in a damn fine fighter. You won't be able to hire anyone else as good for the sort of credits you can pay and the next time the clan are going to hand you your tail. Understand?"

"Your metaphorss sstrange but I undersstand. But you, me good partnerrs, you sstick with me and we go placess yes?"

"Sorry, we go places no. I've got my own business to conduct but take my advice and lay low for awhile. Go trade somewhere safer and stay away from the clans until things calm down. Don't push your luck, I'd hate to read your obituary."

She nodded reluctantly but Corrin suspected the agreement would not last long. He could see the hunger for profit in her eyes and the lure of the easy credit was even more irresistible to Teladi than it was for humans.

"Okay, I tried, now how about my payment?"

"Outwaard journey, Hatikvah's Faith. A Boron sship, Dolphin freighter. Sshe was attacked by Clanss and desstroyed them with drones." She paused dramatically. "Sspecial drones."

"Special, in what way?"

"I know drones, these military. Bigger, fasster - pirates go boom!"

"Drafen, I hope there's more to this else I risked my neck for nothing, go on."

"Ship goes to Aladna Hill and I watch. It heads out of ssector, doess not dock. Odd behaviour no? And I thought, sstrange, examine closer, I have thiss."

The Teladi rummaged in a pouch and produced a data chip. "All my readingss and sscans. Payment made in full. Yess?"

Corrin nodded absently as he fingered the disk. It was actually more information than he was expecting although it wasn't much. A Dolphin with military equipment that headed out into deep space was unusual but not unique. The Special Forces ran many such vessels in support of missions and he had no doubt other races did the same. It would be odd if the Boron were spying on a sector of their close allies but the fact that it was a Boron vessel did not indicate its loyalties. It wasn't much but it was worth checking out.

He slipped the disk into a pocket and quickly finished his drink.

"You take care of yourself Drafen and if you hear anything else you get in touch okay."

"I hope you find what you look for Misster Corrin."

She extended a hand and this time he shook it.

Paskaal wasted no time reviewing the data, playing through the battle between the freighter and the clan fighters several times. The Teladi had been correct; the drones were not the standard commercial variant. It was difficult to tell from the low resolution scan but judging by the attack patterns they looked like the latest mark of the Argon Naval Defence Drone. Only they used the 3 unit V formation these ones were flying. Curious.

The IFF code was not the same as the ship he was looking for but that meant nothing and without access to detailed sector scans and the Clan analysis programs it was difficult to establish if the hull and energy signatures matched. There was no good reason why such a ship would be heading for deep space in an Argon sector on anything approaching legitimate business. He had read no reports suggesting there were clandestine clan facilities hidden in the fringes of the gate system and a Dolphin was not a deep space ship so it could not be heading out into the solar system. Whatever it was up to it would be doing it near the gate sector, probably beyond the range of the sector scans.

Even if it was not related to his current mission it was his duty to investigate possible threats to Argon security so he would have to check it out. It took only a short time to get launch clearance and he set course back to Aladna Hill. The Clan patrol in Hatikvah's Faith gave him a wide berth and he reached the Argon frontier sector without incident.

As soon as he emerged from the gate he transferred the course vectors from the readings the inquisitive Teladi had taken to his auto-pilot. It corrected for orbital drift and displayed a search cone, funnelling out from his current position. The sector readings from his own scanners showed nothing. Neither did the more detailed data-feed from the commercial traffic control sat. There were ways and means to evade both those modes of detection, from power-masking to using stolen access codes to censor out your IFF. Paskaal knew, he had used both techniques more than once. He would have to search, even powered down the Dolphin would not be able to hide from his military scanners if he came within a few hundred klicks.

Assuming of course that it had not left the sector.

There was also another way that was worth trying. Aladna Hill, like all Argon sectors, had a cloaked military Nav-Sat that handled official comm traffic and monitored the system for threats. It's range and sensitivity was considerably more than its cut-down commercial cousins and Paskaal had official access codes. He entered a security clearance and transmitted the code. The reply left him stunned for a moment as the Elite sailed into the darkness.

INVALID CODE. ACCESS DENIED.

He immediately broke off his search and headed for the Light of Heart sector, through the southern jump-gate and accessed the Nav-Sat.

His codes worked fine.

Needing time to think and a shower to get rid of the combat funk he headed for the Trading Station at the centre of the sector.

Daht settled into the command chair, shuffling to adjust his thick tail to a more comfortable position in the groove. The fixture was new and the synthetic smart leather had yet to fully adjust to his spreading bulk. Even so it was so much more comfortable than the cockpit of a Falcon fighter, where he had spent most of his career. Sometimes he missed those days, life was so much more simple without your every waking hour dominated by the pursuit of profit. Honing skills and reflexes, mastering the deadly arts of combat, testing them in battle! There was a joy in that, an addiction strengthened every time they were tempered in struggle against a dangerous foe. Winning was so much more sweet when the stake was your life rather than credits.

He was fiercely proud of the decades he spent as one of the Elite and the ribbons signifying the rank and honours accrued adorned the chest of his expensive hand tailored tunic. It was an affectation and a handicap – a reminder to all he met that he had once taken the Oath of

Renunciation and abjured the pursuit of personal profit. Although it was many years since that life the forces of prejudice were strong and to most Teladi anyone who did not live for personal gain were to be treated with scorn and suspicion.

He could see their point. Anyone not driven by the cultural imperatives of a society were unpredictable and therefore dangerous. The Teladi, like all sentient species, honoured their heroes although the Teladi word was more properly translated as "the valorous, divinely insane." Even that did not fully capture the full schizophrenia of the term, the ambivalence of respect for deeds and fear of the different. He had forced himself into this cultural lacuna, cunningly parleying his spectacular military career into an immense wealth, which still meant little to him except as a means to an end.

With a ruthless exploitation of his credits, contacts and military reputation combined with opportunistic espousals of popular causes had levered himself onto the Board of Directors of the Teladi Trading Company. It was a magnificent achievement for someone of his background, particularly a male and a source of immense pride though it did not temper the frustration.

Command of Scale Plate Green was not a base-camp in the foothills of power, it was a gilded cage, which he paced in frustration while the rest of the Board conspired his downfall with impunity. Established power hates change and "The General" was most emphatically not "one of them," so they feared him and they feared his opaque intentions.

"As well," he thought, "They might."

The governor-ship of one of the most important Teladi sectors had seemed a great prize. It was strategically placed on the colonial frontier and in the front line. The constant Xenon threat offered great opportunity for military success and the wealth of the sector many possibilities for personal gain. He had exerted immense effort, expending many resources and supped with at least one devil pushing at an open door, which his foes had slammed behind him with glee.

Set up for a fall.

He had realised his mistake almost immediately when his demand for the deployment of a frontier fleet was firmly denied. Allies became enemies almost overnight and the deployment of a capital fleet, or even one cruiser, was deemed too "provocative". Planetary defences were strong and the new jump-fleet could respond in minutes should the situation warrant it. There was a specious strategic logic to the argument but many lives could be lost and stations destroyed before reinforcements could arrive.

The Board was confident he had sufficient resources to defend the sector and if not stations could be replaced. And lives? Well, they indicated, no one was expendable.

Not even, he inferred sardonically, the "esteemed" General. Dead heroes were so much easier to control.

It was a trap. The fleet had been an asset he had been counting on, certain that his reputation, wealth and deft grasp of the black art of intrigue would forge from it a reliable tool. Now all he had were the fighter wings based on his Trading Station and the militia squadrons deployed on the other installations. These were good, in fact they were extremely good. The chance to serve under the General was still a powerful magnet and he was confident his fliers were a match for anything in space. But hard-drilled as they were, they could not stop a full Xenon incursion without the weight of a fleet behind them.

And they would come, one day he knew his old adversaries would come, not in the odd wing sent to probe their defences but in force. Overwhelming force.

He was not one to brood on his mistakes, he had erred but granted time he would regain his ground. Meanwhile he had a job to do and the warrior within still relished the challenge.

It was mid-shift and the Command Centre hummed with the subdued murmur of his staff as they efficiently went about their business at the terminals that ringed the large circular room. In the background a dozen comm channels crackled situation reports from flight leaders, intercepts from Nav-Sats, reading from sensors. He ignored them, knowing his officers would alert him to anything unusual and certain his own sub-conscious would pick up on anything significant.

The view-screen dominating the Command Centre scanned the sector, automatically focusing on any new activity according to pre-set priorities. As he watched it focused on the northern jump-gate to record the arrival of a small group of Argon ships. Three freighters and five escort fighters. Tapping controls in the arm of his command station he confirmed they were a scheduled convoy; supplies and munitions for their shipyard in Omicron Lyrae.

Everyone was at their posts, except the Fire Control Officer who hovered nervously at his station unwilling to disturb the creature curled up on the Targeting Scanner. Her caution pleased the General, it had taken him a great deal of time and one brutal example to convey the difference between "snack" and "pet" but now Tiddles the Third could range the station with impunity and knew it.

The cat had been a gift from one of his most useful resources and Daht regarded it with amusement. He could tell from the flattened back ears and the angry twitching of its tail that the beast was feigning sleep in an attempt to prevent eviction from the warmth it was absorbing from the screen. The Teladi did not see the point of pets, in fact the language had no word for it, snack or parasite being the closest. Pets were unproductive and therefore an impediment. In particular they had no time at all for the peculiar Argon mammals. They did nothing but sleep and dole out carefully rationed amounts of affection in return for food, shelter and protection. Their smell and movement also triggered deep predatory instincts.

The General in turn found this attitude odd. It was a very Teladi life-form, indolently extracting all the profit from life it required with the absolute minimum of effort. To him it was a quite fascinating creature and until recently a genetic mystery as it had no antecedents in Argon evolution. Again the Goner sect had been proven correct in its odd theories.

In the absence of a mate, no respectable Teladi family would admit a male of his independence and reputation, it was something he could rely on. The affection might be transferable but so long as it was well treated the feline loved him and that was good for the soul.

At the sound of her name the cat strutted across the room and jumped into his lap. Daht stroked the bundle of white fur as he activated the Command Station side-screen to review reports and deal with correspondence. It was all routine matters; intelligence updates, fuel consumption logs, tactical training scores. Only one thing caught his interest, the signs hidden deep in an otherwise innocuous personal message. The Cat-Man was coming.

He had many names and the General had given up attempting to learn the truth or even keep track so he named him for his gifts. The news that he was on his way filled him with ambivalence. Sometimes the Argon bestowed favours and sometimes he called them in. Most often you did not know which it turned out to be until long after the event. Daht did not like the man, he did not know his agenda or who he represented although they were obviously influential and he would not have reached his position without their help. He disliked being so beholden but for the moment their fortunes were tied.

Since the incident with the lost mercenary pilot he had not heard from him. It had been a small favour but one which he carefully added to the ledger for repayment when the time was right.

His musings were interrupted by the tense tones of the Sector Controller at her station along the left wall of the centre.

"Southern gate activating General, going to Condition 3. Alert fighters launching."

The view-screen flickered momentarily and focused on the exit from the Xenon redoubt.

Around him postures stiffened in anticipation. This was not a routine occurrence but it was far from unusual. Most often all it presaged was a fleet-footed courier, elated by the successful dash through Xenon space. Sometimes it was a wing or two of Xenon fighters, testing defence reaction times before retreating or embarking on a suicidal dash to other sectors. No one knew why they did that as they were always destroyed. Daht surmised they were probably testing new combat algorithms but maybe it was just a terror tactic .

One day though, they would come through the gate in force and the General would do his utmost to ensure they paid a heavy toll.

The Sector Controller breathed deeply to quieten the panic growing beneath her breast-bone as she monitored her scanner. For Chi-lak this was her first command posting and only her third shift since her transfer from Seizewell. It came with a promotion and the extra credits and Company shares were welcome. She would have come without it though for the chance to serve under the Victor of New Income.

The gate winked into life, disgorging waves of Xenon fighters with every blink. She counted them off in what she hoped was a dispassionate voice but there were so many wings. Swarms of the fast, light N Class accelerating ahead to engage the patrolling Bats vectoring towards them. Packs of medium M Class fighters in protective spheres around a hard core of the big L Class strike ships. It was going to be her first combat and it was what she had trained for although she wished she could have benefited from one of the General's legendary battle drills first.

In the background she could hear the General Order Condition 2. Down on the flight decks all the remaining fighters would be scrambling, the 3 defence deploying Bats first. As she transmitted orders to the station militia forces the six laser towers activation signals flashed on her screen. She transferred their control to the junior officer at the Point Defence Station and speaking quietly into her throat mike she formed the militia forces into mixed package wings to intercept the L Class fighters should they strike at a station. They could be carrying the Xenon version of the hornet missile and could not be allowed to get within launch range.

As she designated 2 Bat wings the missile intercept reserve she stole a glance at the General. He evinced nothing but calm as he assessed the situation and issued strategic commands. That the spiteful sharp-clawed creature was still sleeping was a testament to his composure and she took heart from that.

He caught her look and nodded encouragement.

Her monitors showed the Teladi defences forming with admirable efficiency, the outer ring of Bats were already engaging the leading edge of the Xenon attack with the legendary ferocity of those who foreswore the pursuit of profit for the defence of the Company. They wreaked havoc amongst their Xenon equivalents, her sensors keeping track of the kill ratio. Four to one, that was good.

Her command roster showed three Hawk wings transferred to her tactical control from the centre flank. As the Bats disengaged and fell back ahead of the M and L Xenon towards the advancing militia fighters she ordered the Hawks to break high and form a Big Wing. She knew her role and she knew what was happening. The General believed strongly in the doctrine of decentralised command and control and expected his subordinates to be alert to possibilities and take initiatives. As the faster Xenon M's accelerated in pursuit of the retreating Teladi fighters she ordered the Big Wing to fall onto the unprotected rear of the exposed Xenon L's.

The General watched the unfolding battle with satisfaction, his new officer was performing well and had dealt with the powerful thrust at the left flank of the sector defences with skill. The Xenon had split their attack with a similar heavy thrust to the right and he had been forced to transfer more wings from the centre to hold them. A smaller Xenon force, a dozen M's with half as many L's trailing were attempting to force an opening towards the Trading Station but a wing of Hawks were putting up a fierce resistance. With luck he could recall the left flank Hawk wings soon, if not he had a small reserve of Falcons.

Chi-lak resisted the urge to keen in triumph as the Hawks ripped into the slower L Class Xenon, working in pairs to bring down their huge shields. Her forces were taking heavy losses against the numerically superior foe but their aggression was unmatched in her experience and the Xenon strike on her flank was being pulverised between the hammer of the Hawk Big Wing and the anvil of the militia fighters. The right was holding and she committed her small militia reserve to the big dogfight in the centre, confident that the Xenon could not break through her flank in force.

Her first battle and another glorious victory for the General! Perhaps she would be honoured with a medal and shares? The musings on the spoils of victory proved premature as the deep voice of General Daht cut through the Command Centre.

"Go to Condition 1 and transmit Emergency Signal Alpha."

She looked at the main screen, knowing what she would see. A huge Xenon cruiser was emerging from the gate and it was not alone.

From his Dolphin Artur watched in muted horror as a second Xenon cruiser shot from the jump-gate.

As soon as the attack began he had ordered a course change taking the Seera high above the plane of the ecliptic on a heading of 315. It would take him away from the centre of the system clear of the gates. Within minutes Teladi capital ships would be hurling from the northern gate and anything in the way was going to get crushed.

Up until this moment he had believed the battle would be won by the Teladi. Both Intelligence and Scenario Analysis based on predictive algorithms updated with analyses of Xenon behaviour in the Brennan Conflict suggested a full Xenon assault from this sector into Scale Plate Green was unlikely. The Xenon would not risk provoking a new war until they had grown a lot stronger.

The beaten remnants of the Xenon First and Second Order had fought long and stubborn retreats from both directions to this sector. The combined Boron and Teladi Fleets, supplemented by an Argon Carrier Task Force had pushed the machines back sector by sector, station by station and planet by planet in one of the bloodiest campaigns since the Great Retreat of the Boron/Split Conflict.

Rolks Legacy, New Income, Eighteen Billion. They were fighting to reclaim their ancestral worlds, so for the Teladi these names would come to carry as much resonance as Menelaus Frontier and Queens Space did for the Boron. The Teladi triumphed whereas the Boron Empire sustained such damage that it still had not regained its former glory. Rescued from extinction only by the intervention of the Argon Navy at the Battle of the Last Stand in Kingdom End, the Boron spirit took a new course. The drive that at the height of their empire would have rebuilt fleets and reclaimed sectors, including the lost systems beyond Atreus Clouds was directed elsewhere. Planets were sown with new life and terraforming evolved from an engineering problem to a new art form. Art and science exploded in a third Renaissance and the always strong Boron spiritual imperative towards harmony and balance established a firm ascendancy over the martial urges without which no sentient culture could have won their evolutionary struggle for supremacy. Those virtues; honour, duty, sacrifice and loyalty to the Crown remained; feeding into the societal wellspring and as the Xenon, Teladi and the Split had discovered, you underestimated the Boron ability and will to fight at your peril.

The new sensibility also fuelled a new diplomacy where the Argon were essential and firm allies. No other race ever doubted the willingness of the powerful Argon Republic to defend its ally by all necessary means. The alliance had kept the Boron at peace for centuries and their civilisation flourished.

The battle for the New Income system had been particularly costly and General Daht's Profits-Protection Corps had been badly mauled. His fleet too had only beaten back a sustained counter assault by the Xenon fleet with heavy losses. But he pushed on, through the suicidal onslaughts by sector rearguards in Ianamus Zura and Eighteen Billion, determined to match the Argon/Split/Paranid thrust towards Scale Plate Green.

Probes into the enemy sector through the gates did not survive long but the picture they revealed was unexpected. Instead of a handful of cruisers the short-lived Nav-Sats revealed over a dozen cruisers and several bigger battleships of an unknown class. They were unbelievably fast and heavily armed with a power plant sufficient to fire sustained bursts from huge plasma throwers.

It just was not possible to call off the pursuit and riding the elatory wave of victory the two fleets struck into the Xenon sector.

The battle was long and fierce and the Xenon stood their ground, their technical superiority countering the numerical imbalance. The greater speed of the Xenon ships allowed them to conduct constant hit and run attacks on their slower adversaries. It was a grinding war of attrition and their cruisers were running a ferocious gauntlet of plasma broadsides on every pass. They took casualties but for every machine-head ship destroyed, five allied ships were lost. It was not a loss they could sustain and the General ordered all ships to retreat to the nearest gate. His own cruiser formed part of the rear-guard and was the last to leave. It was a point of honour.

Later analysis of the sector revealed the Xenon sector was a fleet base with a Defence Station and Shipyard in a system replete with resources. And there it sat, a tumour on the jump-gate web, getting larger by the year.

It was one to which the Cabal had also given much thought, none more so than the Cat-Man. As the second Xenon cruiser slid to a halt alongside the first and begin launching fighters he was tuning into the Omicron Lyrae sector Nav-Sat and patching a call through the Top Security Command Channel to the Captain of the Athena.

Omicron Lyrae was the stronghold of the Argon frontier sectors. The heavily industrialised sector supported a Shipyard as well as several high technology stations and the Argon Destroyer formed the heart of a large fighter defence force shielding the frontier from the Xenon fleet in the sector beyond Black Hole Sun.

Captain Rieze sank gratefully into the warm scented water, the heat easing the pain of her bruised shoulders and forearm. Either she was slowing down or the new adaptive program of the Combat Droid was as good as the advert said. The ship Battle-Stave tourney was only 10 days away and she had a reputation in the old martial art to protect. A few bruises were, in Errin's reckoning, a small but painful price to pay.

Sighing she slipped beneath the surface only to be blasted by reflex out of the bath across to the comms link as the Top Priority Alert shrieked through her quarters. Nothing good ever happened when a TPA came through on your own personal encrypted command channel. Soaking, she hastily threw on a wrap and entered the counter codes. This had only happened to her once before and then it was..

"Blackmore, I don't believe it?"

"I regret we have not the time for banter Captain. In a few minutes you will receive a call and you will respond appropriately. No time to explain or go through channels, you're just going to have to trust me on this. Besides, you owe me one. Out."

He was right and a small doubting part of her harboured other suspicions. She had completed the mission in spectacular fashion, thanks to the unreported assistance of Blackmore and his shadowy organisation and soon after was made the youngest captain in the fleet. No less than she merited, she knew she was a good officer and her record spoke for itself.

Sometimes though she would wonder, especially when given the Athena as her first command. A third generation hull of the Titan Class destroyer that had been the biggest ships in the Argon fleet for centuries. The Athena had been refitted dozens of times, to keep it at the leading edge. The original design had proven flexible enough to adapt to new technologies and only recently had a new capital class become necessary. She had emerged from one such refit only recently but despite the new 1250 MW power-plant she remained what that class had been for generations, over-gunned and under-powered. Even its 200 mps plus speed no longer gave it an edge over the new Xenon ships.

For the last 2 years it had acquitted itself well in the front-line against the Xenon and her captain had earned a reputation as a tactician that in some eyes marked her as a candidate for Admiral's pips.

Errin hastily pulled on her uniform and had barely had time to begin towelling her hair before the shipwide Yellow Alert sounded. Without stopping to find her boots she sprinted to the Bridge, her long hair dark a streaming comet dripping a soap water trail alongside her wet foot-prints.

The General, aware that showing any sign of the panic he felt growing in sternum could fracture the morale of the Command team, watched the second Xenon cruiser emerge without moving a muscle. He could feel the eyes of the young flank commander on him and he wished he could turn to her and say "End Simulation." This would be just the sort of scenario he would challenge the mettle of a new officer with but it was the real thing and she had acquitted herself with skill and spirit.

"Alpha Ssignal acknowledged General". ETA four minutes."

Four minutes – and it would take them several more to travel from the gates. Longer if the Xenon intercepted them. For his station it might as well be four hours, the powerful and fast Xenon cruisers could be here in moments.

"Execute Gamma 4."

One by one his staff acknowledged the command, implementing the well practiced procedures with sibilant whispers into throat microphones as they activated new defence protocols.

Mine laying Bats would be laying down a concise pattern of Squash Mines to form a 5km screen. This would force capital ships to slow down and give his fighters a chance to engage. Vultures would labour desperately to add a denser backup screen. The remaining wing of Hawks would be scrambling on missile point defence and 2 laser towers would go to pulse mode to give defensive cover and interception fire. The Flank Commanders would be forming Hornet Strike Wings. He would hold the centre to engage the cruisers at the outer perimeter.

The General tallied his resources as reinforcement fighters flooded from the two Xenon ships and knew it wouldn't hold. By the time the Teladi fleet could engage his station would be a ruined shell.

For a second his sense of manifest destiny wrestled with the brute tactical facts. It really could all end like this he realised with disbelief.

When his personal Emergency Comm Channel over-rode his terminal to present the face of the Cat-Man his start was enough to provoke a reproachful glare from the feline.

"Greetings General, you need help, downloading comm data now. Transmit the tactical feed on this channel to the Argon Destroyer Athena and officially request assistance."

"I assume this aid comes with some sort of price?"

"Doesn't it always General." The human looked up. "And I think it just went up."

Daht looked up to see another Xenon ship emerge from the gate. It was one of the big battle-cruisers. Without hesitation he hailed the Argon destroyer.

Captain Reize quickly covered the short distance to the turbo-lift and moments later she hurled onto the Bridge drawing, astonished looks from the duty crew. Her first officer vacated the command chair, a smile creasing his weathered face.

"Thirty seconds Captain, I say that's a new record".

"What've you got me out of a nice warm bath for Commander?"

She sat down and activated her command terminal. It displayed a tactical map of the Scale Plate Green Sector.

"It's a live feed Captain, Xenon capital ships through the southern jump-gate. And we have General Daht on hold for you."

She activated the comm channel on the terminal. She was no xenobiologist but the old lizard looked agitated and in the background she could hear alarms.

"General, this is somewhat unexpected? Official channels blocked?"

"There iss no time. I formally request your immediate assisstance to secure Sector Scale Plate Green from Xenon attack. Your answser iss required now."

There was no mistaking the note of urgency in his voice and quickly scanned the tactical upload. There were no Teladi capital ships and the fighter screen was weak. She doubted very much that her authority extended to making unilateral interventions in other species sectors without formal orders from an Admiral but she would argue the point later.

Errin thumbed open the ship-wide comm channel.

"All hands to battle-stations, prepare to execute attack plan Beta Beta Seven. This is not a drill, good luck."

She turned to her veteran second-in-command as the computer picked up her order and activated the Red Alert siren. Around her the bridge crew exploded into activity and new officers swept in to activate secondary stations.

"Initiate jump-drive." She looked at the tactical feed. "Target southern jump-gate".

Commander Harker raised one greying eyebrow quizzically but repeated her order instantly and the ten second countdown began.

"You have your answer. Athena out."

As the jump-gate opened she issued a stream of commands.

---

Chi-lak stared, fixated by the huge ships emerging from the jump-gate. In her peripheral vision she could see the General whispering urgently into his comm, no doubt trying to summon the jump-fleet by force of will. It might have been her first battle but she had commanded fleets in countless tactical sims and knew to trust the gift of her instincts to sense the ebb and flow of a conflict and judge when most effectively to act. Without waiting for orders she instructed her remaining fighters to form defensive wings around the surviving hornet equipped Falcons and signalled the evacuation of the Flower Farm. It would be the first target if a cruiser came at her flank and her fighters were not fast enough to intercept.

She had read the protocols and knew that the General planned to stall attacking cruisers with a squash mine barrier, giving the defenders the chance to strike. Already the 2 cruisers had launched their fighters. The incoming wave outnumbered the remaining defenders 2 to 1 but those were odds they could handle. Whether the surviving Bat fighters could prevent the fast Xenon N's knocking a path through the mine-field was debatable. If they did there would be nothing to stop the cruisers brushing past the defenders and destroying the Trading Station.

"The Xenon might have the fire-power but we have the General!" That exultant thought kept her cool as she checked load-outs and re-assigned fighters but when a third, juggernaut battle-cruiser entered the sector a palpable wave of despair shuddered through the Command Centre and even her youthful faith faltered.

General Daht regarded the battle-cruiser with a purely outward equanimity as he sought to improvise new tactics. The mines would slow them down but because of their radius of effect they were dispersed and an easy target for the fast Xenon N fighters. Without waiting for the order his commanders were already implementing the correct strategy and redeploying their remaining defences to protect the Trading Station. He allowed himself a moment of fierce pride in his command officers and the pilots fighting and dying with the skill and ferocity he knew was in the Teladi spirit. If freed from the overwhelming obsession with commerce his race could yet claim the premier position in universal affairs. His people were the proof.

The Last Stand tactic left the outlying stations vulnerable to attack and should they choose the Xenon could destroy them all in minutes. He had no choice though, his Falcons were too slow to be able to intercept the cruisers. If they were lucky the jump-fleet would arrive in time to draw the attackers away, if not then may they die with dignity.

The journey through the jump-gate seemed longer subjectively than the elapsed time shown on the chronometer but that was good, it gave her a few spare seconds to curse Blackmore. She hated feeling beholden to him. And although he had helped her out big-time it was his Code Black that had led her into the mess in the first place. She hated the fact that all she knew of the man was he had the authority to issue that code. Most of all though, she hated the fact that he had leaned on her to do something she would have done anyway. Orders or no orders she would have responded to the Teladi distress call and worried about the damn consequences later.

As the destroyer plunged towards the gate exit she checked her terminal. As she knew it would it showed green across the board. All stations staffed and ready with a crew that had practised this battle plan a dozen times. It had been designed for the defence of Black Hole Sun. That Argon frontier sector bordered another Xenon redoubt and she had developed this strategy to counter Xenon numbers with the element of surprise. She was certain that Xenon strategies would not yet have evolved to take account of the new jump-drive and she was equally certain her ship and crew could make them pay dearly for that oversight.

In its heyday the Titan class destroyers were the fastest and most heavily armed ships in space. Now, although it could carry 20 Gamma HEPT's the old frame could not mount the reactors to drive them. The standard load for a Titan was 12 Gammas and 8 Beta HEPT's and even then the 100MW plant could not power them all for any length of time. The Athena had been fitted with an uprated reactor but that only gave it another 20% of power and with the development of the Argon series of battleships fitted with a 200 MW power-plant the days of the Titans were numbered. Several new classes were under test and these would marry the increased power with a new generation of drives said to match those found on the new Xenon capital ships. The Argon class would then be refit to raise its speed above the lumbering 60 mps or so it was currently limited to but until then there was still a role for the remaining under-powered but nimble Titans.

The Athena shot into Scale Plate Green, the Xenon battleship looming ahead in the view-screen. It was moving slowly towards the centre of the sector, letting the other 2 cruisers and its own fighter screen blast a hole through the remaining defences, clearing the way for the kill.

"Predictable."

Her sneer garnered a smile from her Exec. Neither of them had a lot of respect for the tactical abilities of the Xenon, they were generally a crude combination of superior numbers and brute force and today was no exception. It was just what they had drilled for and Errin concentrated on her next moves, confident that her officers and crew would carry out the plan with complete efficiency.

They did. The Xenon ship was completely unprepared for an attack from its own jump-gate and did not even have a skeleton CAP running. The Athena cruised slowly past, only tens of metres from the starboard side of the huge ship. As she did so all her portside turrets opened fire, raking the Xenon with a massive broadside that all but collapsed its shields. Accelerating away to allow her weapons to recharge the Weapons Officer launched 3 hornets from the rear tubes and a rolling series of explosions spreading from the bow to the stern tore the battleship to pieces. The Athena was caught in the fringe of the shockwave of the exploding drive but her shields held and the young officer at the helm rode the wave like a surfer, adding the momentum to his own manoeuvre.

"Rearguard away, LT's away." Harker intoned. A wing of Elites armed with hornets and a couple of the ships laser towers would bloody any other Xenon nose that poked through the gate.

"Good work team, one down two to go. Designate port target Intruder 2, come to a heading of 045 Mark 3, launch missile CAP and one LT Deployer, put 4 around the Trading Station, keep 1 back. Ahead flank speed."

Her superbly trained pilots were launching before she completed the order, 3 of the fast, light Discoverer fighters deploying to take out any Xenon ship-killer missiles and a fourth shooting past the Xenon fighter screen at maximum speed towards the centre of the sector.

———————

For a second Chi-lak thought another Xenon ship had joined the attack but despair turned to hope as the classic curves of an old Argon ship became clear. She was still marvelling at the audacity of the commander as its plasma weapons smashed into the shields of the battle-cruiser. A ragged cheer erupted as the Xenon ship exploded, even the General had a claw firmly clenched in triumph.

She wondered how he had done it.

One of the Xenon cruisers accelerated, breaking high and right, swinging around to challenge the Argon ship. The other kept coming as the Xenon fighter wave crashed onto the remaining defenders.

———————

"Intruder One on an intercept course, closing at 300 MPS." Her Tactical Officer was as emotionless as ever, focused entirely on the moment and wasting no energy on doubt or fear. She wished she felt as confident. The Athena was out-gunned by the approaching cruiser and if the Xenon remained true to form it would use its greater speed to pound her shields down with arcing hit and fade assaults. She needed to limit its room to manoeuvre and had chosen her course astutely.

The cruiser grew larger on the screen, long, thin and elegant in a functional way. Tac-Ops counted down distance and time.

"Arm Mosquito missiles, forward salvo 5, designate Strike 1. Arm 3 hornets rear, designate Strike 2."

The Weapons Officer looked at her quizzically but obeyed without hesitation and waited, her fingers poised over the launch control.

The cruiser adjusted its heading slightly to come head to head with the Athena and decreased speed. Errin could see it planned to pass down her starboard beam forcing her to take the broadside or change course.

"Tac-Ops, Betas on point defence."

"Point Defence Aye."

The two warships hurled towards each other at a combined speed that ate the kilometres. At 3 klicks she ordered speed to Forward One Third.

At two klicks she ordered Strike 1. The mosquito missile was fast but had only a small warhead and was useless against the multiple shields of the Xenon cruiser. As she hoped, the cruiser spotted the fast moving rockets leaping ahead of the Athena and broke away to port expecting a fusillade of hornets. Xenon capital ships often tried to tempt their targets into launching hornets, using their speed and agility to evade them until their prey was toothless.

"Heading 20 Mark 3, all ahead, half. Gamma's fire at will, odd-even break." Firing the energy sapping gamma plasmas in alternate sequence enabled the Athena to keep up a longer burst of fire before the weapons energy drained.

"Intruder 1, shields at 90%, she's coming around, 3 klicks, 2.5, 2 klicks." Hawker's voice was deep and resonant with confidence. He was a 25 year veteran and had served on the Athena for most of his career, turning down his own command more than once to remain with her and he knew what she could do in the right hands.

"Strike 2 launch."

The cruiser broke off the attack run, breaking high to shake off the missiles before looping back down on the Athena.

"Roll and fire, helm come to heading 05 mark 1."

The destroyer rolled, bringing the port turrets to bear. The forward shields of the Xenon flared white but held.

"Rear tubes, 10 silkworm, designate Strike 3, Load Mine Alpha, transfer command to me."

The captain gestured at the Teladi station they were now on course for.

"Helm, get us in a close orbit and try and keep it between us and our bullying friend"

Captain Reizer watched the Xenon on her command screen as it came around for another run.

"All rear turrets 5 second burst on my mark. Mark."

The range was too great for accurate shooting but enough plasma bolts hit home to light up the forward shields. It would disrupt their sensors momentarily.

"Strike 3. All turrets, target Strike 3. Ahead flank."

Ten missiles streaked towards the oncoming cruiser but its tactical algorithms could not be fooled again so easily, despite the attempts to blind its sensors and it plunged towards them, calculating the damage to its shields would be minor.

"Fire!"

At her command the Athena Fire Control Officers fired on the silkworms, detonating them practically simultaneously and blinding the Xenon long enough for it to miss the squash mine. Errin waited for the cruiser to pass beyond it before she sent the activation code.

The Athena was still in the blast radius but close enough to shelter for the helm to ride the outer edge of the shockwave into the lee of the Teladi station.

"Tacs - drop the last LT and launch Strike Group Alpha as soon as the wave passes. Helm, another good job."

She could see the young ensign straighten his back with pride.

"Intruder 1 on-screen, shields 20%." Harker sounded slightly disappointed, like her he had hoped the close range blast would have crippled the ship but she had been forced to delay detonation, to give them a chance of surviving. It had worked but the station had borne the brunt of the shockwave and plasma fires burned in the wreckage on the facing side. She hoped the inhabitants were in the shelters.

"LT away, SG Alpha launching."

Reizer smiled, her Tactical Officer was beginning to sound confident and as she was an avowed pessimist Errin took it to be a good sign.

"Helm, attack pattern Omega 12."

The Xenon ship had taken considerable damage from the blast and as the Athena swept around the station to come onto its tail the view-screen showed it almost dead in space, shield emitters flashing as auto-repair systems struggled to bring them back on line. Three wings of Xenon N fighters had launched to provide point defence and the Athena fired off a salvo of mosquito missiles to keep them occupied.

As she closed to firing range the Xenon cruiser accelerated around the station, masking herself from attack while systems came on line.

The LT blast caught it straight in the face and the three Elite fighters hovering in the shadow of the station launched 2 hornets each at point blank range before looping up and away from the blast. The cruiser disintegrated in a fist of fire, pummelling the already damaged Dream Farm with a flensing storm of debris that sliced through the few intact structures.

Eyes bright Errin stopped herself from cheering. "Status?"

"All systems nominal captain. Retrieving fighters, the LT is gone though. Nicely done captain."

She took Harker's compliment with a smile.

"As I said Commander.."

He finished her sentence for her.

"Predictable!"

———————

The General unclenched his fist as the Argon destroyer accelerated away from the plasma storm that had been the Xenon battleship and grunted approval as it deployed fighters and laser towers to guard the jump-gate. One of the surviving cruisers broke off in pursuit and he kept an in-screen window open on his monitor as he concentrated on the Xenon thrust through his centre.

He could do nothing but watch as the remaining Teladi fighters clashed with the incoming Xenon. They were heavily outnumbered and low on missiles but in open combat he was confident they could triumph. The problem was, winning would not be good enough. They had to protect the mines, prevent any Xenon L's getting within missile range and escort the Falcon counter-strike. It was asking too much even of his elite pilots and despite the tenacity of the Bat fighters they could not stop all the Xenon N's from getting into the minefield.

One by one the mine icons winked out from his display, leaving a gap for the cruiser to exploit.

The Station Defence Officer looked up from her station below his position.

"Argon fighter deploying laser towerss General. She's assigning command codess now. They are on-line."

He acknowledged her report with a curt nod as he added the new factor into his analysis.

The fighter wall was not holding and the few Falcons that could get through to the cruiser with hornet missiles did not survive the point defences long enough to land a killing blow.

"All fighterss dissengage and esstablish a defensive perimeter 2 kilometress around the sstation,"

His commanders busied themselves translating his order into a tactical plan; assigning point defence, interdiction and strike roles to the few remaining fighters.

The General watched intently as his ships disengaged, the slower Falcon's trailing. Xenon fighters pursued each group, relentlessly picking off stragglers.

"Flank Commander order Sstrike Wing 4 to new course, 395, Mark 3."

Chi-lak repeated his command instantly, waited for the acknowledgement and nodded to the General in confirmation. The course took the slow Falcon fighters away from the station into the remnants of the minefield where the pursuing pack of Xenon fighters would cut them to pieces. She could not see the logic but believed in the genius of the General.

Daht watched his display as the fighters broke off. A large contingent of Xenon followed, unwilling to leave a potential threat to the cruiser behind them. As they closed on the Falcon wing the General activated a direct voice-link to the flight.

"Thiss is General Daht, it iss time to sstand and fight your lasst battle. Die well." He put them on the main screen.

The handful of Falcons wheeled around and attacked the mass of pursuing Xenon fighters with fanatical zeal, blasting and ramming with a complete disregard for their own safety, drawing more Xenon to the fray.

"Thesse are real Teladi," he declaimed to the Command Centre, and all eyes were drawn to the sight of the death struggle. "Remember and witness." He touched a control and the remaining squash mines detonated in a flash that overwhelmed the view-screen for a long second. When the picture returned that section of space was empty; the Command Centre fell into a stunned silence.

"All sstations report."

At his command Chi-lak snapped her attention back from the sacrifice she had just witnessed and called out her sit-rep. Others followed suit.

Over half of the Xenon fighters had been destroyed in the blast and the remainder were involved in a frantic battle with the defenders in the very shadow of the station. The laser towers sniped in pulse mode but were having little luck against the hard manoeuvring targets. The cruiser slipped closer and closer, waiting for the moment when the defences were weakened enough for it to move into missile range. Half the laser towers had fallen before the second cruiser fell to the Athena. This time there was no cheering. Argon fighters were rushing to the defence and the Argon destroyer was accelerating towards them. She was minutes away though.

Chi-lak looked at the cruiser as it loomed on the screen. She did not think they had minutes.

The General noted the victory of the Athena but with the other cruiser almost within missile range he had no time to react. He opened the channel to his Directors Wing, standing by in their private launch bay.

His old friend and comrade appeared on screen and they locked eyes for a second.

"It's time?" The General nodded and Charduk saluted. "For the Company."

"Good fortune old friend."

He terminated the contact.

As the Hawk fighters launched Flight Control announced the arrival of the jump-fleet at the northern gate.

They were too late, the first wave of station-killers were already inbound.

The two remaining laser towers switched to point defence and joined the fighters in a last ditch attempt to knock the missiles down. Only five got through but that was enough to severely drain the shields and send plasma feedback surging along damaged relays. A station exploded close to him and the young Flank officer who had displayed so much promise was hurled back. She lay unmoving on the deck, her face bloodied and torn but he had eyes only for the Hawk wing closing on the cruiser.

Two of the three were smashed from space by point defence plasmas as the Xenon launched another 20 missiles. The third, twisting through the incoming fire at full speed, rammed the cruiser, barely denting the shields but his comrade had not died in vain. Daht detonated the squash mine jettisoned as she perished and the cruiser was engulfed in the firestorm. The explosion also triggered the ship killers, completely destroying the cruiser and catching most of the remaining fighters in the expanding shockwave and all but removing the last of the station shields.

When the sensors came back on line barely a dozen fighters had survived.

"Admiral Kulagh ssignalss General."

Daht fixed the Comms Officer with a carrion grin.

"Tell the Admiral that I apologise for dissturbing his resst. He may go. He iss further ordered to transfer a cruiser complement of fighterss to thiss sstation on my authority. Then convey all our thankss to the Captain of the Argon desstroyer."

He stood, cradling the still sleeping cat.

"I exxpect a full damage and operational readiness report in three hourss. I will be in my quarterss and will not be dissturbed, even by the Chair hersself. Undersstood?"

He paused over the body of Flank Commander and saluted before turning back to face his command staff.

"She died well. Witness that."

### *Chapter 27: The Best Laid Plans*

He did not dare let himself speak to the Admiral until his cold fury was safely channelled. The jump-fleet had broken no records deploying to protect the sector, in fact they were 30 seconds outside the reaction time established in drills and simulations. Kulagh would have an iron-hide explanation and the Board would consider the victory a vindication of their policy. The bitter fact was that without the intervention of the Argon destroyer he would be dead even if the sector as a whole survived because of the jump-fleet rescue. His enemies would have won.

He sealed his quarters, locked out all but one comm channel for the call he knew would come and poured himself a large Argon whisky. The fiery spirit barely warmed him but the embrace of the honours, trophies and bonus share issues of his military career that largely comprised the decor, did. He caressed the model of his first Falcon fondly. It was accurate down to the tiny confirmed kill chevrons etched below the cockpit and reminded him of simpler times, when his only enemies appeared in his cross-hairs and his only ambition was to serve and protect the Company. He made a note to ensure a piece of one of the Xenon cruisers was retrieved for his trophy collection.

The feel of warm fur rubbing against his legs pulled him from the trap of nostalgia. The urge to step back into the past was strong but he knew it would lead to pointless dwelling on decisions and actions he could not change and open doors to the blackness that sapped his will and plunged the universe into a gray twilight.

"Doess Tiddless want food? Yess she doess!" He crouched and caressed the creature, running a single claw down its back. It purred with delight and yowled with glee as he moved into the small cooking area and unsealed a food supplement. The small domestic ritual centred him and the darkness haunting the edge of consciousness receded like storm clouds dissipating in a summer dawn.

He drained the whisky and poured another before analysing the consequences and possibilities of the recent events.

On the one hand another triumphal verse had been added to his saga. General Daht, scourge of the Xenon; General Daht, the invincible. Oh, the people would cheer and the Board would be effusive in their praise but he would not get a single cruiser.

On the other hand, his forces had suffered huge losses. They could not deny him a fresh garrison or replacement munitions but they would be young and inexperienced recruits not the keen edged veterans and personally loyal comrades he had lost. It would take months to train them to his own standards and longer still before he could make them his strong right arm. If the Xenon came again the outcome would be different, Argon destroyers or no. He was still in his enemies' trap.

Death he could face, defeat even, but not without a fight.

"No!" He downed the whisky and shattered the clay mug against a wall, enraged. "Not without a fight!"

He took another drink, this time straight from the bottle, and allowed the spirit to kindle his anger and spur him into new and dangerous thinking. As the Argon would say,

"The gloves are off."

It came from their archaic and rather ineffective martial art but it captured his mood. For too long he had been constrained by words such as "duty", "loyalty" and "treason" while his foes conspired with clans to further their own positions.

The Argon had another saying, even more obscure. It had been on his mind since the Cat-Man sent word.

"If you dine with the Devil take a very long spoon."

Knowing he was crossing one of his own lines he waited for the call.

It was not long in coming.

As Artur materialised on the teleport pad the General stepped forward and thrust a mug in his hand. He took a cautious sip, he wasn't worried about being poisoned but he had a palate to protect and sometimes aliens drank the strangest things. It was a vintage Argon whisky, smooth on the tongue but a fire in his stomach.

He raised his mug to the General.

"To those who died well."

General Daht repeated the toast with fervour and drained his mug in one massive gulp before waving Artur to the single armchair designed for humans. The cat conceded it grudgingly and jumped into the Generals' lap where it contentedly absorbed his distracted strokes.

"They almost got you this time General. You were lucky I was about."

"You need not remind me of a debt. All are entered on the ledger."

His words were slightly slurred but his eyes were bright alert.

"You alwayss appear with purposse. Explain."

The meeting went better than Artur had any right to expect. General Daht had always been a resource that bargained hard. Both knew they were using each other for their own ends and where their aims temporarily crossed they could deal. He had been useful, as with dealing with Force, but he was a powerful and cunning man in his own right and the strengths that made him useful limited the opportunities to exploit him.

Artur had worked long and subtly to place the General in his current position and now it had paid off more spectacularly than he could have hoped. He was hurt, enraged and vulnerable. He was ready.

The business with Paskaal was quickly dealt with. Artur handed over a data file.

"In a few days this man will dock at your station going by the name of Corrin. He is an Argon Special Forces operative under cover as a bounty hunter. He will be flying an Elite fighter, you will not be able to miss him. I want him to meet me at the attached co-ordinates, you can let me know the time through the usual channel."

The General took the chip and reviewed the file on his padd.

"I ssee he huntss your man Force. You fear him and wish him desstroyed?"

Artur shook his head. "No, nothing like that - I wish to talk with the man under circumstances of my own choosing. You've read the file, you've got a plausible story. He might not believe you but he will go where you send him."

"Agreed. It is a small favour to ask under the circumstancces. Not as ssmall as it seemss no doubt. You have more?"

Artur smiled, dealing with the General was like playing chess with each of them attempting to manipulate the other to move their pieces so that long term strategies came to fruition. The General was a good strategist, but not as good as he thought. He had a knack for surrounding himself with gifted subordinates in tune with his own thinking and it was they, as much as Daht, who won his battles. He also had one weakness so glaring and it was a wonder he had come as far as he had.

The General was an honest man.

"Actually I have come to offer you aid. What is your biggest handicap on the Board, apart from the lack of a battle-fleet of course?"

Daht's' eyes glittered with anger as he hissed.

"The Clanss."

They were a permanent factor in the Teladi Company affairs as profitable customers, suppliers of cheap resources and most significantly as allies. Allies not of the Company but allies of individual Board members. Those who could draw on the illicit financial and military support of a clan could transmute it into power and the General lacked that resource for personal and practical reasons. Embracing such allies had seemed to him at first, as he clawed himself to his present position, dishonourable. By the time he had come to accept the need for such friends it was too late. Even if he could have lured one into shifting their loyalty none would consider basing themselves in the perilous sector he commanded.

Artur was well aware of the Generals' feelings on the matter and could hear their complexity in the sibilance of his tone.

"Ah yes, I understand your reservations. Some of their activities can be most unsavoury and lacking in honour. What if I said I could arrange an alliance with a new power?"

The General studied the human for a long moment. It was an interesting question and one that confirmed long nurtured suspicions as to the real intentions of his mysterious ally. Aware that the answer he would give was the first step on a darker path with no turnings he waved an impatient claw.

"I bring a long spoon to thiss meeting, you undersstand? Specificss."

When the Cat-Man departed the General spent a long time brooding on what he had heard, what he had agreed. Despite his words it was clear the human Force was little more than a front-man, tied by strings of obligation and personal gain to his ambitious benefactor. Disregard the fine legal niceties and the distinction between pirate and what he had termed "Privateer" vanished like smoke. An independent industrial empire established by a radical interpretation of Company Statutes and Free Trade Agreements in Scale Plate Green and backed by its own mercenary forces was a Clan by any other name.

It was a bold plan. In all the centuries the Company had not issued a Decree of Incorporation to any alien. The right of any corporation to establish facilities in any sector of any species was a theoretical right established by free-trade treaties between the Foundation and Profit Guilds. But it was a right that required the agreement of two parties, one from each Guild. No species had proven willing to expose their own corporations to inter-species competition and like all unexercised rights it had fallen into disuse, considered by all as no more than a well-meaning but pious hope, to be implemented "in the future". Meanwhile trade remained in the hands of quasi-monopolies.

The few attempts that had been made to exercise the right had been met by furious armed responses from the established corporations, although of course their hands remained clean. As a Member of the Board, controlling a Sector, he had a theoretical right to petition for a Decree. With a little persuasion the Board might be willing to agree to avoid an open fight with a figure popular with the shareholders, secure in the knowledge that neither the Argon or Boron governments would agree. The Cat-Man assured him that steps were being taken in this regard and he knew the man well enough to know anything was possible.

It was going to be the political battle of his life but he was fighting now for his own destiny and that made for strange bed-fellows. If one of these was a reformed mercenary human acting as the front man for the establishment of the Cat-Man's Clan then so be it. The Board had forced him into a corner and they would now find out how dangerous that was.

Filling with a renewed vigour he activated the DNA scourers to eliminate all traces of his guest and began plotting.

As the Seera headed for the jump-gate Artur raised his champagne glass to the myriad suns glittering through the flight deck canopy.

"To my lucky stars! Cheers." The sparkling wine was not as cool as he could have wished and he twisted the magnum, burying it deeper into the crushed ice of the antique cooler balancing on the co-pilot seat. When fortune smiled in your direction with such good effect he believed you just had to give thanks immediately, lest her fickle gaze turned elsewhere. He had been saving this bottle for a special occasion and now seemed as good a time as any to get rip-roaringly drunk. To do anything else would be a waste of one of the finest vintages of the last five decades.

"Music Seera, something light but classic. Make it jazz, make it swing." The cabin filled with the sound of a trumpet played by an angel, soaring above the bass and drums and counter-pointed by a light, tinkling piano. It could have been a modern rendition of one of the classics of a musical form the Goner maintained originated on Earth, centuries before gate travel but it was difficult to tell. Familiar snatches of melody surfaced and shone before melding back into the improvised stream of notes. Artur did not care but allowed the music to infuse his soul with a rarely felt joy. The Xenon attack had allowed him to achieve something he dared not hope for despite all his careful planning. He had not seen the General like that before, there was a genuine anger burning behind his carefully banked ambition. The narrowness and circumstance of his victory had demonstrated his self-styled destiny hung by fraying threads. It had made him vulnerable and it had made him reckless and Artur exploited it to the hilt, playing his ambition for his own ends.

Granting a Decree to Force would open up unrivalled opportunities for Max. Artur had envisaged Force establishing himself in the cracks between empires, the sectors claimed by all but dominated by the clans. A rogue privateer among thieves. Now there was the chance of a new corporate empire, spanning the territory of all races, provided one of the members of the Foundation Guild formally agreed. There was of course no possibility that the Argon Senate would agree, the old corporations held the reins of power in a loose grip but would be certain to tighten them should such a fundamental threat to their profits arise.

The Boron though, they were a different matter. Their economy was already dominated by the Argon, their own trading entities no match for the rapacious Teladi or the well-organised humans. And power had other wellsprings than economic muscle. It would take a lot to get a Decree issued in the face of Argon opposition but with his connections, the promising start Max had made and some more luck he could do it. As the Dolphin entered the jump-gate he mulled over several contingency plans. Before he had crossed the new sector he had made his choice. Cradling the tiny vial in a sweaty palm as he went through the heavily protected file of contacts he picked a name and ordered Seera to a new course.

Corrin had put his unexpected return to Light of Heart to good use. The shower had cleared his head of the tail-chasing riddles mixed with combat replays and allowed him to think calmly. The knowledge that his movements were being tracked by someone with the power to alter military Nav-Sat access codes had shaken him. It also confirmed what he had suspected, Marteene had got himself involved with a rogue intelligence operation. The man would not have vanished in the way he did unless he believed he was following legitimate orders, but he was not. The lack of a registered Code Black proved that but someone had done an excellent job of making him think otherwise. Now, whoever this was and whosoever he represented, knew he, Paskaal not Corrin, was looking for him. This was something only the Captain was supposed to know but he had no doubt Trasker would also be aware of it by now. In either case it looked like a conspiracy that may involve either, both or neither.

Whether or not this involved Max Force he could not yet tell but he was certainly being used as the bait to lure him to Scale Plate Green. And bait was only used in traps. It was his only lead so he would have to follow it but it made him feel uncomfortably like prey. This prey though, was aware and had fangs.

## *Chapter 28: ..of Mice and Men*

Paskaal had a long haul to make through the heart of the Split territories. Normally he would have gritted and clenched everything and pushed on through to friendlier sectors but he could not afford to by-pass any sector in his search for the elusive Dolphin.

As a race the Split had a direct attitude that came across as unbearable arrogance and rampant xenophobia and like their allies in the Profit Guild were more than willing to throw up obstacles in the way of traders from other races. They would not even extend docking rights to anyone who had not proven themselves a friend of the Split by risking their lives in victorious combat against their enemies. It deterred aliens from trading and provided a useful backup for sector security forces.

Fortunately the Split had plenty of enemies, chief among them the clans who maintained a heavily defended outpost in Chins Clouds. This resource-rich but sparsely populated sector straddled the eastern route to the New Frontier and saw a great deal of Teladi, Argon and Boron shipping. It was probably because the clans largely confined their depredations to this shipping that the Split tolerated the base. No doubt credits were changing hands in that sector also.

Clan ships were however, fair game, particularly in the surrounding sectors. Their rulers were not benefiting from the clan largesse and saw no need to tolerate clan activities. He had to patrol as far as Chins Fire to find pirates engaging in acts he felt justified his intervention. Three Bayamon fighters and an Orinoco. The Argon piloting the Lifter freighter was grateful for his timely intervention and the authorities grudgingly granted him conditional docking rights throughout Split territories. After docking at the Trading Station Corrin spent a large chunk of his remaining credits renewing his Bounty Hunter license for the Split territories. He planned to replenish these by taking some of the many convoy protection contracts on offer in every Split sector on the route to the New Frontier and with this aim in mind he headed for sector Family Whi. It was off his direct route but it was the jumping off point for Frontier convoys and the fattest contracts could be picked up there. He hoped that arriving in Scale Plate Green as part of a convoy escort would make him less conspicuous and just possibly he could catch his quarry off-guard.

He did not make it that far. As he entered Family Zein only one sector short of his destination, a single clan Mandalay fighter, lurking in the depths beyond the south jump-gate changed course and accelerated towards him. Paskaal watched it approach unconcerned, it was fast but too lightly armed and shielded to pose any threat to his Elite. These fighters were popular with the clans purely for their low cost, which made them affordable for those climbing onto the lower rungs of a clan hierarchy. They were generally only encountered as part of a mixed package defending clan convoys. They fought in packs and they were rarely seen on their own.

Scanning it revealed the Mandalay drive had been fully upgraded. The 230 mps speed suggested it was a courier. Each clan maintained a number of these, despite the cost of the speed upgrade, to function as couriers. They could be found occasionally speeding through hostile sectors but not just hanging around. That suggested it had been waiting for him.

"Okay matey, let's see what you have in mind." Corrin decelerated and banked towards the incoming fighter, using the Zoom function of his HUD to scan the fighter for clues. He had always considered the Mandalay to be one of the better M5 fighters. The cockpit located on top of the hull provided the good all-round vision necessary for a dogfighter; the separation of the two drive units by a short boom gave a clear aft view and the thrusters mounted on spars either side of the nose provided enhanced manoeuvrability. The emergence of the new generation of M5 fighters such as the Argon Discoverer and the Boron Octopus with their superior top speeds threatened to make the Mandalay obsolete but at knife fight velocities a good pilot could still triumph thanks to the greater situational awareness the design bestowed.

Interestingly the fighter bore no clan markings.

At 5 klicks the Mandalay came to a complete stop. Paskaal followed suit but kept a wary eye on the scanner for fighters emerging from the jump-gate behind him. Almost immediately the comm system registered an incoming call and Paskaal activated it. The pilot had his visor unpolarised, revealing an Argon male with deep-set eyes that looked older than his youthful face.

He spoke carefully but his voice was firm and untroubled by the disparity in the capabilities of their craft.

"Am I addressing the bounty hunter known as Corrin?"

It was phrased as a question but delivered with the air of a statement and Paskaal could see no reason to deny it.

"That I am. Is this about the trouble down in Hatikvah's Faith because if it is don't you think you are a little outgunned son?"

The pirate smiled.

"No, nothing to do with that, we've all got to make a living right? Not our clan either but the incident did draw you to our attention. We understand that you hold a commission to find a certain Max Force, is that correct?"

Paskaal considered the question for a second, weighing his words with caution.

"Evidence suggests he died in a Xenon sector. Do you have reason to suspect otherwise?"

"I'd prefer to continue our discussion over a secure channel. May I come alongside and patch in laser comms?"

Corrin nodded. "Since you asked so politely, come on in."

It did not take long for the M5 to pull up off his port side, close enough for him to see the pilot manually operating the comms target system. With a flash of static the emitters synchronised with his own as a clearer, high-resolution link was established.

"Okay, that's better, we don't want anyone listening in on this. We know you have a substantial commission from his former comrades to find him. My employer would like to offer you double that amount to deliver him to us."

"That is a very generous offer son. And your employer is?"

"Clan Stoertebeker." He replied matter-of-factly.

It was not a reply he liked. That clan had a well-earned bad reputation and they were not renowned for taking no for an answer.

"Ah, interesting. You have evidence that Force is still with us?"

The Clan pilot shook his head. "First the agreement."

Paskaal weighed the options. He did not like the thought of working with that particular clan, particularly as he would be forced to double-cross them should they want force dead. On the other hand if they did have information he wanted it. If his suspicions were correct there was some connection between whatever happened to Marteene and Force. Getting directly to Force instead of being led by the nose to Scale Plate Green could be the breakthrough h was looking for.

"That's a lot of credits you are talking about. Why me?"

"A fair question. You are not the only hunter we're approaching but you already hold a commission and like you we want him alive. You've been out of circulation for awhile but you have a good rep on that score. Any thug in an M3 can waste crims, it takes finesse to take them alive. Interested?"

The word almost sounded like a threat.

Corrin nodded.

"Fine. Head for the base in Teladi Gain. Identify yourself and you'll be escorted through the defences. More details will be provided once you dock."

The Mandalay abruptly cut the comm link and accelerated at full speed towards the northern jump-gate. The Elite followed but with a top speed only half that of the light fighter it was left far behind.

Formerly the system of Teladi Gain had been the home of Boron philosophers and visionaries but since falling into the hands of the Teladi during the long Boron Conflict it had become famous for something completely different.

Drug fuelled, unadulterated hedonism.

Where once mystics pondered the meaning of life along solitary shores, the young of all races partied long and hard all the long day of the twin sunned system and throughout the short and infrequent nights too. The Bliss Place established in the sector was one of the most profitable businesses in the Teladi Trading Company and almost all of its production went to sate the voracious appetite of the endless partying planet-side.

The sector itself was run by Jeriak Morn, possibly the richest and single most powerful Director of the Trading Company. General Daht may be feared by his fellows for the threat to the comfortable established order that he represents but Morn was truly hated for her completely ruthless and incessant hunger for the Chair of the Company. Her alliance with the Stoertebeker Clan added terror to the mix. Such was their reputation that none would dare move against her openly and only a fragile alliance of the other Company Directors kept her from claiming the prize the old woman felt was her right.

Paskaal entered the system with some trepidation. He had no previous dealings with this particular Clan but he knew their well-earned reputation for savagery and as a bounty hunter he had a suspicion he would not be welcomed with open arms, even if they did want something from him. The prospect of double-crossing them was not an enticing one.

The Clan Base itself was constructed from the shell of a huge deep space terraformer, dragged in from a long forgotten orbit around the moon of the third planet of the secondary sun. The drives had been refurbished and more equipment and facilities bolted on, giving it a look that was both unfinished but tinged with menace, like a mad cyborg that had torn pieces from other bodies and rammed them bleeding into its own.

He counted 12 Laser Towers and 4 mixed package wings patrolling between them that included the Teladi made Falcon M3 fighter. A scan of them revealed the unmistakable signatures of hornet missiles. Before he had got to within 15 klicks he was intercepted by a flight of 3 Bayamons and a Falcon. The scanner showed another wing moving towards them.

"Elite fighter, identify yoursself."

The sibilant hiss of the flight leader contained the note of barely restrained rage that raised the hackles on the back of his neck and Corrin hastily replied.

"Corrin - I was told to report here and you would be expecting me."

The Falcon had taken up a position on his six and the Bayamons were circling around the Elite like scavengers around a wounded predator. The comm channel cut off for some of the longest seconds of his life before the disappointment tinged hiss of the flight leader returned.

"Confirmed bounty hunter, you may proceed." Two of the Bayamons assumed an escort position while the Falcon remained close on his tail. There was venom in the words and Paskaal could picture the pilot caressing the secondary fire button on her control stick, he could tell that she would like nothing better than send a brace of hornets up his drives and he fought the reflex to roll away and engage. Instead he followed his escort through the station defences and into the docking port where turbo-laser turrets pointedly tracked him every metre of the way. He climbed down from the cockpit on legs he could barely stop from shaking to greet the heavily armed Teladi troops with considerably more bravado than he felt.

"Ay there my lizard lads - I believe you have a job for me."

They said nothing but the leader indicated with his blaster that Corrin should head towards the main exit. Feeling that he may have made a terrible mistake he complied.

———

Two of the soldiers accompanied him. The rest remained in the docking bay, which was busy even for a Clan Base. Launch thrusters roared cacophonously and the twilight gloom was pierced constantly by the arc flash of spot-bonders as maintenance crews replaced damaged hull plates .

Paskaal estimated there were at least 50 fighters in various states of repair docked on the platforms that festooned the cavernous main bay and he had spotted two sets of blast doors on the way in that probably led to secondary docking areas. There were only a few freighters visible, all of them Teladi Vultures.

Groups of Teladi technicians worked with unusual industriousness under the watchful eyes of the guards that constantly patrolled the bay. Corrin was shocked to glimpse Power-Chokes around the necks of a mixed band of Argon, Split and Paranid labouring to remove a drive assembly from a Falcon with a primitive rope and pulley system. For a moment he was not sure what was more shocking, the sight of sentient beings used as slaves or the fact they were performing such heavy work without power assistance. He concluded it must be some form of punishment.

It was a welcome relief for his senses when the bay door slammed shut behind him. He did not have time to do more than glance around the open cargo area before he was bundled into an elevator. In the confines of the small lift the distinctive odour of his Teladi guards became all too noticeable and he concentrated on breathing through his mouth rather than attempt to engage them in fruitless conversation. They were clearly not the talkative type and all the soldiers were much too disciplined for his liking. Paskaal had never been on this station but had experience of several other Clan bases and those tended towards the casual and the anarchic. This base had the oppressive feel of a front-line battle station.

He endured at least a minute of vertical and horizontal lurches through many decks before the lift jerked to a sudden halt. He did not need a gun barrel prodding to make him leave but the guards administered one just the same.

"Okay okay, I get the picture guys. Where to now?"

With an incline of his head one of the soldiers indicated a metal door at the end of the bare narrow hallway he found himself in. It was guarded. A Teladi and a big taciturn human with low furrowed brows who ignored his greeting and ran a small hand scanner over him, removing each weapon he found.

"Theese will be returnned if you leave, enter now." The Teladi activated the door control and it slid open soundlessly. Corrin did not like the sound of that 'if' but had no choice but to step through.

It took his eyes a few seconds to adapt to the low light levels of the long, narrow, high ceiling chamber. It was too warm and clouds of sweet-smelling incense hung in the air. At the far end of the room he could make out the backlit silhouette of a large figure seated in a high-backed chair. Two smaller shapes were crouching at its feet. He took a moment to centre himself back into the Corrin persona before confidently striding the length of the chamber towards the figure.

Seated in what was almost a throne, given the obvious theatrics and the raised dais, was the ugliest man Paskaal had ever seen. At first he was not even sure he was a man. The huge bald head seemed directly affixed to a barrel of a body and it was scarred with a ragged tear of scaled leather running from the lower left jaw up and across his face. The right eye, embedded in the reptilian skin appeared to be electronic. Under a fine green silk shirt powerful muscles rippled beneath layers of fat as he caressed the head of one of the young Argon women cowering at his feet. They were severely under-dressed and looked drugged. He could detect the taint of weed behind the olfactory mask of the incense filling the room from unseen dispensers. Paskaal put the man's age at around 50 but such was the disfigurement it was only a guess.

"Stoertebeker I presume?"

The man laughed, deep and humourless.

"Possibly and possibly not bounty hunter, you may call me Law. Welcome to my little play-room, they are sweet are they not? "

He grasped the jaw of the smaller, blonde woman and jerked her face towards Paskaal. She looked terrified and her eyes couldn't focus. With a shock he realised she was blind and that beneath her long hair she wore a Power Choke. The diaphanous silk singlet left nothing to the imagination and Paskaal deliberately focused on the scarred face of the man, not wanting to contribute in any way to her degradation.

"Ah - you do not approve?" His tone was light and amused but his gaze was a direct challenge, which Corrin met unflinchingly.

"No. Slavery is an affront to every free being and this sort of debauchery is vile. Now do you have a job for me or did you just want to impress the hell out of me with your cheap melodramatics?"

A gloved hand tightened on a chair arm. Knuckles shone white through what Paskaal belatedly realised was not a glove but a Teladi claw.

"You should choose your words more carefully. It is fortunate for you that I have need of your services."

Law extracted a data padd from behind him and flicked it across to Corrin. He caught it with contemptuous ease and activated it.

"You recognise this man?"

Paskaal studied the image for a moment. The helmet masking the lower face made it difficult to tell and the image was low resolution and exhibited enough pixellated artefacts to suggest it had been heavily processed but the eyes and nose looked familiar.

"Difficult to tell, it could be Max Force. Where did you get this?"

"We recovered it from the data recorder of one of our destroyed fighters. It was badly damaged, hence the poor quality. We know from other sources that it is him. You seek this man do you not?"

Corrin nodded.

"Good. He has been causing us a great deal of trouble, interfering in an important business matter. Force has also destroyed many of our fighters and we would like to discuss the matter with him."

"Ah - I get it now. This is the guy that has been running your little blockade for the Boron, I've been reading about that. Max Force! I should have guessed. He's only flying a Lifter, why haven't you just shot him up?"

Law dug sharp claws into the chair arm, scoring fresh grooves.

"We have tried but he has proven most resourceful. He has also repeatedly slipped by our ships into Teladi space and we have no idea how. It's as if he has many different craft. "

The hairs on the back of Paskaal's neck stood on end and he fought to keep his face impassive.

Shadow Skin Technology!

"And," Corrin spoke carefully, "You wish to find out how he does it?"

"Precisely. I have done some checking on you Mr Corrin. You surface periodically, earn a great deal of credits and vanish."

Corrin shrugged. "I like my privacy and I like to enjoy the fruits of my labour. But why hire me?"

"First, you are already looking for him. Second, you appear to be good at what you do and third, you are not a killer. You have a good record of persuading your targets to give themselves up and I'm afraid we are not very good at that sort of thing."

"Yes, I can imagine that. I get the feeling this is an offer I'd be unwise to refuse right?"

Law nodded. "We are accustomed to getting our own way Mr Corrin."

"Okay - 50,000 credits. The Raiders are not going to be pleased with me and I'll need to vanish for a long time."

"That is a somewhat high price but I take your point. Agreed. Do not disappoint me bounty hunter."

Law spoke the words softly but Paskaal had never felt so threatened in his life before.

"Understood. Where should I start?"

"We have resources in Ceo's Buckzoid you may wish to use, the details are on the padd. This is your area of expertise but as he is trading teledanium perhaps that is a clue. Stay out of Boron space though, we do not want to scare him off. Capture him in Teladi territory and bring him to me. Bring him to me soon bounty hunter."

Law fondled the brunette who flinched away from his touch.

"You may go now, I have other matters to attend."

As his Elite shot into open space and away from the station Paskaal knew his life had a new purpose.

He would see Law dead.

## *Chapter 29: Hunters Moon*

In nature there are two kinds of hunter, those who stalk their prey and those that lie in wait.

Corrin by temperament fell into the first camp. He wasted many days prowling Teladi sectors attempting to pry commercial information from un-forthcoming station managers only to discover that the writ of Morn did not run far. The support of Directors whose fiefdoms were most affected by the blockade was lukewarm at best and with profits falling all were willing to sanction trade with Force, reasoning it was the business of the Stoertebeker Clan to prevent safe delivery. That failure, combined with their hatred of Director Morn, emboldened his fellows to shrewdly equivocate when approached for information to aid his search. It left Paskaal chasing shadows in a ship built for combat, not speed. A fully tuned Lifter could just about out-run him and it made the task of tracking down and scanning the many freighters of that design operating in Teladi space a frustrating affair. If Force had acquired shadow skin technology Corrin could fly within 30 metres of him and never know it.

Reluctantly he adopted the alternative strategy.

Ore Mine Beta in Ceo's Buckzoid was the closest station to the western jump-gate to Boron space, which was why the Clan had adopted it as a staging area. The asteroid mine was barely habitable for Teladi let alone Paskaal and he spent many hours in the relative comfort of the Elite cockpit watching the data feeds from the enhanced station scanners and the Clan patrols, whose claw-dragging co-operation came only under direct orders. Worse than killing many of their comrades, Force had made them lose face and Paskaal could smell the desire for revenge and despite their instructions to take Force alive he knew they were just looking for a plausible excuse. It was almost impossible to disable a ship without destroying it once the shields were down and if Force did not eject, well, what else could they do? Let him go?

If he was discovered in the sector Corrin knew he would have to move fast.

---

Artur was also not a man to stay still and he filled his time before the confidently anticipated meeting with Paskaal weaving new strands to his web to subtly support the General in the undertaking he had inspired. When Daht failed to confirm the sometime bounty hunter had been steered in his direction he was forced to make contact. What the General told him he did not want to hear. Not only had Paskaal not arrived at Scale Plate Green; Daht had been able to establish, through his own resources within the camp of his bitter rival that a bounty hunter piloting an Elite had docked at the Stoertebeker base some days previously.

It threw him into a state as near to panic as he ever came. Whether or not Paskaal suspected Force and Marteene were one and the same it would be almost certain to come out if the two met, one way or another. If Paskaal did not recognise him or Marteene did not let on then he was certain that the watching Trasker would figure it out. He had an idea how to neutralise her and although it had not yet hardened into a plan it required Paskaal. He immediately accessed the Menelaus Frontier military Nav-Sat and as he broached the jump-gate penumbra he activated his own jump-drive. Seconds later he emerged into Boron space and ignoring the patrolling Eel and Piranha fighters he arced around to re-enter the jump-gate to Ceo's Buckzoid.

---

For the third time in what, according to his body clock, was the middle of the night, he was summonsed from an uncomfortable sleep by the urgent tone of the sensor alert. His whole body aching he activated the sector scan and forced his tired eyes to focus on the screen, which showed a freighter, had entered through the southern jump-gate. The clan patrol was moving to intercept. It was another Lifter and he ran the IFF code through a validation sub-routine. The check-sum was valid but that only proved it had been generated using the correct algorithm but he had no link to Argon records to run further checks on the registration. Corrin briefly considered launching but he was as tired of the false alarms as the clan patrols were of him stampeding into their midst. Instead he hooked into the powerful station sensors and began scanning the Lifter for signs of shadow skin technology or anything else unusual enough to warrant a closer look.

---

"Bayamon patrol moving on an intercept course Max."

"Got them Xela," Marteene replied as he opened up the throttle and adjusted his heading. The Lifter accelerated to the best speed it could manage with the shadow skin running. "Can you get us any more Zee?"

"Negative Max, 130 mps is all you're getting. I'm juggling energy flows as it is and if I push it any further we will lose systems."

"Okay, time to intercept?"

"Seventy seconds on my mark....... Mark."

"Are we going to make it?"

"Uncertain Max, I've run the calculations dozens of time but there are too many unknown variables."

"What are the odds?"

Uncharacteristically the AI hesitated before replying.

"I don't think you want to know Max."

"That good huh? Well as they say, 'Fortune favours the bold.'"

"And punishes the foolhardy Max. Don't forget that part."

Marteene tried not to let her evident apprehension get to him as he watched the fighters close, they were on a path with no turnings now.

As the pack of Bayamons swept over him the comm system activated and a Teladi, her voice contorted with menace curtly ordered them to heave to. Max judged the distance to the jump-gates and kept going for a few more seconds.

"Lifter, all sstop or be desstroyed."

A hail of plasma bolts streaked around the freighter and Marteene throttled back, bringing the Lifter slowly to a complete halt.

"Status Zee?"

"Signal mask holding Max, all they are getting are the false readings."

Marteene ignored the incoming call for a few seconds and ran a systems check. The reinforced power relays were holding up under the strain of the cycling pulses that Xela was forcing through the shadow-skin tech, but only just. Several were on the brink of failure.

"Okay Zee, get the droids working."

"Acknowledged Max, buy us as much time as you can okay?"

Polarising his visor Max took a deep breath and answered the hail. He did not need an exobiology degree to recognise that the Teladi was dangerously enraged.

"Hi there, anything I can do for you?" Max tried to keep his tone light and hoped the comm did not pick up the tremor he could feel in his voice.

"You will ssubmit your cargo for inspection. Eject podss in units of 10 on my command. The firsst 10 now." The threat in her voice was scarcely implied.

Marteene knew the procedure but stalling for time asked under what authority the search was being carried out. The Lifter rocked under a barrage of fire.

"Authority confirmed it seems, okay, but I'm carrying nothing your scans haven't already shown. A hold full of energy cells, job lot at a bargain price. I can cut you a good deal if you like?"

"I will not assk again." Her sibilant tone hissed with fury. "Begin now."

Max muted the comm. "How's it going Zee?"

"On schedule Max, I think you had best comply."

He moved the first 10 units of energy cells from the subspace hold into the main cargo bay and opened the doors. The jettisoned pods drifted slowly away and on the scanner he noted the fighters swarming in closer to inspect them from short range.

The process was repeated 3 more times at the Teladi's command.

"Nearly ready Max but a dozen relays have blown, we're going to lose our cover anytime soon."

He checked his systems. The Shadow Skin Technology was still functioning but the signal mask was fluctuating. If they were scanned again the pirates might pick up intermittent Teledanium readings. Marteene mentally crossed his fingers, hoping their attention was focusing entirely on the energy cell containers.

---

Paskaal watched the routine unfold on screen. The Lifter had made a half-hearted attempt to run for the western jump-gate but had soon been forced to heave to. His scans of the growing cluster of cargo pods confirmed what his initial scans had shown, the freighter was carrying energy cells not teledanium. It was another false alarm, not the evasive Max Force and if he paid the bribe he would soon be on his way. He was disappointed but the relief he felt at being able to snatch some more sleep won out.

As another slew of energy pods guttered from the Lifter he ran a second scan. There were hundreds more cells in the hold to be checked and it was going to take a long time. Corrin was about to switch the scanner back to standby when the feed from the station sensors showed a slight flicker in the upper EM band. Intrigued he applied a filter to eliminate possible artefacts caused by the interface between Teladi and Argon sensor systems and the anomaly vanished. Narrowing the gain he fine scanned that band range and it returned. The signal was intermittent but definitely there. Quickly he ran a check on the waveform.

It was Teledanium.

A huge jolt of adrenaline scoured away all fatigue as he signalled for an emergency launch.

––––––––––––––––––

The flash of the small explosion behind him briefly illumined the cockpit like a flare before it was plunged into darkness. He switched to his suit air supply as fumes filled the cockpit. Secondary power cut in almost immediately but Max did not need Xela to tell him that the shadow-tech was failing.

"How long Zee?" he asked urgently.

"Seconds Max, we've got to do it now!"

"Status?"

"They're all in range, the Mine is on the fringe and it's just launched another fighter. It's an Elite. Get us out of here Max!"

"Anything else in range?"

"No nothing, a Dolphin has just come through the western gate but it's fine. Now Max, now!"

Marteene hesitated for only a split-second as he weighed his options. He really had none. The timing would have to be so perfect that only Xela could handle it. He gave to word and the AI took control of the pre-planned sequence.

"Go Xela."

She began the countdown from 10 as the jump-drive powered up.

"Ten."

He transferred most of the remaining energy cells into the hold.

"Nine."

He opened the bay doors.

"Eight."

He ejected a cloud of active energy cells.

"Seven."

The first whorls of the artificial wormhole forming in front of him appeared.

"Six, Five, Four."

He ran a final scan of the sector. Through the interference generated by the activated energy cells he noted the clan fighters breaking around to attack.

"Three."

He scanned the Elite closing rapidly on his position, blood freezing at the familiar IFF.

"Two."

"Paskaal, no! Abort, abort!!"

"Request denied Max." Her voice was dull and mechanical.

"One."

The squash mine materialised in the mass of energy cells and exploded, sending the Destiny Star tumbling into the jump singularity.

---

"Faster girl, faster." Paskaal tried to squeeze the last iota of speed from the heavy fighter through will alone. His scanners clearly registered Teledanium now and it would only be a matter of seconds before the Clan pilots noticed the same thing and he had to get there quickly to forestall any rash actions. As he watched the sector scan faded beneath a crosshatched haze interference patterns. He was close enough now to see the freighter had ejected a host of pods.

The explosion, bigger than anything he had ever witnessed, practically blinded him, even through the polarised combat helm. A Second later the leading edge of the shockwave caught the Elite and tossed it like a discarded toy on a storm ravaged sea before pounding it to pieces.

## *Chapter 30: Consequences*

There were two messages in the latest upload. Artur disconnected the link with the Nav-Sat and returned to his office leaving the Seera AI in control as the Dolphin cruised towards the distant jump-gate. The quantum keys on each showed they had not been tampered with and while the decryption sub-routines ran he lit a slim black cigar, savouring the aromatic taste. Such a fine smoke demanded a brandy but he resisted the temptation and turned his attention to the decrypts, digesting each without betraying a hint of emotion.

The first message confirmed Marteene had taken delivery of the data chip. He would have preferred to deliver it in person given the nature of the information but he had other business to attend. The courier was one of his most trusted operatives and only the Xela AI would be able to decode the contents so he was not concerned with security. It would have been useful to meet Marteene face to face again but the last meeting had not gone well. The death of Paskaal was still a raw wound and Marteene was not unreasonably furious that he had not been told that his friend had been searching for both him and Force. He had been forced to grudgingly accept that the "need to know" principle applied in this operation as much as any other but Artur knew he had lost trust he would at some time need to reclaim.

For now Max laboured under a burden of guilt for his death that Artur was not in a position to assuage. The fact that there had been no other choice and Xela had taken the decision from him was no balm. The revelation that the AI had the free will to ignore his orders for the sake of the assignment had come as a shock to him and had strained the growing bond between the two. In truth it was a surprise to Artur also but she was a unique prototype incorporating Xenon technology that was not fully understood. No one really knew what to expect.

The second message was just as welcome, confirming he had followed his instructions and blown his cover to the old mercenary in the Nyana's Hideout sector despite his refusal to tell Marteene the reasoning behind such an insane order.

Marteene did not need to know any of the details of his own private little war with Commander Trasker. Fargas Ryle was one of her minor operatives in the frontier sectors and Artur had expended a great deal of time, credits and ingenuity in turning him. He did not like using double agents, it was an axiom of his profession that they could not be trusted, but with Paskaal out of commission he needed another conduit.

Ryle was a retired veteran turned mercenary who had gambled his pension on his shot reflexes and lost. The Frontier sectors were full of his type, bitter old men living on memories of better times and the few credits they could get for low level intelligence that amounted to little more than bar gossip.

He had fed him significant but utterly false information on several occasions and each time it came straight back to him rather than Trasker. Artur was as confident as you could ever be of the loyalty of this type, especially given the unobtrusive favours he had done and Ryle had dutifully reported the spaceweed ravings of Max straight to him.

He had apparently played the bitter cynic to perfection, which was no surprise, considering what had happened in Ceo's Buckzoid. Artur also controlled the cutout along the route to Trasker's ear should Ryle attempt to double-cross him. He did not think that likely as he had been given an ample understanding of the consequences.

Trasker's network was now primed and in the right circumstances he would pull the trigger.

Artur poured himself that brandy to celebrate, all in all the first 3 months of the improvised operation had gone better than he had any right to expect. His recruit had more than matched the expectations of himself and his dead cousin. He displayed both a pleasing ability to think creatively on his feet and a ruthless will to succeed.

Revenge was indeed a great motivator.

The Ceo's Buckzoid Incident, as it had become known, had proven to be a political earthquake of a magnitude similar to the devastating explosion Max had so cleverly improvised.

The destruction of the large Clan patrol had ended the attempted blockade, not because of the losses as such, but because it demonstrated it was not enforceable. Director Morn had lost much face and at the urging of General Daht the Board had withdrawn their always conditional support. Profits now were preferable to increasingly unlikely monopoly profits later.

With the subtle help of Artur, General Daht had been able to strengthen his position by uniting some of the opponents of Morn under his leadership. It was a small faction but a faction nevertheless and the General, being an honourable being, was further in debt. In the new political landscape the Decree of Incorporation was now less of a spaceweed fantasy and Artur continued to work behind the scenes to that end.

The Boron would have granted it on the spot had Artur not persuaded Max of the wisdom of disappearing. As Marteene had intended the interference generated by the overloading power cells had shielded the jump-drive activation from sector scanners and the explosion had completely overwhelmed them. So far as anyone was concerned Max Force had perished along with everyone else and considering the rage of the Stoertebeker Clan that was a good thing.

The Destiny Star had jumped to the western gate of Menelaus Prime and docked in a private bay in the Trading Station where the Factotum took discreet delivery of the teledanium. Sinas was generous in his gratitude, as was his Captain whose position in the Boron scheme of things had been secured and improved. Max departed with many anonymous credits and more goodwill, held on long-term deposit.

Marteene donned a cloak of anonymity Artur had woven from the Guild Rehabilitation Programme and for the next three months he traded from sector to sector, never staying in one place for too long and rarely leaving his ship. Even so he had managed to make some spectacular deals, many of them legal. The Destiny Star was now fully equipped with combat drones and another 25MW shield and Force had over 250,000 credits in different accounts.

For several weeks now he had hauled ore around the Argon frontier systems where his services were well-rewarded due to the constant threat from the Xenon north of Black Hole Sun. Without Paskaal to follow Trasker had been thrown off the trail, at least until Force resurfaced. The discussion Marteene had just had with one of her former informants was his latest step in dealing with this problem and Artur took a moment to feel pride in the efficacy of the solution.

Artur had spent the months following the Ceo's Buckzoid Incident finalising the construction of a new network he could be sure of. The encrypted details were on the chip now in the hands of Force. The Xela AI had no doubt decoded them and incorporated the information into her knowledge base. It was now up to Max to exploit it and given his resourcefulness the very thought send a tremor of delighted anticipation through his body. Whatever happened now was guaranteed not to be dull.

The wolf was off the lead.

He returned to the cockpit and taking the pilot position programmed a jump sequence. He had another appointment with the unpleasant but useful Doctor Phyrath, many sector distant where he hoped to hear good news.

### *Chapter 31: Running with the Wolf.*

"I hope you're planning to wash that thing before you stick it in me Max?"

"What..? Oh, right."

"I do believe you're blushing Max, pleasant memories?"

Marteene ignored the arched barb as he rummaged through the Emergency Kit for a depolariser to clean the data chip but he was relieved that his partnership with the AI had survived Ceo's Buckzoid. Perhaps a small part of him did still blame Xela for refusing to abandon their plan but when it came down to it the whole scheme was his and with hindsight it was reckless in its disregard for the safety of bystanders.

Of course once Xela had confirmed the practicalities of the proposal they had run simulations to carefully establish the radius of effect. He had made sure they were intercepted far enough away from the jump-gates and any station to ensure they would not be caught in the blast, callously assuming any ship heading in their direction must be Clan. The involvement of Paskaal was not a factor he could have anticipated though.

That did not assuage the guilt, gnawing like a rat on his innards. Neither did it curb the bitterness he felt towards his Cabal controller for failing to keep him informed. This he kept banked behind a wall of cold professionalism and a promise. They both had jobs to do, damn dirty ones and if he had always known Artur would stop at nothing to prevent the Clans getting their hands on advanced technology that knowledge was now visceral.

Blaming Xela, Artur or even himself would not get the job done but extreme pressure has to be channelled lest the vessel splits. Marteene took the hurt, took the rage and focused it like a diamond laser on one target.

The Stoertebeker Clan.

He knew all about them from his previous life. He knew their reputation and their savagery from Intel briefs but that knowledge was not personal. Now he knew he was a marked man for what he had done and as soon as Max Force resurfaced he would have to constantly check his six. More importantly though, he knew they had made Paskaal an offer he could not refuse. That made them culpable, it made them a target and it gave him a goal.

As he ran the depolariser on a low setting over the data chip, causing all the impurities to unbond, he could feel the feral grin beneath his impassive mask. Artur wanted him to get himself a Name so he would get a Name all right. He would tear it from the stinking corpse of the Stoertebeker Clan. Freed from petty legal constraints, unhampered by considerations of policy and with the shadowy Artur in his corner they would soon discover who was the hunter and who was the hunted.

"Those who sow the wind shall reap the whirlwind!" He did not know what dark aspect of his soul he had tapped into but his better angels were howled down by the wild part that exulted in what was to come. He had kept it in check through the long months of anonymous travel but as he scrolled though the new information he could feel it straining at the leash.

"You got all that Xela?"

"Downloaded and incorporated Max. He's been a busy boy again; preferential trading contacts, a whole slew of 'no-questions-asked' types for warm items and this General Daht. You've heard of him?"

It was a rhetorical question. The General was the only Teladi with any military reputation outside of his own race and his exploits against the Xenon were now required reading in the Academy. Knowing the AI had digested a lot more than he could in his skim of the information he replied.

"Sure - big hero, legendary for his aggressive tactics, on the Board of Directors now. Where does he fit in with us?"

"Check this out on your HUD."

Marteene donned the modified shades and Xela flashed up a report she had instantly prepared and with laser monitored flicks of his eyes he read it, following hyperlinks to further information. He was an astute enough observer of politics to appreciate the situation. The General was more than a minor figure in Teladi Company politics but his ambitions over-stretched his reach. It must have been like blood in the water for Artur. Marteene did not care for the vision of a martial Teladi Empire any more than he suspected the Cabal man did. He distrusted fanatics, they tended to get a lot of people killed but any qualms he felt at aiding his cause evaporated like ice in the naked glare of a hot sun. His enemy was another Director called Morn and her allies were the Stoertebeker Clan.

"The friends of my enemy..."

"Did you say something Max?"

"No, just thinking out loud."

"Sure, Max, sure. I don't suppose it's worth pointing to Appendix C: Recommended Strategy is it?"

"Oh you never know, why don't you summarise it for me."

The AI sighed audibly before continuing in a resigned manner.

"Artur recommends you stay well away from the core Teladi sectors and concentrate on quietly building a position of strength out here on the Frontier, bolstering the position of Daht by making Scale Plate Green your centre of operations. He'll be able to provide some measure of protection from Stoertebeker goons and you can help him with Intelligence and the Xenon. Pretty soon he'll be able to swing the Decree and then we'll really be in business."

She paused for a moment.

"If I had any breath I'd be wasting it wouldn't I?"

Marteene grinned and nodded.

"I didn't just have your paint job renewed so we could keep skulking around. We've no idea how long it's going to take whoever is looking to find the alien technology so it's time to up the pace. Take us to the northern gate in Scale Plate Green and do a masked jump to the east gate of Menelaus Frontier. We got enough cells?"

"Plenty. Care to let me in on the plan?"

"It's time we called in a favour and got ourselves some teeth. Then we're going to pay a visit to our old friend Chandus Rarr. That okay with you or are you going to over-rule me?"

He regretted the bitter remark almost immediately.

"Sorry Zee, that was uncalled for."

"That's okay Max, he was your friend. I might be a part Xenon, part human AI but I still understand those things, just don't let revenge cloud your judgement. Rarr isn't one to be trusted."

"Agreed, but he is one looking to make credits and I'm betting he and his associates are not great fans of the Clan, or Director Morn for that matter. Offer them a better deal and back it up with enough muscle and we'll have some new friends. If not we can always just rip off a fat consignment once they trust us. How's that?"

"It is not what is generally understood by the term 'plan' Max, but by your standards it's positively nit-picking in detail. Course laid in, you want me to fly?"

"Yea - I need a strong blast of java and a couple of chocolate bars, those blockers don't quite cut it with that high grade weed!"

Xela laughed. "I'll be sure to include it in our next report to Artur. I'm sure he'll take it up with whatever lab he stole them from. You go and have a sugar jag, I'll call you when we're ready to jump."

Max half expected his channel to the Boron Nav-Sat to have been disabled but Sinas was as good as his word. The comm frequency to his office worked too and although the Factotum could not meet him immediately he specified a time he could be available.

"How discreet does this need to be Max, oh, don't worry this channel is very secure, you can speak freely."

Max thought for a moment. He was tired of clandestine meetings in darkened bars and dives and would welcome the chance to spend an evening in a fancy restaurant with pleasant company but now was possibly not the time.

"Discretion is probably called for Sinas. Do you have a teleport pad in your office?"

The grey haired man nodded.

"Okay then," Max said. "How about contacting me on this channel when you're ready and I'll beam you directly onboard? Until we've talked I don't want to show my face."

"That is acceptable Mr Force, I look forward to meeting you again. Expect my call in a couple of hours. I have a rather fine bottle of Venetarian Red if you would care to provide the food."

Max smiled. "Deal, although I think you've got the shabby end! I'm not a cook, all I can offer is Gourmet Instants."

"Ah well, I've had worse Max. I will contact you soon. Out."

Sinas was punctual and again his word was good. The wine was excellent, full-bodied with a robust bouquet of autumnal fruits and complemented the peasant recipe game and dumpling stew perfectly. By common consent they limited discussion to inconsequentials until the meal was completed, discovering that they shared an exile's passion for the same under-performing Argon Premier soccer team. Having established to their satisfaction that the manager was a bumbling idiot and the urgent need for major close season signings Max bought the conversation to business.

"Sinas, exactly how grateful is your Captain feeling?"

The older man thought for a moment, bringing his steepled fingers to his pursed lips.

"The Boron have a saying they are rather fond of. 'Gratitude is the least of the virtues but ingratitude is the worst of the vices.' Your actions were a great service to him and as you predicted, his star has risen substantially. I understand you also lost a friend and the sacrifice has not gone un-noticed. What is it you have in mind Max?"

"I want to buy a fighter?"

For a moment the Factotum said nothing and then he laughed.

"You help rid the Boron Empire of a thorny trade problem and you want to BUY a fighter? I'm sorry Max, that's just too amusing."

It was not the reaction Marteene had been hoping for and he was too surprised even to get angry.

"Now look, I know you don't just sell military craft to anyone who wanders in off the space lanes but after all I've done. I've got the credits if.."

Still chuckling Sinas cut him off with a wave of his hand.

"No Max, I'm sorry, you've misunderstood. You must think the Boron an ungenerous people to ask so little. If the Decree of Incorporation is passed we'll sell you any ship or piece of equipment you want on the open market but until then I would not dream of taking your credits, not for one fighter anyway. Gratitude is a well that can run dry Max but my Captain will be pleased to gift you a Piranha. In fact I anticipated your request and have arranged for one to be recommissioned from the reserve fleet. It lies, fully upgraded, in the Kingdom End Shipyards."

He passed a data chip across the table. "This has all the information you need to discreetly take possession." He looked Max in the eye. "I've been further appraised of your purpose and I can assure you that whatever aid myself or my Captain can extend, will be. I can't give you a fleet of Eel's but I will help in many other ways, beginning with the Decree. If the Teladi can be persuaded to pass the measure you can be assured of Boron support. Of course if that were suspected beforehand the Teladi Board would not countenance the measure."

"That's good to hear Sinas, I'm going to need people I can count on." He extended his hand and the two men shook.

They finished the wine and discussed other arrangements for several hours before Sinas had to leave. As he stood on the teleport pad he said.

"One more thing, I think I can also arrange further help almost immediately. If so it will be waiting with your new ship. Give me twelve hours."

Marteene turned in feeling more optimistic than he had in a long while.

## *Chapter 32: Boys and Toys*

Max made no attempt to conceal his identity as he spent the next few hours touring the stations to establish trading contacts. News of the return from the dead of the Argon pilot who had smashed the Clan blockade in such a spectacular fashion spread like a virus. He found his name now opened every door and had no trouble arranging the deal he had in mind.

"I like these people Max, they know how to treat a celebrity!" Xela murmured through the shades as he shook on the arrangement with a station manager whose evident joy at dealing with him verged on the obsequious. He made a mental note to pick up a throat mike from the Trading Station. It would be easy enough to tune the device into the personal HUD and at the very least it would enable him to sub vocalise responses to the AI's verbal sallies without appearing insane.

Twelve hours later the Destiny Star docked at the mammoth shipyard orbiting the Boron homeworld.

"What, no marching band? Do these people not know who we are?" Xela complained as he jumped the few feet to the bay floor without waiting for the elevator to deploy.

"Shut up Zee," he murmured inaudibly through clenched teeth. The microphone worked fine.

They had been guided to a small bay off the main docking tunnel. It had enough platforms to host half a dozen craft and from the polished metal gleam and orderly deployment of maintenance equipment he surmised it must be the home of a Boron Navy fighter wing. The platforms were deserted though and only one other ship was docked.

"Reckon that's our new toy Zee?" he asked indicating the Piranha fighter in the adjacent bay. "It's in our colours Max so I'm going to go out on a limb and say yes."

Max walked over to the fighter and caressed the hull. Beneath the fresh crimson and black colour scheme, modelled on that sported by the Star, he could feel the plates were slightly pitted, indicating micro-meteor scoring. A good mechanic could tell the age of a ship from those signs but all it told Marteene was the ship was well used. It would not affect hull integrity though and he continued his inspection, using the data padd sensors to allow Xela to give it an in-depth scan.

"It's great to have a fighter again Zee, isn't she beautiful?"

"In an unintelligent, non-stunning blonde AI sort of way, if you like that sort of thing I suppose," she replied with mock huffiness.

Marteene ignored her jibe; as far as he was concerned an appreciation of the aesthetic of a well-designed fighter was hot-wired into the male brain. He had given up trying to explain it to women, who saw only the deadly purpose.

No one designed better-looking fighters than the Boron as the Piranha demonstrated. Although the basic frame dated from the Boron Campaign it had proven to be such a classic that it had remained the backbone of the Boron fleet ever since. Over the decades the design had been modified to accommodate the evolving drive, combat and computer technologies; becoming sleeker, faster and more deadly with each iteration. The flattened bullet-shaped hull with the gently down swept nose incorporating a long bubble cockpit, just radiated sex and power as far as Marteene was concerned. Wisely he chose not to share these thoughts with the AI.

"Heads up Max, we've got company."

As she spoke the airlock opened to reveal a squad of four Boron soldiers in ornate uniforms he could not identify as they marched across the bay towards him. With a flash of guilt for having forgotten him, he recognised their prisoner.

"Max-Max!" The enthusiastic cry echoed around the bay, it was possibly the loudest sound he had heard uttered by a member of that quietly spoken race.

"Borass Fyi'une," Xela prompted unnecessarily as the young pilot they had rescued months previously bounded towards them.

"Max-Max," he grasped Marteene's hand, pumping it vigorously, "In your debt I am again! An honour it is, truly!"

Nonplussed Max returned the greeting.

"Uh, good to see you again Borass, how you..."

The arrival of the Guard cut short his question. The four soldiers snapped to attention and threw him a perfectly synchronised Argon salute, which was not easy given the bone structure of the Boron arm. One, clearly in command, stepped forward.

"An honour it is to meet you Commander Force." His soft tones did not disguise the formality of the greeting and Marteene returned it with similar gravitas.

The officer flourished a data padd.

"Signing for the prisoner here sir."

Bemused Marteene transferred his digital sig to the indicated data field and with another snappy salute the squad pivoted as one and marched away.

"I think this is our surprise Max," Xela whispered. "You did promise him a job."

"Ah, Borass," he said, turning to the young Boron who was bouncing on the balls of his feet with what was clearly intense enthusiasm, "Can you give us, me, a moment?"

Max wandered back towards the Lifter in muted conversation with Xela.

"What am I supposed to do with this guy Zee? We're spies on a super-secret mission remember?"

"Sinas knew that when he set this up Max, given what we know of Boron mores I think that means we can trust him, to an extent. He's indebted to you for his life and now his freedom, that is a very serious thing for him."

"But he could be some sort of secret service plant, how would we know?"

"We have 2 ships now Max, we need another pilot. If Sinas arranged this we can be pretty sure Artur is in on it. We don't have to tell him the whole story yet, I say we give him a try."

Marteene considered her words as he watched Borass closely inspect the Piranha fighter. Although he had planned to let Xela handle the Star while he flew escort he knew it would be better if they stayed together and sooner or later he would have to recruit more pilots if the plan was to succeed.

"Okay, why not." He strode across to the Boron, who was assiduously examining the starboard thruster ports.

"Borass, do you want to sign up with me or is it just a way out of prison?"

His eyestalks drooped and then focused on him in what was clearly a reproachful manner.

"Max-Max, I almost served term anyway. Short then honourable discharge, family influence you see. No, I want to serve. Owe you much but more I want fun. No, that not your word. Adventure, that is it! I think working for you much thrills and spills eh!"

Max laughed. "Much thrills and spills yes. I'm going up against the Stoertebeker Clan and I'm going to stop at nothing. You understand that means you'll be involved in a whole lot of illegal and dangerous activities? Do you have a problem with that?"

His demeanour serious, Borass looked Max straight in the eye and held the gaze in long seconds of appraisal.

"I not do anything the threaten Empire Max-Max, but I judge you not too. You honourable being, you have code no?"

Max nodded.

"I'm trying to do the right thing Borass and I can't tell you the whole story yet, but yes I have a code."

"The universe is a big evil place Max-Max, full of bad and stupid beings. As we Boron say, 'Cannot make omelette without smashing eggs,' yes?"

Marteene ignored Xela's giggle. "True enough Borass, true enough. If you can swear that nothing we say or do is ever communicated to anyone else, from the Queen herself downwards I'd be honoured to have you aboard."

"My word you have." Borass extended his hand and the two solemnly sealed the deal.

"What are we paying him Max?"

"Damn - I hadn't thought of that. What do you think?" he whispered as Borass continued his scrutiny of the Piranha.

"He's so bright-eyed and bushy-tailed he'd probably pay you. How about nothing?"

"Funny girl - find out what the industry rates are and add 25%."

"You're the boss, boss!"

"Hmmm, I wonder. Hey Borass, you ready to go? Anything you need to do, people to call?"

"Negative Captain, Sir. All arrangements made prior!"

"You're not in the Navy now Borass, Max-Max will do fine in private but best go with Commander on open channels and in public okay?"

"Commander it is Max-Max! Where we go?"

"You ever flown a Lifter?"

"No Max-Max, but how hard it be?"

"Well, you're about to find out. You take the Star, I'll take the M4 and we can both have a new experience. She's fully tuned and needs a light hand and Borass, I've just had her painted so try not to scratch it!"

He caught the crestfallen look.

"That was a joke Borass, I know you'll do fine!"

"Joke? Ha ha, Argon funny guys Max-Max! Let us now boldly go!"

Borass was beginning to bounce again and Max shared his eagerness to try his hand with a new ship. First though he installed Xela in the Piranha and transported the jump-drive across. It took the drones only a short time to adapt it to the Boron systems and while they did so Marteene ran a complete check on his new ship. He could see Borass doing the same.

The Boron had indeed been unstinting in their gratitude.

The M4 had everything he could have expected, including a transporter and a complete complement of trading, navigational and combat systems. The full 80-unit capacity subspace hold was well stocked with an assortment of missiles and the twin Gamma PAC's were backed up with a pair of the lower powered but rapid firing Alpha mark. For defence it had two 5MW shields. Most important of all the drive upgraded to the full 190 mps potential and the manoeuvring thrusters optimised. The fighter would handle in combat like a finely balanced sword and Max was in love even before he launched.

Xela detected his elevated heart rate and ribbed him mercilessly as he continued with the checks. Finally satisfied that everything was ready he looked across to the Star and gave Borass the thumbs up. The Boron just looked puzzled until Max hailed him and explained that it meant all systems were go. Borass grinned and returned the gesture.

"Ready Zee?"

"Always Max, but you're a man aren't you, surely you should be giving this collection of systems a name? Something really macho?"

Marteene thought for a moment before opening a channel.

"This is Force Security fighter Rapier requesting permission to launch."

### *Chapter 33: Cry Havoc*

In deep space, well beyond the confines of the jump-gate sector, Marteene and Borass gave their new charges a thorough shakedown. At first each struggled to adjust to    instrument displays designed for different ocular structures. Marteene found the use of an iris to graphically depict speed needlessly obscure but Borass coped better · with the bar method of the Argon design.

"Or perhaps," Xela opined pointedly, "He just complains less."

Marteene shut up and just revelled in the performance of the fighter as he snapped a high-speed barrel roll around the Lifter. The Piranha was a thoroughbred combat machine.    Fast and skittishly agile it demanded a delicate touch on the stick in a fight.

At first, his reflexes pitched to controls tuned to human strengths and reaction times, Max found it impossible to harness the agility of the Rapier. It responded so quickly to control inputs that the first simulated combats dogfights were quickly reduced to turning battles, won only when he had got onto the drones' tail with an inelegant series of lurching banks and cutbacks.

Once Xela had acquired enough data to reprogram the fly-by-data control systems it handled like a scalpel.

Marteene then found a flying experience that over-shadowed even that of flying the top-of-the-range Argon Elite. The big fighter heavily out-gunned the Piranha and had 5 times the shielding but it could not touch it for sheer speed and handling.   Like a sports speeder, it was a pleasure to fly and with the additional edge the situational awareness Xela provided he felt he could take on a whole Clan squadron.

"I do wish you wouldn't do that Max, really," Xela snapped as he let out another self-congratulatory yelp.  "It's very irritating and makes you sound like a buffoon."

"Sorry Zee, not another sound.  Time to wrap it up anyway." He thumbed the comm button on his stick.  "Borass, recover the drone before it runs out of power and self-destructs."

"On it I am Max-Max, you fly weller even than I hoped."

"Thanks B, you ain't no slouch yourself."

"He means you are good Borass," Xela interjected.

Max had waited until the two ships were well away from prying sensors and as an extra precaution established a laser comm-link before he introduced the Boron to Xela.  Borass took the idea of a 'talking ship' in his stride and they instantly struck up a good working partnership. His aggressive fighter pilot skills and her ability to remote pilot the remaining military combat drones had made the Destiny Star a difficult opponent. More than one simulated combat ended with his gleeful cry of "guns, guns, guns" as he lured Max into drone crossfire that even on the lowest setting rocked the Piranha. Out of pride Marteene would argue but Xela always confirmed the kill. He consoled himself with the suspicion that she was bolstering Borass's confidence and in the real thing he would have evaded the attack.

Borass was more impressed with the shadow-skin technology which at Xela's insistence Marteene had reluctantly revealed, but only after the Boron had again sworn himself to utter secrecy in injured tones.

"Much more going on than meets the eye-stalk, Max-Max. I know, am not stupid. You tell me more when ready. In meantime, we boot much bottom, yes?"

"That's 'kick some butt' Borass," Xela had corrected.

"This really is some ship Zee, the Navy should scrap the Buster and stock up on 'em."

"So you keep saying Max," she replied, plainly bored with his enthusiasm.

Marteene targeted the stationary drone, swiftly inverted the speeding Rapier and pulling the nose up towards the target indicator. In a zero-G environment a lot of pilots failed to lose the instinct to dive towards a target. This left the target beneath the cockpit where a pilot could not watch it and forced them to rely on their scanners.

He preferred to pull up towards a target so he could keep an eye on them and the extra seconds of visual contact made it much easier to snap out of a manoeuvre at the optimum moment. As Max did as he rolled out of the turn with the drone centred in the cross hairs at 500 metres. In his minds eye a Bayamon exploded.

"Bring 'em on, bring 'em on!"

"Excuse me?"

"Nothing Zee, just thinking aloud."

"Your heart-rate and breathing has gone up Max. Fantasising again? Twins?"

"Not this time Zee, Clan."

"I'm sure there must be a word for people like you Max, probably a long medical one. I take it you're keen to play with your new toy?" It was, they both knew, a completely rhetorical question and she received no answer.

"So Borass, what do you think of the Star?" Marteene inquired as the two ships headed back towards the distant jump-gate to Rolk's Drift.

"Fine, fine Max. She big but fast, like a heavy fighter. Would wish for guns and rockets also. You have all fun."

"Stick with us Borass and you'll be looking through gun-sights soon enough. Speaking of which - pick yourself up a sidearm, we keep bad company sometimes. "

"Will do Max-Max, me great with guns too. Quick draw; inhale those bad people; zap, zap, zap!"

"That's 'smoke those bad guys' Borass," Xela interjected. "Knowing ol' Max here, you'll probably get a chance to show us before this is all over."

It took them another half day to complete all their business in Menelaus Frontier as Xela insisted both of them got some sleep

"I don't know what you've got in mind Max but I'll bet it will call for sharp reflexes."

"Not all my plans involve unnecessary violence and destruction of property Zee." His voice was laden with mock hurt.

"Then tell me."

"No, you'd only complain!"

Xela terminated the exchange with a triumphant "Hah!"

While the two organics rested the AI worked on. First she registered Force Security as a legal entity with the Profit and Foundation Guilds. This did not give them the rights associated with the Decree of Incorporation but gave them a credibility lone traders lacked. The cost was, as intended, prohibitive but she deemed it a worthwhile investment and she had all the permissions and codes needed to manage the finances.

The personality-construct welcomed the times Marteene slept. She did not have to maintain a character interface and while docked she was not distracted by dozens of sensor inputs or the need to monitor and fine tune hundreds of sub-systems. Marteene, she was sure, had little understanding of the effort it required to minimise the power-drain of the shadow-skin technology or to keep his ship operating in peak condition during combat. While he was fighting she was busy routing power through the most efficient pathways, monitoring the sensors and extrapolating attack patterns to give him enhanced situational awareness and fine tuning the performance of shields and weapons.

Unconstrained by the limitations of an organic nervous system she was multi-tasking but there were limitations. Xela was still learning her capabilities and it was, as she sometimes complained, "Damn hard work!"

She briefly considered tuning into an entertainment channel and losing herself in something trivial for a few hours. It was fun to take a drama and act out all the parts simultaneously with temporary personality sub routines. Lucid dreaming for AI's, it was better than downtime and possibly, she thought, a new art form.

Looking at the vast amount of data she had stored from the extended practice session she decided against such an indulgence. It all needed analysing and data extracted for two related projects, the development of an effective combat AI program and the ongoing upgrading of the combat drone sub-routines. These were tasks she was uniquely suited for. She had her own knowledge and skills to build upon and her neural network was equipped to self-program by extracting rules from experience.

This was the basis of all neural nets but her special nature raised it to a new level. Being closely integrated into a ship handled by a great combat pilot in real battles gave her data of a quality no other neural network program had. Already she had been able to upgrade the drones to make them much more effective and co-ordinated fighters. She knew that should the opportunity arise she could convert the partition of her neural pathways where the new combat program grew into an extremely effective autopilot upgrade.

She had other ideas too, now that she wore a lethal fighter instead of a freighter for a body, but she needed time and more data before she would be willing to disclose them. Knowing Max she would get this soon enough. There was a hardness to Hela's cousin that her programming did not lead her to think he had in him. It was not just the fine edge of a combat veteran, applied without compassion in a knife-fight. That she expected. It was the manner with which he handled murkier elements. Somehow she had expected more finesse. Instead Max went straight for the jugular of a problem.

As he had once remarked when she chided him on it.

"A smack in the mouth and a kind word will get you farther than a kind word."

It seemed to be true but somehow she doubted his Goner attribution! It sounded like the sort of thing one of the surly and aggressive Split would utter, should they ever discover the art of wit.

Regardless of the origin of the sentiment it had so far worked and in synergy with his emergent entrepreneurial instincts progressed the mission far beyond her or, she suspected, Artur's expectations.

Marteene indeed had darker depths he had successfully concealed from his cousin as well as from the Argon psych profiles.

He was not the only one.

Xela could feel her Shadow, calculating and emotionless. The tendrils of the Xenon template were entwined with her own neural pathways beyond any hope of unweaving, her own personal devil. It was the voice that yearned, in soft whispers driven by its own imperatives for Max to wreak bloody vengeance on their enemies. She kept it under constant watch but did not know if she could always catch the insidious influence.

The question of Paskaal.

Max shadowed the spice-laden Lifter as both ships headed towards the Ceo's Buckzoid jump-gate. Blends of Boron spices were used, as everyone knows, in food production throughout the X-Universe. They could transform almost any ingredient into something palatable for one species or another and was therefore a commodity in great demand.

It is less well known that they are also used in the production of spaceweed. Whilst no varieties of the many spices produced by the Boron had hallucinogenic properties they were used by the Teladi to establish distinctive brands. Different species, different individuals, different tastes. Hot and spicy, sweet and mellow or Split variants that would make any other species gag. Market differentiation; it all helped to shift product.

Max had filled the Destiny Star with an assortment he knew would fetch a good price in Hierophants Joy, the Profit Share Bliss Place where he planned to do more business with Chandus Rarr. At their last meeting he had held out the prospect of lucrative commissions to run the illegal spaceweed to suppliers outside clan networks if Max could prove himself. There was also the question of the concentrate Xela had detected traces of in Star's shielded compartment. Marteene had no problem with spaceweed. He considered the narcotic herb no more dangerous than the alcohol that was available everywhere and like countless others found it relaxing in small doses but while it remained illegal everybody made premium profits.

It was time to take a share.

As they approached the gate Max eased his fighter alongside the Star and linked comm lasers.

"Okay Borass this is the plan, I'm going on ahead to install a Teladi Law Enforcement License subsystem at the Trading Station. You make best speed for the Teladi Gain jump-gate and then head for Seizewell, like we discussed. Clear?"

Borass looked across and saluted, his eyestalks swaying with excitement.

"Understood Commander," he replied, voice soft and business-like.

Max returned the salute.

As the Rapier pulled ahead Xela observed. "Teladi Gain and Seizewell? We are headed for Profit Share still? It was just through the southern jump-gate from Ceo's Buckzoid last time I checked. And Stoertebeker is holed up in Teladi Gain, what happens if they spot.. no Max, don't tell me, the license. You're planning to start a fight aren't you?"

"No, that's up to them but if they do I'll finish it."

Xela remained silent as her net sparked with images of destruction, fleet and blurred. It felt good, a fantasy of the forbidden.

A full flight of six Bayamons were snapping at the heels of the Destiny Star by the time the Rapier mask-jumped into Teladi Gain through the southern jump-gate. Max had done his maths. Given the location of the base the Clan fighters had a long stern chase and as he calculated the Star was only a couple of klicks short of the gate to Seizewell by the time they had almost caught up.

The Rapier closed on the attacking fighters in seconds. Two had broken off to engage the Piranha. Full of the confidence bred of inexperience and easy prey they came head on. Max destroyed one with a sustained burst at maximum range and dancing though the incoming hail of plasma almost ripped away the shields of the other before it twisted away. On Xela's signal Borass launched his drones and two of the advanced models, under her guidance, hounded it to destruction.

The remaining four clan fighters immediately broke off their assault on the Star to engage Marteene. It was a fatal mistake.

The remaining combat drones, empowered by the enhanced AI to fight as a pack, pressed home their attack and quickly destroyed another Bayamon. Realising the threat a single ship broke off to engage the drones. The remaining pair closed on the Rapier, rolling and bobbing through the streaming plasma rings of the Gamma PAC's with an adroitness that marked them as veterans.

Within seconds Max was in a vicious, close-in knife-fight with pilots who knew what they were doing. Although they had only half the shielding of the Piranha the Bayamon fighters had three advantages. They were faster; their weapons were higher velocity and more accurate at long range and there were two of them.

"Bandit Two six o clock low, medium. Five high, four high. One klick, five o clock."

Max listened as he rolled out of the turn on an intercept trajectory with the turning Bandit One. With precise movements of the stick he led the Bayamon with the gun-sights but even as squeezed the trigger, Xela yelled.

"Six O Clock. Incoming missile, break right, break right!"

Rolling and turning in one motion the Piranha broke off the attack. The missile missed by metres but the Rapier took a sustained burst from the quad cannons of Bandit Two as it anticipated his evasion.

"'Drag and Tag', these people are professionals Zee!" he yelled as he snap-rolled to port and pulled a steep turn inside the track of the missile. Bandit One caught him with an oblique burst, taking his shields to 40%.

Keeping a watchful eye on it he attempted to engage the pirates in head on passes where the power of the GPACS would be decisive. They were too experienced to fall for that and would split off before taking damage.

Several more missiles were launched but they were more a nuisance than a threat. Their cheap chemical engines left them in thrall to gravity and inertia and so easily out-manoeuvred by any fighter. One by one they self destructed as their fuel expired. Rolling inverted Max pulled up onto Bandit One as it turned steadily to port. It was a course that would drag him into position for Bandit Two.

Dragging and Tagging, and these two were good at it and could prolong the engagement long enough for the third fighter to overcome the drones and threaten the Lifter. That would force him to break off and engage it and expose him to rear attack.

It was a good plan; un-heroic but professional. Stall for time and wait for your opponent to make a mistake.

Max checked the scanner as Bandit One approached weapons range. Reinforcements were already launching from the clan base. Instead of firing plasmas Max launched two Mosquito missiles and decelerating rapidly, half rolled to port and pulled up towards the Bandit Two. A snapshot of plasmas forced it to bank right and Max hit the afterburners bringing him up onto his six. A 4 second burst of plasma engulfed the fighter as it accelerated away. The Teladi Security License sub-routine intoned the thanks of the Teladi Company and announced the bounty.

The Rapier flew through the blossoming fireball and turned to engage the other Bayamon.

"He's bugging out Max and, there." Another explosion flared in the midst of the raking cross fire of three drones. "That's the other one. I make that three to me and Borass and only two for you hotshot!"

Max checked the scanner before conceding with a smile. The remaining fighter was heading back towards the clan base and although he was certain he could take on the Bayamon reinforcements there were a pair of Teladi Falcon Heavy Fighters close behind them. They were registered to sector security but he was unwilling to test their true loyalties just yet.

"Drones loaded Borass? Good, head straight for Profit Share and I'll catch up in minutes."

Max waited, poised at the jump-gate entrance, until the Bayamon flight was in comm range.

"This is Max Force of Force Security. Attack on company vessels or any under our protection will be taken as a declaration of war by the

Stoertebeker Clan. Stay away from us or you WILL suffer the consequences. Force out."

"Do you really think that will work Max?" Xela questioned as they emerged into Seizewell. "They don't seem the types to scare easily, all you've done is goad them. We won't be able to move through that sector without a fight and who knows what else they'll be mad enough to try. Which was the intention all along I suppose? I take it you have a strategy Max."

"Of course."

"Would you care to share it?"

There's an old Teladi saying Zee.

"Better to have the Split inside the ship pissing out than outside the ship pissing in."

Only a part of her was thrilled with this plan. The rest of her raised half-hearted objections.

## *Chapter 34: The Big Time*

The run to the Hierophants Joy Bliss Place in Profit Share passed uneventfully and on docking Max had made straight for The Split-Split Club, certain his return would have been noted. The place hadn't changed, the same sordid floorshows and the same sweet haze of spaceweed over the redolent fug generated by the crammed mass of revellers. Max pushed his way through the crowd and found Rarr, the corpulent middle-man for the station, at his customary table. The same two Teladi thugs backed him up.

"Hey, like the new nose." Max feinted a combination punch towards the bodyguard whose snout he had smashed on his previous visit, grinning as the Teladi flinched.

"So Mr Force, we meet again."

Max took a seat without waiting for an invitation and smiled.

"Oh please Rarr, tell me I misheard. I told you I'd be back. Damn, you've got me doing it now, one of us is going to have to get a better taste in holo-vids. And you definitely need some new goons."

Rarr did not reply but sneered at the furious looking lizard.

"Good to see Psych-Warfare 101 wasn't wasted on you Max."

He ignored the Xela's remarks transmitted through his shades from the Data-Comm and with a few flicks of an eye initiated a scan for the device that dampened energy weapons. With the lack of imagination he was coming to expect from Rarr it was located inside the dimmed light source on the ceiling directly above.

"Got it Max, it's a modified multi-spectral dampener with a pinprick hole in the upper band. The heavies will be packing needle-guns adapted to that frequency."

"I am given to understand that you have acquired an assistant, a disgraced Boron naval pilot no less. You should have bought him along."

"And expose him to this?" Max gesticulated towards the unsavoury multi-species tableau unfolding on stage. "The company medical plan doesn't cover psycho-therapy."

He snapped his fingers at the seething Teladi guard.

"Cold beer, unopened bottle. No, better make that two. And open me a tab."

Rarr nodded his assent and the Teladi scuttled off, radiating surliness.

"If you've quite finished bullying my staff perhaps we could turn to matters of business. I take it that is the reason for your return?"

"You said establish a cover and we could do real business. Cover established. I even have a Lifter full of legit spices I'm expecting a good price for."

Rarr nodded, his eyes flicking to the stage show as he wiped his perspiring face with a small white cloth. Max did not recognise the fabric but it was obviously remarkably absorbent.

"I don't deal with purchases Mr Force but I'm sure you will be able to obtain a good offer through normal channels. And yes, you have established a cover. I cannot recall my exact words but I am certain that at the very least 'low profile' and 'discreet' were strongly implied. You have acquired a certain notoriety and made a serious enemy of a powerful clan. I'm not sure you are suitable for the task anymore."

Max took the beers from the returned guard and poured the first one straight down. The cool, hop-rich brew cut straight through the dry-mouthed aftertaste of combat and triggered a flush of well-being as his body relaxed.

Taking a smaller pull from the second bottle he replied.

"Sorry Rarr, I don't do 'discreet'. I do, as you have seen, deliver. And correct me if I'm wrong but didn't you say the Clans were an obstacle to profit maximisation, to paraphrase?"

"An accurate summation Max. The Stoertebeker Clan have few friends among the Teladi, even fewer in the light of their failure, but those that they have are powerful and not to be trifled with.."

"Unless there is a big profit to be made?"

"Precisely. But there is the element of risk to be considered. A full hold of the product is worth close to 3 million credits retail and that is a lot to risk in the care of a marked man. How do you answer that Mr Force?"

Max could see the man's point. The station might not be making as much profit as it could due to the Clans but it stood to lose a lot more if a delivery was destroyed.

"Because I'm sitting in front of you now Rarr, despite the best efforts of Clan goons. I'm a hero to the Boron so no one is going to be scanning my holds in their space and I've shown I can out-fly anything the clan wants to put in the sky."

Max took another long swig of cold beer.

Rarr acknowledged his point with a nod.

"Your skills are not in doubt Max but the Stoertebeker Clan have many ships and many pilots. Not all of them fly such small fighters. How would you fare against a wing of Falcon heavy fighters?"

"A lot better than you might think Rarr. Big means slow. The Lifter can outrun them and I can do a lot of damage with my ship. As they say, it's the man not the machine but I can see why you're concerned."

Max had anticipated this objection and had prepared a counter-proposal.

"I'll tell you what Rarr. The station holds are full of spaceweed, production is stalled until your next clan shipments. What they going to pay you? Three nine, four and sell it on to sector distributors for four five? I can do you a better deal."

"You have been doing your home-work Mr Force, What do you have in mind?"

Marteene finished off the second beer as he ran through his pitch. If could get agreement on this it would provide a lucrative short-cut on his quest.

"Okay Rarr, how's this. You have a network of distributors or you wouldn't be hiring people like Panner. You are cutting them a better deal than the clans because you're cutting them out of the deal, say four two, four three on an average production cost of three three. That gives you a profit of around a thousand per unit direct compared to six hundred or so selling to the clans. Your problem is that the six hundred is risk free, once its in their holds but shipping it direct means absorbing the cost of lost shipments to sector security patrols and piracy. If you discount the risk you'd make an extra 400k credits profit per 1000 unit load. How am I doing so far?"

Rarr nodded to him to continue.

"What if I could guarantee delivery in return for a 50% cut of the extra profits?"

The fat man smiled an oily smile that matched his sweat-greased face.

"I would say you have been smoking too much of the product Mr Force but leaving aside your pipe-dream percentage how do you propose to guarantee delivery? You are certain to be scanned by security forces on a regular basis. That is why we are forced to accept the clans as intermediaries. And no, I'm afraid a general air of self-assurance will not suffice. Neither of course would your word."

"But if I gave you the Star if I lost a load? Or if she was impounded, my fighter?"

For the first time he had known him Rarr genuinely smiled but it contained too many poorly hidden layers of calculated avarice to be reassuring.

"Tempting. Tempting enough to possibly turn you in myself, except that I suspect you would have ways of making trouble for me if I did. And how do I know you aren't planning simply to vanish with the whole load?"

"Because," Max replied. "You control the distribution network. The only other people who would buy it are the clans and I'm not their favourite person at the moment."

"A very good point Mr Force, but 50% is quite out of the question. How about 10?"

His looks belied his toughness as a negotiator and Max had to settle on 20% but Rarr agreed to allow Force to purchase up to half of a load at the fixed cost of three eight to sell through the same direct channels. Neither party suggested putting the deal in writing. Both knew the other could make life extremely hard for the other should they fail to honour it.

"Been a pleasure doing business with you Rarr." Max raised the bottle in a casual toast and drained the last of the beer. "I'm ready when you are, how are we going to do this thing?"

"I see no reason to vary the procedure we used with Panner. An access code, which I will have delivered to your ship, will give you a secure access to the Trading System. Delivery destination will be communicated at the time of purchase. You dock normally at the other end and my people will do the rest. Payment will be by anonymous credit transfer. I take it you have a secure account?"

"I'm not an amateur Rarr. How long will it take to set this up?"

"Neither am I Max. You will have the access codes in 3 hours. Until then I suggest you take advantage of the many delights of this establishment. If you see anything you fancy I could arrange a private room."

"No thanks Rarr. It's a little too exotic for my tastes."

"For a mercenary you are a very provincial man Mr Force. Perhaps some other time. Now if you will excuse me I must make the arrangements."

"That was a pretty risky offer Max, one slip and we could blow everything."

Marteene murmured his reply into the sub-vocal throat mike as he returned to the docking bay.

"Calculated risk Zee - we've got to earn big money quick. Rarr was right - Stoertebeker is going to come after us and we're going to need more fire-power. With this arrangement we can make big profits in a short time, provided we don't get caught. I'm going to be relying on you to handle the shadow-tech for that. Do you think you can hide a full load of spaceweed from a close range security scan?"

"No problem Max, provided I'm in the Lifter and nothing is broken. Pulsing false readings through the emitters strains them. Being shot at doesn't help either. I'll get the droids working on them if we're going to be heading out soon."

"Time and profit waits for no man Zee. Let's hope Borass doesn't come over all moral."

Marteene returned to the Star and briefed Borass on the arrangement over a shared meal from ship stores.

"Any problems with that Borass? I'll fly the Star if there is."

The Boron did not reply for a few seconds, masticating his food thoroughly as he thought.

"No Max-Max, not much. So long as cause is good and offence is soft. We at war with Clan, war it makes for strange nestings. Cause is good yes?"

"You have my word on that Borass."

"For me that is good enough Max-Max. When we leave?"

"As soon as we get the access codes and load up. Both of us had better grab some sleep, it could be a long run."

He barely managed 2 hours before Xela woke him.

The self decrypting signal contained the access. Marteene checked his accounts and over the objections of Xela spent almost all of them on 70 units of spaceweed. The rest of the hold was filled with the station delivery.

As soon as the last unit was loaded another signal arrived. Max decrypted it and swore.

"That fat bastard has a bad sense of humour, we don't even have docking rights there. Remind me to break some heads next time we meet."

The destination lay inside Split territory and the direct route led straight back through Teladi Gain.

## *Chapter 35: Spooks*

Captain Trasker sniffed the air again.  She had not been mistaken, her new office stank.  Alcohol and vomit, at least that explained the sticky carpet.  No doubt her predecessor had been celebrating his sudden promotion.  He could not, she mused as she cast a disdainful eye around the cramped space, have had many friends.

As far as she was concerned the office was not the only thing that stank.  Her sudden transfer from the Vigilant stank, the new pip on her collar stank and the belated discovery of wreckage from Marteene's missing Bayamon, impacted on an asteroid in the new Boron mining colony of Rolk's Legacy positively reeked.

No body had been found, she would not have expected one from such a crash, but investigators had found a shadow-skin emitter on a hull fragment.

Case closed.

The fact that no eye witnesses could be traced and the only supporting evidence was a Boron analysis of sector logs may not have bothered her superiors but it worried the hell out of her.  In their haste to wrap up an extremely embarrassing incident she could feel, deep in her bones, they were wilfully ignoring a mountain of unanswered questions.

Top of the list?  What the hell was Marteene doing there in the first place?  The internal inquiry settled on an unknown jump-drive accident and that just begged more questions, as she had forcefully stated.  Three days later she made Captain and transferred to Omicron Lyrae, was still smarting from the ambivalent congratulations of her colleagues back aboard the Vigilant.

Sector Co-ordinator for Xenon Affairs.

It was a position with as much elbow room as her new office.  The previous incumbent had been a junior lieutenant on the way up; they might as well have added "Screw-up" into her personnel file.  For all she knew it was stamped, red-bold, on the cover.  She was now responsible for co-ordinating Xenon related intelligence from the Fleet and the several Special Forces operations monitoring Xenon activity in their redoubt beyond Black Hole Sun.  Without command responsibilities she was little more than a defence analyst.

Her areas of responsibility did not, it had been made emphatically clear, include further investigations into the Marteene affair or the apparent death of Paskaal in the course of his own investigation.  Neither did it include Max Force, the former mercenary fighter, whose actions caused the death.  Apparently any connection to the Marteene investigation was coincidental and his survival of the huge explosion in Ceo's Buckzoid, not to mention of the assassination attempt she had organised, unremarkable.  It had been hinted that he was now a Boron Intelligence asset and on the surface the suggestion was plausible but a foetid miasma of repeated coincidences cloaked the whole affair.

Orders though were orders. The recent Xenon incursion into the Teladi controlled Scale Plate Green sector, showed that there was a job to do, whatever she felt about the circumstances of her arrival. It was a job she would do to the best of her ability but she would not do it here. Hefting her unopened kit bag to her shoulder she strode off in search of the Trading Station Quarter-Master to discuss new offices.

In a far sector Artur was digesting the latest report from the Xela AI and Marteene. It had been transmitted via the Seizewell Commerce Nav-Sat using one of several channels reserved exclusively for the Cabal and encrypted using a quantum key known only to Xela and himself. Not even the Cabal could spy on them, which was good, as he had made no progress in uncovering the presumed traitors in the shadowy organisation.

In the light of this he had endeavoured to make as little use of the organisation as possible but recently had he been forced to pull strings through it to deal with the troublesome Janis Trasker. It was, he knew, expecting too much to hope that she would cease her interference in his affairs but he hoped it would buy him time to implement the more creative solution to the problem he had been working on before Marteene's spectacular actions. There was still a trigger to pull and isolating her from official resources was a necessary step.

Marteene had a gift for improvisation that continually wrong-footed him and Artur was finding it a disconcerting experience to be trailing in the wake of his own scheme. The personal war with the Stoertebeker Clan had become central to Marteene's game-plan but the Cabal lacked a regular source of reliable information on its activities. It was a shortcoming Artur was working hard to remedy, with only minor success so far.

Although Marteene was unaware of the details of the ongoing political struggles within the Teladi Company the outcome of the war was becoming pivotal to the machinations of the General. Defeat for the Stoertebeker Clan would be a massive blow to the power and influence of his rivals on the Board and Artur was now banking on the General to provide the political support Marteene would need to get the Decree of Incorporation passed. Marteene would also need a secure base and again, Artur was relying on the General's support.

The General and his allies were the only players with any assets within the Clan camp. Artur had not, at this stage, been able to subvert any to his particular cause as it would involve a foolhardy visit to the Clan base. All he had was second-hand, low level intelligence provided by the general and his few allies. It wasn't much but it was about to pay-off provided he could get a message through to Xela quickly.

Seera, prepare following message for transmission, same location, same channel, same encryption as last message."

"Acknowledged." the ship AI replied as Artur poured himself a small shot of Argon Whisky. It was a 20 year vintage, brewed planet-side from natural ingredients. The end-result was a thousand light years from the high octane abomination known as Space-Fuel, which was illicitly traded throughout known space.

Although nominally the same beverage the latter was brewed in huge orbital stations from other space manufactured ingredients. No growing medium, however chemically enhanced, could impart to the grain the character of the natural soil of the high latitude islands on Argon Prime whence the drink originated. Neither could ancient ice mined from the permanent shadows of sterile, low gravity worlds replace spring water naturally infused with the taste of the peat over which it flowed and chemically assisted ageing in metallic storage tanks could never impart the grace and character obtained from natural maturation in old hardwood sherry barrels.

The source of most of the space-fuel illegally traded between sectors was the huge distillery located in the Argon sector of Herron's Nebula. Although notionally dedicated to provisioning the vast Argon home market the owners were not interested in the final destination of their product. Anyone with a ship and the requisite credits could fly away with as much of the alcohol as they wanted. Of course they had to take their chances with sector security patrols but such minor obstacles to a very profitable trade were easily circumvented.

The Stoertebeker Clan were by dint of their location major distributors of the product throughout Teladi and Split space. It was one of the major sources of their income and their heavily armed convoys, sloshing with Space Fuel, were a common enough sight throughout the sectors of those races and one of the intelligence assets of the General had access to the flight schedules of the squadron assigned to convoy duty.

Artur accessed the file to confirm his recall, a convoy was scheduled to depart for the Split sector of Family Pride in under two hours. His succinct message to that effect was transmitted immediately. He hoped Xela would check the Nav-Sat before leaving the Seizewell sector. Meanwhile he had more pressing business with Phyrath, the amoral Split physician who had worked the transformation of Marteene into Max Force. Their last meeting had not gone well. The prognosis had been anything but encouraging and it remained to be seen whether the small container buried in the hold full of Soja Husks could tip the balance.

He accessed a plate of a matured cheddar cheese and plain crackers from the galley. It was the perfect accompaniment for the whisky. The simple things in life were often the best.

"Seera. Time on destination?"

"ETA 23 minutes Artur." The timbre of his lost love, almost submerged in the electronic cadence of the AI vocorder, triggered buried memories he had not the luxury of indulging. He finished the whisky and poured another shot.

Two fingers.

He returned to the cockpit with the glass and allowed the beauty of the stars and the tapestry of glowing nebula gases to steal his thoughts as the Dolphin cruised towards the distant cluster of stations.

## *Chapter 36: Fanning the Flames*

"Transmission completed Max-Max." Borass looked across and gave a thumbs down as he disconnected the laser comms. Xela must have said something because as Marteene banked away he could see the Boron pilot of the Star gesticulating wildly. Rolling the Rapier so that the Lifter was above him he acknowledged the frantically waving upward thumb gestures with a smile before dropping back into an escort position.

Following his instructions Borass banked the Destiny Star towards the Space Equipment Dock. The sprawling structure itself was barely visible in the planetary shadow but the almost constant flashing of the twin chain of docking lights clearly marked it. Marteene followed the Lifter through the giant docking port and alighted next to it on a small docking platform high above the main bay. This had cost him several hundred credits extra in docking fees but it was worth it for the security and privacy while Xela refurbished the Lifter power relays.

The eager Boron was already waiting as Marteene climbed down from the cockpit. The bay was barely large enough for both ships and the main lighting was either off or out of order, leaving it in a twilight gloom illumined only by the distant lights of the main bay. The droids though did not need light to work and were already crawling over the hull of the Star.

"Hi Borass, you got.."

The rest of his question was ripped away by the deafening roar of a Teladi Vulture freighter as it passed through the force barrier maintaining the atmosphere of the docking bay area. It seemed the lights were not the only thing not switched on in his bay. Those he could live without but he would have to find and bribe a technician to reactivate the dampening field if only to protect the sensitive ears of Borass.

"I said." He was shouting now through the ringing. "I said, you've got a weapon now?" Borass nodded and went back to the Lifter, returning with a power-wrench. Marteene had to repeat himself twice before Borass understood and produced his firearm from inside his flight-suit.

"Okay, good man. You guard the ships while I go look around. No one is to enter the bay right. Right?"

"Understand. Guard. Yes sir, Max-Max."

The Boron threw another enthusiastic salute, hitting himself in the head with the wrench and staggering backwards.

"You just can't get the staff can you?"

The primitive vocorder of the maintenance droid as it scuttled by did little to soften her sarcastic tone.

"Shut up Zee, how long to complete the work?"

"If you link me into the Destiny Star, an hour or so. Do you think it wise to be hanging around? Someone is bound to tip of the Clan that we're coming through and you're giving them time to set up. I hope you have something better in mind than fighting your way through again but the smart credits say you don't!"

"You don't have any credits Zee. There's some equipment I need to scare up and some poking around I need to do. I'll be gone about an hour and.."

A departing fighter drowned out the rest of his sentence. Max climbed into the Lifter and installed the Xela chip while his hearing returned again.

"Initialised Max. See you in an hour and get the power turned on okay?"

"I'm doing it, I'm doing it!" Max muttered as he checked his pockets but his stash of casino chips was exhausted. It took a couple of minutes to interface the teleporter and the cargo controls so that he could extract a kilogram from one of the containers. This he quickly sliced into smaller blocks with a nano-knife. The molecule thin blade slipped easily though the dense oily resin and he wrapped each piece in clear steri-film.

His flight suit filled with party favours Max left the bay and immediately ran into three saucer-eyed Teladi technicians propping up a bulkhead with their bodies. The discarded butts of spaceweed showed they had been performing their heroic task for some time.

"On the off-chance that the entire station will not collapse if one of you performs a stroke of work is there any chance of getting the power switched on?"

The lizards stared at him with the blank incomprehension of the professionally deaf although one managed to glean enough of the gist to stick out a claw. Max resisted the growing urge to break heads and held up one of the steri-wrapped packages. He slit the film with a thumb-nail and wafted it under their noses. Whatever affliction had removed their power of speech and motion evidently had not affected their sense of smell.

"That's it boys and girls - fresh from the vats and uncut and it's all your if you switch the damn power on and give a few straight answers right?"

"We exisst only to sserve you ssir," the largest of the three hissed as she extracted a data-padd from her coverall. She tapped a couple of keys. "Power restored." She extended a hand and grinned mockingly.

"Not so fast bub - questions too." Marteene indicated what he was looking for. On a Teladi Equipment Dock there was always someone who would sell you what you wanted, it was just a question of finding them.

She called up a station map on her padd and highlighted a section two floors down in the workshop area.

"There, you go there. Give now."

Marteene quickly memorised the direct route and handed over the spaceweed resin.

As he walked away all three of the Teladi were crouching on their haunches arguing in their own language as one filled a small pipe. Miraculously the bulkhead did not collapse.

Marteene had no trouble finding his way to the workshops and experienced only slightly more problems getting what he was looking for. It cost him nearly 2000 credits and almost all of the remaining spaceweed but, true to form, the item was available.

He had to wait while the technicians improvised a servo-mount from a scrapped antenna array and scrounged up a primitive wheeled trolley for him to take it away on.

The three technicians barely moved as he pulled the load past them although their disposition had improved dramatically. He declined the proffered pipe and cleared the snack wrappers from the wheels before manoeuvring the trolley into brightly lit bay.

Borass lowered his gun and rushed over to inspect the package. He was joined immediately by a droid.

"What you got, what you got Max-Max? Something good I bet!"

"Yep, something we've needed for a while. What do you think Zee, any problems fitting it to the Star?"

The droid sensors flickered over the equipment as Xela examined it.

"I will have to replace the upper laser communications array and fashion a retractable dome. Four hours tops. Solid projectiles won't scratch even a 1MW shield so tell me Max, why do we need a mini-gun?"

"So Borass gets to see more than docking bays Zee. You can slave it to the ship sensors and patch the combat AI?"

The second droid joined the first and began sifting through the parts. Xela's half of the discussion switching randomly between them as they began assembling the gun.

"I think so but it will have to be pretty crude. I suggest we program warning shots, no point killing over-eager technicians. Ammunition drums will have to be changed manually and until we get a telescopic mount the field of fire will be limited. Once intruders get close they will be safe."

"Then you'd better not let them get close Zee. Design a mount and I'll get it manufactured. How about auto-reload?"

A droid swivelled its sensors to look at him as it picked up the conversation.

"You would have to reconfigure the upper relays and fit a custom-built turret. I will design one but it will take several days to install and test. We don't plan to hang around here do we?"

Max shook his head.

"No, just long enough for you to get this running. The Split don't have a lot of respect for private property, particularly if it has technology they can steal so if we have to hang out and play with them I want you, the shadow-tech and the jump-drive safe."

"And a Gatling point defence weapon was the first solution that sprang to mind was it Max? If you had consulted me I would have suggested several secure, and here is the key word Max, SUBTLE, electronic counter-measures that would work just as well."

The droid vocorder failed to mask the sarcastic tone.

"Make up a list Zee and we'll get 'em too. I just want something more active and nothings says 'hands off, thieving alien scum', no offence

Borass, like a thousand rounds of live ammo fired in your direction. Just get it fixed and stop bitching."

A droid turned and performed clumsy simulacrum of a bow.

"Your wish is my command oh Master. Toting that barge, hauling that bale now sir."

The two droids, now laden with pieces of machinery, moved away exchanging what sounded suspiciously like murmurs of discontent.

"What do you think Borass?"

The Boron regarded the departing droids with one eye-stalk. The other remained fixed on Marteene as he shrugged.

"You both need professional help?"

While Xela installed the new ground defence system Max cubed some more resin and flew the Rapier across to the main Teladi Trading Station. It took several generous hours of conviviality with off-duty Teladi before he got the information he needed and before he launched he took a stim to clear his head.

The mini-gun tracked him as he walked across the bay to the Lifter.

"Mission accomplished Max-Max?" Borass shouted from the Lifter cockpit.

"Mission accomplished Borass, have you eaten recently?"

Borass shook his head as Marteene climbed the ladder to the airlock.

"Come aft, we've time for a bite and we need to plan our visit to the caring, sharing Split."

Another decrypt from Artur was waiting. Whatever gods existed were smiling upon him and the data it contained dovetailed neatly with the information he had obtained from the Trading Station.

While he ate his steak and tried not to watch in horrified fascination as Borass slurped something gelatinous and fishy Marteene outlined his plan.

"There he goes." Xela activated the sector scan and highlighted a ship.

Borass requested launch clearance without waiting for instructions. He knew the plan and could read the registration of the Argon Lifter launching from the Laser Forge as well as the AI or Max-Max. The Automated Docking System immediately granted permission. It was, Borass thought, typical of the Teladi that they would cut costs on even such an important station as this. Until he joined Max-Max he had little direct experience of that species. The Boron consensus was that the Teladi were a lazy and devious species that were always prone to side with the Split in their almost constant attempt to undermine them. Borass had seen nothing to challenge that opinion.

As soon as the Star exited the Equipment Dock he set a direct course for the southern jump-gate and targeted the Argon Lifter. The female AI was speaking again. It did that a lot, telling him things he could see for himself, offering advice he did not need and assistance he did not require.

As in this case.

He could see the position of the Lifter on the screen and read its velocity. Disgraced Kingdom Navy fighter pilot he may be but he did not need a machine to tell him the correct intercept speed. The Navy would not even accept an application from anyone who could not make such a calculation instantly let alone permit them to graduate.

Borass ignored the computer and it eventually fell silent. He had discovered that this was the best way of dealing with it. Given an opening and it would pratter on relentlessly about everything under any sun you cared to name, as he had found at great cost to his nerves. Now he just tuned it out, responding only to mission critical information. In his opinion it was a serious mistake to even attempt to create artificial life, as the Xenon demonstrated. No race, not even the technically adept Argon, had the requisite wisdom.

He adjusted his heading slightly so as to avoid flying a direct intercept course, planning to make contact as the target slowed to make the jump to Greater Profit. Unlike the Destiny Star the drive of this Lifter had not been fully upgraded. Max-Max had selected it for that reason and it gave him a broad intercept cone to work within.

As the two ships closed Xela reiterated the Shadow-tech drill. Borass listened without comment and as the target slowed to enter the gate he arced onto its tail and closed to within range and activated the system. As the freighter slipped from sight the AI announced what he already knew, the snapshot was complete and the readings stored in memory. Borass banked the Star back towards the northern jump-gate to Teladi Gain, noting the launch of Max-Max in the Piranha. Not for the first time he experienced a pang of envy mixed with loss but consoled himself with the thought that Max-Max had promised him a fighter. He hoped it would be the Rapier, it was what he had joined the Navy to fly.

The fighter reached the gate before him and executed a faultless masked jump. It would now be exiting from the Teladi Gain eastern jump-gate. If there was any reason he could not make the jump it would return to Seizewell in seconds. The Rapier did not reappear and as he guided the Star into the jump-gate he activated the Shadow-Skin. It was not a technology he was familiar with and he purposefully did not speculate how Max-Max had obtained it. He was just thankful that it worked, having no wish to haul a ship full of contraband around Split sectors.

Emerging into Teladi Gain he immediately accelerated to 100 mps and headed straight for the gate into Split space. The sector scan showed no Clan patrols except those flying CAP around the Clan base but he kept a wary eye on the stations along his route, aware that any of them could be hosting a pirate wing. This was one of the riskier parts of the plan, if the shadow-skin ruse failed he would have no back-up as the Rapier was out of communication, a sector away.

It made him nervous but nervous in a good way. Properly harnessed fear kept you alert and thinking clearly and mental disciplines to achieve this was one of the first things the Boron Naval Training Halls taught. His mind fell easily into that state as his mantra pulsed metronomically on the outer fringe of awareness.

With an unhurried glance he absorbed the information on the sector scan, gleaning the rhythms and patterns of ship activity and extrapolating the tactical implications. Only two facts stood out. A pair of Teladi Hawk fighters from Sector Security would soon move to scan him and the Clan Base would soon launch ships. It was obvious from the deceptively casual way Teladi fighters were sweeping the direct route to the eastern gate. It had come as a shock when he realised other races did not have an holistic sense. His instructors claimed that humans possessed something similar called "intuition", which they defined as the ability to draw correct inferences from partial data but if it existed at all it operated intermittently and with uncertain reliability tied in with the personality of the individual. It sounded more trouble than it was worth.

"Heads up Borass, Teladi patrol on intercept course."

Borass acknowledged the computer with a single word and targeted the lead fighter. The drive was fully tuned, meaning it could just about sustain 145 mps and would be able to outrun the Lifter, even without the performance hit the Star was taking from the operating Shadow-Tech. He calculated they would intercept him 10km short of the gate. Not close enough to make a run for it if things went wrong without using the drones.

As he watched an Orinoco left the Clan Base. Two more followed, then a Vulture freighter. They were joined by 5 Bayamons and two Mandalay fighters who assumed an escort formation as the convoy headed towards the gate to Family Whi. If that was the convoy Max-Max was expecting, it was departing early.

As the Star sped through the system he monitored the clan ships and the approaching patrol closely.

"Here they come Borass, entering scan range now. Think innocent thoughts"

He ignored her statement of the obvious and kept a steady course as the Hawk fighters closed.

"Argon Liffter, prepare to be sscanned."

He glanced at the system readouts to confirm that the shadow-skin signals were steady. There were minor fluctuations in the port dorsal emitters but the computer was actively compensating. Long seconds passed during which Borass imagined he could feel the Teladi scanners crawling over his skin.

"No illegal goodss detected. You are freee to proceed."

The pilot sounded bored. So little was actually illegal in Teladi space she had probably had no action in a ten-day. He dipped his wings in acknowledgement as they banked away and he continued towards the jump-gate and continued observing the Clan convoy.

It was still beyond scanner range so he could not detect whether any of the ships were carrying spaceweed as Max-Max believed. The swift Mandalay fighters were sweeping ahead while the Bayamons swarmed around the freighter. The three Orinoco craft loitered behind. They, Borass surmised, would be well equipped with missiles. It was clear from this disposition that only the Vulture carried anything of real value.

To his trained eye the formation was a mistake. The Bayamons should not be pandering to the insecurities of the freighter captain by flying so close. If he had been organising the convoy he would have them flying a wide and fast exclusion zone, intercepting any ship that approached within 2 km of missile range. By sticking so close to their charge they were forced to travel at a slow speed. It would take valuable seconds to come to accelerate to maximum velocity and practically invited a fast opponent to take the first shot.

By the time Borass reached the jump-gate the convoy was still 15km distant although the Mandalay outriders were closing fast. Max-Max had not reappeared so it was safe to make the jump. Either that or he had run into trouble he could not handle.

The instant the Lifter entered Split space Borass accelerated to the maximum speed the Star was capable of with the shadow-skin operational and activated the sector scan.

"Rapier detected Borass - 2.5 klicks from the Family Zein gate."

"Acknowledged computer." he responded as he absorbed the pattern of activity in the sector. Family Zein was more than a border sector, it was, as far as the Split were concerned, the front line of defence against a Boron assault. Many decades before the two species had fought a bitter war which ended only when the Argon Fleet intervened to prevent the destruction of the Boron Homeworld and since then the Split feared retaliation. It was what they would do so the assumption that the Boron would do also had become the bedrock of Split policy. This is what dictated their close alliance with the Teladi, who they saw as both a useful buffer and a counter-balance to the Argon. It also dictated a certain blindness towards the activities of the Clans with powerful allies on the Teladi Board of Directors.

Thus the approaching Clan convoy had little to fear from the huge Python-class destroyer on permanent station in the sector. On the other hand any Boron registered ship could expect to be scanned constantly and most of the trade between the two species went by way of the Teladi.

Borass hoped that as he was flying an Argon registered Lifter the packs of fighters patrolling the sector would leave him alone. As a precaution he set a course towards a station well away from the ecliptic of the system and the main concentration of patrol craft. Only when he was well past the destroyer did he begin angling back towards the southern jump-gate.

He was 25 km short when the Clan convoy entered the sector and he noted that they too chose a circumspect route through it, despite the close alliance of the Split and the Teladi.

Despite his precautions the Destiny Star was scanned twice during its flight through the sector but the shadow-skin disguise held. The Rapier was waiting when Borass entered Family Zein and immediately took up station on his starboard side. He activated the laser comms and a few seconds later Max-Max appeared on screen.

"Hi Borass, hi Zee. Any trouble?"

Borass cut across the computer's attempt to reply.

"All went well Max-Max. The Clan convoy should arrive in 12 minutes. It appears they are not sending scouts through gates first. Transmitting data now."

"Good work Borass, this is a pretty safe sector so there isn't much in the way of security patrols. We'll do it here. I'm going to power down in the lee of that asteroid near the southern jump-gate and wait. You know what to do?"

Borass did. He was to heroically trudge from station to station requesting docking permission. Refusal was of course, a foregone conclusion. Unlike the Boron and the Argon the Split did not grant open access to their stations to aliens, unless they had proven themselves to be friends. The charade would keep the Lifter well away from trouble while Max-Max attempted to violently earn their respect. As pirates were in theory the enemy of all species the Split would be obliged by treaty to reward the destruction of Clan vessels.

Although he burned to be involved in the conflict Borass grudgingly accepted the wisdom of the plan. The Destiny Star and its cargo were simply too valuable to risk, despite its shielding and drones. Even so, the odds would be stacked against Max-Max and Borass wanted to be near enough to intervene if necessary. It was his duty and if there was one thing he had learned from his short time with the Argon adventurer it was that rules were made to be bent, if not completely torn up. This went against all his training and instincts but it was, he had to concede, a liberating perspective.

He examined the sector scan and performed some mental calculations before choosing a trail of stations to visit that would bring him to the one nearest the southern gate by the time he estimated the fighting would commence.

If the computer noticed his intentions it did not comment.

Wiping enough hoar-frost from the canopy to give him a clear view of the jump-gate took only a view seconds but it was enough to chill his hand to the marrow despite the protection offered by the spacesuit gauntlet. Marteene turned up the thermo on his suit another notch and made a mental note to upgrade the environmental sub-system. Xela had not bothered to mention that she had been optimising the settings for humans and without her presence it had reverted to the moisture-rich default settings for the semi aquatic Boron. With the ship systems powered down to avoid the Rapier appearing on the clan convoy gravidars the temperature in the cockpit was plunging steadily towards the absolute zero of space in the shadowed lee of the rock despite the advanced insulation properties of its materials.

He quickly scanned the gate environs for ships, increasing the magnification of the Video Enhancement Goggles to identify each tiny moving dot before his view was again occluded.

"Damn". The convoy was not in sight even though his calculations suggested that the Mandalay outriders should have been approaching the gate if the information from Borass was correct. He ran the maths through in his head again and sheepishly carried an errant 1.

Two minutes.

Marteene set the suit chronometer timer.

Two long minutes, in which Marteene again ran through his battle-plan, taking deep slow breaths to counter both the rising tension in his chest and the zero-g induced nausea in his stomach.

Despite his outward show of confidence he laboured under no illusions as to the scale of the challenge he was about to face. Ten fighters against a single M4. Those were not good odds no matter how good a fighter the Boron Piranha was or how skilled its pilot.

For a moment Marteene considered calling off the attack but Artur's bleak assessment of the consequences of the clans acquiring advanced technology from the alien disk Marteene's own father had scanned demanded risk-taking. He needed docking rights within Split sectors and he needed it now. There really was no other choice if he were to deliver the cargo in the hold of the Destiny Star. The alliance with the Hierophants Joy Bliss Place and by extension with those factions of the Teladi Trading Company who would directly benefit was just too important.

The digits on the timepiece morphed inexorably back to zero.

This time the convoy was clearly in sight, already slowing as they approached the jump-gate.

Marteene gently boosted power to the environmental systems and the thruster's flight controls, hoping that the low level emissions would not be noticed. The frost in the cockpit immediately began to melt forming small drifting globules in the zero gravity. The clan ships continued on their course as he briefly pulsed the rear thrusters, accelerating to 100 mps. Without the loophole provided by the main drive natural laws of momentum held sway and the fighter continued at that speed towards the jump-gate.

Both of the small Mandalay fighters and three of the more threatening M4 Bayamons had entered the winking eye of the gate before the remaining escorts scattered like a startled shoal and vectored towards the approaching Rapier. Marteene immediately powered up all ship systems and accelerated to full speed.

"I've got him. Go get 'em Max!"

Borass had spotted the Rapier as quickly as the excitable computer woman and immediately activated his Video Goggles. The remaining Clan fighters were closing rapidly with the Piranha, the Bayamons speeding ahead of the 3 slower Orinoco heavy fighters.

With characteristic arrogance the Clan ships eschewed tactics in favour of a head-to-head pass. The Rapier weaved through the incoming fire, avoiding most of it and destroying one Bayamon with a concentrated short-range burst that must have drained the weapons bank. The Piranha and the remaining Bayamon exchanged missile salvoes as they passed within metres of each other. The clan fighter immediately went defensive while the Rapier barrelled straight on towards the 3 Orinoco's, relying on speed for safety. Borass noted with some concern that the Rapier had taken enough hits to knock its shields down to below 50%. He hoped Max-Max did not plan to go head to head with the big clan fighters and their devastating Gamma Particle Accelerator Cannons.

The surviving Bayamon adroitly out-manoeuvred the pursuing missiles and swept back round to attack the Piranha as it closed with the other fighters. Borass watched nervously as Max-Max side-stepped and rolled through the snaking plasma of the triple Orinoco onslaught but his speed took him past them with minimal damage to his weakened shields. As he did so he launched another 3 missiles arcing towards the pursuing Bayamon.

The Orinoco wing banked as one and launched a missile salvo. A dozen now tracked the Rapier, closing from 3 sides and forcing it to break high across the sights of the Bayamon. The glancing side shot did minimal damage to its shields as the Piranha rolled 180 degrees and dived towards the jump-gate pursued by the pack of fighters.

"He's going for the freighter Borass." The computer commented. "It's loaded with drones. Stuff orders and get us in there."

Borass did not argue.

Max-Max executed a text book attack on the freighter as it entered the jump-gate, coming in from the starboard aft and raking the length of the hull. It was moving too slowly to avoid the missiles he launched as he banked to avoid the massive structure of the artificial wormhole. As the freighter exploded a dozen combat drones spilled from the hold and targeted him.

Borass watched helplessly as the Star lumbered towards the combat. Max-Max was fully defensive now, it was taking all his skill to avoid the rapid fire lasers of the drones and keep out of the sights of the prowling clan fighters.

"Launching drones now computer." Borass whispered as the Star closed to 3 km.

Xela briskly acknowledged and took control. The 4 small combat drones shot ahead and fell upon the Bayamon. It was a dissipating cloud of plasma before the pilot knew he was under attack. She instructed the 2 military drones to engage their Clan counter-parts and co-ordinated the two commercial variants to attack the Orinoco that had broken off to engage the on-coming Star.

The Rapier was close enough now to get a signal through the interference generated by the mass of weapons fire. It was the centre of attention for the other two fighters and space was full of missiles. Even Marteene's almost supernatural combat awareness was overwhelmed.

"Max, break left break left," she shouted. He responded instantly and a brace of silkworms flashed past. "Now, go ballistic, half roll port and pull up."

In response the Rapier pulled up into a full power climb, rolled and from its cockpit perspective pulled up again onto the six of an Orinoco. It was a classic Air Combat Manoeuvre that allowed a pilot to break from the top of the loop on a heading set by the roll.

Marteene nailed the Orinoco with a concentrated burst and rolled away as its wingman raked him with fire.

"Incoming, incoming at 12 o clock Borass, go evasive. Max, we've got to pull back the drones."

Borass quickly assessed the situation. The attacking Orinoco was being flown by an expert, he had swiftly destroyed one of the two standard drones and launched a head on missile strike. The Star was too slow to outrun them and it would take all of Borass's skill to evade them. Meanwhile the Orinoco was already turning to re-engage Max.

The military drones were systematically eliminating their swarming clan counterparts but the harried Rapier was finding it hard to evade the packs of missiles coming in from all angles. The two Orinoco fighters seemed to have an inexhaustible supply, launching 4 at a time and preventing the Piranha from engaging.

"Jump-gate opening Max, shit - it's the other fighters. Show me some of that fancy flying stuff."

The computer was right, two Mandalays and three Bayamons were emerging from the gate and for the first time Borass experienced a twinge of fear. The combat drones were doing a good job of interdicting the incoming missiles but more were taking their place as the new fighters entered the fray.

"Borass, what the friggin' hell are you doing here. Jump, jump now goddam it. That's a direct order Zee."

She had never heard Max so angry and she didn't argue. They had severely misjudged the skills of their opponents and had not expected the other fighters to get jittery so quickly. The Star was now a burden to Max and the quickest way out was through the gate.

The tone of Max-Max brooked no argument and Borass headed straight for the gate at full speed, relying on the drones to keep the missiles at bay. They were only partially successful and two smashed into the Star, knocking the shields below 30%. As the Lifter plunged directly through the whirling chaos of ships and missiles centred on the Bayamon the Star rocked and shuddered as if under micro-meteor bombardment. Space around them filled with explosions and in near panic Borass checked systems status. As the gate swallowed the freighter they showed green across the board.

"'Way to go Zee." Marteene murmured as the Gatling blasted a swathe through the swarm of unshielded missiles. He quickly plunged through the gap this had created and destroyed a Bayamon in a head on pass. Rolling to starboard he pulled up and caught an over-shooting Mandalay with a reflex snapshot. His Gamma PAC's detonated the fighter instantly.

As the Star and the two combat drones jumped to Family Zein Marteene threw the Piranha into a full power loop, pulling a train of the 2 remaining pairs of Orinoco's and Bayamons. The surviving Mandalay was coming in fast from the left. Satisfied none were pursuing the Star he banked again to avoid a pair of missiles but the move took him straight through the sights of a Bayamon and the Rapier shook under the pummelling.

He was running out of ideas now, the clan pilots were hotter than hot and he had counted on them running once their charge had been destroyed. The clan were not usually so free with expensive missiles and Max would have run himself but could not afford to leave the gate unguarded in case they went after the almost defenceless Star.

The Gravidar showed no sign of the Split coming to his aid although a wing of their heavy fighters loitered a few kilometres from the gate. Marteene rolled and broke low to avoid another salvo of missiles, frantically scanning the skies for fighters. The Bayamons were hot on his tail, plasma fire streamed past his cockpit as he craned his neck to eyeball them. The 2 Spade-heads were coming down from 10 and 2 o clock high, aiming to engulf him in a lethal cross-fire. Marteene flipped the fighter 180 degrees and pulled hard on the stick to avoid the trap. The Bayamons stuck with him through the manoeuvre, splattering his shields with fire. Meanwhile the Mandalay circled, waiting to slip in and administer a stiletto deathblow.

Breaking high and left Marteene headed for the gate at full speed. The Bayamons, with their significant speed advantage, stayed with him. He began weaving and rolling to avoid their concentrated fire dividing his attention between the falling shield levels and the pursuing ships as they closed to point blank range.

They were flying in tight formation now and held their fire for a single devastating close range assault. Marteene kept weaving and watching the fighters. They were close enough now for him to make out the pilots. Both Teladi. He could even make out the broad feral grin of the leader as he lined up the killer shot. As it reached its broadest Max decelerated sharply and executed a double loop barrel-roll as 8 streams of plasma hosed past him.

The clan pilots had no time to react and Marteene rolled out of the manoeuvre on their six. The trailing wingman died instantly but the leader broke hard right, intent on leading Marteene into an Orinoco trap. He spotted it a fraction late and one fighter caught him with an oblique burst that all but removed the last of his shields.

Half dozen different alarms went off and the cockpit filled with the distinctive ozone tang of fried circuitry.

"Shield Generator destroyed." The computer intoned as the remaining Bayamon banked for another pass. The gate was close now and Marteene was tempted to jump to safety, he knew though that at any second the Star would come looking for him. The Spade-heads were also coming in fast so Marteene pulled a wide turn away from the gate and throwing barrel rolls as he continued the turn. The width of the rolls reduced his apparent speed enough for the Spade-heads to close as he headed for the gate.

They weren't wasting energy blasting at a violently manoeuvring target, they were waiting for the faster Bayamon to force him into a fatal error. Once again Marteene cursed himself for the over-confidence that had led him to assume he could take on these odds.

He had one trick left and checked the energy level of his one remaining shield. Fifty percent. It would have to be enough.

As the gate loomed before him Marteene decelerated enough to allow the Orinoco's to close to 100 metres and headed straight for one of the massive columns. As they fired he pulled up sharply, exposing himself to the surviving Bayamon. His shields barely withstood the assault and he knew the Mandalay would be swooping in for the kill but the ploy had worked. The Orinoco's inadvertently strafed the gate and already the Split Mamba wing was moving to intervene. Marteene hoped they were clear who the enemy were.

They were very clear and very, very fast. When the Star emerged from the gate only the Mandalay remained alive and it was running a vengeful gauntlet back to Teladi space.

After replenishing his supply of missiles with the assorted detritus of battle Max escorted the Star to the Space Equipment Dock.  The Split reluctantly granted docking permission.

## *Chapter 37: Split Loyalties*

The Split might have been obliged by treaty to allow his ships to dock and it might have been in their self-interest to cultivate inter-species trade but they did not have to like it. The two ships were guided to a docking bay barely large enough to harbour them and commanded to confine all transactions to automated systems. That suited Marteene. With a hold full of illegal cargo and a Boron pilot he did not want the Split anywhere near his ships.

The bounty earned from the battle covered the immediate maintenance requirements but with all his capital tied up in spaceweed he could not have afford to replace the destroyed shield even if there had been any for sale to aliens. He stood to make 80-90k profit on this run. The new shield would swallow up two thirds of this but it could have been worse. The irreplaceable jump-drive could have been destroyed.

Marteene set his own droids to work on the battered Piranha and took the chance to relax on board the Star while they worked. It was a good time to review his strategy. He'd pushed the Stoertebeker Clan too far now and could expect stiff opposition wherever he flew. They were in a race against time and could not afford to lose large chunks of profits to repairs.

"We need a better fighter Zee. I don't suppose any of Artur's contacts can sell us a second-hand M3 cheap, no questions asked?"

"You wish. There are options though. The Teladi sell their Falcons to anyone with the cash and a commercial variant of the Elite is available from Argon shipyards. They don't have all the flash military electronics but with a hotshot like you who needs them eh?"

"Our own Eel is the finest fighter in all of space Max-Max. Perhaps your well-connected friends could help? I flew one once. Lovely, lovely lovely."

Borass's eyestalks quivered with patriotic enthusiasm but Marteene shook his head.

"They're all too slow for lone wolfing. We need something with a bit more speed, which means either a Paranid Prometheus or the Split Mamba. What do you think Zee?" he said turning to the image of his cousin on the main screen.

Her face screwed in thought and affectation, a lifelike and poignant reminder of his dead cousin.

"The Paranid ship allocates all its energy to speed and defence. It's an attack fighter pure and simple, no cargo capacity to speak of. The Mamba is only commercially available in the interceptor variant. It's extremely fast but can only carry one shield. This version can power a substantial subspace hold but can't fire hornets. The slower, better-shielded assault variant is not for sale. As hornets are illegal and we're not planning to attack any capital ships or stations my vote is for a Mamba. They cost over two million credits though, we will have only 800,000 or so once this load is sold and another shield fitted to the Rapier."

Max performed a quick metal calculation. The deal he had struck with Rarr would net 80-90k gross profit per round trip so it would take 20 or so runs to accrue enough to buy an M3 and retain enough liquid credits for trade. Even assuming the entire Bliss Place production was assigned to this new and risky venture this would take weeks and the newly chastened Marteene feared that their luck would not hold that long in the face of clan opposition.

"Analysis bleak Max-Max but you have plan, no?"

Max shrugged.

"Sorry Borass, I'm clean out. What about you Zee?"

Xela frowned in concentration mixed with indecision. Marteene recognised the expression.

"Spit it out Zee, a half baked idea trumps all at this table."

The AI did not reply. Instead she ran gun camera film from recent dogfights. The two organics watched in silence as each twisting fighter disintegrated.

"I'm just too good but what are we supposed to be seeing Zee? You any clue Borass?"

"I am completely clueless Max-Max and in need of enlightenment." he replied, oblivious to Marteene's suppressed smile.

"It's what you don't see boys. Look again."

Xela displayed the last combat again, dropping to slow motion in the final seconds.

"Here." The playback froze and then jerked forward frame by frame capturing the moment the shields fell and Marteene's plasma bolts boiled away the unprotected hull.

She halted the playback as the drive began to explode and highlighted part of the screen.

"Watch."

They watched as the canopy of the Bayamon tumbled away and the pilot ejected into the plasma maelstrom. He was vaporised before their eyes.

Xela broke the ensuing silence.

"So why did that pilot die?"

To a combat pilot it was almost a rhetorical question and Marteene let Borass take it.

"Because error margin variance in weapon shot output is bigger than safety margin of ejector system."

Xela's smiling face replaced the frozen image on screen.

"Give that boy a gold star. The standard iron man settings of an auto-eject are calculated to ensure the ship is destroyed. Set it too low and space would be littered with abandoned ships and live pilots and set it too high and you die. The energy output of a standard weapon varies up to 5% either way from designed output and smaller variances demand rarer metals and more complicated designs. That would increase the price, making the design uncompetitive. Pilots ego's being what they are, you all fly on iron-man or manual. End result - very few safe ejections and those pilots that do more often than not find themselves on the slavers blocks."

"And," Marteene asked patiently, "This fills my chips with credits how?"

Xela smiled again, a particularly self-satisfied one.

"I'm still working on the details, using data from your flight recorder but I think I know a way around the variance problem, provided I'm wired into the fighter. If I'm right we may be able to get our hands on an intact ship. Admit it - I totally rule!"

That was not a point Marteene was willing to concede until she talked him through the scheme. It would require significant modifications to the weapon power relays to enable Xela to fine tune energy settings and modifications to the short range sensor suite to provide her with the necessary micro-second reaction speed but with a good pilot it just might be possible to trigger some iron-man auto-eject settings without destroying the target ship.

"It does mean I have to be installed though," Xela reiterated. "I'm the only one in the universe smart enough to pull this off. The only one that can be fitted into a fighter anyways. So do I rule or not?"

She did, Marteene conceded, rule.

The journey through Split space to the Trading Station in the Family Pride sector was uneventful apart from an encounter with a pirate convoy in Thurok's Pride. Max ordered Borass to give the convoy a wide berth and to his relief the escort fighters clustering round a single freighter ignored them.

The anonymous transfer of the illicit cargo went exactly as Rarr had stated and with his account now flush again with credits Marteene spent some time on the comm in an attempt to cajole a trade deal from the local Split industrial stations. The only stations willing to sell were the 3 Solar Power Plants. Production rates were high in the twin sun system and energy cells were not considered a strategic item.

"Language Max," Xela admonished as yet another station manager abruptly terminated his transmission. "The Split have no reason to resort to alien traders this deep in their space, particularly unknown and barely tolerated ones. We need that Decree of Incorporation."

Max cursed again in frustration, the thought of running empty back to Teladi space made his traders skin crawl. Xela though, was correct. Family Pride was the Split home sector. The HQ of the Council of All Families was located here and the bulk of the Split navy was thought to lurk in the fringes of the sector although the only visible presence was a huge Raptor-class carrier.

The sector specialised in weapons production; shields, missiles and associated equipment such as warheads and quantum tubes. The Shipyard and Equipment Dock provided a ready market for the finished product although as Marteene had noticed demand for the 1MW shield was currently low, judging by the stock levels held by the production facility.

Despite this the Station Commander had been adamant.

"Split no trade with such as you. You no friend of Split. You go away now."

"Damn them, I'm not leaving with an empty cargo hold Zee, does Artur have any contacts that could help?"

She consulted her records and shook her head.

"No Max I think you are going to have to let this one go. They don't want to trade with you and that's that. Perhaps if you slaughtered a few more pirates?"

"With a single 5MW shield? I think not but you may have solved the problem."

"I have? Oh good. Do you mind telling me how?"

Marteene shook his head and activated the Best Buys Locator. It quickly analysed the sector commercial data-stream and displayed its recommendations.

"Borass, take the Star over to Power Plant Alpha and pick up a full load of energy cells, they're at rock bottom prices, then fly them to the Shield Production Facility and sell them. " The Boron looked at the screen, puzzled. "We make no profit Max-Max, why then we trade?"

Max smiled. "Have faith B, we'll meet you over there."

He removed the Xela chip from the Star and installed it into his Data-Padd. Borass waited until he was back in the cockpit of the Rapier before launching. Max discussed his plan with Xela as he monitored the progress of the Star on the scanner. When it emerged from the Power Plant he requested launch permission and headed for the Shield Production Facility.

The Star docked a few minutes after the Rapier by which time Marteene was ready.

As he had expected the Rapier was routed to a small docking platform and ignored. Taking advantage of the privacy Marteene quickly hooked Xela into the Station database through the public access terminal.

"Any trouble Zee?"

"I'm in Max, I don't think these people seriously want to prevent unauthorised access to their systems."

"How far are you in? Full access?"

"No Max, the command functions are locked out and don't ask me to siphon off a few million credits. I am good but not a miracle worker. You can take it from here, it will be good practice for what I, or Hela taught you."

Using the Data-padd to interface with the station systems Marteene quickly found what he was looking for, the personal data of the station manager and the records of an authorised Split trader who dealt with the station on a regular basis. With Xela's help he installed a temporary transformation filter into the trading sub-system and purchased 170 shield units using the traders identity and the station managers authorisation code.

"Okay Max, we have your precious cargo but unless you leave me hooked up here permanently the station is bound to discover your little ruse and you'll be a marked man throughout the Split territories. Is it worth it?"

"Victimless crime Zee. We are here on legit business, paid good credits for the shields and all we did was borrow an identity for awhile. They make profits, we make profits, everyone will be happy, especially as I'm about to transfer 20k credits into the personal account of the station manager and email him a thank-you note. If you are as good as I think there won't be any evidence their systems have been penetrated and the Split take a dim view of aiding and abetting. As they aren't overly concerned with exacting standards of proof I guess he'll keep quiet about it. If he's really smart he'll do as I 'll suggest in the email and legitimise the deal by granting me trader status for this station."

"I'm better than you think and you Gragore are a wicked boy," Xela said approvingly. "Some day one of your scams is going to blow up in your face. Probably not today though." she conceded.

She was right. The two ships travelled back through Split space to Teladi Gain unhindered, no clan fighters were in a position to harass them as they headed towards the Seizewell jump-gate.

Marteene unloaded the shields at the Equipment Dock where the demand for the Split equipment was always high.

"Fifty thousand credits net profits team, who was it that said crime doesn't pay?"

Borass would have told him but was beginning to grasp the strange Argon concept of rhetorical questions and so kept silent. Xela just presented Marteene with a shopping list and while the station drones installed a new 5MW shield her own helpers modified the weapons and sensor circuits on the Rapier in preparation for a field test of her plan.

### Chapter 38: Take up thy Bed

"So, how is life on the frontier?"

Phyrath regarded the human with disdain. The Split had no need to cloak their feelings or oil interactions with irrelevant social niceties but other species failed to see the need for clear and honest communications at all times. The human knew this yet persisted so the Split doctor gave him an honest answer. From experience he knew this was the best way to terminate such irrelevancies.

Artur listened impassively to the diatribe. He liked frontier sectors such as Rolk's Legacy; things could be easily concealed amidst their expeditious confusion. Things like this small research facility, largely dedicated to developing vaccines to combat the variety of unknown diseases that threatened the new colony.

Largely.

"Make a list of the equipment you need and the luxuries that will make life slightly more bearable and I will do my best to see they are delivered. You'll have to take the gravity the planet deals though. A Gravity Well would be a little hard to smuggle down here."

The irony, like any form of humour more sophisticated than a rock pie in the face, was wasted on the Split.

"The patient?" Artur cut across the complaints as the doctor began to repeat himself.

"Ah, the patient, yes. Always I work for you miracles, for no thanks. You have the device?"

Artur nodded and held up the small silver tube containing the experimental bio-chip he had indirectly acquired from a Boron research station. Phyrath reached out to take it but Artur slipped it back into his pocket and repeated his question.

The Split clicked in exasperation but indicated for the human to follow him. The lab was on the lowest levels of the underground installation, shielded from prying eyes by astronomical security clearance requirements and alarmist warning signs. Like all Cabal facilities of this type it was almost entirely automated. He and Phyrath were the only 2 living beings in the place, unless you counted the patient.

Few would, considering his condition.

Artur inquired the Split ushered him through a door into an antiseptic white Medi-Bay dominated by a modified Intensive Care Unit around which hovered assorted medical droids. The lone occupant lay unmoving, eerily suspended in a Zero-G field to avoid bed sores.

"Has there been any change?" Artur asked.

Phyrath shook his head as he gesticulated towards to life monitors at the foot of the unit. Flat-lines across the board.

"As I say before, humanoid very damaged. Interesting challenge. Damage repaired, cells regenerated but motor functions dead. Brain damaged you see? Patient kept in suspended animation to avoid unnecessary suffering."

Artur did not like the way he said "unnecessary". He handed over the bio-chip. Phyrath carefully opened the tube and placed the tiny silver sphere into a small sterile field generator.

"So much cleverness in so small a ball. You say it was production prototype, how are we sure it functions?"

"It functions." Artur replied abruptly, causing the Split to regard him quizzically.

"So, we are not that different, you and I? How do you humans put it? One careful owner? Hah! Not careful enough I think."

Artur did not respond and Phyrath was a good enough judge of human body language not to press the point.

"I haven't much time Phyrath, how long is this going to take?"

"Using nanoprobes to integrate it into the simple nerve and synaptic structures of your species, no time at all. Once the break in the primitive command and control circuits is repaired it will be just a matter of ending the induced coma. Complete physical recovery? Up to patient."

Phyrath smiled and he reached for a surgical scalpel.

"You wish to watch?"

* * * * * * * * * * * * * * * * * * *

"Bio-readings suggest you should learn to relax Max."

"I'm trying Zee, I'm trying." He took another deep breath and thought calm thoughts. "I'm just worried about Borass."

"And the Star."

"Okay Zee," Marteene conceded. "And the Star. It carries a lot of memories and is pretty key to our plans and Borass can be a little wet behind the ears."

"He's a Boron Max, they are meant to be wet. Besides, how much trouble can he get in hauling cargo around Boron and Argon core sectors?"

Marteene chuckled but conceded the point. The Star had been stripped of the shadow-skin technology and was now just one more legitimately registered trader scraping a living from production overruns and shortfalls while they waited for Rarr to secure another full load of spaceweed. With his high standing among the Boron it had not been difficult to arrange preferential access to contracts in Boron space. The profits would not be high and deals in Argon sectors would be harder to obtain but every credit helped. It would also get security patrols used to seeing the ship and test Borass' trading mettle.

It also left him free to concentrate on testing out Xela's new scheme, which if it worked promised to be a source of almost unlimited capital with which to build an empire. The demand for Clan and Xenon ships was insatiable. Everyone from governments to private collectors would pay top credits on the black market and this was something he had ready access to thanks to Artur's contacts.

Acquiring such craft was not technically illegal, abandoned craft were by treaty considered salvage and anti-piracy laws did not cover pirates or Xenon but selling one openly would draw unwanted official attention.

It had been a long trip but now they were approaching the final gate. Max ordered another systems check and one by one Xela confirmed each sub-system and modification was operating at peak efficiency. Max reduced speed and aimed the nose of his fighter away from the gate and test-fired the Gamma PAC's, causing the Rapier to gently shudder. Satisfied they were fully prepared he accelerated towards the jump-gate to Scale Plate Green.

Knowing a single breath would bring death the swimmer ignored the bursting chest pains and flailed towards the surface in a slow-motion nightmare of leaden, spasmodically jerking limbs. Inch by inch, foot by foot the light grew brighter until, at the cost of one last, strength sapping exertion it engulfed him.

Everything hurt, the light burned and he was unable to move. Worse still, he could not recall who he was. No name, no identity. Just a kaleidoscope of fractured images; faces, names, snatches of events; storming through his brain, inchoate. People, transmuted by tears to blurred shadows, swam in and out of view. There were sounds, he guessed they were speaking. Interrogatory.

Stifling a silent scream he shut his eyes against the glare, it was the only movement he seemed capable of, and attempted to sift the maelstrom for some golden nugget of truth to cling to even as he tried to make sense of the noise around him.

A ship. He could remember an enclosed space with stars all around. A spaceship, possibly a small one. A pilot then, it was something to smother the panic. Something touched his neck, bit and hissed, enfolding his body it in a warm opiate embrace. Everything flooded back, fact and circumstance in one wild, tumbling dam burst.

"Two down. Bayamon 3 and 4 closing, 7 O Clock low."

The Rapier flew through the expanding fireball and swiftly inverted. Craning his neck to keep the clan fighters in view Marteene weaved and rolled through the incoming fire.

"Come on guys, come on, you ain't going to scratch me at that range."

He reduced speed a notch and added full barrel-rolls to his evasive manoeuvres, rapidly reducing his apparent speed relative to the pursuing fighters. They were so close now he could not avoid taking hits. With shields at 75% Marteene sharply decelerated and accelerated through a tight 360 loop that put him close on the tail of the enemy.

The wingman held to the shoulder of the flight leader for a fraction of a second too long before breaking high. The silkworm missiles Marteene launched at close range arced in pursuit, destroying it in 3 consecutive explosions. The remaining escort fighter attempted to extend and escape but like the other in the convoy its drive had not been fully upgraded and it was unable to out-pace the Piranha.

It was an execution not a fight.

"Great flying Max, the target is heading back towards the gate, ETA 4 minutes. Sector security are standing clear."

Marteene had already identified the fleeing Orinoco and gunned the Rapier to full speed. It could not escape.

"Okay Max, remember to watch their shield levels, get them low and keep them low."

"I know the drill Zee." Marteene acknowledged. "Switching to Alpha PAC's." They were less powerful than the standard Gamma variant but keeping the shields low enough to either trigger the safety systems or frighten the pilot into ejecting called for finesse.

A cosh, not a cudgel.

The Orinoco was too slow to escape. The pilot knew it and turned to unleash a barrage of missiles in the hope that he could slip away in the confusion. Marteene decelerated briefly, targeting and destroying each missile in turn before closing onto the six of the fleeing Spade-head.

"Okay Zee, it's show-time."

"Ready when you are Max darling, watch the trigger finger."

The Orinoco gyrated through a series of evasive manoeuvres but could not shake the Rapier from its rear. Marteene held his fire until he was within 100 metres, flicking his eyes constantly between the twisting tail of his prey and the shield display in the bottom right of his HUD. Elegantly simple it displayed the shield strength of a targeted ship as a notched red bar. As shield strength fell the bar shrank. The plan called for Marteene to keep the shield strength as low as possible and allow Xela to micro-manage the power output of his weapons to reduce the shields to a level that would trigger the safety system without destroying the ship itself.

Effortlessly Marteene followed the desperate evasions of the Clan ship, holding fire until it was firmly in his sights.

"Firing in 3, 2 .." Zee, with her digital reflexes, probably didn't need the warning but it focused his concentration. On 1 he strafed the Orinoco with plasma, attention flickering between the shield display, the Orinoco and the other flight systems. The bars on the shield display fell rapidly, before it reached zero he ceased fire.

"Damn." The shield bar still showed two notches, he had terminated fire too soon. He had also concentrated on the shield readings for a fraction of a second too long, allowing the abruptly decelerating Orinoco to twist away.

"Relax Max, you haven't done this before, try again."

It took only seconds to re-acquire the firing solution and fire another short burst into the rear of the Orinoco. This time he made no mistake and disengaging one of the two plasma accelerators Marteene carefully squeezed off single shots that repeatedly knocked the shields down to almost nothing.

At any moment he expected to see the canopy blow away and the pilot eject but nothing happened.

"What's up Zee, he ain't bailing?"

"Inquests later Max, keep on it." Her reply was curt.

He kept on it but the pilot did not budge, instead he stopped his evasive flying and made straight for the nearby eastern jump-gate to Nyana's Hideout.

"He must be onto us Max, or the safety was set to manual. Waste him or let him go."

Without interrupting his firing rhythm Marteene opened a comm channel to the clan ship. The pilot was a human male, middle aged and judging from the lack of panic on his face, a combat veteran.

"What are you waiting for scum-wad? Not got the balls to rip me cold bounty-hunter? Go on, do it you bastard, do it! Do it and see what my friends will do to you."

He was right, Marteene was not a killer and the possibility of becoming the victim of a clan vendetta would be enough to stop most free-lancers simply executing the ship. A dogfight, according to the undefined and nebulous rules of conduct that regulated the grey borders between bounty-hunting and piracy was one thing, executions was another.

Marteene was not a killer, but he knew a man who was.

"This is Max Force of Force Security, surrender your ship no... Holy shit!"

With lightning reactions Max took evasive action to avoid the ejecting pilot.

"Hey, I knew names open doors but yours blows canopies."

Xela's laughter filled the cockpit, merging with his own yelp of triumph.

" Establishing remote control. Control established, we have ourselves a Spade-head Max."

The crescent moon grin threatened to split his face as he called up the remote control interface Xela had designed on the display screen. He ordered it to dock at the big Trading Station at the centre of the sector. There was someone there Artur wanted him to meet, someone who could help dispose of the ship and someone who could help in other ways.

It was time to meet the General.

## *Chapter 39: The Test*

General Daht observed the skirmish in a silence broken only by his own voice commands to the new 3D Tactical Display Holo-Tank installed in his quarters. It was a luxury and an expensive one because the technology was so new. The only visible piece of hardware was the small globular emitter in the centre of the ceiling, which projected images extrapolated from stored data or live sensor readings. Unlike many old warriors, the Teladi war hero knew that there were always new lessons that had to be learnt if you were not to become stale, predictable and defeated. His new toy offered a radical perspective and, striding God-like through the arena, he had learned much from the recent battle with the Xenon.

The General watched as the Boron fighter destroyed the two remaining Bayamon craft, noting with approval the devastating use of missiles at close range. The pilot was good, very good. Daht approved, particularly as the pilot was the man the enigmatic Artur had made the fulcrum upon which both their fortunes would pivot.

He could not yet though discern his intentions. Clearly he had designs on the single surviving Orinoco, he had gone out of his way not to engage that ship and had picked off the escorts one by one. Military scans suggested the hold of the ship was empty so piracy was not the reason. As he had eschewed several chances to destroy the vessel Daht also surmised bounty was not the issue. Time would answer that question and he turned to observe the Orinoco.

It was heading for the jump-gate projected near the standard wall mounted video display, oblivious to the attempts of his increasingly frustrated cat to seize it. Now that it had flown away from any convenient perch the feline was reduced to coiled-spring like leaps that failed to bring the ship within reach of its frantically flailing paws. Daht scooped up his pet and unceremoniously propelled it into the adjacent room, where, if past behaviour was any guide to the unpredictable Argon mammals, it would extract razor-clawed revenge for its humiliation from the furnishing.

The Boron fighter closed rapidly for the kill and Daht immediately noticed it was not using its main armament. The General observed the rest of the combat and as he did so enlightenment dawned, it was an attempt to steal the Clan ship! He ordered the projector to display the shield strength of the target craft, the carefully paced single shots from the Piranha fighter were repeatedly knocking the shields down to zero.

"Curiouser and curiouser." He mused. By all rights one of the shots should have over-powered the shields and destroyed the Orinoco by now. Daht was a warrior and made it his business to be intimately familiar with the technology of his trade even though he no longer flew fighters. He knew it was extremely difficult to regulate weapons power sufficient to avoid accidentally destroy a target. It could be done but the cost was prohibitive. It was far simpler for governments who wanted to study the latest Clan ships to simply buy them on the black market. The seller could make hundreds of thousands of credits, millions for an Orinoco and then spend most of it evading the long arm and remorseless memory of the clans. They did not react well to pilots who abandoned their expensive craft and were merciless to those who betrayed them by selling to their enemies.

Therefore he was surprised when, after several minutes, the Orinoco pilot ejected. Daht shook his head over the disgraceful lack of backbone on display and briefly considered ordering sector security to bring in the pilot for questioning. He was heading for the jump-gate though, and likely to make it before any of the General's patrols could grab him so he let him go. If he survived the jump, and a trip through a wormhole without a ship to shield you from the radiation was to court a long, slow death, he would most likely find himself on the slavers block.

Two questions, Daht thought, needed answering. How did the Piranha pilot manage to force the bail-out, and, more importantly, how could he turn such a talent to his advantage? He was in the process of establishing a private comm link to the Piranha when it became apparent both ships were heading towards his station.

"Docking Control." He did not recognise the young woman who appeared on-screen and made a mental note to review the latest personnel transfers. "Ensure the in-bound Boron fighter and the pirate craft are directed to Bay 12." It was his own private docking bay where a Falcon fighter stood on permanent standby. If this man was to be as important an ally as Artur had suggested they had much to discuss and this was best done in privacy.

He did not know what to expect as he stepped into the docking bay teleporter. Of course Marteene had heard of the General, who in any military hadn't? About the man himself though, he previously knew little beyond rumour and conjecture. A man with a vision, a vision that, if Artur was to be believed, disturbed his fellow directors as much as it disturbed Marteene.

"I don't know about you Zee but I like the Teladi to remain 'money-grubbing lizards', you know where you are then."

She agreed, the words resonating discreetly in his ear from the contact speaker in the arms of the shades. He had debated leaving Zee with the two ships resting either side of the big Falcon fighter but without drones there was little she could do should the Teladi decide to poke around.

A couple of disorientating seconds later he was in the middle of a small, almost unfurnished office that could almost have been a holding cell but for the sophisticated free standing food replicator in one corner and the two seats, one designed for human physiology. Xela shifted the spectrum displayed by the shades to reveal distinctive shimmering patterns of force playing over the walls, floor and ceiling.

"Privacy shield." she added, unnecessarily. "Ah - we're being scanned, weapons and energy sources. Nothing that will finger me but the shades will show."

Seconds later part of a seamless gun metal gray bulkhead slid to one side and a Teladi male entered. Max did not need the uniform to tell him who this was.

"General Daht I presume?" Marteene extended his hand and Daht shook it firmly, his talons scraping his wrists enough to raise weals in what Marteene assumed was some form of Teladi machismo, if that was the correct term for a matriarchally inclined species.

"Max Force, so I am told." Daht looked him straight in the eye and Max returned the alien stare without flinching. "We meet in this ssecrecy, apologies but enemies we have in common, as well as friends. Please, sit."

Daht fiddled with the replicator controls for a few seconds before handing Marteene a steaming mug. It almost smelt like tea. Daht himself took a tall glass of a viscous looking green liquid. Marteene was not sure if or not he saw something moving within it but resisted the temptation to shift his vision into the infra-red. In his opinion good inter-species relations depended on not taking too close an interest in each other's odd habits and practices.

"Be seated, pleasse Mr Forcce. There iss much to disscuss."

There was. The untouched tea-like brew grew cold while the two, tentatively at first but then with more trust and commitment, discussed the foundations of the Force Security privateer empire. An hour later, when the meeting ended, they both shook hands again, this time with enthusiasm. The half a million credits Daht offered for the captured Orinoco Max readily accepted and despite his outward demeanour, inside Daht wore a broad feral grin at the price he had extracted for his help in obtaining the Incorporation decree that would allow Force to expand his mercantile activities throughout the sectors of all the races.

Max had barely materialised in the docking bay before Xela started.

"Thanks Max, I really appreciate being shut down like that. Fill me in."

"The man insisted, as you heard Zee. I guess he's got good reason to be careful, do you want the good news first or the bad news?"

"I'm a good news girl Max, shoot."

"General Daht is only one vote away from confirming the Decree, all we have to do is perform a little favour and that director will swing her faction behind him."

Xela's voice had a dark timbre. "I assume the bad news involves the little favour? What does he want Max? Speak to me Max."

He mumbled a reply.

"I'm sorry Max I didn't quite catch that. It sounded like you said she wanted a Xenon L, but I must have misheard because only an idiot would agree to that and you're not an idiot are you Max?"

Her tone strongly suggested an argument was futile.

## *Chapter 40: Hunt the Xenon*

"Display Tactical again Zee." It had taken Marteene some time to win Xela around. She had many objections, not least of which was there was no evidence that Xenon fighters had any safety system to trigger or that whatever piloted them could be made abandon ship.

"I can offer no guarantee that I can even get a hand-shake with ship systems Max, the technology may be completely alien."

"How's that Zee?" Marteene said quizzically. "From the Intel briefings I understood that Xenon tech tends to be very similar to our own."

"True. Very few Xenon fighters have been captured intact but high-intensity scans and analysis of debris strongly suggest weapons, power and drive systems operate on principles similar to organic technologies and tend to be of the same general level of development. From that Hawks surmise our rate of technological development is just managing to keep pace with the Xenon and to beat them we need to raise defence and research spending. Doves argue that the evidence suggests the Xenon, being machines, lack technological intuition and creativity. Their evolution is based on copying and adapting organic technology. Thus an arms race with the Xenon is an arms race with oneself. Hawks point to the unknown planet-killer and immense capital ships, doves to the inferior performance of the combat AI and our war victories. You pays your credits..."

"But that was not what I was referring to. The technology I can probably figure out. I had a much higher security clearance than you. It is the Xenon machine AI that is alien. Little is known of that and organic research efforts have understandably concentrated on developing complementary intelligences."

"Are you saying you can't do it Zee?" Marteene asked.

"What I am saying is I cannot predict the outcome Max. But we both know you are going to try no matter what I say so let's just assume I'll give it the good ol' Academy try and get on with the planning."

Marteene smiled and called up the Sector Map.

It showed the once extensive Xenon holdings reduced to only 2 isolated sectors. The first, designated Enemy Sector 1 by the Argon Navy, was just though the southern jump-gate of their current sector. The other, designated Enemy Sector 2, was north of the Argon frontier system of Black Hole Sun. There were just 4 sectors where encounters with Xenon craft could be staged.

Marteene and the AI both agreed that the recently established Split colony of Thyn's Abyss, east of ES2, was out of the question. It was still struggling for life against the permanent stranglehold ES2 held on its single trade route to the rest of the X-Universe. The few jump capable Split naval transporters were busy maintaining the defence build up in the adjacent sector of Family Whi. Civilian and industrial life in the 3 Split sectors in this region were sustained through traders making the dangerous dash through ES2 from Black Hole Sun. It was possible if you were bold enough, quick enough or lucky enough and just the challenge itself was enough to ensure a steady trickle of gamblers. The post-war glut of pilots, pushed out to the frontiers by transport cartels in the inner sectors, provided the rest.

It was not strong enough to defend itself against a major Xenon assault and the Split would not look with favour upon anyone who precipitated one.

Sector Eighteen Billion, a Teladi frontier system on the west flank of ES1, was ruled out for diplomatic reasons. That left either Black Hole Sun or Scale Plate Green.

"Black-Hole Sun, no question," Xela reiterated. "When we get into trouble there'll be plenty of help at hand. I've died once already thank you and would prefer not to have to gamble my sentience on the lizards pulling my tail from the furnace. They aren't exactly known for their spirit of self-sacrifice are they?"

Marteene had to concede she had a point. He could easily envisage Teladi Security forces standing idle whilst a single Boron ship was wasted. What profit would there be in intervening? On the other hand they were now unofficial allies of the head honcho and that should count for something.

Black Hole Sun though, that was the front line as far as the Argon were concerned. No capital ships were stationed there, so as not to provoke a pre-emptive strike by the Xenon, but the sector contained an Equipment Dock and such a massive investment for a species was not left undefended. Sector security was provided by several of the best fighter squadrons in the fleet. These Elites and Busters could, at the very least, delay a Xenon advance long enough for reinforcements to arrive from the fleet elements based in Omicron Lyrae. Marteene knew that the odds on them surviving the encounter would be many factors higher if it took place there.

"If we do it here Zee, we won't have to travel through the Argon Frontier. I'm a touch leery about drawing attention to ourselves, especially if Trasker is stationed there. And besides, sector defences may be too damn good and it's going to take you some time to figure out how to get into the Xenon systems. Some hotshot is bound to step in and 'help'."

"This sector has beaten off one Xenon attack recently," he continued. "The Xenon lost a lot of hardware, including capital ships so they can't have too much left. Local forces and the fleet at PTNI Headquarters should be able to cope and if this is going to be our base sector then it can't hurt to show the locals we can dish it out."

By the same token of course it would not hurt to demonstrate the same thing in Argon space, Xela was quick to point out.

"And tactically you can see as well as I that stirring the Xenon up in this section of the frontier would be to our advantage. From chaos comes opportunity, as our new Teladi friends say."

"And you can't make omelettes without breaking eggs." Marteene rejoined. It was not a happy thought. "Okay, Black Hole Sun it is but let's see if we can do this without provoking a war. What options do we have?"

The cockpit was silent for a few seconds as Xela ran possibilities through her tactical sub-routines.

"Logic suggests we either wait for the emergence of one of their irregular armed forays into Black Hole Sun or we employ a subterfuge to lure only a manageable number through the jump-gate. I do not possess enough data upon which to base more detailed options, I suggest we obtain some."

"Couldn't agree more Zee, patch us into the commercial comms and search all species sports, celebrity and crime news banks for 'Xenon', 'races' and 'Black Hole Sun.'

"I'm not an idiot Max, if you want me to find out if any rich play-boys are planning another display of testosterone fuelled idiocy for the benefit of the knuckle-dragging, gambling, masses you only have to ask."

She barely paused.

"And the answer is yes."

"That was quick Zee, even for you. Let's have it."

She flashed the details on screen and Marteene spent a couple of minutes running through the files. Gauntlet, as the entertainment industry quickly labelled it with a dozen copyrighted variants, had rapidly evolved from the exploits of cargo runners though ES1 and ES2.

Xenon activity in these sectors ebbs and flows. Sometimes the vicinity of the gates swarmed with Xenon activity; sometimes it was a few sentry ships; sometimes complete battle groups. It wasn't predictable and probes tended not to survive for long. For transport pilots is was a matter of taking the risk of jumping through for a quick look and judging the odds.

For riders of the Gauntlet it's a matter of judging if it is dangerous enough.

At first it was solo adrenaline junkies but, driven by the twin evolutionary pressures of gambling and mass entertainment it soon metamorphosed into a spectator sport. The Black Hole Sun meets were in almost continuous progress with disparate groups of fighters, wired for sound and vision, waiting for Xenon activity to reach a challenging level. Traders might make runs up to anything like Action 3. Aces might push it to A4 if the price was right. Gauntlet riders would run anything from 6 to 8. Suicides ran at 9.

Action 10 meant a full Xenon task force had swam in from the outer depths of the system and no running was permitted for fear of provoking an attack.

Entrants for the first Flashman Destruction Rampage were already congregating, awaiting an Action 8 notification. The rules were simple. Whoever made it round the eastern jump-gate to Thyn's Abyss and back to Black Hole Sun with the most kills, won.

Xela digested the data in a millisecond. Extrapolating the outcome took even less. She held her electronic tongue, even when her cockpit sensors detected traces of the mind-rotting male hormone.

Flashmans, the Argon Gambling Syndicate sponsoring the race and, a quick cross-reference search through commercial data-stores confirmed, the recipient of tens of millions of credits for network rights, were offering an unprecedented two million credits prize money, winner takes all. For a long nano-second she considered withholding this last factoid but her predictive algorithms strongly indicated that the chance of dissuading Marteene from competing was negligible, regardless of prize-money. Instead she flashed the data onto the screen and compartmentalised a portion of her resources and with the AI equivalent of a deep sigh actuated what she considered her vastly overused "Making the best of another bad situation" sub-routines.

---

The Split was good.

"But not," according to the somewhat dramatic running commentary in her head, "Good enough!"

Anticipating the Mamba's overused deceleration gambit she hung to its six, pounding the shields with her Alpha PAC's as it belatedly engaged afterburners.

Her eyes flickered constantly from target, to instruments, to space; updating her combat awareness with a lightning visual scan. Registering them as posing no immediate threat she noted a Falcon, festooned in shimmering rings of blue plasma from the weapons of the black and red Piranha locked on its tail.

Two drones danced around the dogfight.

Instantly she saw the Falcon pilot had no idea how to shake the fast, agile Piranha and would be dead in seconds.

As would her own victim.

Before the Split heavy fighter could use its superior speed to extend and escape the drive failed with a bright orange flash, through which she observed the pilot safely ejecting. Simultaneously her own weapons cut out, automatically triggering a mental 3 second count as she barrel rolled off excess speed and banked to catch a bushwhacking Hawk, attacking from starboard aft with a snap shot.

The ship flashed through her fire and accelerated away before its shields fell to the level that automatically ended the combat. She cursed briefly, wishing her reflexes remained as acute as her hearing. Almost subconsciously homing on the sound of the Teladi drive from the cacophony of battle conveyed by the Combat Audio Mk 4. A lot of pilots used it for little more than noting incoming fire but she recognised its potential from her first sim training course and assiduously practised its use,

From the Doppler effect she computed its distance, direction and manoeuvre and jinking to avoid the drifting Mamba she banked towards the Hawk, catching it with a brief burst before it rolled and twisted away.

Another quick sit-aware update showed the Piranha had also finished its opponent and was now dancing and rolling through the plasma fire of another Piranha in an aggressive head to head..

There were only 4 ships left in the sky, not counting the Argon Rescue Lifter moving into teleport range of the two recently ejected pilots, and time was almost up. As if on cue the voice of the Combat Co-ordinator, running the session from the Black Hole Sun Sector Control aboard the Trading Station, announced.

"Thirty seconds to disengagement pilots, make, them count."

The Hawk pilot was much too cunning to risk a head on pass and knowing she didn't need the points she just kept her nose pointed at the fast fighter and let the seconds count down.

The Piranha pilot didn't need the points either but he pursued the other Boron fighter with ruthless and often, she had to admit, inspired efficiency. He nailed it on the 15 second mark and was moving to engage her Hawk as Control signalled the end of the contest.

"Good show people, good show." She grated her teeth against the accent she was beginning to think of as 'show biz'. The producer, a small, portly, irritating man whose main talent appeared to be an ability to copiously sweat whatever the temperature, cut into the channel as the controller issued docking orders.

"The great unwashed are lapping it up, record pay-per-view for a qualifying round. Max, you were awesome. You too Telly baby." Seronos Telimar Wodansic IV, merely hissed her displeasure at the barbarian decapitation of her heritage as the Hawk sped back towards the distant gate system.

As usual her own efforts did not merit a mention despite her performance. If she had not spent almost every credit she owned trading up from her old Buster to the Elite at the Omicron Lyrae shipyard, she could have paid the 50k credit entry fee for the position on the starting line her record at other meets merited. If it had not been for the bounties she'd earned escorting the garrulous Boron and his Lifter from Seizewell she would not have been able to meet the asking price at all.

The qualifying rounds were a cakewalk. Team versus team, one on one, all against all; her long experience in private security squadrons and war service in the Argon Naval Reserve, gave her a keen edge over most of the competition. She and the other dozen or so pilots who really knew what they were doing were assured of qualification well before this final session.

A few hours knife fighting for the benefit of couch potatoes of all species was, she reasoned, preferable to running an Action Eight in an M4 class fighter of any species. It would be a target rich environment and the heavier weapons and shields would permit her to more than offset any time penalties incurred with extra kill points.

Joining the straggle of piloted and unpiloted ships heading back towards the gate system she activated the Singularity Time Distortion Drive to make the long, safety dictated journey pass quickly.

Her Elite was one of the last to dock and touched down on the platform adjacent to the black and red Piranha in the bay reserved for Gauntlet Runners. A small multi-species riot appeared to be in progress around the Boron fighter. At the centre of the cacophonous mass, besieged by the swarm of recording devices hovering and darting above the crowd of media reps in an attempt to capture his every word and gesture, was the Piranha pilot.

The media scrum had become a regular feature of the practice rounds as the promoters and media conspired to boost interest in the event by creating minor celebrities from competitors but as usual none of the reporting reptiles separated from the pack to seek her opinions and views.

Her fine-boned beauty had long since matured into handsome and her un-enhanced boyish figure was now, with middle age galloping by with depressing speed, merely plain. Lacking a striking back story to compensate for what the media tacitly deemed 'shortcomings', she became effectively invisible. Watching the pilot at the centre of the media storm she was not sorry. If it was at all possible the younger pilot, impassive behind the aviators shades he rarely removed, seemed even more uncomfortable than usual with the attention, answering all questions with a few short sentences.

A short but fearsome dark haired young woman at his side, fleshed these out whilst shooting him exasperated barbs. A Flying Eye operator said she was some kind of high flier from one of the bigger promotion bureaus on Argon Prime.

"What was her name? Anje something or something Anje?" Whichever it was, she had proven a publicity singularity; a brassy force of nature, demanding attention. With his talent, good looks and an easily romanticised criminal background the woman had a readily marketable product.

"What more could the public want from a star?" She thought as she observed the spectacle.

Anje Dalenari often had the same thought. it was her job and being a professional she had an answer. "A bloody co-operative one!" she muttered as Force summed up his feelings at qualifying for the Gauntlet as "Fine."

"What Max means to say is that he's excited at the prospect of running his very first Gauntlet tomorrow and pretty pleased to be being paid to stick it to the machine-heads!"

Some of the spectators responded with a grunting chant of "Max, Max, Max."

She looked at Max, willing him to respond to her choreographed stunt as she had coached him but he just stood there sporting a strained grin, impervious behind his bloody mirrored glasses to her patented, client-scaring glare.

"I think she's pissed with you again Max, if you didn't want to play ball you really should not have hired her."

"I didn't damn hire the woman, she just turned up as you well know." Max replied sotto-voce as Xela monitored his vocal cords. "Remind me to thank Artur next time we meet."

"It's a good plan, you should be more grateful. And Max, try to smile more. Your constipated ventriloquist act is scaring the children."

"Can we wrap this up Anje, I need a shower?" he said. Hiding her irritation she smiled

"Okay Max, one more question. You." She singled out the Associated Media rep, an ageing sports hack who hopefully hitched his waning star to every passing fad.

"Yes, Max. You've never run a Gauntlet before right, but now you're basically going to be flying through the middle of a Xenon battlegroup in an M4. Are you insane?

A chuckle rippled around the hanger and even Max smiled.

"Probably, yes but I've been in fleet engagements before. This isn't any different, all those competitors, camera drones and decoys – it'll be chaos and as the Teladi say. From chaos comes opportunity."

Under Xela's silent prompting he grinned confidently and held a fist briefly aloft for the holo-cams. The animal chanting resumed as he left.

With what he suspected was a remarkable act of self restraint his unwanted publicist waited until they were ensconced in the privacy of his suite before tasking him.

"Make an effort ... I don't know why I bother ... easier to sell bottled water to the Boron... which I've done.."

Marteene barely listened as he surreptitiously scanned the rooms for bugging devices. He knew her speech by heart and in case he forgot the odd line Xela was helpfully chanting along in wicked imitation, emphasising each "I" with exaggerated self importance.

It took several minutes and as many promises to put on a good show at the pre-race media conference before she could be persuaded to leave.

"Two million credits, I don't know if it's worth it Zee."

Xela did not reply. They had had this conversation and the matter was settled, at least to her satisfaction. The resurrected Max Force had made a significant splash already and was likely to draw even more as he built up the economic empire needed for the plan to penetrate the clan conspiracy to succeed. Given his putative background it was better to control the publicity from the start.

Anje Dalenari was, Artur had assured them both in the encrypted message that presaged her arrival, a master of the black art of spin and so it proved. Max Force, rebel and lone gun; his problems with the Stoertebeker Clan transmuted by her touch into heroic legend.

Max reluctantly agreed with Artur's assessment and allowed himself to be swept along in the tide, consoled by the fact that at least for the time being he was just a growing fish in a small pond; a metaphor he had given up trying to explain to Borass.

The garrulous Boron had flown the Star through Split space to the Argon Frontier as soon as the standard trace he'd placed on the name 'Force' started throwing up minority sports articles, picking up trades and escorts along the way. Max was pleased to see him and even more pleased to see the Star in one piece.

"No perspiration Max-Max, Stoertebeker no angry with me."

That was not entirely true. There had been some trouble in Teladi Gain but the Buster escort fended the attacking Bayamons off long enough for the Star to reach the jump-gate and the rest of the journey had been uneventful, give or take the odd skirmish.

Marteene struggled to get enough rest from a night of fitful sleep punctuated at regular intervals by familiar pre-combat anxiety dreams. In the morning he glided through the pre-race publicity stunts on auto-pilot, responding as best he could to Anje's cues without losing his focus.

The pre-flight briefing told him nothing new. Borass and Xela had worked long into the evening at the Star's Tactical Holo-Display running through strategy, tactics and scenarios and he was as prepared as he had been for any strike mission. The most recent scans confirmed the presence of three Xenon cruisers within the gate system. Two prowled the sector while the third stood station near an unidentified installation. A dozen or so assorted fighters patrolled in 3 ship formations with unknown numbers more poised to launch.

"Two carrier groups jumping in at each gate; Six Elite wings flying strike, half the Buster flying escort, all other fighters on CAP. We could take all 3 caps with only 60% casualties, assuming no reinforcements on either side. Easy."

Her estimate was a little conservative in his opinion but even so he had flown worse ships than a Piranha in such situations and survived. Except, as Borass was quick to point out, there was a universe of difference between implementing sophisticated combined arms tactics with well-trained and disciplined pilots and the free-for-all of a Gauntlet.

"Every being for herself," Xela summarised. "Are you sure you want to do this and I hate to be the one to bring this up but you could get us both killed? Even with the shadow-tech disabled the Rapier will be unable to out-run anything but the L class fighters and ten MW's of shielding will last about 2 seconds if one of the CAP ships target you."

It was a truth that silenced the three of them for a moment. The rest of the discussion was uncharacteristically sombre.

"You could get us both killed."

The words returned unbidden as he held station in the front rank of the ships poised before the jump-gate, thirty appendages hovering over thirty thrust controls.

The gate flashed once as the Pegasus decoy fighter jumped. The tiny Paranid built fighter sacrificed everything for speed and the large single engine protruding from the small main body made it about the fastest thing in space. It would hopefully lure any fighters away from the sector entrance. A second wave, comprised of weaponless decoy drones, followed.

Max swallowed hard, mouth dry.

You could get us both killed.

The starter missile blossomed green beyond the gate and he punched the after-burner.

## *Chapter 41: Break, break, break!*

The jump-gate transit seemed longer than normal, a deceit practiced by a nervous system driven by basic human instinct.

As he had been trained Max registered the fear; the tongue, slightly too large for his arid mouth, the acrid, metal throat, the blood hammering in his temples, the anvil on his chest.

It was the body and it wanted to live.

Marteene stepped away from that body into the calm centre of his being where the fear could be channelled by his rational mind as a turbine harnesses a raging torrent.

As the final seconds crawled by he ran a final, swift systems check.

Gamma PAC's on line?

Check.

Shields up?

Check.

Silkworms active?

Check.

Combat drones primed for launch?

Check.

Emerging from tranquillity into chaos Max hit the afterburners, rolling to narrowly avoid an inverted Hawk re-entering the gate. He noted, in a frozen moment of clarity, the terrified expression of the Teladi pilot as their canopies almost scraped. The smaller fighter careened off the stronger shields of the Piranha, rolling and tumbling into a camera drone as it emerged into normal space. The Hawk slipped sideways into the gate and vanished as the drone smashed into the structure.

Ahead, another Gauntlet Runner was pulling his Mamba into a breaking loop back towards the jump-gate. A glance at the scanner revealed the cause. Pursuing the decoy drone, radiating a cap ship profile, were 4 Xenon caps, colour coded on the display as M1 and M2. A pair of each, 80 klicks and receding.

He left it to Xela to count the cloud of fighters swarming towards them from a station the scanner was unable to identify.

"Heads up Max, 30 fighters incoming, equal numbers L, M and N's. More launching. There are also three mixed wings of 5 interdicting the other jump-gate. This is not a Force Eight Max, this is a strike group. Better part of valour?"

"Negative Zee, the camera drones are deploying and I'm not hearing a recall signal. We're not running away from two million credits, not after all that media crap."

At least not yet, he added silently.

Camera drones, decoys, Runners breaking in every direction; some returning to the gate, some turning to fight and some making a run for the eastern gate; the oncoming red tide of Xenon fighters; the scanner was too full of contacts to be much use.

"Turning to engage, call it Zee!"

The attacking Xenon swarm was now split into class groups by their differing speeds and the boxy, X shaped M5's formed the spearhead.

"Five others are with us Max, all M3's; Elite's and Falcon's."

"Six against thirty eh? Could be better, could be worse, let's, as they say, rock."

"Four clicks and closing Max. Luck."

Having the faster ship Max was the first to engage. Three of the lightly shielded Xenon fighters fell in his first pass, engulfed in three measured bursts of carefully aimed plasma squeezed off as he waltzed through the incoming streams of fire.

"Score, score, score Max!" Xela enthused. "Two others down, three, four. "

Max caught another with a reflex snapshot as it flashed across his nose, smashing the shields almost to zero. A Falcon finished it off.

"Hey, no steal! Second wave 6 klicks, you're clear to engage Max, the other M5's are totally defensive."

Max banked towards the incoming group. Two of the elegant winged Xenon M4's fell to his guns in the head-on pass and again he managed to avoid taking hits. Ten megawatts of shielding offered only a few seconds of protection from the Xenon Alpha PAC's and avoiding incoming fire whilst aggressively prosecuting your own attack was what you learnt flying the M4 Buster in the Argon Navy before you were allowed anywhere near the valuable Elites.

With the all-seeing Xela in the virtual second seat another two fell to his cannons with only minimal damage to his own shields before the imminent arrival of the big, slow L Class forced him to disengage in search of an advantageous tactical position.

Few organics were permitted the luxury to take it in but the Xenon system was possibly the most spectacular arena the X-universe offered. Twin white suns flared diamond white against a massive cloud of interstellar gas, glowing turquoise with the light of the newborn stars flecked through it.

And this was just the backdrop.

A nebula; incandescent rose and eggshell fragile against the turquoise, stood at the aesthetic zenith; an essential honeymoon cruise stopover if it wasn't for the locals.

And if it wasn't for the counterpoint that gave the undesignated sector a savage beauty.

The former Split mining colony was now just chunks of planetary debris. The fusion reactions caused by whatever process destroyed it were still burning, still consuming the larger, moon sized fragments orbiting a common centre of gravity.

Colonisation of this sector and the handful beyond the eastern jump-gate had barely begun following the Brennan War when the Xenon fleet stormed in from deep space. The fifty thousand Split colonists had barely enough time to scream out a static strangled distress call.

"Earthquakes.....massive                    vulcanism.....radiation....dangerous levels....Xenon. Help."

The Nav-Sat went down before the single jump-capable Split battle group could jump in.

Redirected to the adjacent Split colony of Thyn's Abyss it arrived in time to parry a Xenon thrust. The Split won but the immense cost gave victory an ash taint. The Argon faced a similar attack into Black Hole Sun and they too won after a bitterly fought struggle, thanks to the local fleet based a couple of gates away in Omicron Lyrae.

An immediate Argon probe-in-strength was beaten back with 90% casualties, the Xenon clearly had huge resources concealed deep within the gate system. It would take a massive offensive to retake the it and despite its strategic location the price was just too high. The Xenon sector remained a crushing claw around the throat of the New Frontier.

What destroyed the planet remained unknown. A Xenon weapon, a long dormant booby trap, a malfunctioning Xenon mining machine, or, as some wildly speculated, an Artefact from some ancient race? Some kind of fusion process was involved and as the fragments remained in the same orbit, the planet disintegrated rather than exploded.

Despite or perhaps, because of the unknown it represented, the broken planet was a terrible wonder.

Marteene saw none of this as he arced the Rapier around the melee of heavy fighters. He saw lights to blind foes to his approach, energy sources to confuse scanners.

The Runners were outnumbered 2 to 1 by the Xenon L's and the next wave of Xenon N's were moments away. Camera drones and their decoys flashed through the dogfights, drawing some of the Xenon fire and the Runners were holding their own, except for a Falcon pilot suffering a severe case of target fixation, unaware of the pair of L's falling on his tail while he chewed up the rear shields of a third. It was a stock Xenon drag and tag.

Max rolled left, arcing to engage a single Xenon M, twisting his neck constantly to keep both it and the L's in sight.

"Now!"

Banking his fighter Max pulled around and fell out of the flare of the twin suns onto the first of the stalking L's even as it opened up on the Falcon with the devastating twin Alpha HEPT's that made the Xenon heavy fighter so lethal.

Thee superior speed of the Piranha allowed Max to roll out of his attack 50 metres dead on its six.

"Bandits, 8 o clock low. Pair of N's. Contact 4 seconds" Xela called out urgently.

"Fox One, Fox Two, Fox Three, Fox Four." he called out by the book, launching the four Silkworms almost simultaneously and rolling left to force an overshoot on his attackers and continuing the roll back onto the rear of the L.

Four parallel contrails curved after the L as it broke right. The four consecutive explosions kicked the L and in the short seconds it took to regain control Max pulled in to point blank range and pulled the trigger. The plasma burst took away the remaining shields and as the first explosions engulfed the drive unit, causing the heavy fighter to slip and roll into its death throes, Max broke high and right, taking a glancing hit from a camera drone.

"Nice move Max, don't think I've seen it before, break right break right!"

Plasma streamed by, close enough to graze his shields and he rolled back onto the six of the overshooting Xenon M.

"Thanks, a friend taught me it."

Equi-distant target switching. In theory and in a target-rich environment Xenon threat analysis sub-routines would take a split-second longer to react. A very quick and very good pilot could use that time to engage from the rear without taking a fatal punch in the face from the twin Alpha HEPT's. It had been deemed too dangerous a tactic to be officially adopted by the Argon Navy but that had not prevented Paskaal from passing it on to those he deemed capable enough.

How's the Falcon Zee!" he shouted as he took out the retreating fighter with a sustained close range burst that left his weapons drained.

"He's in trouble Max, targeting."

Two more N's and an M sucked Max into a claws-out dust-up that filled the sky around him with missiles. Even with Xela's tactical calls it took him more seconds than the Falcon had to take the Xenon fighters down.

"He's gone Max." Xela announced sombrely.

He caught an M with a pair of dragonfly missiles and finished it with a long plasma burst before making a full speed break, high and right away from the roiling mass of fighters, plasma streams and missiles. The Xenon station had stopped launching ships, a tactical decision Max could not fault as the Runners were outnumbered, out-gunned and not fighting as a unit.

There could be only one outcome and even as Max locked up another target one of the remaining Falcon fighters broke back towards the gate to Black Hole Sun.

As Max finished the M, Xela announced the remaining Runners were also attempting to disengage. The Piranha bladed through the morass, hacking at the N and M fighters attempting to pin the retreating Falcon's for the slower L's, breaking right in response to Xela's cry a split second too late. His shields almost at zero Max rolled 180 and broke high, strafing the belly of an L and forcing it to disengage from the remaining Elite.

"Too close too close Max, get us out of here! Now Max, now!"

Max continued the break, pulling another long high-speed turn that gave him a few seconds to force his body to stop shaking enough to take in the tactical situation. The remaining three Teladi heavy fighters had belatedly formed into a defensive wing to fight their way to safety, drawing most of the remaining Xenon N and M fighters in pursuit. To his relief the remaining L's were falling back towards the station.

"Contest update Zee," he ordered.

"What? Are you crazy? Oh – pardon my rhetorical. Two Mamba's have made it round the eastern gate and are hightailing it back home. They've taken out 3 of the gate guards and the half the rest are in pursuit."

He quickly digested the sector map, it showed he had a clear run at the eastern gate.

"Only 3 L's on station Zee – we could end run those on speed, how about it?"

"You've already decided Max so go for it. You won't be alone."

The Elite pilot also had the same idea and was accelerating towards the gate even as the plasma cloud of the last of her pursuer cooled and dissipated.

### Chapter 42: Counter-strike

"THEY'RE GOING FOR THE GATE, THEY'RE GOING FOR THE GATE! THIS IS THE GREATEST.."

"Mute commentary Seera, shut it up!"

The AI complied and the darkened office was plunged into a silence made eerie by the fractured shadows cast by the two figures prowling around the central holo-tank.

They watched in silence as the two fighters closed on the remaining Xenon fighters surrounding the eastern jump-gate. It was barely a fight. The Elite splashed the first in a head-on pass and Marteene took the second with another equi-distant attack break that positioned him on its six. The Xenon ship died in a hail of missiles and plasma before the AI could react.

"Nicely done, Mr Marteene, very nicely done indeed!" Artur quaffed the rest of his ale in celebration, savouring the dark, nutty flavour.

"I taught him that."

"Indeed?" Artur took another sandwich, proffering the tray to his new pilot.

Paskaal declined.

Artur shrugged and piled the remaining sandwiches onto his own plate as the Elite disengaged and headed for home, leaving Marteene locked on the tail of the remaining L. The shield display showed its shields were almost at zero and every couple of seconds Marteene fired another pulse into its rear, knocking them back down to zero. He wondered what the gibbering buffoon on the tank was making of it but not enough to have to endure any more of his witless utterings. As they watched the Piranha abruptly disengaged on a vector towards the south gate.

"Damn it boy, what are you doing?" Artur muttered, "We need that ship!"

"Out of time, look." Paskaal indicated a timer counting down in the top left of the screen. The decoy drone had emerged from behind the shattered planet and was itself returning to the Black Hole Sun jump-gate, the Xenon capital ships trailing in its wake. "Its too expensive a piece of kit to throw away."

Artur tapped a few keys on the holo-tank controls, displaying relative speeds and time-to-target data. Marteene had timed his disengagement well, at the maximum speed of the L they would arrive at the gate a few seconds before the decoy. He guessed his protégé was planning to lure the Xenon fighter into Argon space where he could capture it at leisure. Artur smiled as he imagined the frenzy that the hijacking of a Xenon heavy fighter on a live net-cast would cause.

Paskaal watched with equanimity, about the only thing in this whole affair he had any confidence in was Marteene's combat ability. Artur had given all the right priority codes and spun a plausible enough tale and given that he did actually owe his life to the man Paskaal was prepared to give him the benefit of the doubt but only one thing would truly convince him.

"When do we meet up?"

"Soon Mr Paskaal, or perhaps I should say, Mr Corrin. Scale Plate Green once the Teladi have passed the decree."

"And that depends on the delivery of an L right?"

Artur nodded, unsurprised at the continuing lack of trust in his tone. He had been as open as he was able with Paskaal concerning Marteene's mission but even so it must have seemed a very tall tale. At his insistence Artur had allowed Paskaal to access his own service record over the Special Forces security channel. It confirmed for Paskaal the facts of his own "death" in an accident whilst working under deep cover and his subsequent transfer to an unspecified Code Black operation. That the latter information was only accessible to those with security clearances several levels higher than that permitted by his own access code, a clearance Artur possessed, went a long way to confirming the story but Paskaal needed to hear it from someone he really trusted.

And that person was not his mysterious benefactor.

"May I?"

Artur surrendered the Holo-tank remote to Paskaal and watched as he assessed the situation.

"Do we have an active spy drone?"

"Another test Mr Corrin? I believe The Argon Navy has one dormant in the asteroid debris surrounding the planet. Why?"

"If you can you'd better get it on-line," Paskaal said evenly as he adjusted the composite feed from the broadcast drones to focus on the east gate. "There." He indicated a bright star with a laser pointer.

It was moving.

---

"Max, disengage. Now, you need to see this."

Marteene instantly complied, using his superior speed to extend and escape from the battered Xenon L.

Her tone brooked no argument.

"I've got something up on long-range scan, coming in at relativistic speed. Something big."

Marteene glanced at the sector display. Xela had already locked up the new target and he pulled a wide turn towards it, careful to deny the L a firing solution.

"Okay fella, let's see what's up. Activating Zooms, max magnification...."

He barely glimpsed the incoming ship before it vanished behind the red glare of massive braking thrusters. Seconds later Xela announced it had entered the gate system and was on an intercept course.

"Better part of valour Max?" Xela suggested evenly.

"Time to intercept Zee?"

"Too soon Max, you might make it but the Elite won't. Too bad, I liked her."

Max shook his head.

"No way Zee, we're not abandoning her. Lock up the L and give me a heads up when the unknown hits 20 klicks."

The target lock shifted instantly. Twenty seconds later the Xenon was nothing but an expanding shell of gas and micro-debris, at the cost of most of his remaining missiles.

"Bogie at 20 klicks, coming in fast. Cap ship. Unidentified."

"I don't like that word Zee, going for a visual."

He liked what he saw even less. It was a monster.

"Who are they Zee? It doesn't look Xenon."

"Configuration matches no known design Max. We might have a new player here."

It was a reasonable inference. The cap ships of all known species, with the exception of the streamlined hulls of the Boron, placed functionality well ahead of aesthetics. This one though, with its long pencil hull and elegant pylon mounted drives, this one looked like it had flown straight off an artist's tablet but fitted no known design philosophy.

"Ten klicks Max, decelerating, I don't think it wants to be our friend."

Max watched the on-coming behemoth and off-set his intercept course another degree to keep from being smashed aside.

At 2 klicks it abruptly decelerated, sweeping past the tiny fighter to take up station 10 klicks from the southern gate.

"Running scans, all frequencies. I'm detecting power surges all over the spectrum. Weapons coming on line, multiple drive signatures. Fighters launching."

The new note of despair may have been his imagination.

" Multiple flights, multiple fighters, inbound. Scanning as Xenon. More are going after the Elite, time to intercept, 30 seconds."

Instinctively Max broke low and left towards the fleeing contestant and it took the longest of minutes to battle through the swarms of Xenon fighters to reach the Elite, which was by now, totally defensive. With Xela acting as an extra pair of eyes for both ships the ensuing battle lasted longer than Marteene imagined possible and he quickly lost count of the number of Xenon ships the two fighters destroyed.

But it could end only one way.

"She's gone Max. Break right, break right! Picking up distress beacon, locking on target."

Max slipped from the foci of the multiple plasma cross-fire and weaved through the firestorm laid down by the big unknown in a desperate attempt to rescue the pilot. She boiled away in the maelstrom, without a sound.

"I didn't even know her name Zee, I didn't even know her name." The words were choked out as a rage, cold and black, stifling every thought except one.

Vengeance.

His shields were down to almost zero and the sector littered with Xenon debris before Xela's exhortations penetrated the red mist. After one final, near suicidal strafing run along the full length of the Xenon mothership, Xela screaming his name, Max disengaged. The Xenon cap did not pursue and only the Xenon N's could keep pace. These he destroyed without conscious thought.

The Piranha entered the gate trailing a swarm of Xenon fighters.

### *Chapter 43: Reunion*

Aboard the Seera, Artur and Paskaal watched the ingress of the huge ship in a silence the net-cast commentator did not feel impelled to share.

"Merde, merde, merde – look at the size of that thing, look!" His voice cracked with rising panic.

"We're looking you gibbering fool, what the damn else would we be doing?" Paskaal muttered, consciously relaxing his white-knuckle grip on a chair arm. "Can we get a close-up?"

Artur quickly flicked through the other channels of the 'cast and shook his head.

"The Gate-Cam's all we got Mr Paskaal."

Paskaal cursed again as the mystery ship disgorged a cloud of fighters.

"Xenon." He spat. "Get out of there laddie, there's too many of them. Break right, break right son!"

Artur cast a sidelong glance at the veteran pilot; unconsciously fighting alongside his embattled friend, fingers twitching on invisible triggers; and allowed himself a moment to envy the comradeship, envy the bond that both his calling and nature denied him.

Reluctantly Artur turned away from the spectacle, activated a side monitor, entered a code and frowned. The encrypted feed from the Argon Spy-Sat hidden among the debris of the shattered planet provided no more information than the public broadcast and a static plagued picture that was considerably worse. Even at long range it should have been picking up load-outs, hull composition and power readings and crisp close-ups.

This was not good.

"This isn't good," Trasker thought as she attempted to filter out the static from the Spy-Sat. "This isn't good at all."

She had warned anyone who would listen that these foolhardy stunts ran the risk of provoking the Xenon and now she feared she was about to be proven correct. To make matters worse, she was completely out of the command loop, cooped up in the Black Hole Sun Intelligence Centre, deep in the bowels of the Trading Station, monitoring events. The real decisions were being made up in the Command Centre by Flag Officers in direct contact with Argon Prime.

A few seconds later the Spy-Sat went off air forcing Janis to switch her attention back to the public net feed where the gravity of the situation was being met with the calm response she would expected from the kind of network that would show this sort of thing.

"They're Xenon, merde, they're Xenon. Hundreds of them., I've never seen so many!"

"Cut him off, cut him off before he says anything stupid." Trasker willed.

"We're all going to die!"

With impeccable timing the public feed flared white, leaving a fading image of a Xenon N burned on the retina of every viewer.

Janis could almost feel the panic she knew would ensue through the soles of her boots.

The Sector Display confirmed the panic had already begun. Dozens of ships, spectators and traders alike were running towards the western jump-gate with more streaming from each station. A quick flick through the internal monitors confirmed her worst fears.

The station was on the verge of mass hysteria, she could smell it.

Going split-screen on the security feeds she confirmed her fear. Fighting had already broken out in the docking bays and several public areas as individuals coalesced into mobs intent on escape.

Belatedly the red alert klaxon sounded and an electronic voice ordered all civilians to remain calm and in their quarters. It may as well have ordered the system primary not to shine.

Pausing only to confirm the Alert One Flight had deployed Trasker checked the charge on her night-stick and headed for the main docking bay.

"I think we are in trouble Mr Paskaal." Artur said, indicating the Sector Display. Even for him it was something of an understatement. Given its proximity to the Xenon strong-hold, the Argon Navy had given much thought to the defence of the sector. The fleet at Omicron Lyrae would already be moving into position and Black Hole Sun itself boasted a large fighter fleet. Jump-capable reserves would be mobilising throughout Argon space and the Teladi fleet at PTNI Headquarters informed of the situation.

The scan indicated that Alert One was already racing towards the northern jump-gate to deploy mines and laser towers.

Unfortunately no one had planned for the Treasure Chest jump-gate to be choked by dozens of small craft.

Paskaal took the tactical situation in with a glance. No capital ship was coming through that jumpgate, the abort call would already be out, and they could not come in through the Xenon gate. The risk of collision with incoming Xenon caps was too great and it would leave the ship in a terrible tactical state; slow and with your rear to an enemy that could jump onto your tail in a second. And most importantly – it would risk destroying the jump-gate and the standing orders of all species dictate that the slamming of one of these precious doors to the universe was to be avoided whatever the cost.

No, the only help coming were couple of jump-capable Tactical Reserve Elite squadrons and even that might be considered too risky.

He scanned the adjacent sectors – fighters were launching, forming streams heading towards Black-Hole Sun. Welcome reinforcements but they'd take time to arrive. And he very much doubted the dozen Bayamon fighters launched from the Clan base in Nyana's Hideout had anything else in their minds than profiting from chaos.

"Open the hatch Artur." Paskaal said quietly.

For you to go where?"

"I'm going to find a fighter."

Artur weighed his options for only a moment. To trust or not to trust? Betrayal versus loss of primary asset? The cost of an un-planned re-appearance someone inconvenient was bound to notice? The cost of putting that right?"

"Seera, grant Mr Paskaal egress. And Mr Corrin," he said, emphasising the identity Paskaal had been using at the time of his supposed death.

"Good luck."

Paskaal picked up his flight helmet and stepped from the Dolphin into a bedlam wall. The main docking bay of the Trading Station resounded with the whine of thrusters as ship after ship launched, with or without clearance. From the main doors the mob roar of panic hardened. Blaster fire and angry screams followed. Beings of all races, singly and in fear-bonded groups, were beginning to trickle onto the deck and he knew this would soon become a flood.

From way down the line came the guttural and utterly unmistakeable thunder of a Gatling cannon followed by a steel lottery of ricochets.

Crouching and briefly wondering what sort of reckless fool would use a solid projectile chain gun inside a docking bay, Paskaal glanced around and spotted a Mamba two bays down, wearing an unfamiliar red and black livery that screamed Merc.

He hurried through the chaos to the Split pilot, who was systematically uncoupling the power relays on the last of the docking clamps preventing take-off.

"Hey laddie, are you heading out there to take on the Xenon?"

"Me fight for credits, me fight when I will win," the pilot retorted angrily, his hand slipping towards his holstered side-arm.

"Split not go splat for Argon."

The Gatling stammered again and the Split crouched reflexively, straight into an ascending flight boot.

"Split go splat." Paskaal sneered as he relieved the unconscious pilot of his access chip. "Coward."

Moments later he was in the cockpit, slamming the hatch on three Teladi, who, unable to break in, were desperately waving credit chips in his direction.

Paskaal ignored them and scanned the controls.

"Pretty standard layout, like the Fleet sims, give or take the odd button and I expect we'll find out what they do soon enough won't we old girl?"

He patted the control panel reassuringly and integrated his flight helm into the flight systems. It took a couple of seconds for the translation matrix to over-ride the standard settings. The HUD reset to the new Argon settings and he activated the comm-link.

"Mamba ready to launch on station defence mission. Permission to launch, over."

The channel was just an inchoate storm of panicked voices.

He shrugged and activated the thrusters, pausing only to wave at the frantically gesticulating Teladi, one of whom was miming something quite disturbing.

"I'll be taking my leave of you now ladies." He waved and smiled his most practiced of Corrin smiles. The Teladi crumpled into the "why-me, can-my-day-get-any-worse" slouch familiar to any pilot who had attempted to get an unbribed mechanic of that species to do her job.

Un-noticed behind them the Split mercenary was regaining consciousness so Paskaal hazarded a guess that it could. It was a cheering thought he chose to take as a good omen.

Trusting to luck and 25 megawatts of shielding, Paskaal muscled the big fighter through the jostling throng of ships funnelling into the launch tunnel.

Marteene hit the after-burners the instant his ship emerged into Black Hole Sun, breaking high and twisting away from incoming fire that all but removed the fighter's remaining shields. A Discover fighter flashed across his nose still firing. A panel exploded to his right and for the few seconds it took the fire-suppressant fields to cut in a white, acrid smoke filled the cockpit.

"Docking computer gone Max and yes the IFF is working." She paused briefly.

"Scanning multiple contacts, Argon fighters, some Teladi, some Split. Three laser towers, back-up screen of squashes. A flight of 12 Bayamon coming in through the west gate, damn buzzards. And Xenon. Three, five, seven. You get the picture."

The scanner filled with red dots and the sky filled with the rapid plasma fire of the LT's.

"I guess we really pissed them off, going defensive, call it Zee."

"We're picking up quite a train Max, two flights of 6, L, M and N. Standard wing-man pairs. A whole lot more fighting round the gate, some going for the LT's, some heading in-system. No caps, either side."

Marteene dodged and twisted desperately, attempting to break away from the gate into deep space as the blue shield strength indicator strip crawled slowly up to full charge.

"You and I are going to have to talk about this self-sacrificial streak of yours Max. N Alpha incoming, break left 25, snapshot."

The move brought the Xenon light fighters across his nose, he took one with a close-range Gamma PAC snap-shot, rolled onto the tail of the fleeing survivor, switched down to alpha's targeted it with a long range burst.

The higher speed but lower powered plasma streams caught the fighter as it accelerated into another attack run.

"Predictable," he jibed.

"And its called Divide and Conquer Zee, basic strategy – I'm surprised you haven't heard of it!"

There was no time for a witty counter-thrust.

The second pair of N's arrived, using their superior speed and agility to tie the Rapier up in harassing fire until first the medium and then the heavy fighters arrived to fill Max's sky with a lethal entanglement of missiles and multi-hued plasma.

Hoisted on the petard of what, he was beginning to realise, was his own recklessness and mentally taking back his earlier crack, Marteene fought the Xenon for his life.

The mob had circumvented the lock-outs and broken through the thin cordon sealing off the main flight deck by the time Trasker arrived. Hefting her night-stick and setting it to Heavy Stun she joined the fray, her enthusiasm for a good, honest fight outweighing the voice that whispered caution. Most of the rioters were bent on either escape or it seemed, running around aimlessly rather than actual murder and mayhem and responded rather well to a stab from her stick, mainly by collapsing in an unconscious, twitching, heap.

Half of the ships had left already and of those remaining, only a handful were freighters capable of carrying large numbers, assuming they had life-support pattern enhancers fitted to their holds. Most of these were the foci of mob attention, except for a nearby Dolphin, whose halo of twitching bodies suggested an unorthodox modification she would have to investigate later.

A chain-gun roared. Down the flight-line and through the crowd she glimpsed a human assaulting the pilot of a Split Mamba. Night-stick flailing she forged herself a path.

"Charge the hull, Seera but try not to kill anyone," Artur ordered as he watched another hysterical tide flood across the deck. "And keep an eye on Mr Paskaal."

The monitor went split-screen and he watched Paskaal make his way towards a Mamba fighter. He also watched as the security forces took off the gloves, or to be more precise, threw them way with enthusiasm. None more so than a lone cop in the foreground, wielding a stun-club with vigour and efficiency. He recognised her the instant before Seera's pattern recognition sub-routines tagged her image.

"Best Buy Locator gone, shields at 25%. Show us some of that seat-of-the-pants stuff Max!"

Max decelerated suddenly, forcing the pair of M's to overshoot. Hitting the after-burner he emptied the remaining weapons charge into a rear shield. It wasn't enough and another racking cross-fire attack forced him to break, taking him through another that blew away almost all his remaining shields.

"There's too many of them Zee and they're too damn good!" he screamed, hearing the panic in his own voice.

"Upgraded AI Max, I can't get a handle on them. Dive dive!!"

The snap-roll and climb took him out of the sights of the converging pair of L's but left him no better off. The scanner showed so many hostiles around him that he could do nothing else but evade and evade, riding a luck that was bound to expire.

"Break left, left, now right, look out Max, look out!"

For minutes only the superior speed of the Piranha and Xela's timely calls kept Marteene alive but he could neither extend and escape nor reduce the odds. Sweating out every iota of skill coded into his nervous system and every learned or invented trick in his book, he battled to survive the co-ordinated Xenon attacks. The high-speed XN fighters prowled the shifting perimeter of the fight, blocking any escape while the XM's sniped and snapped at his heels, chipping away at his energy reserves. And through it all, slow and relentless, came the XL's, stalking heavyweights with primed hay-makers.

"I can't shake 'em Zee, I can't shake 'em!" Sweat poured down his face, warm and slow like blood and Marteene knew, in what remained of the cold rational core of his mind, he was on the point of surrendering to the primal sentient terror of extinction.

"Break high right 45, break left, break left."

Marteene obeyed reflexively; eyes dancing over instruments and scanning the death filled environs to maintain situational awareness. His brain raced to keep up, on the verge of surrender to visceral fear.

And then time, for a micro-second, stopped as Marteene stared his own death in the face. Xela's call was taking them straight into a trap. Two pairs of XN's were vectoring from 10 and 4 to snare him in cross-fire and one of the big, deadly L class fighters was coming in head-to-head.

Frozen now, Max waited for it to fire.

She had gotten him killed.

The XL rolled and broke, juddering under sustained fire. Four missiles slammed into its shields, kicking it across the sky like a broken toy before it died.

Alive again Marteene flew through the gap, almost firing on the Mamba that flashed through his sights.

"I'm on your wing now laddie and I've bought some old friends. Turn and burn, turn and burn."

That voice? Marteene could feel himself slipping into shock.

"Had you going there didn't I Max," Xela interjected, her voice dripping with relief. "Now do what the nice man said."

Through burning tears; his confusion, his relief, his sheer joy, wrapped into one happy parcel to be opened later; a reborn Marteene turned to re-engage in a sky now miraculously filled with Bayamons.

"Good to see you again boss." Marteene did not recognise the taciturn face on the screen or any of the other eleven that flashed similar greetings.

"Your team Max," Xela interjected. "The Raiders – remember the briefing? Time for some quick feet thinking, I'll put together a database. On your tail!"

"I see them Zee." Marteene broke left high and Paskaal right low, pairing up again, on the tails of the two XL's. First one, then the other blossomed fire and disintegrated.

"The first guy was Sarge, he'll be the leader now. Seize the day Max." Zee opened the comm link as Max lined up on a lone XM.

"Ah – Sarge, great to see you guys again. I guess there's a lot of explaining to do."

"That there is Commander, we thought you were dead. Yes!"

Ahead, a Bayamon pirouetted through a flight of XN's, laying waste to each with concentrated fire from its 4 weapons.

"Good kill, good kill, Sarge. Will explain all later," Zee whispered in his ear, a reminder.

"Sarge, no time to explain but I want my sky cleared of everything except one XL. Can do? Copy that, Mamba?"

"Two more machine-head wings inbound Commander, take your pick."

Xela immediately locked up one of the four XL's and transmitted the data to all ships.

"You heard the Commander you rodents," Sarge roared. "Do it!"

The fight developed into a long, fierce whirlwind of chaos but despite being out-numbered and out-gunned the Raiders were not to be beaten.

They were fighting for Max Force.

"Nice work boys and girls. Two ships down sir, no casualties." Sarge was grinning now, wasting Xenon was a black and white good thing, no need to worry about taking sentient life. "One left Commander, what are your orders?"

Max was already on its tail, sticking with the big fighter as it tried to shake him. Paskaal was still on his wing.

"Give me a half squad screen in case any more come through the gate, you take the other half in-sector," Max checked the long-range scan. "Looks like they could do with some help."

"Copy that Commander. Wings Two and Three with me, the rest of you." Sarge paused and checked his display. "The rest of you target the XL's, the Trading Station can't take much more."

It was a good call; station shields were below 50% and with the LT screen gone, the Xenon mark hornets were getting through.

"Mamba." Marteene could not risk using names or ask the one question he really wanted to ask over an unencrypted channel. "Can't explain but I need this XL alive."

"Copy that laddie, you've a delivery to make. Need any help?"

"If we can get the shields down quickly I'd stand a better chance of getting through," Xela said.

"Got it Zee." Max re-opened the channel to Paskaal.

"Mamba – I want those shields down to 10%, stat. Copy?"

"Corrin is onto it lad, consider it done."

The Split fighter, rolled up and away to fall back on the XL with a slashing attack from the right side that left the shields practically at zero. Max took over and with precisely timed single shots, modulated by Xela, kept the shields down while she infiltrated the Xenon systems. Re-routing the self-destruct order through her own matrix and simulating success she probed the alien technology, looking for a way past the lock-outs and protocols designed to prevent this sort of hijack. In many ways it turned out to be easier than she expected, based as she was on a similar template. It took five minutes but because Xenon craft are AI piloted she had a trick that would not work with piloted craft; a core-dump and re-write of the AI algorithms with her own.

The target designator turned from red to blue as Xela remodulated the Xenon IFF and Max stopped firing.

"We've done it Zee!" he yelled in triumph.

"Who's this "we" Max?" Xela joked. "Now how do you propose we deliver this thing?"

She had a good point. Max scanned the circling Xenon, all the shields and weapons were destroyed and the drive system was operating below 50% efficiency. And it was a long way to Teladi space. The IFF now identified the XL as friendly but he had little faith that alone would get it through a war-zone to Scale Plate Green.

"Corrin." He could still barely say the name without choking. "I need to get this to General Daht, Scale Plate Green without some trigger happy kid doing a number." He quickly checked the long-range scan. "The Xenon are bugging out, round up the Raiders as escort and I'll meet you all in Scale Plate Green Trading Station. I have some things to take care of at the station here first. Copy?"

"Consider it done. And Max, it's good to see you again."

"It's good to see you Corrin." He could barely talk. "It's good to see you."

His face was still wet with tears as he disembarked.

## *Chapter 44: Aftermath*

The docking bay reserved for competitors was an eye of calm in the storm of chaos enveloping the station, thanks to its isolation and a private security force enthusiastic in its disregard for the concept of minimum force.

This ended as soon as his feet touched the deck plate, fumbling for his shades. A protective phalanx of guards; cajoled into position by Anje Dalenari, swept in to protect him from the seething mob of reporters, well-wishers and would-be hangers-on.

"Everyone loves a winner?" Max asked, noting his own slurred speech with detached surprise.

"You won Max, if you can call it that. Get those morons back!" For such a small woman she could make a lot of noise.

The security team pushed out, expanding their perimeter, giving Max room to breathe.

Anje studied Max for a moment, whispered to the squad leader, and turned to the roiling crowd.

"Max has no comment at this time, we need to get him to Medical. No comment, no comment."

The crowd bayed its displeasure and pressed forward. The security team rose eagerly to the challenge and the barely functioning Marteene was bundled out of the bay, up a service elevator to the residential level, leaving him and Anje alone in a hotel suite before he could really grasp what was going on.

Sleep, all he wanted to do was sleep.

"Pull yourself together Max, here take this."

He fumbled with the stim and, barely able to restrain her impatience, she snatched the ampoule and triggered it against his neck.

In seconds his head began clearing as the powerful drug ripped new reserves of stamina and strength from his exhausted body.

"You feeling better now Max?" she asked, with uncharacteristic softness.

"Uh, yes, I think so, thanks. Sort of." he murmured.

"Good." The first slap caught him on the left cheek, snapping his head into the second, coming in from the right.

"What the hell do you think you are playing at Max?" she shouted, her eyes blazing. "What the hell do you think you were playing at?"

Max caught the third and fourth blows, restraining both her small wrists in one hand.

"She wants you to kiss her," Xela whispered through the shades. "Do it."

He did.

Moments later he was doubled over in pain.

"Oh for goodness sake Max," Xela laughed. "Do you have to do everything women tell you?"

"Yes?" he replied tentatively.

"What are you burbling about Max?" Anje pushed him across to the sofa. "Sit down and pay attention, hero."

He did as he was told.

"Let me give you a heads-up Max." She sighed theatrically and marshalled her thoughts. The universe had begun bashing her around the head from the moment Force went through the gate and showed little sign of stopping soon.

"You won. Way to go Max."

"Irony alert, irony alert," Xela shouted mechanically into his ear.

"However, as much as the beer-swilling multitude enjoyed the spectacle, the authorities here are, as we in the PR trade say, seriously pissed."

She paused and ordered two drinks from the auto-bar, handed Max a large, steaming mug, and kept the multi-hued frosted glass concoction for herself.

"Thanks Anje." Max sipped the scalding liquid tentatively. The Java was strong and black, no sweetener, just as he liked it. The caffeine jolt felt like an electric current, arcing between his temples, combining with the stim to promise the mother of all headaches later if he didn't get some sleep.

"Don't thank me – it's on your tab. Anyway, there are a few brass hats eager to throw the book at you for provoking the Xenon. There were a whole mess of civilian casualties and the private defence forces also took a beating – and believe me – they ain't happy."

"What about the Navy?" he inquired.

Anje looked puzzled. "What do you mean? Oh, casualties? I've no idea, they can't sue. Try and stay focused Max."

Max stifled a comment as she continued.

"The good news is, neither can anyone else. Not you anyway. Xenon space is outside any legal jurisdiction, even on Lawyer-World. However, the organisers aren't so lucky. Due care and attention and a whole lot of other mumbo-jumbo."

"So, what's the problem?"

"Shut up and listen Max," both females snapped simultaneously. Max removed the shades, hoping if he closed his eyes and opened them again he'd find himself somewhere safer, like back in a Xenon fur-ball.

It didn't work.

"The problem, Max, is appearance, not petty legalities. You messed with that big pointy thing, we all saw that before the pictures went out. Then when you returned you swanned off into deep space, taking your little private army with you, instead of defending the sector."

"Hey, that ain't fair!" Marteene protested, "I lured away several whole strike groups, which with the help of my "private army" as you call it, I destroyed. How much damage do you think they would have caused? Were any stations destroyed?"

"No, why?"

"Well if the civs had stayed docked they'd have been okay wouldn't they?"

Her face brightened beneath the mass of dark curls.

"Contributory negligence, that's very good Max, I think we can use that!" She touched her throat mike and briefly muttered a "note to self" into her data-padd..

"And besides," Max continued, "I was trying to save the Elite."

Her smile grew broader. "Yes, we can use that too! Heroic attempt to rescue comrade ends in tragic failure!"

Her face darkened again.

"Which just leaves the tiny, tiny little question of that machine-head ship you hijacked. I can't but help notice, it isn't here Max, your little friends took it away. The Navy is most unhappy about that and are demanding a debrief."

The coffee cup smashed satisfyingly against the opposite wall, shards like shrapnel. A service-bot scurried from concealment to clean up. Max drew and fired in one smooth motion.

"That goes on your tab too, have you quite finished?" She said icily.

The "little boy" was implied.

Max sheathed the blaster, the barrel warm on his thigh through the leather holster

"Right of salvage, get your lawyers onto the cite," he snapped, donning his shades and reactivating the link to Xela.

"My computer contains a complete record of the combat, including detailed scans of the monster."

And in response to Xela's promptings he added.

"There's also a mirror of the Xenon Combat AI, they've plenty of Xenon fighters, that's all they are after. The ship was obtained on commission for General Daht, THE General Daht and if they want to argue with him about it, fine."

"Okay Max, my people will talk to their people and I'll see if that will do. I don't want you dragged in front of a Tribunal, bad for the image."

"You don't say," Zee whispered. "Good call invoking Daht, Max, verbal contract."

"We shook on the deal, Anje.."

His agent queried her data-padd and read the results.

"I think we're onto a winner here Max, I'm showing plenty of cites for sanctity of contract enshrined in Foundation treaties. Let me run them past my people, if it checks out I'll force a deal that'll keep them out of your hair."

"That would be great Anje, thanks. I need to get out of here, business to attend."

Paskaal, he needed to talk with Paskaal.

"Leave it with me. And Max," she smiled, "I'm not a pilot but that was the gutsiest stuff I've ever seen. Now get some rest."

She left, the guards outside the suite forcing a path through the crowded corridor.

"I think she likes you Max, you should go for it!"

"Don't start that again Zee, she's stronger than she looks," he replied, rubbing a still-stinging cheek ruefully.

The caffeine and the stim precluded rest. Instead he tuned into a live news-feed while Xela compiled edited highlights of the competition coverage. Neither made comforting viewing.

The Seera had launched soon after the all-clear sounded and was many sectors distant, running under a new registry by the time the media conference began.

Marteene looked drawn and haggard, a man running on empty. He barely broke a smile when presented with the outsized chip with 'Two million credits' emblazoned on it. In fact, counting kill-bonuses, the sum was considerably more, and Artur had ensured it had been transferred to the Force Securities account before any of the many legal actions underway forced the freezing of the organiser's funds.

Artur congratulated himself on his own wisdom and foresight as Dalenari aggressively fielded the more hostile questions. The woman might have few morals and no regard whatsoever for the truth, but she knew how to defend a paying client. He had not even needed to pull any strings to prevent the Argon authorities in the sector giving Max the first-degree. The scans of the new Xenon ship and the copy of the XL combat AI were a big enough prize.

"All in all, Seera, that went better than we could have hoped."

His ship agreed, adding, "Your vital signs indicate fatigue Artur. Judgement compromised, recommend rest."

He rubbed his temples wearily, she was right. Artur poured himself a large whisky and knocked it back with a single, sharp tilt of his head, allowing a soporific glow to permeate his body.

Sleep, perchance not to dream.

His guards kept the media at bay as Marteene performed a cursory visual pre-flight check. Apart from scoring around the shield emitters the Rapier looked fine and Xela would spot any real problems once she was plugged back in.

"You take care Max." Anje had to stretch to brush his cheek with an air-kiss. "And you damn well keep in touch. When the Decree of Incorporation is confirmed you'll be news all over again and we'll be wanting a touch of positive spin so try and stay out of trouble for awhile okay?"

Marteene swore he did not even know the meaning of the word and thanked her again for squaring things with the local authorities.

"No problem Max, they had their own troubles anyway. One of their intelligence types died playing cop in the docking bays. They're too busy trying to pin it on someone to bother with you now you gave them their data."

Marteene paused for a final photo-shoot, arms carefully raised in triumph as coached, before sealing himself into the cockpit.

As the Piranha shot from the docking port into bright sunlight a wave of relief swept through him.

"Zee, remind me never to do anything like that again, okay?"

"Max, you have done nothing but lurch from one dangerous situation to another ever since we got together. At least this time we got a big, big pay-day. You have 2.5 million in various accounts now. What is the plan?"

"I'll work on that Zee. For now, fly us to Scale Plate Green. Borass will be there too right?"

"Confirmed Max. Course laid in. Try and grab some rest."

It is hard to sleep through worm-hole jumps but he managed. Xela woke him as the Scale Plate Green Trading Station confirmed docking permission. As the Piranha glided into an isolated docking bay, crowded with Bayamons and a single Mamba, he popped another stim.

## *Chapter 45: The End of the Beginning*

"I think that went rather well, all things considered," Marteene said, slumping against the bulkhead wearily. With the careful deliberation of one who knows he's drunk too much, he placed his shades in a chest pocket. The party, a dozen open kegs on the flight deck, continued to rage in the background, the cavernous docking bay reverberating to the insistent beat of old classics. A sluggish haze of spaceweed extended reluctant tendrils towards hidden recirculators.

"Aye laddie," Paskaal agreed as he joined Max on the floor. It was the first time Marteene had removed those glasses since docking and the first time he had looked him in his new eyes, in a new face. They were moist, red.

"Cheers, Max." They touched pitchers. "Cheers, Corrin. Grief, I thought I'd killed you!"

"It was close, Max – I'd better get used to saying that – I was damn lucky Artur was in transporter range. Even so."

He touched his face and the new skin.

"Comes with the territory." Another toast. "Comes with the territory." Marteene responded.

Ritual, nothing more to be said.

"I forgot to ask – what happened to the XL?"

Paskaal shrugged. "We turned over control before docking. It got siphoned off somewhere in the docking port. I'll tell you what though, that Daht was one happy reptile. I wonder what his game is?"

"I try not to think about it, you've lost the moustache, Mirv."

"Incognito old boy." Corrin tapped his nose and winked theatrically. "Artur is busy filling in the background gaps. You've lost a whole body by the looks. And speaking of Artur?"

They compared stories, each holding nothing back, Marteene's face set grim as Paskaal recounted his dealings with the Stoertebeker Clan and Law.

"Well at least Artur is consistent." Paskaal admitted. "Is he telling the truth?"

"The truth?" Marteene thought for a second. "Yes. All of it? No."

"Our options lad?" Paskaal took a long draught. "Ah, flat and warm, just how ale should be!"

Marteene smiled and put his own glass to one side. "Thanks for the tip. I don't see that we have any choice. The Code Black checks out, he delivers on his promises and his story makes sense."

"But we don't trust him?"

"We don't trust anybody except each other, Zee and Borass and I'm leaving him out of the loop on Artur. We take advantage of who and what we can to build an independent power-base."

"Sounds like a plan to me, laddie, I'm with you all the way on one condition."

Marteene raised a brow. "Stoertebeker?"

"Stoertebeker." Paskaal confirmed.

"We're going to push that sadistic, slave-dealing bastard harder than he's ever been pushed. There's only room for a few players at the Clan table and I'm going to stuff his face so far through the bulkheads he'll be sucking vacuum. Good enough?"

"Ab-so-damn-lutely Max." Paskaal smiled and they high-fived.

"The Fifth!"

"The Fifth." Marteene echoed. "I wish we had our guys with us now, did they all make it back?"

"They did that, laddie." Corrin gestured across at the knots of people surrounding the kegs.

"You've a whole squadron there Max, plus their support crew inbound. I've flown with them; they're better than good. I don't know how you did it but they didn't doubt you're their commander for a second. How did you know all those details?"

"Zee compiled a database from her - Hela's - memories and flashed it on the shades. I just had to act it out."

He was tired now, weary to the bone, making it difficult to think, to see the obvious.

"Grief, I hadn't thought of that, need sleep. How about a strategy session aboard the Star in 8 hours? You, Zee and me."

"Looking forward to meeting her. Where?" Corrin agreed.

"Aboard the Star, it's well equipped and I'll just be able to roll out of bed. I doubt the Teladi have any rooms on offer, there's plenty of space onboard the Star."

Corrin shook his head.

"Thanks for the offer Max but Mirv Corrin can't leave while there's still a party going on! Covers to build, covers to build old boy!"

"Are you sure we're secure here?" Max's gesture encompassed the big side-bay. Four other platforms clung to the inside of the big sphere. They looked deserted.

Paskaal shrugged. "Daht says do. The doors are locked down and guarded by his people. It's all ours for the time being but I got the impression he didn't want us around long. Toodle pip old chap!"

Max watched as Paskaal staggered a little uncertainly back to the party, morphing into Corrin as he went. He was almost too tired to stand now; the stims and the stress of the pretence had taken a toll. It had worked though, as Corrin said. Any oddities in his mannerisms were easily dismissed as tiredness and barring a detailed genetic scan he was to all intents and purposes the commander of a mercenary squadron.

At some point he might have to come clean. Artur's contact had bought his bitter, stoner veteran act. Grief, that seemed a long time ago. A part of the truth hidden in a lie, a cover for a cover in case the Force masquerade was blown.

Ambitious mercenary, renegade agent out for revenge. It could play out either way.

It was good to have options, primed and ready to fire but, as Paskaal had noted, with Artur's finger on the trigger.

That was an interesting thought but not one he could pursue now.

Waving blearily in the direction of the party he stumbled down the flight-line, past the Bayamons and the Mamba to the Destiny Star.

He had been relieved to find it intact. Borass had more courage than sense sometimes but he had resisted the temptation to take the freighter into battle with only a handful of drones. By his own account he had sat out the whole incident in front of the view-screen.

"Max-Max great pilot, silly machines nothing. No worries."

The only trouble he had stemmed from attempts to break into the Star by panicking mobs.

"People stupid cowards." Borass had explained.

"I made them go away," he added, with uncharacteristic restraint. "Is that a new follicular growth shape? Sweat and grease suit you!"

Marteene had thought it best not to pursue the matter.


"It was good to be back behind a stick." The General thought, even if the Falcon cockpit was a little cramped for his ample bulk.

The XL was close off his port wing, flanked by a pair of Falcon fighters. Four Hawks circled protectively and a screen of local Split fighters enforced a 5 klick exclusion zone around the Teladi convoy as it made its way through the intervening Split sectors to Teladi Gain..

Daht scanned the Xenon ship again, to confirm the jury-rigged shields and auto-pilot were holding, despite the doubts of his crew chief.

As the convoy approached the final jumpgate the Split fighters peeled away and General Daht accelerated, eager to get to the Board meeting.

More than eager. With this gift to smooth the way and the Stoertebeker Clan allies of his opponents, tarnished coin; this was a fight he could win. The human would get his decree and he would gain a new resource.

The enemy of my enemy, business did indeed make for strange nestlings.

He was, as he intended, the last to arrive at the Trading Station, knowing all eyes would be upon the alien fighter, seeing it for what it was.

A symbol of his resources, a token of what he could deliver.

To his friends.

Director Morn watched Daht's convoy dock with carefully concealed anger. She saw a threat but not one she could immediately counter without expending much of her own depleted political capital.

"Let the human have his decree," she thought contemptuously. "Let him tie up his capital in targets."

So she was the first to speak in support of Daht's motion. It gave her some small satisfaction to both steal the traction from beneath his claws and sow consternation among her fellow directors around the table.

The stupid ones saw weakness, others sheathed cunning.

"They would find out soon enough," she thought, sourly regarding the coterie gathered around the victor.

Concealed by flowing sleeves, her claws sheathed and unsheathing reflexively.

"Soon enough."

While Marteene slept the news filtered out across the jumpgate network. The Boron confirmation followed shortly and the slightest of chills trembled the corporate spines of the jumpgate system oligopolies.

It was now official, there was a new player in town and his adeptly spun name was Max Force.

"Max Force!" Law's talon grip on the shaven skull of the kneeling young woman calculatingly tightened. Rivulets of blood trickled then flowed down her head. She would have screamed if she could.

"Begone," he commanded, hurling the slave across the polished marble floor with one effortless blow. She smashed into the raised wall of the bath-pool, a rib snapped loudly. Whimpering, she made good her escape.

That name! His leather-scarred face itched at the thought and he fought the urge to tear the alien skin from it. Surgery would be an easy option, even if his own face were lost beyond recovery. But then he would have nothing to show, nothing to remind him that mistakes had consequences. Appearance meant nothing compared to power and wealth and besides, terror gave so many satisfactions, in so many areas.

He read the message again before discarding the data-padd. That man had far more lives than any of his enemies were entitled to and now he had bested the Xenon and got the Teladi to support his bid for a universal trading license. The man was now a direct threat to the mutually beneficial relationship he enjoyed with ruling elements the Teladi Trading Company.

Morn's problems were his problems.

Law considered summoning the injured girl, his aching body demanded the warmth of the pool and it would add a slight frisson but he rejected the idea. He would forego both pleasures as a lesson to himself.

"Problems are the fruit of neglected concerns."

It sounded better in the original Split. He regretted not pursuing his vendetta as soon as Force had resurfaced after rigging the trap that destroyed enough of his pilots to hurt, as well as the bounty hunter he'd set on Force's trail.

The latter mistake was easily remedied. They were here already, the 3 black Prometheus fighters ensconced in a secluded hanger. The pilots had not emerged and the visual scanners in the bay had gone down shortly after their arrival. That was an insult to the Stoertebeker Clan but he would let it pass. These humans warranted respect as necessary and expensive tools he might have use for again.

At the insistence of the leader they negotiated over a scrambled voice link Law found the caution admirable.

"Target?" The voice was mechanical, alien, distorted beyond identification.

"I have a problem with.."

"No grandstanding. Target?"

Law answered, speaking in a slow and deliberate manner.

"Max Force, his properties and associates, himself. Background.."

The robot voice of the mercenary leader interjected.

"We understand the background. You and your Teladi allies don't want Daht and Force messing in your pleasure-pit. Too many cosy deals and monopoly spaceweed profits to lose if old General Rectitude becomes majority shareholder. Right?"

"That is essentially correct." Law replied. "Can you deliver on such a contract?"

"We can deliver Law, if we like the price. Force has a rep and the money to buy a lot of friends."

Law named a price they liked, after a couple of attempts.

"Problem solved," Law stated, taking pleasure in goading fate.

He would not inform the Teladi.

"Morn may favour subtlety," he thought. "But 'Fortune Favours the Fierce.'"

That translated very well.


"Lights, lights. No, dimmer. Okay."

The pounding was not in his head but came from the closed door to his small sleeping area.

"Wait a minute, wait a minute!"

He stumbled into his discarded clothes, pleased he'd actually removed them before crashing out.

He opened the door, Borass bustled in bearing a tray. The big pot of java was a welcome sight, the covered plate, promising.

"Hmmn, smell interesting." The Boron swivelled both eye-stalks so he was looking into his own eyes.

Max held his head – whatever time it was it was too early to even begin thinking what that must feel like.

"You feel bad, this make you feel good." Borass poured the java and handed Max the large mug. He took a lip-burning sip.

"Know all lady she say this good for 'what ails you.' Not as good as not ale-ing in first place I think. Ha – I make Argon joke. Funny, no?"

"No." Max said. "What is it?"

"I look up 'breakfast' in database. It say, egg, bacon, sausage, fried bread, toast, marmalade. Great Fry-Up yes? Good for self-inflicted alcohol poisoning. Then I read about 'sandwich'. Two plus two – voila!"

Borass unveiled the plate with a flourish. Max stared at the mess for a second before succumbing to the tempting bacon smell. Gingerly he took the plate and carefully flattened the greasy sandwich with a palm. The slice of fried bread on top fractured and yellow yolk dribbled down the sides but he managed to take a jaw stretching bite.

"Uh, bacon, sausage and egg. Good combination Borass."

"And marmalade Max, and marmalade."

Max took a second bite. "And marmalade," he agreed, taking a larger gulp of hot, bitter java than was probably wise.

"Do me a favour and find Corrin and bring him back here." He checked the time. "We were meant to meet hours ago."

"Dokerly, okerly Max. " Borass bounded off with altogether too much enthusiasm and Max took the chance to shower and change clothes.

A less experimental breakfast and another mug of java returned him to a state of near humanity by the time Borass returned with Corrin.

Paskaal looked around the luxuriously appointed living area before sinking into an arm-chair.

"Very nice Max, very nice indeed. You look a bit rough though."

"And you look so chipper it sickens me. How do you do it?"

"Years of practice old boy," he grinned. "And a dozen raw eggs, straight down."

"You didn't hear that Borass," Max cautioned as he handed Corrin a fresh cup of java. "Say hello Zee."

"How you doing Corrin?" Her voice came from the view-screen on the far bulkhead, displaying a view of the deserted docking bay. "Heard a lot about you, some of it good."

Paskaal smiled. "Then you've been listening to the wrong people lassie."

Max and Borass listened patiently as the two exchanged banter. It gave him a chance to think and Borass the impression he was deepening his understanding of humanity.

"Okay team," Max tapped his mug with a stylus, "The first board meeting of Force Securities is called to order. Corrin, you want to tell us what you been up to?"

Paskaal succinctly summarised his dealings with the Stoertebeker Clan, glossing over his near death and omitting entirely any reference to Artur.

"So," Xela summarised. "We have coming on to three million credits, a Piranha, a Lifter and a pack of mercs who think Max is their lost leader with which to bust open a putative conspiracy to obtain breakthrough technology by a sub-set of the clans and person or persons unknown, possibly including senior levels of the Teladi Trading Company."

"That's about it Zee," Max agreed. "We also have Daht."

"Who is playing his own game Max," Xela interjected.

"The enemy of my enemy Zee."

"We also have a Mamba, Max," Corrin chipped in. "Just one careless owner!"

"Okay, one heavy fighter in the pot. You and Zee talk about laundering it later. Corrin, how do you feel about the Raiders? They need a leader and if I spend too much time with them I'm bound to slip up."

"It'll be my pleasure Max, they're a good bunch and Payter's a fine second." Paskaal agreed.

"Right, you're Chief of Security. Borass, I'm putting you in charge of the Merchant fleet."

Max cut off the Boron's protestations. " I know one ship is hardly a fleet but give me time. Zee, I want you to co-ordinate everything."

"In that case we're going to need a Nav-Sat network and some heavy duty encryption," Xela replied.

"Okay Zee, make a list for Borass. Corrin, make sure the Star has an escort from now on. I want us ready to move as soon as the Decree comes through."

"Get with the program Max, it's all over the news," Xela replied dryly. "Anje has been a busy girl."

Max and Corrin high fived, Borass jigging around them in his own happy dance.

The group discussed strategies for an hour, reaching a reluctant agreement despite Paskaal's reservations

"Spaceweed Max? I know it's pretty harmless but it's still illegal in most sectors. I know you have the contacts but.."

"It's the fast track to the big money Mirv, legal in Teladi space and we have two clan stations within a two sector radius if we base ourselves here. We can tap into Rarr's distribution network, plus it puts us toe to toe with Stoertebeker."

Corrin smiled. "Consider my objections withdrawn. If we are going up against that scum we're going to need more fire-power. Bayamons are good in large wings but we're going to need something with more solo punch."

"Check," Max replied. "Zee, get Borass through to Sinas later. Make sure we can still get Piranhas."

"With the trading license we can buy commercial variants of most ships Max, but we will confirm."

"Good enough Mirv?" Max asked.

"Good enough Max," Corrin concurred. "A fine, fine ship, we'll need more pilots though. I'll talk with Payter and set up security screening, we don't want Stoertebeker spies. Speaking of which, I've some info on your accident with the Xenon our mutual friend dug up."

He mentioned a name, Xela recognised him as one of the Raiders ground staff.

"Apparently he worked for Trasker. Force and the Raiders were interfering with her operation against the Clan station in Nyana's Hideout."

Both Marteene and Xela were quiet for a long while, digesting the fact that his cousin and Force had died due to an operation by their own side.

"That psycho bitch," Marteene stated finally. "We'll have to watch her."

Paskaal looked surprised.

"You don't know? She was killed in the riots back in Black Hole Sun."

Max looked at Corrin with a brow raised questioningly.

"How?"

"A blaster in the back. There was a lot of shooting, the authorities say they are treating it as an accident."

Max sighed his ambivalent feelings away.

"Corrin, assemble the troops on the deck and get that spy off-station, no killing. We better see if they actually want in and if they'll accept you as CO."

He need not have been concerned. Their loyalty to Force was paramount and Corrin had already earned their respect, fighting at their side against the Xenon thrust into New Income.

Good pay, new ships and the chance to fight for Force. It was all they wanted.

His eyes stinging with tears as they chanted Force's name, Marteene silently vowed to earn that loyalty.

ISBN 141201955-9